Mystery of the Templars

A Novel

MARTINA ANDRÉ

Translated from the German by Yan An Tan

Written by Martina André
Edited by Mairi St Clair
Translated by Yan An Tan
Project editor: Lori Herber
Cover design and illustration: Lukas Mühlbauer

The digital version of this book is distributed by Bastei Entertainment
www.be-ebooks.com

Dedication

I dedicate this book to George and Mairi St Clair, best friends and guardian angels of my Templar novels.
Thank you both for encouraging me to "just do it"!

Edinburgh, June 2018

Contents

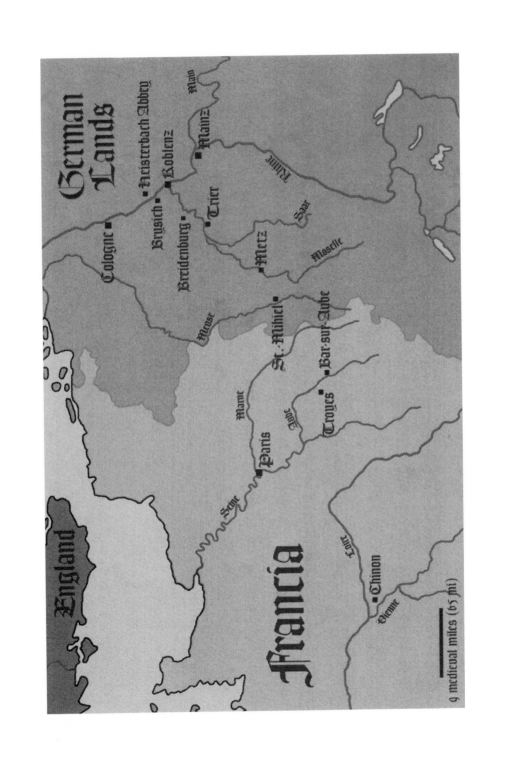

In the year 1156, Bertrand de Blanchefort, sixth Grand Master of the Knights Templar, brought a mysterious object from Jerusalem to his home in France. Those in the know named the unremarkable metallic box 'Caput LVIII' or 'The Head of Wisdom'.

Soon thereafter, Bertrand de Blanchefort became the most successful Grand Master of his time, and under his influence the Order of the Temple established itself as the most important organization the Christian Occident had ever produced.

PROLOGUE

Caput VIII

"The disciples said to Jesus, 'When will the repose of the dead come to pass and when will the new world come?' He said to them, 'What you look forward to has already come, but you do not recognize it.'"

The Gospel of Thomas, Verse 51

Saturday, October 28, 1307
Chinon, France

The wind blew mercilessly over the impenetrable castle of Chinon. Towering storm clouds swept across the high plateau and the subsequent deluge transformed the streets of the fortress into treacherous quagmires. Lightning crackled in the leaden sky, each flash succeeded by deafening rumbles of thunder, and only those condemned to be outside remained in the storm. Today was the day of Saint Simon and Saint Jude Thaddeus. They had been martyred after exposing the ineptitude of Emperor Xerxes's sorcerers, an act that sparked an uprising among the priests who captured Simon and Jude Thaddeus, and – here the scribes differed – beheaded or dismembered them. Soon after, a violent tempest slew the priests and sorcerers, throwing the king and his people into terror.

The day of October 28, 1307, seemed intent on honoring its namesakes – at least as far as the weather was concerned – and the martyrs themselves did not seem too far away.

A small dish of thin barley porridge and a slice of moldy bread marked the start of yet another day in hell for Henri d'Our, Commander of the Templar settlement of Bar-sur-Aube.

On some days, the sprawling limestone catacombs of Fortress Chinon resembled a cattle market. With their whips and bludgeons, emotionless

1

torturers herded hordes of tormented souls through labyrinthine passageways, sieving out the most resilient, only to impose upon them later the most brutal punishments. Yet the day had become eerily quiet after the morning's rations were distributed. Only the distant roll of thunder hinted at impending disaster.

A woman's piercing cry tore through the fragile shroud of silence, confirming Henri d'Our's worst suspicions. He crouched, withdrawn, in the furthest corner of his cell. The once white cloak he wore bore only the faintest resemblance to its original color, and the tattered fabric barely shielded his emaciated body from scornful glances. His matted, silver hair and formerly trimmed, dignified beard were smeared with blood and dirt. His jaw was so excruciatingly painful that he could barely open it and he had to strain his swollen eyes to figure out what was happening around him. Only with great effort could he move his limbs, which were littered with deep blue bruises and painful burns.

Until now, he had stoically endured all sorts of torture, willing his spirit to leave his body so he could face such unbearable agony. And yet, a profound fear was steadily tightening its grip on his heart. What if King Philipp IV of France and Guillaume de Nogaret, Keeper of the Seals and head of the Royal Secret Police, the Gens du Roi, discovered that he belonged to the inner circle of the Templar Order? That, despite his modest post, he had been meeting with the Grand Master and his representatives in France? Was it possible the Gens du Roi had planted spies in the economically insignificant settlement of Bar-sur-Aube? Could they have been sending regular reports back to the court in Paris?

A torturer, ugly as sin, shuffled by. He pulled out his heavy bundle of keys and opened the gigantic iron lock to Henri d'Our's dark cell. His inane grin was dripping with scorn, as if taunting d'Our – whose arms and legs were shackled with chains – to escape.

"So, my good man, off to the next round." The irony in his voice was obvious. "They've been expecting you."

He pulled Henri d'Our to his feet and ruthlessly shoved him out of his cell.

Holy Mother Mary, the Commander of Bar-sur-Aube prayed silently as he struggled to stay on his feet. *Let me remain strong in my honor and keep my faith in the good in the world.*

When he arrived in the large, brightly lit torture chamber, however, his courage withered. A flash of pain cut through his heart like a dagger when he recognized the broken man in front of him. His fellow knight, Francesco de Salazar, had fallen into the hands of the Gens du Roi.

Even worse was the sobbing maiden by Francesco's side. She was, without a doubt, the sister of the once proud Catalan man. She gazed up at d'Our with the same large, hazel eyes as her brother, as if hoping to find salvation there.

Like Jesus on a cross, Francesco hung lifelessly on a slanted, wooden board. Clad only in his tattered remains of his braies, the typical undergarments worn by Knights Templar. Dark welts covered his flat stomach, and burns the size of coins encircled his nipples like grisly roundels. D'Our could hardly believe that Francesco's cracked, bloody lips had once framed his characteristic smile and blindingly white teeth.

Then, as if through a fog, Henri d'Our noticed the elegantly dressed elderly woman. She appeared to have fainted and had been laid on a grimy mattress, her hair freed from the tight wimple women her age often wore. Her dark, silver-streaked curls and olive complexion suggested she was Francesco's mother, the Countess de Salazar. D'Our shivered. The Inquisition showed no mercy in extracting statements from its victims, and certainly made no exceptions for frightened kin.

Groups, mostly of women, had been summoned to the dungeons to weaken the unwavering resolve of the Templar knights. Guillaume de Nogaret and his men knew the captive knights would endure their own suffering to the grave, but not the sobs and screams of the women forced to witness the torment of their sons and brothers.

A medicus stood by the side of the countess. Flitting in and out of the room in his long, black robe, he looked to d'Our like an angel of death. But the commander soon noticed the presence of someone else who fit the description even better: Guillaume Imbert, Grand Inquisitor, Bishop of Paris, personal confessor of Philipp IV, and the unholy ally of Guillaume de Nogaret.

"So, we meet again," said the man softly. His arrogant smile revealed sharp, chiseled teeth as he plucked uneasily at the white lace collar that peeked above his dark gray surcoat.

The portly torturer dropped d'Our against a wooden crate. His limbs in chains, neck stiff, d'Our met the gaze of his tormentor.

"Well, now," Imbert resumed mockingly, glancing casually at Francesco, "if you've finally gotten over your arrogance and have a rational statement to offer me, perhaps you might be able to save this lad's life."

Francesco's sister, who had been following the Inquisitor's remarks with widened eyes, sprang to her feet before throwing herself on the dirt in front of d'Our with her arms outstretched. Her face was hidden under a cascade of flowing locks.

"Noble sir," she wailed, "surely whatever they want from you can't be worth more than my brother's life! I beg you!"

As her body shook violently with sobs, d'Our glared at Imbert accusingly. The Inquisitor stood by the woman, grinning devilishly, making no effort to disguise his perverse pleasure. The commander of the Templars of Bar-sur-Aube could not bring himself to sacrifice his protégé – especially not in front of his mother and sister.

A shadow moved behind Imbert and cleared its throat cautiously. It was the medicus, who had been following the scene with great interest. Imbert's gaze darted between the body of the lifeless countess and the inquisitive doctor.

"Didn't you say the woman would come round again?"

The medicus nodded compliantly.

"Good. Then make yourself scarce. But be ready when I call for you."

The medicus pressed his lips together in disappointment, but, with a servile bow, the black figure vanished as swiftly as it had appeared.

Imbert turned and fetched a nondescript linen sack from under a wooden writing desk against the wall. With a furtive glance, he produced a delicately crafted woman's head. It was only slightly smaller than an actual human head, and wrought from pure silver. It was mounted upon a small pedestal, on which the initials CAPUT LVIII were engraved.

"I don't care if you've feasted on your own freshly-grilled newborns for dinner," Imbert began sharply, "nor whether your novices have to shove their filthy dicks into the Master's ass before they can don the white robe."

For a moment, Imbert savored the horrified expression on the young woman's face as she cowered on her heels, trembling.

"I know you have something much more interesting to me." His voice rose in fiendish pleasure. "Just so we're clear, I'm interested in neither your gold nor where you've hidden it. I'll leave that for others to find out. No. I'm far more interested in the source of your knowledge," he said, stroking the shimmering silver face almost tenderly, "and whether this charming face has anything to do with it."

At this, Imbert affected the expression of a scholar, donning a mask of professional curiosity. "Why, I wonder," he continued in a lecturing tone, "did we find this silver head while searching the Grand Master's private apartment in Paris? This head, whose mysterious existence was whispered of in countless interrogations? In which the message is hidden: *'Go to H d O – only he knows how to make the voice speak?'*"

Imbert chortled. "You see," he exclaimed, "we are capable of deciphering your secret texts! The rest was child's play." He laughed again softly. "Please enlighten me. Why did these three initials match the name of only one person – out of the many we found in the roster of names in Troyes?" The Grand Inquisitor peered at d'Our. "Specifically, your name?"

D'Our remained motionless as he struggled to maintain an expression as clear as pure spring water.

"What are you?" Imbert hissed impatiently. "A sorcerer? Can you make this thing speak?"

He skulked closer to his victim and crouched down in front of him, coming so near to d'Our that the commander, despite his dulled senses, could not help but breathe in the noxious mixture of foul breath and expensive perfumes clouding around Imbert.

"We interrogated your Grand Master four days ago in Corbeil," Imbert continued, sounding remarkably pleased with himself yet not realizing he had just revealed to Henri d'Our where the leader of the Templars was currently imprisoned.

"Jacques de Molay claimed he is but a simple man who never mastered reading and writing, and that he knows nothing of a head. And of course, nothing about a note he supposedly placed, along with this fair visage, in a hiding place completely unknown to him!" Imbert's voice thundered ever more loudly, and fury darkened his pallid face to the shade of a boiled lobster.

He sprang up suddenly. "Do you all take me for a fool?"

In a fit of rage, he threw the head at d'Our. The commander, his arms still in chains, could not catch it, and the small head of solid silver landed in d'Our's lap and struck his testicles, the only part of his body that had thus far been spared from torture.

His face contorted with pain, d'Our held his breath and gulped deeply. All of a sudden, his mouth went dry, and his eyes wandered restlessly between the woman before him and the brutally tortured Francesco, for whom he felt a profound responsibility.

Feverishly, he mulled over how he could escape this trap. He had one small advantage. Imbert wanted something from him, and badly. Till now, his efforts had not seen much success, and King Philipp would probably base the fate of his Grand Inquisitor's career on precisely this task.

"If you would give me a sip of water," d'Our said with a calmness that surprised even himself, "I could consider breaking my silence."

He lowered his eyes and tried to seem disinterested. He could not afford to let Imbert notice how dear the youngster's life was to him.

"Do as he wishes," Imbert said, gesturing to the dungeon's warden to serve d'Our water with a ladle.

D'Our gulped down the cold water like a camel that had been lost in the desert. His remaining teeth hurt terribly, but still, his thoughts cleared with each sip, and his voice sounded clear and firm as he proceeded.

"I will tell you what you want to hear," he began, looking up at the Grand Inquisitor innocently, "on one condition."

"I don't think you're in a position to set conditions," Imbert retorted icily, glancing quickly at the young woman still cowering on the floor.

"And I think you have questions only I can answer?" d'Our countered.

The Inquisitor turned his gaze to Francesco, the young Templar knight.

"You need not take him into consideration at all," d'Our remarked tonelessly. "After all, I haven't told you what you wanted to hear despite all his screaming."

In truth, d'Our had not known who had been screaming till now.

"Then it would certainly not bother you," Imbert responded mercilessly, "if I killed him in front of you."

The young woman pressed her fists against her ears and screamed as if a knife had stabbed her in the stomach. She clung sobbing to d'Our's motionless legs and begged for Francesco's life.

"It troubles me not," feigned d'Our, regarding Francesco's sister as if she were a pitiable lunatic. "But it appears that the life of her brother means something to this young lady. And it would reflect poorly on me if I entrusted such a momentous secret to someone so heartless that he would cause an innocent creature such misery."

"What do you want?" bellowed Imbert, striking the desk with the palm of his hand.

D'Our knew he had baited him. "I guarantee you, you can tortu poor boy until his soul leaves his body. It will be of no use to you. 11c fell silent, and regarded the Grand Inquisitor with an appraising look. "Did you really think that we would trust a child whose tongue works quicker than his brain with our greatest secrets?"

Imbert examined Francesco de Salazar. Bathed in blood and sweat, nearly unconscious from pain, the young Catalan looked nothing like the proud Templar knight who had fought in the Crusades and struck fear into the hearts of all who opposed him.

"Return him to his family," d'Our said, and looked at the young maiden whose eyes darted, half hopeful, half afraid, between him and the beast in elegant robes. "And once I receive notice from his kin that he has arrived home safe and sound, I will reveal to you what you want to hear."

"Good," Imbert agreed brusquely, and signaled to the torturer. "Let them go!"

The torturer received the order with disbelief.

"Two weeks," Imbert snarled, looking down at d'Our in irritation, "and not a day more. Then you will reveal to me the true secrets of your Order." The Grand Inquisitor paused and narrowed his deep-set eyes. "If not, I'll flay you and your remaining comrades alive. Right here, before the Antichrist finally snatches your souls."

PART 1

The Mission

"Lift up a stone and you will find me, split a piece of wood, and I am there."

The Gospel of Thomas, Verse 77

CHAPTER 1

Gregorian Chanting

Wednesday, October 11, 1307
Bar-sur-Aube, France

On this gloriously sunny October afternoon in the year of our Lord 1307, only the refreshing breeze and the first falling leaves gave any hint that autumn had arrived.

A thick cloud of dust rolled down the hill onto the pale limestone road that led from Thors. From the watchtower of the Templar commandery of Bar-sur-Aube, the Brother on duty spotted the black-and-white banner of his Brethren in the distance.

Gradually, the hazy sight became clear: six mighty steeds and their stately riders, Templars, clad in fluttering white cloaks emblazoned with a bright red cross pattée on the shoulder, breast, and back. Their hair and beards were closely shorn, as tradition demanded. The proud bearing of the young men and their open display of weaponry – sword, shield, and knife belt – only reinforced the picture of steely discipline and militant determination.

A group of small boys stood by the side of the road, momentarily awestruck as the cavalcade trotted past them, but the last rider had barely passed them before they began hooting and gesticulating wildly behind the troop.

Gerard of Breydenbach, a knight of German descent from the Trier archdiocese, led the group of riders in white. Gero, as he was known, straightened his back a little more than usual. Alongside his exhaustion, a bothersome pain had plagued him since midday, and only the thought that he could soon exchange his hard saddle for a soft mattress gave him any relief.

Even before early mass, Gero and his companions had set out to deliver a secret message to Thors, which lay two miles away. They had intended to be back around midday, but their return had been unexpectedly delayed. The commander-in-chief of the Bailiwick of Thors, the headquarters of the surrounding Templar settlements, had summoned the Brothers of Bar-sur-Aube to deliver, without delay, additional sealed parchments to each of the five neighboring commanderies.

A ringing laugh jolted Gero out of his thoughts. Not far from the road, three washerwomen were gathering the white, linen sheets they had laid out to dry on the grassy banks of the Dhuys. A gust of wind fluttered both the blonde hair of the women and their thin dresses.

As the warrior monks rode by, the women tried to attract their attention. With a subtle smirk, Gero let his discipline slip as he recognized the women's intentions. The Spanish flag bearer who rode beside him grinned broadly, briefly flashing his snow-white teeth. One of the Brothers behind them let out an appreciative whistle, earning him a ravishing smile from the young women.

"He looked at me!" exclaimed one of the women as she pressed her hands to her breast in utter bliss.

"I told you," announced a second with an enchanted expression, "the troop leader has eyes as blue as the sky."

"I prefer the one with the brown locks ...," the riders heard from behind them. Laughter broke out. It came not from the women, however, but from the Brethren following behind.

Maybe Father Augustinus was right after all, thought Gero. The careworn chaplain's face appeared in his mind, appealing, as he did every Sunday, to the knights' morals:

"We deem it dangerous," *recited the perpetually sour-faced Father*, "for any man of the order to gaze too closely at the face of a woman. Accordingly, no Brother should presume to kiss a widow, a virgin, his mother, sister, aunt, or any other woman. The knighthood of Christ should therefore flee from the kisses of women, through which men often endanger themselves, so that they remain, at all times, in God's sight, pure of conscience, and sure of life."

The mockery that erupted from some of his companions as soon as Augustinus left resounded in Gero's mind. *Who ever said that a man must kiss a woman before he enjoys himself with her ... and he need not necessarily look her in the face either.* Roaring laughter followed these comments, and Gero could only guess how much of it came from personal experience.

Francesco de Salazar, riding to the side of Gero, clicked his tongue and grinned at him as if he'd guessed his thoughts.

Gero closed his eyes for a moment, perhaps to shield them from the afternoon sun's low-lying light or perhaps just to clear his conscience. As he opened them again, the guard on duty in the tower blew his horn – one short blast and one long – the signal for the sergeants in the courtyard below to open the heavy oak gates immediately.

Swiftly, the troop descended into the long, cool shadows of the high fortress walls. The iron horseshoes of the heavy war-horses thundered over the square cobblestones before the noise finally subsided as the riders came to a standstill in front of the stables.

"Dismount!" Gero commanded. Almost simultaneously, the large, broad-shouldered men swung down from their saddles.

The courtyard was bustling with activity. Into the midst of the servants and maids who were scurrying about, flocked a band of young admirers. Boys aged between eleven and eighteen stood ready to take over from their cavaliers the duty of unharnessing and feeding the horses.

With a beaming smile, Matthäus of Bruch, a lanky twelve-year-old with a curly mop of hair, relieved Gero of his gray Percheron's reins. Gero rid himself of his iron-fitted plate gloves, and carelessly tousled his squire's disheveled blonde hair.

"All right there, Mattes?"

Matthäus nodded contentedly and led the enormous horse to a water trough.

Gero headed towards the men's quarters at the other end of the courtyard with his fellow knights. Before they reached the lodgings, he stepped out of line and, despite the need to hurry, indulged himself in two scoops of water from one of the half-full wooden pails by the well. He then hastened up the steep outer staircase of a three-story sandstone building, the sealed parchment in his left hand. He stopped at the first landing and pushed a heavy oak door that creaked softly as it opened. As he headed down the long, dim passageway, he checked the fit of his chlamys to neaten it. These legendary cloaks were constructed from light, unbleached worsted wool and worn exclusively by knights who had sworn their lives to the Templar Order.

At the end of the hall, Brother Claudius was waiting for him. The young, brown-robed administrator noted each visitor calling on his superior with the eye of an eagle lying in wait for an unwary rabbit. No one was allowed entry into the commander's chambers without a prior appointment.

"You can't enter now," warned Claudius, seeing that Gero was heading towards his commander's study. "He is in council with Father Augustinus and doesn't want to be disturbed." The man reached out his scrawny arm and motioned to take the message from Gero.

"I'll wait," said Gero curtly. Claudius nodded briefly and turned sullenly to face his desk, deliberately ignoring his Brother in white.

A short while later, the door to the commander's chamber opened, and, without paying Gero any heed, the chaplain of the commandery darted out toward the exit. Claudius glanced up briefly, and Gero received, with the slightest of nods, permission to enter his superior's study.

Commander Henri d'Our was a wiry figure with the shimmering gray eyes of a wolf and a hooked nose like the beak of a falcon. His height of nearly seven feet ensured that he had the undivided attention of all who crossed his path. His thick, white hair was closely shorn and full of cowlicks, lending him a sympathetically imperfect appearance. D'Our, a descendant of the Duchy of Lorraine, possessed a steely nerve and sharp wit. His heart was full of an inimitable sense of justice, and – when the situation allowed – an odd sense of humor.

For a man who ruled over the hundreds of residents in the commandery, d'Our's study was not particularly large. The two small windows facing the courtyard were unglazed. Instead, when necessary, they were covered with oiled goatskins. They let in almost no light, but at least kept the cold out. Like the rest of the commandery, the furnishings were sparse: a bed, a table with four stools, and a bare dresser.

Gero took a step back, squared his shoulders, and, raising his head slightly, looked his superior firmly in the eye.

"God be with you, Sire!" he saluted d'Our and presented him with the carefully guarded message.

"And with you, Brother Gerard," d'Our replied genially, accepting the sealed parchment. "Shut the door! I have something to discuss with you."

Gero sensed something amiss on his superior's tense face. And he was speaking German – something Gero had only experienced once in his three years at the commandery, on the occasion of his father's visit. Richard of Breydenbach had fought with d'Our in the Holy Land in 1291.

Henri d'Our broke the seal and quickly scanned the parchment's contents.

"Seat yourself," he said, not looking up once as he read. "Our discussion will require some time."

After Gero had settled himself on a stool at the table, he let his eyes roam about the room. A jewel-encrusted Saracen dagger had been mounted and sat on a shelf by the wall, allowing the emir's gift to be marveled at from all angles. Above it, a hand-painted, goat leather map of the Eastern Mediterranean Sea hung on a wooden board. Along with two Oriental rugs that covered the stone floor, they were the only luxury goods the Commander of Bar-sur-Aube had kept from his service in the Outremer, the lost Templar possession in the Holy Land.

D'Our finished reading, went to the fireplace and placed the parchment carefully in the flames.

What is he doing? Gero was bewildered. Paper and parchment were expensive, and in the commandery, a great emphasis was placed on keeping continuous and diligent records that were archived for years to come. As far as he could remember, nothing from these archives had ever been destroyed.

Ignoring his subordinate's look of surprise, d'Our set a carafe of red wine and two cups on the table before he too sat down.

"Would you like a drink?" Without waiting for an answer, d'Our poured the rich, red liquid into two ornately painted stoneware cups and set the carafe aside. "I had this marvelous wine delivered to me from

Provence just two days ago. We should savor it," he said, raising his cup, oddly casual.

Gero mirrored the gesture, catching the tantalizing scent of cherries and blackberries and a heady dose of alcohol as he raised his glass.

"How long have we known each other?" d'Our asked, looking at Gero inquiringly.

Gero shrugged his shoulders. "I've belonged to the Order for about six years, but I was in Cyprus for a long time."

"The fact is, we've known each other far longer than that. You were a child when I first saw you."

Gero suppressed his rising impatience. It was hardly likely that the commander had sat him down just to regale him with tales from his turbulent but otherwise unremarkable youth.

"I value and trust you, not least because of your father. He is a brave man who has always stood loyally by the Order's side, even though he was never one of us." D'Our drank and set his cup down thoughtfully. He stared at Gero with his stone gray eyes, as if reaching into his soul. "You have sworn an oath of secrecy, but still, I would like your reassurance that what I'm about to say will remain in this room – forever." He searched Gero's face for an answer.

"You have my word, Sire," Gero whispered hoarsely.

"Very well," d'Our began, "our sources at court in Paris have learned that King Philipp is planning an attack on all our settlements in France tomorrow night. The orders have supposedly been at Guillaume de Nogaret's headquarters since September. We believe his unexpected appointment to the Keeper of the Seals is not without reason. According to everything we currently know, the orders to attack have been sealed and delivered to all the royal army's command offices throughout the country. Anyone who opens them before tomorrow evening faces the death penalty. That leaves us little time to take the necessary precautions."

Gero stared at his commander in disbelief. "How is that possible?"

"Our official supposition of the king's intentions," d'Our continued with a wry smile, "is that he needs money urgently. And since we won't give it to him freely, he's looking for a reason to seize it in a surprise coup. If he'd announced an investigation, he would have come up against not just locked doors, but locked vaults as well. Due to this unfortunate development, we've received strict orders to immediately take all assets stored in the commanderies to a secure place. Do you understand?"

13

It took a while for Gero to process the momentousness of d'Our's plainly stated words. Fire flooded through his veins.

"I want you," d'Our continued, "to assemble five of your most capable men and take our funds and the local merchants' promissory notes to our depot in the Forest of the Orient tomorrow afternoon. You will meet with Theobald of Thors in Beaulieu beforehand. He's leading the combined march of all our commanderies in the area."

"Do the Pope and the Grand Master know about this?" Gero had completely forgotten that he was not allowed to question an order. "No one except the Pope can meddle in our financial affairs, not even the King – it's a documented right."

"The orders come directly from the Grand Master," d'Our replied tersely. "Besides that, Jacques de Molay has ordered us not to do anything that could tip off the King." The commander looked doubtful.

"In spite of everything, he doesn't believe Philipp would really dare stage such a treacherous attack. Just this morning, our honorable Grand Master and his representative Raymbaud de Charon attended the burial of Philipp's sister-in-law at the invitation of the King himself. As a matter of fact, Molay and our esteemed preceptor from Cyprus are to carry Catherine de Courtenay's burial shroud." D'Our's expression revealed that he found this circumstance just as strange as Gero did.

"I imagine this is a well-calculated move by both sides," he added. "How does the saying go? *You don't tell me that you hate me, and I won't tell you that I know you do.* But I, for one, don't believe the King would give up his attempts to seize the Order, least of all for such a witless gesture.

"As for the Pope ... what he thinks has long been meaningless. Financially, he stands with his back to the wall – something he shares with our fine Philipp – nothing forges such easy bonds as a common sorrow. And he's frightened. After his predecessors Boniface VIII and Benedict XI died so suddenly and mysteriously, he will duly consider every step he takes to ensure he doesn't meet the same fate." D'Our smiled dryly.

"But that's not all," he continued conspiratorially. "There exists a prophecy of a kind," he explained, "about the impending downfall of the Order in the autumn of 1307, and the capture of all Knights Templar in France by King Philipp IV on a Friday the thirteenth."

Gero looked up in shock.

D'Our waved his hand reassuringly. "Which doesn't necessarily mean that our fate is sealed. Molay knows about this, but he believes in the salvation of the Order through the Almighty, even if at the eleventh hour. Therefore, I am neither authorized to undertake anything that would put the members of the Order on alert, nor am I allowed to give the order to flee."

"What does this all mean?" Gero felt his knees go weak.

"Have you ever heard of the High Council?"

"Of course." Gero was beginning to question what other outrageous secrets the simple Commander of Bar-sur-Aube knew. Among the ordinary knights hardly anyone knew anything about the High Council of the Templars. Some joked that it was so secret it probably didn't even exist.

"As far as I know, the council is made up of the most trustworthy of all our Brothers." Gero hesitated when d'Our didn't react immediately. "Chosen by a special codex. No one knows if these faceless figures really exist. They say they advise the Grand Master in all critical affairs of the Order, and they supposedly have visionary powers, although I don't know anyone who has ever met any of them."

"One of them stands before you," d'Our said plainly.

"You?" Gero looked at his commander, and then quickly corrected himself. "Not that I don't think you're worthy enough … "

D'Our smiled faintly. "The selection isn't based on rank. One is chosen for his abilities, and appointed to an unassuming post as a cover."

Gero nodded absently as he pondered who else could belong to the inner circle without anyone having even the faintest idea.

"Are you acquainted with the term Head of Wisdom?"

"Head of Wisdom? Do you mean the infamous Head of Baphomet?" Gero asked hesitantly.

"Baphomet originated from the desire for dangerous half-truths. Higher members of the Order couldn't keep their oaths of secrecy, and boasted about something they themselves had never set sight on." D'Our's expression darkened abruptly and he snorted scornfully. "Unfortunately, it was precisely one of these false replicas of Baphomet that set King Philipp on our path."

"What do you mean?"

"Philipp IV has long believed that all our wisdom springs from a secret magic."

"Is this head holy?" Gero asked haltingly, nursing the vague fear that d'Our would scoff at his ignorance.

Of course, Gero was familiar with all religious teachings of the Orient and Occident. He had read the secret Bible of the Cathari, who were almost completely destroyed in two merciless Crusades for their belief that the Old Testament described the maker of an evil world. And he knew of the *Sefer Yetzirah*, a collection of ancient Hebrew texts in which the secret of how the world is ordered was set forth in numbers and letters. Under strict secrecy he had translated the text into Latin for the commandery's scriptorium – a dangerous undertaking, as the Christian leadership frowned upon anyone who concerned himself with the secret knowledge of the Jews. But until now, he had not seen any evidence to support these fascinating insights.

"No," d'Our chuckled. "Like everything else, it exists within the knowledge of the Almighty. But when it comes to its power, you might suspect it to be an invention of the Antichrist, although it has always served us well."

"What do you mean?" Gero eyed his commander warily.

"Let's not get lost in details. Besides, I'm not allowed to tell you anything beyond what is necessary. Make no mistake, the head has prophesized the destruction of our Order, but it can also help save us. But before we make use of it, we must be sure that the prophecy holds true."

"What do we do now?" Gero felt his composure slipping. He was incensed and searching desperately for an answer that would repair his ruined view of the world.

"Against the will of the Grand Master, the High Council has decided that, without informing their current inhabitants, we should evacuate all commanderies except the fortresses in Paris and Troyes, where the Grand Master currently resides."

Gero looked up, astonished. "How would *that* happen?"

"As much as possible, the knights of the surrounding commanderies will be called on to perform duties that will allow them to return home only after midnight. Should an attack from Philipp's soldiers occur before then, they still stand a chance to escape on their way back. We will take the squires to Clairvaux, with the exception of Matthäus who will ride with you. The servants will remain here so we don't arouse any unnecessary suspicions. We can only hope that Philipp has only the immediate members of the Order in his sight. And now, we come to your actual task."

D'Our took a deep breath and looked at Gero solemnly. "In the event of the High Council's fears holding true, you will proceed promptly to the German lands. Brothers Johan van Elk and Struan MacDhughaill will accompany you, along with the rest of your chosen men. You will deliver Matthäus to safety with the Cistercians in Hemmenrode. I am his only living relative, and it would be too costly a bargain if King Philipp were to capture my nephew."

Before d'Our continued, he drank another hasty gulp of wine, then set the cup aside and reached for a map that lay on a stool beside him. Deftly, he unrolled the stunningly detailed map.

"Along with the two Brothers, you will cross the Rhine and head to the Cistercian Abbey of Heisterbach. I know from your father that you are familiar with the area. Johannes of Heisterbach is Abbot there. After you give him the password – *computatrum quantum* – he will lead you to a middle man who is stationed at the Abbey and who is also a secret brother of the High Council of the Templars," d'Our explained. "Like myself he has been initiated. Afterwards, you will lead only this brother to a hidden chamber under the refectory. Across the adjoining vaulted cellar, you will arrive at an iron door that leads to the sewer. Open it and take twelve steps east. There, the path makes a slight bend facing northeast. Take twelve more steps, and you will find yourselves directly under the cloister graveyard. Turn right, and between the bricks in the wall, you will find a small depression plastered with clay. Break it open and seize the lever that lies under it. With this, you can open a secret door. Behind it is the chamber in which the Head of Wisdom lies hidden."

"I know the path," Gero said softly. "It serves the Brothers as an escape route. When the monks commit a transgression, they have to scrub the drain as punishment. Eight latrine holes lead the excrement directly into it." His face revealed how unlikely he found it that a holy treasure, of all things, would be hidden in that stinking drain.

"When you arrive there," d'Our continued unfazed, "give this middleman another password. Chant the first verse of the second antiphon of 'God's Greatness and Goodness' – *Laudabo Deum meum in vita mea* … am I going too fast for you?"

Too stunned to speak, Gero merely shook his head.

"You will tell Brother Struan and Brother Johan only as much as seems necessary to you. It suffices for them to know they must accompany you to the German lands. They – like you – will learn everything else from a member of the High Council when you are there."

"What happens if the attack on the Order doesn't happen at all?" Gero was visibly confused.

"Then our Grand Master would have been proven right, and the storm will pass right by us," d'Our remarked with a fatalistic undertone in his voice. "Naturally, everything will remain as it is now. You will not flee, and our conversation today never took place. You may not tell anyone the details before we know which path we will have to take. As you know, spies are swarming throughout the kingdom. We cannot allow Philipp to discover the source of our knowledge."

"If we really are attacked, would we be followed out of France?"

"That won't happen," d'Our responded confidently. "They will leave our settlements in the German lands alone for now. You won't be caught in France, I'm sure, but still, you must be on guard."

Gero nodded stiffly. Although he could not grasp the entirety of it, he ultimately had to accept orders whether or not he understood their significance.

"One more thing," d'Our said. "From now on, I would like all knights to take their proofs of origin with them whenever they leave the commandery. Relay that to your Brothers."

The commander rose. "The Holy Virgin shall watch over you, Brother Gerard."

"And over you, Sire." Gero's voice was barely a whisper as he stood up. He felt dizzy, and had to swallow as he looked into his commander's sharp eyes. "What will become of you, Sire?"

"Don't worry about me," replied d'Our, clapping him on the shoulder. "You are my guarantor that I have done all I can to save the Order. I know I can count on you.

"Remember, if the fair Philipp gets what he wants, not just the Order will be in danger. Humanity is at stake. The downfall of our Order would cost the lives of millions, and bring war, hunger, and damnation to the Christian world for hundreds of years to come."

CHAPTER 2

Fin Amor

Wednesday, October 11, 1307, evening

Feeling as if hell itself had spat him straight out onto the stair landing, Gero once again found himself outside in front of the building.

His commander's words had shaken him to his core, but he knew he had to keep a cool head. He steadied himself against the walls for a moment before descending the precisely carved steps.

Gero went straight to the dormitory. Situated opposite the main building, it was a long communal structure that housed the knights' sleeping and living quarters. Once he arrived, he stripped off his cloak, sword, knife-belt and chain mail before collapsing on one of the twelve beech wood beds. The other young men had already dispersed to their respective bunks. Boots and chain mail lay scattered on the polished wooden planks.

Another group of men in white cloaks entered the dormitory.

"Open the window," one of the new arrivals called out.

Stephano de Sapin, a tall, lanky man with an elegant gait, wrinkled his nose. He threw a disapproving glare at the mess of damp, unwashed felt socks laid out to dry on a wooden partition.

As Gero sat up to remove his boots, his eyes fell on Johan van Elk, swearing under his breath as he stumbled over someone's stray chain mail at the door. Like Gero, the red-haired Brother was from the German lands, and was the youngest offspring of a family of counts from the Lower Rhine. Horrific burns distorted his once handsome face. Otherwise, the Brother was tall and athletic as the rest, and only his clumsy movements revealed his true age of barely twenty.

"Jo!" Gero called to him in German. "There you are! Finally!"

The redhead turned his attention to Gero, walking towards him before grinning and clapping him on the shoulder companionably.

"What's bothering you?" he asked. "You look pale."

Gero didn't answer immediately. Whenever he looked at Johan, he was reminded of how swiftly the course of one's destiny could be altered.

Shortly after his acceptance into the Order, the young Brother had stumbled under a machicolation in the forest of Clairvaux. Gero would never forget the bloodcurdling screams of his Brother as the sudden cascade of hot tar entered the eye slits of his helmet and spread over his cheeks and ears. Without hesitation, Gero had grabbed Johan and yanked the helmet along with the hood from his head, dragged the wounded knight to a nearby stream, and plunged him headfirst into the cold water. Only Gero's quick response had allowed the deep burns to cool and saved Johan's life.

"If only I had it as easy as you, and could spend half the day in the scriptorium," Gero replied with a half-hearted smile, "maybe I would be feeling better."

Before Johan could reply, Francesco de Salazar, the dark-haired flag bearer, jumped in.

"How about you repeat whatever you just said in French, Brother Gerard? In case you've forgotten, that's the official language here," the handsome, bronzed Spaniard chided.

"Francesco de Salazar, why don't you lose your Spanish farmer's accent first," Johan retorted in fluent Catalan, making sure to roll his *r*'s with particular relish, "before you dictate how other people should speak to each other?"

The knights within earshot who had understood Johan's riposte laughed in amusement.

Francesco, whose forefathers were counts from the Kingdom of Navarra, drew himself to his full height. "Johan van Elk, do you think I will excuse your insolence just because your mother is a Catalan?"

He circled round Gero's bed and tapped Brother Johan's head sturdily. In a flash, a playful skirmish between the two young knights was underway.

Gero felt a sudden stab in his gut. None of his Brothers had the faintest clue what grisly fate awaited them.

The Brothers were beginning to prepare themselves for the remaining hours of the evening, leaving the dormitory equipped with brushes and linen cloths to wash away the day's grime in the washhouse. Gero looked around.

"Has anyone seen Stru?" he yelled above the din.

"Have any of you seen the lousy Scot?" repeated a pale, blond lad spitefully.

It was Guy de Gislingham, an English Brother who was new to the commandery. And, as far as Gero knew, he was not planning to stay there for much longer either. He was the son of an influential English nobleman, and was in Bar-sur-Aube to further his studies in French and expand his knowledge of the Templars' martial arts in their country of origin. Thereafter, he would head back to his homeland.

According to his own declarations, though, he still intended to take on a high post in the English branch of the Order. His family obviously had enough money, and, because of this, he could rise effortlessly to heights that poorer knights from the lower nobility could only dream of.

Despite his brief stay in the commandery, Gero was not the only knight to question why the arrogant youth hadn't remained in the Order's headquarters in Paris, where his self-importance would have been better received.

"Considering that you want to become a Templar, you have a remarkable lack of discipline, Brother Guy," Gero said with an irritated undertone in his voice.

Struan MacDhughaill nan t-Eilean Ileach was not just Gero's Brother in the Order, but also his best friend. Stru had saved his life five years previously on the island fortress of Antarados in the Syrian sea, shielding him from the lethal blows of the attacking Mamluks. Under a rain of arrows from their assailants, he had carried an unconscious and badly wounded Gero onto a fishing vessel. When Gero finally awoke on the swaying planks of the ship on its the way to Cyprus, the few survivors told him whom he had to thank for his life. Struan had stopped the bleeding from Gero's lacerated shoulder blade with a bandage, and, throughout the journey, shared his meager water rations with him to bring down his fever.

Four months after their arrival in Cyprus, Gero had recovered so well that he and his savior were ordered to join a substitute battalion in France in the spring of 1303. Both knew they were lucky to be assigned to the local commandery together.

Guy de Gislingham knew this story, but it failed to impress him. To him, all Scots were loathsome, and a Scottish hero was unimaginable.

"Everyone in my homeland knows the Scots think washing is unnecessary," he drawled. "They dwell in their damp, windowless stone barracks like savages, always burning peat fires in their hovels until they're as smoked as eels …"

Gislingham's remarks received no agreement. Instead, most of the other men looked at the floor in embarrassment, or busied themselves with other tasks, emboldening the Englishman to go one step further.

"If you don't believe me, Brother Gero, go there yourself. I can't imagine such repulsive conditions exist in the House of Breydenbach." Guy shot Gero an incendiary look, danger flashing in his blue eyes.

"Leave my home out of it, and Struan's, too," Gero hissed furiously. "Let me remind you, in case your arrogance has clouded your mind, we are all equals here, Brother."

Guy shrugged his shoulders and turned away, visibly bored. He punctuated his disinterest by resuming his meticulous cleaning of his chain mail.

"Struan reported that he is sick," Francesco called out, hoping to ease the tension.

Gero raised his eyebrows quizzically.

Guy de Gislingham paused and turned back slowly. His eyes darted over those present. "The lad's been sick for quite a while. He's probably caught a stubborn ailment, the poor thing."

A snide grin slid over his features, which were decidedly less noble than his lineage. He looked from Gero to Johan.

"Perhaps we should ask Father Augustinus if these are the symptoms of the illness he's always warning us of."

Guy's ugly snigger finally made Gero snap. With two mighty strides, he reached the English Brother's bed. His iron fist seized Guy's linen shirt and twisted it into a knot as he pulled the obnoxious Brother to his feet. His glare was murderous.

Guy de Gislingham, a head shorter than Gero, wheezed as his face flushed red and swelled under the pressure. He struggled to loosen Gero's grip with both hands, but he could only stare at the muscles flexing in his opponent's strong arms. He did not have enough air to scream and had the Brothers not feared that Gero would kill him and end up on the gallows, no one might have helped him.

All of a sudden, Gero felt several strong arms tearing him away, and heard Johan van Elk soothing him in German. "Brother, let him go … you'll only get yourself in trouble, and us as well … please!"

With a jerk, Gero shoved the wheezing man to the ground. His nostrils flared. He was tempted to spit at Brother Guy, who was still gasping for air. Abruptly, he turned away and went back to his bunk. Johan lingered for a moment longer, looking down in loathing at the dazed Englishman.

"*Arschloch!*" he spat in German. As Gislingham stared blankly at him, Johan bent down and spelled out the word in English, emphasizing every letter.

"A-s-s-h-o-l-e!"

Then he drew himself up again and left the stunned Brother Guy alone.

Guy crawled laboriously to his bed like a beetle that had lain too long on its back. He massaged his neck as his narrow, hate-filled eyes followed Gero, who stood nearby, not caring to dignify the Englishman with a single glance.

The remaining Brothers observed Gero folding the clothes on his bed nonchalantly as if nothing had happened.

Through the open window, the bells rang, calling the Brothers to their vesper prayers. Gero swiftly pulled on his house habit and looked round at his German Brother, who was already standing next to him.

"Are you coming to vespers?"

Johan nodded.

"I have to recruit a few Brothers for a mission on behalf of the Commander, and you and Struan are coming with me," Gero continued. "After the vesper meal, we will hold a short discussion in the scriptorium."

As the two were leaving the building, someone laid a hand on Gero's shoulder. Gero turned around and found himself face to face with Guy de Gislingham.

"Gisli. It seems you're not satisfied with simply surviving." Gero swept away Gislingham's arm as if ridding himself of a bothersome insect.

Devilish glee flooded Gislingham's voice. "Breydenbach, your Scottish friend is done for, whether you like it or not. I have evidence. By next Sunday, he will bring the noose upon himself. Then he will lose his cloak. And that won't be the only thing he loses, if the rules are followed."

"What on earth are you talking about, you fool?" Gero spat.

Gislingham grinned. "It's come to my attention that your precious friend has given a willing maiden not just his heart, but also the most impressive part of his body ... and I'm not talking about his huge nose." He broke out in laughter.

Gero turned to face Gislingham's foul breath. His muscles tensed in his left forearm, and the fingers of his left hand formed a tight fist as if by their own will.

But before he could knock out all of Brother Guy's remaining teeth, Johan grabbed Gero's habit and dragged him toward the chapel.

The large, pale sandstone building, with its north-facing apsis, was located just outside the commandery. Gero, Johan, and a few other comrades slipped through a nondescript wooden door with iron fittings that afforded the residents a direct path from the inner courtyard to the house of worship. Its main entrance on the western side was only opened on important holidays, when the residents of the nearby city of Bar-sur-Aube were invited to a common mass.

The holy building, still rather new, was an engineering masterpiece. The precise calculations of its construction were reflected in the intricate ceiling of colorfully painted, pointed arches and precisely laid keystones, each chiseled with the Order's cross. The roof was covered with carefully cut wooden shingles, and the six Gothic church windows consisted entirely of ornate painted glass. Above the western side, a magnificent rosette sat enthroned. The last rays of the afternoon sun shone through its colorful circular panes, casting shimmering patterns on the altar stone. Silently, Gero watched the points of rainbow light drift like petals around the base of an impressively large Madonna statue.

The candles in the heavy iron chandelier that hung over the altar on a long chain cast a dim glow on the men who had assembled in a semicircle. The pleasant scent of melting beeswax mingled with the smoldering incense. In turn, the Brothers began to sing, repeating the Latin text in rhythm. Gero listened raptly to his neighbor's sonorous voice as it lulled him into a state of almost mystical calm, and his troubles escaped him for a fleeting moment.

As the Brothers left the chapel, Gero lingered before a smaller altar embedded in the masonry next to the entrance hall. With his head bowed, he made the sign of the cross before a plain wooden cross. First, an Our Father had to be offered in repentance. His slip in the dormitory demanded an indulgence, which Gero could only hope to gain after a hundred and twenty Lord's Prayers. But he had no time for that. Although his appetite had left him after his conversation with d'Our, the evening vesper meal waited in the refectory, and he could not miss it without the Commander's permission.

Gero's fiery temperament had already cost him many a night of penitence on the cold stone floor of the chapel, lying on his belly, stretched out like Jesus on the cross. He had long reconciled himself with the fact that he possessed the battle-readiness of a warrior far more than the gentleness of a monk. As a Templar knight, he should ideally unite the two aspects. But his powerful build and stature alone were a hindrance. His large hands and sinewy arms were made for swordsmanship, and wielded the sword his father had received upon his knighthood with ease, as if it were a stick instead of a six-pound weapon.

With a creak, Gero opened the small door to the courtyard, where Johan was already waiting for him. Gradually, dusk had fallen, and scurrying servants were lighting the torches and fire pits everywhere around them.

The bells rang for the twelfth hour of the day from the nearby city church of St. Pierre, and the scent of oven-warm bread wafted over from the bakery.

Gero stopped in his tracks and caught Johan's arm.

"Thank you," Gero said softly.

"What for?" Johan looked at him, surprised.

"For saving me from doing something stupid for the second time today."

"No problem," Johan responded, then gestured to the half-open courtyard gate. "Look who's coming."

In the light of the burning torches, Gero observed Struan leading his mighty Frisian, black as night, with quick steps to the stalls. The Scottish knight put two fingers to his lips and let out a loud whistle, giving the signal to several lads loitering about to take the animal from him and unharness it.

The evening wind fluttered Struan's knee-length Templar cloak, and even in the twilight, the red cross pattée glowed on his white surcoat.

"There's Struan," Johan said, nodding toward the towering figure.

Gero wondered why his friend was returning so late, and why he had been on the road alone. Struan's clothing – chain mail, leather riding pants, and his scabbard and knife-belt – suggested that he was returning from an external mission.

As a rule, Templar knights rode at least in pairs when they were on a mission, unless it involved a personal concern and the commander had given his explicit permission to leave the commandery unaccompanied for this purpose.

But what did Struan have to settle personally? His relatives never came to visit, and as far as Gero knew, he had no friends who lived outside the commandery. Neither was he sick, despite Guy de Gislingham's claims otherwise.

"I'm going to go greet him quickly," Gero explained to Johan with an apologetic look. "Then I'll be right behind you."

With his head lowered, Struan proceeded to the dormitory. Gero was puzzled. Why was the perpetually hungry Scot ignoring the call for the vesper meal?

Gero had almost caught up with Struan when the Scotsman noticed his footsteps. He stopped and turned around in surprise. He did not seem particularly happy to see Gero. His smile was tired, and he performed the typical Templar crossed handshake only half-heartedly.

Gero sensed that something was troubling Struan but wanted to give the man the chance to bring it up himself, before he began questioning him.

"I missed you during our mission to Thors," Gero remarked simply. "Did our Commander call you up for a special mission again?"

Struan hesitated before he replied, avoiding Gero's questioning gaze. "I was with the eremite at the top of Fire Peak. I had a medicine prepared for me." He paused and rubbed his nose, staring resolutely at the ground. "I haven't been feeling well for a long time. The Commander knows."

"Uh huh."

Gero couldn't help but question why Struan had emphasized that Henri d'Our knew about it. When a knight succumbed to an illness, he first had to report it to the commander. Oddly enough, Struan had never mentioned his ailment. Till now, the Scotsman had been in the peak of health. And as far as Gero could remember, no Brother had ever sought the help of the eremite for anything short of a life-threatening illness. Despite his indisputable healing skills, the methods of the eccentric Templar veteran were better suited for old men on their deathbeds after a lifetime of combat in the Outremer, now fighting their last battles in desperation.

Gero looked at his friend inquiringly.

Struan turned away silently and continued on his way to the dormitory. Determined to weasel out a halfway-satisfactory answer from his reticent friend, Gero held onto the sleeve of Struan's chain mail.

Struan wrested himself free from Gero. "What is it?" he snapped.

Gero refused to be discouraged. "Does the eremite happen to have long, golden hair, doe eyes, and be the daughter of our wine merchant by any chance?"

Struan remained silent, but his light brown face turned dark red.

"I thought so."

Struan sighed tellingly and ran his large hand over his face as if to scour any suspicious evidence from it. He stared into the dark evening sky, seeking an explanation for his deeds.

"Why didn't you confide in me?" Gero's question was spiked with accusation.

Struan pressed his lips together and cleared his throat sheepishly. "Do you doubt our friendship because I didn't tell you about it?"

"You idiot," Gero chided him gently. "Do you think I didn't notice what was going on? I saw her making eyes at you the first time. Since then, I've been asking myself if any good could come of it."

Gero didn't think Struan was the sort of men who fell for just any woman without rhyme or reason. Amelie Bratac was not just a pretty face, although she was blessed with such an ethereal beauty that adhering to certain Order regulations could easily become torture for a Templar. Her father, the wine and ceramic merchant Alphonse Bratac, was a close associate of the Order, and Amelie assisted him with bookkeeping and deliveries. In contrast to the uneducated maidens of her class, she was well versed in reading, writing, and numeracy.

"Are you going to turn me in?" Struan's usually gravelly voice now sounded even more hoarse than usual.

"How could you even think such a thing?" Gero countered indignantly.

Struan swallowed hard. When he looked at Gero, his dark eyes were filled with uncertainty and anguish.

"It definitely wouldn't be a good time for your indiscretion to be exposed," Gero continued. "The Pope and King have been accusing the Templars of having loose morals, and the Order's leaders would hardly be overjoyed if they were proven right. It could cost you your cloak."

A tight chuckle escaped Struan's throat. "That's my least pressing problem at the moment."

Gero shifted closer to Struan and laid a hand on his shoulder confidently. "There's nothing that can't be solved."

"Not here," Struan hissed, running his fingers nervously through his short black hair.

His eyes darted around; making sure no one was hiding in the darkness. Then he turned and headed toward the washrooms. Without a word, Gero followed him.

Struan ducked his head into a low but wide passageway and hurried forward. A beam of light from an outside torch streamed in through an open window, guiding Gero as he followed his friend down the passageway.

Finally, they sat down on the edge of a stone vat. Gero looked expectantly at Struan, who had his hands in his lap and his eyes fixed on a nearby fireplace filled with embers.

At last he cleared his throat, although his voice remained hoarse. "She's expecting a child."

Seconds passed before he looked up at Gero again, shrugging his shoulders in defeat. There was no point in hiding or softening the news.

Gero's eyes widened in shock. "A child? From you?"

"Why else would I have mentioned it, you idiot?" Struan retorted slumping down in resignation.

"How could something like that happen?" Gero asked when he had regained his composure.

"How indeed?" Struan grunted. He scratched himself behind the ear and laughed peevishly. "Just look at her! She has the most magnificent backside, and breasts like ripe peaches. And she has absolutely no shyness in revealing them to me."

"Stru, if you want a woman so badly, why didn't you just go to the whores in Voigny? They are discrete, and an hour with them doesn't cost more than a fat capon."

The Scotsman's eyes widened in outrage. "You can't compare Amelie to any whore," he insisted. "Her beauty is beyond measure, and besides that, I've seldom met such an intelligent woman."

"So intelligent that she's turned your head completely." Gero pressed his lips together and shot his friend a look of confusion. "To be honest, I'd have taken you to be more sensible than that."

"You can't imagine what it is like to feel her soft body, her gentle kisses … how it feels when she touches me, light as a feather … yet as passionate as a hurricane," said Struan, his voice barely louder than a whisper. He gazed distractedly at an abandoned swallow's nest in the dim light. Then, as if waking from a dream, he turned to his best friend, a defiant resolve in his voice. "To lie with her, I would risk everything, not just my honor."

"Even your cloak?"

"Perhaps," Struan replied and dropped his head remorsefully.

A moment later, he looked up again, his eyes darkening. "Damn it, what on earth should I do? She wants me. Show me a man who could escape from such a woman. He's either not right in the head, or a Sodomite."

"Or a Templar knight keeping his vows …" Gero pointed out.

Struan did not utter a single word, but only nodded and sighed deeply.

"How long has this been going on?"

"Since April," Struan answered softly. "Shortly before we set off for Poitiers, I met her in secret for the first time."

"And how long has she been expecting?"

"Five months."

"Who would have guessed your seed would bear fruit so quickly?" Gero shook his head and laughed softly.

"Do you find this funny?" Struan said, squinting at his friend angrily. "I'm in no mood for jokes. Since I found out, I've been racking my brain for a solution that can keep us together."

For a moment, the eyes of the Scot gleamed. He swallowed hard and cleared his throat. "I have dishonored her, and if I don't think of a practical solution, not just I, but also she and the child, will have to atone for it."

"What are you going to do now?" Gero's harmless-sounding question hid his tension. "Do you want to leave the Order?"

"How can I?" Struan shook his head despondently. "The Grand Master won't grant me the honor of agreeing to my discharge. And if I turn my back on the Order, my father and our clan will have me drawn and quartered and hang pieces of my corpse in all four corners of our castle. I joined the Templars for political reasons. If I run, I need not ever look towards home again. What would we live off of, shunned by all, with nowhere to take shelter?"

29

Struan sighed. "Fin Amor. True, eternal love. Damn it." He stared helplessly at his boots.

Gero nodded in sympathy. "I've never spoken about it, but I've been widowed for six years." Despite his strength and courage, the German knight could not hide the leaden pain that still weighed on him.

"Our marriage was not exactly blessed," he continued. "Elisabeth died with our daughter in childbirth. It was my fault. My father always wanted me to join the Templars, but I had other plans. I chose love – despite my father's disapproval, and he disinherited me."

Gero swallowed hard before soldiering on, his voice faltering. "My father thinks I'm a failure. Not just because I impregnated and married my sweetheart against his will, but also because I made him break his vow."

Struan raised his dark eyebrows in surprise. "Which vow?"

Gero's lips twisted bitterly. "My wife was my parents' Jewish foster daughter. In 1291, during the last chaos of the Battle of Acre, my father took her from the broken corpses of her parents, saving her from the invading Mamluks. He made a promise to the Lord that day. If he and his fellow soldiers succeeded in leaving Acre and the Holy Land, he would take care of the child, and hand her over to a cloister when she was twelve. He wanted to send me to the Templars as soon as I was knighted for the same reason.

"His prayers obviously worked, as they escaped Acre but under the harshest conditions. And not just that; they also helped the then Commander of the Temple of Acre flee – none other than our current Grand Master, Jacques de Molay and his faithful, among them our own esteemed commander."

Struan let out a soft, appreciative whistle. "Indeed! Then you do know how I feel." He looked at Gero and his face inadvertently broke out into a small smile.

"You might be right," Gero replied. "My admission to the Templars after my wife's death was more an escape from my grief and my father's outbursts than an act of conviction or obedience." Gero looked at his Brother earnestly. "But there's something else I have to tell you."

"What else, then?" Struan grumbled. "It can't possibly get any worse."

"I'm afraid it can. Apart from the fact that our dear Brother Guy is on your trail and intends to expose you to the counsel, there may be no counsel meeting next Sunday at all. I talked to the old man in private today."

"Henri d'Our? Does he know what I've done?" Fear shot through Struan's limbs.

"If he did," Gero answered calmly, "he wouldn't be trusting you with the Order's fate."

Struan stared at him blankly. "The Order's fate?"

"Promise me you'll keep quiet," Gero whispered.

Struan raised his eyebrows and nodded. Gero quickly summarized what d'Our had told him, leaving out the Head of Wisdom and the mission in Heisterbach. He resolutely ignored the fact that he was defying his commander's order to remain silent. His friend's plight didn't seem any less hopeless than that of the Order, and Gero saw it as an act of kindness to distract Struan with the far greater worry about all their futures. But the Scotsman was not to be deterred.

"And what shall become of Amelie and me?" Struan looked at him for an answer. "Other catastrophes notwithstanding, the child will be born in four months."

"Keep quiet," Gero advised him. "Let us wait and see what happens tomorrow, and find a solution after that."

Struan rose and turned to his Brother, who had stood up as well. He hugged Gero tightly, and then kissed him on the lips.

"It's good to have a friend like you," he said hoarsely. "Whatever happens, you'll always be a part of me."

As Gero crossed the desolate courtyard with Struan, he felt a chill spread through his body. Mercilessly, it ran through his guts, crept up his back with demonic slowness, and seized possession of his thoughts. A feeling was flooding over him that he hated above all others: fear.

All at once the dancing shadows in the cloister appeared to him like devils grinning in the face of death and damnation.

Struan was obviously not feeling any better as he silently followed Gero into the dormitory. The air was stifling. It had cooled down noticeably outside, and, in order to keep out the cold, someone had shut the windows and rolled down the goat-leather window shades.

"Where have you guys been?" Johan asked, looking puzzled. "Everyone noticed your absence at the vesper meal."

He looked around furtively, but in the general confusion, no one noticed him. Grinning, he produced a piece of cheese and two crusts of bread from under his jerkin.

"Here, for the two of you," he said, slipping Struan the food.

The always-hungry Scotsman, however, did not seem particularly pleased. Gero himself ignored the friendly offering, merely clearing his throat and straightening his shoulders.

"Men, may I have your attention, please," he yelled authoritatively.

At this, the bustle died down abruptly as everyone, even Brother Guy, stopped and looked at him.

"The commander has given me the order for a mission. For six of us, this means that we ride out tomorrow afternoon. The following men whose names I call are therefore free from the remaining liturgy of the hours."

Gero scrutinized the faces in the room. Twenty-four pairs of eyes were fixed on him. A stray cough was the only sound to be heard.

"Sergeants, you can rest at ease. This only concerns the Order knights." Beds creaked and blankets rustled as a few of the men returned to their bunks in relief. Gero looked at every one of the chosen few before he called their names.

"Johan van Elk … Francesco de Salazar, Stephano de Sapin, Arnaud de Mirepaux … and Struan MacDhughaill." He continued, "We will meet promptly for a short discussion in the scriptorium. The rest of you can proceed to bed."

"Ah … Arnaud," Gero called to a wiry, dark-haired Brother, whose clipped but unkempt beard lent him an air that better suited a thief than a knight. "Make sure the distribution of weapons takes place at noon tomorrow as quickly as possible, and that the lists are complete so we won't have to waste any time with paperwork afterwards. Besides axes and maces, we will take with us two crossbows and sufficient bolts."

Arnaud nodded. In the day-to-day running of the commandery, he was in charge of the sergeants responsible for the storage and distribution of weapons. Besides that, he wielded the crossbow particularly skillfully, and Gero could see no reason not to bring him along for the mission. For Arnaud, that meant that he would bear much of the responsibility for the mission's preparations. With the litheness of a cat, he weaved through the beds standing in his way and proceeded silently outside.

The other participants of the mission, some of whom had already settled into bed, threw on their Order habits and slipped into the soft, plain leather shoes that were worn within the commandery.

Gero waited until the last of them was ready. None of the other men not selected for the mission seemed to have any objections or questions.

Except one.

Guy de Gislingham rose from his bunk and glared at Gero with loathing. "You might have your reasons, Brother Gero, why you didn't choose me for this mission," he hissed. "But you can be sure that this will not end in your favor. I will take advantage of your absence – you can count on that."

Most of the Brothers looked up in anticipation of Gero's response but he had resolved not to dignify the Englishman with any further attention. Under the shadow of the catastrophe hanging over the entire Order, the offensive conduct of a single Brother was as insignificant as a single drop of water in an impending flood.

Gero gave the signal to depart, leaving Brother Guy behind with his face contorted in scorn. The chosen men followed Gero, walking silently together across the courtyard toward the main building.

In the dim light of the torches in front of the scriptorium, knights and servants carried crates and sacks out from the barred and guarded storeroom, loading them onto a covered wagon stationed directly next to it. Almost noiselessly, the men attended to their tasks.

Johan coughed tentatively. As Gero turned to him, he could not hold back his question.

"Can you tell me what's happening here?"

"Later. The matter is relatively sensitive," Gero whispered. "I will try to tell you as much as I can, but understand that I cannot disclose everything."

Johan nodded his understanding and asked no further questions. He could imagine what Gero was going through. As a commanding officer, he himself was often caught in a quandary where he could not inform his battle comrades of the reasons for a mission.

Struan, who followed behind Johan, remained silent, when they went into the scriptorium. He was far too busy brooding over Gero's words about the Order's fate, and what impact this revelation could have on his own future.

Quickly, a few pine torches were ignited, and the men assembled between the closely packed desks. Gero described the march to the Forest of the Orient without venturing into background information.

"Francesco, it is your duty to instruct the squires," Gero continued with feigned calmness, "to bridle the horses punctually. The Commander wants the warhorses to be saddled. His nephew will accompany us. Matthäus will take care of the pack horses."

The Spaniard, who was responsible for the squires' education and the flag-bearer for the mission, raised his eyebrows quizzically. He had already found it strange that earlier that day d'Our had called for him, and, without further explanation, had given him the order to send the sergeants and the squires to Clairvaux for the following evening and the subsequent night. Why Matthäus, one of the youngest boys, and d'Our's nephew at that, was to follow the knights was equally puzzling to him. Still, it did not cross his mind to question his superior.

"We will set off after None. Our commander wants each of you to take your proof of origin with you," Gero explained.

While the men had been meeting in the scriptorium, a light rain had begun to fall in the courtyard. When the men walked outside again, most of the torches had been extinguished.

Gero was glad no one could see his face. He wouldn't have been able to keep up the act much longer and he cursed his oath of silence. A profound despondency seized him; far more dangerous than any battle he had ever fought. The thought that the Order would be defeated by King Philipp's lust for power twisted his guts so viciously that he let out a gasp.

Johan was at his side immediately. "Are you not feeling well?"

They had stopped in the middle of the dark courtyard. Save for Struan, the others had already disappeared into the dormitory.

"It's nothing," Gero mumbled, breathing heavily and holding his stomach. "I just haven't eaten much today."

"You can fool Gislingham with that, but not me," Johan retorted adamantly. "I've promised not to pester you for details, but I'm worried. Everyone can tell that something is not right."

Gero struggled to straighten himself. Struan moved to help him, but Gero shrugged off his arm impatiently. His eyes fixed forward, he walked on stiffly.

Johan gave Struan a bewildered look, but the Scotsman kept quiet.

Shortly before the entrance to the dormitory, Gero turned around suddenly. He touched Struan's shoulder and nodded toward Johan.

"I'm going to tell him about it. Inform the others we'll come along soon."

"As you like," Struan replied softly and continued on his way, wishing only to stretch out on his bed and shut his eyes.

In furtive whispers, Gero relayed the mission's actual purpose to his countryman.

Johan's eyes widened in disbelief, and he let out a soft whistle. "By all the saints, who would have thought such a thing? And now?"

"I have no idea," Gero replied with a sigh. "Even d'Our doesn't seem to know what to make of it all. Obviously, no one knows what will happen to us."

"But there must be some weight to it. Or we wouldn't be transporting everything in our vaults to the Forest of the Orient, would we?"

"No, of course not," Gero insisted with utter conviction. "Apparently the command comes straight from the top."

"I only question *who* or *what* is at the top," Johan remarked. He was not the only Templar who had begun to doubt the Grand Master Jacques de Molay's ability to give clear orders.

"As always," Gero said resignedly, "we can only hope, and pray. Everything else is futile."

Together, they went into the dormitory where, amid loud conversations, the remaining Brothers were already preparing themselves for sleep.

Gero sat on his bed and took off his shoes and white habit. As an Order rule, the men had to sleep in their undergarments in dimmed light so as to be ready for action in the event of an attack.

Before he stretched his aching limbs out on the soft mattress, he threw the double gray-brown woolen blankets to the side and adjusted the down-filled pillows. Covering himself with the blankets, he felt as if he were under a protective shield.

A moment later, however, his peace was once again disturbed.

"Hey, Gero, your face sure looks like you're being crucified." Gianfranco da Silva, an emaciated sergeant from Lombardy, nudged him cheerfully from the side. "Did a flea hop into your bed?"

"Leave me alone. I'm tired, and we have a long day ahead of us," Gero replied grumpily.

"Hey, Breydenbach, I have something that will cheer you up," Gianfranco whispered, nudging him again. With a grin, he held a small, unfolded piece of parchment under Gero's nose. The extravagantly detailed quill drawing depicted a naked man and woman oddly entwined. Each had their head in between the other's thighs and was pleasuring their partner with their mouths.

"Gian, put that trash away!" Gero growled and rolled onto his side, pulling the blankets up to the tip of his nose to hide his sadness and fear from Gianfranco.

"Oh, pardon me for speaking to you without permission, Sire!" Gianfranco exclaimed in mock deference. He shook his head in bewilderment.

Gero closed his eyes. With relief he noticed that the bustle about him was gradually fading, until only a stray murmur or whisper could be heard.

At last he fell into a restless sleep. Throughout the night, he was haunted by a strange nightmare. Bloodthirsty rats nipped at his heels as he ran for his life. He clung to Matthäus's hand and ran with him across a clearing to get him to safety. Suddenly, an eerie, blue-green light surrounded them and pulled them into darkness. A woman appeared before him, beautiful as the Virgin Mary herself. With her long, chestnut hair and fine features, she looked uncannily like his beloved Elisabeth. She was dead, that he knew, and yet there she was, smiling at him. *So this is what happens when you die*, was his last thought.

Bathed in sweat, Gero woke up. An unceremonious jab in his side pulled him back to reality.

"Get up," whispered Johan van Elk, gently admonishing him. "The night is over."

CHAPTER 3

Forest of the Orient

Thursday, October 12, 1307, afternoon

At None, the ninth hour of the day, the knights of Bar-sur-Aube assembled for prayer in the small chapel. Having everyone present was an extremely rare occurrence. They bowed their heads in deference to Mother Mary as the chaplain said the concluding prayer and let them out into the blazing afternoon sun without the usual final blessings. The Brothers crossed the inner courtyard in silence. A fresh wind blew over the swollen rain clouds that covered the nearby buildings in erratic dances of light and shadow.

Saddled and loaded, the horses stood before the stalls. Most were powerful stallions from the Order's breeding stables.

The wagon had already been set up before the gate, its precious load hidden under a thick layer of grain sacks. The driver, a trustworthy old man who had been working for the Order for decades, sat on his bench seat with a warm blanket around his shoulders, eating a hunk of dry bread while he waited.

Back at his bunk, Gero opened the chest he shared with Johan van Elk. One by one, he retrieved the prescribed field clothes: a quilted undervest; knee-length, hooded chain mail; the white surcoat with the red cross on the breast; and a pair of leather riding pants. As he slipped on a new pair of felt socks and pulled on his rugged riding boots, he suddenly remembered his neck pouch containing his proof of origin and book of heraldry.

Johan sat half-dressed on the bed across from him while Gero searched through his half of the chest.

"What are you missing?" he asked, scratching the back of his neck and yawning.

"My family register and my certificate of admission ... which d'Our told us to bring along."

"I almost forgot," Johan mumbled, heaving himself up from his mattress with considerable effort. He watched his comrade busy himself.

The gap between their beds did not allow the two broad-shouldered men to search through the chest at the same time.

Gero laid aside another shirt then dug out a scuffed leather bag and his neck pouch from under the pile of clothes. If the prophecy came true, Gero still had something to conceal from his attackers. It was his most private and treasured possession: a signet ring his father had given to him on his seventeenth birthday. The ring, which he was not allowed to wear in the Order, bore the Breydenbach family crest. Engraved in silver were wolf-hooks, a rune which bore the likeness of a thunderbolt, above a blue river, from which two curious fish poked their heads. It was meant for sealing documents and letters in the name of the Breydenbachs. Gingerly, Gero unfastened a leather cord and removed his family register proving his noble birth and a yellowed document confirming his admission to the Order. Hidden with them was another piece of paper, wrapped in linen.

Carefully, he untied the red satin ribbon and unrolled the delicate paper. Among soft green tendrils and glowing red roses stood a poem his dead wife had penned in her childish but spirited handwriting.

Gero smiled wistfully as his eyes ran down the lines:

For Gero, my sun, my moon, my evening star
My heart has wings
If you see a little bird in the sky
Know that it flies to you
My love is a wisp of the wind
When it rustles through your hair
Know that I am with you
My desire is the rain
When the droplets fall upon your face
Know that they are my tears of yearning for you

In eternal love, Elisabeth

Johan craned his neck to see what Gero was reading. "What's that?" he asked curiously.

"Nothing," Gero snapped, hastily stashing the letter among his other documents. He fastened the leather cord of his bag and stowed it away under his vest.

As he entered the courtyard booted and spurred, a faint whinny greeted him from afar. Atlas, his gray Percheron, had a coat of shimmering silk and a back as broad and tall as the shoulders of his namesake. The stallion meant more to Gero than he cared to admit. He patted Atlas on the withers and offered him an apple, which the animal accepted in his velvety lips with a snuffle.

Suddenly, a head of blond curls appeared from under the horse's massive head. It was Matthäus, Gero's squire, who was beaming eagerly at him.

"They let me ride with you! And only me!" he announced, his unbridled excitement making his voice break.

Normally, because he was still too young, Matthäus was not allowed to accompany his lord on missions that could lead to combat. Although he had already begun his training in swordplay and horse riding, he could only be admitted into military service at fourteen.

"The others have set off for the Abbey of Clairvaux," the boy announced. "They're going on a retreat there." He scrunched up his freckled button nose. "A day and a night in continuous prayer. I'm glad they let me come with you."

Gero struggled to smile, but the squire barely noticed that his lord did not share his joy.

As if to cheer himself up, Gero ran his hand over his young companion's blond locks. "So, Mattes, has anyone familiarized you with your task yet?"

"Yes," Matthäus answered solemnly. "I am responsible for the pack horses. They're standing ready for the march in the courtyard. You only have to give the order for departure." He looked up at Gero, proud that his knight was the commanding officer for this mission.

This time, Gero could not hold back a smile. Then he snapped back to attention. "Proceed to your horses, boy. The order to mount will take place shortly!"

"At your command, sir," Matthäus replied seriously.

The commander had issued the order to bring battleaxes, crossbows, and maces, along with the regular swords and knives. In the weapon depot, Gero grabbed a crossbow and forty bolts stored in a small chest. The wax-sealed lock guaranteed the number and integrity of the deadly arrows. Ultimately, every shot had to be tallied.

As Gero was returning to the courtyard, d'Our hurried towards him waving a sealed parchment roll, a small leather-bound booklet, and a few sealed letters.

"The letter for the commander of Thors ..." d'Our announced, gasping for breath, "Matthäus's proof of origin, and a letter for his admission in Hemmenrode, should that be his fate."

Pausing to catch his breath, the old man turned to Gero with a serious look. "Whatever happens, Brother Gerard ... promise me you will handle it calmly."

D'Our handed over the documents as well as a deer-leather pouch filled to the brim with clinking coins, and Gero tucked away both objects in his saddlebag. Without a further word, the commander then turned to Matthäus, who was pulling on the cinches of his small mare behind him. He held out his right hand stiffly to his nephew. The boy bowed in deference and kissed the striking Templar signet ring on his uncle's finger.

Gero could see d'Our wrestling to keep his feelings under control as his waxen face twitched. Gero turned away and quickly checked that all his men were present. The knights stood by their horses. Their weapons and shields were secured to their saddles, as were their medical supplies and provisions. Gero waited a second more until the last man had taken his place, then swung himself onto his saddle and called out, "Mount, Brothers. And ... forward march!"

The men rode swiftly around the neighboring city in a southeastern direction. They proceeded on the main road to Troyes along the Aube, a small river, and after half a mile they made their way straight to Bossancourt. Two hours later, they reached the settlement of Beaulieu.

The commandery was a formidable stone building with compact walls and high, round towers that resembled a castle. The gate to the inner courtyard was already open, and the guards let them pass without objection.

The Commander of Thors, Brother Theobald, stood bathed in the golden afternoon light in the middle of the courtyard, coordinating, with the tranquility of a man who is living in tune with the world around him, the ranks of the delegations that had already arrived. He was a tall and slender man. His features and sinewy arms hinted at a resilience won from years of hardship. In contrast, his brown eyes were kind. His dark hair was so short that his scalp gleamed from underneath. He had a full, curly beard that was streaked with silver. Gero knew the man quite well, and, from the stories of the older Brothers, was all too aware that he was a judicious Order knight whose tactical battle skills had saved the lives of many a man.

"Brother Gero!" Theobald welcomed him with a warm smile and extended his hand in greeting. Gero shook it, returning his smile.

"I'm happy to see you," he said earnestly.

The call of a horn rang out from the courtyard – the signal for all the troops of the different commanderies to begin their march.

While Gero waited for his men to assemble, Brother Theobald informed him of the latest orders.

Gero listened closely, then let his gaze sweep over the courtyard. Fifty Templar knights in their white cloaks dotted the walled courtyard. Many of them belonged to the elite combat troops who had fought countless battles under the commanderies and fortresses of the Order, otherwise known as Ordensburgs. They were the favorites for the most dangerous and confidential missions.

Gero and his Brothers from Bar-sur-Aube belonged to this elite. Last spring, they and a few Brothers from other commanderies escorted the Pope and his followers on a journey from the Provençal Carpentras to Poitiers, protecting the Holy Father from surprise attacks. A meeting with the King had been planned there, to which the Grand Master had also been invited. Now the Pope was repaying their loyalty by forsaking them, Gero thought in resignation. He had already harbored doubts even then that Bertrand de Goth, Pope Clement V's actual name, was the right man for the job.

One morning, to his surprise, he found himself dismissed from the side of the Pope. Without any further clarification the commander, a veteran knight of the Templars' headquarters in Troyes, sent him to guard an ostentatiously decorated coach at the very end of the line.

Its occupant, Brunissende de Foix, was among the regular followers of the Holy Father. There were rumors that the Pope's relationship with the woman, the daughter of a count from the south of Provence, was not just of a spiritual nature. Looking at her, it wasn't hard to believe. Her hair was black as night, her eyes dark and seductive as sin, and her lips were as red and moist as the juice of a bursting pomegranate. Gero followed her fancy carriage the entire day, and, now and again, she would poke her head through the opulent curtains and smile at him.

A mile from the next commandery where they were to spend the night, the carriages came to a standstill as a crowd rushed forth to have their children and cattle blessed by the Pope.

Gero rode past the extravagant wagon to take the measure of the distance to their destination. He stood in his stirrups and peered over the procession, but he couldn't see anything. With a sigh, he fell back onto his saddle and turned his stallion around.

"What's wrong, Brother?" a voice as soft as butter asked, unnervingly close to him.

Gero whirled around in shock. He had thought that Brunissende had finally given up trying to badger him. The dark blue brocade curtains that framed the woman's flawless beauty like a painting couldn't hide her determined expression.

"Why are you so cold? Don't I please you?" she purred.

Gero struggled with himself before reluctantly glancing at her. He lowered his head quickly, avoiding her feline stare.

"Madame, I don't want to be impolite," he replied as calmly as he could, "but you should know that I am a knight of the Order. I am not allowed to look at or talk to a woman who is not my kin."

"Well, that's a pity," she responded, sounding not at all sorry. "You have no idea what you're missing."

Her seductive smile made him uneasy. He was a fearless warrior who had been trained to avoid the swiftest strikes on the battlefield, but he staggered under Brunissende's advances.

He had already made a mistake when, instead of retreating immediately, he had bathed in her fathomless gaze a moment too long.

All at once, the curtains parted further, granting Gero a clear view of her lithe, ivory body, wrapped in only a sheer cloth of silk. Gero had heard that these were the preferred garments of prostitutes in the forbidden bathhouses. Her breasts perched round and firm above her slender ribs. Her rosy nipples were stiff in the cold air.

He could not help but stare as she pleasured herself with her delicate fingers, sliding her middle finger into her slit, her face in obvious rapture. Her mouth curled around the index finger of her other hand, sucking on it like a piece of candy.

Gero held his breath unconsciously and swallowed, deeply embarrassed.

"It is all yours," she whispered with an inviting look. Her hands wandered to her breasts. Her fingers began stroking her pert nipples, caressing the tight buds that were straining against the sheer fabric. "Tonight, you could exchange your modest camp bed for the soft pillows of my wagon. Indulge in the delights of carnal lust with me, sir knight. Don't hesitate! I am inviting you into to paradise."

Gero was filled with indignation. He wanted to turn away, but he was no longer a clueless young boy who simply fled from a woman's temptation. He averted his eyes for just a moment and breathed deeply before he met her gaze again.

"If you think that you can lead me into temptation, Madame, I must regretfully disappoint you," he replied with feigned composure.

Her expression, filled with anticipation just moments before, darkened. With a tug, she pulled the curtains to hide her nakedness and smiled at him mockingly.

"Very well," she hissed, her mouth twisted in bitter accusation. "I hadn't thought the rumors about the Templars were true. Even a seasoned man like you obviously prefers to stick his cock in the ass of a Brother than attend to the charms of a beautiful woman. Who would've thought?"

With a stony glare, he turned away and led his horse behind the wagon. Trying to appear unruffled, he inspected his surroundings. His hands were still shaking, however, when a loud fanfare ordered the procession to move again. In the meantime, Brunissende had disappeared within the velvet blue interior of the wagon, like a spider retreating from its web, lying in wait for its next prey.

In his fantasies, Gero would have strangled her. It would never have occurred to him to sleep with the Pope's consort, and, in any case, the consequences of that act far outweighed the dubious pleasure he would receive from it. If they had been discovered, or worse, if she had claimed that he had taken her by force, he would have been thrown into the dungeons, dishonored, and threatened with death. But she had said something that robbed him of far more sleep that night than her beguiling figure ever could have.

She had named the very thing that unsettled all the Order's knights. For months, rumors had circulated that the Pope had received information about the Order's lack of morals. Brothers whispered that the Grand Master had been summoned to Poitiers because of this very subject. Brunissende de Foix was one of the Pope's closest confidants, and her careless words told Gero that she knew something about the meeting between the country's top dignitaries.

The next day, his superior replaced him with a young Italian knight, once again without explanation. Gero could only guess that the Brother was the new victim of Brunissende's game of seduction.

The perpetually sickly Pope, whom Gero accompanied for the rest of the journey, appeared not to have heard anything of it. When his instructions and wishes were not carried out immediately, he behaved like an impatient child.

Contemplatively, Gero watched the activity in the inner courtyard of the Beaulieu commandery. His experience on the journey to Poitiers had given him the impression that they could not rely on the Pope. Clement V, whose name meant "the mild" or "the gracious", and who claimed to be the Lord's representative, was risking the lives of all these brave knights without batting an eyelid. He was not a holy man; he was simply a greedy coward who would betray even his truest followers to the King in order to preserve his life of luxury.

"Brother …?" Gero gave Theobald a timid, questioning glance.

"Yes?"

"Nothing. Forget it." Gero decided it was foolish to ask Theobald what he thought of the Order's fate and the looming possibility of King Philipp's attack.

Theobald looked him squarely in the eye and squeezed Gero's forearm, smiling at him bravely.

"I'm just as afraid as you are," he said gently. "Just like everyone who knows the true reason for this mission. And the Brothers who don't can already sense something. It is a catastrophe of unbelievable proportions. Not only because the Order's continued existence has been called into question, but also because our solidarity itself has been rattled.

"For over a year, we've been split into a few factions. Those who knew something but were doing nothing about it, although they *could*; those who knew something and were not allowed to do anything about it; and the clueless who thought they knew something but were not allowed to voice their concerns.

"Keeping it all secret is the command of the day in an Order that has always prided itself on honesty and justice, and a determination to defend those virtues to the death."

Brother Theobald shook his head, his mouth contorting into a pained smile. "Believe me, Brother, you are not the only one whose heart feels gripped by an iron fist."

Theobald spun around as if nothing had happened, his face, once again, resuming its composure.

"Take your positions!" he yelled across the courtyard.

Within seconds, the first wagon and riders were moving out of the courtyard gateway.

On a hill surrounded by gorse, Brother Theobald gave the signal to stop. The brush, as tall as the men themselves, provided a strategic shield from enemy eyes.

From this point on, only two knights from each commandery would complete the journey on horseback into the swampy woodland where there were no fixed paths. With the help of all men present, the chests and sacks were loaded onto the horses' cargo racks.

The responsibility of transporting the Order's precious assets to the depot now lay with the remaining twelve men under Brother Theobald's command. Among these assets were the entire pensions of many a respectable merchant and the five commanderies' treasures – holy relics from the Outremer and gem-encrusted communion chalices of extraordinary value. Three craftsmen and two architects familiar with the depot's underground tunnels accompanied the knights.

The rest of the Brothers set up camp on the hill to wait for the return of the others from the forest. Gero bid Matthäus goodbye and warned him not to leave the camp until the troop had returned. Johan stood behind Matthäus with his arms placed protectively around the boy's chest.

He smiled. "I'm already making sure nothing happens to our little Brother. Don't worry!"

Gero hurried to follow Struan, who had already disappeared with the troop into the forest.

Late that evening, after the knights had returned from the forest to the camp, Brother Theobald gathered all fifty Templars for a last prayer of thanks.

A large, full moon rose behind the gnarled branches of the oak trees, bathing the area in a ghostly light. Silently, the men gathered around a crackling fire in the middle of the campsite. As if on command, they raised their calloused right hands to make the symbol of the cross then lowered their closely shorn heads in prayer. A raw, throaty chorus chanted the Lord's Prayer and Ave Maria.

Oddly, no personal farewells followed the small ceremony. Only Gero and Theobald extended their hands to each other in the old Templar tradition. Gero's grip was firm as he searched Theobald's clear gaze, deep and unfathomable in the glow of the torches.

"May Mother Mary be with you, my friend," Theobald whispered. "Remember this – we will meet again, and if it comes to that, in paradise."

Gero swallowed hard but could not muster more than a hoarse "yes." The remaining men nodded silently to each other before mounting their horses and riding down their diverging paths.

Haunted by the terrible sense that the worst had already begun, Gero ordered his men to ride without stopping down the road to Dolancourt.

When they arrived at the quiet hamlet, Gero made his decision. Acting against d'Our's order of silence, he informed his comrades of King Philipp's imminent attack on the Templars in France.

An awkward silence followed the announcement.

"Brothers," Gero explained, "I can imagine your horror, but you must decide. If the commanderies have been taken by the French soldiers upon our return, we cannot flee."

"I knew it!" snarled Arnaud de Mirepaux. The temperamental Frenchman was incensed. "Do they think we're stupid? Why didn't d'Our tell us before we left?"

Before Gero could say anything in his commander's defense, Arnaud continued hotly, "Does our good commander have any idea how difficult it is to find a hideout at such short notice? And do the other Brothers in the commandery know about this? What if Philipp rethinks his decision and the whole plan is worthless? Then we would be deserters, and have to answer for ourselves before Jacques de Molay in Troyes!"

"We have to return home." Struan, who had remained in silent contemplation during the entire exchange, suddenly spoke. "How else would we find out how the situation plays out?"

A murmur of agreement ran through the group. After Francesco drew the banner, holding it parallel to the ground like a jousting lance, the troop galloped back at breakneck speed. The street was lit by the bright moonlight. Gero made sure that Matthäus, riding his small mare, remained in the middle. Fear was written all over the boy's face. He asked no questions, perhaps because he would have had to ask for permission,

46

but perhaps also because he sensed that the knights did not have any answers.

Up on the hill before Bar-sur-Aube, the comrades were confronted with a horrific sight that made them rein in their horses momentarily. Towering flames were leaping up the buildings of the commandery.

"The city is burning!" Francesco de Salazar cried.

"That's not the city, you idiot," Arnaud de Mirepaux hissed. "That's the commandery!"

Without waiting for an order, they rode furiously down the slope as if driven by the devil. The troop flew over the wobbly wooden planks of the old bridge that spanned the Aube. Followed by Matthäus on his dainty brown mare, they galloped through the narrow lanes of the city without regard for the fleeing people and animals around them.

The inhabitants of Bar-sur-Aube – nearly four hundred adults and just as many children – were in chaos. Men and women were pouring vats and buckets of water on the relentless flames.

Gero and his comrades reined in their horses and wound their way through the helpers. In the darkness, they almost missed a troop of thirty French soldiers and their horses standing before the main entrance to the commandery. Another contingent of the soldiers had already gained entry into the inner courtyard.

Cautiously, Gero steered his stallion onto a secluded farm road, the rest of his men following him obediently.

Adelard, a young weaponsmith, limped toward Gero, panting. Despite an open leg wound, he had managed to escape.

In the dim light, Adelard recognized the German knight, whose sword, forged from the finest Italian steel, he had long admired.

"Flee!" he cried to the Brothers. "There's nothing you can do! The soldiers have threatened to kill anyone who dares put out the fire! And they will capture you anyway!"

Gero beckoned to his men to follow him southwards, to the commandery's cemetery that lay directly behind the chapel, encircled by a small oak grove.

Between the densely clustered old trees, they gathered to decide their next move. The night sky glowed red from the rising flames.

"It is our duty to save our commander," Gero said to his comrades.

"But how do you know they haven't already captured him?" Johan asked.

"I don't know," Gero answered quickly, "but should we surrender to the soldiers so easily because of a guess?"

"What do you suggest?" Struan looked at Gero quizzically.

"The main gate is surrounded by solders, so we could try to sneak through the graves and enter the chapel from there. As far as I can tell, everything is still dark in there, a good sign that no one has broken in yet." He glanced at the forty graves that lay to the west. Stone crosses surged up like admonishing fingers in the flickering firelight, as if warning Gero and his men of the evil invading the commandery.

Gero thought it quite possible that the soldiers had found it too unsettling to station guards in the cemetery. Among the superstitious, the myth that the Templars haunted after their deaths the places where they spent their time was a common belief.

"And how should we enter the chapel? The entrance is locked, and none of us has a key," Arnaud noted.

"We can get in through one of the side windows and use the small side door to make our way to the courtyard. Then we'll have to see what to do next."

"The eastern tower is already burning," Stephano interrupted. "The mercenaries will have to retreat sooner or later to avoid becoming victims of the flames themselves. If God is with us, they will be far too preoccupied to notice us."

"Then what are we waiting for?" Struan asked impatiently.

"Matthäus will remain here and look after the horses." Gero glanced at the boy, whose face was barely discernable in the darkness.

Some of the horses were neighing and snorting in panic as, with their sensitive ears, they smelled the blood and heard the frantic cries of their fellow animals.

"Tie the horses to the trees so they don't break away," Gero ordered.

He turned to his squire and, grasping him by his slender shoulders, he kneeled before him so that his face was in line with that of the young boy. Matthäus was shaking with fear.

"Listen carefully, Mattes. Do not leave the animals, and wait for us, no matter what happens. I'll come back as soon as possible and collect you. Understand?"

The boy nodded obediently. "You can count on me, Sir."

"Good," Gero said. He continued in a calm voice, "Don't worry. We will rescue your uncle, I promise." Giving him a pat on the shoulder, Gero left his squire in the darkness.

As they did before every battle, each knight made the sign of the cross, and then slipped silently into the shadows of the walls and shrubbery.

They zigzagged across the hundred-foot-wide graveyard, no longer paying attention to where exactly they stepped, making sure only not to stumble over the stone crosses and grave markers. Gero led his steed under one of the church's side windows.

"Johan, you will have the thankless task of looking after Atlas and defending our position until our return."

"Will do, Sire," Johan answered.

Struan had brought along a rope from his saddlebag. He fastened one end to Atlas's saddle, taking the other end between his teeth. Then he swung himself nimbly onto the steely Percheron. Like a tightrope walker, he balanced himself on the back of the horse. The animal stood stiff as a statue, snorting softly just once as if he knew what was expected of him. With the large knob of his broadsword, Struan struck the ornate glass windows in small, precise blows.

Just as Struan intended, only the bottom part of the leaded window broke out, leaving behind a hole just big enough for the men to slip through. Struan led the way, pulling himself onto the window ledge. His armored gloves of thick leather protected him from cutting his hands on the glass shards.

For a moment, he remained poised, crouching on the narrow ridge. He tightened the rope, and then deftly glided into the interior of the building. A soft whistle signaled that the men could begin climbing over the window ledge into the holy building.

Inside the chapel it was considerably quieter than it was outside. The walls had been intentionally thickened to keep out disruptive noises from the courtyard, a refuge for peace and contemplation.

As the Brothers landed one by one in the chapel, Struan counted the echoes of boots hitting on the stone floor.

The fifth in line was Gero, who had been waiting in front of the window to make sure all his men reached their destination safely.

With swords drawn, they crept past the altar, each of them casting a last look at the Madonna, her features peaceful in the candlelight.

As Struan tried to open the small iron door to the inner courtyard, the men finally discovered why no one had fled into the chapel. The Scotsman opened the door just a crack. Suddenly, his entire field of vision was filled with the blue cape of a soldier.

Carefully, Struan closed the door again. To Gero's immeasurable relief, someone had recently greased the hinges.

"What now?" Arnaud whispered.

"Let me take care of it," Struan responded, then added softly to Gero, "I have nothing else to lose anyway."

"Stru!" Gero hissed, holding his comrade back by his chlamys. "What are you up to?"

The Scottish Templar did not reply. He simply gave Gero a piercing stare and gently freed himself from his friend's grip. He opened the iron gate only as wide as he needed for his task and made a single lightning-quick movement with his hunting dagger. Then he dragged the soldier, still wheezing, into the chapel. With his free hand, he closed the small door and laid the dying man in the side corridor.

The scent of fresh blood filled the air, and, in the dim candlelight, the Brothers saw Struan wipe his hands and blade on the dead man's cloak.

Francesco gagged and pressed his hands to his mouth. The rest of the Templars paused, shocked into silence.

"What is it?" Struan asked, looking from one to the other.

"You've defiled the chapel," Arnaud whispered and let his horrified gaze wander from Struan to the dead soldier.

"Arnaud," Gero snorted. "If you really want to see it that way, the entire commandery has been desecrated."

"Are you all going to just stand there?" Struan asked unapologetically. "We are at war, in case you haven't noticed."

In the courtyard, utter chaos reigned. In growing despair a few stable hands attempted to make their way into the burning stables, ignoring the soldiers who were busy indiscriminately arresting other servants of the Order.

As if by some miracle, the entire north side of the commandery had so far been spared from the fire.

In the flickering shadow of the cloister, Gero and his men moved forward, undetected, to the main building where the commander lived. As they reached the stairway leading to the commander's chambers, a blood-soaked figure stumbled into their path. The troop froze in shock.

It was Brother Claudius, who had chosen to remain by his commander's side instead of fleeing to Clairvaux. Gero barely recognize him. The Brother's face was ravaged. Two deep lacerations above his eyes streamed blood. His nose was broken and all his front teeth were missing. When he caught sight of Gero and the others, he fell to his knees, sobbing, and threw his hands in the air.

Only then did the men see that his hands were broken as well.

"In the name of God!" Gero gasped. "What happened?"

Claudius could not lift his head. He sagged forward and pressed his bent arms to his stomach before throwing up with a gurgle. Struan and Gero dropped to their knees and helped him sit up.

"The commander … the commander … " Claudius whispered.

Blood gushed from his mouth. Stephano handed Gero a snow-white linen handkerchief that he kept hidden in the sleeve of his jerkin and Gero gently wiped the Brother's split lip. Claudius hung limply in Gero's arms, his tortured face seeming to plead only for death.

"What happened to the commander?" Gero asked. He had to stop himself from shaking the wounded man.

"They … they are going to kill him … above in his … " Claudius stuttered before he vomited again.

"How many are there?" Gero was determined to suppress his impatience.

"Two," Claudius whispered with the last of his strength.

"Is anyone else there?"

"No."

"Struan and I will go up and have a look," Gero decided. "Arnaud and Stephano, stay with Claudius. Carry him to the chapel, but be careful! Francesco, take shelter in the cloister and wait until we come back with the commander."

The men nodded silently. The horrors that King Philipp's mercenaries had inflicted on Bar-sur-Aube had rendered them speechless.

Gero and Struan slipped unnoticed along the wall and then up the steep staircase. Without a sound they opened the heavy door. Carefully, Gero peered into the long, dark hallway.

Someone could very well be coming towards them. Perhaps the soldiers had followed Claudius as he fled. Gero felt Struan's breath behind him in the darkness.

Swords at the ready, they crept through the open door. A narrow beam of light from the courtyard dimly illuminated their path down the hall. Two surly male voices were arguing with a third. The sound of someone being struck followed. With two fingers, Gero beckoned to Struan, who scurried to the other side of the door to the commander's chamber. On Gero's signal, they stormed into the room.

The soldiers looked up in shock and quickly sprang back towards the furthest corner of the room. Struan bared his teeth in a savage grin. Gero's eyes fell on Henri d'Our. The commander was as badly battered as Claudius had been. His face was darkened with bruises and he had an ugly cut above his right brow. He sat slumped in his armchair with hands and feet bound.

"Damn it, where did these men come from?" a muscular, dark-haired soldier exclaimed to his blond companion.

Fear flickered in the eyes of his companion at the sudden appearance of the knights. With their swords raised, the soldiers braced themselves for the Templars' attack.

Gero noticed that the two men were dressed differently from the other royal soldiers in their blue and yellow cloaks. These men were clad in unremarkable dark brown leather robes and chain mail. This was the uniform of the Gens du Roi – the royal secret police under the command of Guillaume de Nogaret. The fine swords they held confirmed Gero's suspicions. Nogaret was the right-hand man of the King, and, as everyone in the Order knew, he hated the Templars. Rumor had it that his hatred sprang from an old family feud. Supposedly, members of the Order had denounced his grandfather as a Cathar, whereupon he had been burned. Bent on taking revenge, Nogaret gleefully pounced on fallen churchmen, those whose downfall he could hasten even further. Whoever found himself in Nogaret's clutches did not just lose his freedom, but often his life as well.

As if responding to an unheard signal, Gero and Struan fell upon their opponents, charging forth from both sides.

In a heartbeat, steel clashed mercilessly upon steel until sparks sprayed. An expensive Syrian glass carafe fell to the floor with a crash as Struan accidentally cleared the mantelpiece with one blow. Further and further, they drove the Inquisitors into the corner. Their opponents tried desperately to defend themselves. Members of the secret police were generally not trained as fighters, although they were skilled in other areas no less dangerous.

Soon sweat began to run down the officers' faces, and their movements became increasingly erratic. Struan intensified his efforts whereupon his opponent suddenly ducked to stab at the Scotsman's legs.

Struan still had enough strength and focus in him to fight on ferociously. His senses were sharpened to the extreme, and he needed only a skillful leap to the side and a targeted blow to wound his opponent's throat. Mortally wounded, the soldier fell with a groan to the floor.

As his opponent's attention turned momentarily to his fallen comrade, Gero seized his opportunity. With a coldly calculated thrust, he stabbed the man between the ribs. The man's chain mail could not protect him against the vicious blow. The cracking of breaking bones and a puzzled expression on his face preceded the man's quick death.

Relieved that it was over, Gero and Struan wiped their swords on the dead men's clothing and turned to their commander in concern.

Henri d'Our raised his head a mere inch. "In the name of the Almighty," he groaned softly, "you should not be here!"

His arms and feet had been bound to the chair with calving ropes, which Gero carefully cut through with his dagger. His captors had beaten the commander's face with iron-studded leather gloves – a form of torture favored by the Gens du Roi in their interrogations. With two or three well-placed blows, the victim would have his nose broken, lose an eye, or be rendered toothless.

Peering through heavily swollen eyelids, D'Our's gaze lingered on the corpses on the floor.

"They were Nogaret's men," he whispered, his voice cracking. Blood ran over his split lips. "If he catches you, he will behead you or burn you at the stake."

"Then we won't let ourselves get caught," Gero replied stubbornly and gave Struan a sign to help him raise the commander to his feet.

"Come, Sire, let us flee."

"No, Brother," Henri d'Our wheezed. "The prophecy has been fulfilled. The king's arrest warrant for all members of the Order is over there."

Gero snatched the parchment lying half-unrolled on the table. He quickly deciphered the accusations written in Latin. Sodomy, heresy, and blasphemy were the first things that caught his eyes. Without a word he shook his head and passed the text to Struan, who skimmed it before placing it on the table again.

"Yet another reason to flee with us!" Gero exclaimed as he turned to d'Our.

"An admiral remains with his sinking ship. I cannot forsake the commandery."

"Sire," Gero began cautiously, "there's not much left of the commandery. Everything's ablaze."

"Brother Gero," the commander said so softly that Gero could barely hear him, "where are the others?"

"Waiting for us, Sire!"

"And Matthäus?"

"I've left him with Brother Johan in a hiding place behind the cemetery."

"Good. I want you to leave immediately. As we discussed. You, and everyone who can make it. Without me."

"But Sire ... " Gero interjected, and made to lift d'Our out of his seat.

"That is an order!" the commander gasped furiously. "Damn it, are you refusing to obey me?"

"No," Gero stammered.

"Someone's coming," Struan hissed. He stood inside the doorframe and peered tentatively round the corner. His body tensed, waiting for the moment his victim came near enough that he could finish him off without great effort. His hand lingered on his knife-belt as he waited. When nothing moved, he finally dared to venture a glance into the hallway, and almost collided with the head of the soldier.

The mercenary, an older man, let out a cry of horror as Struan stepped halfway out of the door, unintentionally revealing the red cross on his breast. As if stung by a wasp, the man turned around and ran down the hall. Struan pursued him and threw a knife after him. The fleeing man grasped his neck and fell over.

In three steps, Struan was at his side. He seized the body and dragged it into a nearby chamber. As he stepped back into the hallway, he shut the door behind him and began to drag the two remaining corpses out of the commander's office.

Gero looked at him. "What are you doing?"

"I'm removing the evidence." Struan gestured to d'Our with a nod. "Or do you want the Gens du Roi to hold our commander responsible for the deaths of these scumbags?"

"Of course not," Gero answered, turning to his commander again.

Henri d'Our struggled to open his swollen eyes once more. "Damn it, Brother Gerard, what else are you waiting for? You and your comrades are the only ones who can still save the Order. You must leave. Immediately. That is an order!"

For a moment, d'Our's gaze, clouded by pain, lingered on the two knights.

"Farewell, Sire," Gero answered hoarsely. Together with Struan, he hurried to the exit.

"What did he mean, about us being the only ones who can save the Order?" Struan panted, staring at Gero, distraught.

"I'll explain later," Gero answered tersely, though he did not know anything for certain but that their mission would lead them to Heisterbach.

As they made their way from the commander's chamber, smoke filled their mouths and noses, leaving them choking, and Struan pressed his hand against his mouth to stifle his coughs. When they arrived at the foot of the stairs, they saw that the scriptorium was burning. A soldier had probably realized that the other fire was too far away to spread to the rest of the commandery. Sooner or later, the entire building would be up in flames, and d'Our would be burnt alive if no one found him and retrieved him from his chamber.

In the courtyard, it was still chaotic enough for the two knights to reach the cloister unnoticed. There, Gero and Struan searched for the other Brothers but they were nowhere to be seen.

"They've probably taken refuge with Claudius in the chapel," Struan said hopefully.

"I don't know," Gero answered and looked around uncertainly.

With a sinking feeling in his stomach, he slunk behind Struan. They used the protective darkness of the cloister to proceed to the entrance to the chapel, which was still unguarded.

Out of the corner of his eye, Gero saw two more of Nogaret's soldiers running up the stairs to d'Our's room. If he and Struan didn't want to be discovered, they would have to climb out quickly with the other Brothers.

Shortly before they reached the small iron door, they heard a stifled moan coming from a narrow stone alcove where the cloister joined the inner courtyard. Gero paused in the shadows of the exterior walls and listened carefully. As he proceeded forward, he stepped on something soft. A soft cry followed, and he sprang back in shock, holding his sword at the ready.

"Don't hurt me," croaked a thin voice.

Gero's first thought was that it must be a woman but after he peered further into the darkness, he saw a man that he knew all too well crouched on the floor.

"By Holy George," Gero exclaimed. "Struan, come here, you'll never guess who I've found here."

Struan, who had been surveying the area, stepped beside him in the shadows.

"Oh God," the figure at the foot of the wall burst out. "It's you! Thank heaven! Wherever you're going, take me with you. I beg you!"

"Gislingham!" Struan spluttered in surprise.

The contempt he held for the Englishman was unmistakable even under the circumstances.

"We're going straight to hell," Gero said, his voice dripping with irony.

For a moment he was stunned that, like Brother Claudius, the Englishman appeared to have ignored d'Our's command to spend the night in Clairvaux.

"Firstly, I'm not so sure you really want to follow us, and secondly … " He paused before continuing. Guy de Gislingham had stood up, and even in the dim light of their surroundings, Gero and Struan could clearly see that he was dressed sparingly, and had obviously wet his underclothes and shirt from fear.

"And secondly, I'm not sure if you're appropriately dressed for the journey," Gero continued, sighing.

"You do know, Gisli," Struan said with devilish glee, "that pissing in the courtyard is strictly forbidden. Why on earth do you think we have latrines?"

"If you'd seen what I did, you wouldn't have been able to hold it in either," Gislingham snorted disdainfully.

"What did you see?" Gero asked in alarm.

"Nothing!" Gislingham answered brusquely.

Struan seized him firmly by the neckline of his wool undergarments and shook him. "I wonder why you're cowering here like a rabbit, instead of drawing your sword and at least attempting to fight the French dogs!"

"Release him," Gero said calmly. "He couldn't have accomplished anything alone. Even we aren't strong enough to do more."

"How do you know that? Maybe he's partly to blame for this entire catastrophe," Struan hissed.

"Whatever happened," Gero said, "we must leave and find the others."

"What about me?" Brother Gislingham looked uncertainly from Gero to Struan.

"Damn!" Gero snorted irritably. "You're lucky. The rules won't allow us to leave you to the enemy."

He looked at Struan quickly to make sure he had no objections.

Resigned, Struan made the sign of the cross. "In the name of the Lord," he said, although his eyes glittered ominously at Gislingham, "you'll be sorry if you cause trouble on the way, for I'll blow out your lights with one hand!"

"You'll barely notice that I'm here," said Brother Guy, struggling to lend his voice a measure of conviction.

"I'm certain I will," Struan retorted and turned to leave.

Together, they disappeared into the chapel. There was still no sign of the rest of the Brothers, and Gero consoled himself with the thought that they had already gone on ahead to bring Claudius to safety. A little later, he lowered himself down the outer wall of the chapel along with Struan and Guy.

Johan had taken refuge in the forest with Atlas and was waiting impatiently. Matthäus was clinging to him like an infant to its mother.

The boy's trembling had been getting steadily worse, and Johan feared he would crush the boy as he embraced him. But it had helped. After a while, Matthäus had fallen into an uneasy sleep. Very carefully, Johan had covered him with blankets and pelts, then moved to a position not far from the chapel, to await his brothers.

It must have been far past midnight. Thick swathes of smoke rose above the compound. Even in the forest, the smell of smoke filled the air and, involuntarily, Johan inhaled an acrid gust of soot-filled air. Immediately, he was seized by a severe coughing fit. Wheezing, he gasped for breath. Struan hit him firmly on the back and handed him a waterskin.

"Thank you," the Flemish knight croaked hoarsely, letting the water run down his throat.

Meanwhile, the flames had gripped the entire commandery, and Gero began to pray fervently that the commander had managed to leave the building, even if it was with the help of Nogaret's men. The blazing fire lent the ruins of the commandery an unearthly glow.

"Where are the others?" Johan asked apprehensively.

"I thought they were already here," Gero replied, looking around, visibly concerned.

"I've seen no sign of them," Johan frowned.

"We grabbed Gisli," Struan added.

"A poor exchange," Johan snapped. "And where is the commander?" he asked.

"He didn't want to leave the commandery," Gero answered.

"And you really have no idea where the others could be?"

"Right after we sneaked into the inner courtyard, we found Brother Claudius, severely wounded. I ordered Arnaud and Stephano to take him through the chapel to safety," Gero explained softly. "Struan and I went to help d'Our. Two guards of the Gens du Roi had invaded his office and beaten him. Francesco should have hidden the other Brothers in the meantime and been waiting for us in the cloister. But when we returned, no one was there. Something must have gone wrong. I would give anything to find out exactly what happened."

Guy de Gislingham cleared his throat. "I witnessed it," he piped up haltingly.

"And why didn't you tell us that earlier, you fool?" Struan shouted at him.

"Well, I don't know if I saw everything," the Englishman began carefully.

"I saw Brother Stephano and Brother Arnaud dragging Brother Claudius to the chapel. Before they arrived there, a few soldiers noticed them. First, they tried to fight against the mercenaries but more soldiers kept coming, and two of them snatched Claudius, who was lying on the floor, and held a knife to his throat. They threatened to cut it open unless the Brothers surrendered themselves." He faltered for a moment as if he had to think about what happened next.

"Go on!" Gero commanded.

"Then suddenly, Brother Francesco stormed out of the cloister, trying to help the others. I heard the soldiers shout at him, demanding that they give themselves up immediately. As the Brothers raised their swords to fight, the soldiers cut off one of Brother Claudius's ears and threatened to really kill him if they did not surrender. Instantly Francesco threw up in front of his feet, and Stephano let his sword fall. Arnaud could not do much besides follow his lead. Then I heard the Brothers being chained and led away."

"Bloody dogs!" Johan hissed.

"At least we dispatched three of Nogaret's guards in d'Our's office," Struan remarked with a dark smile.

"And what should we do now?" Johan looked helplessly at the rest.

"D'Our gave me the urgent order to flee to the German lands immediately. You will all accompany me. We have a mission to warn the Brothers there. Besides, I have to take the boy to safety," Gero answered.

In Gislingham's presence, he intentionally didn't say exactly where the journey would lead. The English Brother would be left in another commandery no further than the German lands. And who knew? Perhaps Guy himself was eager to return to England as quickly as possible. Philipp's reach certainly did not extend that far.

"In spite of everything, perhaps we should try to free the others first," Johan suggested.

Struan, who otherwise did not shy away from danger, let out a guttural noise. "Judging by how the situation looks now, I'd be mighty curious about your plan!"

"Three against one, goes the rule," Johan justified himself. "Or does that not matter anymore?"

Gero groaned. "Yes, but we're also advised never to go into a hopeless battle intentionally."

"Very well, as you wish." Johan was affronted. "Then we should wait no longer. The longer we wait, the lower our chances of escaping the king's men."

Johan woke Matthäus, who opened his eyes in shock, but when he heard Gero's voice, he sobbed in relief. In the darkness, he felt his way to his chevalier and hugged him fervently.

"Your uncle can't come with us," Gero explained gently, stroking his back to calm him. "He sends his greetings and wishes me to take you to the German lands until he can collect you there." That was a lie, but this was not the right moment to tell the young boy the gruesome details.

"A moment!" Struan grabbed Gero's arm suddenly and pulled him away from Matthäus. "I'm not going anywhere unless I'm assured of Amelie's wellbeing. I can't just desert her. She's all alone at home. Her father is attending a fair in Troyes, and you saw with your own eyes how the soldiers spared no one, not even the attendants. What if someone kidnaps her? Or ... " His voice faltered. "What if I ask her if she wants to flee with us? Would you be against it?"

The despair in Struan's words was unmistakable, and although it went against all reason, Gero could not deny him his request.

"Fine with me," he whispered. "Only, how will I explain it to the others?"

"I don't care what the others think," Struan replied with quiet determination. "Johan will understand, and Gisli doesn't matter."

Gero turned to the other men who were standing like shadows in the dark forest. "Listen up," he said in a quiet voice. "Struan has an important matter to settle on the way out of the city, and we will accompany him." For a moment he wondered if he should add an explanation, but then he decided against it. Curiously, no one protested.

"Can you ride a battle steed?" he asked Matthäus.

"Of course," the boy answered bravely.

Gero had decided to reserve the calm mare of his squire for Struan's sweetheart in case she really wanted to follow them. He helped Matthäus into the saddle of Stephano's well-behaved English Great Horse. The back of the colossal cold blood was so wide that it was impossible for the boy's boots to reach the stirrups. Gero tightened the straps as far as possible, but Matthäus could still only place his feet in the leather loops instead of the iron stirrups. The animal pranced from side to side uneasily as if it sensed that something was wrong.

Guy de Gislingham took over the temperamental Brabant of Arnaud de Mirepaux.

Quickly, Gero gathered the heavy weapons fastened to the saddles of the remaining horses and distributed them to the three other Brothers. Gislingham received Arnaud's shield, as there were no more swords available. In an emergency, the Englishman would have to defend himself with a battle-axe or mace.

After Gero had taken the rest of the provisions from Francesco's saddlebag, he distributed a blanket to everyone from the stock of the missing Brothers. Finally, with a heavy heart, he set the Spaniard's Moorish stallion free.

CHAPTER 4

The Escape

Friday, October 13, 1307, night

With grim determination, Struan led the troop along the Dhuys, through a grove of fruit trees that cast ghostly shadows in the moonlight. The house of the reputable wine merchant Alphonse Bratac, lay on the eastern edge of the city. In complete terror, most residents of Bar-sur-Aube had locked themselves in their homes. Most of the soldiers had already departed. A long procession of burning torches, they rode up the hill behind the city and toward Troyes. In the distance, Gero and his men heard the rattling of wagon wheels and the groans of the soldiers' victims.

While the others waited patiently some distance away, hidden in the shadows of walls and bushes, Gero followed Struan to the back entrance of the house.

Struan opened a window shutter in the basement to peer into the house. "Amelie, can you hear me?" he called out cautiously.

Like a ghost, the young woman, clad only in a white shift and holding an oil lamp, flitted to the door and opened it carefully. When she saw who was standing before her, she set the light on the floor and threw herself on Struan, flinging her arms firmly around his neck and nestling closely to him.

With a deep sigh the Scottish knight returned her embrace and lifted her carefully. Then he kissed her gently on the mouth and set her back on the floor. The next moment, he heard her sobbing.

"What's the matter with you, my darling? Why are you crying?" Struan was alarmed.

"You idiot," Amelie chided. "What do you think? I've been going half-mad with fear. I thought they had you arrested or burnt alive." With both hands, she pulled his head to hers and began to cover his face with kisses.

Gero cleared his throat impatiently.

The woman paused and looked past Struan in shock. "You're not alone?" For the first time, she noticed the shadows of several horses and their riders outside the house.

"Don't worry, Amelie," Struan said, laying his arm soothingly around her narrow shoulders. "This is Gero of Breydenbach. I've already told you about him. Besides him, there's his squire and Johan van Elk, another German Brother. The fourth fellow is not particularly worth mentioning, Guy de Gislingham. You wouldn't have noticed him, I'm sure."

"What happened? Why are they escorting you?"

"Almost all residents of the commandery were captured by the royal soldiers. We must flee to the German lands – tonight. And I ... wanted to ask you ..." he moistened his lips, trying to banish the dryness from his mouth before bringing his sentence breathlessly to an end, "if you wanted to come with me?" His heart pounded like a hammer in fear and excitement. What if she said no? He was grateful she couldn't see the fear in his face.

Amelie did not take long to consider his question. "Wait a moment," she responded and picked up the lamp. "I'll dress myself quickly, pack a few things, and get some money. I'll be back soon."

Gero could feel Struan's relief. Although the woman would be an additional burden on the journey, he could not bear to leave her behind.

"Ask her if she has a pair of pants and a vest for Gisli," he said. "We'll draw attention everywhere with him in his pathetic outfit."

"If I had the choice," Struan growled spitefully, "he would ride to England in his piss-soaked underwear."

It didn't take long for the young woman to reappear in the entrance with a long cloak. She had left her widowed father a short message. The old man did not know that she was expecting, let alone that a knight of the Templar Order was the father. Without doubt her father would murder him should he ever find out. The only thing she wrote was that she had to flee because of the royal soldiers and would return home as soon as possible.

"Everything will be fine," Struan whispered, stroking her already slightly swollen belly.

In the feeble glow of the oil lamp that she still held in her hand, she smiled gratefully.

"One of us had to flee in his underclothes," Struan said reluctantly. "Perhaps you could lend us some clothing from your father, so we won't be noticed everywhere we go?"

"Yes, of course," she answered in surprise. "The only question is whether the clothes will fit. My father does not exactly have the ideal physique of a Templar."

"Not a problem." Struan looked around at Guy de Gislingham, though he was hardly visible in the darkness. "This man has neither the ideal physique, nor is he to be taken seriously as a Templar."

A short time later, Gero received the clothes and a pair of worn boots from Amelie. He went to Gislingham and thrust the bundle into his hands.

"Put this on!" he commanded the surprised Brother.

Grudgingly, Brother Guy took the unexpected gift, a disparaging grunt betraying his displeasure. By the time dawn broke, he would have been laughed at by all.

"We've brought you a horse," Struan said as Amelie shut the door and prepared to go to the stable.

The woman paused, extinguished the oil lamp, and set it on the floor.

"How did you know that I would come with you?"

Struan could hear her smile. "I didn't know," he said mildly, "but I prayed to the Virgin Mary that you would."

"Oh, Struan," she whispered, "I love you."

"And I love you," he whispered to her. "You don't know how much I do." Gently he held her hand and pressed her fingers to his lips before he led her to his horse. "As long as it's still dark, you'll ride with me for safety."

"Gero," Johan whispered, nudging his Brother whose horse stood next to him. "What's Struan's deal with this woman?"

"That's a damn long story. He should tell you himself if he wants to," Gero replied, hoping that Johan would be satisfied with his answer.

"I knew I was right," someone hissed in the background.

Gero turned around abruptly. "Gislingham, shut your impudent mouth," he spat, "or I'll sell you as an indentured servant at the next market."

An unintelligible mumble followed, and then there was silence.

In unspoken agreement, they made their way through the moonlit night, trying their best to travel as silently as possible. Gero prayed that Philipp IV's soldiers had shown the captured Brothers a shred of respect and treated them as fellow Christian men. However, judging by Guy de Gislingham's story, he could not count on them handling their captives humanely. An old enmity existed between the Templars and the royal army and they had often clashed during chance encounters. How much pleasure it must bring the soldiers to march the once proud Templars off in chains! A cold dread settled in Gero's usually fearless heart. Would King Philipp further his interests through the deaths of the Brothers?

Meanwhile, they reached the arterial road to St. Dizier.

Johan rode at Gero's side. "What's your plan?" he whispered. "Do you have any idea where we're heading?"

"First to east, in the direction of Marne. We'll cross the river at St. Dizier and head toward St. Mihiel. There, we'll ride over the Meuse and into the German lands where – God willing – we'll finally be safe." Gero reined in his stallion and slowed down.

"How do you know King Philipp won't follow us beyond the border?" Johan asked.

"I'm only guessing so," Gero replied, omitting the fact that d'Our had told him exactly that. "Firstly, they don't have enough soldiers, and secondly, I can't imagine other Christian rulers allying themselves with such devilry."

"And what do we do when we've arrived in German territory?" Johan asked in a bewildered voice.

"We'll ride to my home," Gero answered as if he had long laid his plan for escape. "My father is an old friend of the Order. Even if he's a tremendous beast otherwise, he can provide us with Writs of Escort that would allow us to continue on our journey without trouble. Besides, he has many connections, so we can gain an overview of the situation of the Order at the Rhine and Mosel and the remaining German lands. King Philipp has an ally in the west of the German Empire. Although he probably doesn't have the support he desires, we must still be wary."

Gero made sure that Guy de Gislingham wasn't near them, and then continued so softly that only Johan could hear him. "I will tell you and Struan about the old man's mission for us in good time when we have reached our destination. Before that, I'll take the boy to the Cistercians in Hemmenrode. Then we'll proceed along the Rhine to Brysich to warn Master Alban."

They rode on silently.

In Ville-sur-Terre, clouds of smoke once again met their eyes. Here, the king's troops had also burnt a small monastery to the ground, as well as its barns and stables. Gero's thoughts turned to Brother Theobald and the other Brothers who had gone into the Forest of the Orient with him. He sent a prayer to the Virgin Mary to protect all the Brothers of the Order tonight and in the future, regardless of how dire their situation might be.

To avoid meeting any roaming soldiers, the troop was forced to go around Soulaines-Dhuys. Behind Anglus, they dipped into a valley with a stream running through it. Gero knew the valley from numerous reconnaissance rides.

Struan, who rode closely behind Gero on his black steed, grumbled, "I suggest we think about where we want to set up camp, so we can rest."

"Wouldn't it be better to ride through the night?" Johan's desire to depart from the traumatic site as quickly as possible was plain in his voice.

"It's a full moon. It makes no great difference whether we ride by day or by night," Gero answered. "On the contrary, it's no accident that Philipp's attack coincides with the full moon. His soldiers can find us better in the still of the night than by day."

"Then we should find a safe sleeping place soon," Struan remarked softly, "if only because of wild animals. There are not just packs of wolves on the prowl, but badgers and lynxes too."

It was neither soldiers nor badgers and wolves that disquieted Struan. Gero knew his concern lay with Amelie. The exertions of a hard, five-hour ride could be quite dangerous for a pregnant woman.

"Dismount!" Gero commanded in hushed tones as the group arrived at a small clearing in a beech forest. Apart from the gurgle of the water and the faint howl of a faraway wolf, nothing else could be heard. When he was certain that there wasn't another soul nearby, Gero gave the command to rest.

Brother Guy was given the instruction to gather brushwood.

Although it probably wasn't wise to start a fire, Gero had little choice, as Struan's pregnant sweetheart was shivering from the cold and desperately needed something warm to drink.

Sullenly, Guy de Gislingham stalked away from the comrades and began to gather deadwood from between the trees, all the while nursing the uneasy feeling that rats and snakes could bite him at any moment. It was a blatant insult to be relegated to such servile tasks. Why had they taken the squire with them if not for this sort of work?

"Are you afraid you'll piss your pants again if you go further into the forest?" Struan shone the burning stump of a torch on Gislingham's tense face.

"Not everyone has a whore like you, holding your hand and your cock …" Guy de Gislingham muttered, full of resentment.

He'd barely uttered the word "whore" before Struan threw the burning stick to the ground where it was snuffed out with a hiss by the damp grass. Before Guy could finish his sentence, Struan punched him forcefully in the face.

Guy de Gislingham could count himself lucky that the Scot had already stored his metal-studded leather gloves in his saddlebag. Nonetheless, a harsh crunch and a groaning cry startled the rest of the group.

Gero was at their side immediately. "Stru, Gisli, what's going on here?" he yelled in alarm, his hand on the pommel of his sword.

Johan hurried towards them with another torch.

"The Celtic pig broke my nose!" Gislingham howled, pressing his hands to his face and rolling on the ground in pain.

"Struan, is that true?" Gero asked sternly.

"Yes, but I had my reasons," Struan defended himself. His eyes still glinted with fury in the flickering glow of the fire.

"He started it," Gislingham snapped as his trembling fingers felt his broken nose. "Johan should give me his sword, and I'll challenge the Scottish dog to a duel. Then we'll see who has God and the truth on his side!"

Amelie stepped up, pale as the moonlight. She had barely seen anything, but had heard their exchange clearly.

"Struan started it," she said calmly to Gero. "He accused him of being a coward. And he," she motioned with her head to Gislingham, "called me Struan's whore. Then I heard the blow."

Struan looked unrepentantly at the ground and said nothing.

Gero was livid. "You two", he said to Struan and Gislingham, "are behaving like half-grown children! Do you really think we should be doing King Philipp's work for him? Massacring each other before they even get to us?"

Feeling slightly ashamed, Struan offered his hand to his opponent, which the Englishman took reluctantly, and pulled him to his feet.

"God have mercy on you, Scot, if we ever meet on an English battlefield," murmured Guy. "That's the only way you'll survive."

The Templars' equipment included sheepskins to keep them warm at night, as well as an iron kettle with handles for boiling water. Despite their quarrels, they sat huddled together around a campfire, resting their backs against the saddles. After a short prayer, they drank hot wine thinned with a little water from their tin cups, while Johan handed out bread and slices of hard-cured sausage.

Gero observed Johan and Matthäus staring furtively at the beautiful young woman who had snuggled herself unabashedly against Struan's strong shoulder. Amelie's eyes were drooping from weariness, and the cup threatened to topple out of her hand. From time to time, she absentmindedly stroked the faint bulge under her woolen surcoat.

Struan nudged her gently when she almost spilled her wine. Amelie looked up at him in surprise and shot him a dazzling smile.

Struan helped her gently to her feet and led her by the hand to one of the improvised beds made of sheepskins. Curiously, Johan watched the behavior of the pair, and then gave Gero a questioning look.

"I'd prefer if he explains who she is himself," Gero answered, fairly certain that Johan was interested in the details.

"I know who she is. I'm not blind, Brother," Johan retorted with a grin that was inevitably askew from his scars. "She's the daughter of old Bratac. And Struan is by no means the only man in the commandery she's blessed with countless wet dreams and trips to the penitence bench. With the tiny difference that he's ventured far beyond just dreams or prayer." Johan smiled sardonically. "Can it be that he's already left his footprints in fresh snow?"

"What do you mean?" Gero's expression betrayed no emotion.

"Is she expecting?'

Gero laughed softly. "Perhaps you should have become a midwife instead."

"I knew it," Johan said triumphantly. "Very brave, our Struan! I'd have expected it of some of the knights, but not him. Although … there was something odd about his behavior during the past few months, wasn't there?"

"What kind of bravery does it take for a wild stallion to mount a mare in heat?" Gislingham grunted. He could still only breathe through his mouth, and was cooling the swelling on his nose with a damp linen cloth.

"I knew from the beginning that he was going behind the back of the commander."

"Then he should be thanking his stars you didn't rat him out," Johan remarked sarcastically.

"I just didn't have enough evidence," Guy hissed. Jealously, he eyed the two lovers, who were exchanging small displays of affection in the distance. "Furthermore, I wonder how these barbarians always manage to breed like rabbits," he added spitefully. "Normally he'd have his cloak revoked for that, at least for a year. And had he deceived the Order, it would cost him his head."

"That's enough," Gero retorted in annoyance. "If my predictions are right, we won't be accountable to the Order any time soon."

Johan's scarred face twisted into a smile. "As long as Struan doesn't start a harem like those damned Mamluks …"

"You don't need to overstate it," Gero whispered with a sidelong look a Matthäus, who tried to look in another direction, but whose red ears betrayed the fact that he'd followed the entire exchange with great interest.

Under cover of darkness, Struan gave his Amelie a lingering kiss as he held her in his arms. As she parted her lips slightly, his tongue ventured forth.

"Not here," she whispered unsteadily as he pressed his body even more firmly against hers so she could feel his hardness.

"Why not?" he asked, smiling, and ran his hand under her cloak until he found her nipples under the thin fabric of her silk chemise. Amelie moaned softly.

Struan bent down to her and brushed her ear with his warm lips.

"Against all odds," he whispered to her, "I could scream with happiness – here, in the middle of this dark forest in front of my Brothers. I'd never dared to hope that I could ever hold your sweet figure in my arms again."

Touched by his words, she nestled her head on his breast where she had always felt safe, though she knew her happiness could not last. But now, everything was different. For a moment, she contemplated asking him what he had planned, where he thought to journey with her, but then she decided to wait. It was still too early for such questions. She put her arms around his neck and pressed herself to him with a sigh.

Struan interpreted her advance in his typical manner. "I will take you, my flower," he whispered, hoarse with desire, as his hand wandered between her thighs, "as soon as we find a proper bed. I promise you."

Amelie took his head between her hands and pressed a kiss on his large nose.

"Well, then, I look forward to exchanging the open field for a decent guesthouse soon," she declared cheekily.

"You can count on that," he said, his voice shaking with amusement. "But it would be difficult. As far as I know, we have absolutely no money."

"Money is hardly the biggest hurdle," Amelie replied. She smiled at him meaningfully, rummaging about in the various layers of her clothes. Eventually, she handed the astounded Struan a leather pouch filled with jingling coins. "Here, take it! I wanted to give it to you earlier. It's definitely safer with you."

"You're deluding yourself there!" Struan let slip a soft laugh. "I've never possessed my own money. What would you do if I went to the next tavern and squandered it all on drink?"

"You won't do that." She looked at him trustfully. "I'm sure of it. My father always says that money is nowhere safer than with the Templars."

Smiling, he hid the purse in his neck pouch. Then he built them a reasonably comfortable bed. The blanket he used was from Stephano de Sapin, so it was definitely free of insects.

Normally, no Templar was allowed to lay his hands on the possessions of another Brother. Every single item – from daggers to bed sheets – had to be accounted for. Once every quarter, the administration would make inventory checks. Losses had to be reported immediately, and punishments were draconic.

As Struan spread the second blanket over Amelie, he thought about how all these rules and procedures had suddenly become insignificant. All the documents that had seemed indispensible to the running of the commandery had been lost in the flames. And Stephano de Sapin was sitting in a prisoner's carriage on the bumpy road to some sinister dungeon, his spotless cloak stained with blood. Or perhaps he was already long dead. Who knew?

Struan embraced Amelie tightly again as if to make sure that she was really at his side. Cheek to cheek, he paused for a moment, then raised himself a little and pressed a kiss to her forehead.

"I'm taking the first shift with Gero," he explained, rising to go back to the fire. "I'll lie with you later," he added somewhat apologetically.

She winked at him and laughed. Then, as if she had read his thoughts, her features darkened.

"Don't worry so much about the other Brothers," she reassured him. "The King can't afford to keep them captive forever – or even kill them. They all come from noble bloodlines. He will be forced to let them go as soon as possible."

Only too readily Struan wanted to believe her, but Amelie hadn't seen what he had.

When Struan returned to the fire, Johan and Matthäus were arranging their sleeping places. Gislingham had buried himself under a blanket some distance away and hidden his face under damp linen cloths.

Struan felt neither remorse nor sympathy when he thought about Gislingham's broken nose. In his eyes, Brother Guy was the epitome of duplicity. All at once a sinister thought came to him. What if Guy de Gislingham was a spy of Nogaret? Their situation was as disorienting as a sandstorm in the desert, and for that reason alone it seemed advisable not to let the Englishman out of sight.

"And?" Gero asked with a slight smile as Struan set himself down next to him with a soft sigh. "Is the little dove sleeping?"

"You've been gossiping, haven't you?" Struan's voice held a subtle, sharp undertone as he slid a rolled-up sheepskin behind his back.

"No, what are you thinking of?" Gero grinned affably. "Johan just expressed his opinion that as long as you don't start a harem, you're in the clear."

"What a loon," Struan exclaimed, but he had to laugh, too, as he looked over at Johan, who had spread out in his improvised bed with relish and grinned a last time at him before closing his eyes.

Swords and daggers within reach, the crossbow lying ready near the fire, Gero and Struan prepared to spend half the night mutually keeping watch and, in the case of an emergency, protecting the others long enough for them to grab their own weapons. In order to enliven the watch slightly, Gero had laid a skin of wine next to them.

With a sideways glance, Gero made sure that Gislingham couldn't hear him. "I can imagine how happy you are that you have Amelie by your side," he said softly to Struan. "But d'Our has given us a mission, and I hope it's clear to you that we cannot involve her in our duties."

Struan gave him a sidelong-glance. "That's what I feared," he replied softly. "But what was I to do? I couldn't just leave her."

Gero turned to Struan with a questioning look. "Do you have any idea where she could find accommodation in the meantime?"

"I'm afraid not," Struan replied solemnly. "I can't possibly send Amelie to my home. The long journey to Scotland is far too dangerous to make alone, and my family's castle isn't exactly what you could call a safe refuge. My father is a tyrant, and as long as our Order still stands in other countries, he will not be sympathetic towards me leaving the Templars to marry Amelie. The word 'love' is best not uttered in front of him. To him, women are less valuable than the cattle on the meadow. After my mother's death, he turned into a godless barbarian, who has married more wives and fathered more children than you can imagine. He would make Amelie his whore even before I could get there to fulfill my promise of marriage.

"And I haven't visited the remaining living relatives of my mother's clan in over ten years. I hardly think I'd be welcome there. Because of some stupid territorial dispute, they've been in a bloody feud with my father's clan for years. Apart from that, the war against England is still raging. From past experience, I know that, regardless of how wealthy a clan is, after the great battles come the great famines." Struan grunted in resignation. "I hardly dare think about how I'll provide a life for Amelie and the child. If I do, I'll be an old man by sunrise."

Gero rose and placed a thick branch in the fire. Then he sank back down next to the Scotsman again and took the skin of wine.

"What about taking Amelie to my family?" he remarked as he loosened the tightly tied cords of the wineskin. "My father's castle lies along our path. Although my father is not a pleasant man, my mother is a kindhearted woman who can hold her own against him. She would be glad to have the young woman as a companion. She could stay with them at least until we know what awaits us in the German lands, and how everything should play out from there." He took a decent gulp of the wine and passed the skin to his Brother.

"You are a true friend, Gero," Struan said. As if to comfort himself, he let the wine flow down his throat in large gulps. Setting the bag down, he gasped for breath and coughed softly. "I count myself lucky to have you as a Brother. I bear all the responsibility for my misery, and don't deserve your support. Even though you told me about the death of your wife, I'm certain you've never broken your oath as a knight of the Order."

Struan gaped when he saw his German comrade smile secretively and look around the dark forest with an unreadable expression, wanting to make sure he could not be overheard.

"During our time in Cyprus," Gero began softly, "before the attack of the Mamluks on Antarados, I had an affair with a Cyprian prostitute, even though I'd sworn never to share a bed with a woman again after Elisabeth's death." He paused for a second to glance at Struan's bewildered face. "She wanted me," he explained with a smile, "and you know as well as I do that no man can resist a beautiful woman who has her eye on him."

Before he continued, he took another gulp of wine. "Her name was Warda. That's Levantine for 'rose'. She was a good few years older than I was. Her features were ripe with a lifetime of experience, but she still had the beauty of the Arabian blooms – hair as black as coal, deep-set, honey-colored eyes, an expressive mouth, olive skin, and a voluptuous body. She spoke French astonishingly well. She later told me that she was the illegitimate daughter of a Brother of the Order who had died in Acre and a Saracen woman who was brought to the island as a serf."

"How long did it last?"

"About half a year; until we were relocated to Antarados."

"Did you love her?" Struan looked at him with an increasingly doubtful expression.

Gero pressed his lips together and stared into the crackling fire. He shrugged his shoulders and turned to Struan again.

"There are several reasons to lie with a woman. One of those is love. Another is the lust for life. When you're clinging desperately to hope but seeing only death before you, you want to leave at least one thing of your own behind in this world. The yearning of a grieving wife or a child with your lover, even if it will never see its father – these needs don't make us any different from other soldiers."

He sighed softly. He himself was no longer sure what he had felt for Warda. After all, he had missed her desperately when she stood alone at the harbor as he departed for Antarados.

"Yes," he said finally. "I loved her."

"But there were the rules?" Struan looked at him, inquisitively.

"Yes, of course," Gero admitted frankly. "The Order has a strict stance on our relations with women. But ultimately, every man decides for himself if he can uphold that standard or not, and who, apart from God the Almighty, is to judge?"

The fire had almost burned out. The lonely call of an owl echoed through the cold night. Struan shivered. In his homeland, the call of an owl foretold the death of a close relative or a friend.

"Do you want to tell me what kind of mission d'Our has given us?" Struan asked, nestling into the warm sheepskin behind him.

"Have you heard about the Head of Wisdom?" Gero replied in a whisper.

"Holy George," Struan uttered softly, evidently shocked. "I first heard of it when I was stationed in Balantrodoch. Our commander demanded that we worship a three-faced head, and no one was allowed to speak a word about it, even though it wasn't the right head. Does d'Our know where it is?"

"'Where' is not the question," Gero responded. "I would be interested in 'what' it is."

"Roger Bacon, the famous English scholar, supposedly saw the head. He said it could speak using the numerals zero and one." Struan raised his brows and looked at his companion expectantly, but before Gero could answer him, he shook his head. "I don't know what to make of that. Bacon also claimed in a letter to the Pope that in the future, there would be carriages without horses that move a hundred times faster than those of our time. And that men would be capable of building a machine that flies." A tired smile played on his lips when he still didn't receive any answer from Gero. "You already think I'm a fool, so don't listen to my nonsense."

"I don't know if it's nonsense, Struan." In the firelight, Gero's features appeared almost like a mask. "But you, Johan, and I are fated to discover it."

A surprised gasp escaped from Struan's mouth.

"Shh ... " Gero laid his index finger on his lips. "Not a word to anyone. I'm only supposed to inform you and Johan about it when we arrive at our destination."

"The head ... will it help us?" Struan made an effort to hide his curiosity.

"I don't know," Gero answered earnestly. "But I would go through hell to find out. Not just to save the Order, but the lives of all our innocent Brothers."

Struan's expression turned brooding, and in response Gero smiled at him. "Go and keep the woman warm. At least one of us should be alert and well rested tomorrow."

In the still of the night, Gero listened closely to the sounds of the forest. D'Our's words rang in his head, and he questioned, not for the first time, whether his secret mission could somehow improve their plight. But he lacked the knowledge and imagination to arrive at an answer.

Sometime later, Johan van Elk got up and took over the watch.

After Gero took off his chain mail, he curled up in a spare saddle blanket and lay down next to Matthäus, who was intermittently murmuring unintelligible things in his sleep. His head resting on a saddlebag, Gero succumbed to his weariness. The obligatory prayer for a peaceful night's sleep resonated in his mind as he finally fell into a deep, dreamless sleep.

CHAPTER 5

Bloodlust

Friday, October 13, 1307, morning

The cold, damp air had settled on Amelie's face like a mask, and she awoke slowly in the soft light of dawn.

Struan, who was snoring blissfully next to her, had unintentionally pulled away her blanket during the night. Now only covered by her cloak, she was exposed to the autumn cold. Shivering, she sat up and pulled the woolen blanket she had worn during the night more tightly around her shoulders.

A comforting stillness lay over the forest; the scent of earth, mushrooms, and fresh leaves mingled in a gentle veil of fog.

Johan van Elk, the young knight with the disfigured features, sat alone by the fire that had burned down to embers, sipping a steaming cup of wine. The gleaming chain mail that stretched across his muscular arms and the silver cross he had fastened to a leather cord around his neck shone with an ethereal light as they were struck by the rays of the rising sun.

Amelie's eyes fell again on Struan, who, with his eyes closed and features relaxed, resembled an innocent boy. Would the child she was expecting look anything like him?

Smiling, Amelie turned to her sleeping protector to kiss him, but a sudden discomfort stopped her. Her full bladder reminded her sharply that she was carrying a baby, and that it was time for her to begin her day. With an effort, she got to her feet and stretched her cramped limbs. She sighed softly and raised her head.

Still holding the cup in his hand, Johan van Elk was gazing into the distance as if something there had caught his attention. For a moment, he appeared tense, but he sat back again and looked in Amelie's direction with a smile, raising his hand in a friendly morning greeting.

It seemed that all the others were sleeping. Amelie decided to take the opportunity to go to the stream to bathe and relieve herself in seclusion. Muttering, Struan turned on his side as she left the pile of blankets and disappeared behind a gorse bush.

After some time, she reached the burbling stream and hurriedly took off her boots. As she waded into the crystal-clear water up to her knees, a fleeting shadow scurried past, moving between the thinning trees. Alarmed, she looked up. With relief, she discovered that it was only Guy de Gislingham, crouching a distance away on the bank and washing out the linen cloth he had used to reduce the swelling on his nose.

The Englishman looked up and eyed her warily. It seemed he hadn't once considered showing her any customary politeness, declining to even greet her. Instead, he merely glowered.

Annoyed, Amelie decided to give up her ideal washing spot. With bare feet, she walked along the sandy bank until she reckoned the Englishman could no longer stare at her so boldly.

Hastily, she crouched at a spot where the water flowed around her calves and the current moved briskly. With both hands, she gathered up her heavy garments to protect them from the water. Blissfully, she shut her eyes as she finally found relief. Then she washed her thighs nimbly. As she made to straighten up and dry herself with her chemise, she suddenly felt hot breath at the back of her neck and a foul odor pervading her nostrils.

Furiously, she turned around quickly to punch the nose of the bold fellow who had obviously followed her. Skillfully, someone snapped up her wrist and pulled her with a swift movement to himself. She felt a sharp blade on her throat, cold and merciless.

"Who do we have here, eh?" asked a deep male voice, letting out a soft, devilish laugh.

Amelie's heart stopped. She didn't recognize the voice.

"Hello, my love," the stranger purred. "What's a pretty girl like you doing all alone in the forest so early in the morning?"

Amelie did not dare swallow, let alone scream, and only when her attacker moved the blade a little to give her the chance to answer, did she dare breathe. Five men in faded blue and yellow cloaks stepped out of the thicket and grinned at her.

They were Philipp IV's hired soldiers, no doubt about it. As they circled her in their rags and tatters, they looked more like godless vagrants or robbers than respectable men.

"Could it be that you are missing from one of the Templar commanderies around here?"

Amelie racked her brains feverishly for a response. They were obviously hunting for Templars on the run, and she could not let them discover that their prey was camping nearby.

"What do you want from me?" she stammered, breathlessly. "I'm just a simple farmer's wife. I have nothing to do with the Templars."

Cautiously, she turned her head and nodded in the direction where she had last seen Guy de Gislingham. Every respectable woman knew it was not advisable to be in the presence of a horde of unscrupulous men without the protection of a brother, father, or husband.

"That's my husband over there," she said, hoping that the soldiers would finally leave her in peace. "We're looking for mushrooms and herbs."

She pointed in the direction to where the Englishman was still licking his wounds, hidden by the bushes.

Gisli was not wearing his chlamys, and looked like a poor farmer in the discarded clothes of her father. Perhaps, if he played along, the soldiers would believe her and let them both go.

"Even better," her captor grunted, and yanked her hair so hard that he snapped her head back. "We'll ask him if he's seen any Order knights recently."

The stranger removed the dagger from her neck and pushed her ruthlessly forward, towards her alleged husband. Feeling as if her bones were made of jelly, she stumbled forward.

Obeying a sign from the man holding her, the five other men moved silently through the bushes.

As she reached the small bend in the stream where Guy de Gislingham had been crouching, she saw a terrifying scene. The five soldiers had rushed ahead to subdue the Englishman. He was bent double on the sandy bank, his hands bound behind his back and a piece of driftwood as a gag between his teeth.

One of the soldiers stepped forward and handed his leader a torn leather cord. On it dangled the silver cross pattée of the Templars.

"I'm certain he's one of the ones we're looking for." The soldier's voice rang with triumphant glee. "He wears the cross of the knights, even if he otherwise looks like a foolish peasant."

"Stand up!" one of the soldiers snarled and kicked Guy de Gislingham in his side.

Brother Guy let out a yelp of pain. Amelie saw that he was trying to say something and struggling to breathe. His nose was swollen as before, and the wood between his teeth made it difficult for him to take in air through his mouth. As he tried to rise from his knees, his face was red from the effort. Amelie was half-mad with fear. Even if he was nursing a broken nose and wearing her father's discarded clothes, Guy de Gislingham was still a Templar. How was it possible that these disheveled soldiers had defeated him so easily?

Tears of despair welled up in her eyes. "You are mistaken," she called out in desperation. "He is no knight of the Order. He won the cross in a game of dice."

Would anyone hear her if she screamed for help? The campsite was at least six hundred feet away. The soldiers would probably slit their throats long before Struan and his remaining Brothers noticed their desperate situation. Why on earth could Struan not simply sense that she needed help?

The man with the foul breath stepped forward, stuck his dagger in his belt, and grabbed Amelie's arm. His rough fingers pressed into her flesh like iron pliers.

The other five rogues – two young and three middle-aged – looked up at him attentively. He was evidently their commander. Before he directed his grim gaze to the pale-faced Gislingham, who was staring dumbly at the ground, he made a barely noticeable movement with his head.

"Jakob, look around the forest nearby," he hissed. "Pons, go to the other side of the stream. Be careful! Make sure there aren't any more of them running about."

Then he turned to Gislingham again. "The whore there claims that you're her husband. Is that true?"

Holy Mary and Joseph, *Amelie prayed in her head,* make him say yes!

As if waking from a deep sleep, Gislingham raised his head and looked at Amelie impassively. Despite the cold, droplets of sweat beaded his forehead; she didn't dare give him a sign.

Slowly, he shook his head, making several grunting noises as though he had something important to say. But the man holding Amelie did not probe any further.

God in Heaven, *Amelie thought,* to hell with you for your utter stupidity!

"No?" the man asked in surprise. "Who is she, then? Your lover?" He looked round the circle of men provocatively, baring his terrible teeth in a grin. "What do you mean? Are you escaped members of the Order, or a pair of harmless turtle doves we've disturbed during a forbidden tryst?"

Cautious laughter made its way around the circle.

"Pull down his pants! A bitch recognizes her master even when she's blind," said one of the men. "If she has no shame taking his cock in her mouth, she's definitely his lover."

"Or a whore!" yelled another, and they all broke into laughter.

Amelie felt she would throw up at any moment. She looked on in shock as one of the men cut through Gisli's waistband.

"What a pathetic sight!" sneered the leader, looking at Gislingham's limp penis.

The Englishman moaned indignantly as a rough hand grasped his penis and began to tug it vigorously.

"Oh, there seems to be some life still in it, comrade. Who would've thought that?" called one of the soldiers.

Gislingham turned red, which amused the gathered men.

"On your knees," the captain grunted, pushing Amelie's shoulder toward the ground with his other hand.

Amelie felt the damp, cold sand under her knees. Desperately, she tried to concentrate on Gislingham's navel, which bulged curiously from under her father's ill-fitting clothes. The Englishman's skin was the color of finely milled wheat, and his hairless groin was covered with birthmarks of various sizes. Her handmaid had once said that every birthmark had a meaning, and the number and texture said something about the person's future. If what the old woman had said were true, Guy de Gislingham would at least survive this gruesome game. In order to fulfill all the prophecies that could be made from these brown spots, he would have to live for at least a hundred years.

A soldier pressed the blade of his sword to Gislingham's neck and his knee in his lower back, so that his semi-erect penis stretched toward Amelie provokingly. Simultaneously, her captor grasped Amelie's blonde locks and directed her head in the right direction until her sensitive nose almost touched Gislingham's penis.

"Go on, take him in your mouth!" the soldier commanded her.

The sight of his clammy member and the powerful smell of unwashed man was a blow to her stomach. Without warning, she threw up noisily on Gislingham's feet. She retched again, like the aftershock of an earthquake, and stopped only when yellow bile was all that she had left.

Swearing, the leader sprang back as the sour-smelling swill flowed between Gislingham's bare toes. Disgusted, the Englishman clenched his teeth into the alder wood gagging him and squeezed his eyes shut.

Before Amelie had regained her senses, a heavy blow struck her on the head.

"Bloody bitch," the man hissed, pushing her into the muck. "You lied. You are escaped members of the Order."

Amelie tasted blood. She dug her fingers into the sand to steady herself.

"Shackle her!" the man growled. "We haven't had this pleasure in quite some time."

Before Amelie could comprehend what he meant, the other men seized her arms and dragged her to a fallen oak log that lay pale and barkless on the bank. They threw her on her stomach over the log, the splintering wood biting mercilessly into her sensitive belly. Someone wrenched her wrists forward and bound them with rough ropes. Still on her knees, her hips were thrust back to the captain against her will. Two strong hands shoved the fabric of her cloak up, exposing her nakedness from the waist down. Her shoulders were pushed down, and her nose struck the sand.

"Bonifaz, come here!" the leader commanded. "It's time for you to learn a new lesson. You're up first!"

To show the youngest of the troop what he meant, the captain stuck his dirty middle finger into her vagina without warning. A burning pain jolted through her, and her body wrenched in agony.

"You must go in there," he laughed bawdily. "I hope you don't disappoint the lady!"

Slowly, he pulled his finger out again, sniffing it appreciatively like a dog picking up an intriguing scent. "Hurry up, Bonifaz," he said hoarsely, "I can hardly wait till it's my turn."

The pimply young man bit his lower lip nervously and looked, dazed, into the expectant faces of his companions. Hesitantly, he opened his waistband and kneeled behind the woman.

"If she doesn't manage to get us going, her faux husband will pay for it with his life," the leader added coldly.

A nod was enough, and the two men who had tied Amelie stood up and forced Guy de Gislingham onto his knees right next to her, pushing his head onto the thick log as if it was a beheading block.

The inexperienced soldier frantically struggled to press his far too soft member into the young woman.

A stinging sensation ran through Amelie, as though she were sitting on an anthill. With certain death before her, she hardly felt fear anymore as a leaden indifference gripped her. The only remaining sensation was a hot beam that ran through her middle and slowed her heartbeat. She thought about Struan and the child who might never see the light of day, and with her last shreds of strength, she filled her lungs with a single deep breath and let out an ear-shattering scream.

Dazzled by the rising morning sun, Gero squinted at the soft blue sky and saw a late flock of migratory birds flying overhead in a V formation. A sudden gurgling noise made him turn around abruptly. It was Johan, suffocating a royal soldier. He seized the struggling man by the neck and forced him down onto the ground.

Before Gero could process what was happening, a monstrous shadow rushed past him, and Gero first mistook it for a belligerent boar. A moment later he saw Struan's mighty figure, with sword in hand, galloping off toward the stream.

Looking around the area for other soldiers, Gero sprang up to help Johan.

The soldier had stopped moving. He lay on his back, staring blankly into the sky.

"I think he's dead," Johan remarked and stood up, breathing heavily. "He would have given us away," he whispered with a haunted look. "It appears he was not traveling alone. There are more of them below on the banks of the stream, and we fear that they've captured Gislingham and Amelie."

Gero glanced quickly at the Scotsman's sleeping-place. Amelie had disappeared, and the Englishman was nowhere to be seen.

Johan grabbed two crossbows and handed one to Gero. Meanwhile, Matthäus had awoken and was yawning widely. When he noticed the dead man, he let out a sharp cry that Gero stifled immediately by holding his hand over the boy's mouth.

"Stand up, Mattes," he whispered to him. "No matter what happens, stay here and saddle the horses. Quickly!"

"Come on, Gero," Johan called softly and swung the quiver with the bolts in the direction that Struan had taken. "There's work to be done."

With his back arched and his comrades goading him wildly, the young soldier thrust his half-hard penis into the rosy crevice of the young woman. Although the act seemed merely uncomfortable to him, he was obviously not sure if he had found the right position to finish the deed.

To help him, his companions had stuffed a handkerchief between the teeth of the screaming maiden. Hesitantly, the boyish soldier, looked to the side one last time.

The last thing he saw was a large shadow that suddenly obscured the warm, morning sun. And the last thing he felt was the impact two large, bare feet making the sandy bank shudder.

Accompanied by an inhuman sound, a Scottish broadsword separated his head from his body.

The head fell with a dull thud and landed directly in front of Amelie's face. Flinching, she drew back as the dead man stared at her with lifeless eyes. A torrent of warm liquid spilled over the nape of her neck, and the smell of blood filled the air. The next moment, the torso that had slumped over her was ripped forcefully away.

"Templars!" shouted a panicked voice.

Although Struan wasn't wearing his cloak, his opponents were experienced enough to recognize him from his jerkin, leather pants, and beard alone.

One of the soldiers attempted to lob off Guy de Gislingham's head. A whirr cut through the silence, however, and interrupted the efforts of the self-appointed executioner.

Gero watched the bolt he had fired pierce the soldier's forehead like a juicy melon. The iron bolt emerged from the back of the man's skull with a spray of blood.

Gislingham rolled to his side after the sword missed him by a hair's breadth, and its owner, a short, powerful man, collapsed on top of him with a groan.

With a second shot, Johan van Elk sent the soul of another soldier straight to damnation.

The remaining men were too shocked to react. They gaped dumbly at their comrade lying halfway into the stream, and stared at the blood that was slowly turning the water bright red.

Struan grabbed Amelie's waist and lifted her to her feet. Hastily, he cut through her fastenings and freed her from the gag. Her hair, arms, and hands were covered in blood. The sight of the fresh blood made her panic even more. Was it her own? Or Struan's?

"Run!" Struan hissed at her.

But Amelie was unable to leave Struan's side by even an inch. In mortal fear, she pressed the palms of her hands to her chest to calm her racing heart.

"Go to the campsite! Damn it, do what I say, woman!" Struan yelled again as he noticed that she had still not moved from the spot.

Meanwhile, Gero had loaded the crossbow again and took aim at the fleeing leader, who ran, changing his direction erratically, like a rabbit being hunted. From a distance of barely sixty feet, however, Gero's bolt missed its target.

With a loud cry and his sword raised, Struan ran after the fleeing man, driven not just by revenge. Like his Brothers, he knew that they could not allow the men to escape alive. To let them escape would mean death for the Scotsman and his companions. In an instant, they would have an entire army of royal soldiers hot on their heels until they reached the border. And even if they managed to cross over to Lorraine, no German ruler would protect them if they killed royal soldiers – leaving them responsible for the murder of Christian souls.

With the ferocity of a lion on the hunt, Struan chased the leader, cornering him on the edge of the small beech forest. When the man realized he had no way out, he turned around quickly, standing tall and pleading with Struan with his cold, gray eyes. Obviously he believed that his furious opponent was prepared to grant him mercy. As if paralyzed, he merely held his sword in his hand, unable to raise it against the Templar.

But Struan knew no mercy. He thought of Amelie and what the men had done to her. With a mighty blow of his broadsword, he sliced the body of the soldier in two clean halves from the crook of his neck to his hips, just as he had learned from the old Order veterans. His heart pounded, and the question of whether he had acted too cruelly floated faintly into his mind as he wiped the stranger's blood from his forehead with his palm.

He pushed the question from his mind when he heard Gero and Johan approaching.

"We can handle this," Gero said to Johan, who had drawn his sword, and was looking at him expectantly. "Look after Matthäus and Amelie. The lad should have prepared the horses."

Following Struan into the forest in search of the last surviving soldier, Gero quickly exchanged the crossbow for his sword.

Silently, the two friends combed through the undergrowth. Broken branches and trodden ferns showed them the path the man had taken.

Suddenly Struan stopped, raised his head, and closed his eyes. He stretched his large nose into the wind. As he slowly opened his coal-black eyes again, he seemed to Gero like a wolf that had picked up the scent of a lamb, and would not give up until he held his prey in his jaws.

Gero avoided making the slightest noise or movement.

Struan looked at him meaningfully and pointed with his head to the left, at a cluster of tall ferns. Lightning-quick, he turned to the side and without hesitation swung his sword into the fern. A piercing cry and a loud moan told him that he had not missed his mark.

As Gero parted the ferns, he found himself staring into the face of a French soldier who could not have been older than eighteen. He lay on his back, his right arm almost severed, his features reflecting a mixture of astonishment, agony, and terror.

Gero was still wondering what to do when Struan made the decision for him. He drew his dagger and dropped to his knees. He put an arm under the boy's neck and lifted him carefully, looking steadily into his brown eyes which were wide with fear. With a soothing smile and a few calming words, he stroked the sweat-damp hair from the forehead of the boy. Then he cut his throat in a quick, fluid movement.

Gero swallowed hard as the boy let out only a quick gasp before a sudden stillness took over. His gaze fell on the blood-smeared hand of the Scotsman, who returned the dead boy to the ferns and closed his eyelids. Struan rose carefully and rubbed the blood from his fingers with a few fern leaves.

In silent understanding, they left the dead soldier to his green tomb and returned to the water with quick strides.

When they arrived at the stream, Gero hastily gathered the bolts still lodged in the bodies of the royal soldiers.

The wooden stems were carved with the Order's symbol, which if discovered, would have immediately pointed to the Templars.

Gero tried in vain to pull the bolt out of one of the dead men, and was forced to lift the unlucky man's head by its brown locks to ease the shot from the back of the head. With a shudder, he studied the face. Staring blankly from half-opened lids, the eyes had lost all human expression. The steel point of the bolt had pierced through the back of the skull like a raw egg and blown out pieces of bone. The contents of the head presented themselves in a bloody pulp, flowing out into the sand. Gero gritted his teeth and closed his eyes briefly as he grasped the bolt by its tip and pulled it backward with a strong tug. A remnant of bloody, gray, brain matter clung to the feathers of the bolt then fell to the ground in one piece. He looked away in disgust. Only his empty stomach saved him from throwing up. Breathing heavily, he stood and went to the water.

Struan followed him. At the stream, the Scotsman washed his hands and face, then pulled his quilted jerkin over his head and attempted to rinse the blood-splattered garment.

In the silence, the feeling came over Gero that they were trying to cleanse not just their bodies and clothes from all traces of the crime, but also their souls. To kill a Christian was a grave sin. The sinner had to beg the Lord's forgiveness even if the act had been committed in self-defense, and, if caught by earthly authorities, he still had to face his mortal punishment.

"We have to move the bodies," Gero remarked. "Anyone could discover them here by the bank."

Struan nodded and looked around thoughtfully. The bodies of the three dead soldiers lay strewn on the sandbank rising out of the stream. A fourth lay cut in two under low bushes, hidden from view, and they did not need to dwell on the whereabouts of the fifth.

"Do you think there are more blueskirts in the area?" Struan asked.

"It's hard to say." Gero scratched his head and squinted at the sun to estimate the hour. "They might've belonged to a troop that's been searching for escaped members of the Order."

"Another reason to cover our tracks as thoroughly as possible," Struan whispered.

Before dragging the corpses into dense clumps of gorse bushes, they removed the cloaks and chain mail from the dead men. They threw the clothing, along with the swords bearing the symbol of the King of France, into a nearby pond, and watched the traces of their crime sink to the bottom of the water.

As Struan bent over to part the tall reeds surrounding the pond, he felt a quick movement by his feet. He stepped back in shock. Roused from its afternoon slumber, an asp viper slithered through the dead plants littering the banks of the pond.

86

"A bad omen!" The Scotsman looked at Gero with a horrified expression as he hastily made the sign of the cross.

Gero shook his head in bewilderment. "Do you really think it could get any worse than this?"

As they returned to the campsite, Gero found a pair of dainty, light brown leather boots on the sandy bank of the stream.

Struan took them from him without asking. "These belong to Amelie," he said, pressing the finely crafted boots firmly to his chest.

When they reached the campsite, they found that Johan had dragged the dead soldier away from the campfire and into some bushes, covering the man with branches and leaves so that Matthäus – and himself – would be spared from looking at the corpses any longer.

The boy crouched by the horses. Fear still haunted his face. Only when he saw his lord and the Scottish Brother emerge uninjured did he spring up, smiling in relief. Gero patted his shoulder.

"You're a brave lad," he said, winking in confidence at the young squire.

Guy de Gislingham was lying on the grass, staring absently into the sky.

Johan, who was packing the last of their possessions, had left the Englishman alone, and only raised his brows when Gero and Struan looked at him for an explanation. With an anxious expression, he gestured to Amelie who was curled up on the ground looking just as listless as Gislingham.

Despite her beauty, she was the picture of sorrow. With her blood-smeared blanket wrapped around her like a cocoon, she sat trembling in the grass, whispering words no one could hear. Her face was pale and her previously golden hair was encrusted with blood. Where her hair had retained its silky shimmer, it gleamed like copper. From time to time, a powerful shudder ran through her entire body.

Struan quickened his pace and kneeled down next to her.

"Mo ghraidh," he murmured in his Gaelic mother tongue, embracing her lovingly. He continued to soothe her in French, as his Brothers usually did with their horses, and lifted her carefully.

"I have to wash her," he said to Gero softly. "She won't calm down as long as she's still covered in blood."

Struan carried the motionless woman like a newborn in his arms.

Johan van Elk nodded respectfully as Gero ordered him to find a dress from the woman's belongings and to follow the Scotsman to the stream.

Dazed and without protest, Amelie let Struan remove her clothes gently and lower her, naked, into the water.

The ice-cold water revived her instantly. Undeterred by her loud whimpers, Struan held her firmly and rubbed the blood steadily from her neck and décolletage. Again and again, in his cupped hand, he scooped water over her matted hair and rinsed it until it regained its natural color. Then, he immersed her head in the water to make sure that every last reminder of the young soldier's death had been washed away in the flowing water. Amelie resurfaced, spluttering and snorting. As he helped her stand up, she lunged at him unexpectedly and gave him a resounding slap.

"Are you trying to drown me?" she screamed at him furiously.

Struan stood up to his knees in the stream, meeting her angry stare with disbelief as water ran in steady rivulets from her wet hair, over her firm breasts, and trickled down her supple thighs.

As if hypnotized, Johan van Elk stared at her heaving bosom and the long, damp locks that barely concealed her slightly swollen belly. Suddenly, she began to sob, and fell readily into Struan's open arms.

Gently, but resolutely, Struan grasped Amelie by the elbow and led her to the bank, where he and Johan helped her into fresh clothes.

"Take me away," she murmured, "to anywhere we can be safe."

CHAPTER 6

Death of a Templar

Friday, October 13, 1307, midday

The sun hung high in the heavens, bathing the autumn foliage in a golden glow. After about six hundred feet, Gero and the rest of the troop arrived at the old Templar route to Souvage-Magny. Before they set off again, Struan, Gero, and Johan took off their surcoats and turned their chlamys inside out to avoid being recognized from afar as Templars. As he waited for the rest of the riders, Gero looked around, making sure they would not meet a royal patrol or any toll keepers unawares again. At his hand signal, they crossed the broad, cobbled road.

It was Friday. If they maintained their pace and met no further obstacles, they should reach the Moselle by Sunday prayers.

Despite the need for haste, Gero gave the signal for rest after they had ridden for another hour. He had long noticed Matthäus sneaking covetous glances at the saddlebags filled with provisions. At a clearing fringed by beech trees, he ordered the troop to dismount.

Still standing, they sank their teeth ravenously into bread and sausages. Struan handed Amelie the skin of water, then took a large gulp himself and passed it to his Brothers.

When they were done, Gero ordered the company to prepare to set off again.

While Johan stored away the remaining provisions, Amelie asked Struan to accompany her while she relieved herself behind a thicket. As she climbed up a slight incline, a stifled gasp rang out from the woods. Amelie wanted to cry out, but Struan was quicker, stopping her scream with a warm hand placed over her mouth. Protectively he pushed her behind his back and stepped forward with his sword drawn. In the shadows of the trees something moved, and the pair heard a soft, steady moan.

Amelie followed Struan, clinging nervously to his sword arm.

"Go to the campsite and alert the others," he whispered to her.

"I can't," she murmured in reply. "I'm scared."

He sighed and pulled her gently into the shadows of a mighty spruce. "Then at least stay back," he whispered, "and let me find out what's going on."

As Amelie cowered next to the sprawling roots, Struan crouched down and worked his way silently through the springy grass carpet to a head-high boulder. As he ventured a cautious look behind the tall rock, the sight struck him like a sudden blow.

Making sure it wasn't a trap, the Scotsman's eyes darted around rapidly before he approached the gravely wounded figure on the ground. A closer look at the young man made all his doubts evaporate. It was a Brother of the Order, and he appeared to be on the verge of death.

"Amelie," Struan called, looking up briefly. "He is one of us! Get Gero and tell him to bring water and the medical bag."

The urgent note in Struan's voice made Amelie overcome her fear.

She hitched up her skirts and ran back to the clearing.

"Keep still, Brother," Struan said as he kneeled down, shooing away a swarm of flies that had already claimed the unknown man's blood-drenched torso for their meal. Carefully, he tried to set the Brother upright, but a stifled cry of pain stopped him from doing so. Struan noticed that even the ground was drenched with blood.

Suddenly Gero was standing behind him with a blanket in one hand and a saddlebag in the other. The goatskin filled with water was clamped under his arm. He had come alone, leaving Johan to protect Matthäus, Amelie, Gislingham, and the horses.

Struan placed the blanket under the injured knight's head while Gero kneeled on the other side and brought the fresh water carefully to the man's parched lips.

The injured Brother was wearing neither his chain mail nor chlamys, but Gero and Struan recognized him by his pants and boots. His face was pale as snow, and deep shadows had settled under his eyes.

Struan thought he had seen the injured man once at a crossbow tournament in the Order. After examining the man's ugly wounds more closely, he exchanged a knowing look with Gero. His jerkin had been slit open on the right side of his torso between his ribs and groin. There, blood had dyed the fabric scarlet, and the tear in the fabric revealed a gaping wound that exposed the damaged coils of his intestines. It was a miracle that the Brother had even survived till now.

"We are from Bar-sur-Aube. To which commandery do you belong?" Gero asked in a hushed voice as he took from the saddlebag a small earthen vial sealed with wax. The vial contained a secret pain-relieving and sleep-inducing tincture. Carefully, he opened the seal of the vial with his teeth and spat out the wax that coated his lips.

"Brother Petrus, from Montier en Der," the man answered, his voice cracking.

"What happened, Brother?" Struan asked.

"Philipp's soldiers ... they attacked us ... before the early mass." He stopped, continuing again only after Gero helped him drink from the waterskin. "When we refused to leave the house, they burned everything to the ground. And they chained anyone who ran outside. I was the only one who stood up to the bastards against the commander's orders. I tried to save my horse from the burning stables ... " He coughed painfully, pausing before he could speak again.

"The soldiers blocked my path, and we fought. Near the end I was defending myself against eight men. I could not keep them all at bay and one of them slashed me open as I fought against the others."

Brother Petrus tried to sit up on his elbows to look at his wounds, but immediately sank back onto the blanket with a groan.

"And how did you manage to make it all the way here?"

"They threw me on one of the carts. They'd run out of chains and ropes, and they probably thought I didn't have long to live anyway. It was dark ... and when no one was looking, I let myself fall from the wagon and dragged myself here."

The Brother closed his eyes. His breathing grew quicker.

"Here, drink this," Gero said quietly, and set the vial to his lips. "It will relieve your pain."

The wounded Templar drank every last drop of the bitter liquid with closed eyes, showing no expression.

The drink would kill him. Any Brother with the slightest medical knowledge knew that the mixture of opium, mandrake, and thorn apple was used not just for pain relief but also, when administered in higher doses, to hasten the process for those at death's door. The small vial was marked with a black cross. The controversial tincture would soon carry the poor Brother into the next realm without further suffering or struggle.

"You know, Brother, it is better to die here, outside, amongst God's creation, than to spend my last hours of existence in a stinking dungeon, where the rats would gnaw the flesh from my bones before my body grew cold."

Gero kneeled next to the man and searched for a way to reassure the Brother. As he touched the man's forehead, a shudder came over him. The cold sweat of death bathed the man's skin. Brother Petrus felt for Gero's hand and grasped it.

"My full name is Petrus de Monet," he panted. "My family comes from Languedoc. Should you ever have the chance, tell them … that I died honorably, and that none of the accusations about us are true."

His words faded away to a whisper as his breathing grew weaker. Gero stroked his sweat-drenched hair.

"You'll be entering paradise, where Saint Peter will welcome you with joy," he said, knowing that it was a promise he couldn't guarantee. He finally managed to meet the gaze of the young Brother. Evidently, Brother Petrus was ready to meet his fate.

"Pray with me … please," the dying man whispered weakly.

Gero nodded silently. "In nomini patris et filii et spiritus sancti …" he chanted, Struan's hoarse voice joining in as they recited the Lord's Prayer, blessing the Brother.

Gero held the dying man's hand, a hand that seemed to him as cold as eternal damnation. Long after the prayer had faded away and Petrus de Monet's soul had departed, he still clutched the stiff fingers as though he were afraid to face the inevitable.

Struan crouched on the other side of the dead man and shut his eyes. As he lowered Brother Petrus's head, a few tears dropped from his large nose onto the corpse's arm. It was the first time that Gero had seen the Scotsman cry.

Silently, they swaddled the Brother's lifeless body in the blanket and bound him carefully with a rope. They had neither enough time nor the equipment to dig him a proper grave, and so, holding his head and feet, they laid the covered body in a shallow depression in the forest floor and covered him with spruce branches. It would take some time until the forest's animals would claim him for themselves.

When Gero and his troop set off again, they rode around the several commanderies that lay on their path, avoiding the larger villages and stations where road tolls were levied. At sunset, they reached the wide banks of the Marne. About half a mile southeast, they saw the looming silhouette of Saint Dizier's church tower transform the dusky blue evening sky into a shadow theatre.

Five hundred feet away, a ferryman sat before his hut enjoying the last rays of the setting sun. The man was obviously alone, and Gero hoped to take at least Amelie and Matthäus across the river with their feet dry.

"Outrageous," Struan murmured after the ferryman had stood up and named his price for a river crossing: six Sous Livres. "You could buy a full-grown sheep with that."

The wizened features of the ferryman's face contorted into a cunning grin.

"Young friend," he began, laying his dirty hand boldly on Struan's shoulder. "You'll die otherwise!"

The Scotsman brushed away the old man's arm as if he had been a leper, lowering his bushy brows in a threatening glare.

"Don't be so hasty," the ferryman countered with unexpected arrogance as he appraised the Brothers' clothes.

"Actually, the price should be higher than that. Even a blind man can see that you are Templars, even if you aren't wearing your cloaks as you usually do. A little bird fluttered past yesterday, and whispered that *someone* would love to see you locked up. A tip-off from me, and crossing a river would be the least of your worries."

Struan seized the man, who was a good measure shorter than him, by the collar of his frayed jacket.

"Listen to me, old man," he hissed as he dragged him mercilessly from his feet. "If you think that a wolf is any less dangerous because a pack of dogs is following it, you're mistaken. That's precisely when it will tear through the throat of anyone standing in its way." The Scotsman bared his impressive teeth in a wicked grin.

Even Amelie found the feral strength of Struan's threat unnerving. She now knew that he was capable of killing someone without flinching, but until this moment, she hadn't imagined he would finish off an adversary with his bare teeth.

"Struan, let him go," Gero commanded.

With a scornful snort, the Scotsman pushed the old man away. Staggering, the ferryman struggled to maintain his balance.

"Tell us the usual price," Gero demanded.

The man gulped, and, with an uncertain look at Struan, he squawked, "A Sous Livres."

"Well, what luck," Johan muttered as he proceeded to the flat boat by the shore and loaded it with some of their belongings.

Gislingham, who could not swim, followed the ferryman. Full of mistrust, the old man had agreed to board the boat first, probably fearing that otherwise they could take off without him.

A little later, Amelie climbed onto the wobbly boat with Matthäus's help.

Gero, Johan, and Struan stripped off their clothes and boots, then secured them to the saddles of their horses. Gero had seen knights crossing a river, who, for whatever reason, had kept on their chain mail and trousers, and drowned mercilessly when they suddenly lost their footing in deep waters. He would take no such chance.

Undaunted, the men advanced into the ice-cold water.

Upon seeing Gero's horrified face, Struan grinned broadly. "If you'd been baptized in a Scottish loch, this wouldn't bother you at all."

"This reminds me of my youth," Johan remarked through chattering teeth, "when I once fell through the ice by the banks of the Rhine and nearly drowned."

Even the horses were reluctant to enter the chilly water, and the three men had to tug hard at the reins to lead them into the river.

After a stretch of about a hundred and fifty feet, they waded with great relief to the other bank. Gero let himself fall into some dry grass and waited until his racing heartbeat slowed down, enjoying the evening sun that, for a fleeting moment, had transformed the river into a glistening ribbon of light.

After dressing and reloading the horses, they decided to search for a safe place to spend the night before it became too dark.

They travelled for about half a mile in the twilight before arriving at a hamlet with several houses and barns.

Gero dismounted and handed Struan his horse's reins while he knocked on the door of the first farmhouse where a dim light still burned. The home seemed relatively large to him, and he guessed that its residents were not particularly poor.

The massive door was carved from oak. Gero's knock sounded perhaps a touch too forceful. When no one answered, he hammered again on the hard wood and waited alertly in the doorway.

Suddenly he heard steps and the door creaked open, revealing only a narrow gap. Someone was holding a flickering candle in front of his nose. At first, he was too blinded to clearly see his surprised counterpart.

"Help me, Jesus and Mary," an unnervingly high voice shrieked. "They are Templars!"

With a creak, the door was shut again, then bolted with a clattering noise.

Despite the fact that they hadn't been received with open arms, it was a good sign that the woman spoke with a noticeably Lorraine accent. The German border could not be far away.

In the house, a heated discussion was taking place.

"The Christian militia boozes, indulges in whores, and rapes women." The farm wife raised her voice in agitation. "If you let the men outside in, I'm taking my daughter and moving to my sister's, tonight!"

Despite these baseless allegations, Gero tried his luck once more.

A moment later, the door was opened again, and this time, an older, corpulent, bald man peered out. He was a good deal shorter than Gero, and wore the typical rugged brown and gray clothes of a farming liegeman.

"How may I be of assistance, Seigneurs?" he asked uncertainly.

"Is that how you welcome a man of God who has fought for the cross?" To reassure the farmer, Gero had intentionally spoken to him in the region's dialect.

"I beg your pardon," the man explained ruefully, "my wife is not entirely herself. She meant no offence."

"We only need lodging for the night," Gero replied patiently. "It's already dark, and the next commandery is miles away."

"How many of you are there?" the man asked, stretching his short neck hesitantly out of the door to assess the situation.

Gero easily recognized that the farmer himself was not completely without fear that a horde of notorious Templars could turn his house upside down and seduce his innocent daughter.

"We have four men, a woman, and a boy."

The farmer raised his oil lamp to verify Gero's claim, simultaneously trying to read the faces of the men to see if they were rogues or trustworthy.

Struan had dismounted to help Gero with the man's concerns. He stepped forward so that the farmer could see him. This was probably not a good idea, as the man's expression quickly turned to fear.

Gero squared his shoulders and assumed the stern face he had often seen his father wear when dealing with evasive liegemen. Ultimately he had no intention of wandering from door to door like Mary, Joseph, and baby Jesus until they finally found someone who would take them in.

"Forgive me for not introducing myself," he said in the calm, deep voice of a father confessor. "My name is Gero of Breydenbach. I come from a respected noble family from the archdiocese of Trier. My mother's family has familial bonds to the House of Lichtenberg."

Gero hoped that his introduction would impress the farmers. The Lords of Lichtenberg were famous in the region. They ruled over half of Alsace, and had occupied the Bishop's seat of Strasburg and Metz until a few years ago.

The farmer's wife, who still stood behind her husband, tried one last time. "We are just poor farmers and surely cannot offer you the accommodations that you are used to. Moreover, I can only offer you simple soup for dinner." In false humility, she lowered her eyes.

"Madame, do not think that we Templars are used to luxurious beds, and the Lord blesses even a simple meal. Where can we shelter our horses?"

With a short, elegant bow, Gero made clear that he had no intention of being rejected again.

The farmer finally conceded defeat. As he let out a loud whistle, a tall, gangly boy, who had already been watching curiously from the barn door, lit a pine pitch torch and led the horses into the stables.

CHAPTER 7

Betrayal

Saturday, October 14, 1307, morning

A sleepy stillness had settled over the thatched roof farmhouse. Matthäus tiptoed quietly through the stable to the latrine. Unbidden, fat Brother Adam, who instructed the squires of the commandery in courtly behavior, appeared in his mind's eye.

"If I catch any of you pissing in the courtyard or washing rooms for convenience's sake, I'll personally make you a eunuch! Should anyone be bolder, and forego a trip to the latrine to attend to even bigger business anywhere near the commandery, I'll lock him in the pig stables for fourteen days, naked as the day he was born."

No one had ever dared to test whether Brother Adam would hold true to his exaggerated threats.

In the dim morning light, Matthäus saw that Johan van Elk had rolled himself in one of the Order's blankets, and was lying between two straw heaps in front of the door to the courtyard. His head resting on his right elbow, he snored softly with his mouth agape, clutching his sword with his right hand so tightly they seemed to have become one.

Guy de Gislingham, however, had apparently already left his bed, as he was nowhere to be seen.

Outside, behind the stables, it was cold and misty. As Matthäus loosened the cords of his trousers to relieve himself, his gaze slid over the surrounding hamlet that rose out of the mist between the fruit trees and isolated oak woods. The discordant squawking of a few crows cut through the early morning silence, but, suddenly, Matthäus realized it was not the only disturbance. Squinting into the distance, he made out a troop of riders coming ever closer down a neighboring hill and, with a jolt, the boy recognized the riders' clothing. The flag-bearer in the front was carrying the crest of Philipp IV of France. He tried to quickly count the men and horses but before he was finished, they had disappeared into the base of a valley.

With a pounding heart, he ran back into the stable to Johan and shook the Brother's arm vigorously.

Startled from his slumber, Johan sprang around quickly and Matthäus almost lost his nose as the Templar's murderous blade missed its target by a hair.

"Mattes, you fool," Johan grunted in shock. "Don't do that again. It could cost you your head."

"If we don't leave soon, it will cost *all* our heads," Matthäus exclaimed fearfully. In his distress, his voice nearly failed him. "It's swarming with French soldiers outside! I saw them! They're coming in droves through the valley. What will we do if they find us here?"

Johan glanced quickly to where Guy de Gislingham had been sleeping the night before, a spot that now lay empty. "Does Gero know?"

"No."

"Run and warn him. I'll saddle the horses!"

"Y-yes sir!" Matthäus stammered, scurrying away.

Upon receiving the news, Gero dressed quickly. In the hallway, he bumped into the farmer's wife, who was approaching him in a woolen, ankle-length shirt. He barely managed to avoid the full chamber pot that she was balancing in one hand.

The Templar pushed open the door to the chamber where he presumed Struan and his lover would be. The Scotsman had spent the night with Amelie away from the eyes of his comrades.

"Damn it," he exclaimed as Gero startled him out of his sleep. He struggled into his pants while Amelie fought with the bands of her surcoat. Struan pulled the half-dressed Amelie behind him, past the bewildered farmer's wife, who was still standing in the hallway gaping at the strange commotion, and followed Gero into the sitting room, where the rest of their belongings lay.

When they were fully clothed, armed, and packed, they ran down the small corridor.

The farmer's wife sprang to the side in shock, letting her chamber pot clatter to the floor.

This ruckus made no impression on Gero, who swung open the door to the stables, allowing Struan and Amelie to pass. He followed them, letting the door shut with a bang.

Shortly thereafter, seemingly roused by the commotion and his wife's shrieks, the man of the house appeared in the stable yawning heartily.

Gero barely noticed his visibly confused host.

"Is there another way out of this village?" he asked the surprised-looking farmer.

"In God's name, why are you in such a rush?"

"Never mind that," Gero snapped impatiently. "Pray tell, how do we get out of here unnoticed?"

With a brief glance, the farmer saw that his unsolicited guests were all ready for the road. He regarded Gero with an odd look. "Where's your servant, then?"

Gero looked around in panic. Servant? Only then did he notice that Guy de Gislingham was nowhere to be seen.

"He took one of your horses with him." With an accusing look, the farmer gestured towards an empty iron rack on the opposite wall. "And if I'm not mistaken, *I'm* missing a saddle and bridle myself!"

Johan van Elk stared in horror at the empty stall where, just yesterday, a piebald Great Horse had stood. Somehow, Brother Guy must have managed not just to vacate his bed during the night, but to steal the horse as well.

"And one of my horse blankets is missing, too," the farmer added. "*You* must account for that. He belonged to you."

Johan was furious with himself. Damn it, why did he not notice that Gislingham had run off?

"It's extremely clear why he's buggered off," Struan grumbled scornfully. "He wants to avoid being caught with us. With his ratty clothes, ragged blanket, and a simple saddle, no one would have any idea he belongs to the Order."

"It does us no good to argue about it," Gero barked in annoyance. "We must leave."

"And what about what happened to my crockery?" the farmer cried out. "I demand that you replace it!"

Amelie, who was huddled against Struan, suddenly started searching under his jerkin until she found her money pouch in his belt bag. Struan looked at her in surprise, but he held his tongue. She opened the small leather pouch and fished out a large silver coin.

"Here," she said to the farmer and held out the coin to him. "With this, you can easily afford a Lombard saddle and a blanket of Flemish brocade, and if you tell me which path leads out of the village without going through the main street, I'll add another two coins to that."

"Well," the farmer grunted. He weighed the coin in his hand with satisfaction. "Come! It's this way."

"Do you think you can ride Arnaud's Brabant?" Gero looked at Matthäus inquiringly. The boy was slight, and the brown steed that Gislingham had left behind was not as well behaved as Stephano de Sapin's Great Horse.

"Of course," Matthäus replied. "I took care of the horse for a while when Brother Arnaud's squire had a fever."

"Very well!" Gero helped the boy into the saddle.

"We must hurry," Johan hissed, pointing into the distance where the group of blueskirts were approaching a distant, neighboring farmhouse.

"Are they looking for you?" The eyes of the farmer flashed with pure terror.

"It seems so," Gero muttered. Did the man want even more money to stay quiet? *he thought.*

But the farmer did not reply. He walked straight to a stand of oak trees behind the barn where he regularly let his pigs graze.

"You should disappear as quickly as you can," he said urgently.

"I hope you are a God-fearing man," Amelie said as she handed the farmer the promised silver. "If you are compassionate, you will not give us away."

The man deliberately evaded her gaze.

"May the Almighty be with you," he murmured apologetically, and, with an ashamed look, stuck the money into the pocket of his coat.

They mounted their horses quickly and rode away between the low trees. The foliage resembled a thick curtain that protected them from the eyes of the steadily approaching royal troops.

Only when they thought they were safe did they spur their horses and gallop away toward the northeast.

When the farmer returned to his farmhouse, a nasty surprise was waiting for him. In his absence the blueskirts had infiltrated the courtyard and turned everything upside down. His wife stood wailing in the doorway, begging the men not to smash their furniture.

"Are you the head of the house?" demanded an imposing officer with sparse brown hair. A bumpy scar ran from his chin to his left eyebrow, making his grim face appear even more fearsome.

"Yes ... captain," the farmer answered uncertainly.

"Is it true that you harbored members of the Knights Templar?"

The farmer exchanged a quick, fearful look with his wife. She nodded dumbly.

"We did not know they were Templars," he attempted to defend himself.

"Where are they?"

"I don't know. They are gone."

The blow came so suddenly that the farmer could not have avoided it. The entire right side of his face burned, and he felt a warm stream of blood flowing from his nose over his lips. His wife began to cry hysterically.

"Silence the blasted woman and search the house and courtyard!" the officer barked at some of the soldiers before turning again to the farmer. A bullish soldier threatened to hit the farmer's wife. Her screams transformed instantly into a suppressed sob as a group of soldiers entered the house.

"So, my good man, try not to lie," the captain said sharply. "Here is someone who can attest to the fact that you knew exactly who you were harboring, and fed them and offered them wine at that."

The farmer gasped. His knees began to tremble as the supposed servant of his escaped guests stepped forward.

"Yes, I told you, this is the man. If they are no longer in the house, he definitely helped them escape," Guy de Gislingham sneered, adopting a lordly manner that ill-suited his shabby clothes.

For a moment the farmer debated whether he should expose the man who had arrived with the others yesterday, and, more than that, had stolen his saddle. But something held him back. The previous evening, he had wondered about this strange servant who had so rudely demanded wine after the guests had only been offered water. In all likelihood, he had long been on the side of the soldiers, and perhaps the Templars hadn't known that a viper lay hidden among them.

"Lord … Lord … " the farmer's wife began to lament. "Tell us, in the name of God, what of the Templars? Since when is it a crime to offer them a place for the night? Don't they stand under the protection of our Holy Father?"

"Foolish cow," the ringleader snorted. "Two days ago his Highness, King Philipp IV, ordered all Templars in France to be arrested. Since yesterday morning, notices have been put up everywhere calling for the people of France to assist in the arrest of fleeing members of the Order. Information that leads to arrests will be rewarded with two pounds of

Tournosen. On the other hand, whoever helps them escape will be thrown into the dungeons, and who knows … " he said, reveling in the woman's horrified look, "perhaps the gallows await your husband, too. Should it be discovered that he has connections to the Order," the soldier continued coldly, "your entire property will be seized on the King's behalf."

Behind the farmers, two figures clad in blue stepped out of the door.

"The wanted men are no longer here. We found only a saddle and a bridle, both bearing the cross pattée of the Templars," a young recruit reported.

A stab of horror ran through the farmer. Damn it, in the hurry, no one had thought of the remaining equipment for the missing horse!

"Shackle him!" the officer yelled to the two men, and the soldiers bound the farmer's hands behind his back.

Stunned, the stocky man fell to the ground. His wrists were bound so tightly that the blood to his fingers was cut off.

In the soft pink light of the rising sun, a few spectators had gathered at a respectful distance, gaping at the strange spectacle.

"Where's my money?" asked the pale-faced man, whom the farmer had mistaken for a servant of the Templars.

"You'll have to settle that with your commissioner, Seigneur Gislingham," the captain grunted. "According to your watchword, you are on the payroll of our Keeper of the Seals. Everything will be paid accordingly."

"Then I hereby request an advance," the agent of Guillaume de Nogaret retorted, holding out his hand impatiently. "Don't forget, my father is the Lord of Gislingham, and the poverty I have endured as part of my mission does not mean that I am accustomed to being penniless."

"I can give you money," the farmer yelled. The budding hope that he could win the favor of his captors drove him to a rash confession. "There are two pieces of silver in my pocket. It's all the money I own. I only beg humbly to buy my freedom with it."

Gislingham raised an eyebrow and looked at the surrounding soldiers in surprise. "Did you forget to search the fool, or did you want to keep the money for yourself?" he hissed.

Faster than the bewildered men could react, Gislingham fished the money out of the farmer's coat pocket with a triumphant smile. "Freedom?" he croaked with a malicious grin. "You should be happy if you survive … without the bribe the Templars gave you for your silence."

He tossed the coin into the air and caught it deftly.

"Thank you for your support," he said, taking a perverse pleasure at the farmer's bewildered face.

As if they had been summoned, a cavalcade of eight riders tore into the courtyard and took their places in front of the captain.

"Ride to the north," the leader of the troop commanded them. "They will try to cross the border to Lombardy. Be careful," he called to his men as they rode off. "They are Templars, not harmless choir boys!"

CHAPTER 8

Beguine Cloister

Saturday, October 14, 1307, afternoon

By midday, Gero and his companions had long since left Bar-le-Duc behind them, a village near the German Lands border in the County of Champagne. If they did not stop, they could reach St. Mihiel in the evening, where they hoped to be safe.

Amelie sat limply in her saddle, completely exhausted. Struan guided his Frisian close to her small mare and studied the clenched features of his lover. She attempted to put on a brave face, forcing a pained smile, and blew him a kiss. He patted her knee as he rode by, then spurred on his horse and rode up to Gero, who was leading the troop.

"Amelie urgently needs a rest, and she's not the only one," Struan remarked, glancing at the glistening coat of his black stallion with concern. "Look at this sweat," he added.

Gero heaved a sigh. "Yes, you're right," he said as he rubbed the damp neck of his own horse with the palm of his hand.

The sun was burning down on them as if determined to win its war against autumn. They desperately needed to find water where they could fill their waterskins, let the horses drink, and find something to satisfy their hunger. The last thing they had eaten was the meager soup from the farmer's wife, and they had no more provisions. With soldiers looking for them, the towns and larger hamlets where they could have purchased some food were too dangerous.

With a sharp pull to the left, Gero steered his steed away from the road and toward a plowed-up grain field surrounded by a small beech forest. He knew this area and that there was a stream not far away.

The troop followed Gero without needing a command. Before they crossed the field, Gero reined in his horse and squinted into the distance. Two deer that were grazing peacefully under the trees led Gero to assume that they themselves had to be the only humans for miles around.

"The way is clear," he said softly, waving to his companions to indicate that they could follow him safely.

Without warning, a pair of crows flew up into the sky and the deer began to flee. Shortly before the troop arrived at the forest edge, a stampede of riders stormed out of the thicket, hooting wildly.

"Mattes, in God's name, stay with me!" Gero yelled to his squire. "No matter what happens!"

Matthäus had no time to answer. Instinctively, he squeezed the sides of the mighty Brabant. The animal reared up, dashed behind Atlas, and galloped north with its rider.

Struan ducked into the woods with Amelie. With two mounted soldiers close behind them, they disappeared into the thick undergrowth.

Johan made his escape across the open field. His horse's hooves pounded across the ground as he fled in full gallop. With his head ducked, he ventured a look behind him. They were definitely royal soldiers. Three men were chasing him alone. Their horses were unbelievably swift, and appeared to be getting closer and closer. Before him, the high plateau ended in a steep, forested valley. Johan clicked his tongue and squeezed the flanks of his steed mercilessly to draw out the last of its strength.

Finally, he reached the first trees. A wooded trail led through a sparse beech grove and steep, rocky precipices. Ruthlessly, he drove his stone-gray stallion forward. He knew he was leaving his tracks in the soft undergrowth, and that sooner or later he would have to confront the soldiers.

Suddenly he noticed something moving among the trees.

With his sword drawn, he approached the spot. Between two firs, he saw a thin female figure appear like an apparition. She was at most twenty years old. Frozen to the spot, she stared at him with large, gentle eyes. Her muddy, green, full-length woolen surcoat blended with the foliage, and her rust-red hair flowed down her back like a shower of autumn leaves, sparkling in the last rays of the afternoon sun. In one hand, she held a wicker basket filled with all sorts of mushrooms, and in the other, a walking stick with a small shovel fastened on one end.

When Johan saw the beautiful young woman open her mouth to scream, he pulled the reins of his Jutlander so hard that the animal pranced two steps back as it came to a stop. He placed his right index finger on his lips to warn her to keep quiet. The woman gaped at him in horror, as everyone did when first confronted with his disfigured features. Relieved that she had remained silent, Johan stuck his sword back in its hilt and drove his horse forward with his heels, still not letting her out of his sight.

As he was riding by, his arm deftly encircled her waist and lifted her onto his horse.

Still clutching the basket, she let the walking stick fall as she found herself sitting in front of Johan on the broad, bespoke Templar saddle. She seemed to be mute, as no word of protest came from her lips.

"Shh … " he calmed her with his low voice. "Don't be afraid. You don't need to fear any harm from me." As if to emphasize his words, he squeezed her waist more firmly. "Can you understand me?"

A timid nod told him that the Almighty had not made her deaf as well.

"Do you have any idea where we can hide near here?" he whispered, his lips nearly touching her ear.

"Over there," she said, so loudly and suddenly that Johan nearly fell off the horse in shock.

The woman was pointing to a rocky overhang at the foot of a great fir tree that had clawed its roots into a steep sloping hillside.

Johan sprang from his horse and lifted the young woman off without warning. He urged his steed toward the towering wall of branches, earth, and stones.

"Who are you?" she asked in a hushed voice.

"Forgive me for grabbing you," he responded with an apologetic bow. "My name is Johan van Elk … I am being followed," he added in explanation as he peered over the edge of their hiding place.

"Soldiers?" she asked, cocking her head. "What was your crime?"

"I belong to the Christian militia," he answered, pushing his cloak aside for a moment so that she could see the red cross of the Order.

"A Templar … Since when has belonging to the Order been a crime?"

"You should ask the King of France," he murmured, glancing back again to watch for the royal soldiers. "Or the Pope."

"All bastards," she murmured.

"What did you say?" Johan looked at her in amazement.

"I belong to the Order of the Beguines, if you know what that means."

"Of course," Johan said as he studied her slender figure more carefully. The communities of the Beguines were almost just as reviled by Philipp as the Templars. But as far as Johan knew, the women were altogether too poor and insignificant for Philipp to waste his war machinery on. There were subtler ways to hurt them. It was far too easy for King Philipp of France to besmirch the name of anyone who displeased him.

"Listen," Johan whispered. "I'd like you to hide here, but keep away from my horse. Understand?"

She nodded, too stunned to answer. A crossbow was fastened tightly to his saddle. With a few tugs, he loosened it, raised it, and inserted a bolt into it. Then he slipped away. Her tense gaze followed him. She preferred not to think of what would happen if he were defeated and the soldiers found her with his horse.

The rustling of foliage and the hushed hoof-beats on the forest floor grew steadily louder. The Beguine woman moved to the edge of her hideout and came to the uneasy realization that she could not see the Templar knight anywhere. Surely he wouldn't have abandoned her? That didn't match with what she'd heard about the Templars. Many said they were brave men who never avoided danger, but there were also those who claimed the Templars were no knights, but barbarians to whom nothing was holy, and whose lives were defined by fighting and drinking. No one, however, had ever called them cowards.

A whirring noise wrenched the young woman out of her thoughts. About 150 feet away, on the other side of a stream that crossed the valley, she saw one of the three approaching riders jerk when a bolt from the crossbow hit him. The soldier grasped his neck and his features contorted with pain. Blood sprayed from between his splayed fingers. He fell from his horse, remaining motionless on the forest path as his horse galloped away in fear. The two other soldiers began to shout. In their panic, they tried to re-orientate themselves. Their heads flailed wildly as their horses pranced in a circle.

Suddenly a loud whistle pierced the air. The massive steed near the woman neighed and threw its head in the air. She dodged the animal just before it took off after a second whistle.

"There he is," one of the pursuers cried, stretching out his arm.

Her heart pounded heavily as she witnessed the two remaining soldiers storm towards the Templar who was standing on a knoll, taunting them with his sword. She watched wide-eyed as the horse rode directly to its master and the Templar swung himself nimbly onto its back. With his sword in one hand and his shield in the other, he steered the piebald colossus only with his thighs.

The attackers could ride only in single file, as the path they tore along was too narrow for two riders – a fact that the Templar used to his advantage. Fearlessly, he galloped toward his adversaries. His first blow was so heavy that he knocked the shield out of the first soldier's hand. With the next blow, the knight struck the soldier's sword arm. Although the chain mail prevented Johan from slicing his skin open, the force of the impact rendered the soldier immobile. In the following strikes, the soldier, now without his shield, lost his head.

The Beguine woman bit her lip at the sight of the headless corpse. She squeezed her eyes so tightly shut that colorful stars danced before them. Only the panicked whinny of a horse made her open her eyes again.

The remaining soldier had turned his horse around and was preparing to flee, but the Templar spurred his battle steed on behind him. The two did not go far. A low-hanging branch wiped the escapee clean off his saddle and, to the woman's surprise, the Templar sprang from his horse as well.

His opponent lay groaning on the forest floor, stretching out his arm in despair to seize his weapon. But the sword and shield lay beyond his grasp.

Just three steps away, the Templar raised the man's deadly blade with the toe of his boot and lobbed it in the direction of the desperate soldier. Obviously, he did not want to just stab him to death like a wild boar with a stick, but was instead challenging him to a fair fight.

"Fight!" he hollered, "if you have the courage. Your life is at stake, and that should be of some worth to you!"

Johan stood expectantly with his legs apart. After the soldier had picked up his sword and shield, he looked around again uncertainly as if he were hoping for help.

But the only person who could have joined the two adversaries in this ill-fated contest stood aside, faint, and feeling as if she would throw up at any moment.

The swords met one another in a violent crash. The bluecoat fought as one already condemned to die. Had Johan van Elk not dodged his blows deftly, the man would have caught the German Templar. The strained, guttural groans from the men made the Beguine woman quiver.

The soldier's movements were becoming increasingly erratic, and Johan parried them with ease. As his opponent aimed for his head, inadvertently wrenching his shield upwards, Johan ducked and turned quickly. Keeping his momentum, he struck the soldier. The blow had such force that Johan's Damascene blade dissected the chain rings like butter, slicing the unfortunate man open at his navel. With a stifled gasp, the soldier slumped forward and fell silently to the ground, where he remained writhing in agony.

Johan waited in front of his victim, still ready for battle, until the wheezing whimpers faded. Then he stepped back, breathing heavily, wiped the sweat from his brow, and looked at his lifeless adversary. Quickly, he made the sign of the cross, a gesture his silent observer did not fail to notice. Carefully, she stepped out of her hiding place. He turned to her as though he had felt her eyes on his back.

"Are you all right?" he called to her.

"Me?" she answered in disbelief from across the stream. "Why me? You were the one who was fighting. I should be asking you that."

Johan bent down and dragged the corpse toward the stream, before letting it fall and shaking his head. She thought he was already returning to her when he once again turned around, walking a few steps up the slope. All the while his mighty steed trotted behind him like a faithful dog following its master.

Johan kneeled down beside the man he had killed with his crossbow. His back was turned to her and the woman could not see exactly what he was doing.

Before he returned to her he retrieved the crossbow, which, in the heat of the skirmish, had been abandoned on the hill.

"Do the Templars always pray by their enemies when they send them into the afterlife?" she asked as he strode toward her.

"Why do you say that?" he asked, surprised.

"Well, I saw you making the sign of the cross over the fallen soldier after your duel, and how you kneeled down by the other two dead men there."

"Maybe I was trying to cleanse my conscience when I made the sign … " he said hesitantly, "and I had to pull the bolt out of the second soldier's neck. It's carved with the Order's symbol. I certainly don't need to announce to the world that a Templar killed him!"

As evidence, he held up the bloody bolt near her face for her to inspect. The woman gagged and quickly cupped her hand over her mouth. She turned away in disgust.

Immediately, Johan hid the bolt behind his back, looking concerned.

"Oh," he gasped, and touched her shoulder with his reasonably clean hand. " … I didn't want to horrify you."

She avoided his gaze and shook her head. "No … don't think that way. It's just that … I've never seen anything like this. Besides, I can't bear the sight of blood. My Sisters in the Order grumble every day that I can't even slaughter a chicken, let alone help deliver a baby."

"I wouldn't want to witness a birth, either," Johan replied truthfully, thinking of his mother's screams during the birth of her third child echoing through every crack in the castle. As a small boy, it had frightened him deeply.

With a soft sigh, he straightened his shoulders. Warily, he peered around the forest. It seemed they were finally alone.

The afternoon had long passed, and the valley already lay fully in the shadows. Shivering, the Beguine Sister kept her arms huddled across her body. Johan briefly removed his sword belt and took off his cloak. Although he longed to look for his Brothers, the gallantry with which he had been brought up did not allow him to leave the young woman alone in the woods with the dead soldiers.

"Come, put this on," he said, draping the dingy white woolen cloak over her shoulders.

She looked at him shyly. "Thank you," she said, and pulled the cloak, which still bore his warmth, closer to her slim figure. "And what do you plan to do now?" she asked softly.

Johan looked back at the corpses, knowing that he should move them. But he did not know where to move them, and regardless, any experienced tracker would find them immediately.

"I will accompany you home," he answered the pretty Beguine.

"I can go alone," she said quickly. "It's not far from here."

"No, it could be dangerous," he protested as he knelt down next to his horse near the stream and washed his hands thoroughly. Finally, he plunged his head into the water to drink and refresh himself. He emerged snorting, shaking himself like a wet dog.

"What if we meet soldiers along the way?" he asked, out of breath. As he rose, he inspected their surroundings casually. "King Philipp's men seem to have multiplied. He's determined to follow us into the farthest corners of his kingdom."

The woman thought for a moment, her gaze fixed on Johan's massive forearms. "It's more my duty to offer you protection. I suggest you take me to the cloister, and I'll see to it that you get some rest and something to eat."

"That's how I always imagined my guardian angel," he replied, looking at her face with smiling eyes.

A winding forest path brought Johan and his companion to a formerly Benedictine cloister. Surrounded by tall chestnut trees and rosehip hedges, the massive building lay well hidden in the densely forested valley. Its former owners had abandoned it years ago, the young woman recounted, as they neared the eight-foot-tall barricade of light sandstone that protected the entire compound. Now it belonged to the Order of the Beguines of Saint Margaret, a loose alliance of devout widows and unmarried women who were not bound by an oath, and were therefore a thorn in the side of many an orthodox representative from the other Orders.

The Sisters had repaired the dilapidated cloister compound as well as they could. Each one contributed to the livelihood of the others with the labor of her hands.

Johan learned with interest that the Sisters were thoroughly loved by the women in the area, and were particularly well known for their midwifery and their treatment of infertility. Although no one spoke about it officially, most knew that they were even versed in helping women avoid becoming with child, a practice that had raised the ire of the church authorities. Under such hostility, they lived isolated lives, remaining as inconspicuous as possible behind the old cloister walls.

When they arrived at the gate, Johan dismounted and helped the woman from the horse. She felt warm, and her soft curves pressed up against his broad chest. Her hair exuded a comforting perfume of lavender and rose oil.

As she gave him back his cloak, she smiled at him. "My name is Freya, just in case we ever meet again."

The cloister gate opened as if by magic, and a pair of shaggy wolfhounds approached them curiously. They eyed Johan and sniffed at his horse, causing the creature to prance uneasily.

Johan's companion seemed to know the formidable beasts well. Eagerly, one of the dogs let her pet its neck.

"We had these dogs, too, when I was a child," Johan said, stretching out his hand cautiously to allow the animals to get used to his smell.

"They guard the property against enemies and vagabonds," Freya explained. Her eyes shone like stars. "You must come in and eat with us. We have a delicious salmon stew, and I could introduce you to our Reverend Mother."

Although he was so hungry he could have devoured a cow, and the air smelled wonderfully of freshly baked bread, he knew he could not accept her invitation.

"I apologize," he responded with great regret. "My Brothers need me. I must search for them."

"A pity," said Freya softly, looking at the ground for a moment, then lifting her head and gazing at him in earnest. "You would not be an honorable knight if you deserted them because of a silly girl."

Tentatively, Johan reached for her hand and kissed it.

"Thank you, Freya," he whispered, his voice hoarse, "and farewell."

He turned around suddenly, swung himself onto his Jutlander, and galloped away.

The afternoon sun was already hanging low as Gero and Matthäus struggled in vain to lose their attackers. They were being driven endlessly in circles. In the forested area to which they had retreated, they could barely conceal themselves. They would have to fight if the soldiers did not give up – a hope that they could not count on.

As they reached another clearing, two of their pursuers rushed forward through the bushes like demons. Matthäus's brown Brabant rose high on its hind legs as it was attacked from the side. In battle, the steed with the shimmering brown coat had a mind of its own, making it unusable for the Templars. But Brother Arnaud loved the animal dearly, and was himself stubborn enough to rival the horse's idiosyncrasies, usually emerging the victor. But Matthäus lost the reins, and had no way to keep himself in the saddle of the anxious horse. Out of the corner of his eye, Gero saw his squire fall to the ground as Arnaud's steed galloped away to the edge of the forest.

Instantly, a royal soldier turned his horse to attack the boy – a provocation aimed only at unsettling the Templar. For as long as he was protecting the boy, Gero would neglect his own defense. The gamble seemed to pay off. Gero pulled Atlas around and spurred him on to fend the soldier off Matthäus. Like two rolling siege towers, the animals launched themselves toward each other.

The soldier's steed was considerably slimmer, and the breast of Gero's dapple gray collided hard against the shoulder of the enemy's horse. It lost its balance and tumbled before its rider could act as a counterbalance. Horse and soldier fell to the ground, and the man was buried under his steed. Gero turned Atlas, who shook himself quickly once, then focused his attention on the second opponent. With his steed, Gero circled round the motionless boy on the ground like an aurochs protecting its young from a rogue wolf. The hooves of his enormous horse came dangerously close to the boy's fragile body. One misstep, and Matthäus's bones would be shattered.

The second soldier, with his sword drawn, attempted to break through Gero's circle and trample the boy lying in the grass, only succeeding in angering his opponent more.

"You miserable cur!" Gero bellowed, trying to force his attacker back by swinging his sword at him. "Are you too cowardly to settle this amongst men?"

The soldier held his shield high and tried to catch Gero's thigh. Moving his leg, Gero dodged the attack and fended his opponent off with a sturdy thrust of his shield. The soldier faltered. Gero seized the opportunity, letting his sword and shield fall and swinging a leg over his saddle in a flash, then straightening himself with the other foot in the stirrup. When he came near enough to the soldier's horse, he lunged at him and, together, both men fell to the ground.

They hit the ground hard, their momentum sending them rolling like tumbleweeds. A fall from this height was dangerous, especially in chain mail. Gero felt every bone in his body, but still he pulled himself abruptly to his feet. The other man had also lost his sword and shield, and was standing up to grab his weapons again. In a few steps, Gero was beside him and seized him by the shoulder.

"So, you filthy dog!" he swore, yanking him around. "Now we'll see if you're still as brave."

The soldier was not inexperienced, and he was strong, but he was no Templar.

With the knowledge that this was his only chance, he drew his dagger, a weapon nearly the length of his forearm, and thrust it toward Gero, but the Templar seized his opponent's wrist and bent it backward. The soldier tried to ram his knee in Gero's belly. Reflexively, Gero raised his thigh and intercepted the attack. In a moment, an intense brawl was underway as Gero tried to keep the dagger at a distance with his left hand.

Fury drove the German as he lunged at an opportune moment, striking the man directly on the nose with his fist, still wearing his iron-plated gloves. Shocked, the soldier dropped to his knees and pressed his free hand to his face. Using the man's distraction, Gero wrested the dagger from his opponent. Quicker than a heartbeat, he thrust the dagger sideways into the unprotected throat of the man. The soldier collapsed in a pool of his own blood.

For what seemed like an eternity, Gero ran through the thicket to reach Matthäus. As he was running, he glanced toward the soldier that had been crushed under his horse. The man's neck had broken and was bent at an unnatural angle, his eyes staring into nothingness.

Matthäus lay motionless on his stomach. Gero's heart pounded violently as he kneeled by the boy and grasped his narrow shoulders. Gingerly, he lifted him and turned him carefully on his back. His limbs were saggy, but he moaned softly. Gero gulped hard as he pulled him onto his lap. He clasped the boy in his arms and held his head to his chest.

"Ouch," a faint voice protested. "My head!"

Gero nearly cried in relief. He ran his fingertips through the thick locks of the boy. Matthäus was sporting a handsome bump behind his right ear. A bruise darkened his elbow, but otherwise he appeared unscathed.

"Boy," Gero whispered, stroking Matthäus's hair again. "Wake up, we must leave."

Grudgingly, Matthäus opened his eyes.

"Where am I?" he asked dazedly.

"Where you belong," Gero answered, smiling, "by the side of your chevalier."

Suddenly, a gray giant burst out of the bushes. Gero was startled for a moment, but saw that it was Johan van Elk with his Jutlander. Relief flooded into the Flemish knight's scarred face when he saw that his comrades were safe.

He was immediately by Matthäus's side. "Hey, Mattes, you all right?"

"You're hurting me," Matthäus yelled angrily as Johan hugged the boy as well, overjoyed that nothing worse had happened to him. "Be careful, I've been wounded in battle."

Johan let him go immediately. "In battle," he repeated, grinning, "and the Almighty was with you. As He should be."

After they had scoured the forest for a while, they bumped into Struan, who was crouched in the middle of a clearing holding Amelie in his arms.

"Is ... is she dead?" Johan asked fearfully.

"No," Struan said, sounding distressed, "she's not injured. She's fainted from fear. And now I'm afraid for her, and above all, the unborn child."

Gero quickly realized what had triggered this shock. Not far away, two dead soldiers lay in the moss. They could hardly be recognized as humans as the Scotsman had hacked them apart so thoroughly. Gero sensed that Struan's actions were his revenge for the misery the men's companions had wrought on Amelie, the dead Brother from Montier-en-Der, and all their other lost Brothers. But the Scotsman showed no regret.

"One of them slipped away from me," Struan growled as he sat up. Then with Johan's help, he pulled his unconscious girlfriend onto the saddle in front him.

Johan led his friends to the cloister where Matthäus and Amelie could receive the medical attention that they needed.

Sister Griselda, the tall, dark-haired abbess of the Beguine nunnery, welcomed them into the sprawling inner courtyard and made sure that Amelie and Matthäus received help in the hospital, a whitewashed wing of the building. The Order Sisters quickly laid Amelie on a soft bed and reassured Struan that she would soon come to.

"I feel sick," Matthäus moaned as one of the young women checked for broken bones.

After she had confirmed Gero's hope that nothing was broken, she tended to the boy's elbow, soaking muslin bandages in vinegar and cool, acetic clay before laying them on his bruise. Finally, she bound the spot with a tight linen bandage.

Johan's breathing faltered for a moment when he looked back at the door. A strikingly beautiful young woman with hip-length, rust-colored hair entered the room.

"The chambers have been arranged," she announced to the group. Gero thought he saw her wink at Johan.

Gero and Matthäus were moved into a spacious room in the main building with two beds, a desk, and two stools. They were even provided with a chamber pot, washbasin, and a bucket of water. The redheaded woman brought a tray with fresh bread and cheese along with a jug of wine and four cups, each filled with goat's milk. Then she left the room again.

Gero undressed Matthäus and laid him on one of the clean beds, swaddling him in a brand new wool blanket, and placing a down pillow under his head. Carefully, he dunked the bread in the milk and helped Matthäus to eat. Johan brought in the saddlebags and placed them next to the door. Then, groaning, he sat down on a stool, ate a piece of bread, and poured himself a cup of wine.

"How did you fare?" Gero asked, looking up momentarily.

"Do you mean to ask if I have more Christian lives on my conscience?"

Gero nodded and continued to feed Matthäus, who opened his mouth like a baby bird.

"There were three," Johan muttered dully.

"I got two of the dogs," Gero said softly. "Can you believe they even went after the boy while he was on the ground?"

Johan shook his head. "The only thing I can believe is that the devil himself has a hand in this game," he whispered, shuddering at the thought. He ran his fingers through his red hair in exhaustion. "I've explained the situation to the Sisters. I told them we have to set off as early as possible tomorrow. If they value their lives, they won't breathe a word about us being here."

"And? Do you think they understood?" Gero asked, wiping Matthäus's mouth with a piece of linen cloth.

"As far as I can tell, they are honorable women," Johan replied.

"What about Amelie? Did the Sisters say whether she can ride with us tomorrow?"

"She's awake," Johan informed him, "but no one knows how great a toll the sight of even more death took on her." He cleared his throat and took another gulp of wine. "You know our scottish Brother, after all. He's a good man, but in battle he's more like a rabid wolf."

Gero sighed. "We will know tomorrow," he said, resigned.

"Good night, then," Johan replied. He stood up and prepared to go to his chamber.

"Sleep well, Jo," Gero replied, "and don't get any stupid ideas with such a bountiful supply of female attention."

Johan grinned and shut the door softly behind him. Afterwards, he headed toward the courtyard again. It was cold, but the clean air and the calm that accompanied the arrival of nightfall cleared his thoughts. A pair of flickering torches provided the only light in the sprawling courtyard.

With his hands on the edge of the well, he leaned in and stared into the dark abyss.

Suddenly, he felt someone touching his arm.

"So contemplative, Brother Johan," said a woman's voice.

Surprised, he looked up into Freya's lovely face. Her eyes glinted with amusement in the glow of the torches.

"What happened this afternoon is weighing heavily on you, isn't it?"

"How do you know that?" Johan asked gently, straightening up.

"I can see it in your face," she said with a smile.

"Then you're far ahead of many people. Most only see my scars and not what's hidden behind them," he replied.

"I'm not interested in your scars," she said. "I find your eyes much more fascinating. I can read them."

Johan felt her gaze rest on his face, and was glad that it was already dark, or she would probably have noticed his face reddening. "What do you read in them?"

"They speak of bravery, kindness, honesty, sorrow, and ..." She hesitated for a moment then looked at him with her brows raised high. "Desire?"

Johan closed his eyes. Her scent, roses, wafted into his nose, and her presence made his heartbeat quicken.

"Shall we walk a little while?" she asked to ease his self-consciousness.

Freya removed a torch from a wall-mounting and linked arms with the redheaded Templar as if it were the most natural thing in the world. Without asking him, she steered him toward a barn door.

"We can talk here undisturbed."

She loosened herself from him and opened a small door that was embedded in the tall wooden door. Doubts about what he was doing ran through Johan's mind as, at Freya's beckoning, he ducked through the door.

"Besides, it's warmer in here," she smiled as she closed the doors behind Johan and latched them from inside.

In the dim barn, she groped around on the ground for an oil lamp and lit it with the torch that she then carefully put out. She led him to a corner at the back of the room, where a ladder led to a loft. Under the ladder, the hay was piled up into a tall stack. With a relaxed sigh, she lowered herself onto the soft heap and carefully set the lamp on the floor.

"Sit," she said, and he saw her teeth flash as they reflected the dim glow of the lamp.

"Won't anyone notice you're not in your room?" John asked as he hesitantly sat down next to her.

"No," she replied, sounding a little surprised, "the vesper prayer is over, and our Reverend Mother has tasked me with taking care of our guests, which I am doing now."

Johan could have sworn that her broad smile hid a certain suggestive spark. Noticing his shocked face, she began to laugh.

"Come, Brother Johan, we've both had a stressful day, and now we shall put an end to our woes."

Before he knew what was happening, he felt the woman's lips on his and her hand on his thigh, boldly making its way up to his groin. He responded to her soft kiss in disbelief and gave himself up willingly to the dexterous fingers of his new companion. A little later, he was lying on his chlamys in the hay, freed from his chain mail and weapon belt and pulling his pants down. With her nimble fingers, the young woman raised the skirts of her garments, under which she wore nothing. She slid a thigh over him and slowly lowered herself until his eager penis had sunk entirely into her hot, wet slit. With a soft moan, she unfastened her dress and exposed her full breasts to the soft light of the oil lamp. The rhythmic movements of her hips made the filigree cross that hung on a thin leather cord between her alluring breasts swing like a pendulum. Softly gasping, Johan thrust into her, losing himself in lust and deep affection. She lowered her head, and her long hair fell over him like a mantle of silk. She ran her moist tongue tenderly over his scarred ear, and her hot breath drove shudders down his back. Moaning, their lips found each other's. As Freya intensified the rocking of her hips, they deepened their kiss. As ecstasy flooded in all at once Johan let out a hoarse cry. He clutched her tightly as he pressed his lips to her shoulder to stop himself from crying out again.

Tenderly, her lips caressed his face. He buried his large nose between her breasts, sniffing like one of the wolfhounds from the courtyard, soaking up her sweet scent. His lips searched for one of her peaked nipples and took it in his mouth. Everything around him seemed to spin, and a deep feeling of joy brought tears into his eyes.

"Shh … " Freya whispered into his ear. She wound her arms firmly around his neck and pressed her cheek against his bristly hair. She felt the wetness of his tears on her breasts and his quivering breath.

Gently, she tried to untangle herself from him, but his strong arms held her like he never wanted to let her go again. Subtly, she pushed her hips against him again.

"Not that it isn't nice to feel you for a while longer," she whispered breathlessly, "but if you don't let me get off you soon, it will be a rather wet affair for both of us."

He loosened his grip and laughed softly. "Hasn't that already happened?" he asked, running the sleeve of his jerkin over his eyes and nose.

Only then did he dare to look her in the face. She lowered her head and brushed his scarred lips in pleasure, showing no revulsion at his disfigured appearance.

"What's your name?" he whispered affectionately.

She smirked and put on a playfully chastising expression.

"I know I was good to you," she said, grinning. "Indeed, it honors me tremendously that I was good enough, you've lost your mind from pleasure." Solemnly, she covered her left nipple with her palm. "Freya. My name is Freya – I believe I already told you that."

He snorted in amusement. "I may be a fool, but even I'm not that foolish. I didn't mean just your first name, but your heritage."

"Ah …" she said, and raised her pretty, chestnut-colored brows. "The good sir wants to know if the maiden who has so unexpectedly commandeered his lap is an equal match for him."

"No, no …" Johan said hurriedly. "I didn't mean it that way."

"If you set me free," she rejoined cheekily, "I will tell you."

With a sheepish expression, Johan released her from his embrace. Letting herself collapse onto the hay next to him, she buttoned her top and rearranged her skirts. Hastily, he pulled up his woolen braies along with his leather trousers and fastened the waistband. With her elbow resting in the hay, she leaned her head on one hand and stretched out another hand curiously. Her slim fingers groped for the knotted leather cords that held his underwear in place.

"Are those the infamous cords of the Templars that all Brothers have to wear after their acceptance, to demonstrate their chastity?"

"Apart from the fact that it's rather inappropriate to remind me of that right now – who told you such nonsense?"

"I heard it somewhere," she said, laying her hand reassuringly on his arm. "I'll forget it again at once. Promise."

With a gruff movement, Johan tugged his quilted jerkin over his waistband.

"Very well," he murmured.

"Freya of Bogenhausen," she said, and held her hand out to him as if she expected him to kiss it. "From the free nobility of Bogenhausen."

Only then did Johan realize what she wanted to tell him. She was an aristocrat like him, and no Lady of easy virtue. He took her slender hand and kissed her softly.

"Johan, second-youngest son of the Count Bechtholt van Elk and his wife Rosanna de Fondarella," he responded, holding her interested gaze. "A pity we hadn't met each other earlier."

"Probably true," she said wistfully.

He moved closer to her, still holding on to her hand firmly. "Why did such a pretty noble maiden like you join the Beguines?"

"I could ask you the same," she replied in surprise.

"Firstly, I've got nothing to do with the Beguines," he responded, grinning. "And secondly, I'm not pretty."

"Oh, but you are," she said, smiling at him. She stroked his neck and ruffled his red hair.

He could not endure her gaze. Quickly he looked down at their entwined hands. Chuckling, he shook his head. As he looked up, all at once she became solemn.

"Both my parents are dead," she said, "and no relatives offered me refuge. In the end, it was a blessing that I could join the Order."

"I'm sorry," Johan answered, searching in vain for comforting words.

"It's not so bad," she said lightly, "I can't remember them at all. My father died during the Battle of Worringen. He fought on the side of the Cologne Archbishop. My mother comes from the county of Luxemburg, but she became depressed after my father's death when we fled to the Dominicans in Cologne. Shortly after, she starved to death. She'd stopped eating from grief. I was only two years old when that happened. I had no siblings, and my uncle, who wanted to seize the inheritance for himself, paid the Sisters a relatively meager sum to keep me with them so he could take over my parents' property, or at least whatever the Duke of Brabant hadn't taken himself. After my novitiate, I ran away. I couldn't bear to hear stories of my mother's death brought up again and again – especially when I didn't follow the rules."

Freya paused for a moment, and Johan stroked the back of her hand with his thumb. "After that, I moved around with some traveling artistes for a while. I danced and read palms. One day, we were robbed, and our wagon was burned with all our possessions. We couldn't perform anymore, and hard-pressed for money, I landed in a house of pleasure in Cologne."

As if struck by lightning, Johan looked up at her in astonishment.

"Do you despise me now?" A heartbreaking uncertainty lay in her question, and Johan immediately banished all budding thoughts about having slept with a professional whore.

"No," he replied, trying hard to hide his shock. "How long were you there?"

"Just half a year, then the Beguines took me in and saved not just my soul, but my body as well. Two years ago, I was sent here from Cologne to help build a new Order house."

After lowering her gaze, she looked up again and peered inquiringly into his eyes. "And from where do your roots grow? De Fondarella doesn't sound like it's from the German lands."

"My mother comes from a Catalonian family of knights. My father met her in Bruges in his uncle's house. She was so beautiful that he asked for her hand immediately. He loved her very much, but she died three years ago in childbirth. It was a great blow to him." A wistful smile flitted over Johan's face as he held Freya's gaze.

"I'm sorry for your loss," she said, stroking his hand tenderly.

"And your father?" she continued finally. "Is he from Flanders?"

"My family lives in the lower Rhine." He hesitated as if he had to think hard. "My father also fought in the Battle of Worringen," he said finally. "He was a vassal of Johann of Brabant … he had no choice but to follow his liege into war."

"Does that mean something?" Freya asked with her brows raised.

"No," Johan said, squeezing her hand gently. "Only that our fathers would have been enemies, and if we had met earlier, we could forget all hopes of being promised to each other."

She looked at him and smiled.

"Then it's better the way it is now," she said, pulling him back on the soft bed.

CHAPTER 9

The White Swan

Sunday, October 15, 1307
Moselle Valley, German Lands

Even before the small bell tolled for early mass, Freya was awoken from her slumber by an uproar in front of the barn door. Removing herself from the strong arms embracing her, she crept to the door.

It was still dark in the barn and Johan stretched himself groggily. Hearing the voices from the courtyard, he sprang to his feet and hastily gathered up his chlamys. He put on his cloak and belted his sword and knife then he stepped close to Freya. She stood with her face against the crack in the small barn door, poking her nose out into the cold. Gently, Johan laid his warm hand on her shoulder.

"What is it?" he asked in a whisper.

"I think we have a problem," she said, turning to face him.

Quickly, she kissed him lightly on the cheek before slipping through the small door and into the morning without another word.

With quick strides, Griselda hurried across the courtyard. Struan carried Amelie, who was covered in a thick woolen cloak, in his strong arms while Gero managed all of their luggage. Together they disappeared behind a large door that led to the cowshed where their horses had been kept. As subtly as possible, Johan blended with the helping hands that followed the group.

"What's happening?" Johan asked when Gero returned from the stables.

"Thank God you're here," Gero called in relief, ignoring Johan's question. The next moment, he paused when he saw the numerous traces of hay on Johan's cloak. "I've been looking for you everywhere," he remarked innocently. "Didn't they give you a chamber?"

Johan scratched his neck in embarrassment.

Before decorum could dictate that Johan answer, Gero continued furiously, "An entire troop of soldiers – at least twenty men – has shown up in the village beyond the cloister. Luckily, a shepherd set out to warn the women in time. Supposedly, besides a few escaped Templars, there are other secrets they're searching for here in the valley."

"Do the Sisters have any idea how we can flee undetected?" Johan scanned the surroundings to see if he could find Freya anywhere, but she was nowhere in sight.

"There's an underground escape tunnel used by the Benedictines. It's probably wide enough for us to take even the horses through. The entrance is located right under the stables."

Quickly, they prepared to depart. Before the Brothers and their companions set off, Griselda handed them a generous pack of provisions and included some powdered medicinal herbs wrapped in parchment for Amelie, to prevent a miscarriage. Gratefully, Struan took the supplies.

Johan looked around, hoping desperately to see Freya at least one more time to say his farewells.

A little later, three slender figures appeared in warm gray cloaks with hoods that hid their faces. A surge of joy flooded through Johan when he saw that one of them had flaming red hair.

"These three Sisters will show you the way out," Griselda announced. "The path is a little over a quarter mile long and leads you directly up the trade route to St. Mihiel. The exit lies in the middle of the woods, and is known only to a few."

Peat torches were ignited, and with the help of a quickly installed pulley, an inconspicuous trap door embedded in the floor was raised. A gently sloping stone staircase led down to a wide, dark corridor, from which a strong, musty smell assaulted their noses.

"It's been some time since the tunnel was last used," Griselda explained apologetically.

"Don't you think we can find the way out ourselves?" Gero asked, looking at the leader of the Beguines, not wishing to burden the Sisters more than necessary.

"With the escorts," Griselda answered, "we can make sure you've reached the exit unscathed and that your escape hasn't been discovered – just in case the soldiers suspect something they can't prove and try to trick us into confessing."

Gero nodded and Johan heaved a sigh of relief knowing that he could enjoy Freya's company for a while longer.

An enormous pounding echoed from the courtyard and the dogs began to bark in warning.

"Open up!" a male voice thundered.

"Go, go, go ... " Griselda urged, shooing the escapees into the tunnel like a flock of geese.

"Windrud, Alheydis!" she called to two Sisters. "Make sure the soldiers aren't let in before we've closed the gate to the vaulted passage and cows are standing there again!"

The secret passageway was too low for anyone to sit on their horses.

As she was too weak to walk, Struan carried Amelie on his back. She nestled her cheek against his broad shoulders, trusting him to protect her. Nevertheless, her fear was profound as the heavy trap door was shut and she and the others were left in near-darkness. Their eerie surroundings, dimly lit by the torches, were like a tomb.

Two of the Beguine Sisters led the way forward, followed by Gero leading two horses, bound to each other, with one hand, and pulling Matthäus on a small handcart with the other. In the middle were Struan and Amelie. Freya and Johan, who was leading the remaining three horses, brought up the rear. As she searched for his right hand, he knew that it was neither destiny nor a coincidence that she was accompanying them. Her left hand played with his fingers as she held a torch at an angle with her other hand.

The underground path ended in a hollow in the woods, where a small door led to freedom. The mighty horses could barely fit through the tiny, man-made opening, and Gero and his Brothers had to remove the baggage and saddles from their backs for them to squeeze through.

A wan light heralded the break of day, and damp morning mist rose over the fir trees.

"Hark!" Freya announced. "From here, it's about a mile more to St. Mihiel. If you hurry, you can reach the Moselle by midday."

Struan lifted Amelie onto his Frisian and swung himself behind her, while Matthäus, warmly wrapped, sat upon Atlas in front of his lord.

"Johan, what are you waiting for?" Gero asked when his comrade made no movement to mount his Jutlander.

"Would you mind if you rode on ahead a little? I'd like to say goodbye to someone." Johan's scarred face turned slightly pink.

"Your wish is my command, Brother," Gero bowed deferentially and shot him a mischievous grin as urged his horse forward.

Before he steered his Percheron to the north, he nodded to the Sisters and raised his right hand in farewell. "Send your abbess my deepest thanks again. The Holy Virgin will reward you for your kindness."

The women raised their hands in return and retreated respectfully into the cave entrance to wait for Freya.

Both Johan and Freya wished they could prolong their farewell, but there was no time for that. Johan looked into her beautiful eyes and swallowed hard, unable to speak. His gaze wandered over her curved brows and slender nose, then over each individual freckle and to her full lips, as though trying to sear her gentle face into his memory.

All at once, she stretched up and pulled his head down to hers. Her kiss was as sweet as a summer peach. A mighty compulsion drove Johan to embrace her tightly. Tears rolled over his scarred cheeks as he searching futilely for words, burying his face in her hair and rocking her from side to side.

"The Sisters say I have the gift of foresight," whispered Freya, "and I know this won't be an eternal farewell."

"Freya, I ..." began Johan with a choked voice, watching her with damp eyes, then swallowed and shook his head, disheartened. He wiped his face with the back of his hand in shame.

She laid her slender index finger on his lips reassuringly – the same gesture he'd made when he met her for the first time. Her gaze was just as imploring, but this time, it was her finger that hushed him.

"You must go," she said firmly, loosening herself from his embrace.

"Yes," he replied in a strained voice, shoving his large hands into his iron-plated gloves. He swung himself onto his mighty steed and rode away without once looking back.

That morning, Gero didn't think that they would be able to cover ten miles. As the main roads were too dangerous, they could only traverse muddy back roads.

But, as they reached the Meuse, they were in luck, for they found a crossing they could ride effortlessly over on horseback. They gave a wide berth to the few villages along their path. Neither toll keepers nor soldiers stood in their way.

By evening, they reached the northernmost tip of the Duchy of Lorraine, which made up a tri-border region with the County of Luxemburg and the Archdiocese of Trier.

As they rode into the steep valley, the bright red sun sank into a violet sea of low-hanging clouds and bathed the mountains in a golden light. The path down to the Moselle was a glorious sight, and the air was cold and clear. From afar, they saw the mighty fortress walls of the Castle Sierck, where the House of Lorraine took refuge.

Despite the fair weather, Amelie was obviously exhausted and cold.

"We must find proper accommodation for the night," Struan said as they stopped for a moment's rest on a rocky outcrop in the middle of the vineyards.

Gero nodded thoughtfully. Matthäus needed a warm bed, too.

"I'll ride ahead and look around for a guesthouse," he said, helping the boy off the horse before dismounting himself.

"What on earth are we going to do?" Johan's gaze was full of doubt.

"I'll explain later," Gero answered, his face tense. "First, we have to see if we're safe here."

"What makes you so sure we won't be followed into German territory?" Struan questioned.

"D'Our told me."

"And why is the commander so sure about that?"

"Trust me," Gero replied. "If I'm not back by sunset, go into the forest and hide. Then go immediately to my father's castle. Understood?"

Johan shook his head silently, but he didn't contradict Gero. Instead, he went to Matthäus, who was nearly in tears as Gero rode away.

After a quarter mile, Gero reached a small village by a shipping pier. From afar, he had already picked up the scent of roasted meat. *Holy Mother Mary*, he prayed silently, *please let there be no soldiers here, and give us a warm meal and a dry bed for the night.*

The riverside road was empty, but thin smoke drifted out of the chimney of a stately timber-framed building, forming the center of a horseshoe with two long farm buildings.

Gero looked around. Two saddled horses were tied outside, but he saw no trace of soldiers. He tied Atlas to a pole and headed to the entrance of the house with one hand resting on his sword pommel. A buxom, middle-aged woman, clad entirely in yellow, was coming through the door towards him. She let out a horrified scream when she suddenly found him blocking her way out. Immediately, a few men stormed out of the taproom behind her. Brandishing the humble knives and clubs they wore on their belts, the peasant figures attempted to intimidate Gero.

Gero couldn't help but laugh as he lowered his sword. He could imagine how he appeared to them in his dirty clothes and with a deadly sword at the ready.

"God in Heaven! You scared me to death!" The woman's gaze was accusatory, but her voice sounded conciliatory.

"Do you have a room free, good woman?" Gero asked, trying to sound as friendly as possible, "and do you perhaps have a warm bath and something to eat?"

The hostess was not pretty, but she had good-natured eyes that twinkled with mischief.

"For a man of the Temple, always," she said with a saucy grin, putting her hands on her hips and swaying her heaving bosom from side to side.

Gero was surprised that she knew who he was. He had deliberately left his cloak behind, as he didn't know who or what awaited him here. But then he saw that her gaze had fallen on the pommel of his sword, where the Order's cross pattée was clearly engraved.

"Are you alone?" the woman asked, raising her brows.

"No," he replied hesitantly, "there are five of us. Three men, a woman, and a child."

"Whatever your desire, you are warmly welcome."

Gero fetched his companions and after a warm meal of chicken broth and bread, the hostess of the White Swan prepared a special surprise for her guests. While she attended to Amelie personally, preparing a warm bath for the exhausted woman, she handed over the care of the men to the remaining residents of the house. Women in translucent garments led Gero and his Brothers into a lavish room, where a few wooden washtubs stood in a row. Gero looked around the room. There were stands with concealing curtains, racks filled with carafes of scented oils, and all varieties of naughty implements, while lewd paintings hung on the wall. An inkling of what kind of establishment this was began to dawn on Gero, who realized he should have already deduced this from their hostesses' revealing clothes.

"A sinful bathhouse," Johan whispered with growing interest after he had settled into a tub filled with hot water.

The alleged chambermaids tended to the Brothers' welfare, scrubbing their backs without instruction. Struan thanked heaven that Amelie had stayed in her room.

Gero fought with his conscience, eyeing the women's ministrations warily, as Johan enjoyed the undivided attention of the pretty helpers. Yet, when the women began to aim for his groin, he, too, began to feel uneasy. Gero raised his voice, ordering the girls to leave and serve the wine and the meal traditionally served during baths in such houses.

After the meal, the knights retired to a common sleeping chamber and swathed in warm woolen blankets. A fireplace gave the room a pleasant warmth. Amelie and Matthäus were already asleep in their respective beds.

In the glow of the fire, the Brothers' gazes turned to Gero, who was sitting on his bed, deep in thought. Finally, he looked up and sighed gently.

"From what I gathered from the guests in the taproom, King Philipp's forces haven't infiltrated the German lands yet. We'll set off for Trier in the morning, as early as possible, to warn the Brothers there. If God so wills, we'll reach the Cistercian abbey of Hemmenrode in the evening. I'll drop off Matthäus there. The next day, we'll leave Amelie with my mother. After we've warned the commandery in Brysich, we will ride on to the Cistercians in Heisterbach. Our actual mission awaits us there."

"What about your father?" Struan looked at Gero expectantly. "Won't he ask about what's happened and what we plan to do?"

"Possibly," Gero explained, "but I swore an oath to d'Our not to speak about our mission with anyone. Even I will only know exactly what our mission is about when we're there."

"By God, so it shall be." At that, Johan made the sign of the cross in prayer.

CHAPTER 10

Marien ad Ponte – Arrival in Trier

Monday, October 16, 1307
German lands

The morning mist hung thickly over the Moselle valley. Small villages of tidy timber houses peeped out where the mist had thinned, dotting the lazy river like a string of pearls.

A barge to Trier stood ready on the jetty, waiting for its passengers to board. Some merchants had already assembled on board with their luggage and a pair of mules. The planks of the barge shook as Gero and his comrades led their battle steeds onto the boat.

"The horses cost extra," a red-cheeked cabin boy called to them.

"Very well, young man," Gero answered off-handedly and handed over the reins of his Percheron to the boy, "if you would lead the animals to the shed."

The boy paused. He barely reached Atlas's shoulder. The usually calm horse was nervous on the gently swaying deck, and snorted nervously, letting out damp clouds of breath. Hesitantly, the boy stood before the colossal beast, not trusting himself to touch it.

"Mattes, show the young man how one handles a warhorse properly," Gero ordered his squire.

As the cabin boy gaped in astonishment, Matthäus serenely led the animals one after the other to the sheds and tied their reins to the wooden border. Arnaud's stubborn Brabant balked as it usually did. Only Amelie's small brown mare complied good-naturedly, trotting obediently behind Matthäus as he led it in front of the group.

"Here," he said, and handed over the reins to the cabin boy. "Maybe you should practice with this one."

Gero fished out a small piece of silver from the precious leather pouch that d'Our had given him for the journey. Unexpectedly, his second trial by fire on German soil awaited him in the form of the weather-beaten Moselle barge captain.

"Forgive us, noble sir," the old man muttered and bowed deeply. "My cabin boy is a silly fool. It appears he does not know that you, as members of the Templar Order, are exempt from river and bridge tariffs."

Johan sighed in relief. The man seemed to harbor no concerns about their membership in the Order, and nothing in his expression revealed anything amiss. After a long, heated debate that morning, the Brothers had finally decided to don their chlamys and surcoats again.

The boatman was still bent in a humble bow when he suddenly shouted for his cabin boy.

"Jodokus! Get your ass over here immediately, or the plague shall get you!"

The wiry, brown-haired boy scurried towards them, fear of punishment already etched on his face.

"Sir?" he panted breathlessly as his confused gaze flitted between his master and the passengers in white.

The old man seized the boy by the nape of his neck and forced his body into a deep bow before Gero.

"Look, Jodokus. These are Templar knights, men of courage and honor. If you see such a red cross in the future, you will offer him your deference and make no impertinent demands. Count yourself lucky the Brothers didn't want you punished."

Struan, who hadn't understood anything, shook his head subtly. Although he himself was used to harsh reprimands, he felt sorry for the boy, who had turned scarlet.

"Let him be," Gero urged the old man.

The whole scene was drawing too much attention to them. The other passengers stood gawking with open mouths. Matthäus had hid himself in embarrassment behind Johan, who himself felt uneasy at the captain's unexpected display.

"You'll pay only half the price," the boatman said magnanimously, "as members of your Order deserve."

Then he let the boy go, pushing him back so fiercely that he almost stumbled into the ice-cold water.

After Gero had paid the man, he observed the ship's crew, which was now raising the sail and tying down the barrels and boxes. The other passengers only showed a casual interest in what was happening around them.

The water splashed against the bow as the crew pushed off from the jetty with long punts, steering the boat slowly into the middle of the river.

The mist lifted gradually and the sun burst forth, making the Moselle glitter like a silver ribbon.

Matthäus stood at the stern, watching two men in a small boat pulling a bulging net of wriggling, shimmering fish on board as their vessel dipped dangerously to the side. The fish leaped and writhed undeterred, fighting desperately for their lives.

Deep in thought, the boy stared at the waves the ship left in its wake. A deep-seated fear gripped him anew. It had haunted him ever since they turned their backs on Bar-sur-Aube. Barred from asking any questions, he was alone with his fears. He was faced with the certainty that if they could no longer return to the idyllic world of the commandery, their own fate would not be too different from that of the fish.

Out of nowhere, their escape had cruelly pulled back the curtain on the gruesome deeds that Christian men were capable of. He was certainly no stranger to violence. When recounting the heroic adventures of the knights and sergeants in the Outremer, the older squires had never spared their younger comrades any details about the massacres of the so-called heathens. Matthäus himself had already received several lessons in swordplay and been reassured that he displayed enough skills to fight one day against the heathens as a knight of the Order.

But now that he had seen the blood spilling from the fallen soldiers and felt the tension and fear of the knights under attack, Matthäus knew it made a difference whether it was real heads or cabbage heads rolling under the sword.

"Hey," called a loud voice.

Startled, Matthäus jumped back. Two mighty hands grabbed him by the shoulders and made to throw him into the water, but held him back at the last second.

"Watch out, you don't want to fall in," Johan van Elk joked.

But Matthäus was in no mood for laughter. The sudden shock sent him suddenly into hiccoughing sobs. Amelie, who had settled herself down with Struan not far away, looked up in surprise.

Filled with shame, Matthäus turned away and crouched down on the planks of the deck.

Johan sat down next to him and laid an arm around his shoulders.

"Mattes, what's going on with you?" he asked in concern as a dim idea of what haunted the boy floated into his mind.

Between sobs the boy shook his head.

"Believe me, Gero isn't abandoning you. I know him far too well."

Johan didn't quite succeed in looking as cheerful as he usually did. Nevertheless, Matthäus sensed that the knight meant him well.

"It's not my lord who worries me, or that I fear the Almighty has denied us his protection," Matthäus sniffed and squinted into the morning sun. "It's … it's Mertin. He's my best friend. What if they've thrown him in a dungeon, too?"

Johan immediately knew who he was talking about. The chubby squire with the brown curly hair was hardly older than Matthäus. One evening, he had met Johan for the first time on the way to the latrine and had run away screaming. Later on, the boy had apologized meekly when he realized that the scar-faced Brother was not as frightening as he had first seemed.

"He's in Clairvaux with the Cistercians," Johan said. "Didn't you know that?"

"Yes, but what if they captured him there?" Matthäus looked at the knight doubtfully

"Gero told me that your uncle sent the squires to Clairvaux because they would be safe there. So you mustn't worry. The abbot there will take care of them, and, if need be, take them on as novices of the convent before King Philipp can lay a bloody finger on them."

Matthäus exhaled audibly. "I thank Mother Mary," he said faintly, "for bestowing my uncle with so much wisdom."

"Indeed," Johan agreed and smiled gently. "Would you like one?" From his leather neck-pouch, he retrieved a honey pearl. Freya had given him an entire bag after their fateful dalliance.

"You know, Mattes," he continued after Matthäus had taken the comforting treat gratefully, "we're all in the same boat, not just because we're journeying into an unknown future on a ship together, but because each of us had to leave behind someone dear to him."

"Does that include women?" Matthäus asked, blinking.

"Nothing escapes you," Johan answered with a laugh.

Right on schedule, in the early afternoon the ship docked near the old Roman bridge in Trier. From afar, Johan and Struan had already admired the imposing silhouette of the episcopal city, which was dotted with churches and tower houses.

To reach Saint Marien ad Ponte, the Order residence of the Brothers in Trier, they had to follow the narrow towpath to the right along the city walls. Through a tangle of lumber cranes and loading ramps, Gero led his companions from the treacherous banks to the bridge.

The path was paved only in certain stretches, and the muddy ground between the cobblestones was littered with rotting kitchen scraps. In the shadows of the walls, a few rats scurried about and gnawed at a dead cat. Amelie and Matthäus wrinkled their noses in disgust and mounted their horses quickly.

The knights followed suit and drove their steeds on to the bridgehead, where the toll stations bustled as goods were transported in and out of the city walls.

The home of the Trier Brothers lay a fair distance away, outside the city gates. On the road there, they passed a few old Roman walls that had served the residents as a rock and limestone quarry. Surrounded by muddy pig stalls that had been furnished with a pair of lopsided shelters to protect the animals, the three-story Order house emerged like a rock in the surf. A broad wooden walkway led from the street, branching off over a putrid ditch to the smooth-walled compound. Beside the main building, there were two stables and a small, enclosed courtyard with an attractive archway. From the street, one could peer into the spacious inner courtyard where a well stood.

"It's not particularly impressive," Johan remarked, noticing that there was no chapel.

Gero raised a brow. "You can't compare it to Bar-sur-Aube," he demurred.

The walkway wobbled alarmingly as the troop rode over it with their horses.

A fat, gray, striped cat sat yawning on a broad gatepost. It paused for a moment as it noticed the approaching riders, but then continued to lick its paws with relish in the gleaming midday sun. Obviously it had decided that the unexpected visitors posed no danger.

Gero dismounted and grasped a tattered rope that dangled from a small wooden bell tower. After ringing it, he waited with his companions until someone opened the massive oak door a crack.

Amelie and Matthäus remained a distance back, and the young Brother, clad in a brown habit, recoiled in alarm when he saw the three unexpected knights in front of him.

"Praise the Lord Jesus Christ," Gero said calmly. "May we enter?"

The Brother nodded distractedly and mumbled something incomprehensible, then pulled the door wide open so the guests could pass through unhindered with their battle steeds.

The house commander was a kind, elderly man with a thinning head of hair. In his brown vestments, he waddled across the courtyard and held his hand out to Gero in greeting.

"I am Brother Godefridus, the commander of this house. How may I be of assistance to you?" he asked, smiling serenely.

Gero knew the mild-mannered Brother from his childhood. In contrast to Henri d'Our, Godefridus had not participated in a Crusade nor undergone training as a knight. Nonetheless, as house commander, he held a high office in the Order and was respected.

"God be with you, good sir," the men called in chorus. Matthäus made a deep bow and Amelie lowered her head graciously.

"Perhaps you might still recognize me," Gero began his introduction. "I am the youngest son of Richard of Breydenbach."

"Of course I recognize you, young Brother," replied the commander joyfully. "Your father was here not all too long ago to audit his accounts."

After the horses had been fed and the small party from Bar-sur-Aube had taken their seats with the commander in the refectory, the Order leader's good mood began to melt like snow in the sun.

"For Heaven's sake," he whispered, his features tightening with fear. "Persecuted? In France? We must dispatch messengers to Roth an der Our and up the Moselle to Koblenz. What about our commandery in Metz?" he asked, scratching behind his ear nervously. "Have you alerted the Brothers there?"

"No, that would have been too great a risk," Gero answered regretfully. "We're glad we made it here. They followed us to Lorraine. If the Bishop of Metz stands in alliance with the King of France or bends to the will of the Pope, we will no longer be safe there, either."

"Holy Mother Mary," Godefridus cried, and his usually friendly eyes filled with tears. "What shall become of us?"

"We are on the way to the commandery in Brysich. We'll warn Master Alban and Master Fredericus there," Gero explained quickly, "so we don't meet the same fate in the German lands as we did in France."

The Brother from Trier nodded without a word. For a moment, they were lost in thought as they pondered what this news could mean for each of them.

CHAPTER 11

Saalholz – Journey into the Unknown

Monday, October 16, 1307

After the meal, Gero excused himself and his friends from the Brothers of Trier. At least the weather hadn't failed them. A glance into the cloudless sky promised that it would remain dry for the rest of the day. The merchants and farmers approaching them on the old Roman bridge as they crossed to the other side of the Moselle gave the majestic battle steeds a wide berth, and a number risked a second look at the dashing riders who wore the legendary red cross on their breasts. It seemed d'Our had been right – the news of the Templars' fate in France had not yet reached Trier. The folk's glances revealed neither contempt nor suspicion.

"What's with the boy?" Johan asked softly, making sure Matthäus, who was some distance away, could not hear him. "Can't he come with us?"

"I don't know what awaits us in Heisterbach, and besides, I promised d'Our I'd bring him to Hemmenrode whether I like it or not. Depending on where we end up, I'll fetch him if the situation allows," Gero answered, glancing behind at the boy.

Matthäus, who knew what awaited him, sat in his saddle with his head bowed as Arnaud's Brabant trotted stoically behind Struan's black horse.

Even Amelie didn't appear particularly happy, although Struan had reassured her that she could be in no better place than with Gero's mother.

The way to the Cistercians' abbey of Hemmenrode was not well constructed. They crossed muddy, rocky valley after valley until they finally reached a lofty mountain range in the early evening, where they could gaze clearly into the lands of Hemmenrode.

"If you don't like it with the Cistercians, I'll make sure that we are reunited," Gero said to Matthäus reassuringly. "Promise."

Amelie regarded the Templar with a critical look. "Don't make promises you can't keep," she remarked quietly, yet clearly enough for everyone to hear.

She had tried to pry Struan's plans for their future out of him the entire time they were on the barge. But he had simply assured her that she would be able to find refuge in the castle fortress of Breydenbach, and that he would wed her as soon as he could be honorably discharged from the Order.

As Gero rode down what he thought was the shortest path to Hemmenrode, dawn was breaking. They ventured through a dense forest, arriving, with a certain sense of relief, at the entrance to an old trade route that had to lead directly to the Cistercians.

Matthäus stuck closely to Atlas's side as the path led into a dark fir wood. Even Amelie on her small mare searched anxiously for Struan's Frisian.

In contrast to the previous woods they had ridden through, the timber in this forest was obviously untouched. *Strange*, Gero thought. He vaguely remembered a territorial dispute among multiple parties over a plot in the woods. Over time, strange rumors had begun to surround the forest. No one from the area dared to pass through it freely, let alone set an axe to the weathered, ancient trees. Locals said the place was bewitched, and that the devil himself had set up his camp there.

Gero was smart enough to know that all this talk was nonsense. His father had always said that the rumors only served to ensure that the most timid squabblers would give up their claims and hand over their land to those who feared neither death nor the devil.

A soft noise prompted Struan, who was riding directly behind Matthäus, to prick up his ears and grab the reins of Amelie's mare.

Did he hear any voices? Was that a whisper he just heard? *He raised his head attentively.*

Matthäus, who had also heard something, hunched his shoulders up around his neck.

The voices whispered again.

"Gero," Johan hissed. "What is that?"

"Robbers," Gero whispered, drawing his sword.

Amelie let out a sharp scream, startling her mare.

The next moment they were surrounded by fifteen men. Five of them were about a hundred feet ahead, while the rest emerged behind them. They were disheveled men, brandishing axes and swords, and their murderous intentions shone in their eyes.

Gero and his brethren knew from experience that the robbers would not be satisfied with just their money and property. At a time when a man could end up in the gallows for a stolen apple, no one was stupid enough to let his victim live. They were probably Lombards, a people who lived in droves in Trier and the surrounding area. The unpopular immigrants were drawn to the fast cash that could be earned along the Moselle and Rhine, if not through honorable means, then through raiding careless merchants and noblemen traveling alone.

Setting one foot in front of the other, swords raised, they encircled Gero and his companions.

"We must try to escape into the woods," Gero hissed, not letting his opponents out of his sight. "We can't get around them on the road."

"Take care of Mattes," Johan said quietly. "I'll keep watch for Struan so he can take Amelie to safety."

"Mattes, hold on tight!"

The boy froze on his horse. Gero grabbed the reins of the Brabant and squeezed his Percheron's flanks gently. In a single bound, Atlas pranced sideways into the bushes, and the imperious Brabant could do little but follow. With that, they unwittingly gave their adversaries the signal to attack.

Struan gave Amelie a few hasty instructions before attempting to break through the ring of attackers with her.

From both sides, shouting fiercely, the robbers ran after the fleeing troop. A second pack lunged at Johan, whose colossal Jutlander stood whinnying loudly on its hind legs, kicking at the approaching mob with its front hooves.

None of the robbers were capable of following a rider on foot and with a raised weapon over long distances, but because of the thick undergrowth and downed trees lying in their path, the animals didn't move as quickly as they would have on the open road. After some time, Gero heard a gasp close behind him.

"Flee to the cloister!" he called to Matthäus. "Straight ahead!"

He let go of the Brabant's reins and hit him on the rear with the flat of his blade, as he held his steed back and forced him into an about-turn to face the men chasing them.

He sliced open the throat of the first attacker. Crimson blood sprayed out from under the man's ear. Moaning, the dark-haired adversary crumpled. Lying on his back, he pressed a hand to the wound in vain. But the rest of the robbers were not deterred by the fate of their companion and set off after Gero and his steed. Again and again Atlas reared, which led to the men intensifying their attacks against the horse.

Gero did not want to risk having his steed injured by an axe or a sword, so at an opportune moment, he sprang out of his saddle and shooed the animal away from him. He faced his attackers on foot. His eyes narrowed with hatred and he slashed at them. Quickly, he drove them back a respectful distance, but the men merely exchanged malicious grins. Gero was confused. Suddenly, he recognized the trap. Another robber had slipped out of the bushes behind him. The Lombard managed to split his chain mail and cut open his arm with his sword in one painful strike. Blood soaked the fabric of his torn sleeve.

Incensed, Gero whipped around and swung his blade into the unprotected back of the man who had wounded his arm. Caught by surprise, the man winced and clutched at his back with a gasp. A rip in the fabric of his two-colored garment revealed a gaping wound. Feeling the warm blood between his fingers, he retreated, yelling. His companions now backed away uncertainly as they shouted at each other in Lombardic. They seemed to be fighting over who would next take on the knight.

Gero used their indecision to search for Matthäus. He didn't know whether the boy had dismounted the horse or been thrown. In any case, the wild Brabant had taken flight, and Matthäus was huddled fearfully against a mighty oak tree not far away.

Gero's Percheron had followed the Brabant and the two horses stood like a happy couple on the opposite edge of the small clearing.

"Come, Mattes, we must leave," Gero yelled to the boy.

Meanwhile, Johan had cut a path through the mob chasing him while Struan took Amelie to safety on the other side of the clearing before hurrying to Johan's aid.

They had already incapacitated two men, and two more, frightened by the gruesomely disfigured redheaded knight, ran in Gero's direction.

Disregarding his injury, Gero ran, wrenching Matthäus to his feet and grasping his thin upper arm like a vice, he pulled the boy with him.

As Matthäus struggled to follow his lord, he became entangled in Gero's chlamys and fell sprawling to the ground. With Gero's help he scrambled to his feet and hurried on, stepping into rabbit holes and stumbling over rootstocks. Gero wanted to at least get the boy on a horse so he could flee into the nearby cloister with Amelie.

140

He had almost crossed the clearing with his squire when a mighty roaring sound suddenly arose, accompanied by an ear-shattering, rhythmic hammering. Gero felt an unusually fierce pressure on his ears, making him feel as if his skull was going to shatter. His face contorted into a painful grimace. He watched as the two horses reared up and raced away, as if struck by lightning. Amelie's mare followed them, the young woman clinging to the animal's mane in terror.

Without realizing that he was still holding the boy's arm, Gero spun around and looked up to see what was causing this chaos. Directly above him, the dark blue of the evening sky was mixing with a glowing green honeycomb pattern at the height of the treetops. Matthäus, who could no longer stand, had fallen on his back, whimpering loudly with pain, his mouth open wide. He stared into the sky, eyes wide with fear, reassuring Gero that he was not the only one who had descended into madness. Increasingly, everything around them was covered by this strange, glowing, blue-green pattern. The original structure of their surroundings seemed to be dissolving and even he and the boy were affected by it.

Instinctively, Gero let his sword fall, dropped to his knees, and pulled Matthäus toward him. As the first tree fell to the ground strangely silently, he shielded his squire beneath him protectively.

"I'm with you ... I'm with you," the Templar gasped. Under him, he felt the rapid breath of his squire, then something hard hit him on the head.

As darkness fell around him, he began a final prayer.

The battle ended abruptly. As if frozen, the rabble stared at the clearing, not moving an inch. In a frenzy Struan took the chance to strike at them, not at all noticing what was happening a mere hundred feet away from him. Only after slaughtering three of his opponents like lambs did he realize that something could be awry. Alarmed, he looked over the clearing to see if Amelie was still at her place. As he noticed the strange light and the silent falling of the trees, it was already too late.

His heart leaping to his throat in fear, he ran toward the mysterious phenomenon to reach Amelie, although he could not see her anywhere. Then he saw Johan kneeling on the ground, injured. With a pained expression, Johan clutched his sword arm and stared at the clearing as if he had gone mad.

A brightly shimmering net spanned the entire area, like a round, glowing cage. From a distance, Struan could see that Gero was also crouching in the middle of the strange phenomenon, hiding Matthäus under him.

Bravely, the Scotsman attempted to penetrate the blue-green shroud with his broadsword, but an extraordinarily strong force made his entire body shudder and robbed him temporarily of his senses, holding him back. He looked on helplessly as the shimmering net struck a tree, slicing through a thick branch, causing it to crash down on to Gero. A second branch fell, striking Johan on the head, cutting a bloody gash on his scalp as the Flemish knight collapsed with a moan.

Shocked, Struan pulled the unconscious Brother away from the clearing as the cage of light steadily solidified. At its boundary, it cut easily through entire tree trunks, no matter how thick.

The Scotsman felt a shudder run through his whole body. Filled with fear, he ran along the outer edge of the glowing circle. All his courage had left him, and he was frantic with worry for Gero, Matthäus, and Amelie. Tears streamed down his face as he screamed in despair in the unnerving silence of the forest. He stretched his hands to the heavens in supplication. Helplessly, he looked on as an entire forest clearing, along with his best friend and an innocent boy, disappeared into nothingness.

CHAPTER 12

Lost Sons

Tuesday, October 17, 1307

All through the night, Struan stared into the dark forest, where no bird sang and no animal rustled. Crouching motionlessly on the ground, only his heartbeat broke the enduring silence that held his soul captive in a boundless, nameless fear.

Amelie was snuggled in his arms in a dazed, helpless heap. He held her so tightly that she could hardly breathe. Her wide-open eyes hid the fact that she had simply lost her mind.

The early morning autumn sun finally breathed new life into Struan, and a soft moan brought him reluctantly back into a world that had been thrown into chaos. His gaze fell on Johan, who stared up at him through blood-encrusted eyes.

"Struan," the Flemish Brother croaked through his dry lips, "Struan, is that you?"

Struan's large hand ran mechanically over his Brother's outstretched arm to reassure him. As he struggled unsuccessfully to sit up, Johan grimaced in pain.

Before he came to Johan's aid, Struan laid Amelie carefully down on his cloak.

"Wait, Brother, I'll help you," he said to Johan softly. Cautiously, he turned his injured comrade onto his side to relieve his pain.

Struan looked up, noticing the horses grazing next to them. It seemed that even the wayward Brabant and Gero's silver dapple gray had sought out familiar faces during the night.

With shaking legs, he went to his black steed to retrieve the dressing material and pain medication from the saddlebags. After covering Amelie in another blanket, he gave Johan something to drink and busied himself with cleaning the wound on his head with a little wine before binding it.

Inevitably his gaze fell on the stage of yesterday's horrific events. The entire clearing had been cut out of the brown earth like a rotten spot on an apple.

"Dear Lord," Struan whispered, struggling to hold back his tears.

Desperately, he scanned the area with his sharp eyes. There was no trace of Gero or Matthäus and even the surviving robbers had fled.

Johan began to retch violently. Struan supported his Brother's head as he emptied his stomach in the damp grass. As Johan looked up, wheezing, his gaze fell on the clearing, and with a sigh of despair, he collapsed and lost consciousness once more.

Feverishly, Struan considered the situation. He had to stay calm and get help, but he could not seek refuge in the cloister. How would he tell anyone what had happened without being ridiculed as a lunatic or accused of collaborating with the devil?

There remained only the Breydenbachs' castle.

The Scotsman recalled that Gero's father, although unpleasant, was an influential man, whose men could certainly assist in the search for Gero and Matthäus.

Despite his doubts, he held onto the faint hope that, in his confusion, Gero could have escaped the strange light unseen and run away with Matthäus. Then again, Struan could not imagine his best friend and comrade ever deserting his Brothers.

Struan decided to leave immediately. Johan's condition was serious, and, like Amelie, he needed urgent medical attention.

The castle of the Breydenbachs sat enthroned on a tall cliff that dropped steeply into the fast-flowing Lieser River. Slowly, Struan led the horses up the serpentine path. He had tied Johan on to the back of the Jutlander, ensuring the man could not slide off the horse accidentally. The wounded Brother was still unconscious, but every time the horse jostled, he moaned softly. Amelie sat listlessly on her mare, clutching the pommel of her saddle tensely and staring blankly into space.

Three tall towers with their wide, defensive corridors and subtly arranged arrow slits soared over massive, turf walls. A fourth tower crowned the main building, which rose high above the walls in the middle of the stately compound. Upon its peak, the banner of the Breydenbachs flew proudly with the colors of the archdiocese of Trier. A wide moat filled with green water protected the front of the castle against invaders.

Struan felt relief wash over him when they finally reached the castle's main gate. The forecourt and sprawling inner courtyard were cobbled with black, angular stones. The lowered drawbridge offered the newcomers a clear view into the courtyard, where they saw children playing, women running around with their washbasins, and servants pulling carts loaded with cattle feed behind them.

A fanfare sounded three times, and the castle sentry admitted entry to the tall, black-haired Templar and his attendants. With five horses, a weary maiden, and a heavily injured comrade in tow, Struan pleaded humbly for refuge.

"Call the steward!" yelled a watchman to a knave scurrying by.

A little later, an imperious voice rumbled over the courtyard. "Woe, if someone there is playing a joke on me!"

With quick steps, an imposing man with a thick belly and a short, graying beard approached the Templars. He paused, his weather-beaten face pail in genuine concern.

The man introduced himself as Roland of Briey and he immediately sent for the castle's lord and his wife.

Jutta of Breydenbach appeared first in the courtyard with her hair shrouded under a snow-white wimple, wearing a brown velvet surcoat with a high neck. She approached Struan to welcome him and take care of her injured guests before her husband arrived. She had a blood-bathed Johan moved to a stretcher, before tending to Amelie, instructing a pair of handmaidens to prepare a herbal brew to soothe her mind. An older maid, skilled in the healing arts, took care of Johan's injuries.

Visibly incensed, the lord of the castle, Richard of Breydenbach, pushed his way through his curious servants. He was followed by a bevy of loyalists, vassals of the archbishop of Trier, who had gathered for a meeting at the Breydenbach castle.

Struan was glad that Richard of Breydenbach spoke French as fluently as his wife. The lord stood, tall and imposing, his silver-blonde hair swirling around his chiseled face. Armed in chain mail, buckskin trousers, and elaborately constructed boots, he wore the red, white, and blue surcoat of the Breydenbachs, as well as the red and gold colors of the archbishop of Trier. Only upon closer inspection did Struan notice he was missing his right hand. Richard of Breydenbach eyed Struan like a bird of prey as he began to speak. The lady of the castle had returned to her husband's side, and was noticeably distraught at the news of her son's disappearance.

Struan tried to break the news as gently as possible. He struggled to find the right words, first speaking only of the Lombards' attack before he started on Philipp's actions in France.In front of all those unknown men, he couldn't tell the whole truth.

"Go back to work," Richard sharply commanded the servants standing around. "You can do nothing here." Then he turned toward the stretcher where Johan lay. "Bring him into one of the bowers."

The imposing man looked appraisingly at the older woman in dark garments, who rose to her feet with an effort as the men carried the stretcher away. "Gertrudis, take care of him," he ordered in a conspiratorial tone. "He must not die, do you hear? He is the son of Count Bechtholt van Elk and an important witness. If necessary, I'll arrange for a medicus from Trier."

The woman nodded, deferential. Laboriously, she followed the injured noble-born who was being carried swiftly toward the castle.

Struan looked on in concern as the lord and his followers conducted a whispered discussion.

Then Richard of Breydenbach turned to his wife calmly. "Don't fret, my love," he said with the same deep voice as his missing son. "Everything will be fine."

She stared at him in outrage. "This concerns our youngest son," she retorted loudly. "What if something has befallen him?"

Before Richard could reply, a fanfare sounded. Struan saw a rider in the Breydenbachs' colors gallop up the horse stairs at breakneck speed on a fox-red stallion. He was followed closely by a boy whose black gelding stumbled on the damp cobblestones.

Before the first horse came to a halt, the knight sprang from its back and ran to the lord and lady of the castle.

It was Eberhard of Breydenbach, Gero's elder brother. If not for his martial clothing and mighty sword scabbard that almost reached to his feet, one could have mistaken him for a woman, because of his lean figure and his delicate facial features. The autumn wind blew thin strands of his shoulder-length, light blond hair into his face.

"Father," he called, bowing breathlessly. "I have peculiar news."

Richard of Breydenbach looked at him with a strange flicker in his eyes. "Speak French!" he ordered with a sideways glance at Struan. "So our guest may also understand."

Eberhard looked up in astonishment, only then noticing Struan.

"The monks are saying that some roaming Lombards sought refuge in the cloister yesterday evening," he continued in flawless French. "They

146

"We were on the way to the Cistercian Abbey of Heisterbach," Struan murmured. "What your son intended to do there, I do not know. He said only that Henri d'Our gave him a secret mission and ordered that Brother Johan and I should help him with it. He said that he could only tell us everything when we reached our destination."

"Heisterbach," Richard whispered absently. "I should have known."

"What are you saying?" Struan squinted at the white-haired nobleman.

"Did Gero say anything else? Perhaps something that you found strange?"

Struan hesitated, debating whether he dared reveal sensitive matters that he himself did not understand.

"He spoke of a 'Head of Wisdom'," he said quickly, and took a quick gulp of the delicious white wine.

Richard took a deep breath. For a moment, all color in his face seemed to vanish. He fixed Struan with a fierce stare and leaned forward in his chair.

"I have to know exactly what d'Our intended with his command."

"I do not know, Sire," Struan replied with despair in his eyes. "Gero only said that it could help us save the Order."

Richard nodded silently and leaned back with his eyes closed.

"Good Sir," Struan said softly, "I've told you everything I know. Would you be so kind as to share your thoughts with me? After all, it's not just your son who is so sorely missed. He's also my Brother in the Order, and the best friend I've ever had."

Richard sat up, sighed, and looked at Struan solemnly. "As you know, I am not a member of your Order," he began, "and yet I feel closely connected to the Templars. When I helped Henri d'Our and your current Grand master flee Acre, I could only sense that it concerned something far more valuable than the lives of a few prized leaders of the Order. My brother-in-law Gerhard of Lichtenberg and I were tasked with guaranteeing Henri d'Our and Jacques de Molay secure passage to their ship during our escape.

"They were carrying a sealed book with them, wrapped in a leather bag, and by the way Brother Henri held it, I could see that it was something more precious than all the gold the Order possessed. Shortly before we reached the harbor, the Mamluks broke through the fortress wall. D'Our lost the bag in the chaos, and, while trying to protect it from the grasp of the Mamluks, we found ourselves in a dire situation. A Jewish merchant hurried to help us, and he succeeded in wresting the bag away from one of the attackers. But the furious mob slaughtered the poor man and his wife in cold blood. Oh, I could kill the Mamluks who attacked them! I tried again to get the bag, which cost me my right hand. My brother-in-law hurried to my aid. Still, he let down his rear guard for just a moment, and one of the Mamluks split his head at that instant. It was Jacques de Molay who killed the assailant. Your Grand Master then took the bag.

"Before we left, I discovered a whimpering girl, cowering by the side of the dead Jewish merchants. She was barely six years old, and obviously their daughter. In the heat of the moment, I swore to Molay and his Brothers that I would not leave the child behind. I promised God Almighty that I would adopt the girl and give her over to the Cistercian convent of Saint Thomas, if only he would let us escape the city with our lives."

Richard of Breydenbach became silent for a moment. Harrowing scenes from long ago seemed to play out in front of his eyes.

"We fled to Cyprus," he continued. "It was there that d'Our revealed to me that he was a member of the Order's High Council, which was responsible for the protection of an ancient artifact called the Head of Wisdom. It contains a kind of prophecy, similar to the apocalypse of Saint John, but the prophecies within aren't wholly evil in nature. Indeed, it has improved the Order's wealth immeasurably. Finally, I accompanied d'Our to southern France, where we sought out a concealed place to hide the sealed book we had saved from Acre, which contained secret information about the Head of Wisdom. There, I discovered that the Head was a mysterious metallic object that Bertrand de Blanchefort, the sixth Grand Master of your Order, brought to southern France from the holy land in 1156 to precisely that location. To my astonishment, I found out that this hiding place had previously been established in a German Cistercian abbey with the knowledge of Saint Bernhard of Clairvaux and the help of the conversi."

Richard of Breydenbach paused as he gathered himself, taking a gulp of wine before continuing.

"D'Our knew that I was trustworthy and connected closely enough to the Cistercians, that he intended to use me as a sort of middleman between the Templars and Cistercians, though I belonged to neither order. That's why I travel to Bar-sur-Aube every now and then, to carry secret messages between the two orders."

Richard continued, "You should know that the Head of Wisdom was transferred under great secrecy from the catacombs in France to the Cistercians in Heisterbach in 1206. They wanted to ensure it was out of reach of those who must not find it. There was a permanent representative under the command of the High Council of the Templars in the abbey there, who, along with the abbot, was responsible for the Head's safekeeping. At that time, it was Brother Cäsarius, the Prior of Heisterbach, in case that name means anything to you."

Struan nodded silently. He had heard the miraculous stories of Cäsarius, the wise Cistercian who had concerned himself with the phenomenon of time and uttered dismal prophecies about the future from his nightly visions.

"Forgive me, Sire, for interrupting you," Struan said. "Have you ever seen the mysterious Head?"

"Not in reality. Only as a painted picture on parchment," Richard said with a tinge of regret in his voice. "It is actually a flat, metallic box, so light that you can carry it in one hand. Nothing about it is conspicuous, and it doesn't look anything like a head. But they assure me that it has magic of unimaginable power, and its wisdom has served the Order since the beginning of its existence. Some even speculate that it can create portals to another time. But d'Our's trust in me didn't extend far enough for him to tell me everything."

"That sounds unbelievable," Struan was quick to admit. "Does Gero know about it?"

"What do you think?" Richard asked with a smile. "I took an oath of silence. No one from my family knows anything about it."

"With all respect, Sire, what would this have to do with Gero's disappearance?"

Richard of Breydenbach sat up straighter with a sigh and stared into the restless flame of the thick hour-candle, which had already burnt down considerably. "Since those days, I've known that there are things between heaven and earth that should only be subject to the will of God, but have been controlled by men," he explained.

"You should know that a Brother has disappeared without a trace in the Saalholz forest once before – a good hundred years ago. The forest belongs to the Hemmenrode Cistercians, who are closely connected to the

Heisterbach convent. The missing Brother, Thomas of Hemmenrode, was a confidant of Cäsarius of Heisterbach, who had taken over the duty of protecting the Head shortly beforehand. I don't know if there is a connection. In any case, the missing Brother was found three weeks later, unharmed but dazed, at the exact spot where Gero disappeared. He told his astonished brethren that he had journeyed hundreds of years into the future. An incredibly elderly Jewish man in strange clothing asked him odd questions. The man assured Brother Thomas that he would be allowed to return home as soon as he had answered all his questions. In hindsight it seems that the young monk spoke of the exact same blue-green light that you mentioned."

Richard shook his head wearily. "I don't know if Gero's disappearance has anything to do with the Head of Wisdom and the secret of Heisterbach, but the monks there conceal more than any faithful person could possibly suspect. Because your mission may very well be connected to the Cistercians of Heisterbach, and neither Gero nor your commander can clarify the circumstances, I see only one way to shed light on the issue. We will bide our time for five days and hope that your Brother Johan regains his strength. Perhaps a miracle will happen before then, and we'll find my son and his squire. Should that not be the case, we will set off for Heisterbach in secret and search for an answer."

PART 2

CENTER OF ACCELERATED PARTICLES IN UNIVERSE AND TIME

"Let him who seeks continue seeking until he finds. When he finds, he will become troubled. When he becomes troubled, he will be astonished, and he will rule over the invisible world."

The Gospel of Thomas, Verse 2

CHAPTER 13

Spangdahlem/Eifel

Wednesday, November 10, 2004
Germany

The constant muffled roar of A-10 and OA-10 Thunderbolt II aircrafts formed the aural backdrop to the U.S. Airbase Spangdahlem's office complex, despite the new structure's soundproofing. And today it was getting on Professor Dietmar Hagen's nerves even more than usual.

For weeks, Hagen had labored over his research at the military compound, where he also lived. He no longer cared about his diet or exercise, much less his alcohol intake. A quick glance in the mirror was all he needed to realize that his toned body would take a beating if he continued living like this.

Yet this was the least of Hagen's problems. With agonizing regularity, he had begun to question whether he really was a scientific genius, or, as his critics claimed, simply out of touch. Even his fame in the field of quantum optics couldn't protect him from the rumor that he was basically insane. Every so often, when his research seemed poised on the verge of enormous leaps forward, the last pieces of the puzzle confirming his theories would simply refuse to fall into place – leaving him to stew in impatience and frustration. In quieter moments, he doubted whether it had been wise to sell his soul to the American military research laboratory instead of staying at the Max Planck Institute for Quantum Optics, where, a few years ago, he had contributed to research in laser physics.

Groaning, Hagen stretched his tired arms and removed his feet from his desk. Meanwhile, the full, decoded text he had received from Beirut a few days ago, in the usual ciphered format, appeared on his screen. It was only thanks to his own genius that he had relatively quickly developed a method to impart some meaning to the apparently incomprehensible combinations of characters. He put on his glasses, squinting as he viewed the final results of his efforts with a mixture of excitement and awe.

In short, we are still stranded in Jerusalem. It is hot and sticky, and the battles outside the city escalate daily. The conquest of Ashkelon persists unabated. The violence is unimaginable. The list of victims on the Christians' side grows constantly. On the coast, ships arrive daily with whole loads of new pilgrims who are thrown into the conflict before they even see the holy city, without regard for career or qualifications. These utterly unprepared and ill-equipped masses are slaughtered like cattle. Not a day goes by that we aren't confronted with death or mutilation. Despite the torrid heat, the dead knights of the Order are brought to the Temple Mount, so they can be buried properly. The stench from the piles of corpses is indescribable. We have not dared to leave our refuge in the headquarters of the Order for a long while. Water is slowly becoming scarcer – and there is the constant risk of hostile Fatimid groups poisoning the well. At regular intervals the drinkability of the precious water is tested on cats and dogs, yet, despite this, there have already been deaths. Although we are vaccinated with antitoxic blockers, unlike the pitiful people of the city, we would rather begin the journey home sooner than later. The fact that all contact with the base has been cut off, however, prevents our return. The last digital exchange with SB 1 took place shortly after our arrival. They've positioned a laser buoy to determine our coordinates. In the meantime, we have come to the conclusion that something unforeseen must have happened during the transfer. How else would such a deviance from the entered time coordinates be possible?

It is a circumstance that hinders our return even further. Until now, there has been absolutely no news. We have received nothing, aside from a fireball, shot outside the city gates by the Egyptians' alleged allies. Almost all our equipment was destroyed in the fire that broke out in our sleeping quarters after nightly shelling. Without drinking water, our energy sources are almost depleted, and as long as we cannot leave our domicile, we have no chance of charging them again. The situation here corresponds with Code Black.

Our hosts, the Christian militia, as they call themselves, have been unexpectedly cooperative, which may be due to the fact that their leader knows some ancient secret wisdom that prophesized our arrival – a useless fact as long as we don't know the source of this knowledge. Unfortunately, we have no historical databases at our disposal. LYN recalled an archive file she had studied in the course of completing an inspection. After that, the next transmission of a person on October 16, 1307 – 18:31 CET from a transmission field in Europe under the coordinates 50° 01' 44.48" N and 6° 45' 18.60" E to 11-13-2004 will occur simultaneously.

I consider it still a rumor that the transferred is supposed to be a member of the Christian militia. Regrettably, LYN is not capable of telling us about the circumstances under which the transmission took place. In any case, it is too late for us. We cannot wait a hundred and fifty years to leave this place. Our only remaining hope is that contact with the base can be re-established.

Until then, we are trapped in space and time without the prospect of completing our mission.

This morning, LYN wrote some formulae and clues on several pieces of parchment and sealed it in small containers. Then, inconspicuously, she deposited the holy messages, as she calls them, in the crypt of five Templar knights when they were buried, with the bold idea that someone in a neighboring time plane would discover the sealed containers and help us return home.

Hope dies last, she said. Still, I think the likelihood that someone will be able to bring us home with the help of this dodgy server and therefore out of this hell is akin to finding a drop of unsalted groundwater in this blasted city. The magnitude of our despair can be measured by the fact that I have to write these lines by hand ...

Here the text broke off. All at once, Hagen noticed that his entire body was trembling with excitement.

It seemed that the author of the incomplete message was stranded on the Temple Mount in Jerusalem, and if radiocarbon dating calculations were correct, this was written in the era of the Crusades. Hagen was sure the words 'server' and 'database' had never crossed the lips of any crusader. That could only mean one thing – someone had succeeded not only in retrieving objects from the past, but even in transporting *themselves* there.

The mention of the coming Saturday and a specific location was Hagen's grand prize lottery win. A quick corroboration of the numbers with their GPS coordinates in a modern navigation system confirmed Hagen's suspicion. The only possible location mentioned in the parchment was his research facility in Himmerod. The secret, underground laboratory, together with a fusion reactor, was housed in a former U.S. military atomic bomb shelter – twenty minutes north of the airbase. Soon he would be able to claim credit for the miracle of transferring a human from the past into the year 2004 – even if he had been lent a huge helping hand.

The last rays of the autumn sun streamed through the half-lowered blinds, throwing patterns of light on the professor's messy workspace. Suddenly, the intercom system buzzed, announcing Dr. Piglet's arrival. Hagen's office was almost hermetically sealed. Visitors first had to identify themselves by their fingerprints before Hagen pressed a button on his writing desk to let them in. Only then would the visitor be allowed to meet the leader of the top-secret research facility, grandly named the Center of Accelerated Particles in Universe and Time – or CAPUT.

A short, unimpressive-looking man in his mid-forties peered cautiously through the crack in the door. In his old-fashioned glasses and even more old-fashioned dove blue suit, the man from Milwaukee always appeared a little eccentric.

"Ah, Mr. Piglet!" Hagen's voice sounded unusually friendly as he greeted his aide. "Take a seat! Would you like a drink? Some coffee, perhaps?"

"No, thank you," Piglet replied, clearly surprised that his boss was offering him anything at all.

"I have news from my friend in Israel," Hagen began with a conspiratorial look.

Piglet had settled down in one of the leather-upholstered guest chairs opposite Hagen. He raised an eyebrow, but otherwise his features remained remarkably neutral.

"And?" he asked simply.

"Another document has appeared. And the tracks lead to Europe."

"That doesn't exactly narrow it down," Piglet responded, flashing his boss the briefest of smiles.

"Hang on, Piglet!" Hagen interjected. "I know from trustworthy sources that this coming Saturday afternoon, we will be achieve an actual quantum leap."

Piglet sent Hagen a look that revealed he had no idea what his boss meant, despite his IQ of 153. "With all due respect for your accomplishments, sir, as far as I know, quantum leaps are a part of your daily work. What's so special about this one?"

"I see," Hagen chuckled. "I'm left with no choice but to go into detail. Surely I don't have to tell you that you are sworn to complete silence." Hagen's gray eyes glimmered. He would hate the National Security Agency, who regularly monitored his work, to poke its nose into this affair.

"Of course not," Piglet assured him, looking slightly put out.

To verify his allegiance to the United States of America, the American's domestic intelligence service had scrutinized every last detail of Piglet's rather dull past. But Hagen had long ago monopolized his aide's loyalty. With Piglet's assistance, behind the backs of his American employers, he had already repeatedly received secret information from the Middle East.

"What are you planning?" A queasy feeling churned in Piglet's stomach.

"I want to transfer a person," Hagen said casually, as if he were merely talking about getting a haircut, instead of an elaborate space-time experiment.

"You want to *what*?" Piglet leaned toward Hagen so quickly that his chair tipped forward dangerously. "But I thought we were still very far from achieving that!"

"That was yesterday," Hagen said dismissively. "Thanks to new findings bestowed upon me ... in a somewhat ... unconventional way, I have decided to expand exponentially the current potential of our experiments."

"You said yourself that we have to adjust the reactor's capacity before we even tried something like this. Or did I misunderstand you?" Piglet was in charge of the approval process for all of Hagen's experiments, and his boss had never before confronted him with a request of this magnitude. "Have you gotten the President's permission?" the aide added, irked that there was only one authority that could stop the professor.

"I'm afraid the red telephone was busy," Hagen answered with a wry smile. "It appears that the President is still preoccupied with his re-election."

"You mean you want to do this ... without approval?"

"Didn't I just say that?" Hagen pressed his lips into an innocent expression of regret and shrugged apologetically.

"Why the devil would you do that?" Piglet cried out in despair.

"Piglet, you're an intelligent fellow, aren't you? We are about to find the only true Holy Grail that has ever existed. We have to make compromises for that." Hagen looked at him seriously. "The future of this facility might very well depend on whether we succeed in transferring a person on Saturday. Imagine what a sensation it would be! Once the person arrives, no one will care how they were brought here, let alone if someone manipulated the system without approval."

Piglet's expression remained doubtful as he studied the professor through narrowed eyes.

"According to the message, the person comes from the beginning of the fourteenth century," Hagen announced coolly. "If we pull this off, Area 51 will be yesterday's news."

Piglet clutched the arms of his chair, shaking his head.

"The person in question will appear on our transmission field at exactly 18:31 CET, and then we spring the trap," Hagen continued. "If it works, the Americans might finally overcome their reservations about experimenting with people, and with their financial support, soon we won't just be able to bring someone out of the past, but also send people there. Do you understand, Piglet? Everything we've accomplished so far will only matter if we succeed on Saturday."

"And what's stopping you from presenting your case to the President for his approval?"

"Piglet, I have no intention of revealing my source. In any case, we don't have enough time to put together an explanation," Hagen said decisively. "I received the message just yesterday. We have less than three days until the window closes, and I don't have the faintest idea if we will ever get a second chance. Our current knowledge suggests that there is a balancing constant, ensuring that external influences can not change the course of history, but ultimately we can't be sure about that."

160

Hagen's voice lowered to a hiss. "Besides, the information comes from my Lebanese informant yet again. How often do I have to explain to you that I want to go into the history books as the inventor of this technology, not its discoverer? Besides, you know well enough how delicate the current political situation is. Even if I put my reputation on the line, we will both be old and gray before the President and his NSA lackeys are done vetting my work for acts of sabotage and making sure our friend isn't an informant for Islamic terrorists."

The professor took a gulp of mineral water, swirling it around his palate as though it were an expensive brandy. After he had swallowed, he glared at Piglet with a look that brooked no argument. "So, Piglet, for organizational reasons, and without my official cooperation, you will alter the schedule for the research staff this Saturday. Put Stevendahl and Colbach on duty. If anything goes wrong, we'll hold them responsible."

Piglet looked like he was fighting with his conscience. "I'd very much like to know," he began, "why you think Stevendahl and Colbach are the best people to send to the slaughterhouse. If the military decides that even one of them re-programmed the computer without authorization, they will both be expelled from the project."

"Well … " Hagen answered slowly, "I'd be sad to see them go, but they are the only ones capable of making such a change in the system's sequence – apart from yours truly, of course."

His look indicated just how little the careers of the two young, aspiring scientists meant to him. In the end, he would do what he wanted, no matter the consequence of his actions, and others would take the fall for him. Of course, he understood that he, too, would be investigated, but he was clever enough to orchestrate the entire affair so that no one would be able to uncover the true scope of his influence.

Piglet had given up trying to locate Hagen's conscience long ago. "Let's suppose you're right, and the person you are expecting appears in our research field. What do we do next?"

"What indeed?" Hagen blustered impatiently. "Our security personnel will arrest them, and the NSA will throw them into a solitary cell and squeeze them dry. I don't care what the President and his Secret Service do to the person after they appear. If everything goes according to plan, in the next few months, I will be busy whipping the equipment into shape for the future. Or should I say – for the past?" Hagen chuckled.

Nervously Piglet adjusted his glasses. "Will the transferred person even speak our language?" He felt like he was hanging over a gaping abyss, grasping desperately at any feeble objections that came to mind.

"Please, Piglet. Have you forgotten where you are? We decode the most complicated genetic codes here. We have databases of speech patterns for every language in the world – even Klingon, for God's sake. Do you honestly think I would have a problem with Middle High German or Old French?"

"And what if all that appears is a lump of flesh? That seems a very likely outcome. That uncertainty, and the fact that no one knows if the space-time continuum will be altered, are the reasons why we currently refrain from such experiments."

"Then that will be a pity for the transferred subject," Hagen said, shaking his head in exasperation. "If the expected fellow accidentally dissolves into his organic components, no one would notice anyway. The only ones who may be annoyed are the cleaning staff." Hagen struck the edge of his desk. "I will never understand you Americans. You have slaughtered thousands of Iraqis, accomplishing nothing, but still worry over the hypothetical death of a time traveler, which no one will even witness and whose mortal remains would, at the very least, benefit science."

"What if the experiment gets out of hand and the reactor overheats?"

"You sure know how to ask questions, Piglet!"

Defiance grew on the aide's timid face. "What makes you think I would support such lunacy?"

Only the slightest twitch of the professor's right eyelid revealed that the question had been a blow to him. He ignored the surge in his adrenaline levels as well as his fantasies of sweeping the desk clean and crucifying his aide on it.

"Because you have no other choice, my friend," Hagen answered, deceptively calm. He rose suddenly, swiftly stepping around his desk. Shortly before he reached Piglet he stopped abruptly and looked down at his aide with narrowed eyes.

"I have made you who you are," he said coldly. Piglet quickly averted his gaze. "And I see no problem in handing over your office to Dr. Karen Baxter." A haughty glare underscored Hagen's arrogance. "Apart from being far more attractive than you are," he said to Piglet, "she's also a worthy successor, just waiting for you to stumble."

162

Silence reigned for a moment. Then Hagen grinned. "And should you think of denouncing me to our employers, I would lose *my* position to Dr. Tom Stevendahl. He's a young man, and he'll hand over your position to Dr. Baxter, too. Besides, what would stop me from claiming that you knew about my plans, but simply got cold feet?"

Before Piglet could respond, the intercom system buzzed again.

Hagen pressed the confirmation button impatiently, causing Tracy Lockwind's round face to appear on the screen.

"You and Dr. Piglet have an appointment with Major Cedric Dan Simmens, the military attaché from the American Embassy, in half an hour. A tour of the facility at Himmerod is planned for 6:00 p.m. and you have a dinner in the private room of the airport casino at 8:00."

"Ah, Tracy, what would I ever do without you? Are my shirts back from the cleaner's?"

"They have already been stored in your dressing room."

"Thank you. You are dismissed for the day. Have a good evening, Tracy."

After a short drive in an armored van, Hagen, Piglet, and the military attaché arrived at the high-security research center, CAPUT. It was built on the former estate of a nearby abbey, whose monks sold the ground to the American government shortly after World War Two. In the research compound's brightly lit lobby, a service assistant from the marine choir was waiting for the professor and his two companions. To Hagen, the insignia on the collar of her navy blue uniform was a depressing reminder that his memory was no longer infallible. Although he had been stationed at the U.S. air base for many years, he still couldn't tell a sergeant from a major – a problem that had occasionally resulted in painful silences with higher ranked military officials, although their subordinates were certainly amused.

With a smile, the infantrywoman took the coats of the distinguished guests and served them cocktails. Hagen's gaze flickered with interest between the brunette marine's long, silk stocking clad legs and the broad-shouldered attaché's uniform. His chest was covered with insignias and accolades in the form of small, colorful rectangles affixed directly over his heart on his perfectly fitted jacket. With his toned, compact figure, he looked every inch the typical ex-marine.

The curvaceous assistant led the men into a small projection room with plush cinema seats. Once the lights were dimmed, a short ten-minute film began to play. With absolute dispassion, the film narrated the individual construction phases of the research facility. It was intended to prepare the unwitting viewers for the complex explanations that would later rain down upon them.

Dr. Piglet squinted nervously as the lights came up and the audience filed out into the brightly lit foyer. The aide followed the attaché and his boss into the elevator that led to the computer servers and the nuclear fusion reactor one level below.

"Why so quiet, Dr. Piglet?" Hagen asked in mock concern as the doors slid open and they walked down the long, fluorescent-lit corridor into the compound's inner sanctum. "I'm sure Major Simmens is interested in how this dream has been financed. After all, his government has paid an arm and a leg and cut down on new missiles and tanks just for this beauty," the professor remarked with a light touch of irony in his voice. "Wouldn't you like to cheer him up with a few statistics?"

"Yes, I'd love to hear them," Simmens agreed, eyeing the flustered-looking aide closely. Seeing Piglet's look of alarm, the major broke into a wide grin. "Surely the figures can't be that scary. After all, the Senate approved them."

Piglet swallowed hard. The entire project had been sold to the Senate as a secret energy research program. Apart from the research team, only the Pentagon and the President's inner circle knew about the true nature of the project – and the attaché should have been aware of that.

"Come on!" Simmens laughed, clapping Piglet on the shoulder. "My colleagues have been asking why their promotions have been delayed for so long, and I'd love to finally have an answer for them."

"Well," Piglet began, "the fusion reactor cost about six billion dollars, which is still four billion less than what the Japanese proposed to spend when they submitted a quote last year for the first ever nuclear fusion test reactor, ITER, at a cost of ten billion dollars and a construction period of ten years. As you've learned today, we took less than two and a half years to construct ours, thanks to the brilliant innovative spirit of our professor here."

With a furtive glance at his audience, Piglet made sure he still had their undivided interest.

"If you've been following the news, you'll have noticed that European scientists are constructing a reactor, as well. They've just started looking at how to control the inner pressure and reduce strain on the reactor walls, which means a longer lifespan for the surrounding hull. Among them are former colleagues of Professor Hagen, who teamed up to investigate the reaction between the wall and the fusion plasma that will be heated to several million degrees. Of course, here in Himmerod, we answered these questions long ago."

"Hats off, Professor," Simmens remarked, gazing at Hagen in awe.

Hagen dismissed him with a casual wave of his hand. "The reactor barely posed a challenge. The real problem was the electromagnet, which generates the necessary field force to advance into the microcosm of quantum mechanics."

"I'm sorry, could you explain that?" Simmens had anticipated that his rudimentary knowledge of physics would not be sufficient to allow him to understand Hagen's work, but that made him all the more eager for an explanation that he could at least partially comprehend.

"Underneath the experimental area we have succeeded in fitting magnetic coils that can generate a magnetic field of nearly 100,000 Tesla in a magnetic pulse that lasts for three seconds. At the moment, the facility uses as much energy as all of Rhineland-Palatinate, Luxembourg, and northern France combined. The amount of energy we use is the main reason why we need the fusion reactor. The magnetic coils are custom fit, encapsulated in special concrete, then cooled with nitrogen so the wires don't melt. As the pulse is initiated, intense laser radiation causes a spike in the field force. With this technology, we can make advances into supposedly bygone time dimensions. Think of them as parallel universes. We have been able to make the existing molecular structures in these dimensions visible. For quite some time now, we have also been able to isolate small parts of the molecular structure we made visible and transplant them into our own dimension."

"That sounds fantastic." Simmens' voice sounded uncertain.

Hagen smirked. "Don't sweat it," he said, ushering the attaché through one of the center's numerous automatic doors. "You're not the only one who finds it hard to understand the depth of our work all at once. At the moment, only a handful of scientists understand this procedure. During the rest of our excursion, I will try to fill you in on all the details. Now, if you would follow me, please." With a jovial smile, Hagen opened another door that led to the lobby of a large hall.

Stepping into the lobby, the attaché peered through a three-meter high shatterproof glass wall at an enclosed area the size of a football field. A special ceramic wall stood waiting, ready to shield the glass during experiments. Above the wall hung a bright red warning sign with a black inscription: *Danger! Beware of Magnetic Pulse.*

"Can we go in?" Simmens asked, marveling at the walls of the experimental hall that towered twenty-five meters high and met overhead in a honeycombed glass roof.

"Of course," Hagen said, and gave one of the technicians on duty an order over the intercom. "As long as the system isn't in operation, nothing can happen to us. Before the reactor is turned on, it has to be locked hermetically. Then cameras, light barriers, radio sensors, and motion detectors ensure that no unauthorized personnel can come anywhere near the field."

A technician, who was wearing white overalls with the research facility's black logo – the letters CAPUT above two intertwined infinity symbols – stitched onto the breast pocket, entered a command into the computer.

With a hiss, the door to the reactor unlocked and slid open.

"Open, sesame." Hagen smiled, gesturing to the Major to enter before him.

As he stepped onto the magenta floor resembling an indoor track, Simmens debated whether he should remove his shoes.

Hagen, who guessed his thoughts, chuckled in amusement. "No worries, Major. The hall is specially cleaned every day. When we carry out our experiments, there is not a molecule in here that doesn't belong in this room."

Simmens spun around once, his head tilted back and his mouth hanging open in astonishment. It was a strange sight, Hagen mused. The heavily decorated military attaché looked like a six-year-old seeing the Christmas tree at Rockefeller Center for the first time.

"How did you arrive at this compound of all places?" the attaché asked the professor a little later.

"As you may know, nuclear warheads have been stored on these grounds since the early 80s. The bunker constructed for this purpose runs several stories deep and is suitably isolated. It offers enough room to accommodate laboratories, storage for replacement parts, and – should it become necessary – a detention center for involuntary time travelers," Hagen said with a smile.

"Do you think that one day we'll be able to transfer a person through time?" Simmens stared at Hagen with wide eyes.

"I don't think anything is impossible in principle," Hagen answered coolly. "But at the moment, we lack clearance from your government to conduct such experiments. Unfortunately, we aren't yet familiar with the underlying physical laws, and, to be honest, these experiments do involve some risks. On the other hand, our research suggests that the technology and the possibilities associated with it are governed by localized constraints. Consequently, the only things that can be transferred must be found within the immediate oscillation radius of the magnetic seeker, and their subatomic processes must have already taken place at the current time."

"So if I understand you correctly, it's impossible to transfer the Queen's crown jewels here from the fifteenth century, unless someone had temporarily buried them on this field, say, five hundred years ago?"

"Well inferred, Major," Hagen confirmed, rewarding the attaché with a pat on the back. "Besides, we stand by the institute's policy of not gambling unnecessarily with the lives of innocent bystanders. If, someday, we get that far, perhaps we could even arrest the thief as he buries the treasure."

Piglet coughed quietly, earning him an angry look from Hagen. On the other hand, Simmens, looked satisfied.

"At this time, we don't have to concern ourselves with such specifics," the professor added hurriedly, pointedly avoiding his aide's piercing gaze. "We are still light years away from the possibility of transferring a person."

"And what does the future look like? Do you think we will be able to travel into the future as well?" the attaché asked.

Hagen shook his head regretfully. "The current status of our research doesn't allow us to transfer something from the future into the present, let alone send anything there. As I've already said, the facility's event horizon cannot be transgressed in the direction of the future."

Simmens remained in awed silence as they strolled across the field, which, now that dusk had fallen, was bathed in gleaming floodlights.

Suddenly Hagen turned around and made a grand gesture with his right arm.

"For the first time, here in this laboratory hall, we have been able to reconstruct complicated magnetic patterns of long-gone atomic movements, making them visible using a laser that glows like the northern lights. About a year and a half ago, we succeeded in entering deeper subatomic particles comprised of vibrating strings of energy. In comparison to an atom, these particles are unimaginably small – imagine, if you will, a single tree in the entire solar system. In mathematical calculations, we begin from the premise that these strings form the primordial matter of which the entire universe is composed. In our field research, we have succeeded in matching atomic particles with strings of different oscillation patterns that account for different mass and charge. These oscillation patterns mean that everything in the universe can be matched to a specific structure. Animals, plants, stones, water ... even music and colors are governed by this principle. Over a year ago, we developed powerful quantum computers that enable us to decode and isolate individual objects out of the jumble of continuous structures."

Simmens was obviously struggling to follow Hagen's lecture. He swallowed, glancing around nervously as he scratched his head.

Noticing the attaché's confusion, Hagen continued in an understanding tone. "I was just as astonished as you are when I realized that the fundamental structures of all existence follow certain energy patterns, like a silent film running continuous pictures while a grand symphony plays." He raised his lanky arms like the conductor of an invisible orchestra. "*Panta rhei,*" he announced with his eyes closed.

Suddenly, as if awoken from a deep slumber, he opened them again.

"Everything flows," he continued, meeting the major's dazed expression with a smile, "said old Heraclitus. And he was right. Invisible to the naked eye, a powerful neuronal net of magnetically ordered, atomic delta connections flooded with an unending, oscillating energy stream organizes the course of space and time. The process repeats itself constantly, and, most importantly, simultaneously. Only through sophisticated formulae and equations is it possible to see beyond the shadows on the wall and to decode their meaning bit by bit. To put it plainly," Hagen said, "we are already able to transfer small organic objects like branches, small rocks, clumps of earth, dead leaves, and even small plants from earlier times into the present by cutting their atomic net sequences out of the space-time continuum – like a gene from a living cell – and implanting the resulting sequence in our current time, right here in this room. And that's not all," he announced with a note of pride, "the pulsating energy stream that is permeating all plains floods through the implanted structures like blood through the veins of a living organism, allowing them to be revived in the current era, solidifying them, and even allowing them to develop further."

"Fascinating," Simmens murmured.

"I'll be happy to accompany you to the botanical garden after this excursion."

"Botanical garden?" Simmens brow furrowed in confusion.

"That's the nickname for our biological research department," Hagen answered with a smile. "The only thing stopping a daisy from the fifteenth century from blooming after its transmission into the current time is if the botanist on duty forgets to water it."

"What if your experiments alter the course of time?" The major narrowed his eyes.

"So far, all test objects have been so insignificant that their disappearances have not brought about any apparent consequences in their actual time patterns, or – better said – on their neighboring time planes." Hagen's tone was decidedly calm, but Simmens would not let the matter rest.

"And what about chaos theory? The famous butterfly effect?"

"If you learn just one thing from me today," Hagen retorted with a touch of arrogance, "let it be to not trust popular theories so blindly. We are moving into uncharted territory. Think of us as Columbus – the first to speak to the Indians. And when we triumph, no longer will anyone doubt that the Americans were the first to plant their flag on the moon. Should that not be the truth, we will rectify it immediately."

Noting that Simmens looked deeply impressed, Hagen reveled secretly in his own dramatic talent, which he regularly deployed against the Americans to obtain the funds he needed for the project, and to dispel any baseless qualms they had about his research. Within his closest working circle, there was still no consensus on the experiments' actual influence on the course of history. One theory claimed that the structure of the net prevented any interference with the past. Until now they had not been able to conduct enough research to prove it. And now, with the introduction of time synchronicity, no one could dispute who had been the first to ram their flag into the moon.

Shortly after 11:00 p.m. that evening, a silver Audi TT rolled up to the entry-control point of the Himmerod research facility. A few feet in front of the guardhouse, the driver turned off the headlights as regulations dictated and rolled down the window.

A serious looking marine in a protective vest stepped into the halogen lights that illuminated the driveway as bright as day. He was followed by a colleague armed with an M-16 assault rifle.

The facility was in operation around the clock to keep the nuclear fusion reactor, which required regular maintenance, running uninterrupted. The computer center required to run the reactor was also staffed 24 hours a day. Important administrative tasks were only allowed to be carried out at night. All employees had their work hours logged, and a computerized scheduling system kept the sentry informed of all work agendas.

The guard looked taken aback when he recognized the leader of the research facility – the man who had created the current security systems. A gray-haired, fifty-year-old man was sitting in the driver's seat in front of him.

"Have a pleasant evening, Professor Hagen," he said politely, and signaled to his colleague to open the roller door.

After Hagen had parked his Audi in a spot reserved for him on deck C, he rode the elevator down to the quantum computer server room in Basement 2. The development and purchase of the computer, which still did not exist on official records, had eaten up half the entire budget the Americans had allotted for the laboratory's construction.

After verifying his fingerprint, inserting a chip card, and entering a code number, Hagen was granted access. Silently he entered the computer room. With its sterile white walls and aluminum furnishings, it resembled an operating room. On this night, five employees were on duty, all hunched silently in front of their computers with their heads lowered. None of them seemed to notice Hagen entering the room.

"Henderson!" A man in his mid-twenties, wearing a white coat over a pair of worn jeans and a garish T-shirt, spun around in shock, sending his blonde dreadlocks flying. Panic filled his eyes. Hagen strode over to him, only to find a sports magazine splayed open in front of his errant employee.

"In case you haven't noticed, you're not being paid to roller-skate here, Henderson, but for the surveillance of a facility whose worth appears to exceed your capacity for judgment!"

"Yes, boss," Henderson mumbled guiltily without looking at Hagen.

During Hagen's lecture, the other four system administrators had hastily taken the chance to hide their coffee, cookies, and magazines filled with pictures of scantily clad women.

"You've signed a contract to give this monitor your undivided attention while you're on duty," Hagen said, his voice growing dangerously soft. "I could fire you."

Henderson's Adam's apple quivered. "Yes, sir," he finally answered.

Hagen turned to the other employees. "That goes for the rest of you," he blustered. "For the money we pay you, I expect you to perform your duties to my satisfaction. The next one of you who doesn't follow the rules can squander his future with Microsoft for all I care!"

His withering glare drove daggers through the pale faces of his frozen audience.

"Have I made myself clear?" he yelled.

He was met with silent nods.

"Now, I want you to prepare a terminal for me."

Geoffrey Henderson looked every inch the computer geek whose only contact with the military was through strategy games. But at Hagen's command, he took on the tense, upright bearing of a soldier, and it almost seemed as if he was going to salute Hagen. After taking a moment to pull himself together, he found the courage to usher the professor to a computer terminal as far away as possible from the employees on duty. Hastily he pulled out the chip card that dangled on his neck from a long chain and unlocked the security mechanism to start the quantum computer.

With an impatient sideways glance, informing Henderson that he could now get lost, Hagen inserted his own chip card in turn. Like a lurking crocodile, the professor's eyes followed Henderson as he slunk away, until his footsteps were lost behind a row of neatly erected dividers.

Only then did Hagen seat himself in the comfortable computer chair and start the program, safe in the knowledge that no one in the room would dare disturb him for the next half hour.

Hagen's fingers flew across the keyboard as he switched one magnetic cartridge after the other. After he had deleted the work protocol, he ejected the chip card and left the hall just as silently as he had entered.

CHAPTER 14

The Accident

Saturday, November 13, 2004

Dr. Tom Stevendahl was due to begin duty at 11:00 a.m. at the US military research institute CAPUT, located about 120 kilometers away, in a remote village in the Eifel. Now it was a quarter to ten, and he was still standing in the hallway of his apartment in Bonn, searching for his car keys in growing desperation. He closed his eyes, entering a sort of meditative state, and remembered his jeans in the laundry room. Amidst a pile of towels and bed sheets, he struck gold when a pocket jingled as he fished out his oldest pair of jeans.

He had often considered moving closer to the Institute, but even though he had grown up in Copenhagen, he had always felt at home in the cozy town on the Rhine. He usually worked from Monday to Friday, unless special shifts came up, which were always announced in plenty of time. And so it had been a surprise that he and his colleague, Paul Colbach, suddenly had to take over their co-workers' shifts for the weekend – and without any apparent reason. Dr. James Piglet, his boss's aide, responsible for managing the research assistants' schedules, had mentioned something about appraisal interviews that their superior, Professor Hagen, wanted to conduct with their other colleagues that afternoon.

As Tom started his silver BMW Z3 Roadster, the engine suddenly stalled, leaving him with little choice but to trouble his neighbor, Leo, who knew as much about automobile electronics as Tom did about quantum physics.

"Can you lend me your Volvo?" Tom asked without preamble when Leo finally appeared, bleary-eyed, and in his underwear at his apartment door.

"Hey, Smørrebrød, don't tell me your ride's taken a little time off," Leo yawned, running a hand through his disheveled hair. "It's Saturday and it's ridiculously early. You know that, right?"

"There's something wrong with the engine," Tom answered. "There might be a cable loose. I'll fix it later. But I've got to get to work, and I'm already late. If you manage to fix it, you can take it for a spin. I'll be back late."

"Fair enough," Leo replied hoarsely, disappearing behind the creaky front door. He re-emerged shortly after and handed Tom the keys to his old Volvo station wagon.

"Thanks," Tom said. "Is there enough gas?"

"It should get you to the Eifel," Leo mumbled.

Tom stepped on the gas in frustration and although he braked quickly, the speedometer still showed 100 mph, when the well-camouflaged speed camera greeted him with a flurry of flashes. *Leo will be overjoyed*, Tom thought in resignation.

Punctually at 10:59 a.m., Tom reached the forested area that surrounded the military base, marking American territory for five miles around. With a nine-foot-high concrete wall, anti-tank barriers, and barbed-wire fences, the facility was completely isolated from the outside world. Armed soldiers with guard dogs patrolled the compound. Entrance to the parking lots could only be gained through an automatic steel roller door in front of a heavily guarded driveway.

After handing the guard his nametag and having his fingerprints scanned, Tom was granted access. But with his neighbor's unregistered rust-bucket of a car, the guard refused to let him park in his regular lot in the underground parking garage, but told him to leave the car next to the guardhouse instead.

Tom took a short walk to another security checkpoint and entered an unimpressive building with a flat roof and a twenty-five-meter-high windowless concrete hall. An intricate dome roof, comprised of innumerable honeycombed glass pieces, crowned the otherwise clunky architecture. The intricate glass dome not only allowed sunlight in, but also prevented any light from escaping.

Tom's workstation resembled an announcer's booth in a football stadium. Eleven yards above the hall's interior, he and his colleagues sat enthroned in a shatterproof glass balcony, where they had an unrestricted view of the field underneath them. The laboratory hall's interior walls were lined with a special ceramic that resembled an eggshell, both in color and texture. The flooring, made of a high-grade material resistant to both heat and cold, was divided into squares, in a shade of magenta that didn't exist in nature. Objects could be located on its surface with electronic precision.

The control room, which often made Tom feel like a goldfish in a bowl, was furnished with an array of screens that made the room resemble an air traffic control room in an international airport. Only the white laboratory coats worn by staff provided any indication that scientific work was carried out here.

Sophisticated internal sound insulation absorbed all disruptive noise. Forbidden in the lab, the small MP3 player that Tom wore on a lanyard under his plaid shirt fed him a steady blast of heavy metal music.

Today, the only deviation from his work routine was his colleague, Paul Colbach, a feisty Luxembourgian with a unique sense of humor. The linguistically gifted thirty-year-old was a brilliant computer scientist who had mastered the revolutionary, top-secret computers quickly. But like all his colleagues working on this project, his talent could only flourish in secret.

"Hello, Tom." Paul grinned at his colleague as the door hissed open. "You look pretty damn exhausted for someone who hasn't been getting any."

"Unlike you, I suppose," Tom retorted with a scowl, "or are you disappointed that you're spending the weekend with me instead of Miss Baxter?"

"Oh, believe me, I'm not disappointed at all. Piglet's switched up my shifts and Karen's so that we can bury ourselves under the blankets together for the next six weekends. Isn't that awesome?"

"Yes, that's magnificent," Tom answered absently as he started up one of the computer terminals.

"Though I wonder why," Tom added casually, his gaze fixed on the undulations of the graph on his screen, "the change was made so suddenly. Hagen has monopolized his beloved Miss Baxter on weekends for the past month without exception. You don't find it suspicious that he's giving her so many weekends off now, right when your first weekend together in a long time has been cancelled?"

"I don't know how the hell you managed to find a connection in all of that." Paul frowned, brooding intently. "Well," he mused, "I had it all planned – candlelight dinner in the penthouse, champagne, and for dessert, black silk panties and little Paul on a silver platter. But then she

174

had to write something up for Hagen, and Piglet sold me on the slave market."

"I rest my case," Tom replied, looking up sharply. The glow of the computer screen bathed his already pale face in a soft green.

"What are you saying?" Paul looked at him in confusion.

"When did she find out about her assignment?"

"Yesterday."

"Does Hagen know about your relationship?"

"I think so."

"Well, then. Don't you find it strange that they're cancelling her free weekend at the same time as yours? And after that, rewarding you for your stoicism, so to speak, with six free weekends together?"

"You're thinking too much! Hagen's just a nice guy."

"That's exactly what makes me wonder."

"Don't dwell on things so much, Tom. Maybe it's time you found yourself a new girlfriend. If you keep going like this, you'll end up a freak. I know a hottie in the finance department. One of Piglet's accountants. She's a little mousy, just like her boss, but she really grills Karen about me whenever Karen and I together. Seems like the needy type, that girl. Those are the most grateful, believe me."

Tom gave Paul a warning look. "Maybe you should concentrate on your work, pal, or I'll be getting in touch with you about my needs," he said.

Unlike Paul, who handled the computer system's hardware and software, Tom was in charge of operating the nuclear fusion reactor and regulating the necessary energy supply in the integrated magnetic field. Along with Paul, he was responsible for mathematically evaluating the objects that regularly materialized during the tests they ran on the field. All further biological and geological investigations were subsequently taken over by scientists from other departments. Even if the current results weren't exactly spectacular, interfering with the space-time continuum at all was anything but safe.

It was now well into the afternoon. Tom's stomach rumbled. Paul stretched his limbs.

"Do you want some coffee?" Tom asked his colleague.

Paul shook his head as he worked on the calculations for the day's trial. "You mean that vile concoction from the vending machine? No, thank you."

Ignoring the rules against bringing food and beverages into the surveillance cockpit, Tom returned a little later with a steaming cup and set it down quickly on a stack of DVD cases as he burned his fingers.

Tom swore softly, but Paul was too busy to pay him any attention. The specifications for the experiment were 10-16-1307, 18:31 CET. Although the time structures they were researching did not follow a human-made calendar, it had proven useful to refer to the respective position of the stars in different time periods in order to fix the time intervals on a horizontal plane. With the help of a program that accounted for both the Julian and Gregorian calendars and transferred the results onto the room's magnetic framework, Paul could calculate to the nanosecond when and where he was cutting out a sequence. Nevertheless, it was a mystery to him why Hagen had insisted on such a precise specification. After all, the only object that should materialize was a small piece of earth, which wouldn't differ much from anything they had transferred so far. Under the circumstances, it hardly mattered whether the transferred material was torn from its regular existence a year earlier or later.

Tom sipped his coffee cautiously, and finally set it down again. The brew was so hot that he could no longer feel his tongue.

"All right, let's go," he said, giving Paul the signal to initiate the transfer process.

An ear-shattering hammering resounded in the insulated hall. In Tom and Paul's refuge, however, and outside the research area, the hall's soundproofing blocked off all sound. Orange warning lights flashed in all the hallways, indicating that a field experiment was about to take place, and that until the all-clear signal was given, all technicians should vacate the research area and assume their assigned positions.

Tom and Paul put on the headsets that they used to communicate with each other and their colleagues in the neighboring reactor center over an intercom system.

After counting down, Tom announced the commencement of the intended transmission.

"Calculation of wave function configured," he said in a monotone.

"Reactor at fifty percent," came the mechanical response from the reactor center.

"Reactor at fifty percent," Tom confirmed. "Paul, what's the magnetic field strength?"

176

"Eighty-five percent."

"That's too early!" Tom yelled frantically. He sprang up and hurried to his colleague's screen to see the numbers for himself.

In the hall, an eerie display was taking place.

Like the swirling northern lights, undulating green and blue light refractions floated through the room. With every second, their frequency increased. Soon, the sky outside the glass ceiling appeared to be darkening, and the iridescent strips of light coalesced into a net that spanned the room from wall to wall, seemingly out of control.

"Something's wrong!" Tom gasped. "Shut down the reactor!" he yelled into his microphone. Beads of sweat pooled on his forehead.

Paul pounded on his keyboard frantically, looking horrified.

"We can't!" someone yelled back, so loudly that Tom thought that his eardrum had burst.

"Son of a bitch!" he swore. "Paul, what's going on?"

"I don't know!" Paul squawked. "The program seems to be going crazy. God knows who messed with it. It sure as hell wasn't me!"

Tom bolted back to his computer. Stealing a quick glance at the hall, he saw that the net structure had already become far too dense to shut down. Desperately, he tried to manipulate the different settings on the computer. But suddenly his efforts were cut off when he knocked over the coffee cup from his tower of DVDs, spilling the hot coffee all over the keyboard.

This can't be happening, he thought. Like mushrooms in a time-lapse video, rough skeletons of trees were sketched in green-blue light, growing so quickly that they seemed to shoot towards the artificial night sky, 30 meters tall, like columns in a gigantic cathedral, smashing through the dome as they materialized. On the outer edge of the hall, oak trunks appeared, so thick that five men could wrap their arms around them. With unbelievable precision, individual blades of grass were being reconstructed. To Tom's amazement, two small figures appeared to be running for their lives across the clearing. One of them was swinging an oblong object around wildly, pulling a smaller figure behind him. The figures paused suddenly. They looked up at the sky and froze for a second. Then Tom saw the larger of the two throw himself onto the smaller one.

"Tom! Get down!"

Paul's shrill scream yanked Tom out of his trance – like state a split second before it was too late. He had just enough time to duck under the console, which was reinforced with lead plates. With outrageous force, a mighty wave of energy shattered the front pane of the control room. Shards as thick as armor plates flew across the room, piercing the opposite wall like a hot knife through butter. An ear-shattering crash rang out in all directions. The entire building creaked and groaned as a roll of thunder tore through the sky like a raging hurricane. Flashes of light danced everywhere, and, for a moment, the ground seemed to quake.

"Are you okay, Tom? We have to get out of here!" Paul cried as he crept out from under the console, looking around for his colleague. Tom was stuck between a shelf and a chair under several fallen monitors. Gripping his arm tightly, Paul pulled him out.

Tom looked around, panting for breath. There was not much left of the hall. Fallen trees burned fiercely. The air smelled of charred plastic, and the entire compound looked as if it had been bombed. The roof had collapsed, its honeycomb glass shards glittering amidst the rubble.

A large hole in the outer wall revealed the visitors' parking lot a good hundred meters away. The inflow of oxygen made the flames flare up, and thick smoke smothered the hall. Tom wasn't sure if anyone had been killed or injured.

"Let's go!" Paul yelled.

Like a sleepwalker, Tom numbly followed his colleague toward the exit.

The main generator had failed, so the sprinklers and emergency lights in the smoke-filled passageways had been triggered. The green and white lights on the floor showed Tom and Paul the way to the emergency exit through the dark smoke. Alarms howled. Here and there, Tom could hear isolated cries that blended into the crackling of the fire.

To Paul's bewilderment, Tom decided not to follow the floor lights, running instead toward the staircase that led down into the hall.

"Are you crazy?" Paul called. "Where are you going?"

"There's still someone down there!" Tom shouted.

"What do you mean there's still someone there?" Paul grabbed Tom's arm firmly and stared at him in confusion.

"We didn't just transfer trees, there were people, too!"

"Tom, what the hell are you talking about?"

"Just come with me! We have to find them before someone else does!"

Without waiting for an answer, Tom sprinted down the five stories, leaving Paul little choice but to follow him. They could hardly see anything, and, again and again, the smoke billowing through every floor made them break out in convulsive coughing. For a moment, Tom wondered how they would get through the double doors in the basement leading to the hall. But the problem solved itself when they arrived at the basement and saw the giant hole in the wall. Along with a mighty spruce, a boulder had breached the inner wall of the field and found its way through to the men's bathroom.

Tom took off his lab coat and ran to the sink, the emergency lights illuminating his path. He and Paul held their coats under the faucet, and then pressed the damp cotton to their mouths and noses to protect themselves against the smoke.

Feverishly, they scoured the field, trying their best to avoid falling glass splinters and tree trunks.

"Here!" Tom yelled, noticing something bright gleaming in the rubble. Under a fallen branch, a tall man was lying on his stomach.

Tom hurriedly pushed aside the debris. Together, he and Paul turned the unconscious man onto his back. To their surprise, they found a second figure in the rubble – a boy about twelve years old. Half of him was lying hidden under the man, who wore a dirty white cloak. Gasping for breath, the boy stared at them with fear-stricken eyes.

"What's up with the man? Is he dead?" Paul asked anxiously.

Tom touched the side of the man's neck. His skin was warm, and Tom could feel his heartbeat pulsing rhythmically.

"No," he said quickly. "He's still alive. We have to move both of them!"

Before Paul and Tom dragged the unconscious man to the outer wall, Paul faced the boy. "Let's go! Come on!" he yelled to him. The child stared at him blankly, but finally followed them.

Together, they headed toward the large hole in the outer wall of the structure. With some effort, they lifted the unconscious man over the crumbling remains of the wall that stood about a yard high. Once outside, they cautiously laid him on the wet asphalt.

Gasping for breath, Tom tried to figure out what was happening outside the ruins of the hall. Darkness was descending, but everything was in chaos. The power lines next to the research grounds crackled, and the awful smell of burning rubber assaulted his sensitive nose. Squinting, he noticed that the heavy cables of the overhead power line had been burned, and sections hung limply to the ground. The reactor was still standing, but in the dim glow of the emergency lights, Tom could see fissures in its hull. From the outside, the hall's glass roof resembled an egg that had been cracked open. The mighty trees had shattered not only the inner wall, but large parts of the outer wall as well. Here and there, people emerged from the rubble in their soiled white overalls. As the sirens began to wail, Tom was reminded of a film he had seen about the Third World War. With their warning lights flashing, the first emergency vehicles were already approaching.

He looked around. In the chaos and misery, no one seemed to notice them.

"What now?" Paul asked breathlessly.

"We have to hide them, Paul. If anyone finds out that we've transferred actual *people from the past*, our jobs won't be the only thing on the line."

"With this disaster, do you really think it still matters that we've transferred people?" Paul asked wearily, scanning the smoky, burning ruins of the research facility.

"Of course it does!" Tom retorted agitatedly. "You know as well as I do that we needed permission from the President of the United States to transfer anyone. Did we have that? Not that I know of!"

"But it wasn't our fault," Paul protested.

"Do you think anyone cares?" Tom snorted. "We're dead. No one knows how something like this could've happened. Just think, the press will be here! Besides, what if Hagen's team catches these two? They they might kill them and freeze them in nitrogen."

"And where do you plan on taking them?" Paul asked. "We can't hide them in my basement."

"I have an idea," Tom said. "I don't know if it'll work, but it's worth a shot. My ex-fiancé lives in a remote farmhouse nearby. Maybe we could house them there for a few days until we can figure out what to do."

"Tom!" Paul shook his head, staring at the man on the floor. "He's huge! And take a look at his sword for God's sake," Paul shuddered. "Who knows what he'll do when he wakes up and finds out where he's landed? What if your ex isn't home, or doesn't want to take him in? Are you just going to dump him on the doorstep with a note tied around his toe saying 'Surprise!'?"

"We don't have time to speculate," Tom said decisively. "Stay here. I'll grab the car."

"Your convertible? How are we going to transport them in your roadster?" Paul, who drove a two-seater as well, eyed his colleague suspiciously.

"I borrowed my neighbor's station wagon this morning because my car wouldn't start." Suddenly, Tom felt a hot flash run through his body. His jacket, where he usually kept his keys, was still hanging in his locker – but then relief flooded over him as he felt the car keys in his right jeans pocket.

A short while later, Tom pulled up in the old Volvo and they began the arduous task of moving two unwitting time travelers into his neighbor's old, beat-up car.

Tom began with the shell-shocked boy. He was light, and didn't struggle as Tom lifted him away from his companion's side. Without a word, Tom set him down in the cargo area at the back of the car, and then returned to help Paul with the injured man.

"What kind of strange outfit is this?" Tom asked, when, with their combined strength, they had heaved the unconscious man into the back of car. He handed Paul a flashlight he had found in the glove compartment. Uncertainly, his Luxembourgian colleague pointed it at the strange-looking man.

"I've no idea," Paul whispered. But all at once the light hit the appliquéd red cross on the man's cloak. "No way," he said slowly, "I don't believe it. He's a Templar knight."

"A Templar knight?" Tom raised an eyebrow.

"Haven't you ever seen *Tombs of the Blind Dead* by Amando de Ossorio?"

"No, I hardly go to the movies."

"Well, it's been a while since they've shown that film," Paul muttered, inspecting the man's striking features. It was then that he saw the blood trickling through the man's short, dark-blonde hair, past his ear to his chin, where it was caught in a neat, trimmed light blonde beard.

"He needs a doctor," Paul said. "Should I come along and help you?"

"No," Tom decided. "I think it's better that you stay here and straighten things out, or the others will think that we've died in the fire."

"What should I say if they ask about you?"

"Just tell them that I'm injured and that I've driven to a hospital because I didn't want to wait for an ambulance. I'll call you when I have news."

Tom took a deep breath, and gave his strange passengers a final look before slamming the rear door shut. "Cross your fingers for me!"

His gaze fell on the guard at the gate. Ambulances were streaming in with sirens whirring, and the roller door was wide open. No one would think to stop them.

CHAPTER 15

An Unexpected Visit

Saturday, November 13, 2004

With a deep sigh, Hannah set down the half-empty glass of Merlot on the small cedar table, pushing aside the tarot cards splayed out in front of her. The Star – meditation and the quest for truth. Ace of Wands – birth and death, dynamic new beginnings in life. Events, staggering and revolutionary, that have yet to occur. Passion – the rise and fall of nations. The root of all actions. Seven of Swords–near complete happiness. Love and marriage. Ideal alliances. Intense, sympathetic friendship. All needs, emotional, physical, and intellectual, shall be satisfied.

"What bullshit," she muttered softly, scratching Heisenberg, her black tomcat, on the neck. In an unusual display of affection, he had sprung into her lap and curled up against her when a slight tremor made the windows shudder. Suddenly the lights went out. With a candle in hand, she went to the fuse box, only to find the electrics of the old timber cottage in perfect working order.

Slightly frustrated, she returned to her plush red sofa and her cat and put the candleholder down to the table. Even the supposedly magic cards could not tell her if someone in her future would free her from her being single and sitting alone at home in the dark.

She watched in disappointment as fat raindrops beat down against the window. Mechanically, her gaze followed the long rivulets of water as they created ceaseless crisscrossing tracks and patterns on the glass panes.

Somewhere in the distance, she could hear sirens. She glanced casually at her mobile phone lying next to the candle stand. Should she call the police just to find out why several ambulances had been deployed?

No, Hannah decided. If it were something important, she would be blocking the line from the officers on duty.

Ruffling Heisenberg's fur, she sat on the couch for what seemed like half an eternity before another sound caught her attention. A car was pulling into the farmyard.

Hannah's friend, Senta, had said that she would pop by at 9:00 p.m. for a card game, but she seldom arrived before the arranged time, and according to the clock on the wall, it was only 7:30 p.m.

Hannah crept across the small hallway to the kitchen window. In the headlights' glare, all she could see was the steadily falling rain. The driver, now storming toward her door, was calling her name. The voice sounded anxious.

"Hannah, are you there? Open up, please! Can you hear me? It's me, Tom."

The surprise visitor hammered on her door, making it shake. It was indeed Tom Stevendahl. Although he spoke perfect German, he had retained a slight Danish accent, for which his friends had nicknamed him Smørrebrød. She hadn't heard from him in months.

"Hannah, if I ever meant anything to you, open the door now!"

Hannah peered at him from behind the door. Tom's hair was drenched, and his face was smeared with soot. He leaned on the doorframe, breathing heavily. When Hannah opened the door a little wider to let him in, she saw that his hands were smeared with blood.

"Tom! What happened? Were you in an accident?" she yelled.

"Please don't ask any questions right now!" he blurted out. "Just say that you'll help me?" He gripped her shoulder with his blood-smeared hand and shook her slightly.

"Yes, of course," she answered worriedly, "if you tell me what you need help with."

"Come to the car. I'll show you."

Hastily, she slipped on her rain boots and stumbled into the heavy rain behind the man who once promised to marry her. The car engine was turned off, but the lights were on, and she saw that the car was a beat-up station wagon with old dents and scratches. Feeling a little surprised, she looked at Tom, who in the past had driven only expensive sports cars.

"Did you rob a bank?" Gradually Hannah's anxiety was subsiding, and she tried to sound breezy. But Tom remained solemn, leading her in grim silence to the rear of the dilapidated car before hesitantly opening its rear door.

Hannah dared not believe her eyes. In the back of the car, a man was lying motionless, bent double and swathed in a cloak or a blanket. In the dim light, his face seemed unnaturally pale and blood was streaming down from his temple to his cheeks. Hannah whipped around and stared at Tom in horror.

"What have you done?" she shouted. Had Tom run over the man, then stowed his victim in his trunk and fled the scene? Or maybe Tom had killed him, and now wanted to bury the corpse behind her house, plant a few carrots over it, and be done with it. No one would ever know the nightmarish crime hidden behind the idyllic façade. Hannah gasped for breath as Tom searched for an explanation.

"I don't know how to explain it to you, but it's definitely not what you think!"

"How do you know what I'm thinking?" she yelled, her voice quivering.

"I'm not responsible for this man's condition," he said enigmatically. "You have to believe me."

"Believe you? I've seen enough!"

"Hannah, damn it, I can explain if you just let me," he replied agitatedly. "But not now," he added quickly as her expression darkened further. "We're dealing with a person's life here. You have to help me carry him into the house. Look, he's badly injured."

Filled with confusion, her gaze darted between Tom and the unconscious man. The rain had grown stronger, and it beat down mercilessly on them.

"What?" she cried loudly, indignant. "You're crazy. You're not bringing him into *my house*. Call an ambulance! Better yet, call the police, too!"

She turned on her heels and started to run into the house, but in a flash, Tom seized her arm, his vice-like grip rooting her to the spot.

"We're calling neither the police nor the hospital," he gasped. "Besides, I'm fairly sure this guy doesn't have an insurance card."

Hannah thought she had misheard him. What did an insurance card have to do with the fact that Tom wanted to drag a half-dead man into her house? Suddenly, she noticed a slight movement in the far corner, behind the man. She flinched back as if she had been shocked. Narrowing her eyes, she tried to make out what was moving in the darkness. At first, she thought that it was a large dog waiting by its owner, but it was no animal. A slender young boy was cowering in the dark corner, stunned with fear. An uneasy shudder ran over Hannah.

Tom touched her shoulder gently. "Hannah ..." His voice was nearly a whisper. "Believe me, I've done nothing wrong. I picked both of them up, so to speak, and now I need someone who can help me help them."

"And why should *I* of all people be this 'someone'?" she retorted, unable to wrench her gaze from the two figures in the car. "I haven't heard from you in months. Why don't you drive to your Institute? It's right around the corner. Your colleagues would certainly help you!"

"That's where I've just come from." Tom's voice faltered. "The entire research facility has been destroyed. And, believe me, it would be unwise to take both of them back there."

Hannah closed her eyes and took a deep breath. When she turned to Tom again, her voice was strained. "Why on earth can't you just call an ambulance? That'll solve everything."

"It's not as simple as you think!" Tom gestured toward the unconscious man. "While we talk instead of actually *doing* something, he's probably bleeding to death."

Finally, nodding in resignation, Hannah relented. Despite the utter insanity of Tom's plea, she couldn't bear to turn away the poor boy, who looked utterly stunned.

"Well," she said, crossing her arms, "how are we going to carry them in? I don't think dumping them in the back of a car did them any good ..."

Ignoring Hannah's objections, Tom instructed her to hold onto the man's feet, while he gripped the man under his arms and tugged at his clothes to turn him in the right direction.

The man exuded a noxious odor of blood, sweat, and wet dog, and Hannah was reluctant to approach him. The boy was still hunkered down in the furthest corner of the car, watching them closely without moving an inch.

Hannah stretched out her hand to the child. Like her shy cat, however, the boy simply retreated further into the interior of the car, resolutely avoiding her gaze. Hannah had the impression that he was holding his breath.

Tom elbowed Hannah. "Hold on tight!" he hissed.

Before he began carrying the man out of the car, Tom glanced at him in the hope that he had regained consciousness, but his arms were limp and his features showed no signs of movement.

He was heavier than Hannah had expected and, as she tried to lift his legs, his feet slipped from her hands.

"Man, watch out, will you?" Tom panted. "You have to do it right, or we'll never get through the door!"

With considerable effort, they carried the man through a dark hallway into Hannah's bedroom, lit only by the weak glow of the car's headlights streaming into the house. Once inside, they dumped him onto Hannah's wrought-iron French bed, which swayed slightly under his weight.

"The electricity is gone," she said.

"I know". Tom crouched down to catch his breath and wiped the rain out of his eyes with his sleeve. Meanwhile, Hannah ran into the living room to fetch a few candles.

After she had lit the candles and placed them around the room, she turned to the injured man. He appeared to be in his early thirties, just as she was, but he could easily have been older.

"Are they father and son?" she asked Tom curiously.

"Beats me," he shrugged. He clambered to his feet and helped her turn the man onto his side. Hannah stole a furtive look at her ex-fiancé. His style hadn't changed in the two years since their separation. He was in his uniform of jeans, checkered shirt, and cowboy boots, although they had never suited him well. In the long years that they had been together, Hannah had never managed to pass on to him her love of horses.

"Do you have anything to help with the bleeding?" he asked. But before she could answer, he had already disappeared outside. "I'll look in the car," he called to her.

Examining him, Hannah was shocked to discover that the man not only had a head injury, but also a wound on his left arm that was bleeding profusely.

"We don't need bandages," she muttered under her breath. "What we need is an ambulance."

Hannah grabbed a terrycloth towel from a cabinet drawer and laid it clumsily on the man's arm. He didn't seem to feel anything. It was then that she noticed his clothes. He was wearing a long sleeveless wrap that reached down to his thighs, over chain mail with wrist-length sleeves. A red cross was emblazoned on his breast. His large hands were hidden under dark leather gloves that were covered with small metal plates. The whole man was shrouded in a dirty cloak, fastened at his throat with a metal clasp. Hannah assumed the cloak had once been white. Another red cross the size of her palm was emblazoned on the left shoulder of his cloak. Like the cross on his breast, it had a distinctive shape, with each bar flaring out at the end. Hannah thought the symbol looked familiar. Vaguely, she recalled that she had seen the same cross in pictures of knights in the Crusades. A wide leather belt with three large knives in elaborate, riveted leather sheaths, encircled the man's waist. The longest knife was over fifteen inches long. The man's dark, tight-fitting leather pants were slightly scuffed and stained. His large leather boots ended just below his knees in a wide cuff. Curiously, Hannah surveyed the metallic bits nailed to his boot soles, but couldn't recall ever seeing anything like them.

Despite being clad in this strange costume, the man didn't seem to be crazy. His curved brows and long straight nose lent his face a powerful profile. A closely cropped blonde beard covered his angular jaw, providing an interesting contrast to his equally short hair, which was a bit darker. As she examined it, Hannah saw the two-inch long wound near the crown of his head, the blood still trickling down his neck in a thin rivulet.

His left arm hung limply over the edge of the bed. As Hannah moved to lift it back onto the mattress, she noticed that even his glove was saturated with blood. Carefully, she removed it from his hand and placed it on the parquet floor. She gripped the man's wrist again and placed the blood-soaked arm against his body.

In a moment, her snow-white blanket was stained red with blood.

His hand was warm, and his breast rose and fell gently with his breath. *At least he's still alive*, Hannah thought.

Hannah was glad when Tom reappeared. He had his arm around the boy, who was trying to fight his way out of Tom's grasp with violent kicks. Gurgling noises escaped his throat as he snapped at Tom like a rabid dog.

Ignoring his protests, Tom threw the rebellious child onto the other side of the bed.

When the boy saw his companion lying on the bed, he fell into a stunned silence. Then he rushed to the man's side and tried to choke back sobs. Hannah looked at Tom in desperation, hoping that he would finally tell her what was going on.

Tom, however, merely frowned and asked, "You have a friend who's a doctor, right?"

"Oh God, Senta!" she yelped. "I almost forgot! How late is it?"

Tom glanced at his watch, looking slightly annoyed. "A quarter past eight."

188

"She was supposed to come over soon," Hannah groaned. Her eyes darted between the boy, the unconscious man, and Tom.

"Can she help us?" Tom was obviously less interested in what Senta would think than whether she could help them.

"As far as I know, she always has her emergency kit with her. But I don't know if I want that!"

"Why not?" Tom asked. "Can we trust her?"

"Tom, what are you talking about? Do you want to drag her into this mess as well?"

"What mess? Do you still think I'm responsible for this?"

"What else should I think?" Hannah cried. "Tell me!"

"Later, I promise. Trust me at least this once."

"Our relationship certainly didn't lack trust, at least not on my part," snapped Hannah.

Ignoring his ex-lover's retort, Tom gestured to the chain mail. "Do you have any spare clothes? He can't possibly keep that on."

"Yes, from my father," she said. "I kept a few things of his after he died."

Of course, the man's outfit seemed odd to her, but she never understood what drove people to wear the strange costumes they did. Suddenly she remembered the cross on the strange man's clothes. *Of course!* St. Martin's Day was taking place this week. At the annual lantern festival, a man dressed as St. Martin would give candy to children. The man must have been on his way to the festival and been hit by a car. Tom must have found them near the air base.

Hannah felt a certain relief at this thought. But why had he brought them to her and not the hospital? There were probably no other witnesses. Perhaps Tom thought that they would blame him for the accident?

She eyed Tom doubtfully. The boy, having stopped crying, was now curled up on the bed in a ball. Noticing her inquiring expression, Tom nodded toward the hallway, signaling that it was probably time he gave her an explanation.

As he pulled her into the dark hallway, Hannah was momentarily surprised. This close to Tom, she could smell the familiar scent of his aftershave. He was still the same, even in his most trivial habits.

"Hannah," he began softly, looking her in the eye, "I hope you understand what I'm about to tell you. You don't know much about my job ... and I bear most of the blame for that. But how would I have explained it all to you? And even if …" He stopped abruptly and turned away. "Oh, damn it, you'll think I'm crazy if I tell you the truth!"

"The one good thing about you is that you can't lie," Hannah said gently, "even if I hated your bluntness sometimes."

Taking a deep breath, Tom began again. "You know that I work in nuclear research."

She nodded. He had earned his doctorate in quantum physics when they were still together.

"We've been running secret experiments that deal with space-time synchronization for quite some time now. Our research is based on the theory that time doesn't run linearly, as we've previously believed, but instead in parallel … and sometimes even in reverse."

Hannah shot him a withering glare. "Is this becoming a lecture on black holes? Or about poor cats in sealed boxes that are both dead and alive?"

Tom continued. "You also know that I work at an American institute nearby. On the outside, it's a regular research laboratory that deals with nuclear disarmament. But inside, there's a department in a high-security wing. Apart from the American government and a small group of scientists who have undergone extensive background checks, no one knows about this special division. Not even the German government."

Hannah fell silent, listening with rapt attention.

"There was an accident this afternoon", he went on with his explanation. "That's probably what caused the power <u>outage</u>. The result of this accident is lying over there in your bed. The two of them probably came from the start of the fourteenth century – our last experiments were focused on that time period. My colleague Paul and I found them after the explosion on the research field. No one else has access to that area – which means they couldn't have wandered in from outside. Right before the accident, I saw something on the computer screen, but I didn't think that it was people." He lowered his head and continued in a whisper so low Hannah had to strain her ears to catch his words. "Hannah, the guy on your bed and his little friend have traveled through time – seven hundred years, at least! They aren't supposed to be here, but somehow they appeared. They might have caused the explosion."

Hannah didn't know whether to laugh or cry. Her look of incredulity seemed to alarm Tom, who grabbed her shoulders and met her gaze squarely. In the darkness, his brown eyes looked like two gleaming black buttons.

"Hannah, you have to believe me. I'm not joking. Paul and I have decided to hide them. If our boss, Professor Hagen, found them, he would condemn them to live their lives as lab rats. Somehow, we have to send them back to where they came from. But until that's possible, they can't afford to be captured by my boss or the American military. Apart from me, you, and Paul, no one knows they exist."

Tom swallowed hard. How could he convince Hannah of something this crazy?

"Imagine if news of their existence got out. The press would be the least of our problems. No one would believe such a ridiculous story this quickly, but the Secret Service, the military, the Vatican ... and who knows who else ... will be scrambling to get their claws on them." Tom stared at Hannah with pleading eyes, an expression that she had given in to all too often.

"And am I supposed to believe you, just like that?" She eyed him doubtfully.

"For now," Tom whispered. He raised his hand, as if to brush away a stray lock of her dark red hair from her face, but then thought better of it and lowered it again. "You're the only one I thought of – because I know I can trust you."

"And by pure chance, I live just around the corner," she said sarcastically.

"Hannah," he implored again. "I'm so sorry for everything ... for us ..."

Hannah cut him off. "Tom, it's not about us. Just promise me you're not making me do anything illegal."

"I promise," he replied earnestly, "unless you consider willingness to help a crime."

"All right," she agreed impatiently before returning to her bedroom. "Whatever the truth is, there are two people in this house who need our help, and I would be the last person to deny them that."

She pulled out an old pair of cotton pajamas that had once belonged to her father from the bottommost drawer of her dresser. Meanwhile, the boy was crouching on the floor next to her closet, half hidden by a heavy velvet curtain, silently observing what was happening to his companion.

She held out the pajamas to Tom. "You can put these on him."

"Well, you'll have to help me," said Tom.

Hannah sighed. And so, as absurd as it seemed, she was to be granted the rare honor of undressing a knight from the Middle Ages on her bed and dressing him in her father's pajamas.

Tom touched the leather scabbard that covered a long dagger, letting a soft whistle escape through his teeth. With some effort, he had pulled the belt out from under the heavy body and laid it on the floor. Warily, he loosened the leather cuff and held the fearsome weapon in his hand. Hannah drew back as Tom held out the blade to her.

"Nice bread knife," he joked, running his finger along the dark metal edge. "Ouch!" he moaned and drew back at once, sticking his finger into his mouth and sucking on it.

"Serves you right", Hannah said, rolling her eyes. "Put that thing away. We don't have time to fool around."

Tom wiped his bleeding finger on his shirt, tossed the blade and belt under Hannah's bed, and then tended to the man's cloak, laboriously loosening the brass fastenings. As he began to pull the thick fabric to the side, something moved in the corner.

The boy had stood up. His face was red with anger. He looked as if he wanted to storm toward them, but then he cried, "Nay, ye noughten do this, ye moste nede me leve the courby!"

He choked on his words in anger, then finally continued, "Hit besemeth not to unclothen myne lorde!"

Hannah was shocked at her small visitor's outburst. She had barely understood him, but he was – without a doubt – speaking Middle High German. Alongside majoring in German Philology, she had taken three semesters worth of classes in medieval history, and a few more classes in Middle High German. It seemed that Tom was telling the truth, for Middle High German was spoken in Germany until at least the end of the fourteenth century.

Looking just as stunned as Hannah, Tom whirled around. "What did you say?"

The boy immediately fell silent again.

"Come on, come over here!" Tom made his way slowly towards him, but the small boy had used his last shred of courage, and retreated fearfully into his corner behind the closet.

Giving up on coaxing the boy, Tom again turned his attention to the man on the bed. With Hannah's help, he finally managed to remove the long, hooded cloak. To allow Tom to get the heavy chain mail over the man's head without scraping his face, Hannah had to lift the stranger's head with both hands. She felt the warmth of his body and the thick, short hair on the back of his head on her fingers.

It took their combined strength and a good minute for them to peel the tight sweater under the chain mail off the stranger.

Tom shoved the bloody, tattered linen undershirt up over the man's chest. He wore a small leather pouch on a thin cord around his neck. Tom removed it and passed the bag to Hannah, who was staring speechlessly at the man's bare torso.

A brightly polished silver cross hung from a braided leather cord around his neck. Upon closer inspection, she realized it was the same shape as the cross on his cloak. Even as he removed the rest of the man's clothing, Tom didn't dare remove this obvious symbol of his faith.

"This probably isn't the first accident that this guy has been in," Tom guessed, inspecting a jagged scar on the man's right shoulder, six inches long and nearly an inch wide. Another scar, twice as long as the first, stretched from the right side of his groin to his ribs, and Hannah and Tom could see that it had been skillfully sewn up.

"That could be from the falling shards of glass," Tom mused as he eyed the fresh wound on the man's well-defined left bicep. "I'm amazed neither of them were burned in the explosion." Tom wound a bandage tightly around the man's arm and began to undo his leather trousers. The fly was tightly secured around his waist by a soft leather band.

"Maybe you should leave his pants on?" Uncertainty flooded Hannah's face.

Tom nodded. "All right, but I think we should take his boots off."

His gaze fell on the leather pouch that Hannah was still holding against her chest. He glanced up at her again. "Look inside," he suggested with a wry smile, "Maybe he has a passport and driver's license in there."

Hannah gingerly loosened a leather cord and set the pouch on her dresser so the contents would not spill out. It smelled strongly of goat leather. With nimble fingers, she retrieved a small, leather-bound book with a worn gold inscription, then a piece of parchment, rolled up and tied with a red ribbon. Something clinked in the depths of the pouch. Fascinated, she fished out a small leather sack filled with coins, and a large, silver ring wrapped in velvet.

"This is a bag of treasures," she exclaimed excitedly, turning the ring about as it gleamed in the candlelight.

Tom took the ring from her and inspected it. "Look," he cried suddenly, "there's a coat of arms engraved on it."

Hannah pulled Tom's hand nearer to the flame and squinted, examining the ring's surface through narrowed eyes. The crest was divided into two halves. In the upper half, there were three intertwined characters, a large *G* and *B*, connected with a thin *V*. In the bottom half, a pair of squiggly arches that looked like two fishes peeked out of several wavy lines that resembled a stream.

Hannah eyed the boy in the corner where he was still sitting on the ground, motionless. Now and then he shot her a stealthy glance, but, beyond that, he made no protest.

Hannah opened the smaller leather sack and retrieved a silver coin and showed it to Tom. "Do you know what this is?" she whispered in awe.

Tom shook his head.

"It's a tornesel from Trier." Hannah held the glistening silver piece closer to the candlelight. "This one here only existed for an extremely short time in the beginning of the fourteenth century."

She laid the coin aside and picked up another, examining it just as closely as the first.

"And this," she continued, "is a French Tournois from Philipp IV's reign."

"Hurry up," Tom urged, glancing at the clock and looking thoroughly unimpressed with her history lecture. "Take a look at the book. Maybe we can figure out who he is before your friend arrives."

Hannah rifled through the small book. She ran her fingers gently over the narrow lines as she read them in the dim candlelight. Ornate crests alternated with neatly written remarks in the margins. Although small, the Latin script was surprisingly legible. Between the last page and the back cover, she found a folded piece of parchment. She unfolded it and smoothed it out on the dresser.

"Can you read it?" Tom asked uncertainly. He felt as if they had just discovered ancient Egyptian hieroglyphics.

"I can try," she replied. Then added apologetically, "It's been a while since my last Latin class."

Two phrases appeared several times throughout the document: *Gerard de Breydenbach* and *Ordo Militie Hierosolimitanis Templi*. A date in

Roman numerals stood next to what was probably the man's name and what Hannah guessed was his birth date.

"From what I can tell, he was born on the Solemnity of the Annunciation of the Lord to Maria in the year of our Lord 1280," she said.

"Go ahead and tell me if you know what day that is." Tom gave her a curious look.

Hannah, however, was too absorbed in her fascinating find. In the dim candlelight, her finger slowly traced the neat, cursive script. Another date, along with a place, was written next to it. "*Datum Nicosie anno incarnationis Redemptoris nostri millesimo tricentesimo primo, festo Joannis baptistae,*" Hannah read aloud.

"And what does that mean?"

"That means ..." Hannah licked her lips in concentration. " ... given in Nicosia in the year of the incarnation of our Savior 1301, at the feast of John the Baptist ... and here's a signature, too ..." Hannah squinted. " ... *Bartholomäus de Chinsi* ..."

Next to it was a seal with two riders on a horse, and a cross, similar to ones on the man's cloak.

"Nicosia," Tom said, looking up at Hannah. "That's in Cyprus. Why would he be in Cyprus?"

"If everything written here is true, these are the papers of a Templar knight who was inducted into the Order of the Temple in Cyprus in the year 1301," Hannah whispered, gazing at the unconscious man in fascination.

"Paul thought he was a Templar knight, too," Tom replied with a nod more to himself.

But before he could continue, they heard a car pull into the farmyard. It had to be Senta. Hastily, Tom shoved the pile of papers and clothes under the bed.

Hannah glanced at the boy before she went to open the front door. He was simply sitting in his corner, staring silently at the ground. "How should we explain all this to Senta?"

"Beats me. I'll think of something."

With a candlestick in hand, Hannah greeted her friend at the door with a hug. "The power's off," Hannah explained apologetically.

As usual, Senta smelled of disinfectant. She had braided her hazelnut brown hair, and it appeared that she had come directly from her medical practice without changing. The doctor was not one to care about fashion.

"Nothing's working at our place, either," Senta answered before quickly kissing her friend on the cheek. "You won't believe what's happening down the road! A building blew up on the American base, near the monastery. Firefighters are arriving from all around. But from what I've heard, the Americans aren't letting anyone on their premises. The entrances have been blocked off, and there are traffic jams everywhere. I had to take a back road to make it here at a halfway decent time."

Hannah felt her knees go weak. No doubt Tom had told the truth. She wanted to blurt out the whole story to Senta, but she knew the woman wouldn't believe her crazy story about a time-travelling knight from the past. With a weak smile, she suppressed the urge to tell her friend everything and ushered Senta in.

"I'm glad you're here," Hannah confessed as she led Senta down the hallway. "An old friend of mine just arrived. He has a serious problem. His colleague injured himself, but he doesn't want to take him to the hospital."

Senta looked surprised. "Where's the patient?" she asked.

"In my bedroom."

"Give me a minute. I'll get my medical kit."

As Senta went to her car, Hannah was glad that she hadn't told her friend about Tom and his unusual career.

Hannah had met her first about a year ago while working at a book convention in Frankfurt. The young doctor had presented an experiential report on aid programs in the Third World. The two women began talking and found out that they didn't live too far away from each other. Since then, they had been meeting at least once a week to play cards.

When Senta entered the bedroom with her medical bag, Tom stood up and introduced himself half-heartedly. The doctor flashed him a cautious smile and shook his hand. Then she turned to the injured man.

"How long has he been unconscious?"

Hannah looked at Tom, but he simply shrugged.

"I think it's been two to three hours," he answered. "I'm not entirely certain."

"How can you not know?" Senta looked annoyed. "Do you at least know what happened?"

It seemed like an eternity to Hannah before Tom began to speak.

"Err … he was helping me renovate my apartment and fell off a ladder," he said feebly.

Hannah couldn't believe her ears. Seeing Tom lie so unabashedly was something new to her. She tried her best to avoid Senta's suspicious stare.

"Got it," Senta said sarcastically. "He has no papers and no insurance, so we can't take him to the hospital, right?"

"No, not exactly." Hannah watched as Tom racked his brain for an explanation. She could only hope that Senta couldn't sense his discomfort.

"He's a student from Latvia who can't afford health insurance."

Hannah looked sternly at Tom before glancing at the boy hiding behind the drapes. To her surprise, he hadn't moved. Hannah feverishly wondered how she could explain his presence to Senta.

The doctor set her bag down and began to give the man a thorough examination.

"Hello? Can you hear me?" she finally asked, gently tapping him on his cheek. He gave no reaction.

Hannah lit another candlestick and set it on the other bedside dresser.

"He doesn't look so good," Senta murmured. Carefully she examined the wound on his head. "What caused the injury?" she asked, eyeing Tom skeptically.

"I don't know," he answered truthfully.

Senta sighed and began to take the man's blood pressure. "110 over 70 – quite normal, actually, if a little on the low side."

Senta glanced up at Hannah and raised a suspicious brow. "I've no choice but to admit him to a hospital. He might have a concussion or even broken his skull, but we can only get a clear diagnosis with a MRI scan. Besides, his head and arm injuries have to be stitched up. We should also make sure he's had a tetanus vaccination."

Hannah sensed that Tom was about to protest and quickly touched his arm before he could say anything.

"I think that's wise, and we'll work something out as far as the costs are concerned. After all, we can't just leave your friend to deal with this on his own, right?" Hannah said with a pointed nod at Tom.

"You're right," he mumbled under his breath.

"Good." Senta fumbled with her bag. "I'll fill out a note of admission for the hospital. We can list one of you as his sponsor. Or does he have any relatives who can pay for him?"

"Not that I know of …" Tom's face was tense.

"What's your friend's name, then?" Senta stared at Tom.

Her simple question was met with mere silence. Hannah saw the uncertainty in Tom's face. He seemed to be debating whether he should use the name that he had found on the papers, or if he should come up with another name.

Hesitantly, he began, "Gera …"

"He is clepid chevaler Gerard of Breydenbach." The child's voice trembled slightly, but it was not to be ignored.

The boy had drawn himself to his full height and was staring at them unblinkingly. It had obviously taken all his courage to speak.

"Eh? Who are you?" Senta looked at the boy in surprise. "I didn't see you at all. What's your name?"

Senta stood up and turned to the boy with a warm, welcoming smile. But obviously he had no intention of returning her kindness.

He remained rooted to the spot and answered her question with utter solemnity. "Myn eme is Matthaeus of Bruch. Myn uncle is Lorde of Our."

Tom broke into a bout of wheezing coughs. Hannah swiftly slapped him on the back. She, too, was amazed that the boy had been able to follow their conversation at all. He had answered in clear Middle High German.

"Are you from around here?" Senta noted the boy's soiled clothing: a dark brown woolen cloak with a hood, and a pair of loose trousers.

"Is that your father?" she asked.

Tom was only too eager to answer on the boy's behalf. "No, he's his ex-girlfriend's son. She's … out of town, and he's taking care of the child for now."

The audacity of Tom's lies rendered Hannah speechless, but it was also clear to her that this was their chance to regain control of the situation.

"Don't worry. Hannah will take care of you," Senta said, trying to cheer the boy up. "She'll call your mother and make sure you're okay."

"My moder is ded," the boy replied.

Tom narrowed his eyes menacingly at the small boy, sending him a clear warning to shut his mouth immediately. Looking a picture of fear and misery, the boy sat down on the floor, not daring to look in Tom's direction a second longer.

"Didn't you just say his mother was out of town?" Frowning, Senta turned to Tom.

Tom didn't know how to respond, and hesitated a moment too long.

"The family's situation is a little confusing," said Hannah, coming to the rescue.

"So it seems," Senta remarked, looking at the boy in sympathy. "Although it's extremely worrying that it seems to be *so* confusing that the child can no longer decide if his mother is dead or out of town. Anyway, someone should make sure the poor child learns some sensible German, or he'll have problems in school."

Senta reached for her cell phone and dialed a number.

"Is this St. Agnes Hospital? I'm Dr. Scheuten. I'd like to call an ambulance."

Tom motioned to Hannah to follow him into the hallway. Once they were outside, he hissed, "Well, that's fantastic. And what do we do now?"

"You're in no position to ask me that," she retorted. "Anyway, we can't just keep him in my bed. I suggest you go to the hospital with him, and I'll take care of the boy. You can come back when everything is under control. I think you owe me more than just that explanation you gave me earlier."

Tom nodded, but something still seemed to be on his mind. "Can we use your name for the hospital bill? It's not about the money. We just can't afford to let any outsiders make a connection between him and me. I don't know what's happened at the Institute since I left. I'll have a lot of questions to answer, that much is clear."

"If you're as quick witted as you usually are, I have no worries," Hannah remarked drily. "Swear to me that we're not doing anything that can land us in jail." She stared into Tom's brown eyes.

"Don't worry. I'll sort it out soon," he muttered wearily.

To her surprise, he gave her a quick hug, followed by a warm kiss on her cheek.

Right then, Senta appeared in the hallway, clearing her throat apologetically.

"Everything's fine. The ambulance will be here any minute. If you want, I can accompany the patient to the hospital."

"That's okay," Hannah replied, struggling to look relaxed as she smiled at her friend. "You've given us enough of your time. Tom will go."

"I guess we won't be playing cards tonight," Senta remarked, patting Hannah on the shoulder regretfully. "Do you want me to stay here with you?"

"No, I'll be fine. And thank you." As much as Hannah wanted her friend's help, it was best that she didn't drag her too deeply into this mess.

It took another fifteen minutes for the ambulance to pull up in the driveway. Senta had been checking the unconscious man's pulse regularly, and she led the paramedics and doctor on duty into the bedroom.

Hannah saw the boy who called himself Matthäus widen his eyes in fear as one of the paramedics slid an IV needle into the back of the patient's hand and lifted him onto a stretcher. The boy sprang to his feet again, looking on in obvious distress as his companion was carried away.

The paramedics had nearly reached the hallway when he shot out of his corner and flung himself onto the stretcher. He clung to the unconscious man in desperation, trying to stop the paramedics from leaving. He whimpered softly, tearing at the thin, silver blanket that his companion was wrapped in, forcing the paramedics to set the stretcher down.

"You'll have to control the little rascal," one of the men said to Tom, nodding impatiently at the boy on the stretcher, "or we can't move him to the ambulance."

With considerable effort, Tom loosened the boy's fingers from the blanket. The child tried his best to scratch and bite his captor as he was dragged back into the bedroom. Hastily, Tom locked the door from the outside.

There was something shameful about the entire scene. Hannah wanted to run to the boy to comfort him, but that would have to wait for now.

Senta raised a questioning eyebrow.

Hannah smiled apologetically as the others left the house. "I have to take care of the boy, so ..."

Tom gave her a meaningful look. "Can you manage?"

"Yes ... I think so," she whispered.

He winked at her as they all left. The front door clicked shut. Hannah heard the roar of engines as the ambulance and her visitors drove off into the night. Then there was silence.

With an uneasy feeling, Hannah unlocked the bedroom door hoping that Tom wouldn't leave her alone for too long.

Matthäus had gathered the man's possessions that Hannah and Tom had left under the bed, and spread them out on the floor. He sat with his back to her in front of the pile of clothes. Clutching the cloak tightly in his small hands, the boy's shoulders shuddered. He hadn't stopped crying.

Hannah approached him carefully. "Hey, Matthäus, don't worry. Your friend will be well again, and everything will be fine. I promise …"

He seemed not to have heard her. She reached out her hand to him.

"Would you like something to drink? Surely you must be thirsty?"

All at once, he sprang to his feet and whirled around.

Hannah drew back with a loud scream. The slender, harmless-looking boy was gripping the leather-bound handle of the long dagger so tightly that his knuckles bulged white. The murderous blade was aimed directly at Hannah's stomach.

"Ye art a sorceresse!" he hissed as he approached. "Wher have ye broughte him? Speke or ye shul deie!"

Hannah retreated in panic, her heart pounding. She had been prepared for nearly anything, but being stabbed by a twelve year-old was something that she had never considered.

"Matthäus," she pleaded, hoping he would understand her. "Put that down immediately. You could kill someone with that."

Trembling, she stood with her back to the wall. Unfortunately, she had shut the bedroom door after entering, and now there was no escape. In her mind, she already saw herself sliced open, lying on the floor, slaughtered by a child.

I could sure use a miracle, she thought, squeezing her eyes shut and waiting for him to ram the glittering blade through her flesh.

Suddenly, she heard a loud clatter. She blinked cautiously. The power had returned, and the ceiling lamp flooded her bedroom with light.

And Matthäus was lying in front of her, his face against the ground and his whole body shaking. He had flung his dagger aside.

"Haff mercy!" he squeaked. "Lat me liven, do not hurten me!"

Too stunned to answer, Hannah slumped against the door. She pressed both hands flat against her stomach, her heart still racing. Taking several deep breaths, she tried to steady her pulse before she bent down to the boy to comfort him.

201

CHAPTER 16

Fish Tank

Saturday, November 13, 2004

Tom felt as if he was driving straight into darkness. Wet from rain, the streets reflected the headlights of the oncoming traffic, robbing him of what little vision he had left. A leaden weariness dulled his concentration, and an annoying lump in his throat made swallowing difficult.

When he'd entered the office this morning, he had been a promising young scientist with an exciting future. He was involved in a secret project with fantastic possibilities at an institute with the kind of first-class facilities that could only be dreamed of by an ambitious young researcher.

Now it had all vanished, and he still had no clue what his next step should be.

Suddenly, his cell phone rang.

"Hello?"

"It's Paul. Tom, where are you?"

"I'm on the way to the hospital."

"The hospital? Did something go wrong?" Paul asked, sounding alarmed.

Tom let out an exasperated sigh. "I'm following the ambulance that's taking our patient to the hospital."

"Ambulance? I thought you wanted to hide the two of them with your friend?"

"Paul, we transferred *people*, not guinea pigs that I can just hand out to eager children. And in case you've forgotten, the guy was unconscious, and he hasn't come to. It was hard enough to convince Hannah to help and unfortunately, I couldn't get her permission to let a stranger die in her bed."

"What have you done with the little one?"

"He's with Hannah. But the situation has become more complicated than I expected."

"I figured as much," Paul said. "Maybe we'll get lucky and the guy will die. Otherwise, we could be in serious trouble."

"What should I do, then? Give him to Hagen?" Tom was annoyed.

"Just be glad you managed to get away!" Paul yelled into the receiver. "You don't even want to know what I've been through. The Institute leadership has called for an investigation and assembled a brain trust for support. The President of the United States was informed immediately. People from the Pentagon are on their way here from Washington tonight. Meanwhile, Hagen himself has been putting me through the wringer. He was not amused that you went missing. I told him that you were in shock and wanted to go home. He wanted me to call you immediately, but luckily, I couldn't reach you."

"Did Hagen say anything else?"

"That we have to report to him by 9:30 a.m. tomorrow at the latest. He wants a detailed report on what happened with the experiments. Their initial calculations estimate the property damage at just under two billion dollars, and there are at least fifteen people injured, three of them critical. The press is all over the compound. God knows how they got wind of this so fast. Piglet's trying to scare them off by telling them that the grounds might possibly be contaminated, and that they need to keep clear for a two-kilometer radius. Colonel Pelham has sealed off everything. I had no idea we had so many soldiers at our disposal. The Americans also have an emergency inquiry by the Green Party to deal with. We're screwed, Tom."

"Okay, I have to hang up now. We've reached the hospital!" Tom yelled. "We should meet up tomorrow before we enter the lion's den. Let's say eight at the McDonalds in Bitburg?"

"All right," Paul answered. "Maybe we can talk again later."

"Sure," Tom said and ended the call.

The ambulance pulled up to a brightly lit roller door. Tom parked his Volvo a few meters away. He ran to the entrance of the building where the man was being transferred from the stretcher to a wheeled gurney, and pushed into an underground hospital wing.

As he was about to follow the paramedics through a frosted glass door, a chirpy voice called out to him, "Are you a relative?"

Tom looked around. A bossy looking middle-aged woman, clad entirely in blue, stared at him expectantly. *Sister Cordula* said her badge. *Was he? Yes*, he decided, *in a manner of speaking.*

"The patient is my brother-in-law," he said.

"Well, come along then," the woman said, sounding a touch friendlier. "You can settle the administrative matters for the patient's admission on the ground floor," she continued.

Tom saw the paramedics and a doctor, who was wearing a stethoscope around his neck, disappear with the injured man behind a swinging door. *Danger: X-rays – Do Not Enter*, said the sign above it.

"Where are they taking him?" Tom asked nervously.

"Don't worry! Your brother-in-law will have to be examined first. You can visit him later. Now, follow me, please." The Sister flashed him a fake smile and gestured toward the stairs.

Handed a form to fill out, Tom threw together a few biographical details that he thought matched the man. He guessed that he was just under thirty, and named him Gerard Schreyber, Hannah's last name, effectively making him her husband, and checked a box allowing him to be treated as a private patient.

"Would you like the patient to be treated by a senior physician, and would you like a single or double room?" the receptionist enquired.

Tom thought for a second. "Definitely a single room," he replied. "It doesn't have to be a senior physician."

He tried to imagine everything that could happen, eventually coming to the unnerving conclusion that this situation followed the laws of quantum physics: everything was possible, and nothing was within his control.

"Could I have Mrs. Schreyber's phone number, please?"

Tom had to check his mobile phone's contact list. Even after all these years, he still didn't know Hannah's number by heart. Something pricked at his conscience. *Should he have dragged her into this mess at all?* He secretly hoped that Hannah wouldn't be too inconvenienced but he could sense that chaos of unknown proportions was looming.

After the paperwork had been completed, Tom was instructed to take a seat in a waiting room.

The large clock hanging above the door read 9:15 p.m. His thoughts turned to Hannah and the boy. It remained to be seen if the boy could give them any information about which exact corner of time and space the two unexpected visitors came from.

Eventually, Tom discovered the fish tank just outside the waiting room. A pair of medium-sized plecos had attached themselves to one of the algae-covered panes, and three or four fat, round fish swam lazily through the dilapidated underwater landscape. Tom felt a spontaneous empathy with these neglected creatures. The sight of them once more made him question who or what was responsible for the place one had in the universe.

A moment later, an attractive blonde doctor appeared at the door and offered him her slender hand in greeting.

"Stevendahl," he said with a firm handshake.

"Sorry for the wait," she said warmly, "but all hell broke loose today. Something in Spangdahlem exploded – apparently it was an American research facility. Strangely enough, we haven't received a single patient from there. But we've had plenty of cases of shock – people think that war's broken out."

Tom turned away sheepishly.

"Hey, have you heard anything about it?"

"No, no, I haven't," he said hurriedly.

"Does your brother-in-law's accident have anything to do with this?"

"No," Tom said resolutely, still not looking her in the eye. "He fell from a ladder while renovating his apartment."

The doctor briefly explained that the X-rays showed that nothing was broken. Casually, she leafed through the new medical records and retrieved a yellow form.

"Ah ... I still need to know if he's had a tetanus shot."

Tom shook his head emphatically.

The doctor looked at him in astonishment. "Any known allergies?"

"No," Tom answered quickly, "not that I know of."

With an understanding smile, she looked up from her paperwork. "Good. We definitely have to give him his vaccination. Tell his wife that we couldn't wait for her consent. I bear responsibility for him right now, and a tetanus infection would be the last thing he needs to deal with." She glanced up again and looked at him almost in sympathy. "The problem is that he still isn't awake, and unfortunately, I can't currently predict how long he will remain unconscious. Maybe he'll be better by morning. We think he's just had a severe concussion."

The doctor paused as she looked at a stack of scans, shaking her head. "To rule out possible internal injuries, we did an MRI. However, the machine was going crazy. These images are as good as trash," she said. "The machine will be repaired tomorrow. After that, I'll run a CAT scan to make sure that we haven't missed anything in the X-rays."

"Of course ..." Tom answered tentatively. The MRI machine placed the body's hydrogen nuclei in a strong magnetic field, which bore certain similarities to the synchronization mechanism of CAPUT's technology. In a series of tests, they had discovered that the atoms of a transferred organism took hours before they began to vibrate at the usual frequency again. As predicted, it seemed human cell structures behaved no differently from plant cell structures. Tom's mind suddenly went blank, and he felt an urgent need to lie down.

Noticing his exhaustion, the doctor patted his shoulder encouragingly as she showed him out. "Everything will soon be fine," she said with a smile. "Tell the patient's wife that we'll call her by tomorrow at the latest."

Tom left the hospital through the front door. It had stopped raining and he greedily breathed in the cold, damp autumn air. It was Saturday, the thirteenth – it could very well have been a Friday.

Fearing another unexpected attack, Hannah touched the boy's shoulder as gently as she could. She had made sure that the dagger really was out of his reach. Finally, she gathered her courage and stroked Matthäus's blonde locks while he was still lying numbly on the floor.

Like his older companion, the boy's clothing was strange. He wore a brown linen tunic with long sleeves, a woolen, gray-brown knitted vest, and a pair of dark brown pants made from thick woolen fabric. His feet were covered by light brown boots, crafted from leather as soft as gloves and folded down over his ankles.

If the boy really was from the Middle Ages, was it any wonder that he reacted with fear and anger? She and Tom must have seemed like two ruthless barbarians who assaulted his unconscious brother, father, uncle, or whoever he was, Hannah mused, and then had him carted away without explanation. Besides, his new surroundings must have appeared frightening and alien to the boy.

At these thoughts, she felt a pang in her heart. She wanted to embrace him, but she knew that her actions might just make things worse.

Hannah walked to the door and switched off the lights. Matthäus hadn't been able to control his curiosity, for when she turned her attention to him again, she saw that he had raised his head slightly and was observing her out of the corner of his eyes. As their eyes accidentally met, his face quickly darkened, and he lowered his head again.

Hannah sat down near the boy on the parquet floor and simply waited. Obviously, he found her behavior so strange that after about five minutes, he raised his head again and stared at her in bewilderment. She attempted a cheery smile and raised her eyebrows questioningly.

Although he didn't smile back, he found the courage to sit up and face her at a respectable distance. He sat with his legs drawn up in front of him, clutching his knees tightly,.

Cautiously, Hannah shifted a little nearer and held out her hand to him. With an effort, she tried to recall the syntax of medieval sentence structure from the three classes in Middle High German she had taken in her college days.

"Myn name is clepid Hannah. Wilcomen in myne hous!"

He said nothing, but he didn't look away.

"Do ye understonden me?" Not ready to give up, she gave him an encouraging look.

He nodded absently. "Ye are michel bele," he whispered suddenly with an expression of admiration.

Hannah swallowed hard. He had called her fair and beautiful. It was a sincere compliment that hit her as unexpectedly as his earlier attack.

His large, blue eyes widened in anticipation. "Are ye a sorceresse?"

Subconsciously, she swept a strand of dark red hair out of her face, making the boy flinch in fear. If the entire affair hadn't been so confusing, she would have laughed at the thought of being mistaken for a sorceress.

Hannah cleared her throat, trying her best to remain serious. In a firm voice, she answered, "nay, I ben neither a sorceresse ne a wicche." She raised her right hand and placed the left on her thigh as if swearing on her honor.

Matthäus relaxed a little. "Thanne are ye a fairye?" He asked as hope lit up his eyes.

Was she a fairy? She felt a little sorry that she had to disappoint the boy again.

"I am wol sori, Matthäus, neither am I a fairye. I am a comon womman." Secretly, she hoped that after being so honest, the boy wouldn't retract his approval.

"What are ye thanne? A bondewomman or a free womman?"

Bonded or free? He seemed to find pleasure in interrogating her. Quickly, she thought about what it meant to be free. In the Middle Ages, it would mean that she was her own master, couldn't be sold like cattle to anybody, and wasn't bound to anyone to perform any sort of service. She wouldn't have to report to anyone when she wanted to marry, and could choose her own partner. By all accounts, she was free. After all, she owned a successful bookstore, and she didn't have to take orders from anyone. As for marriage ... despite all her freedom, she had no suitors to choose from.

"Yea, I am a free womman," she finally said with a smile.

Matthäus cocked his head. "Are ye a sellere? Or are ye a guilde sistere?"

A merchant? That sounded about right. A guild? Well, she did belong to the trade association of German booksellers, but she wasn't going to explain *that* to him.

"Yea, I selle bokes," she answered.

"Bokes?" His forehead wrinkled in disbelief.

"Yea," Hannah reassured him. She was amazed – he really seemed to understand her.

Out of the blue, the thought of her old Professor Marbach popped into her head. "Always remember," he had lectured his German students, "we can try our best to guess how Middle High German originally sounded, but we can never know for sure."

Another smile escaped Hannah's lips, and this time Matthäus smiled back shyly.

The boy's gaze turned to the halogen light on the ceiling that she had turned off earlier. "What is this wunderlice lighte in youre lanterne? It semeth brighter thanne the lighte of a candil."

Hannah pondered for a moment. She was certain that the phrase "electric light" did not exist in Middle High German. But the boy's description moved her. Bizarre light, brighter than a candle – it sounded almost poetic. How should she explain this bizarre light? However she chose, he would not understand it all at once.

She shrugged her shoulders in apology. Maybe it would suffice to reassure the boy that the light would cause no harm. "I knowe not hou I shalle expounden the case. Bot it is full spedeful and not unholsom." Suddenly she thought of something with which she could win the boy's trust. "Artow hungri or thirsti?"

His answer came promptly. "Yea, yif ye had some bred and watir for me?"

Now, finally, the last of her doubts about Tom's story dissipated. What normal child – ignoring for a moment the fact that he spoke fluent Middle High German – would ask for bread and water when offered something to eat?

Hannah rose slowly and winked at the boy. "Come along now, I might have something better than just water and bread."

Uncertainly, he followed her into the living room, where he settled down on the carpet in front of the fireplace. A thick candle was still flickering on the table, and Hannah decided that she should avoid using electric light altogether in case it alarmed the boy again.

The boy's gaze fell on Heisenberg, who had curled up on the armchair as though the day's catastrophes meant nothing to him. With a smile, the boy held out his hand to the cat. He stroked the soft, black fur, and then finally began to scratch the animal behind the ears. Oddly enough, the usually aloof Heisenberg welcomed the boy's touch with loud purrs.

"Stay here," Hannah said. "I'll be right back." Making sure that the boy didn't follow her, Hannah left the room. She only wanted to show him the kitchen, with all its strange technical equipment. But only after he had grown a little more acclimatized to his surroundings.

When she returned to the living room, Matthäus had already made himself comfortable on the sofa. With hungry eyes, he stared at the tray she was carrying, loaded with sandwiches, a red apple, and a large glass of milk.

Hannah was both amused and moved to see the enthusiasm that this humble snack elicited in her guest. Before eating, he made the sign of the cross, folded his hands in prayer, shut his eyes, and prayed silently. Finally, he ate, slowly and with full concentration. Before he bit into the apple, his gaze fell on Hannah's bookshelves.

"You must be a very rich lady," he remarked softly, Hannah translating his words mentally. "Not even my uncle has so many books, and he's the commander of the Templar Order in Bar-sur-Aube."

Bar-sur-Abe, Hannah pondered. *Wasn't that in the Champagne region in France?* So, the strange boy sitting before her lived in France – but why did he speak Middle High German instead of old French, then?

"Besides, you own cups of precious glass," he added after he had devoured the apple to its core. Appreciatively, he lifted the empty milk glass and turned it about in his hand, inspecting it thoroughly. Hannah had to suppress her laughter. It seemed more than a little odd to describe an old mustard jar as precious.

Finally, with a courteous look, the boy thanked her for the exquisite meal. She had to laugh again. Apart from his clothes, he looked like a normal teenager. He had a few pimples on his forehead, and when he smiled, he revealed astonishingly white teeth with edges still jagged like a child's.

A soft knocking that became steadily louder frightened Hannah out of her slumber. Blinking groggily, she looked around to see where it was coming from.

As she turned on the overhead light in the hallway, she glanced at the sofa, and a shock ran through her. The sleeping boy on her sofa was as real as the heart beating in her chest, and the story of how he came to be sleeping on her sofa flooded back into her mind.

"Thank God," she groaned, almost in relief, when she opened the door and found Tom standing before her. "How did it go?"

"Nothing remarkable, apart from the shitty weather." As he squinted at his reflection in the hall mirror and rearranged his damp hair, he smiled. "From now on, you are the wife of a Templar, at least as far as St. Agnes Hospital is concerned. If he does something crazy or bites the dust, they'll call you."

"I'm amazed that you're still in the mood for jokes," Hannah said impatiently. "Do you want something to drink? Or to eat?" she asked as she passed by the kitchen.

"How about a double whiskey?"

"Sorry. The strongest drink I can offer you is a dessert liqueur."

"Wine? Maybe a red?" From their time together, Tom knew that Hannah enjoyed a good bottle of red every now and then. Nodding, she fetched a bottle and two glasses from the kitchen cabinet.

Tom entered the living room, but stopped suddenly when he found the boy sleeping peacefully on the sofa. Taking care not to make a sound, he sat down in one of the armchairs and observed the unexpected guest with a thoughtful look.

"Has he calmed down?"

"Better that you don't ask," Hannah whispered, uncorking a bottle of Cabernet Sauvignon. "He wanted to kill me!"

"Why? With what?"

"Take a guess," she said drily as she poured the dark red wine into the two glasses. Tom was still looking dumbstruck at the harmless-looking boy when Hannah left the room and returned with the dagger, which she placed in Tom's hands.

He weighed the weapon in his hands and looked incredulously at the sleeping child. "Isn't that the knife I cut my finger with? How did he get it?"

"How do you think? You shoved the thing under the bed. He thought I was a sorceress with dark powers who needed to be slain."

"And you ... overpowered him?" Tom's horror was plain to see.

"Not really. As I was savoring the last seconds of my life, the power came on. The lights scared him so badly that he thought it would be better to let me live."

Tom took a hasty gulp of wine and fell silent in embarrassment.

"But on the bright side, we've nearly become friends now," Hannah added, sitting down in the armchair facing Tom. Her arms crossed in front of her, she looked at Tom with her eyes flashing in the darkness. "Don't you think you should explain to me how all *this* happened?"

"Of course," he said, guiltily avoiding her gaze, "but I'm still wondering where I should begin and *how*. It isn't very easy to explain." He coughed, not daring to meet her eyes.

"So you still think I'm too stupid for your scientific pipe-dreams?"

"No ... but ..."

"Then at least *try*."

"Okay." He leaned back, and Hannah could see him struggling for words. It took some time before he began.

"You knew," he said, almost apologetically, "that I was obsessed with my work in Jülich. It was a great opportunity to be able to work on Hagen's team."

Hannah looked at him reproachfully. "Yes, I remember how obsessed you were," she countered grimly. "Nothing else mattered to you – me, our future together ... I didn't have the faintest clue why. Sometimes I thought you were seeing someone else. I felt like a castaway on a deserted island."

"I know I made many mistakes," Tom replied softly, "but now that you know that Hagen was able to build some sort of time machine, maybe you can understand my excitement about working for him."

Hannah laughed nervously. "Time machine," she repeated with a wry smile. "No offence, Tom, but that sounds like a cliché. Doesn't the thing at least have a name that sounds professional enough that I don't think you're mocking me every time you mention it?"

"CAPUT – Center of Accelerated Particles in Universe and Time. That's what Hagen named it."

"Fantastic," Hannah gave Tom a withering look. "Honestly, that doesn't sound much better. And despite your collective ingenuity … how did this disaster happen?"

"I don't know. Neither I, nor my colleague, Paul, altered the programming. We could have, but we're strictly forbidden from doing so. The President of the United States of America has to give the final approval for every change in the procedure. Anyone caught acting unilaterally will be kicked out of the project immediately."

"I understand," Hannah whispered. "So that's why you carted the two of them here – because you thought they would throw you out if unexpected people from another time appeared and it looked like you were responsible for it."

"It's not what you think …" Tom mumbled defensively as he stared at the sleeping boy. "Yes, you're right," he finally conceded when her skeptical glare never wavered. "Those *were* my first thoughts. But it soon became clear to me that someone else could be behind this, and that it was no accident that these two landed on the research field …"

His expression turned imploring. "You have to believe me, Hannah, that my real reasons for not handing them over to the professor and the Americans were humane. I've known my boss long enough to know that life in a gilded cage would be the best fate that the two of them could hope for. The rest of their lives wouldn't be that different from lab rats."

"I'm honored you think that they'll have a better time with me." Hannah laughed drily. "Do you think they have any chance of returning to their own century?"

Instinctively she sensed that the course of her own future, too, hung upon this answer.

"Realistically speaking … not right now," Tom sighed in resignation. "Our technology has been destroyed. And even if everything was functioning perfectly, and I knew what happened in the first place, I don't have the slightest clue how I could send the two of them back to where they came from without anyone noticing."

"What's up with the Americans? Won't they hold you and your colleague responsible for what happened, regardless of whether or not they discover that you've hidden two time travelers?"

"Paul called me when I was on the way to the hospital. For a start, we have to report to Hagen's office in Spangdahlem tomorrow. I know he will put us through the wringer, but if we're clever enough, we'll survive. I think our biggest problem at the moment is concealing their presence. I'm afraid there are logs of the accident. The Americans have all the latest investigation technology at their disposal. All they need are a few skin cells to detect someone's presence – and when they were there – based on organic residue. Our only chance to keep their presence a secret for long is if all suspicious evidence on the field was destroyed by the fire."

"What if they examine your car?"

"I've already thought about that. There must be someone up there who loves me," Tom answered. "The old Volvo outside belongs to my neighbor. I still have to bring it back to Bonn tonight. My BMW wouldn't start this morning, for some reason. It was probably a gift from God, as I could never have brought the knight and his little companion to you in my two-seater."

"To be honest, I was surprised when you drove up in that rusty old thing," Hannah remarked. "So you still haven't given up your flashy sports cars, huh?"

"No," Tom said, looking at his ex-fiancée earnestly. "But as for the rest of me … I think I've changed."

Hannah noticed that he had begun to stroke her hand. Quickly, she drew her hand back and rose to her feet.

"You look pretty tired," she said. "You should probably drive back now. You have a stressful day ahead of you tomorrow."

Tom pursed his lips and stood up. Hannah could sense his disappointment. What did he expect from her, anyway? Was she supposed to fling her arms around his neck? It was already a miracle that she had agreed to help him in this ridiculous affair.

"I'll call you as soon as I can," he said solemnly.

"You'd better!" Hannah exclaimed, glaring at him. "I hope it's absolutely clear to you that from this moment on, I am now responsible for two extra lives. Don't you dare think that you can just dump them with me and pray that your crazy professor doesn't find them."

"If I could've thought of a better alternative," he said, nodding towards the sleeping boy, "I wouldn't have asked you. The two of them won't be safer anywhere else in the world than with you."

Frowning, Tom fumbled in his pockets until he finally found his neighbor's car keys.

Still shaken by the boy's earlier threats from, Hannah stowed the dagger away in a wardrobe drawer before walking Tom to the door.

"Come here," she said to him as he stood in the open doorway. With a quick movement, she pulled Tom's head down to hers and kissed him on the cheek. He smiled weakly.

"Thank you," he said simply, "for everything."

"Drive safely," she replied as he left.

CHAPTER 17

Interrogation

Sunday, November 14, 2004

The only thing impeding Tom's progress was the taxi leisurely winding its way through the narrow streets of the Eifel village like a blood clot through a clogged artery. Tom gritted his teeth and slowed his BMW to a crawl behind it.

After a journey that had taken far too long, he finally glimpsed the golden arches in the distance. Shortly before turning into the entrance to McDonalds, he turned his attention to the eight o'clock news on the local station. But there were no reports of the accident at the American military compound, only of yesterday evening's massive blackout, which had blanketed Germany from Wittlich to Trier, Luxembourg, and even parts of France.

The newscaster reported that the Rhine-Westphalian Electric Company and Vattenfall Europe still hadn't announced how the blackout had happened, and only briefly mentioned that the disturbance was presumably the cause of an explosion on a compound near the U.S. Airbase of Spangdahlem.

It seemed the U.S. Armed Forces had already ensured no one found out that the truth was just the opposite.

Before Tom had even opened the glass doors to the fast food restaurant, he had already spotted his Luxembourgian colleague's strawberry blonde hair.

"There you are! Finally!" Paul exclaimed, sounding nervous. "I was afraid you'd changed your mind and were already on a plane to the Caribbean."

"You sure let your mind run wild," Tom retorted, sitting down across from his co-worker.

"My God, you look like you have one foot in the grave." Paul looked at him in concern.

Dark shadows had appeared under Tom's eyes. He sighed wearily. "I've been awake for exactly thirty-six hours."

"Wait a minute." Paul rose to his feet, and a little later set down a cappuccino and two croissants in front of Tom. "Explain!" he ordered.

Briefly Tom reported what had happened after he had accompanied the unconscious Templar knight to the hospital.

Paul raised his eyebrows. "When he comes round, he'll need something to eat and a roof over his head. And for how long? Is your ex-fiancée clear about the responsibilities she's taking on?"

"She's already agreed to bear all the medical costs until the coast is clear. She was even okay with me passing the guy off as her husband."

"She must still feel something for you. The man and child are complete strangers to her, after all."

Tom slurped his coffee. "We found a leather pouch hanging around his neck. It had an ID of sorts in it."

"And?"

"Hannah helped me to translate the Latin Text. You're right. He is a Knight Templar and was born in 1280 – not far from here."

"So, that blasted machine really worked." Paul shook his head in disbelief. "If only the old professor knew that we caught a crusader!"

"What would Hagen get out of it, anyway, apart from the knowledge that his machine is actually capable of transferring something better than a few bloody pinecones?"

Paul's eyes darted around nervously before he faced his colleague and lowered his voice to a hoarse whisper. "A little bird told me that Hagen didn't develop the technology we're using by himself. Supposedly, someone has been secretly helping him. It seems an old acquaintance of his from Beirut found some clues in Jerusalem during restoration efforts in the Temple Mount, which enabled Hagen to develop the technology in the first place. Understandably, our dear professor has little interest in publicizing this fact."

"*Jerusalem?*" Tom frowned in disbelief.

"The man who gave him the findings is Lebanese, allegedly a cousin of Hagen's property manager in Jülich. Hagen befriended the guy when he was in Germany visiting relatives."

Tom's mouth twisted into a wry smile. "It's hard to believe that our dear professor has any friends at all."

"You can imagine how the Yanks could have a problem with Hagen's Arab friend, and a devout Muslim, at that."

"And which particular *bird* has been spreading such information?" Tom took a bite of his croissant. "It's the first time I've heard about it."

"I have connections!" Paul assured him.

"Come on, spit it out. This is too important – you can't keep your sources from me."

Paul nodded. "Karen," he said simply. "I spoke to her on the phone last night."

"Don't tell me you've already told her everything," Tom's voice darkened.

"No, I only told her that I've been doing well and that she should know that we're innocent, regardless of what the others say. Then she said that she had to tell me something – privately."

Tom grunted in satisfaction. "My, my. Dr. Karen Baxter, Hagen's right hand and confidante! Why doesn't this surprise me?"

"Keep this to yourself. I swore to her that I wouldn't tell anyone."

"That you won't tell anyone what? That the two of you are in a relationship?"

"You idiot," Paul snapped. "I mean the fact that she's told me confidential information. Hagen already smells a rat. She found out about his contact by accident – she had to check the age of two well-preserved sheets of parchment from the Lebanese guy by radiocarbon dating. Under strict secrecy, of course."

"You must be pretty amazing for the Ice Queen to spill her boss's most intimate secrets to you so readily."

"Oh, that's not all, Tom," Paul said in a hushed voice. "Hagen was able to decipher the characters on the parchment – revealing formulae that supposedly bridged crucial gaps in his research. I find it all rather strange. I just can't imagine how an eight hundred-year-old document could help conceptualize technology like ours."

Tom was suddenly wide awake. He felt goose bumps crawl up his skin. "You know what I wonder?"

Paul shook his head.

"Well, I have no idea who could have produced any usable formulae for our technology eight hundred years ago. But is it any coincidence that we transferred a Templar knight? Think about it! Templar, the Temple Mount. Couldn't Hagen himself have something to do with this?"

"I don't know," Paul answered thoughtfully. "The Temple Mount was the Templars' headquarters in Jerusalem eight hundred and fifty years ago. There might be a connection there."

"Our knight would have been born a hundred and fifty years later, though," Tom pointed out.

"Do you think Hagen could have altered the computer settings because he knew a Templar knight would pop up on the field at that specific time?"

"I wouldn't rule it out," Tom answered. "I just wonder how he could have known about that."

"If he knew about it …" said Paul slowly, "that would mean he screwed us over on purpose. But why would he do that?"

"*Why?*" Tom countered grimly. "Because the experiment was illegal? Because he wasn't sure if it would work? Or because he needed scapegoats? Why else?"

"Well, why *us*? I can't recall ever doing anything that didn't impress him."

"I can answer that for you, too!" Tom pursed his lips in agitation. He felt a dark rage rise within him. "Besides Hagen, no one else would be able to alter the program in such a way. And I am the only one who could challenge him for the position of project leader."

"If that's true, I'll kill that pig myself!" Paul roared so loudly that the mothers with small children at the neighboring tables glared at him furiously.

"That sounds wonderful," Tom said drily, "but first, we have to prove it."

"And we will," Paul snorted. "Even if it kills me."

"When's our meeting with him again?" Tom asked.

"Nine thirty."

Tom gave his colleague a roguish grin. "We'll put a hitch in his plans, you can bet your life on that. We'll make him wait for his Templar knight until he's blue in the face!"

"And what are we going to tell him?"

"That the fire broke out, there was smoke everywhere … and we have no idea why. Don't mention a word about the people we transferred. We just have to hope that records from that day have been destroyed."

Paul nodded mutely.

Tom stood up. "Ready, Paul? Let's go."

The American Airbase Spangdahlem was the size of a small town. Only authorized guests were granted entry to the heavily guarded facility. At the gate, Tom and Paul were told to park their cars in the visitors' lot next to the control post and the soldier on duty instructed them to board a beige SUV, which was already waiting for them.

After a half-mile drive across the compound, they arrived at a remote office complex. The five octagonal, double-storied office buildings constructed from matte aluminum and connected by a passageway system resembled a lunar base more than a military compound. Cameras had been installed all along the electric fence, over a mile long, that encircled the compound. Access was granted or denied through a complex identification system.

As a gate rolled aside, an F-16 jet roared overhead. Paul stuck his fingers in his ears, and the security team quickly signaled to Paul and Tom to follow them inside.

After the previous evening's explosion, the Institute's leaders had decided to move all records of their work's progress to a different, secure location outside the actual research compound.

As they walked down the long hallway, Tom felt his knees grow weak. All too quickly, they reached Hagen's office. A gust of stale air hit them as their security escort opened the door. It seemed the air conditioning had broken down. Tom's gaze swept across the room; he counted six people who had obviously been awaiting their arrival. Hagen and his assistant, Piglet, sat behind the professor's desk, which looked unusually tidy.

Two empty chairs sat in front of the desk, and behind them another row of seats, where the Security Officer of the U.S. Airbase Spangdahlem, Colonel Pelham, was seated. Tom greeted him with a nod, but Pelham merely met his gaze with a piercing stare. In the seat next to Pelham's was a bald, highly decorated general from the NSA, who Tom only recognized by sight. The name *Lafour* was engraved on the nametag on his breast. Tom had never seen the third person – a brawny, uniformed man in his late forties. It was Major Cedric Dan Simmens, the new military attaché of the American Embassy in Berlin, whom the American government had sent to act as an observer.

The professor sat like a judge behind his desk, while Piglet leaned close to his boss, every inch the compliant servant. Dr. Karen Baxter, the molecular biologist who headed the Department of Medicine and

Genetics, was standing near Hagen's other side. The good-looking 45-year-old was wearing a light gray ensemble. She sat down, crossing her legs and tugging futilely at the hem of her far-too-short skirt. As she looked up again, she gave Paul and Tom a sympathetic smile.

Tom sat down next to Paul in one of the two chairs that sat front of the desk. He felt as if he had already been handcuffed, with a ball and chain shackled to his ankle. With a quick glance at Paul, he saw that his Luxembourgian colleague felt the same.

After the final military representative had entered the room, Hagen stood up.

"Ladies and gentleman, allow me to welcome you to our extraordinary meeting, and thank you for your kind attention," he began in fluent English. His gaze swept across his audience, although he ignored Tom and Paul even as he introduced them to the other members of the meeting.

"Please, let me introduce you to Dr. Tomas Stevendahl, the acting project leader, and Mr. Paul Colbach, one of our most capable employees from the Department of Informatics," he continued impassively. "We are gathered here to shed light on the circumstances that led to yesterday's catastrophe, and to discuss the first results of our investigation into this matter."

Hagen cleared his throat and finally looked at his two assistants sitting in front of him.

"First, I'd like to give the floor to Dr. Stevendahl who was directly involved in last evening's events, and would surely like to tell us his perspective on how this ... how should I put it ... derailment happened." Hagen looked at Tom expectantly.

Tom suddenly felt as if his collar was tightening like a noose around his neck. He didn't have the slightest clue what traces had been left behind in the research hall. Cautiously he stood up. He could feel his pulse racing. Before he began to speak, he swallowed hastily and it took all his concentration to keep his quivering voice under control.

"So ... Professor, Dr. Baxter ... gentlemen, I regret to inform you that my colleague, Paul Colbach, and I were just as surprised by yesterday's events as everyone else here. There were no signs of any anomalies in the experiment's routine procedures when we began. Contrary to what you might have suspected, we didn't reprogram the system. The reactor suddenly gained a massive energy build-up, and the machine reacted with a corresponding intensification of the magnetic field, which resulted in

220

the unfortunate accident. I regret that I can not offer you any more concrete information at the moment. Naturally, Mr. Colbach and I will be happy to assist you in analyzing what caused the accident. Thank you."

Tom was only too glad to sit down again.

No one made a sound. Hagen's face was twisted into a dissatisfied expression. He cocked his head, propping his right elbow up on the armrest of his chair and restlessly rolled his fountain pen to and fro between his thumb and index finger.

"And you, Mr. Colbach?" he began with a drawl, "do you think you could shine a little more light on the matter?

"No …" Paul's voice wavered and as he looked up, he caught his lover's imploring look. "I can only agree with my colleague's statements. How the accident happened is a complete mystery to me."

Tom sensed what was going on in Paul's mind. He developed a slight stutter when he was nervous, and Tom could only imagine how uncomfortable it must be for him to falter in front of Doctor Baxter.

"Well …" Hagen mused. His features hardened into a look of disdain. "Then we can count ourselves lucky that at least *our* own investigation brought to light something that seems to have escaped your attention in the heat of the moment."

Hagen pressed a button and a picture of a long sword was projected on the screen at the end of the room. Tom's heart was hammering.

"We found this amidst burnt tree trunks and toppled beech trees," the professor continued triumphantly.

A murmur went around the room.

"To our great surprise, there was blood on it. Fresh blood." Hagen said softly. He seemed to enjoy having the undivided attention of every last person in the room. He lowered his head, as if to examine the picture of the blood-smeared sword on his monitor. Suddenly he looked up and fixed his gaze on Paul Colbach, who, unlike Tom, couldn't disguise the apprehension on his face.

"Mr. Colbach," Hagen boomed, "didn't you tell me yesterday that you and Dr. Stevendahl searched the field after you left the control center?"

Paul took a deep breath. "I did," he admitted, giving an involuntary sigh.

"And can you explain how you missed this weapon?"

"I didn't see it, either!" Tom cut in earnestly. After all, they really hadn't seen the sword in the wreckage.

"Very well," Hagen snarled. "Dr. Baxter! The investigation results, please!"

Confidently, Karen Baxter opened the computer program that would accompany her presentation. Tom could sense that she was walking a dangerous tightrope between satisfying her boss and letting her lover off the hook.

After clearing her throat, she began. "The tremendous burst of energy and the subsequent fire destroyed most of the evidence. Only fragments remain, but, using them, we can reconstruct what we think happened."

She paused for a second, looking up to make sure she had Paul's attention. "In order to find precise data on the composition of the transferred mass, we reconstructed the records of the damaged computer used in the experiment," she announced coolly.

"Although the data offers us no information about *who* was transferred during the accident, we can confidently make conclusions about *what* it was."

Hagen sat up in his chair abruptly, gazing at Karen Baxter with a look of utmost admiration.

"To be exact," Dr. Baxter explained, "apart from the trees and the ground, there was a total of 172.39 kilograms of biomass. We registered 15.73 kilograms of clothing, bags, and other such items. Another 142.23 kilograms were of human origin, although we have no information on whether it was one person or several," She continued matter-of-factly. "Finally, there were 14.43 kilograms of steel, presumably from the sword we found and other equipment that the transferred humans had on them."

A murmur rippled through the room again, but Hagen kept his attention was fixed on Tom and Paul. Feeling the professor's piercing stare, Tom tried his best to appear calmer than he actually was.

"The sword found at the scene," Karen continued, "has several noticeable characteristics. Its total length is 125 centimeters, but despite its weight of nearly three kilograms, according to experts called in last night, it is extremely easy to wield. The length of the hilt is 20 centimeters, and the blade is 5 centemeters wide at the cross-guard. This is a rare hand-and-a-half sword, which was presumably forged by one of the most renowned blade-smiths in Italy at the end of the thirteenth century. The pommel is located about 16 centimeters from the cross-guard, which bears a cross imagery that was fashionable then."

Karen Baxter brandished a piece of paper. "This is the report of a heraldist based in southern Germany. It came to us an hour ago by fax. As you can see, there are two identifiable coats of arms engraved on the pommel in a circle. According to our experts, one of them is the coat of arms of a branch of the House of Breydenbach, which has roots in both Hesse and the Rhine. The other is the so-called *Croix Pattée* of the Order of the Temple. There were a few documented crusaders as well as Templars in the Breydenbach family. An investigation into the family's history is already underway."

She took a hasty sip of water before continuing. "On the upper blade of the sword, we found traces of AB+ blood. Further genetic analysis suggested that it must have belonged to a small, black-haired man whose age is estimated at around 20 years. His genetic structure indicates that he came from southern Europe, possibly northern Italy. We managed to extract another blood sample from the sword's hilt. This blood was from the group O+, with the genetic structure of a blonde, fair-skinned man with blue eyes and Celtic-Gaelic origins. Further analysis showed that he must have been about 25 years old and exceptionally tall for his time."

"Based on our findings, we can deduce that a successful transfer of one or two people from the beginning of the fourteenth century into the present took place on the day of the accident. The question remains, however, of where this person ... or these people ... are right now. According to evidence we found at the experimental field, they may have managed to flee from the compound into the surrounding area, an environment unknown to them. As the person, or persons, are obviously injured, we have initiated a search, led by NSA security forces. Understandably, this operation is top-secret. Unfortunately, I cannot give you any further information about the investigation's progress at the moment. Thank you for your attention."

The room was silent. Each of the men appeared to be processing Karen Baxter's statements. Tom was nauseous. He hadn't expected the investigation to uncover so many details this quickly. He was now in far greater trouble than he had anticipated. He felt as if he could hardly breathe.

Hagen took the floor. "Colonel Pelham, you still have a question, don't you?"

The dark-haired colonel from New Orleans stood and drew himself up to his full height. Striding forward in his navy blue uniform decorated with badges and honors, he loomed over Tom and Paul like an angel of vengeance proclaiming their sentence.

"Mr. Stevendahl, Mr. Colbach, the evidence is stacked against you. I only regret the fact that you are not military personnel, or I would've been able to put you under arrest immedeiatly. Alas, I can only pronounce your immediate suspension until the case is closed. Your access authorization codes will be deleted, and as long as your suspension is in effect, you are barred from entering the research compound. You are, however, required to attend any interrogations here at the airbase."

"You are also obligated to maintain absolute confidentiality on this matter. Should you intend to seek legal counsel, which, considering the compensation claims you might have to bear, I highly recommend, you are obliged to engage lawyers of the American military."

Tom did not miss the satisfaction in Hagen's eyes. "I believe it is the accused who has the right to the last word," Tom retorted with biting sarcasm.

"I would be happy if you could present us with any evidence to acquit yourself, Stevendahl." With a smug smile, Hagen rose from his chair and walked round his antique desk. "I cannot for one second comprehend how you were able to defy orders so spectacularly."

"You know that neither Paul nor I altered the programming," Tom said furiously. "And I, too, can't comprehend why you are so willing to betray us."

He glared at Pelham scornfully. "I do not wish to blame you, my dear Colonel, for suspecting us. First, we hardly know each other, and second, I don't think you have any capacity to judge the complex technical links between the individual series of experiments." His eyes ablaze with anger, Tom again turned to the professor. "Professor Hagen, on the other hand, was already my mentor during my university days. All those years, I thought he appreciated my reliable work ethic, and above all else, my integrity. Now, I realize that my knowledge of human nature is even less reliable than quantum physics."

CHAPTER 18

Knights of St. John

Sunday, November 14, 2004

Slowly, Gero's world came into focus. He squinted into the blinding light above him, his head was laced with pain, his nausea nearly unbearable. His first thought was to escape. He ran his fumbling fingers over the soft blanket that covered him. It exuded an unknown scent. Cautiously, he tried to stretch his legs. Long ago, in his knight training, he was taught to first check whether he could move his legs after regaining consciousness on the battlefield.

Gero was relieved when he found that stretching and bending his legs presented no extraordinary challenges. His arms and hands, too, obeyed his commands. Someone had undressed him, but it couldn't have been one of his Brothers, for they had taken even his braies. Cautiously, he pulled up his thin linen shirt. Horror stories of crusaders who had been knocked unconscious during battle and woke as eunuchs left any knight cold with fright, even if he had sworn an oath of celibacy. Although everything appeared to be intact, something felt unsettlingly different.

Gero felt an object next to his genitals that looked like nothing he had ever seen. Immediately, a hot wave of panic shot through his veins. He sat up laboriously. As he attempted to pull away the blanket, he felt a painful resistance from his left hand. His gaze fell on a small, white piece of fabric that was affixed to the back of his hand. He tore at it rabidly, pulling out a finger-length, needle-thin, glass worm that had buried itself under his skin. Blood immediately ran in a thick rivulet down his middle finger and onto the ground. Hastily, he wiped his bleeding hand on the bed sheets and his heart beat wildly as he finally stripped off the blanket with a violent jerk.

He held his breath. There was a transparent cord embedded in his penis. Gero didn't think; his sole impulse was to get rid of the devil's instrument as quickly as possible. He gave the cord a determined tug and immediately a searing pain coursed through his body. It was as if the transparent snake had clawed itself into his intestines. He clenched his teeth and pulled the cord until his tortured penis was stretched taut. Suddenly, the snake gave way. With a jerk, its head appeared and landed between his bare legs. Gero drew back in disgust and stared at the bed in terror. A small puddle of blood and urine spread across the white sheets. Panicking, he held his penis, and slowly, the throbbing pain finally faded.

What sort of hell was this? The Templar didn't dare glance at the rest of his body and the room he was in. What other demonic powers would he have to reckon with? Steeling himself, he stole a look at his surroundings.

At first glance, everything looked harmless. The walls were painted white, and everything looked orderly and clean. But it was all completely foreign to him. A gleaming light shone above him, making his eyes hurt as though he were staring straight into the midday sun. Despite the brightness, there were neither candles nor a fireplace in the room. Even the furniture looked strange. The tables and chairs were made of steel, as was the bed frame, and the floor was made from neither wood nor stone, but from a peculiar glossy material. Gero pulled down his shirt, then summoned all his courage and set his bare feet on the unfamiliar ground. In a few steps he reached a large window. Light streamed in, confirming that evening was still a long way off. Cautiously he stretched out his hand and touched the glass panel in amazement. It was unusually large, and made from a single, thin sheet of glass. He searched in vain for a window latch.

Outside, beneath him, he saw a large garden filled with trees and bushes. The flora, at least, didn't look too different.

Before he could exhale in relief, however, a bewilderingly alien noise rang out. It reminded him vaguely of the buzz of a bumblebee, only a thousand times louder. It came nearer and nearer, becoming so unbearable that he had to press his fists to his ears. Suddenly, something descended from the sky. It resembled a giant insect but was larger than a fully loaded hay cart. It landed on a large, stone surface in the meadow.

Gero was torn between fear and fascination. Although his mind commanded him to retreat immediately, he remained rooted to the spot, spellbound, staring out of the window. The strange creature's wings slowed, and the noise gradually became bearable again. To Gero's astonishment, a door on the miraculous creature's body fell open, and out climbed a few small, oddly clothed creatures. Judging from their movements, they must have been humans.

Yet, as the monstrous insect came to a complete halt, Gero was far more astounded by the white, eight-pointed cross on a field of red that adorned its two wings. It was the symbol of the Order of the Knights of St. John, more commonly known as the Knights Hospitaller. They had been the Templars' rival military order for decades, and their representatives in Bar-sur-Aube had been their immediate neighbors.

What did this mean? Gero broke out in a sweat. Black flecks danced before his eyes as nausea gripped him anew. Despite the throbbing pain, memories were slowly returning to him. There had been a battle, then a strange, hammering noise, followed by a groan and a creak. Everything around him was ablaze. Suddenly, he saw the face of his young squire. *Mattes!* Dear Lord, he was supposed to have looked after the boy and taken him safely to Hemmenrode!

But then, something had hit him hard on the head, and everything had gone dark.

Panicking, Gero looked around the room again. He certainly wouldn't find the answer to all these mysteries here, especially not in this laughable shirt. And whoever had undressed him had taken his weapons and equipment, for they were nowhere in sight.

At that moment, an elderly woman in a bright blue tunic entered the room breezily. As she laid her eyes on Gero, she yelped, looking just as frightened as he was. Hastily, she set down the tray she was holding and addressed him in a loud, stern voice. He could barely understand her, however, for she spoke in a strange dialect that he had never heard before. While he was still stunned with confusion, she strode toward him.

"For God's sake!" she cried in horror, looking down at the transparent snake, its blood-drenched head lying at the foot of the bed. Her features twisted into a pained grimace, and she began a furious tirade that Gero couldn't understand. He followed her movements nervously. She bent down, and he noticed that she was wearing the most unusual gloves he had ever seen. They looked as if they were made of very thin parchment. She touched the back of his left hand with two fingers, then planted her fleshy hands on her hips, clicking her tongue and shaking her head reproachfully.

Much too astonished by her strange behavior, Gero did not protest when she examined the wound on his hand, letting him go only when she was satisfied that the bleeding had stopped.

"You have to lie down now," she said, pushing his shoulder to make him sit down on the bed. The authoritative tone in her voice was unmistakable. Anger rose within him. How dare the woman treat him so disrespectfully, as if he were a servant? Obviously his ridiculous outfit commanded no respect at all.

He squared his shoulders and stepped away from her. But the woman in the tunic and pants just kept on talking. She turned away and began to fiddle with something on the tray she had brought with her. A moment later, she approached Gero once more, this time with a thick needle raised ominously in her right hand.

Gero saw only the sharp needle. He reared back like a stallion, knocking the needle out of the woman's hand with such force that it skidded far across the glossy floor. Then he sprang toward the woman and grabbed her. She was strong, but she was no match for a determined Templar knight who weighed a solid two hundredweights. With lightning speed, he bent her left arm behind her back and encircled her throat with his right arm.

The woman attempted to scream and wriggle out of his grip, but he held her tightly even as his head began to throb again.

"So, woman," he hissed, his deep, smooth voice dark with threats. "Tell me where my squire is, where you've hidden my clothes and my weapons, and the quickest route outside."

The woman obviously couldn't understand him. She kicked and struggled, but then quickly ran out of breath and slumped weakly against his arms. Knowing that he would kill her if he held her any tighter, Gero loosened his grip and immediately a shrill scream rang out from her throat.

"Blasted bitch!" he swore, and tightened his grip again.

Unfortunately for Gero, her cry of despair hadn't gone unheard. A moment later, two young women in white appeared at the door, gaping at the woman and the half-clothed Templar. One of them turned around and ran off, screeching loudly.

Gero realized with regret that he had alarmed his opponent. Shoving the gasping woman to the floor, he stormed past the newcomer and made his escape through the door.

To his disappointment, Gero discovered that he was still inside the building. Countless doors and people dotted the long hallway, making it impossible for him to find his way out. He froze for a moment too long.

228

Suddenly, he found himself surrounded by six men in blue and white garments. As if on command, they lunged forward and seized him. He tossed about madly under their grasp, slipping and falling heavily to the ground like an injured battle steed. He felt his head hit the hard floor.

"Sister Eva, I need a double dose of Disoprivan! Now!" a male voice cried.

Gero felt his strength leave him as the dizziness returned.

"Hurry!" the man snapped, and the next moment, someone was kneeling on Gero's outstretched left forearm. Gero felt a painful prick in the back of his hand, followed by a strong burning sensation. He flinched. Gasping for breath, he summoned the last of his strength and flailed around so fiercely that he managed to shake off his surprised captors. He clambered to his feet and staggered back toward the wall to get a good look at his opponents. To his right were two strong young men in blue tunics, panting heavily, their eyes wide like fearful calves. Three older men in white coats and trousers had jumped aside in shock, and were now approaching him cautiously. For a second, their white garments reminded Gero of his brethren in the Order. One of them bowed to him from a safe distance and tried to calm him, but Gero didn't have the faintest idea what he was saying. Stricken by an unspeakable weariness, the man's face swam before Gero's eyes. Faintly, he felt himself fall. Hanging limply like a speared boar, he let himself be carried onto a stretcher and dumped back onto the bed from which he had tried to escape. Only now, he had been tightly strapped to it.

Hannah had barely slept a wink all night. When the blonde boy on her sofa awoke, blinking innocently into the morning sunlight, she was suddenly struck by the enormity of what she had taken on. When the boy registered where he was, he broke out into hysterical sobs. Hannah hurriedly tried to calm him with all the sympathy she could muster. Everything he had readily accepted the night before now unsettled him again. Only a warm glass of milk, a hearty cheese sandwich, and the presence of her cat managed to soothe the boy.

Matthäus had scribbled his name on a piece of paper with a pencil. It sounded like *Mattes* when he said it aloud, with the stress on the last syllable.

Matthäus seemed like a clever boy. He could read, write, and was fluent in German, French, and Latin. He had effortlessly translated the Angelus prayer engraved on the base of the Madonna statue on Hannah's dinner table into Middle High German. Despite all this, Hannah still found it difficult to believe that he had arrived here from seven hundred years ago. She would never admit it to Tom, but she had only understood fragments of what he had told her about his experiments. She watched the boy out of the corner of her eye. *I hope Tom's experiments haven't caused any dangerous side effects*, she thought as her mind filled with horrifying visions of the poor boy suddenly dissolving into thin air.

Meanwhile, the sun had risen higher and the room brightened. A glance at the clock told her that Tom must already be at his hearing.

"Give me a minute, Matthäus, I'll be right back," she said to the boy, who had his eyes glued to the black cat stretching languorously in front of him. He nodded distractedly.

Hannah headed into her bedroom. She had laid out the man's cloak on her bed, and the neck pouch on the dresser. Before she asked the boy any questions, she wanted to determine who she had let into her house.

Before she examined the assortment of clothing and equipment on her bed, her gaze fell on the bloodstains on the parquet floor. His clothes were flecked with blood as well, and the cloak was covered in grime. She bent down to inspect the different crosses sewn onto it. Hannah didn't know much about needlework, but she gaped in awe at the perfectly stitched appliqués. There definitely weren't any sewing machines around in the 1300s, yet the stitches were so fine that she couldn't see any seams at all. The red crosses seemed to merge with the cloak's cream-colored fabric. Inside the collar, Hannah discovered the owner's name, stitched unbelievably delicately in gray silk thread.

FRATER GERARDUS DE BREYDENBACH ORDO MILITIE HIEROSOLYMITANIS TEMPLI BAR-SUR-AUBE

Frater meant brother. And Bar-sur-Aube … that was the Champagne region of France.

The Order of the Knights Templar of Jerusalem. Hannah racked her brains to dredge up what she knew about this phrase. In the novels that her customers ordered every now and then, the mysterious Templar knights usually assumed the roles of chivalrous heroes. Purposefully, Hannah turned to the leather pouch and tipped out the contents onto the dresser.

The leather coin pouch was the first object to fall out, followed by the book she had glanced at the evening before. Then she noticed a piece of parchment, rolled up and fastened with a red silk ribbon. Hannah loosened the ribbon and spread the yellowed sheet out in front of her. The author had written a poem and drawn tendrils and flowers in glowing green and crimson pigments. *Elsebeten Minnelied,* said the title.

To Gero, myne son, myne moone, myne lucifer,
myne harte is wynged,
yif thou sest a litil byrde in the skie,
thou shalt knowen, hit flies to thee,
myne luf is a bire
yif a breth stroketh thyne haire,
thou shalt knowen, hit is with thee,
myne desir is a reine
yif the droppes fallen on thyne face,
thou shalt knowen, they art teres of myne yerninge for thee.

In luf everlastinge, Elisabeth

Hannah's heart pounded. Thanks to three semesters' worth of Middle High German, she had understood the text. It was a love poem, signed by someone named Elisabeth.

So, *Hannah mused,* there was a woman in love with the poor Templar knight.

Suddenly she heard footsteps in the hallway. Hastily she shoved the objects back into the bag and pushed it aside. Heisenberg scampered into the room and sprang onto her bed. He tried to curl up on the cloak, but then drew back to examine the flecks of blood on the quilted sweater. The boy had followed the cat, and stood at the door, rooted to the spot, staring at the dried blood. Hannah saw him fighting back tears. She strode toward him and held him tightly.

"Everything will be fine," she said, stroking his back as he sobbed softly into her sweater.

After she had calmed him a little, she moved aside the clothing on the bed, sat down, and, patting the space on the mattress next to her, motioned to Matthäus to join her. As he sat down, she put her arm around his shoulders in a motherly gesture. He nestled into the crook of her arm, not daring to look at her.

"Matthäus," she began carefully, "is Sir Gerard ... is he your father?"

The boy looked up in surprise, then shook his head emphatically. "No," he said defensively, as if she had insulted him, "he is my lord."

Well, that certainly cleared things up. "Where is your home?" she asked again.

The boy hesitated. "I'm not allowed to talk about it," he said softly. "I don't know you well. You might try to harm us."

"Would you allow an enemy to put an arm around you?" Hannah asked earnestly.

At this, he shifted away slightly and looked at the ground sheepishly.

"You can trust me, Matthäus. You don't still think I'm evil, do you?"

"You let those strange men carry my lord away, and I still don't know *where* they went! He might be dead, or ..." Tears welled up in his eyes again.

"Hey, Matthäus," Hannah comforted the boy, "your lord isn't dead. He was injured, and we had to take him to the hospital. If you want, we'll visit him today."

As he looked up at her, his blue eyes were filled with hope.

Unexpectedly, her mobile phone, which lay on a dresser in the hallway, started ringing. The boy recoiled as if he had been attacked.

"Don't panic, it's okay," she reassured him quickly, squeezing his arm. "Don't move. I'll be right back," she ordered as she picked up her phone.

"St. Agnes Hospital in Wittlich," a female voice buzzed in her ear. "Hello, may I speak to Ms. Schreyber?"

"Yes, speaking. Who is this?"

"My name's Weidner. I'm the senior physician on duty in the emergency ward. Ms. Schreyber, please come to the ward immediately. We had a few problems with your husband this morning."

"Problems?" It took a moment for Hannah to even realize what husband she was referring to.

"It's nothing serious," the woman at the other end of the line reassured her. "He's regained consciousness, and all his vital functions are stable. Unfortunately, when he woke up, he became agitated and attacked a nurse. We had to give him a sedative shot. I'd like to speak to you about our next course of action."

"I'll come right away," Hannah said.

"Please bring him underwear, a set of pajamas, and some toiletries, too," added the physician before she hung up.

Hannah was glad that she had kept most of her father's clothes after his death. He was a tall, stately man, and she was sure that his black sweat-suit would fit the Templar perfectly.

A little later, Hannah was sitting in her car with the boy by her side, and the sweat-suit, underwear, a pair of slippers, and striped pajamas in a duffel bag in the trunk.

Along the way, she had to stop several times for Matthäus to be carsick. The color of his face reminded her of an unripe green tomato. When they reached the hospital, she quickly pulled the boy out of the car. Heaving violently, he threw up noisily in the roadside ditch.

Pull yourself together, my dear, *she pleaded in her head.*

Thankfully, the fresh air seemed to help him. Casually, Hannah retrieved the duffel from the trunk then, with a click of her keys, she locked the car. The boy recoiled at the noise, and Hannah felt another wave of sympathy for him.

She took him by the hand and flashed him a brave smile. "Listen up, little one, there's a lot you have to get used to, but I'm in the same boat. We can do it together, I promise. Come on, let's go!"

Nodding timidly, the boy let her lead the way to the hospital.

At a kiosk, Hannah bought some mineral water and offered it to the boy, placing the bottle to his lips as if she were feeding a toddler.

"It's just water," she reassured him.

The cashier stared at them in bewilderment, but said nothing.

After a gray-haired receptionist had signed her in to the psychiatric ward, Hannah followed a muscular male nurse down the stairs to the hospital's basement, clutching the duffel bag in one hand and the boy's hand in the other. She had never felt this nervous before.

At the end of the long hallway, Doctor Weidner, the head physician, greeted them with a stilted smile. Directing them to a closed ward, she warned Hannah that the patient had been sedated.

"You'll understand the precautions we took. Your husband not only attacked a nurse, but ripped out his catheter, too. We're extremely lucky that the drainage bag wasn't full, or he could have seriously injured himself."

Hannah glanced into the room through a double window. The bearded man lay motionless on a hospital bed, strapped down with wide leather bands across his feet, torso, and chest. The nurses had replaced the catheter, which was connected to a discharge bag fastened to the side of the bed.

Hannah looked down at Matthäus who seemed to be frozen.

With determination in her voice, she turned to the doctor. "We would like to visit him alone. I hope that won't be a problem."

"Not a problem as long as you don't mind us keeping your husband restrained. While he's a patient in our hospital, we're responsible for his behavior."

"I understand," Hannah sighed.

Still clutching Matthäus's hand tightly, Hannah approached the man nervously. The way he was lying on his back, with his arms and legs stretched out, he reminded Hannah vaguely of famous sculptures of knights from medieval sarcophagi.

They had almost reached the bed when Matthäus broke free from Hannah's grasp and flung himself at his lord, laying his head on his breast. Tears streamed down his eyes when he realized that his companion was beginning to stir.

The boy raised his head excitedly and whispered something Hannah couldn't understand. The Templar cracked open his bleary eyes and she thought she saw a thin smile on his dry lips. He moved his mouth. It sounded to Hannah as if he was speaking French.

"Tell him you're doing well," Hannah said to the boy, touching his arm. "Tell him we'll bring him to my house by tomorrow, okay?"

As if in slow motion, Gerard de Breydenbach turned his head to face her and blinked as if he were looking at her through a fog. Hannah summoned all her courage and stepped forward, a mixture of curiosity and fear ran through her as she stood before the stranger. Despite all her conflicting emotions, she couldn't tear her eyes away and he stared back at her silently. Apart from his unbelievably blue eyes, he looked like any guy on the street. *A pretty good-looking guy on the street*, she corrected herself unwittingly, *even if he is rather pale*.

"The squire?" His lips formed the words softly. Hannah didn't know what he meant, but then saw that his gaze, filled with concern, had fallen on Matthäus. She gripped the man's large, warm hand and squeezed it in sympathy.

"He's with me. I'm taking care of him. You'll be with him again tomorrow. You just have to do me a favor and keep calm, no matter what happens. Trust me – please!" she pleaded.

234

If it had been up to her, she would have taken him home immediately, but it was probably smarter to let him be taken by an ambulance tomorrow, giving her time to take a few precautions. Above all else, she had to call Tom as soon as possible. She still hadn't heard from him, and she was becomingly increasingly worried that something had happened to him.

Taking Matthäus's hand, she led the boy reluctantly out of the room. When they reached the door, he looked back longingly.

Out in the hallway, Hannah made it clear to Dr. Weidner that she wanted her husband – she was surprised how easily the word rolled off her tongue – to be transported to her house the following day. The doctor protested, but quickly fell silent when Hannah added that she couldn't afford any more medical bills.

With an odd smirk, a nurse handed Hannah a small blue bag containing the knight's scuffed leather pants and rough spun underpants.

"We had to remove this." The doctor held out an unadorned cross of Lorraine hanging on a braided leather cord. Gingerly, Hannah took the necklace and examined the silver cross. Struck by a feeling of reverence, she stowed it away in her coat pocket.

CHAPTER 19

Investigation

Monday, November 15, 2004

Suffering from yet another migraine, Professor Dietmar Hagen reached for the open aspirin bottle on his mahogany desk. His hands trembled as he washed down two tablets with a tall glass of water.

Through his office window, he saw an army vehicle approaching. Colonel Pelham, the commander of the Spangdahlem Airbase; General Lafour, the NSA Representative for Europe; and military attaché Major Dan Simmens were coming back from their lunch break. Hagen was still fuming from yesterday's unsuccessful inquiry. He was certain that Stevendahl and Colbach had lied and was all too eager to discuss how to track down the transported people with the three representatives.

He would have loved to begin the search himself, but unfortunately, his American employers had to approve every action he took in this affair, a constraint that the headstrong professor found utterly abhorrent. He hadn't even told his Lebanese informant about the results of his experiments. The nature of this debacle demanded that the fewer people that knew anything, the better. It was impossible to imagine what would happen if further artifacts fell into the hands of an Arab terrorist group. Nor was Hagen interested in working with the Israelis. Not only would they meddle in everything, but they would also strip him unceremoniously of permission for further research, and get into an argument with the Palestinians about territorial claims. No, things were fine as they were. And if possible, nothing about that should change.

Hagen squared his shoulders when the door to his office opened. He had to be careful about what he told Colonel Pelham. He could not afford the vigilant officer developing any suspicions that Hagen was responsible for what had happened.

General Lafour was the first to enter the office. A small, hunched, white-haired man in a beige colored trench coat followed, a laptop bag hanging off his frail shoulder.

The general greeted the professor quickly and introduced the elderly man as the renowned historian, Professor Moshe Hertzberg, from the University of California at Berkeley. The specialist in medieval history had been brought in by the NSA to evaluate the historical artifacts. His specialization, however, was the code of conduct of the Assassins and their effects on the crusaders.

Hagen ushered his guests to a round table at the far end of his office, where Dr. Baxter, another representative from the Pentagon, and the three officers awaited them. After Dr. Piglet had closed the surveillance-proof door behind himself, Hagen sat down.

"So, Professor, how shall we begin?" Major Simmens looked at Hagen expectantly.

"Why are you asking me?" Hagen asked indignantly.

"You *are* the project's leader, after all." Simmens sounded surprised. "I have to write *something* in my report to Washington. The accident will already cost the American taxpayers more than two billion dollars. We can't just come up with that sort of money out of thin air, especially with our present obligations in Iraq."

"As I see it," Colonel Pelham added, "it is less a question of money than of security. No one has been able to explain how the accident happened, and whether Stevendahl and Colbach caused it intentionally. It's definitely possible that they were responsible, but I cannot fathom why they would have manipulated the equipment at that specific moment on Saturday," Pelham said with a pointed look at Hagen.

"They just couldn't wait to transfer a person," the professor answered quickly. "You know how these ambitious young scientists are. They're bloodhounds, always on the hunt, latching onto whatever they catch a whiff of."

Pelham narrowed his eyes. He had a feeling the professor had just come up with that on the spot.

"But the most important thing," Hagen added hurriedly, "is that we are doing damage control. As Dr. Baxter explained, at least one person was transferred even if Stevendahl and Colbach claim they didn't see anything. Surely you can understand that it is in our interests to track this person down immediately."

"I have a completely different question," Simmens declared, peering at Hagen. "What would it mean if we could understand how the people were transferred? Didn't you just tell me that we were years away from accomplishing this?"

Hagen cleared his throat impatiently. "I'm afraid I cannot answer that question yet, Major. First, I'd have to find out how those two pulled it off."

"And when you *do* find out? Who will you transfer next? Jesus Christ or Genghis Khan?"

In the seat next to Hagen, Professor Hertzberg leaned forward with curiosity and watched Major Simmens with gleaming black eyes.

"What are you talking about?" Hagen asked testily.

"I just think the President would be far more interested in the implications of the transfer than how much the damage cost," Simmens stated plainly.

"Tell your President he can rest easy. As long as I'm in charge, nothing will be carried out that hasn't been approved by him beforehand."

"As God as your witness," Simmens quipped. "Although … after everything I've seen here, I'm doubting more and more that God even exists."

"Careful, there," Hagen smirked. "Don't let your boss hear that. He's a God-fearing man."

"I think we have more pressing problems at the moment." Colonel Pelham's gaze swept across the table and settled on Professor Hertzberg. "What about the guy roaming about our streets? What damage could he have done so far?"

The weedy man smiled mysteriously. "Well, gentlemen," he began in an unusually high voice, "I'm not claiming that I have any experience with a situation quite like this, but I'm sure you'll understand that my heart has been racing since I entered this room. When has a historian ever had the chance to look into the eyes of a living person from the distant past?"

Hagen gripped the historian's arm as he looked at Major Simmens. "As you may have inferred from the briefings, dear sir, I'm afraid we can't just offer you the man on a silver platter right now. My assistant, Dr. Baxter, has sent the sword for analysis, to find out who the owner could be. Who knows how many lunatics are wandering around claiming to be from another time? It is vital that you help us to catch the right person."

"Although it may be difficult," Hertzberg said enthusiastically, "we have to put ourselves in the shoes of a knight from the early fourteenth century, and imagine what he would do first."

"He was surely a man skilled in battle," General Lafour added with a grave expression, trying to steer the meeting in the right direction. "Judging by the fact that he was carrying a sword."

"First, we have to consider the danger this person could present to the public," Major Simmens pointed out. "He might have more weapons on him. If there's anything we can't afford, it's publicity."

"I wouldn't worry too much about it," General Lafour responded. "We have madmen threatening people with swords in our time, too. Actually, we'd be lucky if the man committed a crime and was arrested by the German authorities. If he used a sword, his face would be splashed across the papers the next morning – even better if he claims to have come from the fourteenth century. All we'll have to do is to pick him up from the asylum."

"That may be true," Professor Hertzberg remarked with a smile, "but it'd be wise not to underestimate him. Most people think that our ancestors were inferior to us in intelligence and inventiveness. I can only say that assumption is patently false. If anything, the opposite is true. Even if not everyone could read or write, the vast majority of the population was downright linguistically gifted, and because of all the different currencies and units of measurement they had, they could do mental math extremely well. Despite the lack of modern transportation, you'd be surprised at the number of medieval people who were remarkably well traveled. There were the pilgrim routes to Santiago di Compostella, not to mention the Crusades. And they used the positions of the sun and stars for direction. They also had a sophisticated mail system."

Hagen had become restless. "With all due respect, Professor, your reflections are not particularly useful, even if they are enlightening. We should be directing our attention to Stevendahl and Colbach. What if they actually did see something and helped the transferred people escape?"

"Why would they have done that?" Pelham asked. "Didn't you claim that they intentionally transferred people?"

"Let me correct myself," Hagen answered emphatically. "Maybe they were out of their depth and transferred the people unintentionally, then got cold feet when they arrived, and hid them."

"I'll take care of that," General Lafour announced. "We can easily search and bug their houses and have them followed at all times."

"Good," Hagen said with satisfaction. "By the way, I've instructed my assistant, Dr. Piglet, to prepare a breakdown of the total extent of the damage," he said to Major Simmens. "We'll have a complete report by tomorrow at the latest."

"Thank you, Professor Hagen," Simmens replied. "I'm sure the matter is safe in General Lafour's hands. And I am confident that with the support of your investigation team and Professor Hertzberg, we'll soon have results we can use."

As the men rose, Pelham turned to Hagen. "We're having coffee in the clubhouse. Care to join us?"

Hagen shook his head. "I still have things to do," he said.

"Relax, Professor." Colonel Pelham hadn't missed the disappointment in Hagen's voice and gave him a friendly clap on the shoulder. "I was a little faster than the rest of them. Since yesterday afternoon, our forces have been observing your two employees. NSA agents will take over the case once they are operational. I've also taken DNA samples from Stevendahl's and Colbach's cars. Dr. Baxter will share the results with you. We'll find out if they've hidden anyone. If they really are guilty, the noose will only tighten."

CHAPTER 20

Bed and Breakfast

Monday, November 15, 2004

That evening Tom informed Hannah from a payphone that he and Paul had been suspended from duty and were henceforth effectively under arrest as the investigation team had found incriminating evidence that a transfer had taken place. Tom, however, didn't want to tell her what the evidence was, fearing that their call would be wiretapped if the conversation lasted too long.

He had temporarily moved in with Paul at his bachelor pad in Vianden. Since yesterday afternoon, vehicles had been parked in front of his Luxembourgian colleague's front door, perpetually occupied by two men who left only for a change in shifts. The only way Tom could leave the house to call Hannah was by using a secret route.

He told Hannah that he suspected that the National Security Agency was behind this – the American foreign intelligence agency. Equipped with the latest technology, not even the smallest details escaped these agents.

And so, Hannah was left to deal with the two time travelers alone.

The doorbell rang. Hannah's heart raced when she glanced through the window and saw the ambulance that had just brought Templar to her home. On her way to the door, she hastily rearranged her long, dark red hair in front of the small mirror hanging in the hallway, and smoothed the light green woolen fabric of her sweater over her gently curved hips.

One of the paramedics gave her a quick nod in greeting, when she opened the front door. "Where should we put him?" he asked, panting for breath.

The Templar lay calmly on the stretcher with his eyes shut. He was wearing the black sweat-suit that she had given the hospital staff for him to wear. He was still strapped down. Perhaps Hannah's prayers had actually been heard, or perhaps they had given him another sedative shot before leaving the hospital.

"I'll lead the way," she answered, guiding the two paramedics down the narrow hallway into the bedroom. She had prepared everything – as much as she possibly could. She had decided to put her new guest on the ground floor, so that he would have no problem finding the bathroom. The boy, on the other hand, could sleep in the guestroom upstairs, and she would camp on the couch in the living room until she found a better solution.

The paramedics set the stretcher down on a stand next to Hannah's bed and removed the Velcro straps.

"Can he stand up?" Hannah's eyes darted nervously to the supposedly unconscious man.

"Don't worry, we've got this," said the doctor, a man in his mid-fifties with a gray beard, glancing curiously at the unusual clothing covering one of the closet doors. To put her new guest at ease, Hannah had washed and ironed his impressive cloak and hung it up on the closet. She had mended the torn, quilted sweater, and the long, linen shirt the night before and had carefully laid them out with the chain mail and gloves on the dresser. Even his handcrafted boots stood, brightly polished, in front of the dresser. Of course she hadn't forgotten his knife-belt that held the dagger, although she had decided to hide it under the clothing.

The doctor turned to his patient. "Hello, can you hear me? We're here. You can stand up now. Can you manage?"

The Templar blinked. His gaze fell on the cloak, and more quickly than the people around him had anticipated, he got up. But then he started to sway, and held his head.

Hannah held his elbow and led him to her bed to sit down. To her surprise, he didn't protest. Although he was only in socks, he was a good deal taller than she was.

Suddenly, Matthäus appeared. Not caring who saw him, he threw himself at his lord and hugged him so tightly that the Templar staggered. The boy buried his face on the man's broad chest and began to sob.

With trembling hands, the stranger drew the boy into his embrace and held him tightly. He shut his eyes and kissed the boy tenderly on the head.

"Ah …" the doctor coughed awkwardly as he looked at Hannah, who stood with tears in her eyes, moved by her guests' reunion. "We'll be going now. Could you sign the bill, please?"

Hannah laid the paper on the dresser and scrawled her signature distractedly.

After she had escorted the doctor and the paramedics to the door, she returned to the bedroom with her heart pounding. The boy was sitting next to his companion, jiggling his legs cheerfully and looking up at her expectantly. His lord was staring at the floor with his head propped in his hands.

Hannah struggled to think of something to say. The early afternoon sunlight streamed through the patio door, bathing the room in a warm light. Suddenly, the newcomer raised his head and looked at her with a defiant glare, his blue eyes clear as glass.

Hannah lowered her eyes, finding her gaze unintentionally fixed on his broad, muscular throat. For some reason, she thought about what a beheading in the Middle Ages must have been like.

Suddenly she heard a deep, firm voice, and jumped.

"Wher are we? Wher is myn armes? What have ye to doone with the Hospitallers? Is there a manne in the house? Are ye free, or a servaunt?"

It sounded like an interrogation. Time after time, he shot the questions at her and, in vain, Hannah tried to hold his commanding stare. She wasn't sure if she had understood everything he was saying, but she was too stunned to answer him. The man's speech was different from the language of the great poets and bards who she had studied. It sounded far less stilted, more natural somehow, and yet peculiar. And who on earth were the Hospitallers?

With two long strides, the Templar was at her side. Instinctively, Hannah drew back. A large hand darted out towards her; strong fingers encircled her left arm mercilessly and began to shake her roughly. A torrent of words gushed over her, but she felt as if she were paralyzed, unable to understand, let alone answer.

As Hannah tried to free herself from his painful grip, he quickly grabbed her hair with his other hand.

"Nay womman, it is not as ye thinketh!" An ironic laugh followed his words.

Ruthlessly, he turned her head around so that she was forced to look into his intensively blue eyes, which were sparkling dangerously. His chiseled face was etched with an expression both unyielding and reckless. Afraid yet fascinated, she stared at his curved mouth and flawless teeth. *Strange*, she thought, why had she always thought that the people of the Middle Ages had rotten teeth?

"Telleth me now wher we art and who youre maister is!"

Her heart began to race and tears welled up in her eyes. Still, no words came to her lips.

"Speke, womman, or I shal lere thee what it is to disobeye a Lordes kinghte!" Again, the Templar tightened his grip and pulled her hair to emphasize his commands.

Despite her shock and fear, Hannah noticed that he had switched seamlessly from the formal *ye* to the informal *thou or thee* – an unmistakable sign that even he realized that his disrespectful behavior didn't deserve a courtly salutation.

The boy sprang up and clung onto the Templar's arm.

"Leve hir be!" he begged. "She did me wele, herestow me? I praye ye. Sestow not that ye hurt hir?" He pleaded with eyes that could melt the coldest of hearts.

Scowling, his lord loosened his grip, and, with a disdainful grunt, he finally let her go.

"I knowe not what she didde to be werthy of thine bolde wordes for hir, weleful as she is … bot yif min squier desyreth hit," he muttered sullenly.

Gasping for breath, Hannah dragged herself to the patio door to catch some fresh air.

The crusader followed closely after her as if he had sensed her intention to escape. She felt his hot breath on her neck.

"Thinke nat that thou canst scape bifore thou hast answered myne demandes," he hissed.

Then he seized her arm again, spun her around and backed her against the wall, pressing his ribcage uncomfortably against her chest. To look him in the eye, she had to tilt her head back. Invitingly, he raised his perfectly formed eyebrows.

Hannah summoned her courage and her senses, and tried to come up with a halfway logical sentence.

"I have no gilt of youre situation, I cannot chaungen that ye are here and I know nat how thou have comen here," she stammered, in her nervousness choking on her own words.

He looked at her in bewilderment. Loosening his grip, he stepped back from her so that she could breathe again.

"Why spekest thou so straungeli?"

Jesus, did she have to tell him the story about time travel now? Her fear gave way to annoyance. Clumsily, she pushed him aside and went to the

244

dresser, on top of which was lying an old calendar. She beckoned to him. As he stood at her side, she pointed to the numbers and the words on the calendar, making sure that he was following her index finger with his eyes.

"There! You see?" she said, almost triumphantly. "November 2004!"

He looked at her as if she had lost her mind.

Sighing, Hannah took his leather bag that was lying on the dresser. She wanted to show him his documents stating he was from the year 1307, clarifying the difference from the year 2004.

Noticing what she was doing, he seized her hand and pulled her away from the bag. His murderous glower was unmistakable. He obviously had no tolerance for anyone touching his things. Hannah hoped fearfully that he wouldn't open the bag himself and discover that she had already looked through his belongings.

But suddenly he shoved her to the door and ordered her to leave the room. There was nothing Hannah would have loved to do more, and so she obeyed his order with a sigh of relief.

She walked into the kitchen, took a glass from the cupboard, and filled it to the brim with the expensive Cabernet Sauvignon that she had drunk with Tom on Saturday. She was trembling so badly that she had to hold the glass with both hands to bring it to her lips.

Moments later she heard noises, and, stepping into the hallway, she almost bumped into the Templar. He stood upright, fully dressed just as she had first seen him, only now his cloak, freshly washed and pressed, lent him a striking dignity. Immediately, her eyes were drawn to the long dagger that hung on his knife belt.

Gero could sense his hostess's fear. For a moment he enjoyed the advantage he had over her, but then sympathy set in. She reminded him in a painful way of his deceased wife. After all, he was a man of honor, and he already felt sorry that he had treated her so roughly, especially since she seemed to know neither what he was talking about nor what he wanted from her.

Even if he couldn't find his comrades, Gero at least wanted his sword and his horse back. Matthäus had told him that the woman had her own horse, which stood outside in a shed in front of the house. Gero guessed that it wouldn't be too difficult to borrow it, for his squire had also informed him that she was a free, unmarried woman who lived on the farm alone. Nonetheless, he felt obliged to ask her permission instead of simply marching into the stable and riding off on it.

Before he began to speak, he coughed a little to clear his throat and made an effort to look directly into her beautiful green eyes.

"As thou maist see, I am a knight of the Templers, and I can demaunde youre helpe in neede for to fyghten the foes of Christyanytee. Say, womman, wher is thyne hors?"

The woman looked at him in confusion. Obviously, she had not understood his request, and she didn't seem particularly impressed to be standing before a knight of the Order, either.

She shook her head in disbelief. "The horse cannot be ridden," she said simply, in a dialect that he had never heard before.

Gero was annoyed. The woman didn't seem as if she wanted to help him. He felt foolishly reliant on her help, for he hadn't the faintest idea what had happened since escaping from the Lombards.

Very well, Gero thought. If she wouldn't help him, thenMatthäus would. He obviously knew his way around the house and farm. Gero waved to his squire, and, without a second glance at the woman, he opened the door and stepped outside.

As Hannah hurried behind the Templar and the boy, she saw them running to the stable. She stopped and crossed her arms in annoyance. *Okay, you stubborn fool*, she thought, *you'll soon see what you're in for.*

Patiently, she sat down in front of her cottage on a light blue wooden bench. She watched as the knight and his squire saddled the horse. Mona, a usually well-behaved mare that she had saved from the slaughterhouse a few years ago had never been ridden. *Great, I'll finally get to watch a real rodeo*, she thought with a smirk. The sun shone warmly on her face, and for the first time that day, she relaxed a little.

To her astonishment, however, Mona allowed the knight to put the reins on her, and didn't even protest when the Templar led her out of the enclosure. He checked the saddle confidently, speaking to the animal in his deep voice the whole time. Finally, in preparation for mounting the horse, he arranged the stirrups. Hannah sprang to her feet, ready to persuade them that it was not a good idea to leave the farm on their own.

Suddenly even the chirping birds fell silent. The Templar pursed his lips as he tried to make out where a distant rumble was coming from. Without warning, a sustained, sharp buzz broke the midday idyll. Then thunder followed. Two enormous black shadows raced across the sky. The mare balked, rising high on her hind legs, and bolted for the forest, alarmed more by the Templar who had suddenly flung the reins away in shock, than the noise, which she had long gotten used to. The knight and his squire stared mutely into the blue sky, following the two F-16 Fighting Falcons with their mouths wide open.

Hannah simply covered her ears and observed her guests as a second pair of fighter jets followed the first, thundering overhead.

As a second pair of jets sliced through the sky, Gero lunged toward Matthäus and hid the boy under his own body protectively. The two of them landed in a large, muddy puddle. Gero remained in place for a moment longer, until he thought that the danger was gone. His heart raced, his ears hurt, and fear had pooled sweat on his forehead. Even when the noise had long faded away, he wondered whether it wouldn't be better to stay low for a while longer. A shadow fell over his line of vision, and, after a short moment of hesitation, he decided to stand up. Crouching, Matthäus gasped for breath. The brown water in the puddle had dyed the boy's blonde hair dark. Slowly, with his heart still beating wildly, Gero turned around and saw the woman, who appeared unruffled, showing no sign of fear, but the way she was bent over him with concern sent him into a rage. What did she imagine? Did she think she was a heroine and he a coward?

"Milady," he spat, "it may liste oure Lord to sende me to helle, withouten raisouns. Bot I wod knowen why he hast senden me you as aungel!"

Hannah stared at him in bewilderment. How did he ever get the idea that she was his guardian angel? She had to stop herself from grinning. Her guests were soaked to the bone, and the proud knight's face was splattered with dirt, making his eyes appear even bluer than usual.

She stretched out her hand to help him up, but he ignored her kind gesture. Matthäus blinked in confusion. Mona had returned and trotted back towards her enclosure.

"Thou maist followe the example of myne horse," Hannah said snidely as she guided Mona to the stable, leaving the knight and his squire to their own devices.

"I'll draw a bath for both of you,' she announced when she returned a little later. To her astonishment, there was no protest.

"Matthäus!" Gero held back the boy's arm before he could follow the woman into the room next to the hallway. "Did she tell you where we are?"

"No, I can only say that she was friendly to me," the boy whispered with a mysterious expression. "She is beautiful, don't you think? She looks like Mother Mary! Do you think we're in heaven?" He looked at Gero with wide, innocent eyes.

"Nonsense," Gero snapped in annoyance.

This couldn't be paradise. Not with those menacing birds in the sky. He stroked his squire's damp, dirty hair and tried to give him a reassuring smile.

"We'll soon find out where we are, and as long as I am with you, nothing bad will happen to you, I promise."

"Whatever the case, she is a rich woman," Matthäus said, peering at the door behind which she had disappeared. "She has a tub, much lovelier than one in a bathhouse. And the water comes out of her walls. Warm and cold, however you like. You have to see it."

Gero hadn't missed the boy's enthusiasm for their hostess's possessions. The massive sugar bowl and silver spoon, the fine glass, and the elegant crockery had impressed him, too. But as long as they didn't know where they were, and to whom the land belonged, Gero did not feel that he could assess this woman's fortune and social standing. Perhaps she was a rich widow, or a prostitute who took silver from the pockets of influential men.

"Does she wash one's back like the maidens in the bathhouse?" Gero teased.

"No," Matthäus cried, sounding outraged. Despite his troubles, Gero smirked. "She always knocks and asks if she may enter, and if you say yes, she comes in and asks if you need anything. But she has never touched me."

Gero heard water splashing. Matthäus was obviously right. The woman hadn't left the room to fetch anything. Maybe she really had a well that led directly into the house.

The boy took his hand and pulled him toward the half-open door. The room was filled with an unfamiliar but pleasant smell. Unwillingly he followed his squire. As he stepped through the door, he saw the woman bent over a large, white gleaming tub, pouring something into it that began to foam in the water immediately. Was he in a witch's kitchen? He glanced around. The white tiles that adorned all the walls looked like polished glass. His gaze returned to his hostess, landing by accident on her magnificent backside.

Yet, as she turned around and smiled at him, he instantly rejected the suspicion that she could be the devil's assistant.

"I'm almost done," she said in her strange, foreign dialect.

Hesitantly, he let her pull him further into the room. *This has to be witchcraft*, he thought. It was cold outside, but in here it was warm as a summer's day, even though there was neither a fireplace nor stove in sight.

"Doffen youre clothing. I shall wasshe them for you." The woman gave him an encouraging look.

But before he could respond she had already left the room. His gaze followed her with disbelief. Matthäus brushed past him and sat on the edge of the tub. He put his hand into the water, and splashed it about.

"Sir, it's wonderfully warm! Look!" The boy pointed to a metallic pipe that protruded from the smooth, polished wall. Water poured out of it like a fountain.

"Dear Mary, help me understand this," Gero mouthed silently.

Perhaps it was wise to react as Matthäus had, accepting with childish joy all these inexplicable wonders, as long as they weren't unpleasant. Cautiously, the Templar looked around, his eyes falling on a small trough filled with water and connected to the wall. It appeared to be made of the same smooth, snow-white material as the tub.

Matthäus, who had been watching him, sprang up and walked to the strange object.

"That's a toilet!" he said happily. *And*, Gero thought, *a little too insolently*. "Look, you can sit here, and after you've done what you need, you press this lever, and …"

Water rushed into the trough, and Gero took a step back in shock. His squire had already turned away and was fiddling with a small white roll coiled around a narrow, metal rod on the wall.

"And this!" the boy cried triumphantly, his blue eyes gleaming like he had found treasure. "You'll never guess, sir, what this could be …"

With a hasty sideways glance, Gero tried to figure out what on earth Matthäus meant, annoyed that he had let himself be pulled into the boy's little games.

"It's paper," the boy stated confidently with a precocious expression. Then he narrowed his eyes and added in a conspiratorial whisper, "They clean their bottoms with it. And their noses! And their mouths after they eat. Can you believe that?"

"All at once?" Gero raised an eyebrow.

"No!" Matthäus responded impatiently. "One after the other. They use a new piece or even several each time. Pure white paper, as soft as a down feather."

As Matthäus waved the roll about in the air, a long strip broke loose, fluttering down before him like a tired flag.

"I've never seen anything like it," he enthused. "Have you? Here, touch it!" His squire's voice cracked with excitement.

Gero stared speechlessly at the white roll that the boy was holding out to him. Matthäus plucked at individual sheets and let them drift to the floor.

Without a word, Gero left the room. Outside in the hallway, he leaned against the wall, breathing heavily and nervously running his hand over his damp hair and neck.

When he turned around, he almost bumped into the woman who was carrying a stack of towels on her arm and smiling at him cheerfully.

"I stere that ye tak solaas firste, and thanne we shal attempte to speke skylfully." Hannah hoped that the Templar would realize from her friendly tone that she meant him well.

She touched his arm gently. He didn't resist, but instead let her nudge him back into the bathroom. She laid the sweat-suit on the chair next to the tub and handed Matthäus something different to wear. The clothes she had ordered for the boy from a catalog would arrive by tomorrow. Meanwhile, the knight could help himself to her dead father's clothing.

"Here, this is for you," she said, holding out a new toothbrush to the man. He hesitated for a moment, deciding whether he should take it.

Before he could make a decision, Matthäus stepped forward and took the toothbrush from her hand. He smiled knowingly at his lord. Then he turned the bristles to and fro and bared his small teeth.

"It's a miswak …" he mumbled through his clenched teeth. "But you don't have to soak it in water and chew on it before you can use it," he added, smiling thankfully at Hannah.

The lord didn't seem to share his squire's joy. His expression remained opaque, and Hannah chose to leave them alone. Closing the door behind her, she took a deep breath and headed to the kitchen, intending to offer the two of them something to eat after their bath.

Dear God, what were you thinking when you let Tom and his accomplices build this terrible time machine? *she thought to herself.* Tom!

She paused and turned to a small cupboard in the hallway where her cell-phone was.

In the living room, she let herself sink into her cozy sofa. Feeling slightly more relaxed, she propped her feet on the coffee table and dialed Tom's number.

"Hannah!" he sounded stressed.

"Thank God, Tom! I'm glad I could reach you."

"Hannah, you shouldn't call me on my private cellphone. I'll call you as soon as I can. Is the parcel there?"

"Parcel?" Suddenly, she realized that their call might be tapped.

"The parcel arrived today," she replied, slightly ironically.

"Already?" She could hear Tom's surprise. "And were the contents all right?"

"Don't worry, it's all for the best."

"Hannah, I'll fix everything as soon as I can."

"I know."

"That's why I love you …"

"Tom?" she asked, but he had already hung up.

"You have to pull the lever up," Matthäus said after his lord had stepped out of the water and looped a towel around his haunch. He now stood in front of the mirror at the basin to shave.

How does my squire know more than I do? Gero thought in annoyance. When the water shot out of the tap, he drew back instinctively. Quickly, he figured out how to regulate the strength of the stream without being splashed from head to toe. He picked up the piece of soap by the edge of the sink and moistened his face and neck with the foam that smelled of sandalwood. Then he shaved off the stray hair under his chin and along his neck with his parrying dagger. For a moment, he wondered whether he should shave off his beard altogether, but then his pride won. After all, a neat, trimmed beard was to a Templar like a tonsure to a monk.

Hannah recoiled in shock as a large black shadow appeared in the kitchen's doorframe. The statuesque Templar was neatly shaved. He smelled of soap and was wearing the black sweat-suit. Matthäus appeared behind him, looking significantly more cheerful than his lord.

"Tell your lord I've made something for you to eat," Hannah smiled, hoping that this announcement would lighten the mood.

Matthäus looked pleased, but his companion wasn't as enthusiastic. His gaze swept across the various apparatuses in her kitchen with interest, and he approached her very cautiously.

Involuntarily, Hannah drew back. What looked like an apologetic smile crossed his face.

"Womman …" he said hesitantly, " … what is thine name?"

"Hannah … um … Schreyber, with a 'y'," she answered.

"Hannah …?" he paused, looking at her face and her long hair. "Hannah, speke, wher art we? I praye thee."

She thought she saw him give the slightest of bows. "Let's have a drink first. Do you like red wine?"

He nodded although he looked skeptical. Secretly amused at his baffled expression, Hannah uncorked a bottle of Bordeaux and filled two glasses. Matthäus looked at the wine longingly, but Hannah shook her head.

"You're too young for that," she told him in a stern voice, handing him a glass of apple juice that he took without protest.

"Ye art in the Eifel, in Duchelond – hou ye have cummen here is a longe storie to tellen!" She brushed past the astonished knight, who was still examining the delicate glass she had handed him, and motioned for him to follow her into the living room.

Hannah sat down on a couch and he followed her lead uncertainly. She had taken a Middle High German dictionary from her shelf and with this dictionary, a bit of Latin, her ancestors' Moselle Franconian dialect, and a good dose of empathy, she hoped to explain the situation to the clueless man.

"Ande? Hou ben ye clepid?" she asked him bluntly, although she had long known his name from his belongings.

The Templar cleared his throat. "I am Gerard of Breydenbach, yongest sone of the noble Richard of Breydenbach, knight of the archbishop of Trier. Calle me Gero, yif thou liketh."

"Gero," Hannah repeated, tasting the word on her tongue, and raised her glass in a toast. She drank a hasty gulp of wine. Involuntarily her gaze fell on his expressive mouth.

Two bowls of lentil soup and a solid four hours later, she had made enough progress for him to at least accept the unfathomable concept of time travel. As far as she could tell, he was a highly educated man. By chance, she had discovered that he was able to converse with his squire in three different languages, Middle High German, Latin, and something

252

that sounded vaguely like French. She was astonished at how quickly he had been able to adjust to her utterly unique version of Middle High German. He told her that he was twenty-seven years old, which made him five years younger than she was. He had been in the Order of the Temple for six years, and, as Hannah had already guessed, came from a noble family whose castle – or what was left of it – was only twenty minutes away from her house.

The more he spoke, the better she understood what he meant to say, and she was beginning to interpret his words immediately into modern German.

"Can everyone here drive wagons without horses? Or fly, and even travel through time if and when they please? What was the Lord thinking when he gave the people here such power?" Gero asked, standing in front of the patio window. Dusk had just fallen and, as the sky began to dim, the lights outside the house automatically switched on.

"People have been driving cars and flying for a long time now," Hannah responded, "but time travel is something entirely new."

"Why … why me? Why the boy?" Gero looked at Matthäus, who was sitting on the floor playing with the cat.

To see the despair in his eyes was almost unbearable. How could she answer his question?

"I don't know," she said truthfully. "I really don't know."

Naturally the Templar wanted to know who was responsible for his misfortune, and Hannah had been careless enough to mention Tom's name. Seeing the resentment in his eyes, she regretted not blaming God or the devil instead of telling the truth.

"Is he your husband?" Gero asked.

"We were engaged," she said in a tone that was harsher than she intended. Nervously, she twirled a lock of her hair around her finger. "But he didn't really intend to marry me. In any case, he's already married to his job."

The knight looked nearly as distraught as she had when Tom had broken up with her a few weeks after her father's death.

"You know," she tried to explain, "I knew nothing about his experiments, let alone why they were so important to him."

"Will he be able to make up for what he has done?" Gero asked angrily.

"What do you mean?"

"He'll send us home, won't he?"

"I don't know," Hannah answered meekly.

"Damn it!" Gero turned and walked round the table until he was standing right in front of her, glaring down at her. "What *do* you know, then?" he yelled.

Hannah backed into her armchair fearfully. Matthäus, who had fallen asleep on the carpet, sat up unexpectedly and blinked in fright.

"He will definitely try to send you back, but it could take a while ..." she muttered in High German.

Gero crossed his arms in front of his chest, as if to assure her that he didn't want to hurt her. "How long may we take advantage of your hospitality?"

"As long as it takes," Hannah said.

He looked uneasy. He was not a man who could rest comfortably and place his fate in the hands of another person.

"It makes no sense for you to try to find your way back yourself," Hannah remarked cautiously. "In the past centuries, there have been unbelievable changes. Besides, there's still another problem." She dared not meet his inquiring gaze.

"What else?"

"There's a powerful organization behind Tom, which doesn't have particularly good intentions for you. They suspect that you and Matthäus have been transferred to our time, and their ultimate goal now is to seize both of you. They'll imprison you and treat you badly. Tom hid you with me so they wouldn't harm you. If they discover where you are, they'll come and take you, and I don't know if you will survive that."

"If that is true, good lady," the Templar hissed grimly, "things haven't changed as much as you think they have."

"In any case, nothing more can be done today," she replied with a stifled yawn and stole a glance at the small clock on the wall. It was almost midnight. "Instead of you using my bedroom, I've prepared another room upstairs," she said. "If you like, you can sleep there with the boy."

She smiled at Matthäus who, in the meantime, had taken his position next to his lord as if waiting for a command. He looked sleepy.

Gnashing his teeth, the Templar agreed. However, looking at his situation realistically, there wasn't much else he could do.

After having spent the entire evening in candlelight, Hannah now turned on the ceiling lights for the first time. "This is electric light," she said as calmly as she could.

She saw Gero gritting his teeth as his gaze flickered between the light switch and the light fixture.

"No, it's not sorcery," she quipped.

"What makes you think I thought it was sorcery?" he asked.

"Well, Matthäus thought I was a sorceress when he first saw the light …" she said softly so that the boy wouldn't hear her.

"I'm not a child," Gero snapped in annoyance. "Do you think I don't know there's a logical explanation for most things in this world, even when they can't be readily inferred?"

He lowered his face to hers, so close that their noses almost touched. His breath smelled of wine, and his bright eyes blazed defiantly.

"I can't imagine that you would be so silly as to only believe in things that you can see and understand, and dismiss everything else as sorcery. If so, the Almighty and all his workings would be sorcery, and that certainly isn't true."

Hannah swallowed. If he had wanted to surprise her, he had undoubtedly succeeded.

When they went upstairs, Gero of Breydenbach glanced at the modest but comfortable guest bed and nodded in satisfaction.

Hannah fished around in her skirt pocket and retrieved the silver cross on the braided leather cord. She had intended to give it to him earlier, but in the excitement, she had forgotten about it.

His fingers were coarse, warm, and dry as they closed around her hand to take the necklace from her.

"Thank you," he said in his deep voice. The damp shimmer in his eyes revealed that his words meant more than that.

It had taken Hannah hours to fall asleep, but suddenly, the creaking floorboards of the staircase woke her. Bathed in sweat, she bolted up as if from a nightmare.

Her heart pounding, she suddenly remembered that she was no longer the sole occupant of this house.

Anxiously she waited to see if the door to her bedroom would open. What if her new tenant raped her? She heard a dull clatter. It seemed the nighttime wanderer was in her living room. Despite her growing fear, she decided to investigate. On her tiptoes, she crept through the hallway to the living-room door and peered carefully through a narrow gap between the door and the jamb.

To her surprise, she heard a soft, deep voice. It sounded like someone making a secret phone call. She pushed her head a little further through the gap then, bewildered, she paused. The Templar was kneeling on the ground. The silver moonlight filtering in through the patio door transformed his face and upright posture into a collection of sharp, black, and white contours. As he murmured piously to himself with his hands folded, he looked like a life-sized statue of a holy figure in a cathedral.

Hannah strained her ears. It sounded like a Latin liturgy. His gaze was fixed straight ahead, on the large, hand-carved Madonna figure that she had purchased many years ago in a devotional memorabilia shop in Bavaria. It had since stood on a corner shelf above the table.

Although her instincts told her to draw back immediately, she could not turn her gaze away. Suddenly he stopped speaking. He lowered his head to his chest and covered his face with his palms. His shoulders began to shake and soft sobs filled the room. The Templar was crying, there was no doubt about it. She had thought anything was possible – that he could kill her, escape, rob her, wreck her furniture, or even rape her – but she hadn't expected such tenderness.

Hannah retreated quietly. She curled up in her bed, still eavesdropping, and it seemed like an eternity before she heard footsteps again, slowly climbing to the second floor.

CHAPTER 21

The Stake

Tuesday, November 16, 2004

In the morning, like a restless, lonely wolf that had lost its pack, Gero slunk down the stairs while Matthäus was still sleeping. Arriving at the ground floor, he stood motionless, staring at the closed door he guessed his host to be behind. Would she present the same heartrendingly beautiful sight in her sleep as she did when awake?

He slipped into the bathroom. Even in the dim light, a glance at the mirror told him that he still bore traces of his emotional outburst the prevoius night. The woman, or even his squire, should not know that he had cried. He operated the lever as Matthäus had shown him, and held his face with eyes shut under the stream of cold water. Snorting, he straightened himself and removed one of the white towels from the neat stack on the window ledge. He held it under the tap, and after he had wrung it out, he pressed the cool, wet towel to his face.

Fumbling, Gero sat down on the edge of the bathtub and breathed in deeply. Suddenly he recalled Struan and their long conversation in the bathroom at the commandery of Bar-sur-Aube. He sighed, wondering what had befallen his two brothers in arms and the girl. Last night, he had prayed not only for himself and the boy to return home unharmed, but also for his friends. Would they believe him if he told them his story? A child-like curiosity gripped Gero. He wondered if the mysterious Head of Wisdom he was supposed to find would measure up to the miracle of traveling into the future.

Sighing, Gero realized it was a pointless thing to wonder about when he didn't even know if the sewers of Heisterbach and the mysterious artifact still existed.

A fuzzy memory appeared in his mind. Hadn't Caesarius of Heisterbach, the Heisterbach Abbey's former prior, recorded the story of a monk who had disappeared and apparently traveled nearly eight hundred years into the future? Gero tried hard to remember what had happened. Had the monk been able to return to his Brothers in the past

... or had he remained in the future? But how would Caesarius have known what happened to the Brother if he remained in the future? How had the monk even stumbled into the future in the first place?

In the story the monk had doubted God, and fallen asleep. In this regard, Gero thought, there were definitely parallels between his own fate and that of the missing Cistercian Brother. He had already been haunted by doubts about the Lord long before he had fallen unconscious, asking himself how God could turn a blind eye to the King's and the Pope's injustices.

He must go to the Heisterbach Abbey. It was his only hope of finding any answers to his questions. But how would he get there? He wasn't sure if it was wise to inform his hostess of his plans.

He set aside the towel and stepped quietly into the living room. Maybe he had underestimated the woman. Although her German was broken, it was full of words he didn't know, and she even switched to Latin when she didn't know how to explain something in German. She was definitely not simple-minded.

In front of the large glass door, he pushed the latch up to open it, a procedure he had learned yesterday from watching his hostess trying to escape. He fervently hoped she had forgotten what a brutal fool he had been. How fear could change a person's heart!

Slipping out through the gap in the door into the cold morning mist, he took a deep breath. Even the air here smelled different. He was familiar with the smell of charcoal mixed with the scent of damp earth in cold weather, but now there was something else, something that he couldn't identify and which he had already noticed while he was being carted off in the strange wagon.

Although the house stood in the middle of a forest, it wasn't peaceful. Strange noises echoed from every direction. In the fog above him, he heard a distant roll of thunder and a light rolled overhead like a fuzzy star. Involuntarily, he ducked.

His gaze fell on the small, neglected vegetable patch, where sad turnip greens peeped out from the ground. As if to prove to himself that some things hadn't changed, he walked toward to the patch, bent over, and pulled out a wrinkled carrot. He dusted off the dirt and bit into it. Even the vegetable tasted different. Chewing slowly, Gero inspected his surroundings. Lights twinkled in the sky above the bare trees. He shuddered and an uneasy feeling crept over him. Throwing the rest of the carrot into the grass, he headed back to the house.

As the cat brushed past his leg to get into the warmth, he leapt back in shock.

"Damned beast," he hissed at it, knowing very well that he was more annoyed at his own jumpiness than Matthäus's new friend.

Cautiously he locked the door behind him and observed the impressive wall of books in the room. Before he could remove a book from a shelf, he made sure that the owner of the house hadn't appeared at the door unexpectedly. After all, he hadn't asked her permission, as was customary in a scriptorium. Paper seemed to be used lavishly in this house. He ran his finger over the thin pages of a thick book. The typeset script was unbelievably neat and precise. While he was still leafing through the book, his gaze fell on a stack of folded documents. He shut the book and put it back where he had found it then crouched down and retrieved a thin map. The map appeared to be annotated to an extraordinary degree, the likes of which he had seen only in the Templars' secret inventories. It was made of neither paper nor parchment.

Carefully, Gero unfolded the exquisite map and thoughtfully examined a circle adorned with the cardinal directions, squinting to better make them out in the dim light.

He stepped toward the large glass window to get a better look. *Rhineland-Palatinate, Survey Map 1:250,000*, he read, but the words didn't tell him much. He spread the large sheet out on the floor then a sudden noise made him jump.

"Should I turn on the light?" Matthäus stood, barefoot but otherwise fully clothed, in front of him, looking down at him with curiosity.

"Is there a fire striker anywhere here?" Gero asked innocently.

Matthäus smiled. "You don't need a fire striker here," he said, turning around and walking to the door.

"Halt!" Gero wanted to call, but Matthäus had already pressed the panel that turned on the mysterious ceiling lamp like sorcery. In a second, it was as bright as day.

"Turn it off immediately!" he ordered his squire in a whisper.

"Why?" Matthäus stared at him in confusion.

"If you question an order again, you will pay for it," Gero hissed furiously. "Turn it off!"

"Yes, of course," Matthäus muttered, taken aback. "Should I light a candle?" he asked timidly, holding up a long object, which, he explained, could produce a flame with the simple press of a button.

"No," Gero answered gruffly, and folded up the map.

Grumbling, he got to his feet and put the map back on the shelf. He took one of the books instead and sat on a chair by the window, where the rising sun allowed him to decipher the text.

Hours could have passed as he leafed through the pages, then suddenly, some sort of bell rang. Gero looked around and saw only Matthäus, who was studying the bookshelf.

"Is the woman awake?"

Matthäus shook his head.

"Go see who's there," Gero said softly, rising slowly and setting the book aside.

A moment later, Matthäus hurried back.

"There's a man outside," he reported excitedly. "He looks like a Mamluk!"

Gero's hand flew to his knife belt. He hadn't taken it off, not even while he slept. He shoved the boy aside and marched straight into the hallway. Resolutely, he opened the front door.

The young man looked at him in surprise. "Good morning, sir. Here's the mail. Isn't Ms. Schreyber at home?"

Gero didn't pause to consider what the man could have meant. In a flash, he registered the dark complexion, black hair, and muscular body of a Mamluk. In his hand, the stocky man was holding a medium-sized box, as well as an unknown object, which he held out to Gero menacingly.

"Sign here!" the stranger said.

Gero didn't think. Instead, he tore the strange object out of the man's hands and scrutinized it.

"Hey," the voice demanded. "What are you doing? Give that back right now!" The dark-haired man stared at him indignantly without a shred of shame.

Gero threw the unknown object aside and snatched the box out of the man's hands. He pulled out his dagger and stabbed the soft, paper-like material, then, satisfied, he cut open the box. The deliverer of the cargo stared at him in disbelief.

"Give me back my scanner immediately, or I'll call the police!" the man yelled furiously. "What are you even doing here?"

Gero's hand darted up and seized the clueless messenger by the collar. Before the young man could process what was happening, he was pressed, gasping for air, against the whitewashed wall leading into the hallway. With sudden horror, he spied the large knife that was pointed at his throat.

Gero's heart pounded as he scrutinized the young man. God be damned if it wasn't a Mamluk. A Mamluk had given him one of his worst injuries, and another had taken his uncle's life. He would never forget the sight of the men who had been trained to kill French knights. Knights in the Occident had managed to capture several of them and had taken them to France, but even in slavery, they remained unpredictable, and could neither be trusted nor let out of sight.

"So, boy!" Gero snarled. "Tell me what business you have at the house of a woman who lives alone!"

"What is wrong with you?" his prisoner squawked. "Are you crazy or what?" He goggled at the glistening blade. "Hey, don't do anything stupid … okay?"

"Mattes," Gero yelled, "get the lady!"

In her dream, a soft flurry of voices surrounded Hannah like a curtain of shimmering pearls. It sounded like a mixture of Spanish and French. A child's voice snuck into her unconsciousness. "Lady …"

Lady? She squinted. The morning sun was shining painfully into her eyes. The blond-haired boy was bent over her and shaking her shoulder.

"What is it?" Hannah stammered uncertainly when Matthäus shook her again.

"My lord sends me," he said plainly. "There's a Mamluk outside who speaks a strange language."

"A what?" Hannah cast a frantic glance at the small, silver, radio-controlled alarm clock. Without another thought about what a Mamluk was, she sprang out of bed and stormed past Matthäus in her nightgown, toward the front door.

Between the coat rack and the front door, stood Ferhad Yildis, the delivery boy from the German Parcel Service, pinned against the wall, while Gerard of Breydenbach held a dagger to his throat.

Hannah blinked in disbelief, when she saw twenty-three-year-old Ferhad, whose parents came from Turkey to Germany thirty years ago. The young man – who was born in a local village and spoke flawless German – delivered her book shipments once a week to her house.

"What are you doing?" she shouted at the Templar.

Gero turned his attention to her briefly without letting Ferhad out of his sight.

"He is a Mamluk," he announced calmly. "I asked him who sent him, and what he wants from you." The Templar squared his shoulders. "He was being impertinent," he added solemnly, "shoving this strange box under my nose and babbling something about a signature."

Hannah's gaze followed Gero's finger with horror. The cardboard box on the floor was hopelessly shredded.

"In my homeland, we do not sign for anything that we cannot see. So I slit open the box to make sure that the Mamluk wasn't hiding anything that could hurt you. He became angry and swore at me. I told him that he's lucky he didn't pay for his behavior with his life."

Gero's expression relaxed a little, and his voice took on a smug tone. "I wanted to let you decide whether we should detain him until his lord fetches him and he's received his punishment, or if I should teach him a lesson right here in front of your eyes." He straightened his broad shoulders.

"Put down the knife immediately!" Although Hannah's voice was calm, she was trembling.

Gero avoided her stare. Shaking his head irritably, he lowered his fearsome weapon and stepped away from his victim. Matthäus gave his lord a surprised glance, and looked at Hannah as if he were annoyed that Gero had followed her order so promptly.

The young delivery boy let out a loud sigh of relief.

"You may leave," Hannah hissed at her two roommates, earning disbelieving looks from both Ferhad and her guests.

Gero leaned down toward Hannah until his mouth nearly touched her ear. "You should reconsider rejecting my protection," he murmured. "His people are seldom trustworthy. Even if he isn't particularly tall, it doesn't mean that he's harmless. If he gets the chance, he'll kill you faster than you can imagine."

Hannah didn't budge. Instead of answering, she shut her eyes in exasperation.

"As you wish," Gero muttered, annoyed. "But don't say I didn't warn you."

Without another word, he turned away. With a commanding nod, he motioned to Matthäus to follow him. Hannah heard both of them climbing the stairs.

"Ferhad … I …" she stammered, wishing that the ground would swallow her up, along with her shame.

The young man glanced at her nightgown, then in despair at the shredded cardboard box. It was plain to see he had no idea what to make of what had just happened.

"I'd like to formally apologize to you," Hannah continued. "My brother and nephew are here to visit, and … and sometimes my brother … likes to joke around," she concluded lamely.

She shrugged apologetically, her gaze falling on the light-brown leather backpack on the dresser. Almost casually, she reached for it and fished a twenty-euro bill out of her wallet. "You know, for some people, the world's a stage," she said, giving him a pained smile. She hoped vaguely that the young man would forget Gero's attack as soon as possible and keep quiet about it at that.

"Ms. Schreyber …" he said, retrieving his hand-held scanner from under the coat rack. Luckily, the delicate device had survived the attack without damage. "You still have to sign … for the package. Or should I say, for what's left of it?" An uncertain smile flickered over his face.

Thank God, Hannah thought. He was taking it with a bit of humor. Nonetheless, his hand was shaking as he held out the small device to her, on which she scrawled her digital signature.

"What country is your brother from?" Ferhad asked, regaining his old curiosity surprisingly quickly. "His German is worse than my dad's."

Hannah looked up for a moment, but gave him no answer. Instead, she shook his hand in parting. He looked baffled at the formality, but then a look of understanding dawned on him as she loosened her grip, leaving him with a crumpled bill in his hand.

"For your patience, and for not spreading this story around," she said quietly.

Hannah took a deep breath before picking up the shredded box and placing it on a couch in the living room. Fortunately, the contents hadn't suffered the same fate as the box. Satisfied, she spread out two different colored sweatshirts and two pairs of dark jeans that she had ordered for Matthäus by express mail. She had also ordered a set of modern socks and underwear for Gero.

Hastily, she went to her bedroom and slipped into a lilac-colored woolen skirt and a short, lime-green sweater. After that, she went to the kitchen, and began to prepare breakfast. When she delivered the clothing to the guestroom a little later, she was met with an icy glare.

"Are my leather pants dry?" Gero asked as he held up the jeans meant for Matthäus with his fingertips. With a nod, he passed them to the boy.

"I'll go check on them," Hannah answered. Before she left, she paused next to Gero and wrinkled her nose as she scrutinized him. "You can't possibly run around here in a cloak and chain mail," she decided. "You'll draw attention to yourself, and that's far too dangerous."

"I don't intend to parade around like a peacock either," he retorted as he turned his attention to her father's clothes, which lay neatly folded on the floor.

Hannah frowend, annoyed. If she didn't succeed in convincing him of the realities of the twenty-first century, their situation could become far more dangerous. The incident at the door would be just the beginning.

"Well," he relented, eyeing the rest of the clothing. "The underclothes and hosiery look fairly decent. If it pleases you, I'll wear them."

Hannah smiled involuntarily. Could the man read her thoughts? How did he know that she had a problem with his medieval braies?

"Breakfast is ready," she remarked casually.

When Gero appeared at the door to the living room two minutes later, he was still wearing the baggy black sweatsuit. He circled the breakfast table and let his gaze glide over it as if he were searching for something in particular. Just Monday morning, Hannah had acquainted herself with what people in the fourteenth century ate, and at the organic grocery store she had bought a loaf of crusty bread, raw milk, comb honey in a stoneware jar, a piece of unpasteurized French cheese, and fruit preserves. She had prepared a large pot of porridge made from barley grits and fried a few free-range eggs. She had even found bacon from pigs that had been fed in the traditional way. She was certain her guests would be satisfied with the sumptuous spread.

"What day is it today?" Gero asked, a bit confused.

"November 16," Hannah answered.

He shook his head impatiently. "I didn't mean the date. I meant, is it Monday, Tuesday, or Sunday?"

"Tuesday. Why?"

"Then today's a meat day. Do you have any hard-cured sausage?" he asked politely.

"Hard-cured sausage?" she repeated disbelievingly. "Um … no, sorry. I'll get some tomorrow. Tea?" She raised a pot of glazed stoneware.

"Beer?" He looked unsettled. "Or wine?"

"Beer?" she cried in astonishment. "Tea would be better, just for the boy," she decided finally, and handed him a steaming cup.

While the scent of peppermint and lemon balm wafted into his nose, he still looked skeptical.

"Sugar?"

He paused for a moment before declining, staring with a dazed expression at the sugar bowl and the large silver spoon buried in it.

Just then Matthäus entered the room. Proudly he presented his new trousers, which were a little too large for him, and his new dark blue sweater. He was obviously pleased that it looked exactly like his lord's. After he had filled his plate, he took his seat and began to eat without hesitation. Gero shook his head disapprovingly and addressed the boy in sharp tones.

He had obviously spoken Old French, for Hannah could not understand him, but she could see the message must have been unpleasant, as Matthäus put his bread down on his plate and lowered his eyes sheepishly. Hannah decided to ignore the oppressive silence and began to butter her bread. But Gero didn't pay her any attention. Out of the corner of her eye, she watched as her guests sat up straight. When she saw them fold their hands on the edge of the table, she abruptly stopped eating and swallowed the unchewed piece of bread that she had bitten off, coughing as it nearly became stuck in her throat. Embarrassed, she laid her utensils down next to her plate, and folded her hands as well.

Matthäus began to recite a prayer in Latin. "In nomine Patris, et Fili, et Spiritus Sancti. Benedic, Domine, nos et haec tua dona, quae de tua largitate sumus sumpturi per Christum Dominum nostrum …"

Hannah's high school Latin was good enough for her to recognize that it was a benediction. While the prayers her grandmother had taught her lasted ten seconds, this litany stretched on for at least five minutes.

"Amen," said Matthäus finally, and looked expectantly at Gero.

With a benevolent nod, the Templar let him know that he could now begin to eat.

While they were eating, no word was spoken, and not even Hannah was tempted to say anything. A short time later, however, she jumped as the doorbell rang, announcing yet another visitor.

"Excuse me," she mumbled, rising to her feet.

Through the kitchen window, she spied her employee from the bookstore. *Damn it*, she thought. She had forgotten that just yesterday, she had asked Judith to order some books about the Templars and bring them by her place today.

"Good morning!" called the familiar voice from outside, and as Hannah hesitantly cracked opened the door, Judith squeezed past her into the hallway, her teeth chattering, a pained grin plastered on her face. "It's freezing outside. We can talk inside, can't we?"

She was carrying a thick stack of books in her arm.

"Is this an inconvenient time?" Judith smiled politely, but she didn't wait for an answer. Before Hannah knew it, Judith was heading into the dining room.

"Oh!" She paused when she saw Gero and Matthäus eating calmly.

Only Matthäus looked up curiously as the two women suddenly entered the room. Gero, who had a clear view of the front door, didn't react.

Judith placed the books on the coffee table and marched toward the dining table.

"Judith Stein," she said plainly.

Pointedly, she held out her hand to Gero, accidently brushing against the empty plate he had just set down on the tabletop.

With lightning reflexes, he caught the dish before it fell to the floor. He set it down on the table, and his gaze panned to the source of this mishap.

"Are you coming into the kitchen with me?" Hannah asked, gently nudging her employee and friend in the ribs.

"Of course, but aren't you going to introduce us first?" Judith didn't seem to notice that Gero wasn't particularly eager to meet her. But then he seemed to remember his good manners, and finally rose slowly. He was a good two heads taller than Judith. He placed his right hand on his chest and bowed slightly.

"Gerard of Breydenbach," he announced in his sonorous voice.

Stunned, Judith stared up at him and mechanically extended her right hand to him. He didn't react. "J ... Judith ... Stein," she stuttered, and, with an embarrassed expression on her face, she let her hand drop.

Gero seemed to be waiting for an explanation as to why she had disturbed his breakfast but Judith was looking at him as though she had been hypnotized.

Hannah tugged at her friend's sleeve and dragged her away.

"Excuse us for a second," she said to Gero.

Like an obedient horse, Judith trotted after her boss, and only seemed to snap out of her trance after Hannah had shut the kitchen door behind her.

"My God, that dude has some eyes. They're amazing. Where did you pick him up?" Judith squeaked.

"I'm glad you've finally calmed down," Hannah teased. "He's not really all that amazing."

Judith was still breathless. "Does he live with you?"

"He's a friend of Tom's, my ex, and is looking for an apartment. Tom couldn't put him up, so he asked me to help him out. But only temporarily, and anyway, my new roommate has baggage that you may have missed when you were gawking at him."

"Baggage?"

"The twelve-year-old sitting at the other end of the table."

"Even if he had a hundred-year-old grandma in tow, that wouldn't stop me from giving him refuge."

Giving him refuge ... If you only knew how right you are, *Hannah thought wryly.*

"When will I see you in the store?"

"I need a few days off to settle some things. If it's okay with you, I'll compensate you and Carolin with twenty percent of the sales while I'm away."

"Oh ... yes!" Judith grinned. "It's a deal! Tell the dreamboat we say thank you. He can live with you as long as he wants, under the condition that you let us have a good look at him in the store every now and then." Judith winked at Hannah suggestively.

"Like hell I will!" Hannah retorted. She smiled apologetically as she led Judith to the front door.

"Thank you again for the books, but I'm afraid I have to go now," she said in a firm voice. "I still have a lot to do today."

"I have something else for you," Judith said, whipping out an envelope made from colorful wrapping paper. "My brother is inviting you to his store's opening on Thursday. He'd like you to be there. Firstly, because you're my boss, but also because he'd like to get to know the lady with such a deep interest in the Templars."

"Thanks," Hannah said, surprised, "but I don't know if I can make it. After all, I have guests."

"Just bring them along," Judith smiled broadly. "They might enjoy it."

After Hannah had bid Judith goodbye, she found Gero sitting on the sofa, engrossed in one of the books that Judith had brought.

She stood behind him, looking over his shoulder.

"All right, there?" she asked meekly.

She had not actually intended to confront them with the material about the Templars. Till now, she had hardly had time to explain their current situation in greater detail, let alone what had happened in the last seven hundred years since their disappearance.

Matthäus was playing with Heisenberg, and Hannah was glad that he at least had found a friend in the shy cat so quickly.

"These are strange letters," Gero remarked casually as he leafed through a page in a Templar encyclopedia. "And yet they resemble our own. None of your books are handwritten," he muttered, more to himself than to Hannah. "Everything looks printed."

"You're familiar with the printing press? It's only been around since the fifteenth century," Hannah gaped at him.

Her comment seemed to have wounded his pride. "Do you think I'm a fool? Even if one has never printed books, it doesn't mean that he doesn't know about them. We had printed books from the Orient in our scriptorium. The Saracens printed books, even if they weren't numerous." His blue eyes blazed belligerently. "And the residents of Cathay were no less acquainted with the printing press ... if Marco Polo's reports were true ..." he lectured, without pausing to consider that Hannah already knew that Marco Polo had written the truth in his tales of his travels in Asia.

"Can you read the text, then?" Hannah asked.

"Haven't you already asked me if I can read? If I tell you that I've read Chrétien de Troyes, Eschenbach, von der Aue, Strassbourg, and Türheim, would you believe me?" Gero shook his closely shaved head testily.

"Although I imagine," he said irritably, "that you've never even *heard* of those writers."

"Believe it or not," Hannah said sharply, "I never doubted that you could read, and believe it or not, I read *Parzival* when I was studying at university." She awaited his reaction with a touch of haughtiness. She knew that in the Middle Ages, nearly no women had been allowed to study at universities.

"You studied at a university?" His voice was more than surprised.

It was as if he had suddenly begun to see her through new eyes. Hannah allowed herself a satisfied, almost benevolent smile.

"Where?" Gero could hardly believe it.

"In Bonn," she said airily.

"Since when has there been a university in Bonn?" he asked in disbelief.

"Since the eighteenth century," she answered.

"Good," he said, nodding appreciatively. "If I can't decipher something or understand a word, I'll ask you."

Hannah sensed that his impression of her had changed. He looked up from his text, and with his clear blue eyes, seemed to ask if she might lend him her help from now on.

Bitterly, Gero acknowledged that his Order had been destroyed over seven long years at the behest of Philipp IV of France, whose soldiers had slain countless numbers of his Brethren. The Templars in France had been persecuted, tortured, and forced to make implausible confessions.

"What's a 'Baphomet'?" Hannah asked as she reached a passage in one of the books on idol worship.

Gero looked up in shock. "Nothing," he said curtly. "It's just as nonsensical as the claim that we all had carnal knowledge of one another."

Hannah raised an eyebrow and noticed he was evading her gaze with a certain air of embarrassment.

"Of all things holy," he muttered, glancing up from his text and looking flabbergasted. "They wanted to burn him at the stake."

He stared at Hannah with a look of incomprehension. It was a moment before she realized that he was talking about Jacques de Molay, the last Grand Master of the Order of the Temple.

"Are you sure that these books tell the truth?" Gero asked, looking at her as though he were pleading with her to tell him they were full of lies.

"I'm sorry," she whispered sympathetically. "But I'm afraid they're true. As far as I know, their findings are well-researched."

269

"Do you know what it means to be burned to death? Have you ever been to an execution?" The color had drained from Gero's face.

"No, we don't have those any more," she answered truthfully.

"First, the skin on the legs splits open, and then you can barely see anything through the smoke. If the person is lucky, they'll pass out from the unspeakable pain, or the smoke will suffocate them before the flames devour him. But until then, they still have some time to scream until the very last bit of breath is out of their lungs. The stench is terrible. It invades your senses like a rabid animal and doesn't let go. Even months later, you'll be thinking about it, and some it stays with for their whole lives."

A shudder of horror ran down Hannah's spine.

"If I could, I would save them. Molay and my comrades. Damn it …"

Hannah saw his jaw clench as if he wanted to crush something.

"I have to go back …" Gero whispered absently. "Whatever it takes …"

Hannah was sitting next to him, and she felt as if she could physically feel his torment.

"I've left all my Brothers behind," he mumbled with a desperate sigh. "What if they've been captured? Or they've been killed or have to live the rest of their lives like animals in caves, just to avoid being discovered?"

"Can't they find somewhere to hide, lie low, and start anew?" Hannah asked in disbelief. Surely it couldn't have been that difficult to escape the authorities' grasp in the Middle Ages?

"Lie low?" Gero shook his head. "As sensible as that sounds, you seem to forget that you have to resurface at some point. Or at least you did in my time. Without the proper documents legitimizing your heritage, you are a bondsman and can be sold on the slave market or killed at anytime. Things may be different now."

"Well, the Pope exculpated your Order of all these allegations not too long ago," Hannah said, trying to cheer him up. She pointed to a paperback with references to more recent developments concerning the Templars.

"How wonderful!" Gero smiled bitterly. "Only seven hundred years too late. We should be so thankful that the subsequent generations are still concerned about our fate."

After reviewing the research material all day, Hannah served her guests a hearty dinner of bread, lentil soup, and cured ham. Later Gero dived into the documentation about the fate of his Order.

Suppressing a tired yawn, Hannah glanced up at the clock. It was midnight.

"Let's continue reading tomorrow," she suggested. "If you want, I'll travel to Paris with you. There are apparently archives there that can produce far more detailed reports, papers, and documents about your Order than all these books here."

Gero nodded thankfully. His gaze fell on Matthäus who had fallen asleep on the carpet. "Is there a way back?" he asked softly, not daring to look at Hannah. "Be honest ... please," he added.

"I think so," she answered, trying to lend her words a note of confidence. "I just can't tell you when. Only Tom will know."

"When will I see him?" Gero's expression was fearful. Dark shadows lay under his luminous eyes.

"Maybe tomorrow," she replied sleepily. Her heart ached as she saw him go to his knees, gingerly lifting the sleeping child from the floor and cradling him against his chest.

She felt a yearning to follow Gero as he began to climb the steps and tuck Matthäus into bed.

"Can I do anything ... for you or the boy?" she asked.

"No," he said. "I'll manage. I wouldn't know ... no ... thank you." Gero smiled at her for the first time that day, and, unless she was mistaken, for the first time since he had entered her house.

CHAPTER 22

Breydenburg Castle

Wednesday, November 17, 2004

Hannah had gotten out of bed around 7:30 a.m. to feed her animals and prepare breakfast for Gero and the boy. As she stood before Mona's empty stall, a feeling of dread washed over her. Her eyes fell to the hook on the wall where the saddle and bridle usually hung. Breathlessly, she ran back into the house.

There, lying neatly on the bed, she found the sweatshirt and jeans that Matthäus had been wearing the day before. All Gero's clothing, the cloak, the knife belt, and even the small, leather pouch were gone. The Templar and his squire had left. But where had they gone?

Feverishly, she tried to think. Should she call Tom? But what would that even accomplish? He couldn't help her look for them. Hadn't he said that he was being observed by the American military? Filing a missing person report about her husband who had lost his mind and had ridden away with her horse was out of the question too.

Her heart hammering wildly, she ran down the stairs into the living room and looked around. Frantically, she examined the bookshelf. Her gaze fell on the stack of maps on the bottom left shelf. *Why didn't I notice that immediately?* She thought. The collection, usually so neatly arranged, was askew. One of the hiking maps of the Lieser River and a city map of Wittlich were missing.

The thought of her medieval charges heading to the former ancestral home of the free nobles of Breydenbach on her wayward mare made Hannah shudder.

Shaking her head, she put on her coat, grabbed her car keys, and went out into the freezing cold. The man must be insane. Neither he nor the boy had jackets with them, and they would hardly be able to find their bearings in the morning rush-hour traffic. Skillfully, Hannah reversed her car backwards into the garage and connected the horse trailer to it before driving off.

Gero had no intention of waiting for some *Tom* he didn't know to decide his fate. He wanted to find out for himself if anything from his world still existed, and then travel to Heisterbach. Maybe there, he would find the answers to all his questions.

Hannah wouldn't mind him riding her horse, even if she would disapprove of him leaving her house by himself. And even though she was friendly and helpful, and though the sight of her pleased him more than he would have liked to admit, he didn't want to burden her any longer. If he and Matthäus could succeed in reaching Heisterbach Abbey, perhaps they could seek shelter there.

The mare was more trusting than he had expected. She seemed to sense that the man sitting on her back knew how to handle her. Obediently, she trotted across the farm roads they turned onto after they had left the forest. Matthäus, on the other hand, had protested lightly when Gero had instructed him to put on his old clothing and follow him into the stable. Shivering from the cold, Matthäus had taken his place behind Gero on the horse's broad back and pressed himself to him as if seeking protection.

It had taken Gero all his might not to appear frightened on their journey, although the erratic lights and the foreign sounds startled him. Now and then, Gero allowed himself to glance up at the sky that was steadily brightening. The most important thing was that the large, threatening birds were nowhere to be seen. Thanks to the maps, Gero knew roughly where he was headed. Even though the landscape looked entirely different, the rivers, plains, and hills hadn't changed. Along the way, he realized that it wasn't wise to ride across the plains, as most of them had been enclosed with spiked iron fences.

He made sure to avoid the smooth, stone streets that he had seen here for the first time in his life, as the wagons without horses raced along them at furious speeds.

In less than two hours, he reached the Lieser valley. At least the small stream that rushed past looked just as it had in his memories. Apprehensively, he approached the hill that led to the castle of his ancestors. After everything that he had seen, he knew that Hannah had spoken the truth. If seven hundred years really had passed since the last time he had ridden on this path, his family couldn't be alive anymore. But what would be awaiting him instead? He pulled the reins and looked at his plated leather gloves. Hidden under them, on the ring finger of his right hand, was the signet ring that his father had had made for him.

Unexpectedly, Gero felt the mare begin to prance. Something must have unsettled it. He squinted into the undergrowth. All at once, a dreadful yapping began. The horse recoiled so strongly that it rose on its hind legs. Matthäus barely managed to tighten his grip to avoid being thrown off. Out of the thick fog, a figure clad in dark green appeared. A man, wearing a wide-brimmed green hat on his head and a peculiar cane on his back, looked at him grumpily. The small dachshund, which was responsible for the loud barking, pulled madly on a leather leash.

Gero calmed the horse down, and laid his hand on his knife-belt as a precaution.

"You can't ride here!" the man in green shouted at him sharply. His speech was as strange as Hannah's, but when Gero concentrated, he could understand most of it.

"Out of the way, rogue!" Gero snarled, not prepared to be scolded on his own land. He clicked his tongue and gave the mare a light kick in the flanks to instruct it to continue on its way.

"Dismount immediately and tell me your name and address, or I shall report you," demanded the man when he realized that his instructions had not been heeded.

Gero had decided to ignore him, but suddenly, the furious man pulled his left leg.

In a flash, Gero drew his cutlass and seized his antagonist by his collar, then he held the blade to his throat.

"This," he hissed darkly, "is the land of the free nobles of Breydenbach. If you value your life, you will keep your silence and flee!" He regarded the man with a piercing glare. Even the dog had put its tail between its legs and hid, whimpering, behind its master's feet.

With a contemptuous snort, Gero let the man go and returned the knife to its sheath. Coolly, he continued on his way.

Around nine, Hannah turned her car onto a narrow gravel road. Between tall trees that were slowly losing their leaves, she drove up a hill to an unpaved, abandoned parking lot. In the entrance, a sign still stood. Breydenburgweg – Route 23.

She couldn't care less at the moment that she was blocking the road with her Ford Focus and horse trailer.

As she shut the car door, lost in her thoughts, she turned her gaze to the misty forest. Far and wide, there was no one to be seen, and, besides the harsh cawing of a few crows, there was nothing to be heard either. The silence and the bare silhouettes of the wraithlike oak trees formed a sinister backdrop. Freezing, she raised her shivering shoulders and headed up the path to the castle ruins.

Gero and his squire had almost reached their destination.

"What are we doing here?" Matthäus asked, still clinging fearfully onto his lord.

"I don't know yet," Gero answered honestly.

Slowly, the suspicion crept over him that it hadn't been a good idea to ignore Hannah's advice and ride off without warning. Not only could he see the castle from here, but he could also smell the burning wood used for heating and smoking all the way down at the Lieser. Back then, the castle was teeming with servants and maids, with horses and carts and traveling merchants who all used this path to reach Breydenburg Castle, as well as the celebrations of the lords of Manderscheid.

A low-hanging cloud had shrouded the forbidding castle in an impenetrable fog. Making his way blindly forward, Gero recoiled in shock when a wall suddenly appeared in front of him.

As if turned to stone, he sat in the saddle, unable to move.

"Have we arrived?" Matthäus asked helplessly.

The boy looked at his lord and slid smoothly off the horse's back. He seized the mare's reins and sat down on a fallen tree trunk. He looked as if he was about to burst into tears, but Gero ignored him and marched ahead.

Breathlessly, he took in what had once been his home.

"Good God. Let it not be true," Gero murmured at the sight of what remained of the once proud noble estate. He slowly dismounted from the horse. The ground swayed and threatened to give way under his feet. With both hands, he picked up a piece of the rubble that was strewn across the ground and, full of despair, threw it against the remnants of a wall. Like a missile, the heavy stone collided with the ancient wall, knocking loose several stones that fell noisily to the ground.

Somewhere, something rumbled. Hannah stood still and looked around, searching for the sound. She had known the castle ruins since her childhood days. Only the remnants of red sandstone walls and gray slate remained, belying the fact that a lordly structure had ever stood here. Nonetheless, it was a romantic, magical place that had evolved into an insider's tip among the many tourists who came to this region in the summer to visit the well-preserved castle of Manderscheid nearby. The history of Breydenburg Castle was shrouded in mystery. No one seemed to know anything about the family of knights who had once lived here.

Anxiously, Hannah hurried further along the path. Suddenly, her mare, Mona, appeared in front of her, and, next to her on a tree trunk, was Matthäus, staring at her as if she were an apparition. Swiftly she took off her coat and draped it around the shivering boy.

"Wait here. I'll be right back," she said, and stumbled over the rocks through the fog.

Gero was standing in front of an immense cliff, propping himself up against a slender birch tree. Slowly, Hannah approached him.

Without thinking, she offered him a tissue. "Here – you can wipe your face or clean your nose with it – if you want."

He accepted her offering and ran it over his red-rimmed eyes in a sheepish gesture, snuffling noisily.

"Should we sit down for a moment?"

"No."

"Gero …" she began warily. "I mean, it …"

"Forget about it," he said. "I didn't want to believe it … you're not to blame. On the contrary, it's to your credit that you knew exactly what awaited me here and wanted to hide it from me. But I would have been drawn here sooner or later anyway. You understand, don't you? Are you angry at me?"

"Why should I be angry?" Hannah stared at him in confusion.

"Because I didn't listen to your advice and took your horse?"

"No. Did you think that I was?"

Gero was tempted to touch her hand in gratitude, but then drew it back.

"What would you have done if I hadn't found you?"

"I don't know," he said, then paused before asking, "even if the castle is gone, is the Heisterbach Abbey still standing?"

Hannah knew of the eight-hundred-year-old ruins from her time in Bonn. She didn't want to disappoint him again, but in truth, not much remained of the once monumental church. It was nothing like the grand Cistercian abbey that Heisterbach had once been. A few nuns still lived there, but Hannah didn't think that their presence would comfort Gero.

"There's not much left of Heisterbach, either," she answered cautiously.

"What do you mean there isn't much left?" Gero's voice trembled.

"Well," Hannah said, "only the apse still stands."

He pursed his lips and nodded silently.

"Would you like me to drive you and the boy there?"

"Maybe tomorrow," he said, taking a deep breath, "if the weather clears up and I've recovered from this evil."

He placed an unthinking hand on her back and pushed her in the direction of the former castle gates.

Despite the terrible cold, Hannah felt the warmth between her shoulder blades like a crackling fire.

When he saw Hannah and his lord appear from behind the remains of one of the walls, the boy jumped to his feet and ran toward them in relief.

Gero was surprised when, in an outburst of emotion, the boy embraced Hannah and not him. Only when Matthäus loosened himself from her did Gero notice that the boy was wearing her coat.

"I was a fool not to listen to you," he said, his eyes fixed on the shivering boy. "I'm glad you followed us."

"But of course," Hannah smiled understandingly.

"Are you cold?" he asked. Without waiting for an answer, he loosened the metal clasp of his cloak, took it off, and draped it around her shoulders. Immediately she felt the warmth emanating from the cloth. Although the woolen fabric should have been thoroughly drenched, it was so densely woven that even the constant mist could not penetrate it. She peered at the red cross that adorned the left breast. The Templar's cloak nearly reached her feet.

It was a strange feeling, she thought. At that moment, she was gripped by a strange unrest.

"Come on, let's go," she said softly, and turned around.

"To whom does the land belong today?" Gero asked after he had taken the mare's reins in his hands and lifted Matthäus onto Mona's back.

"I've no idea," Hannah answered. "To the state of Rhineland-Palatinate or the Archdiocese of Trier?"

"So the Archbishop of Trier still exists?" His eyes were suddenly filled with hope.

"Yes, the current one has been in office for three years," she answered, happy that she could at least present Gero with something that was familiar to him.

"Is he a powerful man?"

"Well, he's just the archbishop. He doesn't have much power, at least not as much as in your time … He'll be lucky if his followers don't all desert him."

Gero stared at her in astonishment. "A lot seems to have changed since then," he remarked tersely, and shrugged.

Hannah hesitated for a moment before she spoke. "We have to take another way. I have a trailer we can transport the horse in."

"I brought the horse here, and I can ride it back," Gero argued stubbornly.

"I believe you," Hannah said hurriedly as she didn't want to give him the impression that she thought he was unable to find his way back to her house. "But it's better if no one sees you. We have to tread carefully. Tom's people are after you. They would take away your freedom and the child's, too, and …"

"Freedom …" Gero said, and laughed disparagingly. "Can a man lose what he never had? This Tom and his master best stay out of my sight," he growled softly, "or I'll break their necks with my own hands."

"Tom didn't intend to snatch you from your normal lives," Hannah countered. "He suspects that his master is responsible."

Gero frowned impatiently. "And who's making sure we go home again? Tom's master?"

"At the moment, no one," she replied carefully. "The machine that Tom and his master were using was destroyed. Until your appearance, no one has ever succeeded in transferring people from the past."

"Does that mean we're trapped here until Tom saves us?" Gero looked horrified. "It's bad enough that seven hundred years have gone by and the Lord still hasn't decided to end the world. Do you know what it means to have no prospect of ever seeing the ones you love again, either on earth or in paradise?

Hannah sighed. Holding the horse by its reins, Gero increased the pace of his wide strides and Hannah had to struggle to keep up.

By mistake, they had walked in the wrong direction, and now found themselves a good distance beneath the actual castle, where the impressive foundations of the old masonry melded with the rocks.

"Dear Lord!" he gasped.

Hannah followed him as Gero hurried on. At the place where he stood, small trees and saplings had been snapped off recklessly, and soaring climbing plants had been pulled down. Someone had come through with large machinery, and dug a deep hole into the side of the steep hill.

Most of the excavation site had been buried again, but a hole, about three feet wide, hadn't been filled in, exposing a gap, just large enough for a man to pass through, in the foundations of the outer walls. Hastily, Gero tied the mare's reins to a branch. Before Hannah could object, he had disappeared into the hole headfirst. Hannah thought quickly. She ran back to Matthäus, who looked at her in confusion, and fished out a lighter from her coat pocket. Then she took off the Templar's cloak and ran back to the wall. When she reached the interior of the chamber, her eyes had become accustomed to the darkness. It smelled of decay, and in the dim light that streamed in through the entrance, she had to strain her eyes to recognize where she was. The flame from her lighter brightened the room only slightly. The arch of the underground room was so low that Gero nearly hit his head on the ceiling. Alcoves, in which stone coffins lay, had been carved in the rock walls. There might have been eight or ten, and in the darkness, she couldn't tell if there were more ahead. Hannah wasn't keen on finding out.

Some distance away, Gero stood with his back to her, staring at the ground. Before him, a heavy stone slab had been pushed aside, revealing an opening. A staircase led down into a crypt.

As she stepped toward him, she felt something was wrong.

Cautiously, she illuminated the stone passageway.

"What is it?" she asked fearfully. "Did you know someone who was buried here?" When the Templar didn't answer, she glanced at the weather-beaten stone sarcophagus. New scrape marks on the heavy lid hinted that it had been opened recently and then carelessly shut again.

"My wife," he answered so softly that she could hardly hear him.

Hannah gaped at him in shock. "Your *wife*? You're married? I thought you were a Templar knight?"

He turned around to look at her. "She died before I joined the Order."

"I'm sorry," Hannah whispered sincerely.

Suddenly, the dismal place became too much for her to bear and she hastily climbed outside. On her knees, she slipped through the narrow opening without caring that she was getting dirty and cutting her hands on the sharp stones.

Outside, she leaned, panting, against the brittle foundation. Her throat felt constricted. She'd had an inkling of what it might mean to be thrown so suddenly into another time, but it was entirely different to be confronted with the crumbling stones of your home or graves etched with names you knew by heart. It took a few minutes for Gero to appear next to her.

"What's wrong?" he asked defiantly. "Did you not think that I had a life before I came here?" He sniffed disdainfully.

Hannah looked at him imploringly. "I will do anything I can do to help you and Matthäus."

"I know," he acknowledged gruffly. He took a step back and eyed her closely. "But you can't actually do much to help us go home, can you?"

In resignation Hannah looked up at the old walls. "You know, I find it strange that there was an excavation here in the middle of autumn. There's been no word that a burial chamber was found. I have a hunch that something here isn't right."

"You know," he repeated, mimicking her tone, "I find it rather reprehensible for anyone to desecrate the graves of my ancestors ... no matter what time of the year it is."

Hannah sighed and bit her lower lip.

The mare was suddenly startled. "Quiet, girl," Gero soothed, patting her neck.

At Hannah's pleading, he followed her back to the car before leading the animal into the trailer with reassuring words. Then he helped her shut the heavy hatch.

"Would you mind taking off your chain mail and surcoat?"

"Why?" he asked indignantly.

"Because it's not normal to dress like that here." She handed him a black Jack Wolfskin jacket that had once belonged to her father. Without a word but with a contemptuous expression, he pulled his surcoat over his head and begrudgingly loosened the leather belt on his chain mail.

After Hannah had taken his things from him, he slipped into the black jacket that, as she expected, fit him well, making his shoulders appear even broader.

General Lafour had appointed Jack Tanner, a long-serving agent of the NSA, as the Chief Investigator of the Himmerod case. Jack had been specially flown in from Maryland as he had spent some time as a Marine in Germany, and had not only learnt the German language, but had also become familiar with the terrain between Bitburg and Frankfurt. He looked like the stereotypical NSA agent: a toned body, a curious, piercing stare, and a head of thinning hair that had been buzzed into a crew cut. He always had a slight spring in his step, and his gait was a little too self-conscious.

With long strides, Tanner crossed the hastily assembled investigation office in the basement of the administration building at the Himmerod compound, a heavily guarded part of the US Airbase Spangdahlem. Altogether, eight staff members and twenty field observation agents were supporting him in his efforts to shine a light on last Saturday's accident. For up to seventeen hours a day he was busy, not just with ensuring that Dr. Tom Stevendahl and Paul Colbach were shadowed around the clock, but also with the search for the man who the two scientists had supposedly transferred seven hundred years into the future.

Tanner was still skeptical that a human being had actually been transferred from another time dimension. The statements from Stevendahl and Colbach that such a thing wasn't possible with current technology seemed logical. Additionally, Professor Hagen, the impetuous leader of the research facility, who distrusted his colleagues so vehemently, appeared a little unhinged to him. Tanner couldn't shrug off the feeling that Hagen was hiding something.

"Jack?" The voice came from one of the computers behind him. Tanner turned around.

Forty-year-old Mike Tapleton, who was a little on the chubby side, had risen from his office chair and was beckoning to him.

"I believe I have something," he said with a touch of triumph flashing in his brown eyes.

Tanner headed over to his colleague. So far, the investigation results had been rather unfruitful. Stevendahl and Colbach were hiding in Colbach's apartment in Vianden, barely moving from their positions, apart from the two times they had made phone calls from different phone booths. In the apartment, they spoke only of trivialities. Colbach could not be underestimated. He specialized in operating quantum computers, after all. For him, hacking into any known system must be a piece of cake. Hell, he might even be able to gain access to the NSA's investigation records if he knew about their surveillance.

"What do you have, Mike?" Jack asked.

"I've gained access to the police records of the state of Rhineland-Palatinate – and look … there was a report this morning. A ranger alleged he met a man on a horse in the forest under the castle that we investigated yesterday. The man had a boy with him, too."

"And?" Jack asked impatiently. "I don't find that very meaningful."

"Just wait," Mike replied, sounding offended. "The guy was wearing a white cloak with a red cross on it, and he was obviously on his way to our castle. He held a large knife to the ranger's throat and claimed that the land they were on belonged to the free nobles of Breydenbach, and told him to get lost if his life meant anything to him."

"Have you already told Colonel Pelham this?"

"No, not yet."

"Send the boys down. Tell them to search the area. They might still be there. But be careful – the man could be dangerous."

"Do you think they really are our time travelers?" Mike grabbed the telephone and dialed a number before he looked at Jack again.

"I've no idea," Jack mumbled absently. Then he looked up suddenly.

"Have you been able to compare the DNA results from Stevendahl's car with those from the catacombs and the blood from the sword?"

Mike never replied. Someone had answered the phone at the other end of the line.

Hannah helped Matthäus buckle his seatbelt, ignoring Gero's dubious look as she started the car. Slowly it rolled down the gravel road. Hannah could just make out the paved main road when a silver-gray BMW blocked her path. Two men sprang out of the vehicle, hastily parked on the side of the road, and hurried up to her, gesticulating wildly. Instinctively, she grabbed Gero's Templar cloak from the back seat and stashed it under the front passenger seat.

"Not a word," she hissed as the two men came nearer. Then she locked the doors and rolled down her window.

"Yes?" she asked cautiously.

"Apologies for the disturbance." The shorter of the two had an unmistakable American accent. "We're looking for a man on a horse wearing a knight's costume."

Hannah didn't dare to look away. "A knight's costume?" she asked with exaggerated disbelief.

"It's a friend of ours," the man explained with a smile. "He belongs to a troupe of re-enactors who've set up camp right around the corner from here. Knights' Games. Ever heard of that?"

Hannah shook her head. Her heart pounded when she saw that the other man was scrutinizing the trailer, and Gero and the boy as well.

"I'm sorry," she said tersely, "we don't have time for this. We're on the way to the vet. Would you mind moving out of the way?"

"No problem!" said the shorter man, waving as Hannah drove off.

"What did those men want?" Gero asked, noticing that Hannah had gone as pale as chalk.

"I don't know," she said truthfully, turning onto the main road. "Did anyone talk to you on your way to the castle, or did anything unusual happen?"

Gero fell silent.

"There was a strange man with a stick and a dog," Matthäus piped up.

"And?" Hannah shifted into the wrong gear in her impatience, and as the engine wailed in protest, Gero recoiled in shock.

"And my lord threatened to kill him if he didn't get lost," Matthäus blurted out innocently.

"You did *what?*" Hannah whipped her head to the side to face Gero as she jerked the steering wheel, almost losing control of the car.

"You're trying to kill us, too!" Gero yelled, desperately clawing his fingers into his seat. Hannah turned her attention back to the road and stopped the car.

"I want to know exactly what happened. Right now," she said firmly.

"There was a man," Gero began uneasily. "He was telling me what path I could or could not take – on my own family's land. Surely you understand I couldn't permit that."

Hannah sighed. "He probably ran to the police right away. And now they're looking for a man in a knight's outfit who threatens innocent passersby." She shook her head. "I only wonder if Tom's Americans were the ones who just stopped us."

For the rest of the journey, Gero stared straight ahead, shrouding himself in a steely silence. After Hannah parked the car in front of her house, he led the mare out of the trailer and back into the stable, giving it hay and water without uttering a word. Meanwhile, Hannah drew a bath for the freezing boy. Finally, she tucked him into bed and sat next to him.

The boy barely moved. He felt weak and his forehead burned.

Soon Gero appeared to check on his squire. He had stripped off his wet clothing and slipped into the black sweat-suit.

"He has a fever," Gero said softly, laying his hand on the boy's forehead and cheeks. "We have to brew medicinal herbs. Are you familiar with that?"

Hannah noticed the unease in his eyes. She stood up and offered him her place by the boy's side.

"Don't worry," she said confidently. "He'll be fine. To be on the safe side, I'll call my friend. She's a doctor."

"No doctors," he said absently. "They often make a sick person worse than they already are."

"My friend is very capable," Hannah tried to reassure him. "Besides, medicine has improved significantly in the last seven hundred years. She will give him some medicine and he'll be better by morning."

Twenty minutes later, Senta was standing in the room. She already knew Matthäus, and she recognized Gero from the same night. She was astonished that the doctors at the hospital had agreed to release him so early.

Gero, who had no memory of the woman, didn't respond to her greeting with enthusiasm. He stood up, bowing slightly and avoided giving her his hand.

"Well, let's see," Senta said. Gently, she pulled back the blanket and pushed up the boy's shirt so that she could feel his pale belly. Then she carefully pressed a digital thermometer in his ear.

"Almost Forty," she murmured. "He's developing something."

Hannah watched as Gero followed the doctor's actions with a tense expression. The boy let her examine him without protest. At her command, he widened his mouth with a long "ahhh" like a hungry baby bird.

"He might be developing tonsillitis, but it could just as well be the beginning of diphtheria. Do you know if he has been vaccinated?" Senta's gaze darted from Hannah to Gero.

"I don't think he's been vaccinated against anything," Hannah answered hesitantly.

"That should be rectified as soon as possible," Senta decided. "I'll give him some antibiotics and I'll also have to draw some blood. That's the only way we can be certain if it's infectious or not."

"Very well, if you think that it's necessary," Hannah decided, not wanting to delay the matter unnecessarily. "But try not to hurt him. I don't know if anyone's ever drawn blood from him."

As Senta exposed the boy's thin, white arm, she looked around for help. Matthäus lay with his eyes shut, and didn't move. Senta knew from experience that most children reacted strongly when they felt the needle pricking them.

"It would be better if someone held on to him," she said, looking at Gero.

"I'll do it," Hannah said and sat down on the other side of the bed, placing a hand onto Matthäus's shoulder to restrain him if he drew back or moved in surprise. She stroked his hair reassuringly.

Gero hadn't moved the entire time, but the moment that the needle began to pierce the boy's arm, he bolted over to Senta. As he was trying to pull her back, he lost his balance and fell on top of her.

"No bloodletting," he gasped, staring at the doctor under him with a fierce look.

"She's just doing her job, Gero, let her go!" Hannah cried in horror.

He got up reluctantly. The doctor had almost stabbed herself while still balancing the needle in her hand.

"No bloodletting. Understood?" His commanding voice left no doubt that he would enforce his order with violence if necessary.

"Bloodletting? That sounds like something out of the Middle Ages. I just want to draw some blood from him to do a blood test," Senta explained, more baffled than terrified by the attack. Shaking her head, she decided to put the needle away in her bag again.

As she said goodbye to Hannah at the door, she handed her a prescription.

"I'm sorry," Hannah said apologetically. "I didn't know that he would behave so oddly."

"As long as he doesn't treat you that way, I have no problems with it," Senta answered drily and smiled. "This isn't my business, but … are the two of them living with you now?"

"Only temporarily, until Tom's found an apartment for his friend." Hannah bit her lip.

"Well, you'll have peace in the house again soon, then." Senta smiled sympathetically, and promptly became solemn again. "If anything's wrong with the boy … if he gets worse or if he can't stomach the medicine, call me immediately, okay?"

"Thank you," Hannah said, embracing Senta as she left.

"Can you explain why you made such a big fuss back there?" Hannah demanded when she returned to Gero, who was sitting on the bed and holding the boys hand.

"Templars are not allowed to undergo bloodletting without the permission of our commander. It weakens the sick person more than it helps them," Gero responded indignantly.

"But you're not with the Templars anymore! You're in the twenty-first century. And could you trust me just once?"

"As you wish," he mumbled, lowering his gaze and looked at Matthäus who had fallen to sleep again.

The sky had already begun to darken, and Hannah quickly lit two candles, one on the windowsill and another on the bedside table. Gero still hadn't taken to modern electric lighting.

"I have to leave for a short while," she said, "to fetch the medicine."

Gero nodded silently.

"Wait here for me," she said.

Slowly, he turned around and stared at her angrily through narrowed eyes. "Where else would I go?"

Without a word, Hannah left the house.

Absentmindedly, Gero looked at the red spots on the otherwise pale face of the boy.

"Damn it," he murmured. Matthäus was running a high fever. Gero's elder sister had died from a fever. A mixture of helplessness and sorrow overwhelmed him. Silently, he began to pray.

He wasn't sure what made his heart beat faster when Hannah returned some time later with a cup in her hand.

"What do you have there?" he asked as she brought the medicine to Matthäus.

"Would you like to smell it?" She held out the pink-colored brew to him without waiting for an answer.

It smelled faintly of raspberries and, surprisingly, of something else that reminded him uncomfortably of a terrible time in his life.

"Mold potion," he said, wrinkling his nose.

"What?" Hannah stared at him in astonishment.

"It smells like the medicine our eremite used to brew. He prepared noxious potions from molding cocoons. He used them to aid in expelling pus."

"Surely you aren't telling me there was already penicillin in your time? As far as I know, this substance was first discovered in the middle of the twentieth century."

"Call it whatever you want." Gero glared at the syrup in disgust. "I only know that it tastes atrocious. I always had to vomit after they poured it down my throat."

He could still clearly remember his first experience with the disgusting brew in Cyprus when his shoulder had been abscessed. Back then, he had begged for beer or red wine to drink afterward, but he had only been allowed to drink sweetened lemon water.

Filled with sympathy, he watched as Matthäus stirred and Hannah put the cup to his lips.

"It'll be all right," she said, gently stroking the boy's forehead after he had shut his eyes again. Gero could have used the same reassurance.

"Are you joining me downstairs?" Hannah asked.

"No, I'd like to stay by the boy," he replied softly.

"Then I'll stay, too," she answered, adding, "if it's okay with you?"

He nodded quickly and felt a deep gratitude that she hadn't left him alone.

A little later, she appeared with two glasses and a bottle of Merlot under her arm. In one hand, she held a tray of sandwiches. She set the tray on the floor and looked at him encouragingly.

"You should eat something, or you'll get sick, too."

She sat down on the floor, crossed her legs, and leaned back against the wall.

"Do you want to sit with me?" she asked.

Sighing, he accepted her invitation. They sat with their shoulders touching.

With an uncertain smile, he took one of the delicate glasses and watched in fascination as the shimmering red wine created a dancing whirlpool as Hannah poured it into the glass. Wearily, he shut his eyes, enjoying a feeling of warmth against his back. He turned around to look at the source of his comfort, a flat box that was mounted on the wall. In his father's castle, there had been a green-tiled stove that spanned the height of the room and provided the same warmth in the cold seasons.

"Is that a stove?"

"Yes, something like that," Hannah answered, and poured herself a glass of red wine. "There's a boiler in the basement of this house that heats up a certain amount of water. It's then pumped through the piping installed throughout the house and into these metallic cases that we have in every room."

"I believe the Romans had something similar, yes?" He looked at her inquiringly as he bit into his cheese sandwich.

Hannah nodded in amazement.

As she chewed on her sandwich, she said, "Tell me something about your family."

Gero pondered what to say for a moment, gazing at her auburn hair.

"The free nobles of Breydenbach are widely dispersed," he began in a low voice. "One branch lives across the Main River. Another lives north of here, near the Rhine, and yet another where we were today. Long ago, the Archbishop of Trier gave my father a piece of land and the castle as a fiefdom, not far from the Hemmenrode Abbey. My mother is descended from the House of Eltz." He cleared his throat and turned to the sleeping boy

"Was your wife sick before she died?" Hannah asked unexpectedly. The thought of the crypt hadn't left her mind, and perhaps his wife's early death could explain why he reacted so fearfully to the boy's fever.

"No, she died during childbirth. The child was too large. She couldn't deliver her in the normal way. We tried everything. Finally, we had to cut her open so that the child could at least be baptized while it was still alive."

Hannah stared at Gero in horror. The idea of bringing a child into the world without professional medical help seemed utterly barbaric to her.

"Did you say we?" she asked breathlessly.

"I held her as the midwife did what she had to. I couldn't leave her alone." Hannah thought she saw pain flash in his eyes. "It was clear that she would die," he continued tonelessly. "Elisabeth screamed until she had no strength left. The midwife tried to turn the child, but that wasn't the problem. The child's head couldn't fit through her bones. On the evening, the midwife gave my wife a strong medicine that made her fall asleep, in a way. Then, the midwife had the priest called in and they explained to me that she had to cut open Elisabeth's belly. They reminded me of what St. Augustine taught us. An unborn child who died unbaptized would forever burn in hell. After that, the midwife went to work. The priest rushed out for a moment, as he couldn't stand the sight of blood, and the midwife whispered to me, asking me for permission to press another sleeping sponge onto Elisabeth's face – in case she couldn't be saved – so that the medicine it was soaked in could grant her a quick, painless death."

Gero took a deep breath.

"I don't know where I got the strength to agree to that," he whispered absently. "I only know that I never gave up hoping for a miracle … and praying that she and the child would survive."

"But it didn't help, did it?" Hannah said softly, stroking his arm.

"No. The child, a girl, was already dead. Strangled with its own cord, and Elisabeth …" He looked down at his now empty wine glass and cleared his throat. "She couldn't be saved."

Hannah herself was near tears. She wanted badly to put her arms around him to comfort him. She held up the wine bottle instead. "Would you like some more?"

"Yes, please." Gero raised his head and smiled thankfully. As she refilled his glass, he gazed at her inquiringly. *A moment too long,* she thought. She turned her gaze away.

"What about you?" he asked, surprising her. "Where is *your* family? Surely you don't live here all by yourself?"

"Actually, I do," she said. "My father is dead, and my mother eloped with an Italian."

He looked shocked.

"She went away," Hannah explained, "to Australia. That's really far away … at the other end of the world. I haven't heard from her in ages. And I have no siblings."

"Nor a husband," he said, before her nod encouraged him to enquire further. "Don't you ever think about marrying someone? It's a dangerous life for a woman without a man. You have no one to protect you and no one to do the difficult tasks for you. Unless you're hiding behind cloister walls."

"No," she replied with a smile. "I'm actually sick of men. Tom was my last boyfriend, but he wasn't serious about marriage. His work was more important to him than a wife or children."

"Isn't it normal here for an honorable man to have both?"

"Yes, of course." Hannah smiled wistfully. "But Tom was a little different. He's married to his work. There's no place for a wife in the grand scheme of things."

"Like with a warrior monk," Gero mused.

Hannah wasn't sure what to make of his comment.

"There are no warrior monks left today," she said firmly, not knowing why she had even said it, let alone why she felt so strongly about it.

"Tell me something about the German lands," he said. All at once, a child-like curiosity filled his eyes. "It certainly is very different from the land I left behind."

"Yes, quite a few things have changed," Hannah answered slowly, wondering how she was supposed to explain the history of the last seven hundred years.

Late into the night, after answering an endless marathon of questions, she fell asleep on Gero's shoulder.

When she awoke, she found to her astonishment that he had carried her to the bed and laid her down next to Matthäus. The sole candle on the bedside table was still burning, and it cast an eerily long shadow against the opposite wall.

"I'm thirsty," Matthäus stammered.

A moment later, Hannah saw Gero appear with a cup. Carefully, he moistened the boy's dried lips with the water that Hannah had set down on the bedside table. Then he felt the boy's forehead with his thumb and index finger and made the sign of the cross. He folded his hands and appeared to be praying silently.

Hannah blinked and raised her head.

"Go back to sleep," he whispered, smiling. "I'll keep watch."

CHAPTER 23

Confrontation

Thursday, November 18, 2004

A tickle on her nose and the distinctive smell of sweaty child's hair greeted Hannah as she awoke. Slowly, she raised her head. Matthäus had cuddled up to her, pressing his back against her like a puppy seeking its mother's warmth. His breath was calm and even, and his features were relaxed. She stretched out her hand and held it to his forehead.

The fever must have receded. Curiously she craned her neck over the side of the bed.

Gero had lain down on the soft, carpeted floor, sleeping soundly on his stomach with his head resting on his right arm. He was still fully dressed, even still wearing his boots.

Hannah rose silently and slipped through the door. After a hot shower, she walked to the living room, wearing only a white satin bathrobe and with her hair piled high in a turban she had fashioned from a towel. Heisenberg was already waiting for her, meowing loudly. She opened the patio door and let him out. For a moment, she shut her eyes and breathed in the cool, damp air. It was still dark outside, and so foggy that she could no longer make out the vegetable patch behind her house, despite the outside lights.

On her way back to her bedroom, she jumped in shock when she saw Gero coming down the stairs. Clad only in his leather trousers, he stopped abruptly on the lowest stair and stared at her attire in surprise. His eyes were open wide and fixed on the slightly askew neckline of her bathrobe. For a moment Hannah held her breath, feeling inexplicably drawn to her new roommate. Her gaze turned involuntarily to the numerous scars that ran over his impressive muscles. He must have suffered far more than he had admitted yesterday.

Hannah cleared her throat to end the tense moment. "Is Matthäus better?" she asked.

"Yes, thank the Lord ... and you, for your help," he answered softly without looking at her. Hannah sensed that he still had something to say, but then he tore his gaze away from her and disappeared into the bathroom without a word.

Matthäus didn't come down to breakfast. On the guest room's bedside table, Hannah set down a large glass of apple juice and a bowl of oatmeal that she had sweetened with honey. Tenderly she stroked Matthäus's hair as he slept.

Gero had crept into the room. His eyes bore a soft expression as he smiled at her. "You would be a good mother to him," he remarked in a husky voice. Then he coughed suddenly. "We should have breakfast downstairs, so we don't disturb him."

When the doorbell rang a little later, Hannah jumped up so quickly that she spilled her tea onto the dining table.

Gero looked up in surprise. "Are you expecting someone?"

Tom! was her next thought, but she didn't say it aloud.

When she cracked open the door, she saw that it really was Tom.

"Why didn't you call me?" Hannah exclaimed in surprise.

Tom looked at her in confusion. "I did tell you we were being shadowed, and possibly wiretapped," he explained. "That's why I couldn't get in touch earlier. I thought you'd be relieved to see me." He sounded agitated.

"And? What do you want? Or have you found out how to send them back?" Hannah asked hopefully.

Tom shook his head. "I wanted to see how you and our visitors were doing. I've brought my colleague Paul with me. He's just as involved in this mess as I am. Are you going to let us in?"

"Of course," she said, gesturing apologetically as she stepped aside to allow them to enter. "How's it going with you?"

Only then did she notice Tom's strange outfit. The legs of the gray overalls he was wearing were at least six inches too short. She stared.

"Hey, we had to outwit the National Security Agency in order to come here at all," Tom said indignantly. "Paul's brother was kind enough to lend us his company car and uniforms."

Tom introduced his Luxembourgian colleague. Wearing the hideous light gray overalls labeled *Colbach: Transports Luxembourgeois*, the wiry redhead could not have looked any odder. In contrast to Tom, Paul's uniform engulfed his slight frame.

"My name's Paul. Nice to meet you," he said politely, holding out his right hand to Hannah and winking at her with friendly blue-green eyes.

"I told you," Agent Jack Tanner muttered to himself. "Old Jack isn't so easily fooled." He craned his neck to get a better view as his silver Mercedes C200 rolled past the perfectly restored farm cottage into which Stevendahl and Colbach had disappeared.

"Check the address, Mike," Jack ordered his colleague as he steered his service car a few feet furtherbefore pulling off and parking alongside the forested road.

Agent Mike Tapleton typed a few details into the computer on the car's dashboard, which was connected to the database of the local Resident Registration Office.

"Hannah Schreyber, born in Koblenz in 1972, residing in … Binsfeld since August 2002. Lived on Maxstraße in Bonn, until August 2002 …"

"Wait a minute," Jack cut in as he shoved another stick of gum between his teeth. "Isn't that Stevendahl's address?"

"You're right," Mike answered, looking at his colleague in surprise.

"It looks as if the two lived together for a while."

"A while?" Jack Tanner countered, peering at the computer screen. "Four years is nearly a lifetime to me. No one lives with the same woman for so long. They must have been in a serious relationship." He turned and began to bark into the dashboard's microphone, "C1 to base. Tell the boys to get ready – things are getting exciting. Stevendahl's with his ex-girlfriend, who lives five miles southwest of the facility. She could be an accomplice."

"Should we prepare to seize them?" came the reply from the loudspeaker.

"We don't have anything that we can seize yet," Tanner answered impatiently. "Besides, we can only spring the trap when we are absolutely sure that our targets are there. Nevertheless, we should get one of our operations teams to bug the house. Only when the birds have left the nest, of course. Till then, block the area off. This is the only road that runs by here. If you guys don't mess things up, no one in this house will be able to escape us. Also, get me a surveillance van with a thermal camera and a directional microphone immediately."

"Tom," Hannah whispered, catching his arm before he and his colleague could enter the living room.

Tom paused. "What is it?"

"Please, watch what you say in front of them. Our time traveler is rather pissed off at you, and he can't understand everything you say. He speaks only Middle High German and Old French."

"What do you mean *watch what you say* …?" Tom retorted sourly.

"All I'm saying is, imagine if someone grabbed you from your normal life and transferred you …"

Tom glared at her through narrowed eyes. "I thought you explained to him that I saved his life – from the press, the Americans, and from Hagen and his pack of researches?"

"Where did you get *that* idea? I was happy he even understood that he landed in the twenty-first century."

"Well, he should be thankful," Tom snapped. "I bet his life in his goddamn Middle Ages was worse than this! Where is the guy anyway?"

"In the dining room."

Before Hannah could utter another warning, Tom marched toward the dining room and Hannah followed him with a bad feeling in her stomach.

By the time Tom entered the dining room, Gero had already sprung to his feet.

Hannah suppressed an amused grin when she saw her ex-fiancé stop dead in his tracks. It wasn't just the crusader's muscled figure that filled Tom and Paul with respect. His upright posture and his piercing blue eyes rendered Tom Stevendahl, who wasn't fazed by much, at a loss for words.

"Gero, this is Tom and Paul," Hannah said as casually as possible.

Gero looked unimpressed. He scanned the two men from head to toe. He crossed his brawny arms in front of his chest and turned directly to Tom.

"Greetings," he said, when Tom made no attempt to make the first move. "So, you are the one who experiments on innocent people and then abandons them to their fate – regardless of the consequences!"

Tom turned to Hannah for help. "What did he say?"

"That in his humble opinion, you've botched things up," Paul replied with a grin. His Luxembourgish mother tongue obviously helped him understand Gero's medieval Eifel dialect.

"Excuse me?" Tom said, offended. "What does he know?"

Before Hannah could stop him, he had marched up to Gero and glared furiously at the man from the past, obviously trying to intimidate him.

Gero forced a tired smile. "Be quiet, boy," he snarled at Tom dismissively. "The only thing I want from you is your promise that you'll send us back to where you took us from. And soon!" He gave Hannah, who hardly dared to breathe, a sideways glance. "Or even better, since you seem to be the master of time, you can send me and my squire back two weeks before our disappearance."

Tom stared at him in disbelief. Gero had spoken softly but slowly, and he had understood most of it.

"Did I hear him correctly?" Tom turned around and looked at Paul doubtfully. "He wants us to transfer him back two weeks before the time of his disappearance?"

"Sounds like it," Paul confirmed, as he settled into a dark red armchair. "Well, try your best!" He grinned, and said to Hannah, "Does your visitor know that we don't know exactly how he arrived here, let alone how we can return him?"

Hannah shrugged. "I tried to tell him, but I don't think he was satisfied with my explanation."

"What is all this nonsense?" Tom grumbled. With a livid expression, he turned to the Templar. "Do you think I want to have you here? If it were up to me, you would be gone by tomorrow! Count yourself lucky that we found you and your little friend and brought you here!" Tom planted his hands on his hips and stared defiantly into the face of the knight. "If I'd left the two of you there, where I found you, they would have frozen you in nitrogen long ago and hacked you into tiny pieces."

Hannah was shocked. How could Tom be so spiteful?

But instead of calming him down, his words only seemed to have stoked his fury, and, while he was speaking, he stepped dangerously close to Gero. "Besides, millions of people died of the plague in your goddamn Middle Ages. Just looking at the statistics, you'll probably live a few years longer here than in the squalor from which you were taken! So, you have every reason to be thankful!"

Tom had come near enough for Gero to seize him effortlessly by the collar of his overalls and grab his throat.

With one hand, Tom attempted to free himself from his opponent's grip, and when he didn't succeed, he tried to hit the Templar in the face with his other fist. A split second later, Tom landed on his back. The crusader had rammed his knee into his stomach and was now holding a knife to his throat. Tom went stiff.

Paul had leapt to his feet, but obviously he still wasn't sure if it was a good idea to help his friend.

The man's eyes glittered dangerously above him, and as if from a distance, Tom heard Hannah's voice begging the Templar to let him go.

"Swear, you malefactor!" hissed the man holding him down mercilessly. "Swear by all the saints, by the holy Virgin, St. Michael, and St. George, that you will send us home soon. Otherwise I'll cut out your heart and feed it to the rats!"

Tom nodded quickly, fearing that the blade would be stabbed into his chest any second.

"Yes … I swear," he gasped, barely audible.

Gero felt his heart pounding in his chest. The ravenous urge to kill took several long moments to subside. Like many of his Brethren, it struck him to his core when he was confronted by the dark side of his soul.

He shut his eyes and took a deep breath before he felt a tentative hand on his shoulder.

"Please," Hannah said gently, "let him go, he didn't mean those things. If you hurt him, he certainly won't be able to help you anymore."

Gero looked up. Two clear green eyes were fixed on his, so near and so intimate that he felt a sharp pang in his heart. Groaning, he rose and stuck his knife back into his belt. He felt dizzy. Abruptly he turned to the patio door and disappeared outside without looking back once.

"Gero?" Hannah called halfheartedly. Uncertain if she should follow him, she stood motionless for a moment before coming to the conclusion that it would be better if she first tended to Tom.

Tom was lying on the floor as if he was dead. But then he raised his head and opened his eyes. Shuddering with horror, he touched his neck where the edge of the knife had been.

Hannah tried to help him up.

Impatiently he shook off her hand. "Leave me alone!" he yelled. "I can stand up by myself!"

His face pale, he struggled to his feet, looking around furiously, visibly relieved that the Templar had gone outside.

"Sit down," Hannah suggested in a conciliatory tone. "I'll get you something to drink."

"I don't want to sit down," Tom answered sullenly.

"Hey, Tom," Paul said. He touched his friend's arm reassuringly. "It's not Hannah's fault the guy flipped out. What did you expect? That you

296

could discuss this civilly with a modern man? The guy is desperate, and he reacts as he's been taught. Anyhow, I can understand where he's coming from. We've turned his world upside down, and he has a right to demand that we straighten it out again."

Tom sighed in frustration.

"Extraordinary problems demand extraordinary solutions," Paul added. "That's always been your motto, after all. Acting like a sulky ten-year-old doesn't help."

"You're right," Tom admitted. "I shouldn't have provoked him. After all, he's an uncultured barbarian."

Hannah swallowed the retort that was on the tip of her tongue. Tom certainly wouldn't understand that she was fairly sure Gero was more civilized than Tom would ever be.

"You better leave now," she said to Tom, "before there's any more trouble."

"Be careful, all right?" Tom said, stroking her hair as he said goodbye to her at the door. "I would jump off the Moselle Bridge if he raped you … or killed you."

"He's a monk," she replied testily. "He won't do anything to me."

"He sure doesn't act like one," Tom said, gripping her shoulders and forcing her to look him in the eye. "If he touches so much as a hair on your head, I'll make sure he won't survive it. You can tell him that."

Hannah looked up in shock, and he smiled cynically. "What do you think would happen if the Americans got ahold of our precious knight?" Tom asked. "They would crucify him in the name of research and examine his every last cell, or lock him up in a cage in one of the high-security NSA jails to study his behavior for the rest of his existence."

Hannah ran a hand reassuringly through his thick, brown locks. "You'll think of a way to turn back the clock. I'm sure of that." Her words sounded like a prayer.

"Before I forget," Tom said suddenly. He quickly strode to the car, where Paul was already waiting for him. A moment later, he returned to her. "Here," he said, handing her a brand new cell phone, "a prepaid phone for you. I have the same. Paul's brother bought them for us. My number is the only one saved. If you need me, just call that number so we can be sure that we're not being wiretapped."

With a sigh, Hannah looked down at the cell phone, a small comfort, considering the scope of the disaster they found themselves in.

"If there's nothing fishy going on here, I'll eat my hat!" Tanner declared. He watched in satisfaction as the gray delivery car left the house.

"Agent Hannon." Without waiting for an answer, he turned his attention again to the two-way radio. "Follow Stevendahl and Colbach! We'll attend to the lady of the house."

Gero caught Hannah by the stairs. "I'm sorry," he said, so quietly that she could barely hear him. Obviously, his temper had cooled in the garden behind the house, and had only now emerged after Tom had left.

"You don't have to be sorry," she said, handing him a mug of tea. "It wasn't your fault."

"Thank you," he said simply, and turned back to the stairs.

"Are you checking in on Matthäus?"

He nodded.

"Let me do it. He needs his medicine," Hannah said with a smile, "and a little consolation."

"Matthäus likes you. You have a kind heart, and … you're very beautiful." Hannah was taken aback by the way he said it. She glanced away and felt blood rushing to her cheeks.

She took the penicillin syrup from the fridge and followed Gero up the stairs. For some reason her knees had gone weak.

Matthäus was awake. The penicillin and a good night's sleep had worked wonders. Gero beamed as his squire prattled on to his lord and hostess. He was delighted to see the poor boy in such good spirits.

Hannah observed the knight gazing tenderly at his squire. *There are two entirely different sides to Gero of Breydenbach's soul.* She sat down next to Matthäus and handed him his breakfast.

After Matthäus had eaten his oatmeal, he snuggled back into the blankets and blinked at his lord.

"You have it real good here, my boy," Gero teased him with a smile. "Don't get too used to it, or you'll be disappointed when we return home."

Hannah suddenly had an idea. "If you're still feeling well later," she said to the boy, "and if your lord agrees to my suggestion, you may accompany us to a party this evening."

"A party?" the boy asked with wide, innocent eyes.

"Yes," Hannah answered, "there'll be music and dancing, and probably something good to eat, too."

298

Gero looked interested. "What kind of party? You never mentioned it."

"Judith's brother invited us to celebrate his new business. I hadn't planned on going, but after everything that happened today, I believe it's time that you see a little more of our world than these four walls."

CHAPTER 24

Modern Swordplay

Thursday, November 18, 2004

With bated breath, Gero clutched the back of the chair he was straddling, following every movement Hannah made with wide eyes. She stood in front of the dining table, wrapping a potted fern in colorful paper. These people from the future were either all crazy or just unbelievably wealthy. Gero would never have dreamed of wrapping a potted plant in painted paper. He shuddered as he imagined how much it must have cost.

Watching her fasten the ends of the paper together with a sticky, transparent strip of something, he felt utterly lost again. So much in this world was different from his own, though he was glad that there were at least a few things that hadn't changed.

Gero smiled silently to himself and looked over Hannah appraisingly. His gaze lingered on the white lace blouse that stretched across the subtle arc of her back, then wandered down the remarkable curves under her ankle-length, leather skirt. He imagined how lovely she would look in a surcoat, but then his mind went down a darker, more dangerous path, and he caught himself picturing her completely naked.

Gero felt as if he had been caught red-handed as Hannah turned around and looked straight at him. Abruptly he leapt to his feet, as if preparing to escape. Perhaps he really was mad. The devil must have taken his soul a long time ago. Why else would his lust for his hostess have grown so monstrous? He could no longer keep her sweet body out of his mind, and he had been seized by a terrible desire to hold her in his arms.

"Is the party nearby?" Gero tried to sound casual as he turned to the glass patio doors. It was nearly dark outside, and in his time it was not common to walk for long distances at night if it were not necessary.

"No, it's about a quarter mile from here," she answered with a tinge of pride in her voice. No one today knew that a mile in the Middle Ages meant a distance of about ten to twelve kilometers, and on horseback the journey would take nearly an hour. "In any case, we're taking the car."

The Templar's expression darkened. The thought of Hannah's horseless steel wagon made him sick.

"It won't be a long journey," Hannah said to reassure him.

She had never met Anselm Stein, but she had heard plenty about him from Judith. Anselm had moved here from Stuttgart and bought a house not far from Binsfeld. The invitation had been a kind gesture, and Hannah thought it was a good opportunity to give Gero and Matthäus a taste of their new environment.

As things stood, Hannah feared that the two time travelers would never make it home. Besides, she couldn't hide them both forever; Binsfeld was far too small a town for that. Moreover, she reasoned, the Americans probably wouldn't be looking for someone who had integrated so quickly into modern life. In a pair of jeans and a sweatshirt, Gero looked like any other attractive man on the street. No one in their wildest dreams would ever imagine that he was an actual Templar knight. Hannah let her mind race. They could start a new life here and create new identities for themselves with forged passports. *That shouldn't be too hard to arrange*, she mused, *money could buy nearly anything*.

Gero looked pensive. He stood close to the windows, arms crossed over his chest, staring into the twilight. He had asked her just yesterday if the lights he saw outside were will-o'-the-wisps.

Hannah wasn't sure how to help the knight understand everything about her world that confused him. She herself didn't understand the inner workings of her clothes iron, let alone airplanes, cars, televisions, or refrigerators. Perhaps, she mused, the clothes iron wasn't the problem at all, but the social norms of her time. Would he even believe that nowadays a thief didn't deserve to be hanged for his crime?

Gero turned around suddenly. "I'll get Matthäus," he said, already making his way upstairs.

"You look beautiful," the boy said as he descended the stairs, surprising Hannah as she stood before the mirror in the hallway, loosening a few strands of hair from her updo.

"You're a sweetheart," she thanked Matthäus with a smile.

Gero was suddenly standing behind her. He was wearing his leather pants and boots, along with a navy blue sweatshirt and her father's jacket. He stared at her just as appreciatively as the boy had, although far less innocently.

As he helped her into her coat, his warm hands brushed her neck. A shudder ran down her back. Courteously, he opened the front door for her, stepping outside to check that there was no danger before offering her his hand.

According to the invitation, the host's house was an old building with a few stables surrounding a medium-sized inner courtyard. Hannah parked her car on the side of the road some distance away from the house, and joined a group of other guests who were making their way to the party.

"Targets are approaching the site," crackled a voice from Jack's radio. "There's a party going on. Looks like it'll be a long night."

Satisfied, Jack Tanner leaned back in his car seat. "One of you should go in with them. I want to know what kind of guy she's dragged along." He broke into a smug grin. "And … action!" he remarked drily into his cell-phone, giving his team the signal to begin bugging Hannah Schreyber's house, while the two agents who had followed the suspects installed a GPS tracking device under her car.

"You know what I wonder, Mike?" Jack remarked as he watched the team approach Schreyber's house on the small screen of the dashboard computer.

"No," Mike said, biting into a donut with obvious pleasure.

"If the guy accompanying her really is a time traveler as Hagen claims. I mean, he's already found a date in a week – and Stevendahl's ex-girlfriend, at that?" Shaking his head, he opened the car door. "If you ask me, that's just impossible."

Before Mike could reply, Tanner had already stepped out of the car. "I'll go check whether the boys are doing things right," he said as he turned on his LED flashlight. Without another word, he strode into the darkness.

"What's up?" One of the men shone his flashlight at Jack's face and peered at him inquiringly. Like the other men with him, he was wearing light gray overalls with the label *Municipal Sewer Cleaning* on the breast pocket.

Tanner shook his head. "Nothing, Greg. Make sure you get results."

Holding up his light, Tanner observed his team as they cracked open the deadbolt and opened the cast-iron outer door.

Before they entered the house, the men pulled light, plastic coverings over their damp, muddy shoes. The last thing they needed was to leave footprints all over the woman's house.

With practiced speed, Greg inserted a flexible fiberglass camera into a ceiling panel. A small LED lamp that he had placed beside him lit the area as bright as day. He was wearing cream-colored surgical gloves. With his fingertips, he attached an inconspicuous listening device, running his tongue over his lips in concentration. He then he placed a small, white, mesh cap over it to disguise the cavity. With his index finger, he activated his earpiece.

"Camera is on," he said simply. "Have you gone into the bedroom?" he asked Jack.

"What awaits me there?" Jack grinned.

"Have a look around," Greg replied seriously. "After all the things I've learned about this case so far, I thought it would be of interest to our investigation."

Curiously, Jack stepped into the room that usually roused the greatest interest among his colleagues. A white cloak with a red cross on it lay on the romantic iron bed with the flouncy white canopy. Swiftly, he whipped out his digital camera and sent the picture to his control center.

"Tell the boys to verify whether this object matches the ranger's description, and what exactly it means."

Stowing his cell phone in his breast pocket, Jack took a last look around the room.

"Did you take any hair samples?" he asked, heading to the basement exit.

"Of course," came the reply just before the last agent shut the door carefully behind him.

Nothing could go wrong now. By the end of this evening, they would know if the tale of the time-traveler had been the dream of a mad, old German professor, or the start of an unbelievable new reality that Jack barely dared to imagine.

Guests streamed in through an open courtyard gate, most of them dressed in strange costumes. The women wore long, flowing robes, while the men looked even stranger with their plaited hair, tunics, and long, pointed shoes. She tried hard to remember if there had been a dress code in the invitation.

Gero and Matthäus looked around with interest.

"Stay close to me, and don't talk to anyone," Hannah said softly with a pleading look at the both of them.

"If we have to behave like serfs," Gero growled, "why did you bring us here at all?"

The house was ancient, but it had been newly restored and lavishly furnished. Thick, freshly painted timber beams and decorative gable carvings lent the building a rustic charm. Two peat torches blazed in their wall mountings on either side of the grand entrance.

Along with the other guests, they entered a vast hall lit only by torches.

At that moment, Judith charged toward them in a flowing, dark red satin dress, not letting Gero out of her sight for a second. Hesitantly, Matthäus hid behind his lord.

"Hello, you three! I'm glad you came," Judith exclaimed a little too loudly.

"So, be honest," she whispered as Hannah greeted her with an embrace. "Your new friend has something animalistic about him. I'd love to know what he's like." She grinned suggestively and poked Hannah in the side. "You know what I mean."

Hannah had already begun to regret accepting the invitation. With a terse smile, she handed Judith the present she had brought.

"Tell me, Judith, what kind of party is this?" she asked.

Judith raised her eyebrows in astonishment. "A medieval festival," she replied, as if the facts were plain to see. "Didn't you know my brother is heavily involved in medieval markets and knight tournaments? He's one of Germany's foremost experts on medieval swordplay. He also trades in antique weapons. Today, he's celebrating not just his housewarming but his store opening, too. About a month ago, he established the headquarters of his new online shop here," Judith smiled proudly. "Most of the people you'll see are important clients and friends from the scene."

There really are no coincidences in this world, *Hannah thought.*

"How would I have known?" she asked, sounding slightly annoyed. The bad feeling that had dogged her since she stepped into the hall grew stronger. "You didn't mentioned it before. How much does your brother know about the Middle Ages?"

"Oh, he knows a good deal, all right," Judith answered proudly. "He speaks Middle High German, and is one of the few people in Germany who speaks nearly flawless Old French. He also owns an impressive collection of books on the Early and High Middle Ages. Why did you think he had so many books about the Templars?"

At the word Templar, Gero pricked up his ears, narrowing his eyes and raising his head like a wolf that had found the scent.

Judith hadn't missed Gero's look. "Would you like a drink?" she asked nervously.

"Yes ... do you have any red wine?" Hannah answered, uncertain if alcohol would really help in this unforeseen situation.

"We have red wine, mead, cloister beer ... anything you want," Judith answered with amusement before leading them into a large room.

Thick ceiling beams that had been painted brown lent the room an air of rustic comfort. The floor was covered with green patterned tiles. Small groups, obviously familiar with each other, dotted the room, greeting each newcomer with warm embraces and pecks on the cheek.

Only the host was nowhere to be found.

"I'll go look for him and introduce him to you," Judith excused herself before slipping away.

"Jack?" buzzed the radio set.

Mike Tapleton, who was sitting in the front passenger seat waiting for his boss, responded with a whisper. "Jack is in the surveillance van. What's up?"

Agent Piet Hannon sat in a silver BMW with his partner, watching the courtyard entrance into which the targets had disappeared.

"Listen, Mike," Piet responded in a slightly agitated voice, "you have to call Jack. We've checked the host's address. He's the weapon expert who examined the sword for Hagen! That's an odd coincidence, isn't it?"

A moment later, Jack Tanner's command came over the radio.

"Piet, proceed into the location and mingle with the other guests. You won't be noticed among a hundred people. Find out what connection Stevendahl's ex has with our weapon freak."

"Yes, sir," came the words from the loudspeaker. "I'll report back as soon as I find anything."

A sumptuous buffet had been set up at the end of the hall. Crossed swords and shields hung on the wall above it, while the other walls were adorned with tapestries of medieval hunting scenes.

Gero smiled wistfully. "One feels almost at home here," he said.

"We have to be careful," Hannah whispered to him. "The man who owns the house is supposedly an expert in your era and culture."

"How do you know?" The Templar asked, his tone oddly neutral.

"Just look around you! Haven't you noticed that most of the guests here are dressed like the people of your time?"

"No one in my time walked around looking like that," Gero replied indignantly. "In my time, any self-respecting man wore his hair down, and never past the shoulders. Some even set curls in their hair. And for some, like members of my Order, short hair was required." As if to prove his point, he ran a hand over his shorn head.

"But the clothing looked like this, didn't it?"

"Hmm," Gero mused, the corners of his mouth curling into a contemptuous smirk. "I suppose they could pass as beggars or day laborers."

Hannah recalled that the workmanship of his cloak, which she had already washed twice, was exquisite. Not for the first time, the thought floated through her mind that it was utterly incorrect to think that medieval people were barely out of the Stone Age.

Judith had given up searching for her brother and returned with a glass of red wine, which she handed to Hannah, and a mug of cloister beer for Gero. For the boy she quickly rustled up a glass of apple juice. Gripping the glass tightly in her hand, Hannah stood near the buffet table with a tense expression. Gero stood next to her, sniffing at the beer like a sommelier before taking a large gulp. He hummed in approval and emptied half the mug in one go.

"It's rare to come by such good beer," he said, sounding impressed, after he had taken yet another mighty gulp. Hannah hoped fervently that he could handle his drink. Uneasily, she watched as he absorbed their surroundings. Curiously, he stared at the crossed swords and the shields on the wall.

She smiled as Gero licked the foam from his lips with relish and wiped his mouth and nose on his forearm. When he noticed that she was observing him, he looked at her apologetically. His manners were usually impeccable. She had heard rumors that knights were slovenly eaters, belching and farting at the table with abandon, and thoughtlessly throwing their leftovers behind them. Gero of Breydenbach and his squire Matthäus of Bruch were nothing like that.

The boy had sat down on the floor with his legs crossed. To Hannah's great astonishment, Gero had given a glass of wine to him, which a waiter had served. It was common to give boys of his age wine, the Templar had claimed matter-of-factly. Even younger children drank wine mixed with water.

Hannah tried to hint to Gero that giving children wine wasn't acceptable in the twenty-first century, but then she gave up, concluding that it made no sense to quarrel with him in front of a room full of medieval enthusiasts, whom she feared would realize that Gero was speaking Middle High German.

Suddenly, Gero's attention was captivated by the sight of a woman sucking on a cigarette, exhaling the clouds of smoke through her nose and mouth. He was so fascinated by this peculiar sight that he let his mouth hang open for a moment before he finally turned away and emptied his mug of beer, drinking every last drop.

Hannah took a deep breath. She must have been crazy taking such risks, she thought, bringing the two of them to the party.

Suddenly someone tugged at her arm and she almost spilled her wine.

A head with dark, curly hair appeared next to her. It was Carolin, her part-time employee from the bookstore, dressed in a gaudy hippie costume.

She had scrutinized Hannah's new roommate from afar, and was just as curious about the mysterious man as Judith was.

"If he ever gets his own apartment, you can ask if you can move in with him," Hannah remarked with annoyance.

"Really?" Carolin squealed. She craned her neck to look for him again. "Where is he? I don't see him anymore."

"What?" Hannah looked around in shock.

Gero had disappeared. She glanced at Matthäus, who, thankfully, was still sitting on the floor.

"Excuse me," she said, pushing Carolin aside.

She bent down to Matthäus quickly. "Wait here for me. Don't move. I'll be right back."

Breathlessly, she wandered around, pushing her way through the sea of guests. Suddenly, her heart lurched when she saw Gero conversing animatedly with a stranger. His partner had plaited his long brown hair. He was a good head shorter than Gero, but his shoulders were nearly as broad. Hannah couldn't believe her eyes, it seemed like he possessed the ability to conduct a fluent conversation with Gero.

He was far more flamboyantly costumed than the other guests. Over a black sweatshirt, he was wearing short-sleeved chain mail, a yellow tabard with an upright black lion on the breast, form-fitting black pants, and rugged, dark brown leather boots. A full, dark, neatly trimmed beard framed his friendly face. The impressive-looking man probably didn't have a clue that he was standing opposite a real knight.

Suddenly the long-haired man turned around as if he sensed that he was being watched. Apologetically, he gave Gero a nod before approaching Hannah then broke into a broad smile, revealing the dimples in his cheeks.

"I don't believe I've had the pleasure," he said, holding out his hand to her. "Anselm Stein. I am your host for the night."

"Hannah Schreyber," she said distractedly, giving Gero an uncertain look.

"It's a pleasure to meet you. Judith has told me a lot about you."

Hannah swayed slightly, and forgot to shake his hand altogether.

"Are you feeling unwell?" Anselm Stein asked, looking anxiously at her pale face. "Would you like something to drink?" He laid a concerned hand on her shoulder.

Gero, too, had noticed that something wasn't right. In one long step, he was next to her, holding onto her elbows and trying to calm her.

"Ah," Anselm said in surprise. "You're together?"

Hannah cleared her throat and looked at him apprehensively. "You could say so."

"Do you speak the *langue d'oil*, too?" The host raised his bushy eyebrows curiously.

"Excuse me?" she blinked.

"No, she doesn't speak the language at all," Gero explained to Anselm.

Anselm noticed that Hannah looked agitated.

"Don't worry," he chimed hurriedly in modern German. "Old French isn't an easy language. Hardly anyone today can still speak it fluently, especially since there are several dialects. Gero is the one and only person I have ever met who speaks it better than I do," Anselm said with an encouraging smile. "Can I bring you something to drink?" he asked Hannah.

"A large glass of red wine, please," she replied promptly, deciding she no longer cared how much she drank. She would walk home if she had to – that would give her enough time to lecture Gero and blow off some steam.

After Anselm had left the room, Gero smirked at her. "I've always wanted to drink with the Count of Jülich."

After some initial confusion, he quickly learned that the people around him were acting out some sort of fantasy version of the past.

It was the first time in a long while that he had felt so unburdened. Perhaps it was the delicious beer that was putting him in such a good mood, or the discovery that although this world was so markedly different from his own, not everything was entirely unfamiliar.

As his spirits rose, Hannah appeared even more desirable than usual. He yearned so badly to touch her, to brush her dark red hair out of her face, or even better, to kiss her lips ... But at that moment, he was suddenly yanked out of his fantasies.

"Have you gone mad?" she spat at him. "I thought we had an agreement!"

"I am my own master," he retorted brusquely, angered by her insubordinate tone.

Hannah felt like a lion-tamer standing in the middle of the circus ring without her chair and whip.

Before Gero could say anything else, Anselm returned and handed him a mug of beer filled to the brim, and Hannah another glass of red wine. He clinked glasses with them merrily, and Gero recited a lengthy text in Old French.

Anselm shook with enthusiastic laughter as Hannah scowled.

"That was a fabliau. A medieval blonde joke, so to speak. But I haven't heard that one anywhere else yet. It's a rather suggestive rhyme about drinking men and nagging wives," the host enlightened Hannah. "Your friend has a bawdy sense of humor. I hope you don't mind if I spare us both the translation. I'm sure he didn't mean it personally."

Hannah forced a pained smile. She felt as if her worst nightmares were coming true.

A young man with a thin, blonde ponytail, wearing brown bloomers and a hooded shirt, hurried toward Anselm. He whispered in Anselm's ear, loud enough for Gero and Hannah to hear that the host wasn't tending to his other guests enough.

Hannah pricked up her ears as Anselm whispered back to the man. "Look at the guy next to me, Stefan. Can you believe it? Someone who speaks both Middle High German and Old French, and is perfectly skilled

in swordplay? He must be an absolute freak in the re-enactment industry."
Anselm's eyes glittered.

His friend glared suspiciously at Gero and turned away without a
word.

"Excuse me for a minute," Anselm said to Hannah and Gero. "I have
to greet a few guests. Please, help yourselves to the food."

Hannah handed Gero and Matthäus plastic plates and cutlery. *A harsh
departure from the night's theme*, Hannah thought.

The Templar squinted at the knife and fork that he was holding
clumsily in one hand. Pensively, he lowered his lids before giving Hannah
a pained look. "Things really have changed more than I thought," he
remarked softly, "except for the beer and beautiful women," he added
with a wistful smile.

Gero decided on a slice of beef and a piece of bread. Matthäus had
loaded his plate with fried potatoes and bacon, a dish that he had not
known before, as potatoes hadn't arrived in Europe until the fifteenth
century.

As the three of them sat down at one of the free tables, a passerby could
have mistaken them for a family.

Hannah noticed that some of the guests were staring in bewilderment
as Gero and Matthäus made the sign of the cross, then folded their hands
for a few long minutes as they murmured a prayer before finally eating
silently.

After he had polished off his food, Gero whispered something into his
squire's ear.

Hannah looked up curiously. As Matthäus grinned at her, his ears went
red and he left the table with Gero following him.

Hannah deduced that the boy was showing Gero the toilet. Sighing,
she realized to her great unease that she couldn't follow them everywhere.

Gero stood before the latrine, looking helplessly to his right. The man
next to him peed uninhibitedly into one of three basins fastened to the
wall. Unlike the other men at the party, he was wearing everyday twenty-
first century clothes. Gero loosened the cords of his pants and aimed into
the drain just as his neighbor had done. For a moment, the man watched
Gero fasten his pants again, turning away with a grin only when he caught
Gero's irritated glare. Gero followed the man into a small antechamber
where he washed his hands while whistling softly. The stranger, who
looked somehow familiar, left the bathroom, still whistling.

Gero had stepped out into the small passage leading to the hall to wait for Matthäus, when the man with the blonde ponytail suddenly appeared next to him.

"Hey, you," he called to Gero disrespectfully, seizing him by the arm. Feeling more puzzled than angry, Gero looked down at the man. "Anselm is waiting for you. You're signed up for a swordfight."

Although the guy didn't speak Middle High German, Gero understood what he had said but could hardly believe what he had heard. Had the man really said something about a swordfight?

"No," Gero said simply as the man beckoned him to follow.

But the other man would not accept his answer, and pulled him along impatiently. "It is customary for a guest to take on Anselm in an exhibition fight, and this year, you're the chosen one."

As the blond man pulled him toward the courtyard, Gero glanced around, searching for Hannah and Matthäus. He had no idea what Anselm had in store for him. Yet it would be impolite to refuse him.

Gero squinted in confusion as he stepped into the courtyard. From the barn roof, a gleaming bright light flooded a section of the courtyard demarcated with colorful ribbons.

Someone grabbed his wrist and pulled him into a large storeroom.

It was Anselm, who smiled and gestured with pride at a hodgepodge of battle equipment. Shields, swords, and chain mail of all sizes lay on long shelves. Surcoats in fantastic colors hung on clothes hangers. Gero was reminded of the weapon chamber of Bar-sur-Aube, although everything they had, came only in black, white and red.

"Help yourself," Anselm encouraged him.

When Gero hesitated, Anselm reached up to one of the shelves and threw him some chain mail that he thought would fit him. He handed the Templar a colorful, patterned cape, a pot helmet, and a sword.

Gero reminded himself that he, as a Templar, was forbidden from engaging in any form of tournament, but then, he concluded, this world was governed by different rules anyway.

Hannah waited for Gero and Matthäus for fifteen minutes. The hall had begun to empty out and guests were putting on their jackets and heading for the exit. A fanfare sounded from outside, and cheers rang out. Hannah stood up uncertainly.

Suddenly Carolin hurried to her side. "You have to see this!" she yelled with wide eyes. "Your friend is challenging Judith's brother to a swordfight, in full gear. Both of them look like real knights!"

"What?" Hannah couldn't believe her ears.

Judith appeared in the door and flailed her arms excitedly. "I had no idea that your new friend was from Anselm's industry," she exclaimed.

"Neither did I," Hannah answered bitterly. "Where is he?"

"Come on," Judith called, pulling Hannah outside.

Long ribbons fastened to colorful poles created a square the size of a boxing ring. The audience pushed forward against the barriers, already drunk with excitement.

Desperately, Hannah searched for Gero, but he was nowhere in sight. Suddenly, the spectators parted, forming a small lane in the middle of the crowd. Two men entered the ring, clad in chain mail and colorful surcoats appliquéd with different coats of arms. Each held a shield in one hand and a sword in the other. They wore iron helmets with only narrow slits to see out of. Hannah couldn't see their faces, but she knew exactly which one Gero was.

A sinking feeling washed over her. Where the devil was Matthäus hiding?

Pushing the other spectators aside, she wove her way through the crowd toward Judith, the only one who could stop this madness.

"Judith! Tell your brother to stop immediately! It's far too dangerous," she yelled at her from some distance, but Judith merely laughed and waved her hand dismissively.

The sound of steel hitting steel sent Hannah into a panic. What if Gero killed Anselm? How would he know that people today fought according to different rules? She didn't know much about medieval tournaments, but she knew enough to know that death was more than just a rare occurrence.

The fine-grained gravel that covered almost the entire courtyard didn't appear to be ideal ground for a swordfight. With every other lunge that Gero made, the small black stones sprayed high into the air like tiny missiles.

Anselm was struggling to evade his remarkably nimble opponent. Even Hannah could see that he was pitifully inferior to Gero. The blows rained down on his shield with such force and speed that Anselm could barely defend himself.

The audience cheered, but a leaden fear fell over Hannah. If anything happened to Anselm, how would she explain to the authorities why Gero hadn't held back?

Anselm ducked to evade Gero's next blow then he pulled off his helmet and flung it to the ground looking completely exhausted.

Gero hesitated, unsure whether to finish his opponent off altogether, but he followed Anselm's lead and threw his own helmet aside.

The audience shouted their approval.

Anselm's blonde friend suddenly popped up beside Hannah.

"What sort of man is your friend, eh?" he asked sharply. "The European champion in swordplay?"

"Do me a favor. Stop talking nonsense and make the two of them stop!" Hannah replied hotly.

"I'd love to, but you don't know Anselm. He'll only stop when one of them is on the ground."

Hannah's heart pounded as she watched Gero strike Anselm's sword with one decisive blow. It shattered down the middle. Anselm dropped the sword as if he had been struck by lightning and stumbled backward before falling to the ground. The crowd cried out. With a pained expression, Anselm clutched his arm.

With his sword still in his left hand, Gero walked up to Anselm and held out his right hand.

Hannah breathed a sigh of relief as Anselm looked up at Gero and gave him an exhausted smile before taking his hand and letting his opponent help him to his feet.

The spectators broke into applause.

"Good God," Anselm croaked breathlessly. He looked up at Gero with a look of reverence as he wiped the sweat off his brow. "Even I have found my master in you! Do you give lessons?"

"No, he doesn't!" Hannah had shoved her way forward. "Take off that costume!" she ordered Gero. "We're leaving!"

Gero turned around slowly and regarded her with a mixture of amusement and annoyance. His eyes blazed, and he drew himself up to his full height, still holding his weapon ready.

As he approached her, she stepped back involuntarily.

"Woman, I don't recall allowing you to speak," he said in fluent Middle High German, his deep voice so icy it made Hannah shudder. "I

313

favor obedient women. If you don't like being chastised, I advise you to think before you speak in future!"

The few men around them who had understood him broke into laughter, but Hannah was furious. "Fine!" she snarled, turning on her heels. "Have it your own way."

"Hey," Anselm said as he caught her arm. "It was just a bit of fun. You don't have to get angry."

With a jerk, she pulled out of his grasp and gave him a fiery glare. "Fun? I don't think you have the faintest clue what you're dealing with here," she snapped. "Nonetheless … thank you for your invitation. We have to go home."

She turned away and looked around for Matthäus. She felt like crying.

Matthäus appeared next to Gero and looked at Hannah curiously. He had seen Hannah choking back tears before walking off.

"What's wrong with her?" the boy asked softly in French.

"I don't know," Gero answered cautiously, "but I will find out." Then, staring at Hannah who was hurrying toward the house, he added under his breath, "I think I made a mistake."

Resolutely, he took off his battle gear and handed it silently to Anselm, who looked amazed that Gero and the boy had spoken Old French.

Gero caught up with Hannah as she emerged from the coatroom holding Matthäus's jacket in her hand. At least she wasn't prepared to go home without the boy, Gero thought.

He grabbed her wrist and forced her to look him in the eye. Her eyes were red and bleary, and red splotches covered her neck.

"What?" he asked urgently. "What did I do wrong?"

She lowered her gaze. "I'm not feeling well," she said, taking a deep breath. "Let's go home. I need fresh air."

Matthäus looked up at Hannah. "Aren't we driving?"

"No," Hannah answered with an exhausted smile. "I've drunk too much wine. It isn't safe to drive in my condition."

"A rational decision," Gero said approvingly with a look at Matthäus. "Do you still remember old Bratac's assistant?" he asked his squire.

"Yes," the boy answered guilelessly. "Didn't he die a while ago?"

"He was drunk all the time," Gero continued. "In the end, he had a terrible accident with a wagon. In his stupor, he drove the horses too hard, lost the reins, and drove off a cliff. One of the horses broke a leg and had to be slaughtered while the poor man had a full load of barrels roll over him. Three months later, he was dead."

"Nice comparison," Hannah muttered.

"Should I call a taxi for you?" Judith had appeared in the coatroom, looking concerned.

"We're fine," Hannah replied. "We're walking. My place isn't too far away."

"You won't believe what just happened!" Piet yelled to his colleague as he climbed into the car. Still shaking his head, he activated the handset attached to the radio.

"Jack," he croaked breathlessly, buckling up.

"Come in," buzzed the radio.

"What do you think of the pictures I sent you?"

"Very interesting," his boss answered sarcastically. "The guy doesn't look like how I imagined a medieval person to be. I'm almost afraid that, like our weapons expert, he's a part of the so-called re-enactor scene, where they re-enact historical eras with battles and costumes. Unless we have the guy's DNA samples, we can forget about arresting him."

"You could have told me that earlier," Piet complained as he started the engine. "I would've asked him for a urine sample in the bathroom."

"You were with him in the bathroom?"

"Yes," Piet said with amusement. "The size of his dick is rather respectable."

"And how does that observation help us?" Jack asked.

"Jack, I'm sure he is our man. I swear he's never stood in front of a modern urinal in his life. He looked absolutely confounded when the sensor set the flush in motion. If it were up to me, I'd arrest him immediately!"

"No, Piet. We can't just act on a hunch. Stay on their tail until they've arrived home. Be careful they don't notice you. Then come back to base for debriefing."

"As you wish," Piet said grudgingly, and steered the car onto the dark village street.

"What are you up to?" his colleague asked softly when he noticed that Piet seemed to be plotting something.

"I'm going to have a little chat with them. I'm positively certain they're the same people we saw two days ago by the castle. I thought the car looked familiar. Besides, I'd never forget the guy's blue eyes."

Without a word, Hannah marched swiftly down the dark street with Gero and Matthäus trailing behind. A car whizzed toward them, its blinding headlights shining directly into their eyes.

As Hannah tried to pull her two guests away from the road, she tripped, and would have fallen into the roadside ditch had Gero not caught her in time. For a second, he held her in his arms. She felt the warmth of his body, and his light musk scent clouded her senses. His chest rose and fell in regular movements, and she felt calmed by his touch.

"I'm fine," she said as she recovered from her accident and pulled away from Gero. "I think I'm tipsy," she chuckled, and the next moment, a mighty hiccup seized her.

"You have to hold your breath and say at least three Hail Marys," Matthäus piped up from behind.

Helplessly Hannah turned around to her young advisor. "I have no idea what the words are," she admitted helplessly. "If you lead the prayer, I'll try."

"You don't know how to pray the Hail Mary?" the boy asked, his eyes widening in disbelief. "I thought you were a Christian. Every child learns this prayer before he is seven years old."

"I've heard of it," Hannah said, "but I can't recite it by heart."

"We'll help," Gero decided. Hannah would have wagered good money that behind that deep voice lay a missionary.

They must be a strange sight, Hannah thought, walking down the street in the middle of the night praying loudly in Latin. Lost in her thoughts, she didn't notice that a silver BMW had stopped ahead of them on the other side of the street. Suddenly, she saw the rear lights of the car as the driver rolled down his window.

"We're headed to Binsfeld," the man called, sticking his head out. "We've gotten lost."

Hannah felt her heart pounding. The car had a Trier license plate, but the driver had a distinctly American accent. This fact by itself wasn't unusual, since thousands of Americans lived in the area surrounding the airbase. But Hannah sensed that the man was lying. About five hundred meters behind them was a junction with an unmissable sign: *Binsfeld: 2km.*

Gero stood so closely behind her that Hannah could feel his hand slowly wandering to his knife-belt.

"Keep driving straight on. You can't possibly miss it," she told the driver curtly, then turned to her two companions again.

But the man called to her once more. "Don't we know each other?"

She glared at him. "Even if we do, it's hardly the right time to ask that sort of question. It's dark, and I'm standing in the middle of the street. Have a good journey."

"Maybe we could drive you somewhere?"

"No, thank you," she replied shortly. "We're taking a walk."

"No problem!" the stranger said, raising his hand to bid them goodbye before driving away.

"That seemed fishy," she said nervously.

"What do you mean?" Gero looked at her curiously. He had hardly understood the conversation.

"I've seen that guy before," she said softly. "But I don't know where."

"I do," Gero said. "He was the man who spoke to you by the castle, and if I remember correctly, I saw him in the latrines this evening."

"Shit!" Hannah swore. "They could be from the NSA. I knew this wasn't going to go well!"

"What are you talking about?" Gero grabbed her arm.

Hannah tore away from him. "I told you from the start that you shouldn't talk to anyone at the party because it's far too dangerous! But no, the noble lord isn't used to taking advice from a woman. And why should he? Women don't know anything anyway."

Without waiting for an answer, she set off down the road.

"What is so wrong with talking to Anselm or having a training match with him? The people there didn't find it unusual, anyway, or they wouldn't have applauded us!"

"You know ..." Hannah began, "you can't just speak Old French to random strangers here or engage them in swordfights. You have to stop drawing attention to yourself."

Gero lost his patience. "You know ..." he mimicked Hannah as the fury and despair of the past few days bubbled to the surface. "I'm sick of running after you like a little lap-dog and asking your permission for everything I do!" He caught up with Hannah and planted himself in front of her menacingly.

She stopped all of a sudden. "I'm sorry," she replied regretfully in her voice. "We can't change that at the moment."

"You're sorry!" he barked back and grabbed his head in despair. "What are you sorry about? Me losing my home? Leaving all my Brethren behind? My life? That I'm stuck somewhere in a world completely alien to me, without the prospect of ever feeling familiar ground under my feet, let alone seeing a familiar face?" He sounded utterly broken.

"What can I do about that?" Hannah retorted. "Have you any idea what the Americans could do to you if they caught you?" Determinedly, she strode ahead.

In the moonlight, she could already see some distance away the tall beeches that marked the driveway to her courtyard.

"No one will capture us so easily!" Gero declared. "I am a Templar knight, not a blundering farmer. If anyone comes too near me he will feel my wrath, and before anyone touches the boy, he first has to kill me."

"You're an idiot," she blurted, but the words had barely left her mouth before regret set in.

When they reached her house the lights turned on automatically, and she became aware of Gero's hurt expression.

"I'm sorry," she said softly. "I didn't mean that but sometimes even I forget where you came from. You just have to realize that the customs and traditions of your time can't be compared to ours at all."

As she groped for her key in her bag, he approached her slowly.

"I'll try to call Tom," she said without glancing up at Gero, "and tell him that he has to come up with something."

"So that's what it is," he hissed darkly. "You think that malefactor is smarter than I am."

Hannah paused and looked up in alarm. His blue eyes were blazing. "Gero …"

"Admit it," he said, squaring his shoulders angrily. "You think I'm a poor fool who can't count to three."

"Can you tell me why you're suddenly going on about such nonsense?" she asked breathlessly. "I'm doing whatever's in my power to help you. Till now, both of you have been in good hands with me, and, to some extent, Tom was right. We don't torture people or burn them at the stake here, and nobody has died of the plague in centuries."

"That remains to be seen," Gero retorted.

Sitting in front of the door, stroking the cat, Matthäus looked up at them fearfully.

"What can a man like me expect in a world like this," Gero yelled furiously, "where I can't live without depending on a woman? What would become of Matthäus and me if you decided to turn your back on us? Or what will happen to us if you are drawn back into the bed of that sorcerer?"

Hannah had to admit that it had been a mistake to mention Tom's name twice in a row.

"Sometimes I ask myself," Gero said, dangerously soft, "whether I'll be brave enough to stop myself from plunging my dagger into my own heart if your good friend doesn't manage to send us home."

Hannah gasped involuntarily. "Then, my dear," she began calmly, "according to everything you've taught me about your time and your beliefs, you will burn in hell. For all eternity!" Unimpressed, she turned her key in the lock and opened the door. Matthäus ran after the cat, and the two of them disappeared up the stairs to the second floor.

For a moment Hannah's reply rendered Gero speechless. He had hurt her feelings; there was no doubt about that. Silently, she hung up her coat and disappeared behind her bedroom door without a second glance at him.

Gero felt like punching himself. Helplessly, he crept into the living room. With a glance at the wooden Madonna, he prayed for forgiveness. The smile of the Holy Virgin seemed to suggest that it was time to ask someone else for atonement.

On his way to Hannah's bedroom, he rehearsed his apology in his head.

Politely, he knocked on the door. There was no answer. He knocked again, but again, he was greeted by silence. He felt anger rising in him once more.

Hannah simply *had* to understand him. If she didn't, who would? He flung the door open, but she had her back turned to him. As cool as ice, she lit a second candle without turning to him. She had changed, and was wearing only her white shimmering silk dressing gown. His gaze fell on her bare calves and feet, and her well-rounded backside outlined under the thin fabric. To his disgust, he felt an unholy desire to take her creep over him. She had cursed him. It couldn't be anything else.

Without even looking up, Hannah bent over her dresser. In two long strides, he was next to her. He seized her upper arm and spun her around. The desire to hit her was nearly overpowering. He despised men who bent women to their will with force, yet he felt himself doing the same. It was pathetic to feel so utterly dependent on someone. He touched Hannah's chin and forced her to look him in the eyes.

"Damn it, woman," he hissed with pure desperation in his voice. "What are you doing to me? Maybe you really *are* a sorceress."

He shook her again as if it would somehow make the answer fall from her lips.

Hannah was too shocked to answer. As he raised his hand in threat, she ducked her head.

"Tell me!" he roared. His grip was so tight that it cut off the blood in her upper arm. "I have to know!"

Suddenly, she began to cry and he was overcome with shame. He let her go and turned away sheepishly. Breathing heavily, he sat down on her bed and buried his face in his hands.

His shoulders shook and Hannah sensed that it wasn't just his hurt pride or exhaustion, what led him cry; his world had fallen to pieces. Suddenly, she realized how unfair it had been to assume he was endangering himself and the boy on purpose. He knew nothing about the modern world apart from the little she had told him. She sat down next to him and touched his shoulder.

Uncertainly he looked up, his face was wet with tears. In the candlelight, his features were as soft as a child's.

"Come here …" she said softly and opened her arms, "please." Gero looked at her uncertainly then noticed the sincerity in her eyes. He shut his eyes and rested his damp cheek on her head.

They sat like that for a while, neither able to say a word.

Eventually Hannah removed her arms. Gero looked at her as he wiped his face with his forearm.

"Do you forgive me?" he whispered hoarsely.

Hannah stroked his bearded cheek.

"I have to apologize for being so insensitive, too," she answered gently.

Instead of replying, he took her into his arms, lowered his head, and pressed his lips to hers.

As if electrified, she returned his kiss as its urgency steadily grew. She opened her lips, and his tongue explored her mouth while he pulled her ever closer to himself.

Hannah decided not to think about what had just happened. She knew only one thing: it was exactly what she had desired for days.

320

She ran her fingers through his short, dark-blonde hair and as he removed his lips from hers to catch his breath, she loosened the belt of her satin robe, under which she was naked.

"Forgive me for behaving like a blundering idiot," he whispered hoarsely. "I haven't held a woman in my arms for years, let alone shared a bed with one."

"You smell so damn good," he continued softly as he kissed her again. His hands caressed her breasts and wandered down to her thighs.

"You're so beautiful," he whispered. "I ... I ..." His voice died under Hannah's outstretched index finger which she placed on his lips with a commanding look in her eyes. Determinedly, she shoved her hands under his sweatshirt. When she touched his knife-belt, she drew back for a second.

Flashing her an apologetic smile, he quickly pulled the navy blue sweatshirt over his head and removed the belt with his weapons. Casually, he shoved the belt under the bed. Then, he took her hand and pulled her to him. Lying back with her on the soft pillows, he kicked off his boots and unfastened the cords of his pants.

Eagerly, Hannah helped him undress, and finally allowed him to slide her satin robe from her shoulders. Tentatively, she caressed his flat stomach as he enjoyed her tenderness with his eyes closed. The plain silver cross hanging from a leather cord on his chest made her pause for a moment. Guilty feelings welled up, which she pushed aside resolutely. His breath stopped as her fingertips wandered increasingly lower.

Gently but firmly, he held her wrist and directed it towards safer territory. With his mouth, he stroked her sensitive neck. Eventually, he sat up.

In the flickering candlelight, Hannah observed the fluid movements of his muscles as he kneeled above her, naked and without shame.

He bent over her in bliss, brushing her nipples with his lips. When he opened his lips and took one in his mouth, she began to moan.

"Virgin Mary, stay with me ..." he whispered hoarsely, not knowing what he should do next.

Hannah twisted herself until she was sitting in front of him. She bent down and left a trail of kisses on his muscular chest.

When he looked down, his gaze fell on her shaved vulva, which, during his time, differentiated noblewomen from Levantine prostitutes. With her lips pressing into him, she began to glide down to his loins, leaving a hot, wet trail on his body. Throwing his head back, he shut his eyes and breathed in and out as her tongue brushed his penis. In the next moment, a hot wave swept over him. He guided her gently to lie down on the bed beside him. She let his lips explore her body before he spread her thighs with skillful fingers and kissed playfully between her legs.

Finally he entered her, pushing further with each thrust. Hannah put her arms around his neck and pressed her breasts against him. With his right hand, he cradled her head, tucking his bearded face against her cheek and propping himself up on an elbow so that he wouldn't crush her beneath him.

For a moment, his conscience pricked him. What would happen if he let his lust run free? His old fear of impregnating a woman, with all its terrible consequences, welled up in him. But in the next moment, all his thoughts deserted him. Slowly, he moved in her, hard and thrusting, savoring every inch and second. He marveled at her long eyelashes, and, as she held her eyes shut, she purred like a contented kitten. He whispered ceaselessly of his affection for her in the *langue d'oil*, the words sliding off his tongue like poetry.

As they reached their climax, Hannah pulled him down to her, gasping, holding him close as she let out a muffled moan. He felt her heart pounding hard against his chest. A surge of pleasure and deep love washed over him, a feeling he hadn't experienced in forever. Unable to move, he breathed in the scent of her hair and listened to the sound of his own heartbeat.

His body was bathed in sweat. Their passion had taken more out of him than the swordfight, Hannah thought, with an involuntary smile.

She yearned to lie with him like that forever, but suddenly, he drew away without a word and lay down on his back, shutting his eyes in exhaustion. *Or was it embarrassment?* Hannah wondered. He pulled up the rumpled sheets to cover his nakedness.

Hannah lay on her side, her head resting on her upper arm, and looked at him. In the candlelight, small pearls of sweat still shimmered on his forehead. Without saying a word, she took the tip of the sheet and wiped them away. "That was brilliant," she whispered.

Gero laughed softly as he finally turned to face her.

"*You* are brilliant, milady," he replied, smiling in admiration. Unexpectedly, he pulled her to himself to kiss her again.

With one foot, Hannah fished for the soft duvet that had landed at the end of the bed during their lovemaking. She picked it up and spread it over herself and Gero, then snuggled into his side.

She felt the distinct ridges of his scar under her left cheek. She drew back a little and ran her index finger gently over the uneven skin.

"Where did you get that?" she asked in a whisper, looking up at him.

He sighed. "I don't know if you'll understand me if I explain it in my language?"

"Just try," she said, nestling back into the crook of his arm.

"Have you heard of the isle of Antaradus?"

"Antaradus?"

"Antaradus is a tiny rocky isle in the Mediterranean Sea just off of Tartus, between Cyprus and the Holy Land."

"Yes," she answered, "I know where Cyprus is, and the Holy Land is in the Middle East today."

"After the Mamluks and the Saracens seized our territories in the Holy Land, Antaradus was our only base left standing. On Easter in the year of our Lord 1302, I was transferred from Cyprus to the island, along with another fifty of my Brethren."

In the candlelight, she thought she saw a wistful smile on his lips.

"I remember it well. It was a week after St. Benedict's Day. Days before, I had finally been inducted into the Order as a knight, after serving as a novice for a year. To celebrate, I had a drinking session with a few of my Brothers. The next day, I suffered from a terrible headache. As you can imagine, the voyage by ship to the island was no fun at all. I felt as if my head would roll off my shoulders at any minute." He grinned, but in a heartbeat, he had become serious again. "At the command of our Grand Master, we set off on a mission to chart the Mamluks' shipping routes. After that, we were to capture their galleys, and if we had the chance, launch a surprise attack on their settlements. From the island, one could observe the commerce on Tartus, and, with time, gain information about what kinds of ships the enemy had. Apart from that, the Order leadership wanted to use our presence on the island as a declaration that we would not surrender, and to use the island as a supply base for our troops in a Crusade. But that never came to pass. Before we had fulfilled even one of our missions, we were attacked by the Mamluks and nearly destroyed altogether. They killed hundreds of soldiers, and the few remaining survivors were sold into slavery."

"And you couldn't defend yourselves?" Hannah asked.

"It was already late summer," he continued quietly. "Though an army from the East had announced their support, they never came. In the previous months, our enemies had repeatedly tried to cut off our supplies and we were struggling to preserve our water supply. The few wells in our castle supplied only a little water, and for weeks, we had only flatbread, dried meat, and dried fruit to eat. Some of us even tried to drink the blood of the horses and eat their oats. We hardly had anything to defend ourselves with. They knew our weak spots, and we had too few ships to defend our two piers for long. We would have had to have battle-ready galleys, but most of them were docked either at La Rochelle or in the Strait of Messina. And we could never have withstood a siege, for we lacked both weapons and provisions."

Gero cleared his throat softly, and absently stroked her hand. "One day, several galleys attacked us from the southwest at sunrise and we realized that we were trapped with nearly nine hundred people on the island."

"How did you survive?"

"I was in a reconnaissance unit and at the time of the attack, we were in a lookout tower in the western part of the island. We only saw the ships when they attacked us in the early morning fog. There was no time to warn our brethren in the fortress as everything happened so quickly, and they could only shut the gates. Later we discovered what had taken place during our absence when we crept close to the enemy. It was impossible to penetrate their troops – for the place was swarming with bloodthirsty Mamluks. Like rats in a flood, we hid ourselves in the cellars of the surrounding houses as the Mamluks combed the town. With a few residents of the island, we hid for two days in an underground den, brewing plans to outfox the enemy. When we finally dared to venture outside, we found that our comrades in the fortress had succumbed to the Mamluks' treachery. They had been promised safe conduct if they gave themselves up, but, of course, those Mamluk dogs didn't keep their promise. We witnessed what they had done to our poor Syrian archers, who were Christians like us. A hundred and fifty men, whom the Order had commissioned to defend the island, had been condemned to death right there and then by the heathens – only because they didn't think the men would fetch any ransom money."

Gero's voice faltered. As Hannah stroked his chest in reassurance, her gaze fell on his shimmering silver cross again.

"You don't have to tell me the rest if it's too difficult for you. I've heard enough," she said gently.

As if he hadn't heard her, he continued. "In the courtyard in front of the fortress, the executioner stood in the blood of the Syrians as heads thumped like a steady heartbeat. The villains had even chained Bartholomäus de Chinsi, our commander in chief, to a stake in front of the fortress."

For a moment, he seemed to stare blankly into space.

"We respected him deeply," he explained. "And now the Mamluks were humiliating him by making him witness the deaths of the lives entrusted to him, as he himself slowly died a wretched death. The worst part was that we couldn't do anything at all. It was as if the devil himself was giving us a preview of hell. Whether we fought or surrendered, we couldn't help anyone."

Hannah held his hand reassuringly. "How did you manage to escape the island?"

"After four days had passed, we realized that there was no hope of salvation. We didn't have a drop of water left, and no one was left in the city besides our troop and the few residents who were hiding with us. We decided to slip away in the moonlight, either to die or find a way to escape with God's help. Most Muslims slept at this time, and the shoreline was not as strictly patrolled as it was during the day. Their guard was down, for they hadn't counted on the possibility of survivors. The corpses of the Syrians had been thrown into the sea. Sharks circled the bay, and the prisoners had been carried away on ships days before. But there was still a tiny fishing boat that the Mamluks had left intact and unguarded. Near the beach, we bumped into a group of galley guards. We fought with the courage of desperate people who had nothing to look forward to but death. As we dueled, a heathen sliced open my shoulder. But with the help of the Almighty, I managed to subdue him. Still there was a second attacker who was aiming for my head. His mace hit my helmet, and from there on, I only know what happened from what others told me. I have Struan to thank who is my most trusted friend and Brother. He was the one who beheaded the Mamluk fast enough to save my life."

Beheaded ... Shuddering, Hannah recalled her morbid childhood memories of beheaded chickens running around her grandmother's farmyard after being butchered.

"Struan later told me," Gero continued, "that he and the others prayed ceaselessly to St. Christopher and to the Virgin Mary to grant them a safe journey to Cyprus. The Mamluks could have overtaken us effortlessly with their fast ships, but they probably allowed us to escape so someone could inform the defeated Christians of their triumph."

As Hannah stroked his stomach, her fingertips touched the second long scar. "Do all your wounds hide such terrible stories?" she asked in awe.

"I'm afraid so," he answered, and pulled her closer to him.

As if she were trying to alleviate his old wounds, she raised her head and pressed gentle kisses onto his scarred shoulder.

As she continued stroking his broad chest, he stretched with pleasure.

"Have I ever told you," he whispered to her, "that you remind me of my dead wife?"

In confusion, Hannah remained silent.

"I know that women probably don't like hearing such things," he added hastily, "especially not from a man she's lying with, but I wanted you to know. Don't ask me why."

"If that's the case ... does it bother you?"

"No," he answered hurriedly, brushing a strand of her hair from her face. "But it *is* peculiar. She was Jewish. Before my father adopted her into our family and baptized her with the name Elisabeth, her name was Hannah." Gently, Gero stroked her cheek. "Do you believe in the Almighty's providence?"

"Yes," Hannah said softly. "I do. At least since I met you."

Later, he fell asleep in her arms. Almost reverently, she listened to his breathing. In the darkness, she felt for her dressing gown and tiptoed into the dark hallway. With shaking hands, she fished out the mobile phone from her purse that Tom had given her and chose the only number that was saved in it.

Tom picked up almost immediately.

"We have to meet," she said hoarsely. "At best, tomorrow."

"Why?"

"I don't know exactly. It might just be a feeling. But I think your friends know about us."

326

"What happened?"

"Not now. Are you coming over?"

"I'll see what I can do."

"I need an ice pack," Tanner groaned. He was busy analyzing the video footage of the two targets who were currently enjoying themselves in the large canopy bed.

Even Mike, his colleague, was fighting to keep his breathing steady.

"What are you doing?" he yelled in alarm as, against all the rules, Jack opened the back door of the van and jumped out onto the dark forest floor.

Jack ran around the car once. Surveillance personnel were not usually allowed to leave the vehicle in the middle of a mission, but here, deep in the forest and in the dead of night, it was unlikely that anyone would notice them. In any case, there had already been an incident that evening.

Around 11:30 p.m., a local man had parked his car directly behind the van. It seemed he had mistaken the NSA's vehicle for an opportunity to purchase some feminine attention. The driver, Nicole Norton, war a former member of the US Marine Corps. With her buzzed blonde hair and blue-gray overalls, she looked absolutely nothing like the prostitute the man had apparently been expecting in this desolate area. The would-be suitor had drawn back in shock, and hurried to his car after the burly American woman rolled down her window and flung a demanding "What?" in his direction.

"Headquarters wants to know what language the two of them were conversing in," Mike said as Jack returned to his seat at the back of the van. Jack leaned back and fiddled with various instruments. "The sound was faulty for a while," Mike said in explanation.

"How the devil would we hear anything else in the middle of such a scene?" Jack answered, throwing his hands up in despair. "Just tell the idiots that it was gibberish and sounded nothing like German."

Mike played the disputed part of the DVD again. Besides a constant murmur and a few other distinct noises, there was nothing to be heard.

"Fast forward some more," Jack instructed him. "The woman made a call after that. Maybe she has another toy boy in waiting."

With a sigh, Mike played the recording gain.

"The guy is full of scars," Mike remarked as he gazed at the images on the surveillance video.

Jack looked up and saw the man rise from the pillows.

"Maybe he was in a war?" Mike whispered.

"Which war?" asked his colleague with an ironic laugh. "And with which army?"

"Probably not the German army," Mike teased. "If Hagen was right, he might have been in a Crusade."

"And to unwind, he fucks a German in her canopy bed!" Jack snorted in amusement. He still couldn't believe that the crazy professor's allegations could be true.

"You can cut it off. We're done for the day," a voice buzzed over the radio, relieving them all of their torment.

"Why now?" Mike asked in disbelief. "Why don't we just grab the guy?"

Jack shook his head. "As long as we don't have a final translation and a thorough genetic analysis, you can forget about it. Don't worry. They won't get away."

Jack shut his laptop and signaled to Nicole.

Less than fifteen minutes later, they arrived at the mission's headquarters at the airbase.

CHAPTER 25

Cross Pattée

Friday, November 19, 2004

Groggily, Hannah glanced over at the other side of the bed. In the dim morning light, she saw Gero lying on his back with his arms flush against his sides and his eyes shut.

She felt around for her alarm clock. It was nine forty-eight. *Damn it,* she had overslept. Matthäus would be awake by now, and she hadn't prepared any breakfast for the hungry boy.

Hannah heard a soft moan behind her and turned around. Gero had buried his face beneath a pillow, and only his short hair peeked out from beneath the white pillowcase.

Recalling what she had done last night with the handsome man sprawled on her bed, Hannah was suddenly flooded with embarrassment. Yes, it had definitely been wild, unabashed sex. And yet, despite her embarrassment, she felt a strange familiarity that she hadn't before experienced with any other man.

Quickly she pulled a warm nightgown over her bare skin, both to keep out the chilly morning air and to hide her nakedness. She walked round the bed and sat down next to Gero. With a bemused smile, she pulled at the pillow that he was gripping tightly. Gero grudgingly relented and squinted up at her as if he were looking directly at the sun.

"Do you have anything for headaches in your time?" he whispered hoarsely.

"Yes," Hannah answered, glad that she could finally help him with something. She stood up and opened the patio door to let in some fresh air. A little while later, she returned with a glass of bubbling water, in which she had dissolved an effervescent aspirin tablet.

"Drink up," she ordered, smiling at him in encouragement.

With a pained expression, Gero took the glass from her and emptied it in a single gulp.

"I won't turn into a toad, will I?"

Hannah laughed. "No, your headache will be gone in half an hour. Have you heard of willow bark tea?"

"Yes."

"This is something similar. Just lie down for a minute longer."

Hannah stood up, intending to go tend to Matthäus, but Gero seized her wrist firmly, refusing to let her go.

"I … I," he stammered sheepishly, finding it difficult to look her in the eye. "What must you think of me?"

It took Hannah a moment to puzzle out why he had asked her that, then her face broke into a wide grin.

"I think you're a crazy monk who let himself be seduced by a lustful she-devil. Maybe you should start praying for our souls now."

Gero gaped at her in horror. "That's not something you joke about," he hissed.

"Do you regret what we did last night?"

"No … I don't," he replied hesitantly, pulling her gently to his side. He sat up, holding her face tenderly in both hands, and kissing her first on the forehead, then on the mouth. "It was so wonderful that I would even risk the Order's condemnation to do it again."

"Is that a great risk?" she asked. "I'd like to know what being with me is worth to you."

He was so close that she could feel his breath on her lips.

"It would definitely mean that my cloak would be confiscated – for a year at the very least," he said softly. "Not to mention corporal punishment and performing menial duties … and if I were with you over a longer period of time and lied to the Order about it, I would be stripped of my knighthood, and perhaps even thrown in the dungeons for life."

Hannah touched his cheek gently and smiled. "You don't have to worry about all that here."

"There's still something else …" he said sheepishly, lowering his gaze.

"Just tell me," she encouraged him gently "If I need to, I'll get my dictionary."

Gero summoned his courage and looked her in the eye. "Last night … did you … take anything so that you don't … conceive?"

Hannah didn't know whether to be outraged or simply laugh. That was the last question she had expected of him. No man she had ever slept with – not that there were so terribly many of them – had ever asked her this question.

"Don't you think that it's a little late to be asking me this?" His anxious expression amused her. "Don't worry," she then explained. "I can't … conceive."

"I'm very sorry for you," he answered with obvious sympathy, if not a touch of relief.

"No, no, don't be," she added hastily. "That's not what I meant. I can conceive children, but I use something so that I'm not fertile."

Gero looked at her inquiringly. She took his hand and led his index finger to a spot on the underside of her left arm. Beneath Hannah's soft skin, he felt a small, oblong object.

He pulled back in surprise. "What is that?"

Hannah had already begun to regret explaining as much as she had. Suddenly, she found herself in the odd position of figuring out how to explain to a man from the Middle Ages how a hormone implant functioned.

"It was implanted by a doctor, and prevents me from being fertile until it's taken out again."

His face twisted in disgust and stared at Hannah's arm in utter confusion.

"You must be a very brave woman," he said, then paused. "Do you have many suitors?"

She sensed what he was getting at. He had used the word "wouer" for suitors – a medieval word with two meanings: an honorable lover, or a dishonorable seducer.

"No," she said emphatically, then added under her breath, "that position is still up for grabs."

Before he could reply, the doorbell rang. Hannah glanced at the clock in alarm, and gently loosened herself from his embrace.

"Give me a minute."

Tom had arrived. He and his redheaded colleague had parked their dark green rented Audi in the driveway. A wave of cold, damp air brushed against Hannah's skin as she cracked open the front door.

"Come in," she said, craning her neck to see if they were being followed. The yard was empty.

"They've arrived," buzzed the radio set.

"Take your positions," Jack Tanner barked in reply. He had parked on a dirt road a short distance away from the Schreyber residence. Following

Stevendahl and Colbach hadn't been difficult. They had rented a car in Trier and driven directly here. "Are we broadcasting?"

"Affirmative, sir," buzzed the receiver. Piet had parked the surveillance van about five hundred yards away from the house.

"Our knight seems to have gotten sick overnight," he continued.

Jack grinned at Mike who was sitting in the passenger seat next to him slurping his cup of coffee. "What, he can't go anymore?"

"No," said Piet, "she gave him aspirin."

"Why is that a big deal?" Jack shook his head, not understanding why his colleague was reporting something so insignificant.

"I just received the first part of the translation," Piet explained in excitement. "You won't believe it – the guy asked her point blank if she was going to turn him into a toad!"

"If the DNA sample hadn't been positive, I would've thought that they were messing with us," Jack chuckled. He paused theatrically, then barked, "Stay vigilant. I want results soon. Over and out."

Tom gaped when he saw Hannah at the door in her dressing gown.

"Sorry," she muttered. "I woke up late. I couldn't sleep all night." She glanced up at Tom apologetically, desperately hoping that his meeting with Gero would be a little less eventful this time. She took a step back to let her ex-fiancé in.

"And I thought you had something urgent to tell me," Tom said impatiently, peering around cautiously.

"I do," Hannah replied grimly. "Did you notice anything on your way here? Were you being followed?"

Tom shook his head. "It looks as if the Americans have stopped watching us. They've withdrawn all their vehicles since yesterday, it seems. When we drove off this morning to rent this car, they definitely weren't following us, or I wouldn't be here."

"Strange," Hannah murmured. For a moment, she had actually believed that Tom's employers were even targeting *her*.

"Well, that calls for a celebration! We thought you'd be making breakfast," Paul chuckled, holding up a bag full of bread rolls.

"You can set the table," Hannah remarked before disappearing into the bathroom.

Paul sat down in a chair and studied the daily paper, while Tom turned on the radio to his favorite music station before heading into the kitchen. He rummaged through Hannah's provisions like a dog looking for a bone.

Wholegrain bread, butter, honey … no Nutella or Choco Pops in sight. Sighing, Tom gave up his search and went to return to the dining room. But as he stepped out of the small foyer that connected the kitchen and the living room, he jumped back in shock.

The dreaded knight, clad only in his leather trousers, was slipping calmly out of Hannah's bedroom and heading toward the staircase. He was holding his sweatshirt casually in one hand, and in the other – as if it were the most normal thing in the world – his fearsome-looking knife-belt.

Tom had already suspected that the man was a deadly fighting machine, and that he would do well to forget any romanticized notions about knights when dealing with him. By chance, their eyes met.

For a second, Tom wondered whether he should wish his opponent good morning, but the Templar's face didn't look as though its owner was in the mood for niceties. Turning his gaze away, Tom hurried into the dining room to join his co-worker at the table. *What, in God's name, was that primitive man doing in Hannah's bedroom?*

Tom cranked up the radio to full blast, ignoring the look of annoyance that Paul flashed him.

A little later, Hannah reappeared in jeans and a T-shirt with a towel coiled around her head and turned off the radio. Gero didn't like hearing constant noises whose origin he couldn't determine.

"And I thought you had it all taken care of," she taunted the Luxembourgian, glancing down at the empty dining table.

Tom stood at the patio door and was glaring at the frost-covered grass in Hannah's garden as if he wanted to murder every blade of it.

Hannah joined him, idly watching as Heisenberg chased down a small rat before running off to the stables with his prize swaying lifelessly from his jaws.

"What's up with you, Tom?" Hannah asked, undoing her turban and rubbing her hair dry. "Is something bothering you?"

"I would reconsider letting him into my bed," Tom remarked with unusual acidity. "I don't think he has the same hygiene standards as us."

"Heisenberg doesn't sleep in my bed. He has his own basket in the living room," she pointed out, sounding hurt. She pointed to a wicker basket behind the sofa that was covered with old blankets.

"I wasn't talking about the cat."

"What are you trying to say, then?" she asked defensively, but she couldn't stop the obvious redness that was flooding her face.

"I wonder," Tom said through gritted teeth, "what on earth the barbarian could have lost in your bedroom."

"Jesus, Tom, why is that any of your business?" Hannah burst out. "Besides, I recall *you* being the one to dump him on my bed when he was injured. Why do you suddenly care about what happens on my mattress? What the hell has gotten into you?"

Paul tried to save the day with humor. "Don't worry, Tom. As a knight of the Order, he's sworn an oath of celibacy. Anyway, yesterday I read somewhere that everyone in his Order was gay."

Hannah glared at Paul indignantly. "What are you talking about? He isn't gay. I should know!"

She turned away from her two annoying visitors, ready to head back into the kitchen.

Tom narrowed his eyes. "What do you mean by *that*?"

At his words, Hannah stopped dead in her tracks. Slowly, she turned around, glowering at Tom with as much loathing as she could muster.

Her ex-fiancé didn't look any less livid. "You slept with him!" His voice cracked like a teenage boy's.

"And so what if I did?" Defiantly, Hannah met Tom's glare.

"Are you insane?" Tom cried, sounding utterly scandalized. "You don't know anything about him! He could have fucked his way through a million whorehouses. What if he has leprosy? Or the plague, syphilis, gonorrhea, scabies ... and God knows what else!"

"The only sick one here is *you*! You're out of your goddamn mind," Hannah replied, dangerously quiet. "You better be thankful that I'm excusing your outburst as a result of intense stress and that it doesn't occur to me to take you seriously. Now, please spare me any more of your ridiculous presumptions."

Like a departing hurricane, Hannah disappeared behind the kitchen door, slamming it shut behind her.

"Bingo!" Jack Tanner slapped his thigh in glee. He had taken over from Piet in the surveillance van. As he spoke German well, he had effortlessly understood the altercation between Stevendahl and his ex-girlfriend. "Even though I still can't believe it, it looks like Hagen was right."

"Good work, Tanner," said Colonel Pelham over the radio.

"Before we seize them, I want to know what Stevendahl and Colbach plan to do with that guy. Until then, our dear esteemed professor has to be patient for a little while longer."

Upon seeing Hannah's guests in the dining room, Matthäus, in a huff, had decided to take his breakfast into his room. He didn't trust Tom, and no matter what Hannah said, she couldn't change his mind.

"They're the devil's henchmen," he hissed indignantly, and his usually trusting face darkened as he looked up at Hannah. "I don't understand why you're in league with these men."

"Mattes!" Gero said sharply. "You're forgetting your manners. No squire talks to a lady like that!"

"No, Matthäus … they're not evil," Hannah said soothingly. "They're just regular people like you and me. We can't just shun them because they did something wrong. They'll take you back home and make things right again, even if it takes a while for them to figure out how."

"Oh help us, St. Christopher," Gero muttered under his breath and rolled his eyes, before he put on a black sweater.

"If you like, Matthäus," Hannah added, "you can go to the stables after breakfast and help groom Mona. She'll be glad to see you."

Matthäus answered with the slightest of nods, but he seemed appeased. Hannah patted him on the shoulder and stood up.

"Will you at least accompany me to breakfast?" she asked Gero on her way to the door.

Gero winced and looked away.

"Come on, it won't last long," she pleaded.

Reluctantly, he rose, smoothing down his leathertrousers with a soft sigh, and followed Hannah. When they reached the stair landing, he pulled her into his arms without warning and held her flush against his chest. When she looked up at him in surprise, he kissed her gently on the mouth.

"What was that for?" she asked breathlessly when he finally let her go again.

"For taking care of Matthäus and his wayward lord," he said, smiling at her gratefully. Before she could reply, he descended the stairs, the old wooden boards creaking under his weight.

The breakfast table was painfully silent as Hannah and Gero sat down. Barely acknowledging his new companions, Paul chewed listlessly on his roll with honey. On the other hand, Tom ignored them altogether, his gaze never shifting from his teacup.

Gero dunked a piece of bread into his tea and bit it off. Every now and then, he stared at Tom while skewering a piece of sausage with the long dagger that he had held against the other man's throat just yesterday.

Men, *Hannah thought,* always ready to provoke each other, no matter which century they're from.

"So," Hannah turned to Tom, finally breaking the uncomfortable silence, "we have to talk."

Tom coughed, and exchanged a quick glance with Paul. "Before you begin ... I have news, too. We've found out from a rather reliable source that Professor Hagen has ... a very special interest ... in our friend here," he said, making sure to neither look at Gero nor utter his name.

Gero's face hardened.

Hannah looked at Tom in annoyance. "What do you mean by *special interest?*"

"Hagen must have known *before* the transfer took place that someone would appear on the field with the coordinates that we used – and it appears that he tried to keep this information secret."

"Are you trying to say that he tinkered with your computer because he was expecting Gero?"

"Expecting isn't exactly the right word. With the right information, one could transfer anyone at any time. We don't know why Hagen picked Saturday of all days."

"And why on earth did he pick Gero?" Hannah was more than puzzled. "He has no clue how he even arrived here. How could he help Hagen?"

"We don't know, either," Paul said. "That's why we're hoping," he added with a cautious glance at the knight, "that Gero can tell us if he knows anything we don't."

Tom had crushed an eggshell from a hard-boiled egg into tiny fragments, which he was now shoving around his plate as though he were trying to piece together a puzzle. "If we don't find out what's going on, and figure out what the Americans – and Hagen – want, we have no chance of protecting our time travelers, let alone of sending them back home."

"I don't understand," Hannah sighed. "Didn't you say it was an accident?"

Paul sat up straight and ran a nervous hand through his red hair. "I have an informant," he announced with a tinge of pride. "She's been keeping us in the loop for quite some time now. None of us knows how Hagen developed the theories for our research facility, but it seems that he's not quite the genius he makes himself out to be. The foundations of his research were actually based on eight-hundred year-old parchments that a good acquaintance of Hagen's found during excavations at the Temple Mount in Jerusalem."

"What? How is *that* possible? Do you think it has something to do with the Templars, then?" Hannah knew that the Templars owed their name to the Temple of Solomon, which once stood in Jerusalem. During the crusades the Templars had their headquater there.

"I've no idea," Paul said as he glanced at Gero and shrugged, but his expression remained unreadable. "Despite this secret source, Hagen has been acting recklessly. He knew that the reactor risked being overloaded and that we would get into serious trouble if we transferred anything larger than a dog. There has to be a reason why he would take such a great risk without the Americans knowing."

"This is where the fun starts," Jack muttered, whipping out his cell phone. "Colonel?"

"Yes, Tanner?" Pelham was still in Spangdahlem, impatiently awaiting further news.

"Is Hagen nearby?"

"No."

"Good. It seems our dear professor knows more than he's let on. I just overheard Stevendahl and Colbach saying that it was most likely *Hagen* who caused the accident."

"Let the translators do their job," Pelham said uneasily. "Before acting I want to be absolutely certain what's behind these allegations."

"What shall we do with this information?"

"Don't mention it in the official report until we get more information. I'll stave Hagen off and tell him that we'll be ready to seize the targets by tomorrow."

Hannah shook her head in disgust. "As if his damn invention hasn't caused enough trouble! What else does this professor of yours want?"

Tom looked Hannah straight in the eye before nodding in Gero's direction. "Maybe your friend here can help us answer that question. Ask

337

him if he knows why he was traveling through this region and what kind of mission he was on."

"Ask him yourself!" Hannah snapped, sick of Tom and his colleague treating Gero like an imbecile.

Tom sighed and, with a pained smile, he turned to Gero. "Good sir," he began with exaggerated politeness, "could you kindly tell us what mission you were entrusted with before you were cast away into our world?"

Gero didn't seem to hear him. Leaning back casually in his seat, still chewing his bread and sausage, he turned to the Madonna figure on the corner shelf. Suddenly he met Tom's gaze with his cold blue eyes.

"No," he said firmly.

"*No?* What the hell does that mean?" Tom looked at Hannah in annoyance. "Did that idiot even understand what I said?"

"Tom!" she gasped.

"Very well," Tom said bitterly, "tell him that he'll never go home if he keeps being this stubborn."

Hannah turned to Gero, but he spoke first. "I can't reveal my mission to him. I have sworn an oath of silence – not even torture could move me."

"Well, that's just fantastic," Tom grumbled. He had understood most of what Gero had said and was quickly losing his patience. "You idiot!" he exclaimed, leaning over the table so suddenly that he nearly knocked over a pot of tea. "Whoever you swore your oath to has been dead for seven hundred years!"

Gero narrowed his eyes. "Didn't you say that time only exists in the heads of men? If that's the truth, it doesn't matter whether my oath was sworn yesterday or seven hundred years ago. And my commander, whom I had given this oath, was already as good as dead then. As a Templar, one is forever bound to an oath – beyond even death!"

"We're not going to get anywhere like this," Tom sighed, shaking his head.

Hannah gave Gero a pleading look. *Do it for me*, she seemed to say.

Gero pressed his lips into a thin line. "Very well then" he began in a low voice, "I was on the way to the German lands from Bar-sur-Aube with my two brethren. We were heading for the Cistercian abbey of Heisterbach on the other side of the Rhine. I was to wait there until I met a Brother of the High Council and give him a secret password. Then we were to find the place where a secret was hidden, whereupon the Brother of the High Council would confer upon us another mission."

"You weren't alone?" Hannah looked at him in surprise.

Gero shook his head hardly noticeable.

"How come only you and Matthäus were transferred?" she asked.

"You'll have to ask *him* that," Gero answered testily, with an ironically look at Tom.

"Maybe the others weren't on the field," Paul piped up. "Do you think what you were looking for in Heisterbach is still there?"

"How should *I* know?" Gero spat. "So far I've not seen the abbey."

Hadn't he asked her about the abbey, Hannah suddenly recalled, *at his ancestors' castle ruins a couple of days ago?* He hadn't mentioned it again after that day, not even after they had slept together.

"The Templar High Command were hiding something from King Philipp of France … something that must have been of great importance to the Order," Gero continued, staring blankly at the tabletop, as if he were replaying those dreadful scenes in his mind. "It's called the 'Head of Wisdom', and it seems to be the source of the Order's wealth and influence." He looked up uncertainly. "If all your roads are as good as the ones I've seen, surely you can reach Heisterbach easily with your fast wagons."

"And?" Tom prompted. "What does this Head of Wisdom look like?"

"I don't know," said Gero irritably. "I was only told as much as my mission required of me."

"What sort of idiot goes on a mission not knowing what it's about?"

Gero narrowed his eyes. "If I'm not mistaken, you're not any less of an idiot, or we wouldn't be sitting here wondering why your master didn't tell you about everything he's orchestrated, would we?"

It took a moment before Tom's expression revealed that he had understood Gero perfectly.

"A hundred points to the knight," Paul grinned.

"Jesus Christ, it just keeps getting better," Tanner exclaimed after he had received the translation. "Get the entire surveillance team into position immediately and prepare to follow them, wherever they're heading."

"Code Red activated with immediate effect," confirmed Colonel Pelham after he had consulted with General Lafour. "Inform only your men directly involved in the mission. And mobilize Hertzberg. Tell him to come to the command center. I need a historian's perspective."

A dark blue Land Rover rolled slowly into Hannah's driveway and stopped directly in front of the garage. Anselm Stein had been on his way to a business meeting when a curious compulsion drove him to pay his new acquaintances a visit. Lying on the back seat was something he was all too eager to show Hannah's friend, a sword whose age and origin he had been commissioned to assess. Strangely enough, it looked brand new. Perhaps he could ask Gero for his judgment before returning it to his client.

Anselm clambered out of the vehicle and shut the door, then stood in front of it, basking in the warm morning sunlight as he drank in the picturesque landscape. At the edge of the paddock, someone was grooming a sturdy brown mare tied to a wooden fence. Anselm squinted. It was the boy from last night, who, like Gero, appeared to be fluent in the *langue d'oïl*.

Anselm slowly approached the boy in the paddock.

"Hey, you!" he yelled.

The boy looked up in shock.

"Come here!"

Anselm had deliberately spoken to him in Old French. If the boy understood him and could converse fluently, he would have many questions for both Hannah and her friend.

The boy patted the horse on the neck, carefully laid aside his grooming tools, and then strolled over to Anselm.

"What's your name, boy?" Anselm asked affably.

"My name is Matthäus," the boy replied, looking around uncertainly. "How may I be of service, Seigneur?"

Anselm couldn't believe what he had heard. The boy had answered in slightly accented Old French, as if it were the most natural thing in the world. *Now*, thought Anselm, *I just have to ask the right questions.*

"What are you doing here?" he began casually.

"I'm brushing the horse," Matthäus answered, sounding annoyed.

"Uh huh. And where is your father?"

"Father?" Matthäus stared at him in confusion.

"Isn't Gero your father?"

"No, he is my lord," Matthäus answered guilelessly.

Anselm smiled. This Gero and his family had either gone completely mad, or there was another compelling reason why the boy had called him his *lord* and had mastered a language that not even an expert could ever hope to speak so fluently.

"Why do you speak such fluent French? Did you grow up in France?"

"No," Matthäus frowned. He hesitated for a moment before adding, "my family is from Trier, and my father was a vassal of the Archbishop. Why do you want to know?"

Anselm suddenly felt his heart pounding hard against his chest. He eyed the boy from head to toe – blonde curls, freckles, a red sweatshirt, a pair of jeans, and sneakers. He looked like any other twelve year old. Perhaps he was one of those child prodigies who could teach themselves things that, for any normal adult, took years of study.

He smiled at Matthäus uncertainly. "Just asking. No worries. I'm just going to pop by the house. I brought something for your ... lord to look at," he said, tapping the oblong cardboard box he was carrying.

Matthäus craned his neck to catch a glimpse of it. "What's that? Can I see it?" he asked, his blue eyes gleaming with childlike curiosity.

"But of course!" Anselm laid the bulky package on the ground and opened it. A long wooden sheath appeared. The leather-bound handle of a battle sword peaked out at one end.

"Oh!" Matthäus cried.

"Amazed, eh?" Anselm chuckled.

"Can I touch it?"

"Yes, but be careful. It's terribly sharp." Anselm pulled the long sword out from the sheath. "Go ahead, hold it – but please don't drop it! I don't want the blade to get any more scratches."

Matthäus gripped the handle in his small hand and executed a few turns with astonishing certainty. As he was about to return the precious weapon, his gaze fell on the engraving on the sword pommel. He narrowed his eyes and frowned, then looked up at Anselm in horror.

"How did you get this?" he demanded.

"Why do you want to know?" Anselm asked in surprise.

"This is my lord's sword. It was stolen from him!"

Anselm took a step back. "Stolen?"

Matthäus held out the pommel to him. "See the coat of arms here?"

The Templar cross was engraved on the bottom. Above it, the curved wolf-hook symbol hung over a river with two fish.

"Why, yes!" Anselm had to suppress his excitement. "What is it?"

"It's the symbol of the Breydenbach family! There are only three swords in the world that bear this coat of arms: my lord's, his brother's, and his father's. So, tell me. Where did you get it?" Matthäus demanded again furiously.

"Slow down, boy!" Anselm held his hands up, trying to calm the boy down. "Why don't we go to Hannah's house and clear up this misunderstanding?"

"Good," Matthäus huffed, clutching the sword tightly in his hand. He didn't look as if he had any intention of giving it back.

"We have a visitor," Piet Hannon announced from the other end of the radio set.

"Who is it?"

"You'll never guess, Jack! A dark blue Land Rover just turned into the Schreyber residence. It's our weapon expert from last night! He's brought the sword we found in the wreckage. Karen Baxter gave it to him to analyze."

"*What?*" Tanner couldn't believe what he was hearing. "How does he know Stevendahl and Colbach?"

"Baxter must've spilled. How else?"

"Did you wiretap Dr. Baxter's phone?"

"No," Piet answered. "Hagen didn't want us to monitor her. I've no idea why."

"Listen up!" Colonel Pelham said angrily after Jack had briefed him. "From now on, everyone will be monitored, including Professor Hagen himself. I'll clear this with General Lafour. And send an investigation team to the weapon expert's house. Have it bugged as long as he's hanging out with Stevendahl's girlfriend."

"Yes, sir."

"Install a GPS tracker under his car. Understood?"

Matthäus' sudden appearance in the house with the long, gleaming sword in his hand sent the breakfast table into a frenzy. Hannah recoiled in fright, while Gero sprang to his feet as if he were ready for battle.

Anselm, who had been trailing behind Matthäus, stepped forward and greeted Gero in Old French. Bowing slightly as he placed his right hand over his heart, the knight returned the greeting.

Tom gave Hannah a look of incomprehension. "Who are you?" he asked the man with the ponytail.

"Tom, may I introduce you to Anselm Stein?" Hannah cut in. "He was kind enough to invite us to a party celebrating the opening of his store last evening."

"You were at a party? All three of you?" asked Tom incredulously.

"Yes," said Hannah tersely.

"You took him with you?" Tom eyed Gero as if he were a savage beast that had to be locked up in a cage.

"I thought it would be good for them to familiarize themselves with their new surroundings as soon as possible," Hannah explained.

"But that doesn't mean setting them loose in front of dozens of people! What if he had gotten drunk? Do you have any idea how great a risk you took? You saw what he did to me. He could easily have killed someone!"

"That was your fault!" Hannah shot back. "You provoked him and treated him like a stupid child. And it looks like you haven't changed at all!"

"Oh, yeah?" Tom raised his dark eyebrows in provocation. "And you slept with him to apologize for my poor behavior, did you?"

"You bloody bastard!" Too furious to care who was watching, Hannah leapt to her feet and gave Tom a resounding slap, making even Gero flinch.

Tom nursed his reddening cheek. "I honestly wonder how I could have been naive enough to believe that this savage could adapt to civilization within a week when he can't even keep his hands to himself."

Hannah's eyes blazed with rage, but she kept silent.

Anselm stared at the madness in front of him. His first impulse was to turn on his heel and run. He wondered why Judith hadn't mentioned that her boss and her family were this dysfunctional.

Clearing his throat, Matthäus chose this moment to step forward and hand the sword to Gero. Gero's expression darkened immediately as he weighed the sword in his hands. He stared at Anselm, his eyes flickering with a mixture of confusion and anger.

"Where did you get that?" he barked at Anselm in Old French.

"From a client." Anselm was taken aback. "I was commissioned to analyze how old it was. I thought you could give me a second opinion."

Gero ran his fingertip across the blade as he inspected the weapon. "By my own calculations … it is more than seven hundred years old," he said, licking the blood from his fingertip unblinkingly. With the weapon in his left hand, he took a step toward Anselm, who retreated uneasily.

Meanwhile, Paul had been scrutinizing the ornate weapon, too. "Tom," he said quietly, "that's the sword Hagen showed during the presentation."

"Wait a minute!" Tom stood up and turned to Anselm. "Who are you, and how did you get this sword?"

Anselm stared at Hannah. "Do me a favor and tell me, what film set have I stumbled onto?"

"Gero lost his sword," she explained cautiously, "and Tom would like to know how it came into your possession."

"An American lady gave it to me," Anselm replied, sounding distraught. "Her name was Baxter. She wanted me to analyze it."

"You work for Hagen?" cried Tom furiously.

"Who is Hagen?" Anselm asked in despair. "If it was stolen, I didn't know anything about it. The woman called me in the middle of the night sounding desperate. She claimed to be an archeologist who found the sword during an excavation. I'll be happy to give you her address, and you can get in touch with her yourself if you want it back."

"We won't be able to give it back to you," Hannah remarked with a sideways glance at Gero.

"I'm really sorry," Anselm answered regretfully, "but I can't possibly leave it here. Its value is immeasurable. I was on the way to Himmerod to return it to the client this afternoon. If anything is amiss, I insist that you alert the police."

"No one is calling the police!" Tom decided.

"What do you mean?" Anselm demanded. "Surely you don't believe that I can simply leave the sword here?"

He turned to Hannah for help. "Before I lose my mind, tell me what's going on here! Why don't Gero and the boy speak regular German? And why does your other friend keep blurting out incoherent things that make no sense at all?"

"Fair enough," Hannah said. "I think we should all sit down first. Nothing will be solved by standing around and talking over each other."

She offered Anselm a chair and reluctantly he took his seat. Gero sat down nearby, the sword still tightly gripped in his fist.

Anselm felt uneasy in the company of Hannah's other guests. They all seemed as if they had escaped from an asylum. Cautiously, he made sure that his cell phone was safe in his coat pocket – just in case.

344

"Have you heard about the American base in Himmerod?" Hannah began.

"Are you going to tell him the truth?" Tom's eyes widened in panic.

"What else can I do?" Hannah retorted angrily. "Do you want him to go running to the police? Or tell the Americans where the owner of the sword is?"

"No," Tom said grimly, "but maybe we can lock him in your cellar until we've solved all our other problems."

Anselm, who was becoming increasingly certain that Tom was unhinged, turned to Hannah again. "Of course I know about it," he said, lifting his chin confidently. "I was a representative of the Green party on the city council a few years ago. We tried to prevent its construction because the Americans are using it to secretly store their atomic warheads."

"Oh, not that as well!" Tom groaned.

"I'd be careful about what I tell him," Paul warned, casting a doubtful glance at Hannah.

Hannah, however, was not to be deterred. "So you think you know what goes on in there?"

"Yes," Anselm retorted, sounding slightly annoyed. "Atomic bombs that were removed from other bases are stored there and gradually exchanged for new ones."

"And what makes you so sure about that?"

"My information comes directly from the inner circle of the American military," Anselm continued. "Naturally, I can't give you any names."

He eyed Hannah warily. "Why are you interested in the American base?"

"I'm afraid your informants have set you on the wrong track," Hannah said. "Their nuclear division is harmless in comparison to what else goes on in there."

"What is it, then?"

"The two of them can explain it better than I can." Hannah pointed to Tom and Paul. "It's your call, Tom."

"Hannah, what are you doing? How can I explain everything to him?" Tom exclaimed. "He won't understand, and it'll just make everything even worse."

Just when he thought that he was off the hook, he now had to explain how he was to blame for a catastrophe that only a Nobel Prize nominee in Physics would understand. Sighing deeply, he began.

"Do you think I'm an idiot?" cried Anselm, after Tom had explained CAPUT's research into altering the space-time continuum as simply as he could manage.

"It really is true," Hannah confirmed. "And if you don't believe it, we can prove it to you."

"Prove it?" Anselm stared at her with wide eyes. "How? Are you going to drive me there and take me on a field trip to the Roman Empire?"

His features hardened. "Either hand me the sword now and let me go, or I'll call the police." He stood up and headed to the door.

"Gero, stop him!" Hannah cried.

Swiftly, Gero moved in front of Anselm, blocking his way out.

With a quick sideways glance, Anselm tried to judge how far his captors would go. "I honestly wonder whether you're crazy enough to kill for this bullshit."

"Anselm!" Hannah stood up and walked toward him with a pleading expression. "Aren't you an expert in medieval paraphernalia?"

"Yes, I should think so," he said peevishly.

"And what if I ask you to inspect something that proves Tom is telling the truth?"

"Very well, if you swear to God that you will let me leave after that."

Anselm watched tensely as Hannah returned with a white cloak, and spread it out on her sofa.

As he laid his eyes on the cloak and saw the red cross, he gasped. He couldn't tear his gaze away.

Hannah looked at him, waiting for him to realize the truth. "Can you determine which era this piece of clothing is from?"

"Of course," Anselm answered softly as he examined the fibers, running his fingers over the coarse fabric. "But this can't possibly be real. It's far too well preserved."

"It's a linen-wool blend, made of worsted wool, lined on both sides," he whispered to himself. "This style of weaving was used until the middle of the fourteenth century, but it died out after that … I've never seen anything like this. I've only read about it in books." Gingerly, he stroked the delicately affixed appliqué of bright red wool. "A cross pattée," he said, staring at Hannah in amazement. "This can't be real."

She took a step toward Anselm and pointed out the embroidery on the cloak's collar to him. "And what about this?"

Fascinated, Anselm read the name and the toponym. "Surely you aren't telling me that this is an original chlamys of a Templar knight? Not a shred of this sort of clothing has been found to date. We only know what it looks like from pictures and reports."

"If that's not enough for you … I have something else." She gestured to Gero to step forward, then pressed the leather pouch into his hand. "Gero, would you show him your documents, please?"

Anselm followed Gero's every movement breathlessly as he took out a parchment and a small leather-bound book, and spread out both objects on the low cedar-wood table. With a nod, he gave Anselm his permission to look through the documents.

"Can someone turn on a light?" Anselm asked, sounding flustered.

He's taken the bait, Hannah thought. Now, they could only hope that he made the connections, and was willing to help them.

Through narrowed eyes, Anselm deciphered the script on the extraordinarily well-preserved parchment.

"I can't believe it. Whom do they belong to?" he asked in awe.

"I'll give you three guesses," Hannah answered with a victorious smile.

"They belong to me," said Gero plainly.

"No," Anselm said slowly. It was clear that he was beginning to doubt his own sanity. "How is that possible?"

Gero held out the silver signet ring on his right hand. "This is a present from my father," he explained, "just like the sword."

"You are a Breydenbach?" Anselm's gaze slowly wandered up from the ring to Gero's face. "I thought they'd all died out," he murmured, "the earlier branch of the Eifel line that bears this coat of arms, in any case."

"What exactly do you know about the Breydenbachs?" Hannah wanted to know.

"Breydenburg Castle was located directly on the border to the County of Manderscheid. Today, only a pile of stones remains. Things were going really well for the free nobles of Breydenbach for a while. But sometime at the beginning of the fourteenth century, they seemed to fall into a dispute with the Archbishop of Trier, Balduin of Luxemburg. He took away their fiefdom, and after that, all traces of the family fizzled out – historically speaking."

Silence fell over the room. Hannah stood with her back to the wall, nervously observing Gero's expressions, which revealed no emotion. Anselm wasn't certain if he should continue, but nonetheless, he did.

"As for the Hessian line of the Breydenbachs …"

"Be quiet!" Gero cut him off gruffly. "I don't want to hear it. Anyway, you've already told me more than I wanted to know." He bit his lip.

Gero's face had become pale, and his eyes were filled with tears. He turned away and stared out of the window.

"But …" Anselm stuttered. "Surely you're not telling me that he's an actual Templar knight from the fourteenth century?"

He smiled uncertainly. What was happening here? Hannah's friend fluently spoke two languages that hadn't been in use for centuries. The papers and clothing appeared to be authentic artifacts. And why would they stage such a ridiculous act, in the first place?

Gero turned around indignantly. "What's so special about that? Several men in my family belonged to the Order. My father's cousin, for instance. He was from the Gelnhausen line, and died in 1303, when I returned from Antaradus."

"*What?* You know what happened in Ruad?" Anselm asked in surprise. Ruad was the name later used for Antaradus. Anselm had read all about the Mamluks' attack on the island's Templar base. "Even if this insanity actually corresponds to reality, that is not possible. Every halfway historically-educated person knows that after the attack of the Mamluks, not one Templar left the island as a free man. He was either beheaded or made a slave for life."

"Obviously your historians don't know everything," Gero answered darkly.

"I can't believe it," Anselm gasped. He sank down into an armchair, never once taking his eyes off Gero, who, despite his impressive stature and build, looked like a surprisingly normal man.

"He's real – every pixel of him," chuckled Paul who had followed the conversation with interest. "That's CAPUT's quality guarantee."

Anselm spun around. "CAPUT? Isn't that what the French found when they arrested Jacques de Molay in the Templars' Parisian headquarters?"

"That's the name of our research facility," Tom explained. "It stands for *Center of Accelerated Particles in Universe and Time.*"

"Strange." Anselm shook his head in disbelief. "Surely that can't be a coincidence?"

His gaze fell on Gero again. "Did you conjure him up intentionally?"

"We didn't *conjure* him," Tom retorted. "He was suddenly there. We don't know how it happened."

"What do you mean you don't know?"

Hannah quickly explained what had happened. "Apart from us, nobody knows that the two of them are here. That's why I am begging you to please keep quiet, no matter what happens," she pleaded.

"And what are you going to do now?"

"We were going to drive to Heisterbach today. Perhaps it'll help us understand the situation better."

"Heisterbach? Where the ruins of the old Cistercian abbey are? What are you going to do there?"

"We're hoping that we'll find some answers there," Paul answered. "For instance, why Hagen was so eager to carry out the experiment precisely last Saturday, why he didn't tell anyone else about it, and whether he had his sights on Gero and the boy."

"The boy, too?" Anselm stared at Matthäus incredulously.

"Gero was on a mission before he was transferred here," Paul continued. "He was traveling to Heisterbach after the attack on the Templars in France. I can hardly imagine what this mission has to do with Hagen, though."

"Wait a minute," Anselm said, his brown eyes flashing with excitement. "Have you heard of Caesarius of Heisterbach's story of the sleeping monk?"

"No," Tom replied coolly. He still wasn't sure if it had been a good idea to let Anselm in on the secret.

"I know the story," Gero said softly.

"I thought so," Anselm smiled, lapsing into Old French again. "The *Dialogus miraculorum* … it must have been required reading for you."

"What are you talking about?" Hannah asked.

Looking suddenly solemn, Gero cleared his throat. "According to a legend, there was once a monk in Heisterbach who travelled through time. Caesarius of Heisterbach recorded his story."

"What does that mean?" Tom peered at Anselm with interest.

"Caesarius of Heisterbach was a Cistercian who lived in Heisterbach from 1199 to about 1240," the medieval expert, clearly in his element, eagerly explained. "He was the abbey's prior, and found fame as a talented writer. He also made apocalyptic prophecies. Some even claim that he foresaw the current environmental catastrophe and a third World War, and that he was a forerunner of Nostradamus. In any case, among his numerous works, there is a legend that concerns a monk who fell asleep in a cloister forest and then awoke on the exact same spot. He found to his surprise that no one in his abbey recognized him anymore, and he had fallen asleep not just for an afternoon, but for a few hundred years."

"Interesting." Paul sipped his tea and looked at Anselm encouragingly. "Maybe it's not a myth at all. The story might have originated from a truth that was hard to believe until recently."

Hannah looked around the rest of the room curiously. "But I still don't understand what Gero has to do with this. After all, this Caesarius would have long been dead when Gero was given his mission to look for the abbey."

"There is a deep connection between the Cistercians and the Order of the Temple," Anselm explained. "They were both founded by the very same man. Some even claimed that the Cistercians functioned as a sort of secret service of the Templars. After the Order's destruction, many Templars sought refuge in Cistercian abbeys. Moreover, St. Bernhard founded the Himmerod Abbey, and Heisterbach was originally comprised of eight monks from Himmerod. Delegates from the abbeys in Clairvaux, Himmerod, and Heisterbach attended the annual chapter assembly at the Cistercian headquarters in Citeaux, Burgundy. I don't know if any of that is related, but the fact that your facility is located right next to the Himmerod Abbey, bearing the distinct name *CAPUT*, leads me to guess that your professor knows something he isn't letting on. He might've just had a hunch, but I can't explain why else he would target Gero. Anyhow, as a Templar knight, Gero has a connection to all three – the Order of the Temple, the Cistercians, and Heisterbach Abbey."

At this, all eyes in the room fell on Gero again.

"Don't look at me like that," he said self-consciously. "I can only say that Anselm is right. There were already rumors during my time that Caesarius' tale was based on a true story. There was indeed a monk named Thomas who disappeared in a forest near the Himmerod Abbey. It was as if he had been swallowed by the ground for three weeks before he suddenly reappeared, claiming that he had fallen asleep and woken up a thousand years into the future. Naturally, nobody believed him. He went somewhat mad after that, and he was sent to Heisterbach to cleanse his soul. He might have met Caesarius during this time, and finally found someone who believed his story."

Gero lowered his head for a second. "Since I arrived here, I've been wondering whether there was a connection between his story and mine," he whispered.

He raised his head and looked Paul directly in the eye. "What if the Brother from Himmerod met the same fate as me and Matthäus?"

"If that's the case," Paul said, "then he was clearly luckier than you guys. Whoever picked him up was able to send him back home."

"And that …" Tom mused, " … would mean we're not the only ones experimenting with space and time …"

CHAPTER 26

Heisterbach Abbey

Friday, November 19, 2004

To make sure they didn't lose their target vehicle, Tanner's team had affixed a GPS tracking device the size of a pack of cigarettes to Anselm's car, which enabled them to locate the vehicle within a ten-foot radius.

The entire team of five NSA observation vehicles began following the dark blue Land Rover at 1600 hours. While Mike drove the silver Mercedes along the A1 toward Cologne, Tanner reached for his cell phone. Colonel Pelham and General Lafour were leading Operation Heisterbach from the headquarters in Spangdahlem.

Every now and then, Gero cast a doubtful look at Anselm. He drove like the devil himself, weaving his way wildly through the other steel wagons. Without warning, the car careened around a bend onto an impressive bridge over the Rhine. Gero gaped at the river, glittering in the late afternoon sun, then at the seven mountains rising in the distance, beyond the water.

Shuddering with fear and fascination, Gero turned his attention to the monstrous ships plowing through the gray water like giant steel fish. They reminded him of the conversation about Roger Bacon he had with Struan in the forest. In the middle of the thirteenth century, the Franciscan English scholar had prophesized flying machines, steel wagons a hundred times faster than horse carts, and ships, no longer dependent on sails and rudders, steered by a single man. Perhaps Bacon had seen into the future like Gero had. How else could he have predicted these incredible inventions?

Gero gasped at the sudden sight of a tower of reflective glass, soaring up from the Rhine's left bank like the Tower of Babel. Its innumerable windows caught the gleaming sunlight, and, for a moment, it looked as if the building had begun to glow.

"That's the Post Tower of Bonn," Anselm remarked, smiling at Gero. "480 feet tall, but still no match for your Gothic cathedrals."

"Did you see that, Sir?" Matthäus exclaimed from the back seat. "How did the Lord Almighty ever allow something like *that*?" The boy's mouth was agape. He stared in disbelief as a massive flying machine suddenly appeared above their heads and crossed the Rhine toward the west.

When Anselm finally pulled into the visitors' parking lot of the Heisterbach Abbey, Gero was struck by a feeling of familiarity, even though pitifully little remained of the church he had known.

"Dear Lord, please spare me from further ruin," Gero whispered, shutting his eyes as a profound sorrow welled up within him. His fingers were numb from clutching the car's upholstery throughout the entire journey. His stomach was churning and he wasn't sure whether it was because of the anxiety, Anselm's driving, or simply the vegetable soup that Hannah had served her guests before they had set off.

As the car came to a halt, Gero unfastened his seatbelt, flung the door open, and stormed outside. He ran to the first tree he saw before throwing up noisily in the grass. He staggered a few steps, finally propping himself up on the branch of a young poplar tree. There he slumped, until the urge to vomit ebbed.

Hannah had followed him, looking concerned. She held out a tissue and a bottle of water she had taken from her backpack. Gero rinsed his mouth and handed the bottle back to Hannah with a nod of relief. For a moment, he planted his hands on his hips, raised his face up to the sky, and drew deep breaths with his eyes shut. When he opened his eyes again, his gaze fell on Tom and Paul, who were standing by the car, observing him from a safe distance. Scowling, he spat at the ground.

Before they set off for the abbey, Hannah convinced him to leave his precious sword behind in the locked car.

It was freezing. The last few rays of the afternoon sun fell gently on the old abbey which lay in a meadow, half hidden by trees. Only the ruins of the abbey wall hinted at how vast the compound must have been. There were other buildings, but they appeared to be newer.

Gero stood closely behind Hannah, gently stroking her back. He yearned to be near to her. Since last night, he had felt far more affection for her than was good for him. As if he had sensed his lord's thoughts, Matthäus nestled against Hannah like a puppy and looked up at her expectantly. Smiling, she laid an arm around his shoulder.

Tom and Paul joined them hesitantly. "Maybe we should look around the area first," Paul suggested. "We can discuss what we find afterwards."

Looking like a monk in his navy hooded coat, Tom nodded. In silence they walked up the road that led to the abbey.

A plaque with the inscription *La route des Abbayes Cisterciennes* – "Road of the Cistercians" – hung on the old abbey gate. As dusk fell, Gero paused for a second to take in the sight of the ruins. In its heyday, the towering church could have rivaled the Cologne Cathedral. After a checkered history, however, it had fallen to the French in 1802. The arrogant victors declared the building a stone quarry, although miraculously the choir apse had been left intact.

A wide path led them to the sprawling compound lined with ancient trees and several large stone markings. At the far end, the sacral ruins towered over a lawn that had been cut with exacting precision.

Gero's stomach churned and he turned away to fight back the tears welling in his eyes. While Hannah waited for him, Tom, Paul, and Anselm marched resolutely toward the ruins. Meanwhile, Matthäus, who seemed to have discovered something interesting, ran to the forest that bordered the ruins.

"Tell me what it used to look like," Hannah said gently, with an encouraging look at Gero. He paused. It was nearly impossible to describe the opulence and splendor of the old abbey, especially when seeing it in its pitiful state today.

His eyes swept across the grounds. "The first time I was here, it was the second day of April in the Year of our Lord 1297. I was with my father, four other knights, and eight Cistercian monks. Seven days before on the Solemnity of the Annunciation of Mary was my seventeenth birthday. The Archbishop of Trier had commissioned us to escort the monks, and I was proud that I was allowed to come along."

In his mind's eye, he reconstructed the walls and ramparts, the refectory and the dormitory above it, as well as the large dining halls and scriptorium, brimming with books and writings on every shelf. All at once, the scene was filled with life. Shrouded figures in light gray habits appeared from the fog of his memory. In rows of two and with torches in their stiff, frozen fingers, they followed the call of the vigils, the prayers that robbed every devotee of sleep, lasting until daybreak. In the darkness, their feet, clad in well-worn sandals and woolen socks, slipped into a peculiar rhythm. They shuffled forward on the cold, damp floor, keeping their shoulders hunched high and their faces buried deep within their hoods, shuddering in the cold.

Gero could still feel the leaden weariness that he had felt walking by his father's side at four in the morning. The elder Breydenbach had insisted that, as guests, they were obliged to take part in the monks' morning prayers. Tightly wrapped in a thick travel cloak, Gero sat down on one of the church's many wooden benches, muttering the Latin chant over and over again. It served just one purpose – to keep him awake while he waited for the time to pass, hopefully quickly, so he could return to his bed.

Gero draped a protective arm around Hannah's shoulder, and, with his outstretched finger, directed her gaze toward a graceful statue of Mary in front of a dense hedge.

"See the stone Madonna over there?"

Hannah nodded, nestling her cold cheek against Gero's warm chest. She smelled ridiculously good, and all he wanted to do was to pull her closer to himself.

"The guests' sleeping quarters were there," he continued softly. "They were just as modest as the monks' quarters, but the food was good and abundant." For one blissful second, he shut his eyes and a smile crept across his face.

"What was there to eat?" she asked.

"Hmm, let me think about that ..." he said with a smirk, glancing at where the kitchen and bakery had been. "The Cistercians seldom ate meat, but they roasted an ox on a spit in our honor. Mostly, there was boiled carp or baked trout, although whether it was enjoyable or not was debatable. Besides that, there were pickled beans and turnips, and a puree of winter apples with honey and nuts, and of course, fresh bread." Gero's mouth began to water.

"And from what I know about monks, water was definitely not their drink of choice," Hannah said casually.

"The people of Heisterbach had their own vineyards," he explained. "They weren't extraordinarily fruitful, but they yielded a decent cup. And they had beer in barrels directly from Cologne. That was almost even better than the wine."

"I think," Hannah remarked with a smile, "that's something that still hasn't changed."

"It's good to know that not everything changes," he said. He lowered his head and kissed her. She took his hand in silence, and they followed the others along the outer wall and toward the ruins.

"Do you have any idea where we should look?" Hannah asked in concern.

"I might," he answered absently, letting his eyes glide over the foliage that had colonized the abandoned terrain. It was an odd feeling, comparing the pathetic ruins before them with his memories, still fresh in his mind, of the abbey.

"I'm just worried that the passage leading to the Head might have collapsed," he remarked thoughtfully.

Beneath a beech tree, Gero held Hannah's hand gently before bending down to kiss her.

A loud cough behind them made Gero spin around, ready to attack.

Tom took a step back in shock. "Beware the kisses of the Templar," he said to Hannah viciously. "I didn't come up with the saying, but whoever did must have had his reasons."

Blood flooded into Hannah's cheeks.

"Are you two going to set up camp here?" Tom asked snippily. "Aren't we searching for the Holy Grail or something?"

With an apologetic shrug, Hannah untangled herself from Gero's embrace and he felt the cold emptiness where her warm body had been. He followed the rest of the group, doubting even more that he would find anything here that would lead him home. None of the clues d'Our had given him still existed, and it seemed foolish to hope that there was anything to be found among the ruins seven hundred years later.

In the evening light, Gero imagined stepping through the mighty doorway that had once stood on the spot, its pointed arches marking the entrance to paradise. He had been young and impetuous when he had first stood here. Despite that – or because of it – the proud arches had filled him with a deep sense of awe and humility in the knowledge of the Lord's greatness. This recognition had comforted him, and given him the courage not to fear anything in the mortal world, for his fate was in the Almighty's hands.

Gero lifted his gaze to the evening sky and made the sign of the cross. He then took a large step forward, until his body was flush against Hannah's. He lifted her chin with his finger and surprised her with a deep, warm kiss, not caring if anyone was watching.

Paul waved to him and Hannah. Tom had already disappeared behind the apse. Hannah took Gero's hand, and all at once, he felt light-hearted.

"Did you find anything?" Hannah asked the Luxembourgian curiously.

"Yes, I think there's an entrance there, south of the apse, about a hundred yards away in the forest."

Paul pointed toward a short wall, overgrown with ivy, between two beech trees, in the middle of which stood a small iron door.

"The entrance is locked, though," Paul added.

He crouched and typed something into a small laptop he had set down on a flat stone. "I found a map on the Internet that confirms that there's a vast network of underground passages right under us that was discovered just two years ago. There are still some unexplored areas down there."

Gero suppressed his bewilderment at the strange machine which produced letters at the press of a button, and made images appear as if by magic. Suddenly, d'Our's words rang through his mind. The Head is located in a secret chamber underneath the refectory. Across the vaulted cellar that lies under it, you will arrive at an iron door that leads to the sewer. Open it and take twelve steps east. There, the path makes a slight bend facing northeast. Take twelve more steps, and you will find yourselves directly under the abbey's graveyard. Turn right, and between the bricks in the wall, you will find a small depression plastered with clay. Break it open and seize the lever that lies under it. With this, you can open a secret door. Behind it is the chamber in which the Head of Wisdom lies hidden.

"Wait," Gero said. His gaze followed the layout of the church and the refectory he knew from memory, and finally landed on the small iron door.

"That *is* the entrance," he said. "If my memory hasn't failed me, it used to lead to the cellar. Apparently, there's a door there that leads to the sewer." He looked at Hannah triumphantly. "The latrines are a little further ahead. The drains lead directly into the passageway."

"How appetizing," Hannah remarked, wrinkling her nose involuntarily.

"Anselm!" Paul called. A moment later, Anselm appeared behind a fragment of the wall.

"Be a good boy and fetch our tooling equipment from the car," Paul said to him. "And tell Tom. This will interest him."

"We have to go to Heisterbach," Hagen decided.

Piglet looked confused in his beige-colored suit.

"Right now?"

"Yes, now!"

"But … why?" Piglet eyed his boss doubtfully. "I thought the NSA had everything under control." He rubbed his neck nervously under his tight collar.

"Hertzberg has analyzed the man's language, and Dr. Baxter's determined his DNA profile. Besides, the suspects' conversations prove beyond a doubt that we are right. Can you tell me, dear Piglet, why the NSA is still letting the man run about freely?"

"No?" Piglet squeaked.

"Well, neither can I. And that's why the two of us will have to go on a little field trip."

As Hagen packed up his laptop and stuffed a few documents into a folder, Piglet watched uneasily. But then his eyes opened wide in alarm. Hagen had unlocked his safe, removed the pistol he kept in it along with a full magazine, and finally slipped them both into his briefcase.

Piglet knew that Hagen didn't have any experience with weapons. Although the NSA recommended that important personnel affiliated with the organization carry a weapon with them, no one actually checked that the training units provided had been completed.

The professor removed his black trench coat from the rack. Then, pausing as if he had forgotten something, he returned to his writing desk and pressed the intercom button.

A female voice answered. "Yes, Professor Hagen?"

"Tracy, if anyone asks where I am, tell them I've gone to my house in Jülich for the afternoon. I have important documents to collect. If there's an emergency, I can be reached by mobile phone. Mr. Piglet will be accompanying me."

Tom and Paul stumbled along in the darkness, keeping close to the church wall. The group had waited a good half hour in the car until it had become so dark that nobody would notice them creeping into the abbey. The only light they had to orientate themselves by were the headlights of the occasional car that sped past them. Anselm followed closely behind the two scientists, grunting softly as he lugged his heavy toolbox along.

With light footsteps Gero followed the men at some distance. His eyes had quickly adjusted to the darkness. He now held his sword in one hand and urged Hannah and the boy forward like a sheepdog herding its flock.

They reached a small wooden gate in the wall. Anselm snipped the padlock with a pair of bolt cutters. Glancing around to make sure no one was watching them, they slipped behind the apse and hurried through several rows of trees to the entrance of the sewer system. Finally Paul switched on the powerful LED lamp he had brought with him that lit the path over three hundred feet ahead. Hannah could see snowflakes dancing in the bright cone of light. She shivered. In the absence of the sun, it had become even colder, and clouds covered the sky overhead. Now that it was dark, she smelled withered leaves, earth, and mildew. The abbey's cemetery hadn't been far from here. Two ancient gravestones, dated 1624 and 1733, stood in front of two mighty beech trees. They were the only grisly evidence that people had once been buried here.

A loud snap made Hannah jump back with a gasp. She looked up. Matthäus had stepped on a dry twig, and he looked just as frightened as she did.

"They're all here, even the boy. Our weapon expert has a toolbox with him," NSA Agent Robert Fowler reported as he leaned over the abbey wall and adjusted his night vision binoculars. "What's that our suspect is holding?"

"If you're asking me, it looks like a sword in its scabbard," Greg answered as he crept along the wall after Agent Fowler.

"A *sword*?" Tanner grunted over the radio. He ran his hand over his Kevlar bulletproof vest as if making sure it hadn't dissolved into thin air. "Didn't Pelham say our man from the past would be easy to subdue?"

"Be gentle," Paul warned as Anselm pressed a crowbar against the rusty doorframe. The medieval expert paused, then tried again. He fished out a ragged kitchen towel from his toolbox, and wrapped the crowbar with it to muffle the sound of his efforts.

With all his might, Anselm tried to force the door open, but it refused to budge. He re-positioned the lever and pushed in the opposite direction. Nothing happened.

Gero stepped forward and placed his hand on the iron rod. "Should I attempt it?"

Anselm eyed the knight's chiseled biceps. "Please do," he said with a nod.

On his first try, Gero ripped the door off its hinges and it fell to the floor with a dull clang. Tom pointed his lamp into the gaping abyss.

Gero stepped aside and handed the crowbar back to Anselm. Straightening his posture, he let his gaze sweep across the area. Everything seemed peaceful.

The stench of dampness and mold became stronger.

Anselm turned to Hannah. "Normally, I'd say 'ladies first', but …" he looked around at the dimly lit faces before him. "Who wants to go first?"

"Let our knight go," Tom piped up hurriedly.

Without a word, Gero stepped forward. He held out his hand to Tom expectantly.

"What, am I supposed to hold your hand?" Tom asked impatiently.

"No!" Gero exclaimed with some annoyance. "I need light. Do you think I can see in the dark?"

Paul, who had understood Gero immediately, took the LED lamp out of Tom's hand and handed it to the knight. Without a second's hesitation, the crusader climbed down into the dark abyss.

Instinctively, Gero ducked his head, even though the stone-tiled ceiling was at least seven and a half feet high. The walls were built with quarry stones. The path was not particularly wide, and the ground was damp and slippery. The stone tiles on the ground had been laid in a V formation so that they formed a tapered gutter, which, over time, had become clogged with filth. On either side of it was a plastered tread one could walk on. Holding up the lamp, Gero lit the tunnel ahead. *It is far brighter than any peat torch*, he thought wryly. Steadily, the bright rays devoured the darkness and illuminated a wall about thirty feet away. If d'Our was correct, that was where he had to turn left. As he moved cautiously forward, water dripped from the ceiling. Gero let the cone of light glide over the floor. Even the rats, which had swarmed through the sewers in his time, had disappeared.

"This is the passageway," he called back toward the entrance.

Anselm picked up his toolbox. He gave Tom the second lamp before hurrying after Gero, and Paul followed him without a word.

Tom paused and turned to Hannah. "You better stay outside with the boy and wait for us."

"No way," Hannah replied. "Matthäus and I are coming along."

"As you wish," Tom muttered, and stepped aside to let her and the boy walk ahead of him.

Their steps echoed dully off the walls. Hannah was glad that she had put on her jeans and flat, mid-calf leather boots. The darkness encouraged her imagination to run wild, and in her mind, the place was teeming with spiders. She squeezed Matthäus's hand. The boy never let go.

Mike killed the engine and turned off the headlights before the car rolled silently into the parking lot.

"Jack?" said a voice over the radio.

Agent Tanner sat up in the seat next to Mike. "Come in," he said softly with a quick glance at the abbey.

A few street lamps dimly lit the main path between the old abbey and the new residential and farm buildings. Gates and walls blocked their view of the ruins.

"This is Robert. Our suspects have disappeared through a door to a passageway heading underground. I've no idea where it leads. What are your instructions, sir?"

"Wait," Jack replied. "I have to inform the Colonel." He grabbed his mobile phone. More forces were waiting, camouflaged in the bushes. Others stood a good distance away from the abbey on a forest path.

"Colonel Pelham, it's Tanner," Jack said. "The targets have entered an underground area through an entrance right next to the ruins. What is your command?"

"Is there another exit?"

"Beats me. I suggest that we have our team in Spangdahlem search their databases. They should be able to find out if there is one."

"I'll give the command immediately. Can you follow them?"

"I don't think that's a good idea. They may be anticipating a confrontation. In any case, our time traveler seems to have brought his sword with him."

"Be careful, Tanner. The last thing I want is a bloodbath in a German nunnery. Wait near the door until all targets have emerged again, then strike. If they take anything with them …" Jack heard the colonel laugh softly, "say, a heavy chest filled with gold …"

"Jack?" someone yelled over the radio.

"Just a minute, Colonel. Something's going on."

Tanner lowered his phone.

"Jack," the voice hissed again. It sounded urgent.

"What's going on, Robert?"

"You won't believe it. Two other people have just left the apse and are running to the door. Guess who they are!"

The next second, Tanner received a painful jab on the shoulder, and Mike Tapleton pointed to an Audi TT with its lights turned off, parked at the other end of the lot.

"Hagen!" Jack exclaimed in disbelief. "Damn it, what's the professor doing here?"

"What?" came the voice from the telephone.

"It's the professor and Dr. Piglet," Robert confirmed.

"Hagen is holding a weapon."

"Tanner, I want to know what's happening," Pelham yelled so loudly through the speaker that even Mike could hear him.

"I don't know, sir, but I will find out," Jack responded haltingly and turned around to take his coat from the back seat. As he stepped out of the car, his phone's connection with Pelham abruptly ended.

"How could Hagen have slipped through our fingers?" Jack hissed.

"I'm guessing he came here before we took up our position," said Mike who had clambered out of the car as well, automatically checking the fit of his Beretta in its shoulder-holster and casually pulling on his army jacket.

Jack's mobile phone rang furiously.

"Tanner! This is Pelham. We were cut off. What in the devil's name is going on over there?"

"Hagen and Piglet have appeared. It looks like the professor is armed."

"Shit," Pelham swore. "Is he out of his fucking mind?"

"Don't worry, Colonel. We'll get it under control." Jack hung up and turned his mobile phone to Push-to-talk mode. In the darkness, he tried to make out if there was any movement near the ruins.

"Robert?"

"Yes, Jack?"

"Tell the boys to get ready. When the others appear, we'll seize them."

Gero had arrived at the spot that d'Our had described to him. The small, plastered depression in the wall hinted that the room had miraculously remained untouched for seven hundred years. His pulse quickened at the thought that what he should have protected so long ago still existed in the same place.

"Is this it?" Anselm asked with a reverent falter in his voice.

"Presumably," Gero said, in a voice much calmer than his emotions.

Anselm opened his tool kit and removed something from one of the side compartments.

"What are you doing?" Gero asked when he saw that Anselm was busying himself with the steel point of his tool in the depression.

"I'll be careful, I promise," Anselm said and pushed him gently to the side.

The rest of the group looked on breathlessly as Anselm carefully worked on the wall with his battery-powered drill. Like an archeologist uncovering dinosaur bones, he freed a lever from the clay, which had hardened like stone.

"I don't believe it," Paul gasped. "The chamber really exists."

For a moment, no one dared to speak. Then Gero broke the reverent silence and firmly turned the lever.

The wall shuddered. A section the size and shape of a door emerged from the rest of the wall. As Gero pushed the door inward for roughly four inches, the stones made a grinding sound. Then, with considerable effort, he pushed the door to the left. The front of the door was composed of precisely hewn quarry stones that had been affixed with cement on a continuous granite slab six-and-a-half feet high.

Pieces of plaster fell to the ground as Gero managed to open a gap wide enough for him slip through.

The room on the other side was about the same height as the passageway and could fit twenty to fifty people. The walls, ceiling, and ground were all covered with polished granite slabs. Unlike the musty passageway, the air in the chamber was dry.

Hannah could clearly see the fear in Matthäus's eyes as he craned his neck to look for his lord. They were all waiting for Gero's signal. Before someone could stop him, the boy pushed his way forward to follow his lord into the chamber.

The boy's sudden scream made all of them jump. Hannah wove her way past Tom and the others and through the narrow door opening.

Gero was standing motionless in front of some sort of altar – there was no other way to describe the heavy, oblong granite stone – and staring at a mummified skeleton on the ground. With its arms crossed across its chest, it looked almost peaceful.

Tom had hit his head on his way in, and swore angrily before stopping abruptly in front of the skeleton.

"Good God!" he exclaimed as his foot accidentally brushed the skull.

Gero ignored the corpse and stepped up to the altar. Warily, he ran his fingertips over a cleanly carved circle.

"It's the Temple's stonemason mark," he said to himself. Brows furrowed, he examined the small, commonplace chest that sat enthroned in the middle of the immense masterpiece.

After a moment's hesitation, Paul and Anselm slowly joined the rest in the chamber.

"It looks as if we aren't the first ones to enter," Paul said after he had looked around the room.

Only then did they notice a flat object that looked remarkably like a laptop the size of a cigar box.

Tom bent over the metal box. After handing Paul the LED lamp, he stretched out his hand to touch the smooth surface of the unadorned box.

"Don't touch it, Tom!" Hannah yelled with a sideways glance at the skeleton. "As long as we don't know how this person died, we better not touch anything."

"There's a knife stuck in his throat," Gero explained.

Tom had heard neither Hannah's warning nor Gero's explanation, for a sudden clicking noise made him jump back in shock. The others, too, hadn't missed the noise. Together, they stared at the small box in stunned silence.

A piece of the box retracted, revealing its contents in the form of a flat, dark gray colored object that reminded Hannah of an ultra-flat LCD monitor.

"Remove your hand!" Gero hissed seeing that Tom was trying to touch the object again. He had drawn his knife. "It belongs to the Order," he warned as he took a step toward Tom.

Tom stepped back in surprise. "What are you doing? Are you going to kill me?" His gaze flicked between Paul, Hannah, and Anselm for help.

"Gero led us down here," Hannah remarked in a surprisingly calm voice. "He has the right to do what he wants with this ... thing."

"Why don't we all calm down first?" Paul suggested.

"Am I surrounded by idiots?" Tom was livid. "Our dear crusader doesn't know what on earth to do with this thing!"

Hannah had taken the lamp from Gero, and now shone it directly into Tom's face. "But *you* know, do you?" she asked sarcastically.

"Silence!" Gero commanded.

Taking a few long steps forward, he stood directly in front of the strange artifact, gazing straight ahead before closing his eyes in concentration. Then he raised his sonorous voice. *"Laudabo Deum meum in Vita mea ... I will sing praise to my God as long as I live."*

Dead silence followed Gero's words. Anselm had folded his hands in prayer and Tom was about to make a snide remark when something suddenly made his jaw drop.

While the edges of the artifact remained dark, the rest of the surface had begun to glow a bright blue-green. As if out of nowhere, a foot-high, iridescent, blue-green screen of smoke appeared above the smooth, dark surface.

Matthäus clung to Hannah's coat in fright, hiding his face in the crook of her arm, and even Gero stepped back in shock.

Suddenly, a multicolored, holographic projection of a woman's head appeared. Only a little smaller than a real head, it had distinctly Asian features and a dark complexion. The angle from which they looked at the three dimensional image didn't matter, the woman always seemed to be looking directly into their eyes. Her well-proportioned, bodiless face hovered above the illuminated platform.

"Greetings, esteemed participants," she said in a pleasant voice, her sleek, black, chin-length hair fluttering slightly as she spoke, as if a gentle breeze was blowing through it. *"You are connected to Time Project Server 58. To establish a connection to another time plane, place your hand directly over the blue SCAN field and wait until the server has recognized your specific network structure and has processed it."*

The Head of Wisdom – how fitting, Gero thought. Never had he dreamed that this was the truth behind the mystery. As he inspected the woman's eyes in fascination, he was reminded of people he had seen from the Mongol Empire. He couldn't believe that this was what d'Our had entrusted to him.

The head dissolved into millions of specks of light that fell back to the flat surface, only to be replaced with a lurid, turquoise-blue fog of dancing light particles, which then solidified into a hand revolving around an axis. Three flashing, wedge-shaped arrows pointed to where one had to position one's fingers.

"I understand what she's saying." Anselm said. Gero's surprised gaze fell on the man.

"Me, too," Hannah added. "But I don't think she's speaking aloud at all. It's some kind of telepathy."

Matthäus looked up at her in confusion, and she stroked his blonde hair soothingly.

"It's like I'm hearing it in my head," Paul remarked in bewilderment.

Slowly, he stepped forward from his position at the chamber's entrance to inspect a symbol on the edge of the display: two intertwined figures of eight.

"CAPUT?" he gasped as the surprise in his eyes grew. "That's our logo. What does that mean? Tom, do you think Hagen actually has something to do with this?"

"Beats me," Tom answered absently, as though he were in a trance. "But it seems like this device works analogously to our own technology. The analysis of the magnetic net structure of the object to be transferred is required for a successful transmission. I was right in my suspicion that not every pattern can be transferred everywhere, but first, every compact object must go through a test to check if it is even able to be transferred."

"Do you mean it comes from the future?" Paul was breathless with excitement.

Tom smiled secretively. "Didn't you say that time and space have been suspended since we started our research? This here is the final proof that you were right."

"And now?" Hannah asked uncertainly.

"Tell our time traveler to place his hand on the field," Tom said softly, fixing his gaze on Gero.

Hannah didn't like the way he looked at Gero at all. "He's not a lab rat," she yelled furiously. "Have you still not grasped that fact?"

Gero laid a reassuring hand on Hannah's shoulder.

Tom's expression grew haughty as he met Hannah's accusing glare. "You just said that this thing belongs to him. You don't actually believe that I would risk having his dagger at my throat again, do you?"

"Tom," Paul stepped in. "Do you have any idea what will happen if he places his hand in the light?"

"Even if we assume that this thing here can really replace our technology, we still can't know if he will be accepted in the chosen time plane. But even if he is, how are you going to determine if the transfer was successful or not?

"What's the worst that could happen, Paul? The device works by calculating all eventualities. If we don't try, we'll never find out." Tom gave Gero a piercing look. "And he wants to go home. Or am I mistaken?"

To Hannah's horror, Gero had understood Tom's invitation. Decisively, he stuck his large hand into the blue-green fog of light.

"Calculating ..." the voice said. "Enter target coordinates below the current time plane."

"Eureka!" Paul cried.

He bent over and marveled at Gero's hand that was now encased in iridescent, blue-green light particles. Then he stood up straight and looked Tom in the eye. "It really looks like this little thing will replace our entire research facility."

He pursed his lips and shook his head in disbelief as he circled the futuristic-looking object reverently. "I wonder where it gets the energy from. And how does it manage to enter our minds?" he asked excitedly.

"What does this all mean?" Hannah asked, holding onto Matthäus's hand tightly.

Suddenly, Tom turned around, seized the boy by his upper arm and pulled him away from Hannah, who was too stunned to defend the boy from Tom.

Gero swiftly drew his hand out from the fog and clawed his fingers into the collar of Tom's navy blue down jacket.

"Let him go right now!" he yelled as he pulled Tom toward him.

Straight away, Tom loosened his grip and raised his hands in defeat. Matthäus rubbed his pained arm.

"Tom!" Hannah shouted. "Are you completely out of your mind? What are you doing?"

"Don't we all want both of them to go home?" he retorted aggressively. "Now is their chance. Go, Templar, tell it where you want to go. It looks like it's your lucky day. This nice little device is ready to fulfill your humble wish to go back home."

Gero didn't contemplate long. "What about the boy?" he asked. "I can't leave him here."

"That's what I meant," Tom said snidely. "Both of you, place your hands in it, and we'll see what happens."

Cautiously, Gero gripped his squire's ice-cold fingers. All at once, the boy seemed to comprehend what was happening and tears filled his eyes as he met Hannah's sad gaze. Gero didn't dare glance at her.

"Calculation recalibrated," the voice said. "Enter time coordinates."

"I believe you can now enter which moment in time you'd like to return to," Tom said with a smile. "However, you should take note that this moment – according to our research findings so far – can't be earlier than the time of your disappearance. Perhaps you should give yourselves a few days to be completely sure. Let's say October 19, 1307."

Tom's serene expression made Hannah's anger flare. Anselm translated Tom's explanation into Old French.

"I am choosing the 18th day of October in the year of our Lord 1307," Gero said firmly. The earlier he could meet the Templar of the High Council he had been ordered to find, the better.

"Approval of transmission granted," the voice said.

The fog dissolved and sank into the bottom of the flat device.

The woman's head reappeared. She smiled subtly. Simultaneously, a garish, glowing light stabbed Gero in the eyes and robbed him of his vision. Instinctively, he turned his head to the side and raised his hand.

"Show's over!" yelled someone from the entrance.

Tom whipped around. "Professor Hagen!" he exclaimed. "Let me guess! An entire regiment of NSA agents are standing outside waiting for us, am I right?"

"One could say so," Hagen replied with an arrogant smirk.

Shocked, Hannah noticed that the professor was holding a pistol in his hand.

"I just wonder ..." Tom said, glancing casually at a miserable looking Dr. Piglet who had appeared behind Hagen's back " ... why they've sent both of you here to arrest us instead of Colonel Pelham's men. Could it be that you want to avoid the attention of our esteemed colonel?"

"That doesn't concern you, Stevendahl. You have something that belongs to me!" The professor's gaze fell on the server that had powered itself down at that same second. "Don't make things difficult for yourself. Hand me the device."

"And what if I don't?" Tom asked in a remarkably calm voice. "Are you going to shoot me? I guess then you could get rid of your only true competition. And you can tell the Americans that you've developed this marvelous machine completely on your own."

"Tom," Paul exclaimed urgently. "Shut up!"

"Paul, are you saying that I should let this bastard have his moment of triumph? Over my dead body! And you wouldn't go that far, would you, Professor?"

Gero's gaze darted between Tom and the grim-looking elderly man.

"Professor Hagen!" Piglet squealed in English. "For God's sake, put down the gun!" His voice trembled. "Murder is *not* an option. As far as I know, you don't even know how to use that weapon."

"Shut up!" Hagen snapped at his aide, who had backed into the doorframe in fright. "Go, Piglet, go over and take the thing!"

With the pistol in one hand and a flashlight in the other, Hagen pointed toward the granite block.

After a moment's hesitation, Piglet stumbled toward the flat metallic object.

Tom blocked his path. "Piglet, I'd have thought that you would be the last person to take part in such a conspiracy. I'm sorry, but if your boss wants to have the device, he has to get it himself."

Piglet looked around helplessly.

Hagen's face turned red with rage. "Stevendahl, do you think I'm holding a banana in my hand?" Suddenly, the professor raised the weapon and fired twice.

Two ear-shattering shots resounded through the room. Everyone ducked their heads, even Hagen himself, who was thoroughly surprised by the pistol's recoil.

Piglet fell to the floor with a thud. A ricocheting bullet had pierced his neck, which was now streaming blood.

Hannah saw Gero feeling around under his jacket. In a flash, she pulled Matthäus to herself and fell to the ground with him. Hagen was waving his weapon at the people standing around, but before he could release a third shot, a giant knife split open his skull. Stiff as a pole, the professor fell backward to the ground.

Hannah let out a scream of horror.

"There's been shots fired," Jack thundered into the radio set. "Calling all forces. Seize them now."

Swiftly, all the agents gathered at the entrance near the apse. Lights began to flicker on in the nearby nuns' dormitory.

The men in dark uniforms disappeared into the underground passageway. Jack checked the fit of his body armor again. Stooping low, equipped only with a night-vision device and with Colt 45s at the ready, they slipped into the dark, forbidding tunnel.

"Someone's coming," Paul whispered into the deathly silence.

"Damn it, we have to leave," Tom hissed. "If it's Pelham's men, they'll think *we* killed both of them. The Americans will arrest us or gun us down like rabbits."

Anselm looked up at Gero, who had withdrawn his dagger from the dead man's head without blinking. "Do you have any idea how we can get out of here?" he asked in a wavering voice.

"Follow me!" Gero answered. "This isn't just a sewer, but an escape route as well." Calmly, he took the server with him.

Tom made no protest. Obediently, they followed the knight to the exit in the sewer.

"Watch out," Jack whispered as he saw a few figures creeping through the passageway some distance away. "There's something going on up ahead ... stay back. If we shoot now, we could be hit by our own ricochet. We have to get our target in sight."

Gero had noticed the men approaching from a good forty feet away. "Down here," he said softly and pushed Hannah, who had exited the chamber after him, right, into the tunnel.

"Take this thing!" he said, and passed her the server.

A brief, blue-green glow almost stopped her from taking the device from Gero. It was as if she could hear the strange voice in her head again.

"*Recalibrating,*" she thought she heard it say. Her heart was pounding. She was so frightened that she felt like she couldn't breathe. Anselm walked some distance ahead and illuminated the path for her. Matthäus stumbled after him.

"Can you take this from me?" she asked hoarsely, handing Anselm the flat box over the boy's head without waiting for an answer.

"Yes, sure," Anselm agreed, trudging bravely forward.

The box glowed again, and Hannah was relieved that she hadn't been seeing things. She heard Gero's heavy footsteps behind her. But where were Tom and Paul?

"Seize them," someone thundered in English, and somewhere far behind her, a flurry of voices rose.

"Run!" Gero cried, shoving her forward.

Cries rang through the tunnel and Hannah thought she heard Tom's panicked voice.

"Stop!" someone yelled. "We are unarmed."

"Fifteen feet more," Gero yelled, giving Hannah a slight push.

MYSTERY OF THE TEMPLARS

"Hey," Anselm said breathlessly, "I could be mistaken, but this thing in my hand is babbling something about '*Destination activated*'!"

He stopped running and looked spellbound at the blue-green lights that had suddenly risen like a vapor under his hands, covering part of his body with a glowing green net structure. Matthäus collided with him and became penned between Hannah and Anselm. Speechlessly, Anselm watched as the net enveloped Matthäus and Hannah. She now heard the voice, too.

Gero stopped directly behind her. He turned his back to Hannah and peered into the darkness. Slowly, the glowing net stretched across the back of his head and broad shoulders. But in his search for their pursuers, he didn't seem to notice any of it.

Hearing a flurry of footsteps approaching rapidly, he silently drew his sword from its sheath.

Agent Jack Tanner stopped abruptly in his tracks. The man's eyes glittered like a wild animal's in the viewfinder of his night-vision goggles. The deadly blade of his opponent glowed green like a futuristic laser sword. Resolutely, Jack aimed his Beretta 92 FS Brigadier equipped with a laser sight at the man.

Just as he was about to press the trigger, a gleaming light blinded him. For a moment, he felt as if someone had stuck hot needles straight into his pupils. He squeezed his eyes shut from pain and sucked in air through his teeth in agony. Unintentionally, he fired. An ear-shattering bang echoed from the walls.

As Tanner slowly opened his eyes again, it took a while until the glowing spots disappeared from his vision.

His colleagues didn't seem to be in better shape.

"Where is he? Shit!"

"I must have gotten him," Jack called, desperately trying to listen for movement in the hallway. "Damn it, I need light."

As if on command, the men turned off their night-vision. Shortly afterwards, an LED spotlight lit the tunnel.

"He's gone," Jack said to himself. "Right into thin air."

Tom wanted to scream, but no sound would escape his throat. An NSA agent had his knee pressed down hard between Tom's shoulder blades. Distantly, he heard frantic murmurs.

"Do you have him, Robert? I'll put his handcuffs on."

"Jack?"

"Yes?"

Tom heard muffled steps.

"Update from Position One. The German police are advancing. Joe is asking what he should do."

"Make sure the Germans don't hear a word of what happened," someone hissed in Tom's ear as both his arms were pulled behind his back.

"Tell them to stage an accident. That'll keep them busy for a while."

"Come on! Stand up, you joker," Tom's captor hissed and pulled him to his knees.

Paul wasn't in any better state. He had been handcuffed as well, and he stood motionless, staring into space. Apart from some swelling on the bridge of his nose, he seemed to be unharmed.

"Move the corpses!" someone urged in a commanding tone.

"What about the skeleton, Jack?"

"Leave it, we'll get it later. Shut the door to the chamber and give me the floodlight."

One of the agents handed Jack the LED light, which, at the press of a button, lit up the sewer like broad daylight. Apart from weathered stones and a dirty sewage drain, however, nothing was to be seen.

"There's nothing here," Jack confirmed in disbelief.

"Where did your friends go?" the man behind Tom demanded.

"I don't know," Tom said slowly. "They're gone. As if they never existed."

Paul nodded mutely, still staring into space.

"There's something on the ground there," one of the Americans said. "Looks like a mini laptop."

The agents combed the sewers for the escapees, but they were nowhere to be found. The exit that the monks had used as an escape had long been buried.

After they arrived at Spangdahlem, and were brought to the temporary headquarters of the NSA, the agents led Tom and Paul, still handcuffed, into a windowless interrogation room.

Despite their remote location, the muffled roars of aircraft still streamed in from the base outside. Although they were currently alone, Tom was certain that an entire troop of interrogation specialists would soon appear to put them through the wringer. He glanced over at his colleague, who seemed to have lost his mind. Paul was silently rocking back and forth in his seat.

The door burst open, and General Lafour entered the sparse interrogation room along with Colonel Pelham and another NSA agent.

A little later, Dr. Karen Baxter followed. Her dark blue pantsuit contrasted sharply with her pale face and her expression was filled with concern.

"Are you ready to work with us?" the General asked Tom and Paul in a cutting voice.

"Of course," Tom said hoarsely. "We, too, are interested in knowing what is actually going on here."

Paul had composed his tortured features and nodded in agreement.

At a wave of the General's hand, the NSA agent stepped forward and released Tom and Paul from their plastic handcuffs. They rubbed their pained wrists in relief.

"Then tell us how Professor Hagen and his aide, Dr. Piglet, died," Colonel Pelham said. "We would also be highly interested in knowing where your girlfriend and her companions have gone."

Haltingly, Tom tried to summarize what had happened since last Saturday. His explanation had just one goal: to prove that he and Paul Colbach were not to blame for either the accident at the Institute, or for the evening's events.

Pelham, however, was not easily convinced. It was only when Karen Baxter intervened, informing the colonel of the professor's computer that no one else had access to, that he began to listen.

"We'll look into the matter," he said coolly.

"What about the small laptop that the NSA took from Heisterbach?" Tom asked, hoping that it could be a way to incriminate the professor.

"The device is in the laboratory," Lafour answered. "But I fear we have a small problem. Now that our professor is dead, nobody else, except the two of you, can get any sign of life from the device." Pausing to clear his throat, he continued, "Even if it pains me to say this, we are now dependent on you, for better or for worse."

Tom sighed in relief. "Well, I can only guess that the mysterious artifact is some type of highly advanced quantum computer, with which our process of time synchronization can be accomplished far less problematically than with our current, modest methods. I don't know if Hagen was aware of its existence, let alone how it landed in the sewers and how exactly it functions." Nervously, he rubbed his face with his hand. "It was a coincidence that the device was turned on. If I had known exactly how it functions, my friend and her companions would definitely not have disappeared. You can believe me."

"What about the knight? Do you think he knew what the device could do?" Pelham gave Tom a piercing stare.

"No," Tom answered, "he was just as clueless as we were."

"And do you have any idea where your friends could have disappeared to?" General Lafour asked.

Tom shook his head helplessly and buried his face in his hands. "Maybe the box catapulted them into the year 1307. Or maybe the transfer dissolved them into individual atoms. I do not have the slightest idea."

PART 3

DEATH AND HONOR

"One day is with the Lord as a thousand years,and a thousand years as one day."

2 Peter 3:8

CHAPTER 27

On the Other Side of Reality

Wednesday, October 18, 1307
Heisterbach Abbey, German Lands

"What was that?" Hannah's eyes darted about fearfully, and, for a moment, she couldn't see anything at all. She felt as if her body was dissolving, but quickly put that brief sensation down to the flurry of emotions she was experiencing.

"I don't know," Anselm whispered nervously. In the commotion, he had dropped the lamp and, as he bent down to pick it up, wet fur brushed against his hand. "Rats!" he shrieked, nearly dropping the light again.

Hannah backed against the wall in fright but when she saw Gero leaning against the damp brick wall near her, she heaved a sigh of relief. Swaying slightly, he held his sword in his left hand and his forehead in his right and was turning to look at where their pursuers had been.

Hannah could have sworn she had just seen someone there. But now, as far as her eyes could see, there was only darkness ahead. She had been too stunned to notice it before, but now the nauseating stench of the sewers, urine mingling with decay, assaulted her nose, almost making her retch.

"Where's the server?" Anselm called, scanning the floor for the missing artifact. "Did *you* take it?" His questioning gaze fell on Hannah.

"What, me?" she answered in surprise.

"Matthäus?" Anselm shone the light in the boy's eyes. Shivering with cold and fear, he huddled close to Hannah, and silently shook his head.

"We have to get out of here," declared Gero, the first to come to his senses. Calmly, he stuck his sword back into its sheath on his belt, and, with a quick glance, made sure his companions were unharmed.

"What in the world stinks so damn badly here?" Hannah gasped, barely able to breathe. "And where are Tom and Paul?" she asked, peering into the darkness where the noises had been, but she still couldn't see anything.

"It looks like the Americans got them," Anselm answered.

"And why didn't they arrest us?" Hannah asked. "They were right on our heels."

"No matter what's happened to them, they're gone now," Gero said. He touched Hannah's shoulder gently as he squeezed past her in the sewers. "Follow me to the exit." He nodded at Anselm. "You can light the path for me."

After trudging forward for nearly 300 feet, they came upon a massive wooden door. Gero unbolted the ancient-looking iron latch, and pushed against the oak planks. The door slowly gave way, and they finally burst out of the noxious sewers. Hannah greedily drank in the fresh air. For a moment, the unbearable stench of human waste lingered, but it was blown away almost immediately by a gust of wind, leaving behind the fine scent of clean air. Hannah was reminded of a night, long ago, when her grandfather had taken her for a walk through the woods.

Outside it was dark and cool, although there was no longer a biting wind like there was before they entered the sewers. A few bright clouds rolled across the sky, now and then revealing the luminous, waning moon. Anselm shone the LED lamp on the surface of a pond that spread out in front of their feet like a dark, shifting abyss.

"*What?* We're *here?*" Hannah gasped in astonishment, realization slowly dawning upon her. As she took a step back, the soles of her boots made a squishing noise. "But it can't be," she said, looking up at Gero.

"We went down, and the pond is much farther away. How is that possible?"

Gero, his eyes strangely glassy, didn't answer, and, bewildered, she followed his gaze southwest.

"No!" she exclaimed. A sudden wave of dizziness hit her, and, staggering, she would have fallen into the water had Gero not caught her in his arms.

"Good God!" Anselm blurted.

With wide eyes, he gaped at the shadowy silhouette of the massive church rising out of the darkness ahead. A seemingly endless row of dimly lit round windows hinted at how astonishingly long the building must be.

Just then, a sudden chiming made them all turn around in shock. In the darkness, they could just make out the small bell tower above the apse. It was as if someone had been expecting their arrival.

"Where are we?" Anselm asked.

"Heisterbach Abbey," Gero answered quietly. "The bells are ringing for the evening's Angelus prayer."

He sat down on the damp bank and pulled Hannah, shivering convulsively, down onto his lap. Stroking her hair, he whispered something in her ear in Old French and his velvety voice and warm hands gradually calmed her down. Hannah's gaze fell on the symbol of a wolf's paw stitched onto Gero's breast pocket. Never had she thought that the simple emblem of a sportswear company would make her yearn so badly for home.

"Tell me I'm dreaming," she whispered.

"Where did that goddamned server go?" Anselm stood rooted to the spot, gaping helplessly into the unfamiliar night.

Matthäus hunkered down next to Gero. "How did the chapel suddenly appear?" he murmured, sounding uneasy.

Gero didn't answer their questions. "We have to seek shelter in the abbey," he said simply. "That's the only way we can find out if we've arrived at our chosen destination."

He quickly squeezed Hannah's hand twice to let her know that he was about to stand up. "Hand me the lamp!" he said to Anselm. "I'm going back to see if the Head is still in the same place."

After helping Hannah to her feet, he turned to Anselm again. "Wait here for me," he said as Anselm handed him the LED lamp. "I'll be right back."

"*Wait here for me*," Anselm repeated in resignation after Gero had shut the weather-beaten oak door behind him and disappeared into the sewers. "Where would we go without him, anyway?"

It took mere minutes for Gero to return.

"There's nothing there," he panted, crouching low and gasping for breath. "I couldn't find the machine, and the entrance to the chamber was untouched, just as we found it before Anselm broke it open."

"But there is absolutely no doubt," Hannah said slowly as she eyed the proud abbey, "that we've landed in the past. Right?"

"Who knows?" Anselm remarked with a touch of irony in his voice. "Maybe we're stranded in a parallel universe. I no longer think anything's impossible after what's happened to us."

"Parallel universe?" Hannah grimaced. "Do me a favor, Anselm, and don't make things any worse than they already are. I'm reaching the end of my tether."

"Everything looks just as I remembered it," Gero reassured her. As if to confirm his statement, he inspected his surroundings again.

Anselm scratched his head in confusion, but suddenly a light dawned in his eyes. "Could we open the chamber," he began hopefully, "and check if the server is still inside? Maybe we can use it to return to the 21st century."

"Let me stop you right there," Hannah cut in, unable to suppress the hopelessness in her voice. "If the server functions according to the same principle as Tom's stupid machine, we'll only be able to travel *back* in time. If you want to travel *forward*, you'll have to be picked up from the future. So, it might be better to set off for Himmerod, to spend at least every other day at the place where the research hall will be, and to hope that Tom and the Americans are working on bringing us back."

Gero shook his head reluctantly. "Before we break into the chamber again, I want to know what day it is today."

He wasn't interested in any further experiments with the Head. If he had actually been transported back into his own era, he first had to continue with his mission. Maybe, if everything went according to plan, the knight from the High Council of the Templars was already waiting for him here, and could help send Hannah and Anselm back into the twenty-first century. Gero had long questioned what the Order hoped to accomplish by using the Head, and he had no idea whether he should be angry at d'Our for sending him and his comrades on this mission completely unprepared.

Anselm seemed to have guessed his thoughts. "Assuming that we've arrived at your intended destination, isn't there someone here who can help us? I mean, even if you don't know how the server functions, surely there's someone in your organization who is familiar with it, right?"

"I think so," Gero agreed. "There's a man who knows how the Head works. And if my commander was right, I'll be meeting him here in the abbey. Still, speculating is useless before we know that we've arrived at the right point in time."

He held onto Hannah's arm reassuringly and headed down the narrow pathway that led across a levee to the abbey gates. Anselm and Matthäus marched behind them like obedient soldiers.

The chiming stopped, and the lights behind the windows dimmed. When they reached the last few feet of the long quarry stone wall, Anselm turned off his LED lamp and hid it underneath his coat.

With a queasy feeling, Hannah watched as Gero strode ahead and pulled himself up onto the wall. Perched on the ledge, he peered over the stony wall. Then he let himself down again and casually pulled on a long rope, making the bell on the abbey gates ring out into the night.

"Someone's coming," he said after a moment.

Squaring his shoulders, he turned to the small door that was embedded in a much larger wooden gate and his proud bearing revealed that he was once again in control. There was no sign of the flustered Templar that he had been mere minutes, or even centuries ago. The rest of the group stayed behind at a respectful distance.

Hannah suddenly noticed that Gero was still wearing his sweater and the black jacket, and wondered whether their outfits were even appropriate for the Middle Ages. Her eyes fell on Anselm who would probably be the least conspicuous of them all. His brown leather coat nearly grazed the floor, and with his long hair and rugged boots, he could easily have blended into several different historical periods without attracting much attention.

Hannah looked down and scrutinized her own outfit. Luckily, her ankle-length camel hair coat hid her skintight jeans. She felt for the backpack she had taken with her into the underground passageway and breathed a sigh of relief when she found it still firmly strapped on her back. Even though she was certain no one here would be interested in her credit cards, carrying a few familiar objects from home everywhere she went made her feel safe: her migraine tablets, mints, comb, nail scissors, and even a toothbrush and a travel-sized toothpaste tube.

With a soft creak, the door opened. Hannah wasn't sure if the entrance was still in the same place in the twenty-first century. The asphalt road had disappeared; in its place was a trampled dirt path.

A man stepped forward holding a burning torch in his hand, his tonsure and light gray habit revealing he was a monk. Gero spoke to him, gesticulating insistently the whole time. The monk's eyes kept wandering back to Hannah, and he looked uncertain whether to accede to Gero's requests. As they talked, Gero whipped out his leather neck-pouch.

Surely not, Hannah thought. He had actually taken his papers with him before they had set off – as if he had anticipated what would happen.

Like a customs officer at the border control, the monk raised his torch and shone it on the documents Gero was holding out. He craned his neck and nodded in Hannah's direction. Gero waved to the rest of the group to enter.

"Don't worry," he whispered, a triumphant grin flitting across his face.

"Today is Wednesday, the 18th day of October, in the year of the Lord 1307."

"Well, at least we now know that the server works," Anselm remarked with a touch of sarcasm. "I'm not sure that makes me feel any better, though."

Uneasily, Hannah watched the young monk hurry forward. The pale oval of his tonsure gleamed in the moonlight as he crossed a courtyard paved with round stones, nimbly sidestepping a splashing fountain. Worn sandals adorned his feet, which were covered in thick, felt, ankle-length socks to protect him from the cold.

As they followed the monk, Hannah marveled at the large, ornate, stone fountain, which sat like an oversized chalice in the middle of the sprawling inner courtyard, spraying a steady stream of water that cascaded back down into the base. Hannah wondered how it could function without an electric pump.

Gero's strides were so long that even Anselm struggled to follow him, and Hannah and Matthäus had to break into a trot.

"Where's he taking us?" Hannah asked breathlessly.

Noticing his companions struggling to keep up, Gero stopped and waited until Hannah had reached his side. "To the abbey," he answered putting his arm around her shoulder. "The Cistercians have to announce our arrival."

They climbed up a steep sandstone staircase that led to the building's second floor and Gero stayed by her side until they arrived there. The young monk was holding a heavy oak door open for the newcomers while he waited for them to catch up. When they had all passed through the doorway, he led them down a long hallway into the abbey's hermitage.

The monk knocked on a closed door. After receiving permission to enter, he invited the unannounced visitors into the spartan room. With his head bowed, Gero took the first step in, and Hannah and Anselm followed hesitantly. Matthäus, however, chose to wait outside in the hallway.

Abbot Johannes of Heisterbach was a gaunt man with small, cunning eyes that flickered with curiosity. When he saw the woman among the visitors, he rose from his armchair, smoothed down his light gray habit, and bowed slightly. Then he slowly stepped forward from behind the heavy beech desk and turned to Gero, eyeing his visitor's strange outfit suspiciously.

"Ah, the young lord of Breydenbach and his charming guests, at so late an hour!" The abbot's smile was a little too suggestive for Gero's taste, but his expression quickly became serious again.

"*Pax vobiscum*," Gero said softly, kneeling slightly before the abbot and kissing the ring that the man held out to him expectantly.

"*Pax vobiscum*, Brother Gerard," the abbot answered solemnly, repeating the gesture with the ring to Hannah, who realized an embarrassing moment too late what was expected of her. Nervously, she imitated Gero, but her voice failed her as she opened her mouth to repeat the greeting. Anselm, however, almost fell to his knees to bestow the customary honor upon the abbot.

After the clergyman had returned to his seat behind the gigantic writing desk, Gero turned to him once more. "Father Johannes, may I speak with you in private?"

The abbot looked at him with a strange expression. "Of course," he agreed.

He waved to the young monk to lead Hannah and Anselm out into the hallway.

Gero winked at them. "It won't take long," he whispered.

After the door had been shut, Abbot Johannes peered at Gero with interest.

Gero stepped nearer to him and bowed. "*Computatrum quantum*," he announced ceremoniously.

The abbot's initial bewilderment was quickly replaced by an understanding look. "If I'm not mistaken, you are already expected," he murmured, "although I was told that two of your Brothers from the Temple would be accompanying you. No one ever mentioned a woman and a boy."

"In all his mysterious grace and wisdom, The Almighty, has chosen a different path for me than the one my commander intended," Gero answered calmly, hiding his surprise that Abbot Johannes seemed to know the details of his mission. "I was separated from my Brethren on our way here," he added. "I have my current companions to thank for being able to continue my mission despite the adversities we encountered. They, along with my squire, are under my protection. I therefore ask your grace to extend to them the same hospitality that you would to me."

The abbot cleared his throat. "It is our duty as Christians, Brother Gerard, to offer wanderers refuge for one night, although you know as well as I do that we cannot accommodate women in the presence of the other Brothers. In light of these special circumstances, however, and because it is you, I'll make an exception. You should also know that your Order's representative, Brother Rowan, hinted that you and your Brethren would be going on a journey after your arrival. You'll have to discuss what happens to your companions with him."

The abbot's eyes gleamed curiously from beneath his bushy eyebrows, but Gero offered no explanation. He himself didn't know what the abbot was hinting at.

The abbot stood up and gestured to the door. "Then let us escort our guests to their humble quarters."

After they had stepped outside into the hallway, the abbot exchanged a few whispered words with his subordinate.

"Brother Jodokus will escort your friends to their quarters," he said to Gero. Then he looked him in the eye, and his voice became softer. "After that, he'll take you to Brother Rowan."

The young monk first led Gero and his companions to an isolated, timber-framed building behind the refectory. The structure usually housed the abbey's invalids, though it was empty at the moment. Hannah was to spend the night in a small, whitewashed chamber apart from the men. Noting her fearful expression, Gero gave her a confident wink after the Cistercian had left the room.

"Don't worry," he said softly. "As soon as I've spoken to the representative from my Order, I'll come back. In the meantime, Anselm will take care of you and the boy."

With a discreet nod, Gero turned to his friend from the future and handed him his sword. "They don't look too favorably on anyone wandering the hallways fully armed," he explained. "Could you keep this for me? If someone tries to do any of you harm, you have my permission to use it."

As he took the precious weapon from Gero, Anselm looked baffled. Gero stroked Hannah's arm reassuringly. "Everything will be fine," he said with a smile.

He followed the Cistercian through the unlit cloister to a ground-level hermitage, where a gate stood in a wide, arched passageway to the courtyard. His escort knocked on a door set in the gate, and, after a moment, a solemn voice granted them access.

Unlike the damp and chilly dormitories, this room had its own fireplace where a cozy fire was crackling. Brother Rowan stood at the window with his back to the door. His shoulders were broad, and he was wearing the habit of the Cistercians. Only after the young monk had shut the door behind him did he turn around.

Rowan's piercing eyes were just as gray as his hair, which must have once been jet black but was now marbled with silver. Gero guessed that he was nearly fifty, but he couldn't recall ever seeing him before. With a slight shudder, he bowed before the unfamiliar knight.

"May God be with you, *beau sire*," he greeted him solemnly.

"You're early," the stranger said in a peculiar dialect that resembled Struan's. "Where are your comrades?"

"I don't know," Gero admitted frankly. "A number of unforeseen things happened on the way here."

The unfamiliar Brother looked at him questioningly and began to speak. "My name is Rowan of Tradoch. As you may have assumed, I am a member of the High Council, just like your esteemed commander."

He gestured for Gero to take a seat on one of the two stools that sat around a small, square table. "Sit! We have a number of matters to discuss.

Your presence assures me that the unthinkable has happened, and Philipp, that French bastard, has fulfilled his destiny, and ours along with it. I'm sure you have quite a lot to tell me. Speak freely. I know more about what has happened to you in the last few days than you can imagine."

Gero was bewildered, but he dared not question Brother Rowan. Could he possibly know that Gero had traveled to the future? He supposed it wasn't all that unlikely. Ultimately, someone in the Order must have had an idea of how the Head of Wisdom worked. He began to describe in detail what he had experienced in the past few days – or, more accurately, in the next few centuries.

When he finished his story, he was surprised to see Brother Rowan's expression of disbelief.

"And am I to believe what you say?" he asked simply.

"If not you, then who?" Gero felt his desperation growing.

"And how is the Order doing?" Rowan asked in a tone that suggested that Gero was trying to make a fool of him. "What do the people from the future know about its fate?"

"The Order no longer exists in that time," Gero replied. "Under the current circumstances, it won't survive."

"Your experiences are further evidence that we have to take our fate into our own hands," Rowan muttered grimly.

"With all due respect, Sire," Gero said, sounding distraught, "what are you implying?"

Rowan removed a gray habit from one of the hooks on the wall and handed it to Gero. "Put this on!" he ordered without a word of explanation.

Gero mustered his courage. "What will happen to the people from the future who came here with me? Will we be able to help them return home?"

"We don't have time for that," Rowan said curtly. "You have a mission to fulfill, Brother Gerard. Nothing else matters. They'll find their own way home soon enough. Now, follow me!"

Gero longed to protest, but nonetheless he rose in soldierly obedience. As he removed his doublet, Rowan's gaze fell on his knife-belt.

"You can leave your belt here for now," he remarked. "We need different weapons for where we're going."

Gero unbuckled his belt and slipped reluctantly into the scratchy, gray woolen habit.

384

"Now, lead me to the Head!" Rowan ordered.

Hesitantly, Gero opened the door that led into the cloister. He still hadn't given up hope that he could convince Rowan to help his comrades return home after he let him have his way. Gero and Rowan headed toward the sewer through the wine cellar under the refectory. With his torch, Rowan lit the way to make sure that no one was following them. Together, they stepped into the darkness of the sewer, and Rowan held his hand to his mouth, gasping. Gero, who was already used to the stench, went ahead readily. When they arrived in front of the chamber, he glanced around. He didn't have a knife to break the clay out of the wall and uncover the handle, but Rowan seemed to sense what Gero was searching for. He pulled out a long hunting knife from under his robes and handed it to him.

Just as Anselm had done, Gero chipped away the dry clay and small stones to free the metal handle, praying all the while that the Head of Wisdom was still in the same spot. He handed the knife back to Rowan and, with considerable force, pushed open the secret door.

Stepping ahead of Gero to enter the room, Brother Rowan looked around in amazement as if he had never been down here before. Everything was in the place where Gero had found it in the future, except for one thing. The dead man, who had been lying on the floor like a mummy, was missing.

"The password," Rowan said coolly. His eyes were glued impatiently to the flat metallic artifact.

Gero cleared his throat before he began to sing: *Laudabo Deum meum in vita mea ...*

To his surprise, Rowan didn't jump in fright when, unexpectedly, the small box opened with a click and a shimmering head appeared surrounded by blue-green light. Then the head faded and five wraithlike fingers materialized. With a strange gleam in his eyes, Rowan passed the flaming torch to Gero. "The two of us will now embark on a journey, Brother Gerard," he murmured ambiguously.

"What do you mean by that?" Gero looked at him, thunderstruck.

"We shall both travel to the year 1268 of the Lord's Incarnation, and ensure that the second son of King Philipp III and his bride Isabella of Aragon will never see the light of this world."

Gero felt an icy jolt run down his spine. "How?"

"Brother Gerard," Rowan snapped, "you are a knight of the Temple, and you have sworn obedience to the Order. And I command you to accompany me and do what I tell you!"

"With all respect, Sire," Gero's voice sounded almost pleading, "you know that I am responsible for three people. I can't just leave them behind here, and apart from that … yes, I am a Templar, but I am not an assassin. I will not kill women or children just to reach our goal."

In the greenish twilight glow of the Head, Rowan's face looked positively demonic. "There is no price too great to pay for the salvation of the Christian Occident, Brother Gerard. Never forget that! We are dealing with something far greater than your honor here."

"No," Gero answered resolutely. "Never!"

Suddenly, Rowan raised the hunting knife threateningly in his right hand, and glared at Gero.

"I'm most surprised, Brother Gerard," he declared. "As a knight of the Red Cross, you should know that one must be ready to sacrifice his conscience at any time when the survival of Christendom is at stake."

"I've seen enough to know that the survival of Christendom isn't what's at stake here," Gero retorted defiantly.

"You know nothing at all!" Rowan snapped. "I honestly wonder how your commander could have chosen a fool like you for such an important mission. Preventing the birth of Philipp IV is our only chance of changing the world's fate, not just of saving the Order. We must not just exterminate Philipp IV, but his mother and father as well, so that both of them have no chance to give life to a second or third bastard who could grow up to be like her firstborn son."

Gero shook his head. "If I allow something like that to happen," he whispered, "then it will no longer be the Order that I know."

"Very well," Rowan hissed through gritted teeth, "then I'll go alone. I'll spare myself the assistance of an idiot like you." Grim-faced, he turned around and placed his left hand in the blue-green vapor.

Gero sprang forward and pulled the gray-haired Brother back. "In the name of the Lord," he gasped, "you cannot do this!"

Before he knew it, Rowan had pulled out his knife again and thrust it at him.

Instead of defending himself, Gero dropped the torch in shock. Rowan was no less experienced in combat than he was, and he struggled to avoid his Brother's deadly blade. But Rowan knew no mercy, and there was no question that he would kill him.

Again and again, the Brother of the High Council lunged at him. Gero tried to grab the blade in Rowan's hand, but was instead rewarded with a deep cut on his forearm. At the next blow, he ducked, and, as he fell to the ground, he flung out his leg and brought Rowan, in his floor-grazing habit, down with him. Quickly, he seized the Brother's wrist and pinned the hand with the knife to the floor.

With unbelievable strength, Rowan tried to wrench himself free from Gero's grip. For a moment it seemed as if Gero would succumb. But suddenly, Rowan flailed too close to the torch, and the long sleeve of his habit caught fire.

Gero let his opponent go as Rowan began to thrash about like a madman. With a jerk, Gero threw him aside to escape the flames.

Rowan's habit was blazing fiercely, and as Gero hastily took off his own frock and beat at the fire, Rowan began to writhe violently, clutching at his throat.

The fire was relentless, and before the last flame had been smothered, Rowan died a wretched death.

Gero stared numbly at the corpse. The hunting knife that Rowan had aimed at Gero's heart just moments before was now plunged into the man's neck.

Lord Almighty, *Gero thought,* what have I done?

Panting, he turned around, and in the weak glow from the torch he had dropped, he saw the Head, which had switched itself off and now lay untouched.

Gero had thwarted the High Council's shameful scheme, but he also knew that he had endangered his Order's existence. He couldn't imagine Henri d'Our allowing the lives of an innocent woman and her unborn child to be taken so callously to save the Order. Perhaps d'Our himself hadn't known about the High Council's actual plan. Why else would he have chosen Gero for such a mission? The commander knew that he himself had lost his wife and child under terrible circumstances.

Utterly exhausted, Gero dragged the charred corpse behind the granite block. All at once, he remembered the exact moment, seven hundred years in the future, when he had seen the dead man as a skeleton.

"May your soul rest in peace, my Brother," he murmured. "This chamber will be a worthy tomb for you."

After some hasty deliberation, Gero decided to take the Head of Wisdom with him. As things now stood, he had no choice but to search for d'Our. The Commander of Bar-sur-Aube was the only member of the High Council whom Gero knew personally. He was certain that as long as d'Our was alive, he would be the most likely person to make a wise decision about what to do with the Head, and perhaps he could even help Hannah and Anselm to return home as well. Carefully, he wrapped the Head in his habit.

Hannah looked up as the door opened. To her disappointment, however, it was not Gero who entered the room, but the young Cistercian, who smiled shyly at her as he knelt down to set a freshly cleaned chamber pot on the floor. In his other hand, he was balancing a wooden tray with four cups, a large, rust-colored stoneware jug of white wine, a loaf of bread, some cheese, and a small basket of ripe apples. He set the tray down on a small side table, wished Hannah and the others a blessed night, then left the room without turning back.

The oil candle in the brass cup near the wine jug provided the room's only feeble light. The small, flickering flame hinted that from somewhere, a draft was streaming into the room.

"Where on earth is Gero?" Hannah moaned, glancing around the room uneasily.

The only window had no glass panes, only a leather roller blind, and wooden hinged doors that could be shut from the inside. She stood up reluctantly.

"What are you doing?" Anselm asked in alarm. Since Gero left, he hadn't taken his hand off the sword.

"Checking if the window is shut," Hannah answered, inspecting the lock. "I don't want anyone to climb in." Before she returned to the bed, she sliced some bread and cheese and handed it to a frightened-looking Matthäus.

Suddenly, Gero was standing in the door, soot-blackened and blood-smeared.

Hannah sprang to her feet and ran to him. "What in God's name happened to you?" she cried in horror.

Anselm stood up too, clutching the sword even more tightly than before.

"Don't worry," Gero answered quietly. "I'm fine."

"I can see that," Hannah replied flatly as she eyed Gero's forearm. He had fashioned himself a tourniquet from a scrap of dirty fabric, which was already soaked with blood. Glancing around quickly, she spotted a clean linen towel on a rack next to a dresser with a washbasin. As Hannah approached him with the towel, Gero sank down wearily on a stool. Without a word, he handed Anselm a bundle of woolen fabric that smelled unmistakably of smoke and fire.

"What is that?" Anselm asked in shock.

"The Head of Wisdom," Gero said. "We'll have to find a safe place for it."

"The server?" Anselm stared at Gero curiously. "So it really *was* there. And where is the knight from the High Council?"

Gero shook his head. "I'll tell you soon," he said evasively.

He held out his bleeding arm to Hannah, quickly instructing her on how to clean the wound with water and wine. Hannah was relieved that he had been immunized at the hospital, as Tom had informed her, and couldn't become infected with tetanus.

After she had dressed his wound, Gero briefly described what had happened in the sewers.

"This means that the High Council knows what the timeserver is capable of," Anselm commented. "But it doesn't necessarily mean any of their attempts were successful," he added thoughtfully.

Gero took a large gulp of wine. "Yes, you're probably right," he agreed.

"You know what I wonder?" Hannah said. "If you took the Head with you, how can we find it in the same place seven hundred years later?"

"Good question!" Anselm interjected, turning to Gero with interest.

"That doesn't really matter to me," Gero said in a tone of resignation. "I don't even understand how all this could happen. Any more questions like that, and I'll go insane before I can come up with a single rational plan to help us."

"And what plans do you have?" Anselm probed.

"We will look for my commander. I don't know anyone else besides him who would know how the Head works, so he is the only one who can help us save the Order and send both of you home again."

"What if the abbey asks about where the dead Brother has gone?" Anselm asked.

"Let that be my cross to bear," Gero reassured him. "I've sealed off the chamber and hidden the depression with earth and clay from the pond.

Apart from myself, I doubt anyone else knows the exact spot where it's hidden, and now, Rowan can no longer reveal the secret," he added, sounding almost remorseful.

"We should go to bed. In the morning, I'll try to convince Abbot Johannes that Brother Rowan left on his journey without me – wherever that may be."

"Which is the truth, in a manner of speaking," Anselm chimed in with a fatalistic shrug.

Turning to face Hannah, Gero ignored Anselm's remark. "We will set off on foot and rent a few horses in the village. Then we'll ride to my father's castle. He'll help us. Besides, I want to find out what has become of my Brothers."

Gero stowed the Head of Wisdom in Hannah's backpack and hid it under her bed, then he escorted Anselm and the boy into the monks' dormitory where they would be safe for the time being. Under the pretense of having to use the latrine, he slipped away from the Cistercians' curious eyes and, clad only in a short, black doublet, leather pants, and boots, he hurried through the dimly lit cloister.

After he entered Hannah's chamber, he pushed the back of a chair under the handle to bolt the door. Hannah welcomed him with a tender embrace.

"We should go to bed," he said softly, kissing her hair.

Next to God's love, Hannah's was the best comfort he could imagine at the moment.

"Could they blame you for the death of your Brother?" Hannah asked in concern as Gero led her to her narrow plank bed.

"As long as no one finds him, it would be unlikely," Gero replied, sinking down on the bed to remove his boots. Then he stood up again, and calmly unfastened the cords of his trousers and draped them over a chair without a second thought. Finally he pulled his doublet over his head, unbuckled the knife-belt that he had retrieved from Rowan's chamber, and casually hid it under the pillow.

Now completely naked, he made sure that the blinds were shut before returning to the bed and slipping under the coarse bedding with a smile. Hannah had been watching him silently and now stood indecisively in front of the bed.

"Come lie with me," he said, raising the woolen blanket, "so I can warm you up."

Clad only in her underwear, she lay down beside him. As he held her in his arms, he kissed her, hard and urgently.

Panting, she freed herself from his embrace. "What if someone catches us?" she asked breathlessly. "They didn't put me far away from the monks for nothing."

"Don't worry," he answered with a reassuring smile. "Whoever dares trespass here will have to answer to me, not I to them. Besides, Anselm knows that I'm spending the night with you, and he'll keep an eye on Matthäus while I'm here."

Undeterred, Gero continued to caress her neck, but Hannah stopped him again. "Should we be doing this right now? Someone died today, and somehow I still can't grasp the fact that I've found myself seven hundred years away from home."

"Forgive me," he muttered, looking at her guiltily. "I just thought a little distraction would ease your worries." He shifted away from her with an apologetic shrug.

"I didn't mean it like that," Hannah said running her fingers through his short hair. "I just keep thinking about what happened down in the sewers. Your Brother could easily have killed you. I don't dare imagine what would have happened if you had obeyed his orders. If I haven't misunderstood Tom, there is still great uncertainty about whether the course of time can be changed. Maybe it's possible with the Head of Wisdom, but what if it isn't?"

"One should never give up hope," Gero answered.

She shifted closer to him and gently kissed him on the cheek. "Come what may, I'm happy that we're together," she said. "The thought of not seeing you and Matthäus ever again was far worse for me than traveling through time with you."

For a moment, a happiness that he had long forgotten flooded through his veins. But as the blissful moment passed, cruel reality caught up with him again.

"Hannah ..." Gero struggled to find the right words. "We haven't had time to talk about it yet, but I think it's too dangerous for you stay with me in the long run. I'll have to find a way for you and Anselm to go back to your own time."

"Why are you suddenly trying to get rid of me?" she asked, sounding hurt.

Gero sighed. "It's not about what *I* want at all. Don't you understand?"

391

"But you still want to sleep with me," Hannah said, staring at him defiantly. "Right?"

"I'm concerned about your wellbeing, and nothing else!"

"What if I get pregnant?"

He stiffened, and stared at her in confusion. "But you said that couldn't happen."

"Oh, yeah?" Her eyes flashed at him. "Did I say that?"

He groaned loudly. "Oh, Hannah … I'm sorry."

"What are you sorry about? That you have to be responsible for me?"

"I love you," he declared. "Do you think it's easy for me to send you back? It's precisely because I love you and feel responsible for you that you can't stay here." He pulled her close, driven by a need he couldn't articulate. "Hannah," he sighed. "Even if I can never see you again, my heart will still belong to you forever."

"No one has ever said something like that to me before," she whispered. "But if I were to believe anyone, it would be you."

"I can't imagine anything more wonderful than being next to you," he continued in a whisper, playing with her auburn hair, "every day and night until the end of my life."

"What's stopping you?" Hannah replied with a smile and lay back down on the pillow.

Gero bent his head down to her and touched her ear with his lips. "I am a Templar," he answered bitterly. "Nothing can change that. And apart from the fact that I've sworn an oath to remain unmarried, it appears as though my future leaves much to be desired. The Order is as good as dead. And I now bear responsibility for the fact that this fate might very well be irreversible. Even if Philipp's manhunt extends only to the edges of the German lands, they could still be looking for me. If word gets out that I've killed members of the Royal Secret Service, I'll be regarded as a murderer of Christians, and not even my family will be safe from dishonor and persecution. In any case, I'm already considered a heretic when it comes to Philipp IV and the Pope. Even if fate grants me mercy and no one's interested in my whereabouts, as my father's second-born son, the best I can hope for is to join the Teutonic Order under a false name. That means marching off into the eastern parts of the land where one can only travel in winter, as that's the only time the marshes are traversable." He shook his head. "With such prospects, can you tell me how I could take care of a woman from an unimaginably distant future?"

"We have a saying for that," Hannah answered calmly. "Just when you think you can't go on, a little light comes on somewhere."

"I know that saying," Gero said in surprise. "When I was a young boy, my mother would comfort me with the same phrase in my language whenever I felt hopeless: "Gif hit you thinketh lif is sette at noght, a lighte be comen hider."

"You see?" Hannah raised her head and kissed him tenderly.

"Words change over time, but they convey the same meaning. We aren't so different after all."

"No, just by seven hundred years and my foolishness," he replied with a smile, returning her kiss.

"If a thousand years is like a day to God," she continued in a whisper, "then seven hundred years is hardly worth mentioning."

CHAPTER 28

Brysich

Thursday, October 19, 1307
Headquarters of the Templars in the Rhinelands

Early in the morning, Gero slipped back into the monks' dormitory. After the nighttime vigils, the monks had once again fallen into a deep sleep. Anselm, too, was lying on his back and snoring soundly, as if the monks' liturgies had been all but a dream.

Exhausted, Gero lay down on his uncomfortable plank bed. Unlike Anselm, he hadn't had a wink of sleep all night. After he had made love to Hannah and held her in his arms until she had fallen asleep, his thoughts returned, again and again, to what had happened earlier that evening.

The existence of the Head was unfathomable enough, but Brother Rowan's order to go back in time and kill the future parents of Philipp IV seemed as if it had come from the devil himself. He still wondered how the Order had even come to possess the Head, and if d'Our had really known Rowan's plans.

His eyes rested on Matthäus, who was snuggled under a coarse woolen blanket on the bed next to Anselm's. Gero thanked the Lord that he had made the right decision, not just with his head, but also his heart. He would never have been able to leave the boy behind to embark on such a shameful mission.

Gero felt a deep affection for the boy, for Hannah, and for all his friends. In his eyes, there was nothing holier than love, no matter whether it was for a comrade, a woman, or a child. Why should he only love the Order, and why was it a sin to want more than that? Who made the rules? Saint Bernard, or God? Where was it written that a man was only pious if he renounced the love of a woman and the joy that a family brought? Maybe it was God who had sent him an epiphany in the form of this fantastical journey, just when the Order was fighting against its own destruction. All at once, he realized that he was no longer driven by battle and honor. What he wished for most fervently was a family of his own. A wife, children, and a modest property that would sustain their peaceful lives.

Gero shut his eyes and began to pray, doubtful that his wish would ever be granted. As things stood, it wasn't all that likely.

"Where is Brother Rowan?" asked Abbot Johannes when Gero entered his office to bid him farewell. He registered Gero's injury with a quick glance.

"He left last night," Gero lied, "and he decided not to take me on his journey."

The abbot nodded. "That's a matter to be settled amongst your Brethren. It doesn't concern me," he said, and then added, "We Cistercians were always just the nest for the Temple's eggs, anyway."

Returning to the dormitory, Gero gently shook Anselm out of his sleep. "We have to leave as soon as possible," he whispered.

Anselm blinked at him in disbelief. "Damn it," he exclaimed, "you're actually serious."

As he rose from his hard bed groaning, he looked around in astonishment, shocked to find that he hadn't simply dreamed up their journey into the fourteenth century. His eyes wandered across the austere dormitory unable to comprehend what they were seeing.

Golden rays of morning light shone through the thin oil-soaked parchments that covered a row of narrow windows. The monks' beds were lined up neatly underneath, separated in the middle by a passageway that connected two large doors on either side of the hall. The air was moist and heavy.

With a mixture of curiosity and dismay, Anselm regarded Gero's outfit. As a disguise, he was wearing a brown, ankle-length, hooded cloak that he had bought from one of the monks.

"Let's go," Gero said, slapping his thighs before standing up.

They left the dormitory, with Matthäus hopping impatiently behind them, plagued by an urgent need to pee. The cold air was making matters even more urgent, but before he ran off to relieve himself, he made Gero swear by the Lord's name that he wouldn't leave him behind.

In the morning mist, a pair of squawking crows took off from a tall beech tree, its yellowing leaves announcing the arrival of winter. Anselm's eyes followed the birds' flight with interest.

"So," Gero began cautiously, "it looks like you and Hannah will have to put up with my company for a while. At the moment, I don't see any possibility of taking you back to your world."

Anselm's eyes flickered with doubt, and Gero wondered how the man from the future would receive his fate. After all, he himself had nearly lost his mind at the thought that he would never be able to return home.

"There are worse things," Anselm replied with a fatalistic smile.

Oddly enough, the clouds of breath that rose steadily from his own mouth as he spoke seemed to be what fascinated him most. "It's all real," he whispered, still disbelieving.

"We'll travel to the commandery of Brysich first," Gero continued. "I'll find out if they know what's happened in France since I've been gone and I might even be able to meet my Brothers who accompanied me from Bar-sur-Aube. They could very well be searching for me and the boy."

A mass of gray tunics wandered through the morning mist, past Anselm and Gero, occasionally muttering a greeting of "Praise the Lord Jesus Christ". Shrouded by their hoods, the men's faces were unrecognizable. The pious monks disappeared down the cloister that led to the refectory, where breakfast was waiting for them.

Anselm looked longingly at the mighty church. Its main doors stood open, just as before.

"Before we leave, I'd like to pray first," Gero said softly. "Will you join me?"

Anselm followed Gero to the church entrance where they were immediately greeted by the scent of frankincense and beeswax. As Anselm stepped into the monumental pillared hall, he was overcome by the feeling that for the second time this week, he was crossing a border into another reality.

Every step they took echoed off the gigantic ceiling arches. The ornate church was alight with a blaze of painted colors. Several wooden benches had been set up in the inner hall, and where the benches ended, two long rows of choir pews lined either side of the mighty walls, ending at the apse. The slim pillars, which were still standing in Anselm's time, curved around the altar stone in a semicircle. The altar itself was covered in an expensive cloth adorned with gold and precious stones, which shimmered in a riot of colors in the glow of the thick candles. Above the altar was a large statue of Mary. With a serene smile on her face, the mother of God looked almost real. Other life-like statues of different saints stood on stone pedestals along the corridors and oriels, as if they were in a long, deep slumber.

Anselm took a seat next to Gero on one of the wooden benches and folded his hands in prayer. The red, morning sun danced amongst the clouds of frankincense, enveloping the colorful church in a warm, apricot glow.

"It hurts to know," Anselm said as they left the building, "that one day, nearly all of this splendor will be gone."

Gero nodded with a deep sigh, and excused himself to collect Hannah and the boy for the journey ahead.

Quietly they left the abbey courtyard, and after a short journey, they reached the small, picturesque village of Dollendorf with its timbered houses and colorful Romanesque church.

It was market day and Gero bought bread, cheese, and wine so his companions could enjoy a small breakfast under the shade of a large linden tree. Taking a deep drink of the freshly made sparkling wine, Hannah felt as if she had never drunk anything more delicious.

After breakfast, Gero sought out the best animals from a groom not far from the Rhine, paying the elderly man a few coins from his leather pouch. When the horses were saddled and bridled, Gero removed the Head from Hannah's backpack and stored it in one of his own saddlebags.

Fortunately, both Hannah and Anselm were experienced riders, and soon they reached a trade route along the Rhine. The sun was shining, and the air was intoxicatingly pure. Meadows and fields unfurled before them, parted by a deep blue river. The wind whispered through the tall reeds on the edge of the riverbank.

A gentle veil of mist floated over the glistening water. Two wooden sailboats glided silently down the Rhine. With steady wing beats, a massive flock of storks took flight and vanished toward the south. Hannah looked into the distance across the riverbank. There were far fewer trees in the world of 1307, but far more castles on the mountains. A fortress crowned nearly every hill, and, on the opposite bank, on top of a bare mountain, the Godesburg castle towered into the sky like a big trigger finger.

Gero headed south, and Hannah glanced around again before following the rest of the group.

A rider was approaching from the north at tremendous speed. He was perched on his dun horse like a jockey, and flew past them so quickly that

Hannah was only aware of a multi-colored blur. Dust swirled up around them, and about ten yards later, the rider, without looking around once, raised his gloved hand in greeting. His jacket and the satchels bobbing at his hips were adorned with a black and white cross emblem. Then he disappeared just as swiftly as he had appeared.

"What was *that* all about?" Anselm asked.

"A messenger of the Archbishop of Cologne," Gero explained. "They're always rushing along the Rhine here, day and night."

In Königswinter, the next small town, Gero dismounted to buy Hannah some clothing appropriate for the Middle Ages, leaving his companions to wait for him in front of the city gates.

"A woman as beautiful as you causes enough of a stir," he teased, "without them thinking you're a Mussulman in your strange pants."

When Gero returned, he handed her a spring green silk dress, a dark green velvet surcoat, and a dark brown hooded woolen travel cloak.

"Thank you," she said with a smile, taking the clothing from him. The soft fabric smelled of wool and herbs.

"It's the least I can do to thank you for what you've done for me," Gero replied.

Smiling, he fished out a finely woven, light green silk veil from a side pocket of his cloak and held it out to Hannah, who carefully took the delicate cloth from him. Seeing the excitement in her face, he beamed in satisfaction.

Anselm was fascinated by the flawless workmanship and quality of the fabric. "What about me?" He gave Gero a questioning look. "Do you reckon I can keep my old clothes on?"

Gero inspected Anselm as if he were seeing him for the first time, and laughed softly. "You look like a well-heeled merchant, apart from your boots, which look more like they belong to a vagabond soldier."

Anselm relaxed and re-examined his boots.

"Well ... come to think of it," Gero remarked, and circled the man while rubbing his chin thoughtfully.

"What?" Anselm asked, looking up anxiously.

"Your hair ..."

"What's wrong with my hair?"

Gero took one of his knives and minutes later, Anselm was sporting the typical hairstyle of a knight, a straight, chin-length bob that looked as if it had been cut with a ruler.

Anselm's new look made Hannah burst out laughing. The medieval expert gave her a warning glare.

"What's so funny?" Gero asked innocently. "He looks like a nobleman."

Hannah was still choking with laughter and shaking her head. "He looks like Prince Valiant," she gasped breathlessly.

"Prince Valiant?" Gero stared at her in confusion.

"Forget it," Anselm grumbled, and mounted his horse.

Beneath the towering castle of Lewenberg, they found an empty shelter for sheep where Hannah could change unobserved.

"How did you know the clothes would fit me?" She paused for a second before stripping down to her underwear in front of Gero.

"My dear," he said with a small smirk, letting his gaze wander over her naked body. "I've shared a bed with you. What sort of fool would I be if I didn't know what figure you had?"

Hannah laughed and shook her head, then clumsily stepped into the open chemise that was fastened in the front with silk laces. "Are all the men here as attentive as you are?"

"I don't know," he answered in amusement. "I rarely go out as a woman."

For a moment Gero forced himself to tear his eyes away from Hannah in order to peer through the doors, which were slightly ajar. When he turned back again, he was practically speechless.

"Despite the plain dress," he said, admiringly, "you look like a queen."

The slim cut of the chemise accentuated her breasts and hips, and the color of the tight-fitting surcoat perfectly highlighted her chestnut colored hair, fair skin, and green eyes.

"Don't look at me like that," she said shyly. "Help me with this veil. I haven't the faintest idea how to wear it."

"I know what it looks like when it's on," Gero said, and began a clumsy attempt to fasten the delicate fabric over her stubborn curls, "but I can't help you any further than that." He examined his unsuccessful efforts in exasperation.

"Let me try." Hannah took the copper-colored hairpin out of his hand. A little later, she had skillfully pinned up her dark locks. With two more hairpins, she affixed the soft fabric above her temples so that it hung down on both sides.

"Well?"

"It looks something like that," he concluded, nodding in satisfaction.

After he had helped her into the cloak and shown her how to fasten the clasp, he took her into his arms and kissed her bare neck. Her skin tingled. Out of the corner of her eye, she could see that his eyes were shut. He inhaled with relish before reluctantly releasing her from his embrace.

Hannah gathered her old clothes from the fence and folded them neatly while Gero watched her in silence. His face, cheerful just moments ago, darkened.

"Is anything wrong?" she asked.

"No," he replied quietly. "I'm just wondering how I'll explain everything to my family."

"Surely you aren't going to tell them that you traveled through time?"

"Never," Gero said, taking the bundle of clothes from her. "They would never believe me." As he opened the shelter doors, his eyes were filled with sorrow. "There's so much I don't understand. I have no idea why the Order leadership didn't warn us earlier about Philipp. From what I've learned, the Brothers of the High Council already knew of our impending destruction long ago. Why weren't the protectors of the Head able to act against King Philip and his troops in time?"

"Maybe they tried?" Hannah suggested tentatively.

Gero raised an eyebrow. "Well, I seem to have ruined our last possible chance of saving the Order, and now I don't know if even the Almighty Lord can help us change our destiny."

The rest of their journey led them down a dusty road along the Rhine, past smaller fortresses and castles, which mostly turned out to be toll stations. They had to stop at every station where they should have been subject to intensive questioning, but because Gero was a member of the Knights Templar, they were allowed to continue on their journey unchallenged.

At the small Templar commandery in Hönningen, they were greeted by loud bleating. Hundreds of sheep were clogging the road, blocking the path of an approaching horse and carriage.

Hoyngen, as Gero called the place, had its own ferry station. "We can cross the river for free," he explained after showing the sharp-eyed boatman his papers. "The ferry belongs to the Order."

The far larger commandery of Brysich stood on the other bank and Hannah marveled at the long, impressive walls that met at the river bank in a large archway. Tall, shady, sycamore trees surrounded the entire compound.

After a quarter of an hour's journey from the opposite bank, the ferry docked near where Gero and his companions stood waiting. As they climbed in, the boatman called for them to hurry. In answer to Gero's questioning look, he gestured to the north, where a group of at least fifteen horses was trudging up the towpath, towing a large vessel on thick ropes.

Gero took his companions' own horses by the reins, and, with Matthäus's help, pulled them into a wooden shed where he tethered them so they couldn't shift too much on the swaying boat.

When Hannah tried to lean against the wooden rail, it wobbled dangerously, and she took a step back in fright. Yet the water was much calmer than it was in her own time, and the bank appeared wider and shallower. A gust of wind stinking of fish and stagnant water, blew against her face.

With their united strength, the crew pushed the ferry into the current, and the moment its hull drifted free from the river bottom, they jumped aboard. A thick rope in a wooden guide that spanned the Rhine ensured that the boat didn't drift too far away.

Anselm took the opportunity to take a closer look at the people on board the boat. It was difficult to guess most of their ages. With their suntanned skin, the six ferry crew members, all men of about twenty, and the ship's master, a tough, gray-haired fellow with only one eye, looked little like the pale-faced figures of medieval artwork. The men's short-sleeved surcoats displayed their impressively muscular arms and although most of them had to perform hard labor, none of them appreared dissatisfied.

With the men's swift rowing, the wooden boat glided through the river before it was steered toward the other bank by the current and with the aid of long punts. In Brysich, the boatman pushed himself up to the edge of the pier and a few men hurried over to secure the ferry with the ropes a shipmate had thrown to them.

A sailing ship was anchored right next to them. Another ship, with a steadily turning waterwheel, which Gero identified as a ship mill, was secured in the current by four anchors.

Matthäus helped unload the horses before the group rode slowly up the path to the commandery. The water gate, as Gero called the wide archway that opened onto the Rhine, connected the commandery and the jetty, and was meant only for transporting goods. A huge wooden crane lurked nearby. To reach the commandery, visitors had to go around the water gate, through a picturesque apple orchard. From afar, Hannah could see the weathered walls of the neighboring village that hundreds of years later would bear the name Bad Breisig.

A large, round gate, framed by fragrant, dark red roses, marked the main entrance to the commandery, which consisted of a few stables and farm buildings of smooth sandstone. Gero halted his horse and waited until his companions had come to a stop by his side

An older man, dressed in a black habit embellished with red crosses on his breast and equipped with a fearsome-looking sword, controlled who was allowed to enter the headquarters of the Templars in the Rhinelands. The guardhouse was set in an oriel next to the entrance, where the officer on watch stood, flanked by three younger men in similar habits, and armed just as fearsomely as the main guard. They were nervously watching their surroundings.

Gero produced his parchments once again.

"Ah," the old man exclaimed, and a smile cracked his weather-beaten face. "The young Lord of Breydenbach. Your father was here just two weeks ago to deposit his quarterly earnings. Have you come from Metz with the troops?"

"No," Gero said, pricking up his ears with interest. "We came from Bar-sur-Aube. We're on the run."

The old man looked at them contemptuously. "Name me a Brother from France who isn't on the run. May the devil rip King Philip's balls off and stuff them down his throat until he chokes on them!" He spat out angrily before continuing. "Just yesterday we learned of what happened and since then, we've been receiving an endless stream of Brothers fleeing from France. Some have even come from Lorraine. They say that things are going poorly even there."

Gero's unease increased. "Have you had any news of Brother Johan van Elk and Struan MacDhughaill? I was separated from them along the way."

The old man shook his head. "I can't remember everyone's names. You'll have to ask the administration if they've been registered here."

Then his gaze fell on Gero's company. "And who do we have here?" he asked in a slightly suggestive tone, eyeing Hannah a little more closely.

"The woman and the other two belong with me," Gero answered a touch hastily. "They're followers of the Order from Bar-sur-Aube."

Anselm bowed slightly. "Anselmo de Caillou. If I may introduce myself."

"Hmm," muttered the old man who obviously didn't understand French. "You may proceed," he said to Gero, signaling the young guards to lift the wooden barriers that blocked the path.

"De Caillou?" Hannah whispered to Anselm as they crossed through the archway.

"Pebble in French," Anselm smiled. "It sounds a little more refined than 'Anselm Stein'."

The commandery's spacious courtyard was paved with pale trachyte. Just like at the Heisterbach Abbey, a chalice-shaped fountain stood in the middle of the courtyard, reminding Hannah of an old baptismal font. Brownish spring water spluttered out of a clay pipe in the middle of the chalice. The water spread out in ripples, flowed over the edge into a gutter embedded in the ground, and then finally down into an underground run-off. Someone had thrown an iron hook over the edge of the stone fountain and secured a metal ladle to it on a leather band. Anselm couldn't resist ladling a scoop of water and tasting it.

"It tastes like iron," he said, raising his bushy eyebrows in surprise.

"You better be careful," Hannah warned. "The last thing we need is one of us getting the runs and requiring medical attention."

Gero let his eyes drift down the long row of stables, the adjoining men's quarters, and finally to St. Donatus' chapel, which was dedicated to the wandering Frankish monk. When he was younger, Gero and his father had prayed here in honor of the local Crusade relic. From behind the smooth walls, monastic chants resounded; the midday Sexta prayer was in full swing. The courtyard itself was empty, and the horses stood at designated poles, with their lids half-shut patiently waiting for their owners.

Anselm noticed that the steeds all bore the Templars' brand mark. He smiled wistfully as he dismounted his comparatively mangy gelding, and handed the reins to Matthäus.

"What's my old nag compared to these stately mounts?" he remarked, approaching one of the magnificent white beasts. "Perfect," he said appreciatively, stroking the broad leather saddle stamped with Latin numerals. The white horse whinnied softly. Its neck was damp with sweat.

"You need to towel off this sweat," Anselm said to Gero, "or the horse will get a cold."

Gero put two fingers between his teeth and whistled loudly. Shortly after, two boys, only slightly older than Matthäus, showed up at the stable door.

"Come on," Gero called to them, "don't just stand there. Get the saddles off the horses and rub them dry!"

The two boys stared at Gero as if he were out of his mind. Matthäus sniggered at their looks of disbelief, promptly earning him a chastising glare from his lord. The boys eyed the strange looking man mistrustfully, but his towering stature and the short hair and beard that all Templars wore finally convinced them to follow his orders.

Gero ordered Matthäus to tend to the group's own horses and wait for him outside. Turning to Anselm and Hannah, he motioned for them to follow him and together they entered a three-story building. As they entered the antechamber the air was thick with the scent of frankincense, beeswax, and stew. A three-foot tall stone Madonna stood on a marble base in the corner, a gracious smile adorning her face.

"Brysich is the second-largest commandery in the Rhinelands," Gero explained proudly. "Before I entered the Order, I often used to come here with my father since he usually makes his monetary exchanges here."

Anselm nodded, looking a little surprised. "So it's true that the Templar commandery in Bad Breisig was some sort of medieval bank."

Gero registered himself and his guests with a young man with thinning blonde hair. The young monk examined Gero's papers thoroughly, then leaned on his lectern and scribbled something on a yellow piece of paper, which he tore into two clean halves. He handed the bottom half to Gero and dropped the other half into a small box. Gero asked about his missing comrades, but the monk simply shook his head.

Gero was still holding the paper in his hand when the bells began to chime loudly. Amidst a flurry of voices, at least fifteen men streamed into the hallway. A side door to an adjoining room was opened, and the men entered a bright hall, where two long rows of tables awaited the hungry knights.

As the sea of long white cloaks streamed past her, Hannah felt as if she were being carried away in a current. Anxiously, she looked around for Gero, but when she finally found him, she wasn't the only one to do so.

"Brother Gero!" someone in the crowd called. The voice was deep and raw, and belonged to a middle-aged man with short, dark hair and a thick, dark-gray beard.

Hannah saw Gero's blue eyes light up when he recognized the man who had called his name. "Theobald! God in heaven, Brother, what are you doing here?"

The two men fell into a hearty embrace, delightedly slapping each on the back, while other men in white cloaks looked on with interest. Meanwhile, Anselm had backed against the wall, and Hannah saw him furtively whip out his cell phone. If they ever returned home, he would be the only person to own a photograph of two members of the fearsome Knights Templar sobbing with joy.

"Gero, *mon frère*," the stranger whispered in a choked voice and Hannah noticed that he had sounded the 'G' in Gero's name like a 'J'. Then, after a second's pause, he unexpectedly kissed Gero on the mouth.

"Brother Theobald," Gero said, his voice rich with emotion. "Thank the Lord, you're alive!" To Hannah's great surprise, Gero returned the man's kiss with an intensity that annoyed her.

When several other knights recognized Gero, the men broke into a frenzied flurry of Old French and to Hannah's surprise, it seemed it was not at all unusual for men here to kiss each other on the mouth.

"Not here," the man with the dark beard said to Gero, glancing around as if he were searching for something. "We should let the commander assign us a room where we can talk undisturbed."

"I'm not alone," Gero replied. "Let me first show my companions to the refectory so they can nourish themselves, and then we'll have some time to talk."

Stealthily, Anselm stowed his cell phone in his coat pocket when he saw Gero striding toward him. The knight gave him a few short instructions, and, with a confidential wink, excused himself from Hannah before disappearing through a side door with the unknown knight.

With Gero gone, Anselm led Hannah to the dining hall. The day's two mealtimes were announced in chalk on a black slate slab at the entrance to the dining room. Silently, the hungry warrior monks fell into a long line in front of a brick serving-counter at the other end of the room. Each of them was equipped with a wooden dish and spoon. From large iron pots, several men behind the counter distributed meat and vegetable stew and grain pudding sweetened with applesauce and honey. Earthenware dishes of fresh apples and grapes were laid out on the tables.

By midday, the wine was already flowing. But before they began to eat or drink, the men rose for a prayer that must have lasted at least ten minutes. Matthäus, too, had joined them, and stood with his hands folded devoutly in front of his soup.

Hannah was pleased to discover that she still remembered the Latin version of the Lord's Prayer, but was lost again as the monks launched into a second prayer, which they recited repeatedly in turns. After half an eternity, the men finally sat down and devoted themselves to their meals in silence, communicating only with hand signals when asking for bread or a jug of wine. The occasional slurping or clinking of spoons and cups echoed loudly in the silence.

A tall knight with a curly brown beard gave Hannah a fleeting smile when he noticed her staring absently at his hands after the main course. With a large knife that he had removed from his belt, he was carefully cutting a few apples. The slender hand that held the dagger's hilt was neatly groomed, but covered with scars of various sizes. The man stole another glance at her from the corner of his eye as he handed his Brothers the apple slices. Hannah quickly lowered her gaze to stare at the tabletop in front of her. How could the knight know that when she looked at the knife, she was thinking of one of his Brothers, standing half-naked in her bathroom, shaving his beard, or of a dead professor with exactly the same blade plunged into his forehead?

Unexpectedly, the man held half of an apple out to her, speared on the tip of the murderously sharp blade. It was a friendly gesture and he had even removed the core from the fruit. Hannah dared not reject the offering, thanking him with a nod as she hastily took the apple.

She sensed that the apple-parer seemed amused by her behavior, and the other rakish knights at his table didn't look any less thrilled. As she looked up without thinking, friendly grins went around the table. She chewed her apple slowly to deter the man with the curly beard from offering her any more fruit.

Anselm, however, didn't seem to have noticed anything. His attention was fixed squarely on a Brother in brown, reading in his best Latin from a Bible on a lectern in the middle of the hall.

After he had left his companions in the refectory, Gero first spoke with the commander of Brysich, Heinrich of Blauenstein, and obtained a new chlamys, chain mail, and surcoat. The commander was adamant that the Templars in the German lands shouldn't have to disguise themselves by not wearing their usual uniform just because the King of France had gone mad. On the contrary, he was convinced that the knights had to fight to preserve the Order's honor until the very end.

After that, Gero and Brother Theobald retreated into the scriptorium, where they could talk undisturbed. They sat down on a bench next to a small tracing table strewn with several colorful, ornamental pieces.

"Do you know where they've taken Henri d'Our and my Brothers from Bar-sur-Aube?" Gero asked anxiously. He still felt responsible for his Brethren's fate.

"A stonemason from Troyes told me that Henri d'Our and three other comrades from Bar-sur-Aube were transported to the fortress in Chinon. He'd seen the distribution lists and wondered why. No one else was sent there."

"*Chinon?*" Gero looked distraught. "How will we ever get them out of there?'

"Get them out?" Theobald croaked in disbelief. "No one gets out of there, except when they're dead. You should stop entertaining such impossible thoughts and follow us south instead. We're going to the commandery in Mainz to organize the resistance with Brother Alban of Randecke and Brother Fredericus Sylvester."

"Do you know how the German rulers will react to what Philipp has done, then?" Gero asked.

"No," Theobald replied, sounding uncharacteristically unsure of himself. "The Bishops of Cologne and Trier have been on our side up to now, and as they've often shown unity with the Bishop of Mainz, we hope that will also be the case this time, too. Unfortunately Theobald of Lorraine, despite his usual political leanings, is on the side of the French King, at least as far as the Order is concerned."

"How do you know?" Although Gero had read in Hannah's books about the Duke's scheming against the Order, he was still desperately clinging to the hope that the historians were wrong. His heart began racing. Without realising it, Theobald had begun to turn Gero's vague and hypothetical knowledge of the future into something real and concrete.

"First of all, the Duke has issued an edict that henceforth, all goods under the management of the Order cannot be sold without his approval,"

Theobald explained. "Secondly, he's announced that every Templar who leaves his territory unauthorized will be imprisoned as soon as he's caught. Despite this, we, along with the Brothers from Metz, managed to escape. They know just as little as we do about the stance of the bishop there. At the moment, nobody knows how things will turn out, or if it's true that we'll be safe in the dioceses there."

"What I'm about to tell you is for your ears only," Gero said in a strange voice. "You have to believe me, even if it sounds bizarre to you." With increasing certainty that the stories in Hannah's books were true, he found himself faced with the decision of what, and who, he should tell about the future without letting his Brothers in on the true secret of the Head of Wisdom. If he was already burdened with failing to carry out the High Council's mission, the least he could do was to use his own knowledge to spare his Brothers from the worst of their fates.

"You will be safe here," Gero said softly, "and in Mainz, too, although there will come a time when we have to show the Archbishop that there's a limit to what we'll put up with. No matter what happens, the Order and its Brothers will be granted no peace. Within five years, the Order of the Temple will be dissolved through a papal bull. All property will be relinquished to the Hospitallers and the Teutonics. In most cases, our Brothers will be given the chance to switch Orders, but none of us should return to France without good reason – it's still extremely dangerous there."

"How do you know all this?" Theobald asked, his eyes wide with shock.

"Let's just say that I do," Gero answered, staring stubbornly at the colorful letter designs on the table next to them.

"What if," Theobald asked apprehensively, "Philipp prevails over King Albert and manages to expand his borders eastward? Will we be in danger once again?"

"That won't happen," Gero said, wondering for a second if he had gone too far with his prophecies. "King Albert won't survive the next summer, and his successor will not be Charles of Valois, as King Philipp expects, but the Count of Luxembourg, the brother of Baldwin of Trier."

"Baldwin of Trier?" Theobald wrinkled his forehead incredulously.

"Before the end of the year, Pope Clement and King Philipp will have appointed a new Archbishop of Trier."

"Mother Mary," Theobald whispered. "What happened to you? Have you turned into a mystic?"

"I had a vision, of a sort," Gero said, and stood up quickly. "I can't tell you anything more."

"So it isn't just a myth," Theobald remarked quietly, looking up at the colorful glass windows that depicted Saint John surrounded by the seven riders of the apocalypse. "The High Council ... the council actually exists, and you belong to it. Who would've thought?" He gave Gero a wry smile. "Anyway ..." he muttered, and for a moment, his eyes were fixed blankly ahead. "Thank you," he said firmly, and embraced Gero so suddenly and tightly that he could hardly breathe.

Gero avoided Theobald's searching gaze after he had let him go and whispered: "You know, Brother the mystics were right. There is a world hidden behind the reality we know. Nothing is as it seems. Our fate is determined by providence, and there can be no escape from it."

"I found out where they've taken my commander," Gero said quietly to Anselm and Hannah as they headed across the courtyard to the stables. Matthäus had run ahead to scoop some water from the well. Gero didn't want to mention d'Our's terrible fate in the boy's presence.

"And where is he?" Anselm asked.

"Chinon," Gero said simply.

"Isn't that where the Grand Master was imprisoned?" Hannah looked from Anselm to Gero.

"Yes," Anselm answered, and raised an eyebrow. "He might as well have said ... Alcatraz."

"Where are you headed?" asked the guard as he opened the gate.

"Home," Gero said simply.

"Today?" the old man inquired, squinting at the low-lying, late afternoon sun.

"We're spending the night in Mayen," Gero explained to satisfy the gatekeeper's curiosity. "The castle bailiff is my mother's stepbrother and my God uncle," he added, pulling the reins to steer his horse southward, onto the road.

Before the road to castle Rheineck began its ascent up the hill, they turned right into a narrow valley and rode past farmyards and castles, into the setting sun.

They had long since left the abbey behind them when dusk began to fall, and the defensive tower of the thirteenth century Genovevaburg castle came into sight.

The cold evening wind cut through Hannah's medieval clothing, making her shiver. Matthäus was riding close by her side, and he gave her an encouraging smile.

A million thoughts were wandering through her mind. The German lands in this era were actually very tranquil, and the people seemed to be more civilized than she had expected. Even the food tasted delicious, although the soup in the commandery could have used a little less salt for her taste.

A loud whinny tore Hannah from her thoughts as Matthäus' horse threw its head back and lunged forward. From nowhere, a black shadow sprang out of the bushes and whipped the reins out of her hands.

Before she could react, a foul-smelling stranger was sitting behind her and spurring her horse on. Hannah tried to scream, but the shock had rendered her speechless, and only when the man grabbed her waist and turned the horse around could she let out a pitiful cry for help. Swiftly they galloped through a ravine and down the mountain.

"Hannah!" Gero cried her name like a warning. But what could she do? Her abductor was holding onto her with steely determination. Should she try to make the man fall from the horse? But what would happen if she broke a leg or an arm?

The man steered the animal away, across a stream, and into a thick forest. Only then did Hannah notice that they were not riding alone into the deepening darkness. A second man had wrestled Matthäus' horse from him, but, to her relief, he hadn't dragged the boy along with him.

Hannah's heart pounded. What was going on? Were they taking her hostage, or were they going to kill her?

"Shit!" Gero swore as he spurred his horse on. He now regretted not accepting the offer to take one of the commandery's battle steeds with him.

As Matthäus had fallen off his horse during the strangers' attack, Anselm helped him onto the saddle behind him Shivering with fright, he clung to Anselm's coat while they struggled to follow Gero into the night.

Gero pushed his horse to its limit, guiding himself solely by sound, the stamping of hooves and rustling of leaves and branches keeping him on the right path. As they crossed a clearing, he saw Hannah and her abductors for the first time since the chase began. He felt for his knife-belt and pulled out his dagger, urging his horse further on with his other hand. Steadily, he closed in on them. He narrowed his eyes as he took aim. Without another moment's hesitation, he hurled his hunting dagger at the nearest man, striking him squarely in the back.

Suddenly Hannah's abductor moaned and tightened his grip on her. She was so surprised that she nearly fell from the horse. With the last of her strength, she grasped the horse's mane. Suddenly, Gero appeared by her side. Steering his horse only with his thighs, he held his sword aimed at her abductor.

But the man was not about to give up without a fight. All at once, the blade of a broad sword glistened against Hannah's throat. The next second, however, the blade was gone, and all that was left of the hand holding the sword was a bloody stump, the hand cleanly severed above the wrist. Hannah felt the man tip from the saddle, threatening to pull her down with him. Instinctively, she leaned forward and clung to the horse's neck with both arms. While the animal circled in confusion with only her on its back, she stopped thinking and held her arms clenched around its neck so tightly that she felt she couldn't let go even if she wanted to.

Anselm broke through the thicket and stopped his horse not far from where Gero was standing over a motionless man. Matthäus leapt off the horse and ran to Gero. After tying his reins to a shrub, Anselm followed the boy. Hastily, he pulled out the flashlight that he always carried with him, and shone it on the man on the floor. He was lying on his side and moaning softly. His right hand was missing, and a knife was plunged into his back. Without saying a word, Gero pulled it out of his victim. Anselm swallowed hard as the smell of fresh blood made him take a step back and nausea overwhelmed him.

"What … happened?" he asked in a faltering voice.

"Keep him at bay," Gero replied handing him the knife. Anselm had to force himself to take the blood-smeared handle from the knight.

Gero ran across the clearing towards Hannah, whose horse had finally slowed to a halt, but she was still cowering over the horse's withers.

Anselm knelt down next to the wounded man, and, disobeying Gero's instructions, laid the knife in the grass. From his coat pocket, he fished out the small leather strip he had tied his hair with that morning. He positioned the flashlight on his lap and gritted his teeth as he held the slackened arm with the bleeding stump between his thumb and index finger, and carefully lifted it up. He began to bind the wound until the veins stopped pulsing. The man had lost consciousness. Anselm picked up the flashlight and stood, pensively shining it on his handiwork.

"We'll let him lie here," Gero decided grimly when he returned with Hannah, who had calmed down a little but still looked frightened as she sat in her saddle. "His friend can take care of him," he added without sympathy.

"What if he doesn't come back?" Anselm pointed out. "He'll definitely die if no one takes care of him."

"I should have killed him anyway," Gero remarked darkly. "He would have deserved it, and every fair court in the land would have ruled in my favor. But since Hannah's with us, I'll spare him."

A cold shudder ran down Anselm's spine when he met Gero's eyes.

"Come along," said the Templar, pulling fiercely on the reins of Hannah's horse.

After they had returned to their original path, Gero swung himself onto the saddle behind Hannah. Her entire body was shaking and Gero held her tightly to keep her warm and to reassure her that she was safe.

When they had almost reached Genoveva castle, Hannah finally found her voice. "My backpack," she cried, touching her shoulder. "Where is my backpack?"

"I'm afraid one of the robbers stole it," Gero said, helping her down from the horse.

Without warning, she burst into tears. And so, the castle guard, who had opened a small peephole in the gate to see who had arrived at such a late hour, was greeted by the strange sight of a sobbing young woman in the arms of a Templar knight.

After Gero had produced his papers and the group had been escorted into the castle, they were warmly welcomed by Wilhelm of Eltz, the Bishop of Trier's ministry official and castle's custodian. As Gero later explained, he considered the man in the plush, velvet surcoat a godfather of sorts. They'd always been close when Gero was a child. Now the older man listened attentively to his godson's story of the assault. Occasionally he asked a question, and the lively movement of his eyes hinted that he was not only thoroughly analyzing the events, but was obviously also interested in the underlying reason for Gero's visit, and the presence of his companions. Gero, however, could only say that he and his friends were on a mission for the Order.

Hannah's gaze settled on the castle lord's curly gray beard and lush mustache, which bobbed up and down peculiarly when he began to speak.

"I will prepare a suitable chamber for you," he said in a steady voice. "We'll take it from there."

A little later, a handmaid led them into a spacious guestroom with smooth, plastered walls and a spotless wooden floor. In the middle stood a beautifully carved bed with a green brocade canopy. Hannah resisted her first impulse to fall onto the mattress, and contented herself instead with stroking the bedspread, which was made of the same precious brocade fabric.

"Come, lady," said the handmaid, curling her cold, bony fingers around Hannah's wrist. "Your bed is at the other end of the hallway."

Instinctively, Hannah yanked her hand out of the maid's grasp and looked at Gero pleadingly. "In the name of the devil, don't leave me alone," she cried out. In her fear of being separated from the men, she forgot that she was speaking modern German, and that even a listener from the fourteenth century could understand the word 'devil'.

"Let her be," Gero said to the baffled servant. "We will spend the night in this chamber together. The lady will sleep in the bed, and you'll bring a few straw mattresses and blankets for the boy and us men."

The woman, who still dared not tear her gaze away from Hannah, nodded before hastily turning around and leaving.

Shortly afterwards, a man entered the room. After giving them a subservient bow, he went silently to a fireplace that spanned an entire wall of the room and knelt down. With some burning kindling, he lit the pile of beech wood, and then just as silently left the room. The crackling fire quickly made the room warm and cozy.

As Gero and Anselm took off their cloaks, Hannah looked down at herself. Gradually, she realized where the metallic scent she had smelled was coming from. Gero, who had followed her gaze, quickly removed her blood-smeared cloak and threw it into the fire without a word. Anselm stepped back in surprise as the cloak went up in flames.

"I'll get you a new one," Gero said with a smile of regret.

When the servant returned to light a candle, he too, wrinkled his nose at the smell, but said nothing. Another servant carried in a tray loaded with an appetizing spread of sliced bread, a large piece of soft cheese, and a tall earthenware jug of white wine. He set down the tray and four cups on a small table.

After both men had shut the door behind them, Matthäus took a piece of bread and sat down on a sheepskin rug that lay directly in front of the warm, blazing fire. As he chewed on his bread, he gazed pensively into the flames. Gero, who normally would have insisted on saying grace and on table manners, refrained from chastising the boy.

Heavy footsteps in the hallway made Anselm prick up his ears. Matthäus jumped up in fright as a heavy pounding made the massive oak door shudder.

"Come in," Gero called loudly.

A bearded man with short brown hair, dressed in a surcoat of the Archbishop of Trier, entered the room and snapped to attention in front of Gero. The stout man was armed to his teeth with his chain mail, knife, sword, and war hammer. "The Lord of Eltz requests you, noble Sir, to aid in the arrest of the robber vermin," he began. "We have assembled in the courtyard. Please, if you would take your sword and follow me."

"I'm coming, too," Anselm said without hesitation.

"Let it be, Anselm," Gero said to him in Old French so that the soldier wouldn't understand him. "You have neither a weapon nor the right armor, and one of us has to stay here with Hannah. We can't leave her here all alone with Matthäus."

"But ..." Anselm didn't want to give in, even though his knees were quivering nervously.

"No buts," Gero said firmly. "I don't think you've ever participated in something like this. It's pitch dark outside. They hunt with torches and dogs, and nobody knows how many robbers are lurking outside. I don't want someone to stab you in the middle of the night."

Anselm wasn't sure whether to be annoyed or relieved by Gero's decision. Gero gave Hannah an encouraging wink.

"I'll be back soon," he said casually, as if he was heading out to a bar for the evening. He took two slices of bread and a piece of cheese he had hastily cut off with his cutlass, and then finally left the room.

The night stretched on endlessly. Hannah wasn't able to sleep a wink, and three cups of fine Moselle wine hadn't helped at all. Hours must have passed without Gero's return. The candle on the iron stand had burned down to half its length. After Matthäus and Anselm had fallen asleep on the thick straw mats in front of the warm fireplace, she reluctantly used the chamber pot under the bed, covering herself with her dress, so that she didn't have to brave her way through the windy hallway to reach the latrine outside.

Early in the morning, when it was still dark outside and the fire had long since died down, Hannah sensed someone cautiously lifting the blankets behind her. She had dozed off from exhaustion, and at first she was shocked, but then she smelled Gero's familiar scent. Even unwashed, Gero smelled comforting, and the desire to be close to him welled up in her again. He was naked save for his braies.

"Is it over?" Hannah whispered in a choked voice as she allowed him to slide his icy hands under her warm armpits.

"Yes," he said softly. He said nothing further. Instead, he pulled her flush against his sculpted stomach.

"Did you catch them?" she asked breathlessly.

"Yes," he answered again. "I've even brought back your backpack," he murmured as he buried his nose in her hair.

Hannah raised her head in confusion, and Gero took the opportunity to kiss the exposed nape of her neck.

"I'm sorry," he said softly. "There was nothing left in it."

"Damn it," she sighed, letting her head sink onto his outstretched arm. "What will I do without my toothbrush?"

"You won't be in need of anything, I promise you," he whispered as he caressed her ear with his tongue. "We don't have the toothbrushes you're familiar with, but we Templars use willow roots with fringed ends instead – it keeps your teeth wonderfully clean. We learned it from the Saracens. They even have something like toothpaste. My father brought the recipe with him from the Outremer. It's a mixture of alum, salt, and pulverized chamomile blossoms." He laughed softly. "The heathens must be good for *something*, after all. And at the market in Trier tomorrow, I'll buy you combs, brushes, and whatever else a woman needs to make herself beautiful."

Hannah turned to him and hugged him tightly, pressing her warm bosom against his cool chest.

"You saved my life," she whispered in the darkness.

"By helping you keep your teeth clean?" he asked, sounding amused.

"No. You know what I mean."

"I would have done it for any other woman," he muttered. "I once swore an oath to protect with my life the poor, the sick, children ..." again, he laughed, " ... and even women."

"You don't say," she said dryly. "Thanks, anyway."

She nestled her face into the crook of his neck and inhaled deeply before she fell asleep again moments later.

CHAPTER 29

A Glimmer of Hope

Saturday, November 20, 2004
Spangdahlem

The next morning Tom insisted on driving to Hannah's house as someone had to take care of the animals she had left behind. With the wrench Jack Tanner had given him, he forced open the front door.

When he stepped into the narrow hallway Tom was glad that Paul was with him. The thought of Hannah, who had greeted him in her nightgown at the same spot just yesterday, now wrenched his heart with sadness and guilt. *It feels like it happened a thousand years ago,* he thought.

Paul scooped the meowing black cat into his arms. "Here, boy," he said with a smile as he scratched the neck of the momentarily confused feline.

"We should take Heisenberg to your place," Tom remarked softly. "It doesn't look like we're going to get his mistress back anytime soon. By next week, all hell will have broken loose. I have no idea how to explain Hannah's sudden disappearance to her co-workers and friends, let alone to the medieval expert."

"Don't worry about it," Paul said, glancing sideways at Pelham's men, two ex-marines, who were waiting for them in a silver Mercedes parked in Hannah's driveway. "Agent Tanner said the NSA will come up with something. Maybe Anselm and Hannah spontaneously decided to travel the world. They'll send postcards, e-mails, even make calls on their travels. No problem."

Tom shook his head in disbelief. Just then the cat sprang out of Paul's arms and ran into the bedroom, where it crawled under the bed. Paul went down on his knees to look for it and after a few minutes of coaxing, he finally lured the recalcitrant feline out. When Paul rose to his feet, he showed Tom a coin he had found under the bed.

It was an ancient coin, but it gleamed as if it had been freshly minted. At the sight of it, Tom finally broke down. Completely baffled, Paul gaped at him in incomprehension as his colleague sat down on the bed, sobbing uncontrollably and burying his face in his hands.

"Shit," Tom groaned, trying to stem his tears, and Paul held out a tissue to him, which he gratefully accepted.

"We'll find them," Paul said, trying to look confident. "And then we'll bring them back. The only thing we need is time."

"Which is exactly what we *don't* have!" Tom cried almost angrily. "Every goddamn day may cost them their lives. And if they die wherever they are, it's likely that no one will be able to bring them back anymore. Do you have any idea what the fourteenth century was like? I asked Hertzberg. Life was full of war, pestilence, and instability! You might as well call it Russian roulette!"

After they had left Hannah's house, Tom and Paul headed to Karen Baxter's laboratory, where all the transferred historical objects had been catalogued and meticulously analyzed before being frozen in nitrogen and stored in a special safe. To her frustration, she had come to the conclusion that the supposed timeserver from the future must be damaged. No matter what they did, the holographic woman's head never once reappeared.

Obviously, the ancient chant sung by the Templar knight was needed to activate the timeserver, but neither Tom nor Paul was able to piece together the text and melody in the right order. Besides, the sensitive machine had fallen to the ground, so even if they did find the correct combination of words and melody, the server could be so damaged it wouldn't matter.

Defeated, they took a break from their work and headed into a large conference hall, where a meeting with everyone directly involved in the case was taking place. Apart from the American ambassador, his military attaché, Colonel Simmens, and General Lafour, several other important members of the Pentagon were present. Professor Hertzberg, the appointed historical expert, sat with Tom, Paul, and Dr. Baxter on the other side of the conference table. The empty chairs left by Hagen and Piglet could not be ignored.

Standing before his audience, the ambassador held a short memorial for the two men, and then introduced Dr. Tom Stevendahl, Paul Colbach, and Dr. Karen Baxter as the new leaders of CAPUT.

When General Lafour took the floor, he reported that an analysis of Hagen's laptop data showed that the professor himself had manipulated the main computer, thereby proving Tom's and Paul's innocence.

"In line with our investigations, we've taken the liberty of questioning Hagen's secret informant, an architect with a PhD, from Lebanon," the General said with an odd smile. "It took a little persuasion and a couple of bucks before he was prepared to speak to us, but unfortunately, he couldn't tell us as much as we had hoped. He could only confirm that he had found mysterious parchments in sealed caskets during the excavations while he was part of an Arab construction team that had refurbished parts of the West Wall near the former Jerusalem headquarters of the Knights Templar. Curious to find out what the parchments meant he then sent them secretly to his friend Dietmar Hagen. He didn't know what the professor found out. In the meantime, we were able to keep the parchments safe. They are written in an unknown language and are at least eight hundred years old. Professor Hagen obviously built our facility here by translating these documents."

Lafour cleared his throat and took a sip of mineral water before looking at the spellbound faces of his audience again. "I'll let Professor Hertzberg explain to us how this could be possible."

Hertzberg rose from his chair and bowed politely before addressing the room. "Do you have any idea," he began, "what it would mean if one could prove that the Templars had made contact with a distant future?"

"What do you mean by '*could*'?" Tom retorted. "Aren't the two people that stayed with my friend enough evidence that it's already happened?"

"Don't get me wrong," Hertzberg answered calmly. "I still don't have any information proving that your knight and his companion really did come from the year 1307, or that they actually belonged to the Order of the Temple, let alone that they knew about such momentous secrets." Hertzberg cleared his throat sheepishly when he noticed Tom's impatient glare.

"But there's no doubt that the knight and his boy came from the past," Tom insisted. "The knight knew that the server was located in the sewers of Heisterbach, and how to activate it."

"May I suggest," declared the ambassador, giving Tom and Hertzberg an inquiring look, "that you do everything necessary to finally discover the truth of this matter – immediately. We've not a second to waste. Seek out historically inexplicable phenomena, and test them for possible connections with time travel."

"Perhaps we should first investigate the general subject of these supposed knights," Hertzberg suggested. "Four days should be enough to search the archives of Troyes and Paris, and survey the remains in Bar-sur-Aube." His gaze rested on Tom. "Dr. Stevendahl, we will speak again in further detail, and you can tell me everything you know about the man."

"I will assemble a team to assist Professor Hertzberg as soon as possible," General Lafour announced, nodding agreeably at the ambassador.

"It would be great," the ambassador added, "if we could present the President with our initial findings by next Thursday."

"I can't promise anything," Hertzberg said, rising from his chair and placing a hand on Tom's shoulder. The historian seemed to enjoy the fact that, for the moment, he found himself at eye level with the lanky scientist. "But together, we'll work it out somehow," he said, winking at Tom.

"Good," the ambassador said. "As the Pentagon is urgently waiting for a report, we will meet again next Wednesday. I do hope, Dr. Stevendahl, that you and your colleagues will be able to clarify the technical components of our findings by then."

Tom nodded absently. He was now paying the price for being stubborn and avoiding every possible interaction with the medieval knight. Guiltily he pushed aside the nagging anxiety that he wouldn't be able to transfer Hannah safely back into the present.

CHAPTER 30

Breydenburg Castle – The Confession

Friday, October 20, 1307

Early the next morning, Gero bought Hannah a new travel cloak. Gratefully, she accepted the hooded blue velvet cape without asking where it came from. As he helped her fasten the silver clasps, she silently inspected the signet ring that he hadn't taken off since their visit to the ruins.

"You're a real sweetheart," she whispered with a smile, giving him a quick kiss before following him into the knights' hall along with Anselm and Matthäus.

In his white Templar regalia, Gero was the morning's star attraction. Be they men or women, soldiers or servants, all eyes were fixed admiringly on him. As they walked across the hall, some of the uniformed men addressed Gero and exchanged a few words with him, but they spoke too quickly and quietly for Hannah to understand anything.

Before they left around midmorning, Wilhelm of Eltz insisted on personally bidding Gero and his friends farewell, and escorting them to their horses, which had already been saddled.

On their way to the lower chambers, they could see the fortress walls through an open window in the stairway. In the cool morning wind, high up on the wall-walks, soldiers patrolled under the jaunty banner of the Archbishop of Trier. Hannah was surprised by how sophisticated everything looked but, as they stepped into the cobbled inner courtyard, an unexpected sight made her gasp in horror.

"My God," Hannah whispered in disgust and disbelief.

The naked, blood-bathed corpse of her attacker was hanging on a hook next to the castle gate. The unspeakable pain that must have accompanied his last breath was etched deeply into his gaunt features.

"Don't look!" Hannah shouted when she saw Matthäus staring, horrified at the dead man with wide eyes.

Three other figures were cowering on the wet, gleaming cobblestones, half-naked, and their lips blue from the cold. They had been locked up in

421

individual iron cages that looked like rabbit hutches, barely large enough to contain their prisoners. Two of the captives wore cuffs around their necks and wrists that were connected to a heavy chain, preventing them from moving more than an inch.

Hannah stared at the younger of the two in horror. He was barely seventeen. A blood-encrusted wound on his forehead extended into his dirty blonde hair. His face was oddly swollen, and his back was covered in countless welts, raw flesh bulging out of the fresh wounds. The second captive, a man with dark, matted hair, stared blankly at Hannah.

The third cage contained a young woman. Strands of blonde hair had come loose from the braid that adorned her head like a crown of thorns. With tattered clothing and bare feet, she sat on the hard, stone ground, shivering with cold and fear. Fortunately for her, she had been spared the iron chains, but her hands were tightly tied behind her back, and her lips were smeared with clotted blood.

Hannah looked uncomprehendingly at Gero, who had not even glanced at the captives once.

"What's going to happen to them?" Anselm asked anxiously, unable to tear his gaze away from the leather strip that had once belonged to him, and now was tied around the arm stump of the dead man on the hook.

"The gallows await them," Gero answered without an ounce of sympathy in his voice. "They will be hanged there until the crows let their bones see daylight, to deter anyone else from committing the same crimes."

"But only two of them attacked us, and one is already dead," Hannah protested. "And what does the woman have to do with it? Surely you can't let them kill her!"

"There was an entire band of robbers. She belongs with them," Gero said calmly. "We weren't the first people they attacked, but some of our predecessors didn't survive their assaults."

Hannah gave him an incredulous look. How could this man, who had been so gentle to her this morning, permit such inhumane deeds?

As he bade him farewell, Wilhelm of Eltz gave Gero a peculiar look, then he glanced at Hannah suspiciously. Gero helped her onto her horse, his stony face betraying his annoyance at Hannah's interference.

"Send your parents my warmest greetings," the castellan said pointedly to Gero as he mounted his horse.

"Thank you for your hospitality, dear Godfather," Gero replied, tightening the reins.

When they finally set off, Anselm was visibly relieved. With a clattering noise, the large outer gate was raised on a mighty chain to let them pass. The guards snapped to solemn attention and saluted them, holding up lances adorned with banners as they passed.

As they rode by, Hannah knew that she would never forget the sight of the corpse hanging on the hook.

It drizzled the entire morning, but Hannah was amazed that her hair stayed dry under the hood of her new cloak. Gero didn't seem at all bothered by the rain, leaving his head uncovered even as the downpour grew steadily stronger.

On the way, Hannah tried to see if the surroundings were familiar to her, but it was no use. Occasionally, she thought she recognized mountain ranges and streams, but as she had already noticed, there were far fewer forests in this time, and the small villages were located close to picturesque castles that she had never seen before, not even as ruins. Fields and meadows dotted with large herds of sheep completed the foreign landscape. The partially cobbled streets were crowded with traffic and they overtook several horse carriages and ox-drawn carts carrying piglets, chickens, stones, straw, wood, and barrels of wine.

At one point, Gero left the path and rode into a field. His companions had no choice but to follow him. Since they had left the Genovevaburg castle, he hadn't uttered a single word and only now and then did he glance at them to make sure that the group was still complete.

Matthäus, who formed the rear guard, sat in his saddle with his head bowed and, smiling, Hannah reined her horse in to wait for him.

"What's wrong?" she asked. "Aren't you glad you're home again?"

"I don't have a home," Matthäus replied quietly.

"Isn't your home with Gero?" Hannah tried to look encouraging while wondering what would happen to the boy if his lord really did decide to head for France to search for his commander. She had learned, at least since this morning, that Gero could be downright ruthless.

"I think he's taking me to the Cistercians in Hemmenrode," Matthäus replied softly.

"He won't do that," Hannah announced with certainty.

"How do you know that?" The boy's eyes lit up with hope.

"He said it himself," Hannah lied.

"Really?" An expression of joy shone on the boy's young face.

I hope I'm right, Hannah thought, glancing at Gero's back. The red cross on his Templar cloak was visible from afar, and all at once, it appeared to her like a target.

On the way to the ancestral home of the free nobles of Breydenbach, the group had to conquer one set of hills after another, and ride past cattle pastures and harvested fields. Narrow paths divided the individual plots of land, and at every larger fork in the road stood a wooden cross of thick beams or a small brick chapel with a carved Madonna in it. Gero made the sign of the cross when they rode past every sacred shrine, and Matthäus imitated him dutifully.

It was already late afternoon when a tall, fortified tower appeared on the horizon, its impressive height hinting at the proud grandeur of Breydenburg Castle that stood behind it.

"I had documents made in Brysich," Gero said casually to Anselm. "The parchments will identify both of you as siblings, and as dependents of the Order." He sat up in his saddle and turned around to face Hannah. "Your name is Hannah de Caillou, as Anselm suggested."

Hannah squeezed her mare's flanks with her feet and rode up to Gero. "Maybe you should have asked Anselm in advance?" she asked, wrinkling her forehead.

"Not a problem at all, little sister," Anselm said with an agreeable smile.

Gero regarded her seriously. "It's a question of honor, that a woman should have a male guardian with her. Some men see women traveling without male protection as easy prey."

"Didn't you say that *you* would protect me?" Hannah demanded defiantly.

"Yes … I did say that," he replied. "But it wouldn't be wise to introduce you to my parents as my ward. They could get the wrong idea."

"And is that a question of honor as well?" Hannah raised an eyebrow.

"Maybe we should get there first before worrying about introduction rituals?" Anselm looked at both of them impatiently.

Without a word, Hannah drove her mare on and settled into a light trot. Breydenburg Castle was built on the edge of a cliff that led directly down to the river Lieser in a steep slope. Hannah was overwhelmed by the scale and beauty of the castle that suddenly appeared after they had conquered the last hill. From where they stood, a cobbled path led straight through a brick archway into the proud castle compound. The walls and turrets were brightly plastered, while the battlements, oriels, and window ledges were adorned with blue and rust-colored ornaments. A few hundred yards away, small, timber-framed cottages with thatch roofs clustered around the grand masonry, surrounded by old fruit trees and man-made ponds.

Not far ahead, a boy was driving a herd of goats toward the castle with a long stick. A large man trotted listlessly behind, his head and shoulders hunched as if he were supporting a yoke.

When the boy heard the riders approach, he turned around curiously, not moving from the middle of the path. The elderly man, whose gaze had followed the boy's, quickened his steps and roughly pulled his young companion from the road.

"Bow down!" Hannah heard him hiss at the boy. He hit the nape of his neck and pushed him down violently. But suddenly, the man's features changed, and he released the boy momentarily.

"No!" he cried, and fell so suddenly to his knees in front of Gero's horse that the animal was startled. "Sir, I beg you." The man stretched his hands to the heavens as if in prayer. "Is that really you?"

Gero looked down at him with a smile. "What are you going on about, Ludger? Don't you recognize the son of your lord anymore?"

"Forgive me, sir," the man stuttered, lowering his arms. "They said you were probably dead. Just yesterday, your mother had a mass read to plead to the Almighty for your salvation. I thank the Lord for his mercy," he declared, hastily making the sign of the cross.

"You may rise!" Gero gestured quickly to the man and Hannah saw his Adam's apple bob as he swallowed nervously. "We shouldn't waste any more time," he said to his companions in a raw voice.

At full gallop, they rode the last five hundred feet to the castle. The forest around the mighty walls had been cleared, apart from a few remaining fruit trees, allowing the guard to observe effortlessly who was approaching the tall, ringed walls. Additional solders in colorful surcoats patrolled the wall-walks in between them.

In order to reach the palace, the living quarters of the castle lord and his family, they had to pass over a wide, water-filled moat before they were allowed through the defensive walls. Upon seeing the visitors, the guards raised the iron portcullis and lowered a wooden drawbridge.

The guard on duty snapped to attention when he recognized the red cross on Gero's chlamys. As Hannah passed through the first gate closely behind Gero, she ducked instinctively at the sight of the sharp iron spikes that hung from the arched gate. A cobbled path led up the so-called horse stairs, which led to a second gate guarded by two uniformed men.

When they recognized who had entered the castle, the guards' spears clattered to the ground in shock. A wild-looking man in chain mail and a surcoat, the guardian of the defensive tower, excitedly blew a fanfares.

Hannah's heart raced in nervous excitement as they arrived at the sprawling inner courtyard, a fairytale-like setting of oriels, turrets, and colorful windows. All at once, they were greeted by a sea of shocked faces. A few women let their wash baskets fall to the ground. A group of men in scuffed leather aprons froze in the midst of shoeing a massive cold blood stallion, and then hurriedly sprang to the side in terror when the horse unexpectedly reared. Children, too, suddenly paused in the middle of their games. The crowd fell silent, as if the castle and all its inhabitants had fallen under an enchantment.

Finally, a young boy shook himself out of his shocked state and ran over to take the horse from Gero with a deep bow. Hannah, who had likewise dismounted, watched as more helpers followed to take the other horses from them, until a throng of at least twenty people were clustered around them. Suddenly, the mood of the crowd changed, and they retreated.

The last rays of the setting sun pierced through the clouds, blinding Hannah for a second. She raised her hand to shield her eyes and squinted at the entrance to the main house, which had been flung open.

A man stepped into the courtyard. He was tall and broad-shouldered, with thin, white-blond hair and a slimmer figure than Gero. Upon closer inspection, Hannah saw that his right hand was missing. With his athletic build, he resembled a damaged Greek statue. He was dressed in dark-green leather pants, knee-length brown leather boots, a tapered dark green doublet with a standing collar, light chain mail, and a colorful tabard that fell to his knees, emblazoned with the same crest as on Gero's signet ring. A sky-blue stone, set in an ostentatious gold ring, adorned his remaining hand.

While she marveled at this impressive figure, Hannah barely noticed Gero handing the saddlebag containing the Head of Wisdom to Anselm before facing the older man and kneeling before him with an uncharacteristically humble demeanor.

"May the Lord be with you, Father," he said in a solemn voice, bowing his head respectfully the entire time. "I am happy to have found you in good health."

The lord of the castle rested his only hand on Gero's hair. For a moment, the two of them remained poised in this position. Then the older man murmured something, and Gero slowly rose. Father and son stood eye to eye with each other, and Hannah became aware of their striking resemblance. Something told her that they did not have an easy relationship. Gero flinched slightly when his father unexpectedly drew him into a hearty embrace.

Someone in the crowd started shouting joyfully, and the other inhabitants of the castle soon followed his lead. Throughout the courtyard cheers for the house of Breydenbach resounded, followed by several more for the Archbishop and the King.

Someone behind Hannah cried in despair.

"Oh Lord, how will the Lady take this news?"

Curiously, she turned around and saw a young maid biting her fist nervously among the rest of the anxious-looking women in starched white bonnets and headscarves.

Gero's father stepped aside, and a woman in a shimmering, green, floor-length dress and a white, starched bonnet stepped out of the crowd that had gathered at the entrance to the main building. When she saw Gero, she ran to him and flung her arms around his neck. Fighting tears, she held him silently and pressed her cheek against his chest, her eyes shut. Again and again, she stroked Gero's broad back. He held her tightly and rocked her like a child. Finally, she loosened herself from him and wiped the tears from her face. With a sheepish expression, Gero looked around until he spotted Hannah, and waved her forward.

Just then, his father raised his voice and addressed his subjects.

"You may go back to work now," he announced loudly. "Tommorow I will throw a feast in honor of my son's return and so that we can all celebrate, the cellarman will be opening two barrels of our best wine."

Muffled cheers of approval sounded, then the crowd dispersed just as quickly as it had gathered.

Hannah sensed Gero's mother scrutinizing her face. The lady of the castle was a beautiful woman with pale skin, and only a few wrinkles

427

around her deep blue eyes hinted at her real age. From the subtle but decisive curve at the corners of her mouth, Hannah concluded she must be rather assertive. *An essential character trait*, she thought as she glanced at Gero's father.

As if the lord of the castle had noticed her interest, he turned around and fixed Hannah with an odd, piercing look. "Pray tell, maiden," he said. "Where is your family from?"

Hannah was too startled to answer, but Anselm came to her rescue.

"Allow me," he said in Middle High German, and executed a perfect bow. "My name is Anselmo de Caillou, and this is my sister, Hannah." He laid a protective arm around Hannah's shoulder. "We accompanied your son for part of his journey, but I'm sure he will tell you about that himself."

"Hannah?" Gero's father asked evenly. "Are you a Christian?"

"Of course," Anselm replied, and bowed again.

"As friends of my son, I welcome you to my home," Richard of Breydenbach declared.

Then he turned to Gero, who was standing behind him with a tense expression on his face. The conversation that his father had begun so unexpectedly with Anselm and Hannah had obviously unnerved him.

"Your mother will instruct the maids to prepare the guest chambers on the upper floor for your friends," his father said to him.

Gero nodded in relief. "Thank you, Father, for your hospitality."

"He's probably glad his old man didn't throw us into the dungeon," Hannah whispered with a sideways glance at Anselm.

Suddenly, a slender figure in a flowing, dark blue robe broke away from the masses. Hannah wondered for a moment if she had ever seen a more beautiful person. With her fair, even complexion and golden blonde curls that cascaded down to her waist, the young woman could have won any modern beauty contest. A translucent, light blue veil covered her flood of hair, and was held in place by a golden circlet that crowned her forehead like a halo.

The woman said something in Old French and smiled at Gero with gleaming white teeth.

"Amelie?" he answered, but despite returning her captivating smile, he seemed not to know whether he should be glad to see her. His searching gaze wandered through the crowd. Then he turned to the pretty girl again.

"Struan?" he asked hesitantly.

The girl chattered away chirpily, and Hannah glanced at Anselm, hoping that he could translate what she was saying, but he was standing too far away to see or hear her.

A horse's whinny made Gero prick up his ears. A tall, broad-shouldered man with short, black hair, clad in full Templar regalia entered from a nearby wing, leading a massive silver horse by the reins. Hannah didn't know what fascinated her more – the huge dapple-gray steed or the dazzling Templar. When the horse saw Gero, it neighed loudly and pawed the ground with its front hooves.

"Atlas! Thank the Lord," Gero yelled, running up to the magnificent horse, which, amidst soft whinnies, nuzzled him with its soft, velvety lips.

Matthäus ran towards the horse as well. Both knight and squire patted the stallion, their faces contorted with emotion.

"Take him into the stable and give him three bushels of oats and apples, whatever you have," Gero said to Matthäus with an encouraging clap on the shoulder.

Then to another boy standing near them he added, "Show my squire where the horse stables are."

Finally, he turned to the other knight, and drew him into a hearty embrace.

"This is Struan," Gero introduced the man with the black hair and dark eyes. Hannah was surprised to learn that he was Scottish and not a fiery Spaniard as she had expected. "He's my best friend," Gero continued with a smile, slapping him hard on the back as if to prove his point.

The rough gesture didn't seem to bother the Scotsman. He bowed, placing his left hand on the pommel of his sword and his right on his heart.

"Madame, it is an honor," he said in Middle High German in a decisively hoarse voice.

Anselm, who was no less impressed by Struan, could not tear his gaze away from the Scotsman's bulging biceps.

Struan looked at Gero apprehensively when neither Hannah nor Anselm said anything in reply.

"This is Hannah and Anselmo de Caillou," Gero explained in French. "To them, I owe my life."

Struan looked quizzically and the blonde woman who had snuggled up to his side stared at Hannah in confusion. Then, with a friendly smile, she held out both hands to her.

"Amelie Bratac," she said, giving Hannah a slightly awkward hug. To Anselm, she simply nodded. Then she added in French-accented Middle High German, "It is a pleasure to meet you."

"Where's Johan?" Gero asked. He hadn't stopped fearing for his two comrades since he had been separated from them.

"He's doing fine," Struan replied in a serious voice. "He was injured. He wanted to save you and Matthäus before the strange light swallowed you up, but he was hit on the head by a falling branch. He'll be able to stand up soon enough, though."

"Where is he?" Gero glanced around in concern.

"Let us go inside first," the lady of the castle decided. "Instead of mourning, we now have something to celebrate." Gero's mother had a radiant smile on her face. "You must tell us where you've been all this time."

Gero cleared his throat and glanced sideways at Hannah. "Yes," he said simply.

"Your Flemish brother," his father began to speak, "was in terrible shape, but now that you're back amongst us, I am convinced that he will recover all the more quickly."

"Praise the Lord," Gero looked at his father.

The lord of the castle nodded slowly.

Gero's mother took Hannah's hand and led her into the large knights' hall where diligent servants were already setting up tables and benches. Gero nodded to Anselm, instructing him to follow the two women.

Along with his father and Struan, Gero climbed up the narrow spiral staircase to the women's quarters. A young servant holding a chamber pot darted past the men in the carpet adorned hallway, leaving the door to a chamber open.

With an uneasy feeling in his heart, Gero entered the chamber, his father and Struan following behind him.

"Gero! Mon frère!" came a cry of unrestrained joy.

"Johan!" Gero gasped. Without paying the injured man's condition any heed, he stormed up to the bed and hugged him tightly.

The Flemish Brother's head was wrapped in white linen bandages. Johan looked even paler than usual despite, the red scars that ran across his waxen face. With effort, he hooked his left arm around Gero's neck and, sobbing, he pulled Gero down toward himself. "Gero! Thank heavens you're alive."

"Of course I'm alive," Gero whispered, patting him reassuringly on the back. "And no harm has come to me. So there's no reason to cry, is there?"

"No, no …" Johan replied softly, running his large hands over his face and trying to fight back the tears in his eyes. "I just thought … I was sure … that it killed you."

"It?" Gero looked at Johan uncertainly.

"The green light. It cut through the trees like cheese."

"We have to talk about that," said a sharp voice from behind.

Gero's father shut the door. With his arms crossed, he leaned against an open window. Gero turned to his father, who was watching him with a strange glint in his eyes that somehow reminded him of Henri d'Our.

"Speak!" Richard of Breydenbach demanded a little too loudly.

Gero tried to ignore his father's stern tone. "I don't know what you want to hear from me, Father." With feigned composure, he rose from the sick bed and went to the open window before turning around again to face his father.

"Give us a good reason," Richard hissed, "why you frightened us so badly with your disappearance." He paused, searching Gero's face for a sign of regret. "As if what's happening in France isn't bad enough," he continued, "you disappeared with your young squire and abandoned your Brothers. Four days later, you appear, hale and hearty, in the company of two complete strangers, and behave as if nothing has happened."

"As your son, I owe you the respect you deserve," Gero began in a calm voice. "I will not lie to you, no matter what. I owe my life to the woman who arrived here with me. She took me in when I was unconscious, and made sure I could return home."

"Ha!" Richard snorted. "And why couldn't they send us a message so we wouldn't worry? Your sword bears the crest of our family, and there's not a soul who doesn't know us for ten miles around. Or were you further away?"

"No," Gero said truthfully.

His father's face flared red. "So you're playing me for a fool in front of your Brothers?"

"Have I ever told you a lie?" Gero asked.

Richard paused. "No," he said curtly, narrowing his eyes. "But prove yourself! Who is Anselmo de Caillou? Why do I know neither this man nor his sister?"

"He arrived in this area just recently," Gero answered. "He's a free trader from the South."

Gero's father wasn't prepared to let the matter rest so easily. "And how do you explain what happened in the Hemmenrode forest?"

"I can't tell you exactly what happened to me," Gero replied, sounding slightly frustrated. "It was like a bad dream. We were attacked by Lombards." His gaze darted between Struan and Johan, who were looking at him no less expectantly than his father. "My two comrades here can bear witness to that. After trying to fend them off, I was bringing Matthäus to safety when a storm came, and I was hit on the head." To prove it, he lowered his head to show his father the scabbed wound that had been stitched up at the hospital and had already begun to heal. "If I tell you what happened after that, you would doubt me even more."

"I was there in Saalholz," Richard answered, "and your Brothers saw you disappear, along with your squire, and a large clearing. So spare me your old wives' tales!"

Gero's eyes widened in surprise. What else did his father know about his disappearance? Maybe if he convinced his father that the story of the time-traveling monk from Heisterbach was true, he could safely keep the Head of Wisdom a secret.

"Well?" Richard was still waiting for an answer.

Furiously, he stormed past Gero to lean out of the open window and breathe in the cool autumn air. Then he turned again to his son.

"If you haven't seen it, you should ride there and take a look for yourself! The whole clearing is gone – every tree and bush. Can you explain what happened?"

"No," Gero answered, "but don't people say the devil is at work there?"

"Sure," Richard said, with a sarcastic laugh, before sitting down in a folding chair. "That's what they say." With his only hand, he picked up a rosary that was lying on a small side table, and let the black pearls glide silently through his fingers. "Did he send you?"

"The devil?"

"No, you idiot," Richard snarled. "Henri d'Our."

"What?" Gero felt his mouth go dry.

Richard's gaze fell on Struan MacDhughaill. When he spoke again, it was in French, so that the Scotsman could also understand him. "Your Scottish comrade here told me that you were going to Heisterbach to fulfill a mission. Is that true?"

432

Gero looked at Struan in horror. "Damn it, Struan, I trusted you!"

"It's not what you think," Struan protested, turning to Gero's father for help.

Richard of Breydenbach looked his son in the eye. "It's not his fault. In truth, I am the one who should feel guilty. I've long known where the Head of Wisdom was hidden," Richard explained quietly. "D'Our entrusted it to me after we retrieved some secret documents from Acre containing records with an explanation of the Head."

"What ...?" Gero shook his head in disbelief.

Richard of Breydenbach looked down at the rosary again. "I don't know if d'Our ever mentioned it to you. We were ambushed when we left Acre. D'Our lost his bag containing the sealed book of the Head's secrets. The knowledge must have been very valuable. Nearly a hundred and fifty years earlier, Bertrand de Blanchefort hid the documents in a secret depot in the South of France. I was told that they contained legendary plans far ahead of our time – they formed the basis of the Order's entire financial system, hitherto unknown medical methods, and some inventions that far surpass even the Saracens' knowledge. All of this nearly fell into the hands of our enemies, but Henri d'Our has your uncle and me to thank for recovering it. Your uncle paid for it with his life, and I with my right hand. Elisabeth's parents, who rushed to our aid, were brutally murdered in front of our eyes."

For a moment, Gero was at a lost for words.

"Do you know how the Head works?" he finally asked, hopefully.

"I don't have a clue as to what it looks like," Richard of Breydenbach admitted. "Word has it that this thing conquers space and time, and even opens up a secret world to whomever owns it. But those who know about it, like Henri d'Our, would never use it unless it was an emergency." He looked at Gero solemnly. "The Head comes from a very far away place. Anything ever written about it is safely hidden in dozens of underground depots scattered across France, England, and Scotland. And although I know only part of the story, I know that it can help the Order in its greatest time of need. But if you ask me, this is all the work of the devil. It will bring blessings to neither the Order nor to us mere mortals. And contrary to what I've claimed so far, I've known since those days that this devil has been causing trouble in Saalholz."

All at once, Gero understood why his father had been so cynical all these years. It was the pain of the ignorant, torn between loyalty to an organization not his own, and his doubts about God, whose workings he could no longer understand.

"I was there," Gero said quietly.

"Where?" Richard asked in alarm.

"In this secret world," Gero answered. "I was in the future, over seven hundred years from now. And I can tell you that what happened in Saalholz is connected to the Head of Wisdom."

"And you came back?" his father asked. "How?"

"With the very same Head that was hidden in Heisterbach," Gero answered softly. "It is in the shape of a small, metallic box. After you sing it the password, the head of a beautiful woman appears. An evil man in the future, who made the clearing in Saalholz disappear, knew nothing about the Head, and couldn't even explain it. I don't know how he was able to suspend God's laws despite this. In the future, many things we dare not even dream of today will be possible. But there is yet another misfortune."

"The woman and her brother?"

Gero nodded hesitantly. "They come from the future. It was not our intention for them to accompany Matthäus and me. And now I don't know how to help them back into their own time."

"How did you know that the Head of Wisdom would still be in the abbey in the future? Someone else could very well have stolen it in the hundreds of years that had passed." Richard of Breydenbach was still gaping at his son in astonishment.

"I didn't know," Gero answered sighing. "I was lucky, if nothing else." Overcome with exhaustion, he sat down by Johan's side again.

Tentatively, he began to tell his father about Henri d'Our's secret mission for him, and what had happened after. "In the year of our Lord 2004, only the apse of the Heisterbach Abbey remains standing. The rest of it is a pathetic ruin that you would never recognize. But the underground passageways are fully preserved, and the Head was in its hiding place, completely untouched. I sang the password, and then I landed beneath the abbey on the eighteenth day of this month, together with Matthäus and the pair from the future."

"And then?"

"I actually met the Brother from the High Council d'Our wanted me to find," he said weakly. His eyes fell on Struan who was shaking his head in disbelief. "If I tell you what they wanted me to do, you'd think I was lying."

"Tell us!" Johan cried, far too worked up to keep his voice down.

Gero calmly explained what Brother Rowan had ordered him to do. He did not omit the fact that matters had culminated in a fight, during which he had unintentionally killed the Brother, and that he had taken the Head with him to Breydenburg Castle.

"Jesus Christ be with me," Richard of Breydenbach groaned. "And now what? What if you were followed and someone else takes the Head?"

"Who would be after me?" Gero answered. "Brother Rowan is dead. It seems he was the only one who knew how the Head worked."

"We can't possibly keep it," Struan pointed out. "It belongs to the Order, no matter who knows about it and what the High Council intends to do with it."

"You did the right thing," Johan said, looking at Gero sympathetically. "I can't bear to think that d'Our knew they wanted to assassinate the Queen and her husband."

"We'll have to find out," Gero said calmly before recounting just a few fragments of the knowledge he had gained when he was in the future. To explain everything in full detail would have been too confusing for his audience. Nonetheless, he was determined to tell his Brothers of the Order's fate.

"Barring a miracle," Gero explained his eyes downcast, "in the year of our Lord 1312, Pope Clement will universally dissolve the Order through the Papal Bulls Vox clamatis and Vox in excelso. Two years before that, fifty-four Brothers will be burned at the stake in Paris, and in 1314, Jacques de Molay and Gottfried de Charney will be burned after years of imprisonment. A fair number of us will spend our lives on the run. Only a few will manage to begin a new life under the banner of the Scottish or Portuguese kings."

"Lord Almighty," Johan gasped. "You think all this will happen?"

"I'm afraid so," Gero said solemnly. "After the death of the Brother in Heisterbach, Henri d'Our seems like the only one who can help us save the Order. Additionally, I am responsible for Hannah and Anselm. They have to return to where they came from. Even though I haven't seen much of their world, I know it's very different from ours and, sooner or later, they would go mad. Maybe d'Our can help us send them back."

For a moment, the room was silent, save for the soft crackling of wood in the fireplace.

"Who told you d'Our was still alive?" Richard wrinkled his forehead.

"On the way here, I met Brother Theobald from Thors. He told me that they took our commander to Chinon."

"Holy Mother of God! I can't imagine a worse fate," Richard of Breydenbach exclaimed, and then looked his son squarely in the eye. "No matter what you decide, I will do anything I can to help you. I alone am to blame for all your misfortune. And I dare not hope for your forgiveness."

"What are you saying, Father?" Gero felt his heart pounding in confusion.

"I swore an oath in Acre," his father sighed. "The salvation of those damned documents was so important to the Order, and I felt more of a connection to the Templars than to the Archbishop of Trier. And Elisabeth caused me such sorrow, cowering next to her parents' slain bodies, covered in blood. It was a miracle that she was unharmed, and no word of complaint crossed her lips. I thought to myself that if God protected this child, he would protect us, too. To gain God's mercy, I swore to Him that I would hand her over to a Cistercian convent when we returned to the German lands. But your mother didn't want to send her to a Nunnery before she had turned sixteen. She loved her as if she was her own daughter. And so I relented. But I swore another oath. Out of my devotion to the Order, I wanted to send you to the Templars as soon as you had been knighted. As you know, things turned out rather differently. But I want to tell you that I am truly sorry," Richard of Breydenbach added hoarsely, "for you and Elisabeth and your child. And you, my boy, bear no blame for all the terrible things that have happened."

His father's words went straight to Gero's heart, and he fought back his tears for the belated confession.

"You are forgiven, Father," he murmured.

After a prayer in the castle's chapel, to which only close relatives, friends, and high-ranking officials were invited, the castle lord asked everyone to a banquet in the hall of knights. The return of their missing son was far too joyous an occasion to allow the political catastrophes in France to dampen spirits in the House of Breydenbach. Not a word was uttered about the conversation between Richard of Breydenbach and the three Templars.

Night had already fallen when Hannah stepped outside with Gero for a moment to get some fresh air. The burning torches bathed the upper castle court in a dramatic light. Suddenly a fanfare sounded, and two riders raced through the second gate with torches in hand, swerving at the last moment to avoid running over two children who were running around.

"My brother," Gero said with a sigh that could have meant anything.

Eberhard, as Gero later addressed him, swung himself gracefully down from his saddle. He was smaller and slimmer than Gero, and his shoulder-length, white-blonde hair shimmered like his father's.

"Praise the Lord," he exclaimed, hurrying towards Gero with open arms. His deep voice, which resembled his brother's, seemed a little too mature for his boyish figure. "You're alive!" he cried, hugging Gero tightly.

He stepped back a little and inspected his visibly confused brother with a relieved smile. "Our father lost sleep over nothing." Laughing, he clapped Gero on the shoulder. "I knew you would outwit even the devil himself."

Gero's expression remained unreadable.

"And who is this?" Eberhard of Breydenbach asked, eyeing Hannah with interest. "A pretty Templar maiden?"

Gero looked slightly exasperated. "This is Hannah de Caillou, sister of the merchant Anselmo de Caillou. They arrived here with me today." It was clear that no one in his family, apart from his father, should know the whole truth.

Eberhard pulled off his glove and bowed courteously as he took Hannah's fingers and kissed the back of her hand.

"Madame," he said, smiling up at her. With his chain mail and surcoat, he looked like a warrior, despite his slim figure.

"She looks like Elisabeth," he remarked, staring at Hannah so blatantly that she felt her face go red, and she realized instinctively that Elisabeth must have been Gero's dead wife.

After the meal, Gero insisted on showing his guests to their quarters. Anselm and Matthäus were to share a room on the second floor, where the men of the house usually stayed. After that, he escorted Hannah to her chamber. At the top of the stairway, they ran into Gero's mother, holding a candle in her hand.

"Shouldn't I call a maid instead to lead your guest to her quarters?"

The look that Jutta of Breydenbach gave her son was unmistakable.

"Don't trouble yourself, mother," Gero said with a smile, taking the candle from his puzzled mother. "I know where our guest is sleeping."

The colorful, painted room on the third floor, near the women's quarters, had a large canopy bed and a warm fireplace.

"Well, what did your parents say about us showing up?" Hannah asked, looking around the cozily furnished chamber.

"My father knows what happened."

"You didn't tell him about us time-traveling, did you?" Hannah gasped at Gero.

"It's a long story," Gero replied, and shut the light cherry wood door adorned with carved flowers and vines. "It seems as if your maleficus and his master left their tracks behind in Saalholz several times. Anyway, my father knows about the Order's secret, although, unfortunately, he doesn't know enough to help us. As I've said, we will have to return to France to search for our commander."

Instead of saying any more, he walked to the fireplace, knelt down, and lit the stacked firewood. As it began to crackle, he looked up. "Besides my comrades and my father, no one knows where you came from. So, please, keep silent about this matter."

Hannah nodded, sinking down onto the comfortable bed with a sigh. She freed her hair from the pins that had confined it and took off her veil. As she ran both her hands through her hair, she noticed Gero's odd expression. In two steps, he was by her side, sinking to his knees in front of her and grasping her boots.

"Let me do it," he said, and pulled off the dirty boots.

Without meeting her eyes, he pulled off her stockings as well and gently massaged her feet.

"What have I done to deserve this?" Hannah whispered.

His palms lightly ran up her bare legs. Quicker than she thought possible, he shoved up her chemise and surcoat as he gently, but firmly pressed her onto the bed.

"Gero," she gasped. "What …?"

Instead of letting her finish her question, he kissed her and pulled down her chemise. Just as quickly, he undid the cords of his pants.

"Not so fast," she chided, placing a hand on his chest to stop him. "At least let me get out of my dress."

Sheepishly, he paused. "Forgive me," he murmured and took a step back. "I completely forgot myself."

He helped her pull her clothes over her head. While he took off the rest of his own clothing, she slipped under the silk sheets, naked.

The unfamiliar surroundings made every action seem surreal to her. The oil lamp's flame was reflected in the room's single glass window. The room's sharp, Gothic ceiling made Hannah feel as if she was in an old church, while statues of Christ hanging on the cross, a colorfully painted Madonna with the Christ Child, and a silver holy water font on the opposite wall completed the illusion. The walls were covered in painted green vines, leaves, and flowers. The scent of rose oil wafted from the luxurious sheets. Nothing in this room resembled the musty sitting rooms of the old castles that had been turned into tourist attractions.

"Hold me," he pleaded as he crawled into the bed beside her, as naked as she was.

It seemed like a cry of despair to Hannah and she obliged without a further word. When he penetrated her, gasping, she squeezed her thighs against his hips and clutched his back with both hands as though she never wanted to let him go.

Later, as he lay next to her with his eyes shut and a blissful smile on his lips, she kissed his bearded cheek. "Could it be," she asked slowly, "that you were thinking of someone else when you were sleeping with me?"

"No," he replied quickly – a little too quickly for Hannah's liking. "What makes you think that?" He sat up straight, staring at her uneasily.

"Forget it," she said, and stared at the dark-blue canopy where a circle with twelve star signs was embroidered in shimmering gold thread.

"Tell me what's on your mind," he urged her. "We come from two different worlds. I can only understand you if you tell me."

"Everyone here is looking at me so oddly. Could it be that I resemble your wife more than you would like to admit?"

"Perhaps," Gero said, and looked at her silently for a moment. She could see him searching for familiar traces in her face. "Yes, you do look similar to her," he concluded truthfully, "but I know the difference between the two of you. Have no fear. The woman I love isn't dead; in fact, she isn't even born yet," he said with a smile.

CHAPTER 31

Sea of Possibilities

Wednesday, November 24, 2004

"Despite intensive research, I could not find any historical data in France about the persons in question," Professor Hertzberg announced with great regret. "Unfortunately, information about the Templars in France is patchy, to say the least. A lot of historical materials that survived the Revolution and Napoleon were later destroyed in the Second World War. Besides, one had to be rather famous to leave behind any record in 1307."

The scientists and representatives of the American government and military couldn't hide their disappointment at Hertzberg's words. Tom Stevendahl was no exception. He had hoped so badly for a sign of life from his missing friend, no matter where it came from. At least he would have known where exactly she was, and he could narrow down his efforts to locate her to a specific year. So far, they had not made any progress with their sensational find from the future.

"The only documents that we found relating to the commandery in Bar-sur-Aube," Hertzberg continued, "testify that, for unknown reasons, the building was sold to the Hospitallers in 1288." The historian paused and drank some water. "Anyway, I discovered a few other interesting clues that suggest a new Templar commandery was later constructed about a mile southeast of the city."

"What do you think, Professor?" the American ambassador asked. "Is there a possibility that the Templars really had contact with a civilization from the distant future?"

Hertzberg smiled enigmatically. "When you begin to examine the Templars' history, a number of strange clues appear. Just think of the numerous theories surrounding the Holy Grail that have made their way into popular culture. I honestly believe we are on the trail of something huge, which may even shine new light on the so-called Holy Grail."

"What do you mean?" General Lafour asked, his eyes wide with interest.

"Well, for one, the Templars had a remarkably sophisticated financial system," Hertzberg answered. "To date, no historian dares say where the Templars got this knowledge. Some claim that it came from the Saracens, others that it came from the Jews. But the fact is that the Templars created financial systems that no one had ever used before, such as bills of exchange and coding of money transfers. They perfected inventions like the magnetic compass, and some even claim that they were already experimenting with penicillin in their hospitals. Last but not least, rumor has it they had trade relations with South America. Don't forget, even Columbus sailed under the Order of the Red Cross – an organization that was a successor of the Templars and he most likely discovered the New World using Templar knowledge. Perhaps he knew about the New World because he got his hands on some ancient maps with future knowledge?"

"Are you seriously claiming," Major Simmens cut in doubtfully, "that the Templars got their knowledge from the future?"

"Why not?" Hertzberg challenged. "After all that Dr. Stevendahl has reported, we can even explain the mysterious head idol that crops up in countless interrogation records from the Middle Ages. It seems they may have been referring to the holographic image of a woman's head that appears when the device is activated. I only regret that we cannot personally behold this sight. Its existence would lend credit to the legend that Jacques de Molay, the Order's last Grand Master, predicted Pope Clement's and King Philipp's dates of death at the stake. If he had access to the device, the legend could be true."

"Do you think other nations might know about this?" General Lafour, a military intelligence officer to the bone, could not be moved from his fundamental belief that anyone was capable of anything. The thought of the Russians or the Chinese having access to similar technology disturbed him deeply.

Hertzberg scratched his right ear and straightened his glasses. "Ah, General. I've often asked myself this very question. What if there are more records of the time-traveling device? Or, what if there are other servers in long-forgotten catacombs only waiting to be discovered? After all, there have been countless documented mysteries throughout history, which the device could explain ... In 1885, a respectable clergyman who lived near Perpignan was reported to have found a legendary Templar treasure, although no one ever saw it. He became immeasurably rich after his discovery, but no one knew why. Reportedly, he received the money for his lavish lifestyle from a rich German noble, but in exchange for what?

"And then there was the famous English scholar Roger Bacon, who lived between 1220 and 1292. Bacon once sent the Pope a secret essay in which he wrote about strange wagons that were driven extremely fast without horses. Flying machines and underwater boats appeared in his reports as well. He, too, spoke of a speaking head that the Templars possessed. Where would he have gotten such visions?

"Or think of Leonardo Da Vinci and his futuristic drawings. He was rumored to have connections with the organizations that succeeded the Templars. I could go on forever," Hertzberg said with a sparkle in his eye. "And possibilities for further research appear just as boundless. What if, all this while, we've been heading in the wrong direction regarding many of history's unsolved mysteries?"

The professor paused and cleared his throat theatrically. "But that's not all … Not by a long shot. What if we could prove beyond a doubt that the Bible was written recently? Can you imagine how explosive that would be?"

Major Dan Simmens couldn't stay in his seat any longer. He jumped up and strode towards Hertzberg, all the while eyeing him like a hawk. "My dear Professor, I agree with you on all counts. It can't be denied that our findings possess tremendous political, and even military, potential. What could be more explosive than having control over a time machine?" Simmens planted his feet and looked from one person to the next. "But shouldn't we first analyze what dangers such a machine could present to humanity? What if this groundbreaking invention can permanently alter what has happened in the past, present, or even future?"

Tom coughed timidly.

"Yes, Dr. Stevendahl?" Simmens whirled around and addressed him in a provocative tone. "Do you want to add something?"

"Er …" Tom began uncertainly. "As far as we can tell, a change in the space-time constant isn't possible. Regardless of how you meddle with it, our experiments seem to have absolutely no effect on future events. It's almost as if all our experiments are simply parts of the whole. That is to say, they are integrated in the total flow of current events. As far as we can tell, the programming of our existence fundamentally cannot be influenced."

"Well, that is far worse than if something could be changed," the American ambassador cut in. "Imagine if people realize that they can do whatever they want, because whatever will happen will happen, anyway. How will we hold murderers or terrorists accountable for their actions? With this theory, you're giving every criminal on earth the perfect excuse because whatever crimes they commit are fundamentally predetermined!"

"Maybe we should get some advice from a famous philosopher of physics," Hertzberg suggested with a sigh.

"Interesting approach," General Lafour remarked. "For me, the question is where God stands in this matter."

"I'm afraid that there is no longer a place for God in this game," Paul said. "What we call life is nothing more than a computer simulation, with the one flaw being that until now, we have not been able to find out who owns the source code. As far as I'm concerned, you can call the fellow in question God. But don't be disappointed if you find out that his name is Lucifer, or that he doesn't even have a name, or – what some believers would consider far worse – that it is a *she* who steers our fate. I know only this. Whoever is responsible for our existence doesn't seem to discriminate between Christians, Jews, Muslims, Buddhists, or whatever earthworms believe in. In this system, everyone is equal."

Lafour gave Colbach a poisonous glare.

Hertzberg simply smiled wisely. "God has many names," he said. "What it is really isn't that important."

CHAPTER 32

Death Sentence

Saturday, October 21, 1307

When Hannah awoke, she had lost all sense of time. She felt around for Gero, but the other half of the bed was empty. A second later she let out a bloodcurdling scream. A woman dressed in pale clothes was standing before her, the candle in her hand bathing the unfamiliar room in a ghostly glow. Framed by her white headdress, the stranger's bulging eyes were fixed on Hannah's face. She drew back in horror and screamed as well, pressing her free hand to her breast.

"I'm sorry," Hannah mumbled, suddenly realizing that the woman was simply a servant.

A large stoneware dish and jug now stood on the sideboard and a few blue towels and a bar of soap lay on a wooden shelf nearby. The woman composed herself, and, turning to the fireplace, she stacked some wood that she had taken out of a wicker basket.

Hannah had a feeling that her new maid had no interest in morning conversation. She felt likewise. Understanding and speaking Middle High German were two entirely different things.

The maid, rapidly overcoming her initial shyness, stepped towards Hannah's bed again. Without asking, she pulled away her blanket. Although a cozy fire had begun to crackle in the fireplace, it was still far too cold for Hannah's liking. Shivering, and dressed only in a knee-length gown, she allowed the pale-faced woman to take her by the elbow and help her to her feet. The woman probably thought that Hannah was mute or came from a distant land, for she only communicated with her in a rudimentary form of sign language.

Like Alice in Wonderland, Hannah allowed herself to be seated in a chair before having her hair brushed and her face, hands, and even feet washed then massaged with a salve that smelled of lavender and rose oil. Without a word the woman left the chamber.

Hannah used the opportunity to inspect the washbasin. Hidden behind the blue-green ceramic jug was a small cup of fired clay. The brownish liquid and the small wooden twig sticking out of it reminded her of milky coffee with a swizzle stick. Hannah picked up the cup and tentatively sipped the liquid, struck by the strangely familiar taste of chewing gum. Taking out the small twig, she saw that it was fringed on one end. It smelled of wine, chamomile, and sage. Suddenly, it dawned on her that it was the ancient toothbrush set that Gero had told her about.

The door opened again, making Hannah jump. Hastily she put the cup back in its place, spilling some of the liquid onto the wooden table in the process. The maid handed her a light-blue silk undercoat and a dark-blue embroidered brocade surcoat, but made no mention of Hannah's mishap, simply wiping away the spilled liquid with a rag on her belt. Despite Hannah's doubts that the clothes would fit her, her silent attendant helped her tighten the hidden laces with skillful fingers, allowing the outer tunic to fit her figure perfectly. Light, thigh-length silk stockings fastened with a garter and pointed shoes of soft, dark-blue leather completed Hannah's odd outfit.

"Thank you," Hannah said after she had finally plucked up her courage to speak to the woman in Middle High German. "What is your name?"

The maid looked bewildered, and Hannah feared that she had said something wrong. Just then, the woman let out an unintelligible sound, but it was only when she parted her lips and revealed her tongue, cut off so that only a stump remained, that Hannah realized the true reason for her silence.

She flinched, but the maid seemed merely amused, and broke out into a throaty giggle, which only made the entire situation seem even more surreal.

Hastily, Hannah gathered her surcoat, desperate to get out to find Gero or Anselm, or anyone who could get her out of this nightmare.

She discovered one of the many pitfalls of her medieval clothing when she stumbled down the spiral staircase. If she wasn't careful the long tips of her shoes folded over, making her trip as she walked, but, miraculously, she reached the kinghts' hall unscathed. Momentarily, Hannah was overwhelmed with panic. Everything looked unfamiliar to her, and she couldn't see anyone she knew. Under the black timber ceiling stood rows of heraldic shields, displaying the many branches of the House of Breydenbach. Below them, a warm fire blazed, providing the room with comforting warmth, along with two large Oriental tapestries.

Finally, she spotted Gero. He was standing under an iron chandelier near the entrance, waiting for her. Instead of his Templar cloak, he was wearing an ankle-length, golden-brown surcoat, and a snow-white shirt with starched sleeves and collar. It took Hannah a moment to get used to the sight of his aristocratic clothing. She longed to fall into his arms in relief, but in front of all these people she had to restrain herself. Then she saw Struan and his fair lover. He, too, wasn't wearing his chlamys, but instead a pair of fitted black pants and a knee-length tabard with red and gold embroidery.

The tables and benches in the great hall had been re-arranged. Massive tankards of wine and beer stood ready for the thirsty castle residents. Gero yelled something to a stately-looking man with a beard threaded with silver, who was laughing freely, and led Hannah to his table. She had already noticed the portly elderly man's booming voice the night before.

"Lady Hannah, may I introduce you to the steward of Breydenburg Castle?" In the presence of his family, Gero consciously spoke to her formally to avoid stoking any rumors. With the steward, however, he spoke informally.

"Roland, this is Hannah de Caillou. She took me in after I was attacked, and cared for me and Matthäus while I was unconscious."

Gero made the effort to remain truthful although the steward still looked at him with a certain degree of doubt. Hannah tried to imagine what would happen if he told the truth.

"Roland of Briey." The steward rose and bowed elegantly despite his size. "It is an honor, milady," he said with a hearty laugh. "So we have something in common – I've saved his ass a few times, too."

Hannah smiled uncertainly.

"He taught me horse-riding and swordplay," Gero told her.

With a cheerful grin, he motioned for her to take a seat next to Roland. The steward poured himself a mug of beer from a large pitcher that stood in the middle of the table, and emptied it in one go. With the tip of his tongue, he licked the foam from his thick red moustache, reminding Hannah of a walrus.

"Wine?" Gero asked Hannah.

She shook her head. "Not so early in the morning."

Roland stared at her in bewilderment.

"Milk? Or some herbal brew?" she asked in embarrassment, realizing that she had forgotten to alter both her pronunciation and word choice.

446

Gero stood up to search for a jug of hot milk.

"You're probably not from around here," Roland said through a mouthful of bloodwurst he had sliced with his dagger.

"Why are you drinking herbal brew for breakfast?" he continued when Hannah failed to respond. "Are you ill? You don't look as if you're wasting away."

"No, no," Hannah answered lowering her eyes. "I'm fine." Perhaps the steward would leave her in peace if she pretended to be shy. She hadn't yet agreed with Gero what she should say about her ancestry.

Roland smacked his lips with pleasure and dunked his remaining piece of sausage in a pot of mustard while continuing to watch Hannah with interest. From far away, she could see that Gero was detained at his mother's table, and so she was glad when Anselm suddenly appeared, striding towards her table. He, too, was wearing a colorful tabard. Proudly, he smoothed down the ornately embroidered garment when Hannah eyed him questioningly.

"Not bad, eh? It's from the castle lord's discarded clothing stock."

He introduced himself to their tablemate with his new French-sounding name, and, after a slight bow, he sat down, to Hannah's relief, between her and the burly steward.

"Roland of Briey," the man introduced himself in his deep voice, and then chuckled. "Is that your wife?" he asked brazenly, gesturing towards Hannah.

"My sister," Anselm said, smiling at Hannah innocently. Hardly anything could surprise her anymore. Anselm was a remarkable actor, and had immersed himself in his new situation more quickly than Hannah had expected. A short while later, the Lord of Briey had already offered him the informal "thou", and the newly-born friendship was toasted with two large mugs of beer.

The piercing call of fanfares yanked them all out of their conversations. Gero's brother was the first to spring to his feet. With frightening speed, the men grabbed their weapons, and the room erupted into a frenzy of glittering steel blades, toppled-over benches, and rattling crockery.

Roland patted Anselm's shoulder reassuringly. Anselm had also risen to his feet, but he still didn't have a weapon. "Wait here and take care of your sister," Roland said to Anselm in a hushed tone before drawing his sword from a sheath decorated with precious stones and heading to the door.

Richard of Breydenbach opened the door to the courtyard. With a group of heavily armed men following behind him, among them his own two sons and the forbidding Scotsman, he walked outside. The fog had cleared a bit, and a few timid sunbeams snuck through the gaps in the clouds.

The women and children who had remained inside fell into an eerie silence. Through the open window, Hannah could hear a second fanfare sounding, and she saw a soldier on watch run breathlessly down from the tower and, with a deep bow, stop in front of Gero's father.

The castle lord gave him an order. The man ran back up and a little later gave a hand-signal from the tower. A troop of six armed riders dashed into the courtyard on large, gleaming black cold bloods, the sound of galloping hooves echoing from the castle walls before the beasts came to a stop. The foremost rider sprang off his horse and, with a short bow, handed the castle lord a sealed roll of parchment. Only then did the bearer appear to deliver an explanation for his sudden arrival. Richard of Breydenbach looked stunned.

"What's going on?" Hannah whispered to Anselm.

"I don't know," he admitted. "But something tells me there's a problem here. The old man doesn't look too enthused."

"But the men who arrived bear the same crest as the Breydenbachs. They must be allies," Hannah said uneasily.

"Do you have any idea how complicated alliances were in the Middle Ages?" Anselm grinned sardonically. "One day they could be friends, the next day they could just as easily be enemies. That's what my history professor always said about the medieval noble houses' shifting alliances."

The fearful faces of the castle residents however, hinted that this peculiar surprise visit was far more troubling than Anselm had anticipated. He pricked up his ears and heard one of the servants in the hall wondering why the castle lord wasn't inviting his feudal lords' followers in for a drink as usual. Instead, a heated battle of words arose outside. Surprisingly, the men of the Archbishop of Trier reacted not with their swords, but simply retreated wordlessly.

A murmur went round the room when the riders disappeared and the men returned to the women, children, and servants in the hall. No one said a word, but it was clear that everyone was eager for an explanation from their leader.

"Don't let this spoil our meal," Richard of Breydenbach declared. "Nothing of any significance has happened."

Even the simplest of them could tell from his stony face that he wasn't speaking the truth. With a nod, he ordered his sons, the Scotsman, and his castle steward to follow him, and, together, the five men left the hall. Hannah glanced at Gero's mother to see that the usually stately lady of the castle was fighting back tears.

The massive oak door of the lord's chamber slammed shut. Richard of Breydenbach's blue eyes flashed, ready for battle.

"That bastard from France wants your heads," he said, giving Gero and Struan a mirthless smile. "Philipp IV of France has issued a request for your extradition to the representatives of the Archbishop of Trier." Unrolling the parchment that he had been holding in his hands, he read the Latin text aloud, so that Gero and the others, who were fluent in the language, could decipher the text for themselves.

In nomine Dei Amen Notû ſit omnib qui prefentes litteras patentes ſeu inſtrumentum legunt vel legere audiunt Milites Ordinis Templi Gerard de Breydenbach & Struan MacDhughaill jnveſtigandi & accuſandi ſunt d hêreſia ſodomia homicidiaq militû Chriſtianorû Regis Francorû Si notû fuerit vbi ſunt nulla mora interpoſita Curti Regali a Principe quocûq tradendi ſunt Habem vnûquêq qui tali hoſpitiû daberit jn eodê modo d flagitijs nefarijs côſortê esse & ſeculariter atq ſpiritaliter minime carcere p totâ vitâ abiudicatione cunctorû libertatû atq retentione omniû bonorû puniendû esse
Dat Pariſijs Anno Jncarnationis 1307 jn feſto Bi Lucê Evangeliſtę
Vt hęc prêſcriptio firmi ſit Ego Guilelm d Nogareto Cuſtos Sigilli Summ Philippi Quarti Regis Francorû ſigillû meû ad litteras prêſentas adfixi

As Gero listened to his father's baritone voice, he quickly translated the Latin in his mind: In the name of the Lord, Amen. Let it be known by all unto whom this letter shall come: The knights of the Temple, Gerard of Breydenbach and Struan MacDhughaill, are to be tracked down and prosecuted for heresy, sodomy, and the murder of the French King's Christian soldiers. If it becomes known where they are, they are to be immediately delivered to the Royal Court by the ruler in question. We consider anyone who grants shelter to one of those named above to be accomplices of the villainous crimes, and such persons will be sentenced to a minimum of lifelong imprisonment, renunciation of all freedoms, and confiscation of all assets in both the mortal and divine worlds. Given in Paris in the year of the incarnation of the Lord 1307 on the Feast of St. Luke the Evangelist.

So that this commandment is all the more secure, I, Guillaume de Nogaret, Keeper of the Seals of Philipp IV, King of the French, have attached my seal to this letter.]

"Guy de Gislingham – I bet we have our English friend to thank for this," Gero said, pursing his lips and looking at his Scottish Brother. 'Only he knew that we wanted to flee into the German lands together.'"

"What does that mean, murder of Christian soldiers?" Richard gave his son a piercing stare.

"When we were trying to protect Henri d'Our from Nogaret's soldiers, we were left with little choice but to kill two soldiers of the Gens du Roi. Later, we had to fend off our French pursuers. One of the Brothers who had accompanied us on our escape, Guy de Gislingham, is apparently an agent of Nogaret's. One morning, he fled." Gero's voice was filled with bitterness. "We think he walked right into the enemy camp after that. Why else would we have been ambushed by an entire troop of French soldiers near Bar-le-Duc? We got into a skirmish with them, and had no option but to send them all to hell. Otherwise, they wouldn't have been satisfied with just killing us, but instead, we would have been turned over to King Philipp."

"As long as there are no other eye-witnesses, it's our word against his," Richard said firmly. "And if he claims to have been there, he could be accused of not interfering, and he would be suspected of assisting you. Should there be a trial, they would first have to prove that you killed the men."

"And what if they make us swear an oath of truth?" Gero looked at his father in confusion.

"It won't come to that," Richard said, and, with a glance at Struan, switched to French again. "Do you honestly think I would allow my son and his friends to be delivered to Philipp IV like dogs?"

"Father, I don't want you to have conflicting loyalties with the Archbishop because of me. He is our liege," Gero replied softly. "I have already caused you enough worry."

"Diether of Nassau has been in delirium for weeks, and his subdeacon, Baldwin of Luxembourg, presumably doesn't dare to carry out the King of France's orders without receiving support from a Papal letter. And from what I understood of the delegation's explanations, that hasn't yet happened."

"Diether of Nassau will soon die. In December, Baldwin will become his successor," Gero let slip.

"How do you know that?" Roland stared at him in utter astonishment.

"That doesn't matter," Richard said curtly. He had a hunch about where his son had acquired this knowledge. "You can't return to France under these circumstances – it would be certain death. Tomorrow, first thing, I will send a message to the leaders of the Teutonic Order in Koblenz to request an audience with them."

"I don't intend to join the Teutonic Knights," Gero responded calmly. "And neither do my comrades. You already knew that. We are going to free Henri d'Our."

"Gero, listen to your father's advice for once," Roland of Briey said. "A well-planned escape is the only choice you have left. The Teutons are anything but easily intimidated, and will pay the King of France no heed. They don't care what lives you have on your conscience, as long as you are a good soldier. You can easily find shelter there."

"Roland is right," Richard decided, having composed himself again after his initial shock. "But you need a completely new identity, a new name, writs of escort and freedom papers, badges, and documents that prove your nobility."

"And how will you get all of this together so quickly, Father?" Gero stared at him in confusion.

"You know I have my connections. Give me two days, and we will have everything ready."

"Then I beseech you to arrange for the papers for our journey to France with the same care," Gero said.

"In God's name, you're as stubborn as a mule!" Gero's elder brother jumped in furiously. "You're dragging us all down into this misfortune! If we aren't extremely careful, the Archbishop will take our castle. There are still rich profits to be made in the East with the Teutonic Order. They are planning a Crusade to penetrate further into Wendish territory, and they would be happy to take any qualified fighter they can."

"Forgive me, brother, but you have spoken in vain," Gero replied defiantly. "Only our father and my comrades know why."

"You are mad, boy," Richard groaned, his eyes full of despair.

"What do we have to lose, anyway?" Gero asked.

"Your lives," Richard snapped.

"If we don't succeed in saving the Order, we won't have them, anyway," Gero answered flatly. "If we aren't even allowed to bear our own names anymore, what meaning does life have?"

He glanced at Struan for his support, but the Scotsman had only been able to partially understand the conversation in French and German.

"This devil in France has on his conscience everything that is dear and precious to me," Gero added in French quietly but resolutely, "and I will do everything I can to stop him."

It was clear to Richard of Breydenbach that he could not stop his youngest son from trying to change the fate of his Order and all the Brothers he had left behind in France. The castle lord also knew that the welfare of his friends from the future was close to his heart.

"Very well," Richard said reluctantly. "No matter what your plans, you have my support."

"Stay with my mother, please," Gero whispered when he returned to Hannah in the knights' hall. "We have something to discuss amongst men."

Hannah's eyes widened when he signaled for Anselm to follow him. All day, she had been left behind, first when the Archbishop's soldiers appeared, and then again when Richard of Breydenbach hurriedly left to speak with the Templars, and now Gero was leaving her here under the pretext of an important discussion in which Anselm, but not she, could participate.

Anselm followed Gero with rapid steps, not turning back to look at her even once. Although Hannah didn't know exactly what this hastily organized meeting was about, she had a faint inkling. Having made up her mind, she stood up. Amelie, the young woman with blonde curls, was sitting at a neighboring table, and Hannah had seen her black-haired lover whisper something to her before he too left the hall. But unlike Hannah, her face had gone pale instead of red with rage. Nervously, Amelie sipped her milk, staring over the rim of the cup she was holding to her mouth. A woman like her was probably used to holding her tongue when, without a second thought, her lover strode down the road to ruin.

Hannah wanted to take the woman by the hand and ask her to join her in searching for the men, but she was afraid Amelie wouldn't understand, and she didn't want to put her in the difficult position of facing Struan's displeasure. The two of them already had enough difficulties in any case. Gero had told Hannah the night before that the girl was pregnant with the Scotsman's child, and a marriage was momentarily out of the question because her lover was a knight of the Order.

Ignoring her surroundings, Hannah left the table and ran past Gero's mother, across a wide hallway, and toward the spiral staircase. With her skirt hitched high, she hastened up the narrow steps to the topmost floor. When she reached the chamber of the Flemish knight, she stopped. According to Gero, he was still sick and bed-ridden, and for reasons unbeknown to her, he hadn't yet introduced her to him. She was sure that Gero would not leave his sick Brother out of any important new developments.

She could hear a few male voices from behind the thick oak door. Tentatively, Hannah pushed the heavy latch downward.

When she entered the room Gero looked up in surprise. "Didn't I tell you to wait for me downstairs?" he asked.

His comrades turned to face her curiously. The guilt on Anselm's face at leaving her behind was plain to see.

Out of the corner of her eye, Hannah saw a young, broad-shouldered man in a white nightgown. With his forehead bandaged, he sat between silk sheets and down pillows in a large canopy bed, looking like a baby bird that had stumbled into a nest too large for it. Short, red hair peeked out from beneath the white linen bandages, and his sparse red beard failed to cover the burn scars on his badly disfigured face. He looked as if he had had a terrible accident.

"Oh," the man exclaimed cheerfully without an ounce of shyness when Hannah turned to look directly into his clear, blue-green eyes. "Who do we have here?"

"Pardon the disturbance," Hannah said, turning away from him and smiling uncertainly at the men. "I'm afraid I left something here that I need."

Anselm looked at the floor and remained silent. *Coward*, she thought, and, despite Gero's objections, she pushed her way into the room, shutting the door behind her.

"Hannah," Gero began imploringly, "I told you that our plans are far too dangerous for a woman. You should get to know my mother instead, as I will have to leave you behind with my family for a rather long time."

"Ah, so you honestly think you can leave me behind so easily?" she retorted. "Then there's one thing you haven't reckoned with. I'm coming along, no matter where you intend to go."

"Holy Virgin." With a groan, Gero turned his pleading gaze to the ceiling. "Make this woman understand!"

"What does she want?" Struan had spoken in French, but even without much knowledge of the language, Hannah knew that the Scottish Templar disapproved of her presence.

Gero didn't answer the question, but instead turned with a wary smile to his redheaded friend. "This is Hannah," he said, introducing her as if he were announcing a thunderstorm. "She is the woman who traveled through time with me and Anselm."

"Johan van Elk – it is an honor," said the knight, giving her a slight bow, and flashing his flawless teeth in a winning smile.

"We should tell her our plans," Gero said with a sigh. "She is no less affected by this than Anselm. The two of them come from an unimaginably faraway future. Her return is nearly as important as the salvation of the Order."

Hannah felt the men's eyes rest on her. Johan stared at her as if she had turned into a creature he had never seen before. "She looks like an angel," he remarked with a smile. "Does she really come from the future?"

"Yes," Gero answered, "just like Anselm."

"Perhaps the venerable Brothers of the High Council have made a mistake," Johan murmured thoughtfully. "If she and her companion come from the future, and everything you have told us about the Order's annihilation is true, the future must already be written. Doesn't that mean that nothing more can be changed? Have you ever thought of that, Brother?"

"Yes," Gero muttered, "I've thought of that, too. But that would also mean that prayer is meaningless, as God no longer has any influence over the world."

A crushing silence suddenly filled the room.

Finally, Hannah broke the silence. "What on earth is going on here?" she demanded, as she turned to look at Anselm, who was standing at the window and periodically glancing down at the castle courtyard.

"The King of France has issued an extradition order to the Archbishop of Trier," Anselm answered flatly. "As of this morning, Struan and Gero are amongst the most wanted criminals in Europe. Lord have mercy on them if they are ever captured by the French king."

"What are you saying?" Hannah asked, looking thunderstruck.

Gero slowly walked towards her. "Don't you remember? I told you in Heisterbach that Struan and I killed soldiers of the royal Keeper of the Seals in France. Somehow, Philipp has got wind of it, and now he's on the hunt to find and kill us."

Hannah felt the blood drain from her face. "And what now?" she asked helplessly. "What are you going to do?"

Gero's lips curled into a wretched smile. "Our only option is to disappear from here as quickly as possible and to set off on a secret mission to France. Apart from our commander, I don't know anyone who could help us avert the end of our Order."

Hannah peered over Gero's shoulder at the rest of the men. "And what if your friend is right, and the course of time can't be changed?"

"We will find a solution," Gero replied. He sounded fairly confident, but his expression betrayed how desperate he was.

"I have an idea," Johan said. Awkwardly, he began to unravel his head bandages. "We'll dress up as minstrels, with wagons, horses, and costumes. Each of us can play an instrument. We know love songs well enough. And if we shave off our beards, no one will ever think that we are Templars."

"And what about Struan? He can neither sing nor play the lute," Gero pointed out.

Johan smiled and felt his freshly stitched head wounds. "He could compete in wrestling matches for coins. Or he could split an apple on people's heads with his knife."

Gero snorted and shook his head, looking over at Struan, amused.

The Scotsman regarded him curiously, obviously not understanding Johan's suggestion. "You should be glad, Johan, that he hardly speaks any German, or you'd be in danger."

Johan smirked. "But isn't it a good idea? As minstrels, we could move about freely. Anyway, we wouldn't look suspicious, because our profession would make us vagabonds. No one would guess the true nature of our mission."

"Minstrels!" Gero glanced at Anselm. He knew the time traveler loved to dress up. "Why not?" he mused. "When I was younger, I would have loved to travel through the lands as a juggler – always free, surrounded by pretty maidens."

"Yes, maidens," Johan said with a grin. "To disguise ourselves, we need a few good women."

Hannah noticed Gero's redheaded friend scrutinizing her.

"Can you dance, darling?" he asked in Middle High German.

Gero, who caught Hannah's confused look, jumped in with an answer. "Absolutely out of the question! That's far too dangerous. She's staying here."

"I don't want to meddle," Anselm said hesitantly, "but we can't simply leave Hannah behind. I can't imagine how it would feel to sit here and wait for a sign of life from us. If we succeed in freeing your commander, and he really knows how to operate the timeserver, he could probably show Hannah and me a way back into the future right then and there, and we would be spared the dangerous journey back to Breyden."

Hannah flashed Gero a triumphant smile, and crossed her arms resolutely in front of her chest. "There is no way I'm staying at this castle, and I'll follow you myself if I have to."

"If I wanted to, I could command you to stay!" Gero glared at her with eyes blazing. "Even if Anselm's opinion has some merit, I still think it's too dangerous!"

"I am a free woman. I didn't know you had the authority to tell me what to do," she countered.

"Your alleged freedom can quickly be diminished," he replied in a foreboding voice. "It would be easy for me to throw you into our dungeon until you regain your senses."

Instead of evading his gaze, Hannah glared up at him belligerently. "You're deluding yourself, *Frater Gerard*," she said firmly, deliberately pronouncing the "G" in his name like a "J", "if you think that your carnal knowledge allows you to treat me like an underage concubine."

Gero was at a loss for words. All he could muster was a sheepish cough.

"And the lady wins this round," said Johan, who had understood every word.

CHAPTER 33

Setting off for France

Wednesday, October 25, 1307

Four days had passed since the Archbishop's riders had appeared at Breydenburg Castle. During that time, Rotgunde, the Breydenbachs' seamstress, and her team of girls had sewn two dozen colorful minstrels' costumes, all embellished with little bells.

Anselm was overwhelmed with excitement. Never before had he come across such perfectly hand-stitched clothing in brocade, velvet, and silk. The seamstresses had raided the storeroom for fabrics from Bruges, Paris, and Cologne. Riders were sent to Trier to buy flutes and fiddles, a few drums, and a symphonia, as well as dice shakers, divination cards, torches, balls, and cones. Although most of the equipment would not be used, it was necessary for a convincing disguise. The wagon that was supposed to transport the minstrels' accessories was prepared for deployment half a mile west of the castle, on a secluded liege farmstead.

On his way to the rooms upstairs, Struan bumped into Amelie, his lover who had fallen into a deep depression since learning of their plan to return to France. Quickly, he took off his plated gloves to embrace her and Amelie forced a strained smile as he pulled her into his arms.

"How are you and our child doing?" he asked tenderly.

"Well," she said, her voice choked with tears.

With a sigh, she buried her face in his chest. Struan stroked her cheek. He lifted her chin with his hand and looked into her eyes with concern.

"Amelie, please," he said gently, brushing her blonde locks aside. "Let's talk upstairs, okay?"

She nodded, and followed him into their shared sleeping quarters. Amelie cried all the way to their bed, then let herself fall face first into the soft pillows. Struan sat down next to her and cautiously touched her shoulder.

"You've always been so strong," he pleaded helplessly. "Think of our child, Amelie. What will he think of his mother if she's always so sad?"

457

Hesitantly, Struan brushed away a strand of her untamed hair as she looked at him with red-rimmed eyes.

"And what about his father?" she demanded. "Why are you going back into that hellhole when you know they're looking for you? Think about what happened to us in that forest! Your Brother and his squire are cursed, and his companions, too. Damn it, Struan, if Gero and his friends want to go on this suicide mission, let them. The French soldiers will kill you when they catch you!"

"This is not about Gero, nor his companions," the Scotsman declared passionately. "It is about our Order, and our Brothers in France who were helplessly put at the mercy of the Royal Secret Police. I told you from the start that I must do everything I can to protect my Order and commander from harm. Only then can I plead for an honorable discharge so that I can take you as my wife in front of the Almighty Lord."

"What good does that do us now?" she cried, her voice cracking. "You have been outlawed. You can't live anywhere under your real name anyway. But Richard of Breydenbach is a powerful man who could easily get you a new name, and then I wouldn't have to wait to become your bride."

She shifted closer to him and folded her hands as if in prayer.

"Please, Struan," she whispered with quivering lips. "I beg you. Don't go to France with Gero. For me, and for the love of our child!"

When he looked into her tear-filled eyes, Struan's heart melted. But he knew he couldn't fulfill her wish. He had sworn an oath to the Order, and had an obligation to do anything he could to save it. Besides, Gero was his Brother and his best friend, and to the deepest part of his heart, he felt responsible for him, even if he only understood a little of what Gero had planned. He couldn't tell Amelie about the Head of Wisdom, yet he still had to convince her that he had no choice but to follow his conscience.

"Amelie, I love you so much," he said, carefully wiping a few tears from her cheek. "But I have to stand by Gero's side. He won't succeed in rescuing our comrades and commander by himself," he added as she turned away. "So please understand. It is my duty."

She took a deep breath. When she lifted her head and looked him in the eyes again, her features were expressionless. "Very well," she said. "It seems to be our fate that we won't see our child be born and grow up, together."

"Amelie, what are you talking about? I'm going to come back and marry you, I swear on my honor and my mother's grave. Until that day, you will be safe here."

"I'm only telling you what I think," she defended herself. "If you go to France, we will not see each other again in this lifetime. I am certain of that."

He reached out his arms to pull her towards him, but she shrugged him off and stood up. She hurried to the windowsill, where the sunlight were slanting through the open window. There she stood, gazing out at the autumn landscape of the Lieser valley.

Struan followed her, and embraced her from behind. Like a statue, she stood motionless and let him caress her, but even when he stroked her swollen belly, she didn't react.

"I had a dream last night," she whispered absently. "I saw the King's guards torture you … and when you were dead, an enormous black gryphon came and carried you away."

"Amelie," he said, trying to placate her, "no gryphon is capable of carrying me away. That was only a dream."

She turned around slowly. "If you think that making jests would comfort me, you don't know me very well." She lowered her head before continuing in a soft voice, "I can't bear the thought of never seeing you again, so, please leave now, and don't bother me again before you leave for France."

"You can't be serious," Struan said darkly.

"I've never been more serious in my life. Leave!"

A blow from a sword could not have hurt him more. Slowly he let his hands drop.

"Just leave," she repeated in a choked voice.

Wounded, Struan left the chamber.

That evening, they sat together in silence for what might be their last meal together. Matthäus hung his head, and when he was ordered to say grace, it sounded more like a bleak murmur than a prayer of thanks for their daily bread.

Gero's mother had taken her seat next to her husband at the head of the table, and was pushing around a piece of salmon pastry with a silver spoon, unable to eat. She looked up only now and then to sip her wine. Richard and Roland drank their beer in silence. Hannah shuddered slowly, just beginning to realize what she had gotten herself into. It seemed their plan was actually far more dangerous than she had thought.

Struan looked so forbidding that no one dared speak to him. To everyone's surprise, his French girlfriend had excused herself from dinner under the pretext of not feeling well. It was, after all, the last evening the two of them could spend together before the departure. Even Johan, who was always up for a joke, simply drank his wine, deep in thought, only glancing absent-mindedly at the juicy roast. Despite the cook's best efforts, it had barely attracted any attention from the diners.

Only Anselm was enjoying his meal, as he was completely preoccupied with observing every minute detail that he experienced here. He seemed to Hannah like a large child with a free ticket to a magical adventure land he had been dreaming of his entire life. He had recently even begun carrying his own sword, which Gero had found for him in the armory. Like a peacock, he paraded around with the gleaming weapon, forged by a famous Flemish blacksmith, a flaming star engraved on its pommel. Roland had shown Anselm a few feints that had impressed him greatly. The steward had told him that hardly anyone fought according to the rules. In the everyday life of a warrior, survival, not elegance, was the only thing that mattered. Hannah sensed that Anselm was itching to finally fight a real battle.

Unlike Anselm, Gero looked just as brooding as the rest of his comrades. The only time he spoke was to ask Eberhard to pass the salt or wine. Hannah could tell that he was making a conscious effort not to look in her direction. But it was Matthäus, not she, whom he was avoiding. The boy was sitting in the seat next to her.

"Please, let me come with you," he pleaded meekly, after summoning the courage to look his lord in the eye.

"It is too dangerous," Gero muttered edgily. "You will stay here at the castle with Amelie. You will be in good hands with Roland of Briey. He'll give you the necessary polish that you need to become a reputable fighter. When I am back, we'll see how far you've progressed."

Matthäus asked for permission to leave the table and tersely excused himself for the night.

A little later, Hannah left to find the lavatory, and found the boy sitting on a stair landing outside the banquet hall. He had one of the many cats that lived in the castle on his lap, which he was stroking as he sobbed. The cat reminded Hannah of Heisenberg, bringing on a momentary pang of homesickness. Suddenly, the animal noticed that it was being watched, and sprang out of the boy's lap in fright. Matthäus looked up in astonishment and wiped his wet nose on his sleeve when he saw Hannah walking towards him. She sat down next to him on the stone steps, draped an arm around his shoulders, and pulled him close to her. When he looked up at her with sorrowful eyes, she knew she couldn't possibly leave him behind.

Tenderly, she pressed her cheek against his damp face, and he flung his arms around her neck, burying his curly blonde head in the crook of her neck.

"You know where the wagon is?" she whispered.

"Yes," he answered breathlessly, and hesitantly released himself. "I helped to load it yesterday."

"Be there tomorrow morning before dawn. Don't get caught before you leave the castle, and hide yourself there until we arrive."

The boy lowered his head shyly and nodded.

Hannah smiled at him in encouragement. "We can do it."

CHAPTER 34

The Code

Saturday, November 27, 2004

"Open sesame, God damn it!" Tom's voice echoed through the high security wing of the makeshift research facility in Himmerod.

He thought of Professor Dietmar Hagen, whose uneventful burial had taken place two days earlier. Perhaps the professor could have helped him crack this peculiar case. But it was no use. Hagen was dead, and the timeserver was like a stubborn oyster that could only be opened with brute force. For nearly twenty hours, Paul, Tom, and a few other computer scientists had been trying to elicit a sign of life from the artifact. *If only I could remember how the Templar brought this thing to life*, Tom thought desperately.

"Surely we must be able to figure out what password your knight used?" Dr. Karen Baxter, who had just appeared through the secure door, seemed to be able to read minds. She raised her carefully plucked eyebrows with interest and looked at him with a smile.

"He sang something," Tom answered thoughtfully. "After that, the program booted up all by itself."

"It must to function by way of a specific language code," Karen remarked helpfully. "What did he sing, then?"

"It was a monastic chant," Paul explained.

Karen shook her head in disbelief. "Do you mean Gregorian chants? Why don't you make an inquiry with the monks in the neighboring Himmerod Abbey?" she suggested. "I'm sure they have plenty of knowledge about these chants."

"That's a nice idea, sure, but how would we do that?" Paul stared at her in confusion. "Are you saying they'll give us private lessons?"

"Why don't you just listen to the vesper chants as audience members?" Karen suggested. "As far as I know, they sing for the public every Saturday evening around 5:00 p.m. Gregorian chants are ancient. Maybe you'll find something familiar in their performance?"

"And then? Are we supposed to memorize everything?" Paul looked her in disbelief.

"Hmm," Karen pondered, "well, unless I'm mistaken, a recording won't accomplish much. I believe there is a vibrational difference between real human voices and recordings. If the box really is calibrated to respond to direct vocal input, then it must be sung live." Deep in thought, she looked at Paul and Tom for a second. "Just take the server with you into the abbey," she finally decided, "and see if anything happens."

"I don't know if this is a good idea," Paul muttered as he and Tom entered the main door of the Himmerod Abbey that evening.

In his right hand, Tom was carrying a small, unremarkable, shatterproof aluminum suitcase in which the precious artifact had been stored. They were not the only audience members sitting under the soaring choir arch that evening. A few elderly men and women huddled in the front rows of the pews, marveling at the beauty of the Baroque church.

A little later, a line of hooded men in white robes entered through the side entrance of the apse. When they arrived at the altar, they removed their hoods and took their places in two long rows on either side of a beautiful Madonna statue enthroned on a crescent moon.

Paul sat in one of the pews at the back, tensely glancing between the singing monks and the suitcase that stood between the kneeling bench and Tom's feet.

Time passed. One song flowed into another without the timeserver inside the suitcase making even the faintest of sounds.

"I don't think there's much point in staying any longer," Tom sighed in resignation. "Let's go."

Just then, the monks began a new song. "*Laudabo Deum meum in vita mea ...*"

A soft click sounded.

"Shit! Something's happening!" Paul yelled frantically.

A few churchgoers in the front rows turned around in annoyance, but the two scientists paid them no heed. Tom stormed toward the exit with the suitcase in his hand, and Paul ran ahead to yank open the heavy door. They ran to the car. Tom fished out his car keys with trembling fingers.

"I have to admit," he gasped as he struggled to open the door, "I didn't think about what we would do if our plan worked."

Paul flinched when Tom tried to push the suitcase into his hands.

"Here, take it," Tom ordered him. "I can't drive and keep the thing under control at the same time."

"Under control!" Paul nearly screamed. "What do you mean under control? I'm just as clueless as you are about what to do with this thing."

"Just look inside," Tom suggested.

Unlike Paul, he seemed to know what he wanted. He started the car and steered it onto the road. Nervously, Paul opened the metal suitcase. Inside, a greenish light shimmered, and something momentarily took control of his thoughts.

"User mode calibrated. Enter coordinates. Retrieval mechanism activated."

"It's talking to me!" Paul cried, and raised his hands as he balanced the open suitcase on his lap. "What should I do?"

"I hear it, too," Tom replied nervously. "Maybe we should just pull over."

The sky had already become dark, and in the headlights, they could see that they were in the middle of the Himmerod forest. The Institute was still a few minutes away, but Tom could no longer concentrate on the road. The car skidded as he pulled suddenly onto a side road and braked hard.

Paul was thrown forward against his seatbelt, and in the last moment before it collided with the dashboard, he caught the suitcase.

Tom flung open the driver's door and hurried over to Paul. The timeserver had started to warm up, and the familiar female voice made a few more announcements. With visible relief, Paul handed the gray object to Tom.

"Call the base!" Tom yelled. "Tell them to send out a security team as soon as possible. The devil only knows what else this thing may do."

"Yes, sir," Paul answered. Hastily, he pulled out his cellphone but his thoughts were dominated by the strange voice in his head, and he had to summon all his concentration to enter the number of the operations center: 01 01 12 21.

"They're coming right away," Paul gasped.

Although the other members of their team would be just as ill equipped to control the mechanism, it would be comforting to have a few steely marines at his side before the possible appearance of the next time-traveling knight.

The device glowed brightly, bathing everything within a hundred-foot radius in a greenish, glowing haze. An ear-piercing scream made Tom recoil, and he nearly dropped the server in horror. Against his first instinct to hide in the car, Paul stepped out. His heart pounding with panic, he shone his flashlight around the surrounding terrain. He wasn't sure if what he had heard had been Tom's scream, but his colleague was crouching, motionless and silent, on the forest floor, the server on his lap. His eyes were wide with fear.

"Behind you!" he gasped breathlessly. "There's something behind there!"

About ten feet away, a shadow moved. Paul moved the flashlight, thinking they had startled a deer, but the beam of light hit a nearly bald young man. Startled, Paul shone the light on the slender figure. He was wearing a light-colored, coarsely woven habit, and stood still with a shocked expression that mirrored Paul's own. Moving the beam of the flashlight down to the ground, he saw the man's bare feet in worn leather sandals that were definitely too breezy for this time of year.

"Tom," Paul said in a choked voice, "I think we have a new problem."

CHAPTER 35

Stowaway

Thursday, October 26, 1307

Just three days after the arrival of the Archbishop's edict, Richard of Breydenbach had acquired all the documents needed for a safe journey to France. The Caillou siblings, as Anselm and Hannah were known, were given papers that secured their free status, and a writ of escort for the German lands and France issued by the City Council of Trier, identifying them as members of a minstrel guild. Similar documents had been prepared for Struan MacDhughaill, who was now known as Stefan the Black, and John van Elk, who had been renamed Hannes of Melk.

Gero was to follow in the footsteps of his dead uncle, and now bore the name Gerhard of Lichtenberg. Even Matthäus had not been left out, although he wasn't to be taken on the journey to France. Without protest, Roland had acknowledged him as his illegitimate son, lending him his name so that his real heritage would remain hidden from the spies of Philipp IV. According to Gero's knowledge from the future, it was entirely likely that King Philip had sent spies to the German lands to search for members of the Order. Judging from experience, Nogaret's soldiers would not spare even a young boy from their gruesome torture methods if they thought he might know something of the whereabouts of the wanted Templars.

And there was something else that Gero had discussed only with his parents. If he didn't return, they were to raise the boy and see to it that he became a knight at the appropriate age. Gero was hunting for Matthäus to bid him farewell when he ran into his mother in the castle courtyard.

"What should we tell the boy if you don't return?" she asked quietly

"Tell him that I will always love him like a son, and that I am proud of him, no matter what he does," Gero replied hoarsely.

Jutta of Breydenbach could not hold back her tears. Sobbing, she laid her head on her son's chest.

"I'm sorry," she whispered as Gero held her tightly in his arms. "I didn't mean to cry."

"Don't worry," Gero said gently. "The Almighty will watch over us. He alone knows the right path for us."

Hannah stepped out into the courtyard wearing the light blue travel cloak that Gero had bought for her at Genovevaburg Castle. Matthäus was right, Gero thought. With her curly, chestnut hair peeping out of the hood, and her soft, dainty features, she looked like the mother of God herself.

The cold wind tore mercilessly at their cloaks and blew Hannah's hair into her face. She looked around, searching for something. When she spotted Gero, she gave him a fleeting smile.

Somehow, Gero felt naked without his beard. He and his two Brothers had shaved the day before. It was the last symbol of his membership in the Order. Since their argument, Hannah had been terse in her responses to him and had largely stayed out of his way. She still seemed to be offended that he had wanted to leave her behind at the castle, though she knew he had only meant her well. The fear that a terrible fate could befall her was far worse for him than any fear for his own death.

"What's going on with you and this woman?" his mother suddenly asked, noticing that he still hadn't torn his eyes away from Hannah.

"She has become a friend to me," he said without a second thought.

"A friend?" His mother smiled knowingly. "Has she let you into her bed?"

Blood flooded into Gero's cheeks. "Mother! You know I am a knight of the Order," he replied, sounding outraged.

"That doesn't answer my question."

"Please," he answered softly, gripping his mother's hands. "I don't want to lie to you."

"You couldn't possibly do that," she replied with a wistful smile. Out of the corner of her eye, she looked at Hannah, who was still standing indecisively in an archway. "Do you love her?"

Gero looked down uncomfortably. "Yes," he whispered.

"I will pray every day," his mother said, "that no harm will come to you and your friends. Remember that, wherever you are my son."

"We're ready," said a deep voice from behind them. Gero's father had entered the courtyard.

Gero nodded. With difficulty, he met his mother's gaze, but turned away again as if it were too much for him to bear. He walked over to Hannah and offered her his arm before leading her to the stables.

Richard of Breydenbach, Geros brother Eberhard , and Roland of Briey accompanied them to the secluded farmyard where Gero and his friends would change into their minstrels' costumes. But unlike other traveling artistes and troubadours, they were secretly armed to the teeth, ready to fend off attackers at any moment.

Knowing that she might never see the castle in its magnificent state again, Hannah gazed at it one last time. Struan rode ahead with shoulders slumped, his face stony. His pregnant lover had not come out to the courtyard to bid him a last goodbye. Hannah watched Gero drive his Percheron forward to the sullen-looking Scotsman and pat him sympathetically on the shoulder as he rode by.

Their journey led them through a rugged valley and up onto a dusty farm path bordered by harvested fields. Thick morning mist hung over them, and only the dull plodding of hooves and the squawking of the crows broke through the ghostly silence. Hannah was getting used to the fact that in this world, horses were necessary for every significant journey and she patted the neck of her well-behaved mare appreciatively. Suddenly, a stone-gray horse appeared next to her, and with an imperious snort, the mighty Jutlander demanded her attention. Lost in her thoughts, Hannah was startled at the sound, and when she looked up, she noticed the rider on the imposing cold blood. It was Johan van Elk, who was regarding her with interest.

"I didn't mean to scare you," he said apologetically. "I just wanted to ask you some questions."

Hannah smiled at him. Although he spoke an unusual dialect, which was different from Gero's Moselle-Frankish, she could still understand him fairly well.

"Be my guest," she replied with an encouraging nod to dispel the shyness that, despite his fearsome appearance, he displayed when he was alone with her.

"I'd like to ask … do you like it here?" Johan said quietly, looking around to make sure that no one could hear their conversation.

"What do you mean?" she asked in surprise.

"Not this horrible situation that we're in, nobody likes that, of course," he hurried to add. "I mean … is it very different where you're from … in the future?"

"A little," she answered vaguely.

He narrowed his eyes. "I wish I could imagine what it was like," he said.

"It's definitely not as beautiful as it is here," Hannah began. "The divine quietness here is unique, and you have different animals. The pigs we have are almost naked. The aurochs have died out, and wolves and bears only live in remote areas, or else they're locked up in enclosures. And the air is seldom so fresh and sweet-smelling. Even the stars in your night sky are brighter than ours. Where I come from, there are unbelievable noises roaring from every corner. There are machines everywhere, even in the sky. And I've only realized how badly it stinks since I've been here. I used to think it would be the reverse."

"It stinks here, too," Johan replied in astonishment. "Just wait for winter, and then you won't be able to ride through a village without smelling the stench of burnt wood and peat." He gave her a crooked smile. "Somehow I thought that life where you came from might be better than it is here. Isn't it?"

"No," Hannah replied, surprising herself at how quickly this answer came to her lips. "Life is easier in some aspects, but certainly not in all aspects, not by far. Although we have eradicated several illnesses, we have in their place numerous new ones that are no less terrible than their predecessors. And there are other things that haven't changed at all."

Johan looked pointedly at Gero who was leading the cavalcade and, at the moment, deep in conversation with Roland and Anselm.

The knight's good-natured eyes lit up as he looked at Hannah again. "How about men and women? Are things the same as they are here? I mean … do they desire, love, and marry one other?"

Hannah smiled in amusement. "Hopefully nothing about that will ever change, although I'm surprised that you're asking me a question like that."

"Why are you surprised?" he asked hesitantly, and Hannah had the feeling that he had misunderstood her.

"Well," she answered slowly, "I'm surprised that a knight of the Order, of all people, is asking me such a question. I'm afraid I had a completely different impression of men like you and Gero."

Johan tilted his head. "And what was that?"

"I didn't think you would be so … normal," Hannah began with a smile, but quickly became serious when she saw how important her answer was to him. "Besides, I thought that women didn't feature in your lives.

My image of a crusader was a man whose only concern was the unconditional fulfillment of his duty, praying and killing in the name of the Lord, without thinking too much about it."

"You thought we were cruel and dim-witted?" He looked horrified. "What made you think that? Did you have bad experiences with us? Did one of us harm you?"

"No, no," she said hurriedly. "I'm sorry. I hope I didn't say anything wrong."

With a sigh, Johan shook his head. "You're not the only one who has these prejudices against us. But none of it is true." His voice became emphatic. "There are always a few black sheep, but they are simply aberrations. We have strict rules that we normally follow. And if one of us looks at a pretty girl," he added with a smile, "surely that isn't a sin against the Lord, right?"

"No," Hannah said. She was riding close enough to Johan to touch his left arm. "I didn't mean it like that, either. I like you and your Brothers very much."

"And I you," he said, squeezing his horse's flanks so that the mighty animal suddenly dashed forward.

After a short journey they arrived at a pine grove where a barn and three stately timber-framed houses stood. Before they reached the main gate, the men sprang off their horses and walked towards a portly old man who greeted them courteously.

As Gero had told Hannah earlier, the wagon and horses would be exchanged here. The precious battle-steeds bore the brand mark of the Templars, and they had been advised to travel with special horses bred to handle long journeys.

Gero and his comrades exchanged their fine surcoats for everyday clothing and harnessed four new horses. Three more horses were tied to the wagon in case any of the other horses became tired or went lame.

As the men headed into the house to get provisions for the journey and hay for the animals, Hannah looked around. Suddenly, Anselm was standing next to her.

"What are you looking for?" he asked.

"Nothing," Hannah said hurriedly. "I just wanted to take a look around. Every day here is a new experience for me."

"Tell me about it," Anselm agreed. "But all I want to know now is where the bathroom is."

470

"Go ask Gero," Hannah responded. "This place belongs to the Breydenbachs, after all. He would probably know where you can relieve yourself."

Without another word, Anselm marched away towards the house.

Hannah promptly resumed her search and discovered Matthäus between the chicken coop and the beehive.

"Quick," she called to the boy in a cautious voice, hastily pulling him to the wagon that would be their home for the time being. The structure had stable wooden walls, and with the colorful garlands and drapery that adorned two small windows, it resembled a circus wagon. The low entrance was located in the back of the wagon. Everything they needed for the journey was stored there: clothing, tents, blankets, entertainers' props … and beneath were deadly weapons, stored in a hidden space beneath the wooden planks. Immediately after their arrival, Gero had hidden the timeserver in the same place, and Hannah had seen that there was just enough space remaining for a stowaway.

Matthäus looked appalled when he saw how narrow his hiding place was.

"If you have to pee, do it now," advised Hannah, who was feeling just as nervous as the boy.

Matthäus shook his head and pursed his lips, then slipped into the narrow gap. His face looked fearful as Hannah lowered the wooden boards back over him.

"I'll let you out as soon as we're far enough away that they can't send you back," she promised. "Also, I'll lift up the boards every now and then so you can get some fresh air."

That evening, they were about two miles away from St. Mihiel, when Matthäus could no longer take his narrow enclosure and made his presence known through shouts and banging. Finally, Hannah relented to his pleas to be let out of his hiding place.

Gero, who was sitting on the coachman's bench, abruptly stopped when he noticed the commotion in the wagon behind him.

"Both of you must be mad," he bellowed from a small window, through which he could see into the interior of the wagon from the coachman's seat.

Hannah whirled around in shock. To her horror, Gero stormed into the wagon a second later, seized the boy by his hair, and pulled his head back against the nape of his neck.

"What should I do with you, huh?" The Templar's face flared red with fury, and his eyes blazed terrifyingly. "I should thrash you until you can no longer walk. And then I should send you home, on foot, so that you can think about what an idiot you are for every damn mile you walk!"

"Let him go!" Hannah yelled in outrage, shaking Gero's arm. "Don't you see that you're hurting him?"

"I don't know what you're doing, woman," Gero replied darkly. "You're in league with him, aren't you? If he is hurt or killed, it will have been *you* who lured him into danger."

Hannah took a deep breath and squared her shoulders before she addressed Gero once again.

"How can you send him home when he doesn't even know where his home is?" she demanded

Gero snorted scornfully, but at least he let the boy's hair go. Tears welled up in Matthäus' eyes, not from pain, but from shame and sorrow.

Johan had come down into the wagon as well. Hannah could see that he felt sorry for Matthäus, but still, he didn't say a word.

Gero glared at Hannah with a hostile expression. "You have absolutely no idea, woman," he snarled, "what danger you've placed the boy in. If your life isn't worth anything to you, that's your own concern, but I am responsible for Matthäus. He has no identification papers with him. At every damn checkpoint that we go through, we'll be trapped in tedious explanations of who he is and where he comes from. If Nogaret's secret police are looking for him, his life will be in danger, and you had better not think that the Gens du Roi will refrain from torturing him just because he is still a child!"

A little later, Gero stopped the wagon and chose a place some distance away from the road to set up camp for the night. They couldn't enter the safety of the city walls because they needed to avoid the city's sentries. Instead, they would have to take turns keeping watch that night.

Johan lit a fire from the supply of beech logs they had brought with them. The wagon provided some privacy from the road, where fewer and fewer riders and horse carts appeared as the evening wore on. They had to make do with a few sheepskins and blankets for comfort. Bread, wine, and cheese were passed around, but Gero didn't utter a word the entire time. He sat in the grass some distance away from Hannah, not dignifying her with a single glance. Finally, she couldn't stand it any longer. She rose silently and marched off into the darkness.

472

Anselm looked up, disturbed, unsure if he should follow her. Finally, it was Johan who stood up with a sigh and headed after her with his hand on his knife-belt.

Hannah recoiled in shock when he silently appeared next to her as she was sitting under an old oak tree.

"It's me, Johan," he said in a whisper, laying a reassuring hand on her shoulder. "Did I scare you again?"

"Don't worry about it," she answered.

Johan could tell from her voice that she had been crying. He sat next to her and felt for her hand. He squeezed it gently.

"He didn't mean it so harshly," he said gently. "He's afraid, just like the rest of us. He's worried for you, and now for Matthäus, too."

"I couldn't leave the boy behind," Hannah defended herself. "I know how dearly he clings to Gero."

"You've really warmed to him, haven't you?"

"Who?"

Johan burst out laughing. "Both of them. The lord and his squire."

"Am I that obvious?"

"I may be just a knight of the Order, but I still recognize love between two people."

"Is there by any chance someone who's sharpened your senses?" Although it was dark, she could hear from Johan's sheepish cough that she had hit her mark.

"Yes," he said quietly. "She even lives near here."

"Why don't you go to her?" Hannah asked.

"First, it is too dangerous, and second, it wouldn't be right to draw her into this mess. Besides, it makes no sense for us to see each other again. She belongs to the Order of the Beguines, and I am still a Templar knight. What would become of us?"

"Don't you think it's worth it to fight for love?"

"I don't know..." he answered evasively, and pulled her to her feet. "Come. We should head back."

CHAPTER 36

St. Mihiel

Saturday, October 28, 1307

The next morning, Hannah awoke to hear a few fragments of Old French from outside the wagon. She didn't have time to get up before the wagon door opened and Gero climbed in. Carefully, he stepped over her and the boy who had moved closer to her during the night. While he searched through a pile of clothes she pretended she was asleep.

Opening her eyes very slightly, Hannah saw Gero lovingly stroking Matthäus's head and, sensing that he was looking at her, she couldn't bring herself to deceive him anymore. To her surprise, he bent down and kissed her gently on the forehead.

"To hell with this," Gero said, suddenly standing up and giving a deep sigh. He turned away from her, pulled a jingling pouch out of his leather bag and went outside without another word.

"Johan will ride to Saint Mihiel this morning to survey the area," Gero announced when he returned to the campfire where the rest were having their breakfast. "We can't go in if the city is teeming with French soldiers. We will have to find another place we can cross the Meuse without a bridge."

It was still early, and cold mist was swirling despite the bright morning sun. Already on their way to the city, traders and farmers drove past them with loud rattling carts pulled by oxen and mules.

"May I accompany Johan?" Anselm looked at Gero who was warming his hands on a steaming cup of wine.

"Fine with me," Gero said. "If he agrees."

"Why would I object?" Johan asked innocently, before biting into a piece of dark rye bread.

"You are not to let him out of your sight at any time," Gero insisted. "The world he knows is completely different from ours." He took the ladle and poured some more of the warm red wine into his tin cup before sitting down next to Johan. "Most importantly, make sure you stay clear of any sort of conflict. Anselm has no idea how quickly things can escalate into a fight."

"I think I'll just buy some bread and look around a little," Johan replied after washing down his last bite with a gulp of red wine. "What could go wrong?"

He stood up and stored his cup in a leather bag lying on the floor. Finally he picked up his saddle that had served as his pillow the night before, and turned to face the horses grazing near the wagon.

"Come along, *compagnon*," he said, smiling at Anselm encouragingly. "We're going on an excursion."

Anselm knew Saint Mihiel – in the twenty-first century. With its imposing church that stood in the central square, the medieval version seemed, surprisingly, only slightly smaller than its modern counterpart. In fact, the city center in the year 1307 was far livelier. After they had shown the guard their documents and passed the toll station, they entered a colorful Oriental bazaar.

Johan handed the horses over to an exchange stable, where, for a few small coins, they would be watched over and given hay. Wooden market stalls had been set up everywhere, offering fresh vegetables and fruit: mostly turnips, cabbage, and apples at this time of year. In another small street, mountains of freshly slaughtered meat had been laid out in piles, neatly chopped and sorted by size. With a fly swatter, the butcher's wife struggled to shoo away the many flies buzzing near the meat. At the side of the stall were the less appetizing parts, whole lungs still attached to windpipes, tripe, and pig and sheep heads on iron hooks hanging from wooden rods. Underneath them stood earthen bowls filled with innards. It was not just the ghastly sight, but the stench, that left Anselm gasping for breath.

Strange-looking figures were loitering about between the stalls. They were dressed in rags, and wore odd metallic badges on long cords around their dirty necks.

"Who are they?" Anselm looked at Johan for an answer.

"Beadsmen," Johan snorted. "Don't tell me you don't have such people? I always wonder how they manage to exploit the merchants' benevolence. See the badges they wear? Each one stands for a visit to a pilgrimage site far away. None of them ever dreams of pursuing a reputable job. Instead, they promise that they'll put in a good word for their patrons with the numerous saints whose holy sites they visit."

As if on command, one of the butchers threw a pig's eye to a waiting beadsman who caught it skillfully and promptly popped it into his mouth. He tossed the second eye to another pleading man and to the other men who were stretching out their hands beseechingly, he handed large pieces of fat.

Anselm was struck so suddenly by the urge to retch that he could hardly suppress the reflex. Johan, who had noticed that Anselm was feeling sick, quickly pulled him into a side street where bakers were peddling their wares.

Suddenly, somewhere in the thick crowd around the stalls, a commotion broke out.

"Hold on to her!" bellowed a red-cheeked man as he shoved his way through the crowd with his fat potbelly.

He grabbed the long red hair of a young woman and yanked her around brutally. She howled miserably and was trying in vain to free herself when a second man hit her hard in the face.

"She is a thief," croaked a toothless old woman from beneath her dirty, once-white headdress.

Thrashing about wildly, the young woman tried to defend herself from the blows.

"To the pillory with her!" yelled a third man from one of the neighboring stands.

"What does that mean?" Anselm whispered. He felt adrenaline surge into his veins when one of the men brandished a long knife and set it against the woman's sumptuous breasts.

Johan did not reply. Instead, he elbowed his way forward to the unfortunate maiden. Onlookers turned around indignantly as he pushed them aside, but fell silent when they noticed his scarred face and his imposing stature.

"Let the woman go!" he boomed, withdrawing a cutlass that he had hidden under his brown leather doublet.

The baker recoiled, and even the man with the knife momentarily let the girl go. Anselm glanced around nervously. His heart pounded furiously when he noticed another man behind Johan pull out his knife. As if in a trance, his hand felt for his belt and found the dagger that Roland had given him for close combat. He silently crept behind the man. Lightly, he held his dagger under the man's left armpit. The man twitched and froze.

476

"Toss that thing away!" Anselm whispered into his surprised victim's ear.

His voice nearly failed him, and he was dizzy with disbelief when the man actually did as he was told. Johan hadn't noticed any of it, and Anselm wondered doubtfully if it had been a good idea to add to the chaos. The scarred Templar was still grimly eyeing the bickering merchants.

"She tried to steal my bread," the baker protested.

"I'm sure she wanted to buy it," Johan said in a calm, deep voice as he slowly lowered his cutlass.

"She has no money at all," the old woman with the dirty wimple shrieked. "Just look at her. She's in rags and tatters. How could she pay for it? In services?"

Ugly laughter rang out as the baker made a lewd gesture behind the old woman.

"What does she owe you?" yelled Johan above the noise.

"Nothing," said the baker, who still had his eye fixed on the blade that the disfigured man held. "She just touched the bread rolls."

Johan snorted contemptuously and threw him a coin. "That should cover the touching," he snarled.

With one hand, the Templar seized the young woman's slender upper arm and pulled her along with him. She was too dazed to protest. From afar, two city guards, who seemed to have been alerted by the commotion, were approaching.

"Let's go," he whispered to Anselm as he walked past him. He was surprised at how readily the pretty redhead let Johan steer her away.

In front of a tavern, not far from where the altercation had taken place, they finally stopped.

"Johan," the young woman suddenly gasped. She gulped back her tears and threw her arms around his neck in relief. "Heaven sent you! I thought you were already in the German lands."

Johan pulled her closer and pressed his lips to hers. With their eyes shut, the two of them remained in this position until he reluctantly let go, but the young woman slung her arms around his neck again, pushing herself against him as if trying to make their separate bodies one.

Anselm gaped at them in confusion. How could it be that every Order knight he had met had a relationship with a woman?

"Allow me to introduce you to someone," Johan said a little later, nodding at Anselm. "This is my friend, Anselmo de Caillou. Anselmo, this is Lady Freya of Bogenhausen."

Anselm greeted the woman with a slight bow, although he was puzzled by the fact that neither her clothing nor the pitiful plight they had found her in bore any hint of her supposed nobility.

Instead of buying bread, Johan took them into a guesthouse. Anselm watched in fascination as Freya of Bogenhausen devoured several portions of beef stew. While chewing and swallowing incessantly, she recounted her story.

After she and her Beguine sisters had helped Gero and his comrades escape, the soldiers of the French King had stormed the cloister.

All the women were arrested and sent to Troyes, except for the three who had helped the Templars escape through the underground catacombs. Upon their return, they found that the soldiers had burned the entire abbey to the ground, and residents of the surrounding area were far too fearful of the King's revenge for them to take in any of the women. The two other Sisters who had accompanied the Templars into the tunnel had been able to find shelter with their relatives, but Freya had neither kin nor acquaintance for miles around. She fled into the city to search for ways to travel to Metz or Trier, where she could find shelter with another Beguine community.

"They were looking everywhere for escaped Templars," she whispered to Johan conspiratorially, mopping up the rest of the dark sauce from her plate with a piece of bread. "I don't know if it's brave or stupid that you've come back." She stared at him as she shoved the last bite into her mouth. "This place is crawling with French spies."

"It is fate," Johan replied with a dreamy smile, looking into her green eyes.

"Fate," Freya repeated thoughtfully, and took a sip of the red wine from the pitcher he had ordered.

"Come with me," he said, taking her hand. "I'll do everything I can to protect you."

"I'll believe you," she answered with a mischievous smile. Nodding at Anselm, she continued, "but what will your Brothers say about you dragging along a Beguine on the run, who, without her papers, has been forced to scrape by like a common woodlouse?"

Anselm could guess what the pretty woman was getting at. "Is there a shop here where someone can purchase writing materials?" he asked Johan suddenly.

"Why are you asking?" Johan asked in surprise.

"There's a Jew who sells paper and parchment. He lives down by the river," Freya told them. "He mixes ink and peddles goose quills, too."

"Good," Anselm decided. "I also need red and yellow sealing wax, and fine tools, a small hammer and a very small chisel. Oh, and lead."

"What on earth are you planning?" Johan wrinkled his forehead.

"Well," Anselm began, "you lack documents. We can forge those quite easily. Back where I'm from, I'm known for copying seals and old writings. It would be easy for me to reproduce a document. I just have to know what it should look like."

Freya pushed her wooden plate aside and leaned forward, gazing into Anselm's eyes. "What was your name again?" she asked sarcastically. "I didn't know there were forgers and fraudsters among the Templars. I doff my cap to you, sir – we can still learn a thing or two from you."

"He isn't a Templar," Johan answered a touch too quickly, but when he saw Anselm's disappointed face, he added, "but he is still an honorable man, who very much wants to help us."

"Well, then," Anselm said, smiling conciliatorily, "what are we waiting for?"

Stealthy as a fox, Freya slipped out of the city. Under the bridge, where the riverbank was overgrown with reeds, she took off her shoes, held them in her hand, and gathered up her dress. Then she waded through the Meuse, icy cold water lapping at her thighs.

The guards at the gate had their backs turned as Anselm and Johan paid the export toll for their bread, grain, cheese, and fresh beer. They had hidden their other purchases under their clothes.

All three met up again near the bridge. Johan heaved a sigh of relief that Freya had remained undiscovered and pulled her up onto his horse. Anselm noticed the red-haired Templar closing his eyes for one blissful moment when the girl nestled herself against his chest as she sat in front of him in the saddle.

"Who do we have here, then?" Gero exclaimed when he saw whom Johan had returned with.

Quickly he scrambled up from the spot at the campfire where he was roasting on the spit a few trout he had caught. Struan, on the other hand, glanced up for only a moment before continuing to sharpen the blade of his broadsword with a grindstone.

"So, we meet again," Freya replied, tossing back her flaming red hair after Johan had helped her down from the horse. With a smile, she walked up to Gero. "I thought you had reached safety long ago," she continued. "But now it seems you've all gone mad, and are walking right back into hell."

Gero examined Freya from head to toe, shocked by her ragged appearance.

"Looking at you, I'm afraid you may be right," he replied half joking. "What happened to you?"

Quickly Freya recounted what had happened to her.

"I'm so sorry," he said regretfully when she had finished her story. "It's our fault that you've had such misfortune."

"Save your sympathy for yourself and your own men," Freya said solemnly. "Heralds are announcing the arrest of your Brothers everywhere, and notices are fastened to every church door that anyone who helps a Templar escape or hide will pay heavily."

Freya looked around and noticed Hannah sitting some distance away under the shade of an oak tree, obviously listening attentively. With a suspicious look, Freya examined the unknown woman, and finally gave her a friendly nod.

"If Philipp's soldiers catch you," she continued, "they will flay and quarter every one of you, men and women alike."

Gero sighed, pleased that Hannah couldn't understand French. "There is no way back for us. We have a mission to fulfill. But if we can help you find a safe refuge first, we'll gladly do so."

His eyes fell on the holes in Freya's surcoat. "Perhaps you could use some money? Or a few new clothes?"

A smile played on Freya's lips. "If you don't have anything against it, I'd be happy to join you. Ultimately, we share the same enemy." With a yearning glance at Johan, which escaped no one's attention, she continued, "I heard you want to disguise yourselves as minstrels in order to enter the fortress of Chinon and free your comrades. Believe me, I know what to do. If you really want to distract the soldiers at the fortress, you need dancers who can move with absolutely no trace of shame – or you can forget about all your plans now."

Struan stepped forward, breaking his silence for the first time on their journey. "And you know how one can accomplish that?"

Freya gave the Scotsman a broad smile. "Two years with a troupe of traveling musicians and one year in a well-managed house of pleasure in Cologne should be enough to learn how to make a man lose his mind."

Struan froze for a moment with his mouth hanging open, and Johan, who had been drinking from a goatskin, developed such a mighty coughing fit that his Scottish comrade had to pound him on the back.

"You've convinced me," Gero said with a smile. "But be warned! Know that this may cost us our heads."

"Why would that scare me?" Freya said with a sad smile. "I've already lost everything in life that one can possibly lose." Suddenly she looked up again and turned to face Johan who hadn't taken his eyes off her the entire time. "Let's just say that I'm following my heart. And as you know, there is no price too high to pay for that."

Late that afternoon, Anselm hunkered down over a wooden board in the wagon. With a quill in his hand, and biting his lip in concentration, he scribbled nonstop over the parchment that he had spread out on the board. "I need more sealing wax," he said after he had inscribed the last stroke with a flourish, and stretched out his hand without looking up. Johan handed him the small, heated iron pan of liquid wax.

Gero stared in amazement as the man from the future produced a document of similar quality to the writs of escort his father had procured. The certificates from the minstrels' guild gave Freya and Matthäus each their own identities and certified their authorization to be employed as jongleurs.

"Perfect," Johan declared in amazement as he eyed the results that had been laid out to dry. "Someone like you would be welcomed into the Order with open arms."

Anselm beamed. One could not have given him a higher compliment.

"Now we just have to wait and see whether the guards are as enthusiastic," Gero remarked. "Mattes, hitch the horses!" he yelled.

With that, the troupe set off for Saint Mihiel.

CHAPTER 37

Thomas of Hemmenrode

Sunday, November 28, 2004

"Damn it all," Tom swore as he hurried down the hallway lined with fluorescent lighting toward the laboratory. "The last thing we need is a Cistercian monk from the year 1221. Why couldn't he have at least come from 1307?"

"Well," said Professor Hertzberg, who was struggling to keep up with the scientist's long strides. "At least now we know that the machine works. And if I'm being honest, you've done me a huge favor with the appearance of this young man." A broad smile spread across the Jewish historian's face.

"That's probably true for you, since you're interested in anything that comes from the past," Tom answered slowing down his pace. "But for the poor guy inside there, it's a nightmare. I'm not sure if he'll appreciate being interviewed right now."

"I just have a few harmless questions," Hertzberg reassured him. "Then you can safely throw that goldfish back into the water."

"That's the problem, though," Tom retorted agitatedly, pressing his thumb to a scanner on the wall to activate the automatic door. "I don't have the faintest idea if it will work. If we actually manage to send him back, that would mean, for one, that my friend and her companions have arrived in the past safe and sound, and that we can also retrieve them with the timeserver. But for now, we have no idea how and why it's brought this person here."

Thomas of Hemmenrode sat in dazed silence on the white-tiled floor of an isolated cell. With his back to the wall, the twenty-year-old had retreated into the furthest corner of the room. He had lowered his tonsured head so far that his nose almost touched his knees.

As the door to his spartan cell opened with a hiss, he recoiled in fear.

"Has anyone offered him something to eat or drink?" Hertzberg asked. The young man in his sterile surroundings reminded him of his childhood, when he had trapped insects in mason jars just to find out how long they could survive in there without air or nourishment.

"No," a female voice rang out from behind. "After he told us his name, age, ancestry, and the year he came from, in his initial confusion, he became agitated and rejected all food and water. As long as his vital signs stay stable, we don't have to worry."

"Do you think I can ask him a few questions?" Hertzberg said to Dr. Karen Baxter, who was responsible for the research subject's medical care.

"Of course. I'll administer some of our truth serum," the attractive scientist smiled. "It's made everyone talk. Still, I've called in a few of our strongest men, in the unlikely event that the visitor develops superhuman powers."

Two marines were standing at the door brandishing sophisticated looking tasers. Dr. Baxter brushed past the shorter historian as she approached the time traveler with a device that resembled a futuristic space-age pistol.

With a soft hiss, she injected the truth serum into the monk from the thirteenth century and a shudder ran through his bony body. The serum, normally only used on stubborn prisoners of war, was guaranteed to make him talk.

Readily, the monk reported that he had come from the Himmerod Abbey in 1221. He had been in the woods gathering wormwood, which was used by the Order's own hospital to cure various maladies.

Hertzberg's knowledge of Yiddish allowed him to understand the man from the Middle Ages effortlessly. He was amazed as the young monk asked repeatedly about the Last Judgment, obviously believing that, at the sight of the white-haired Hertzberg, he was sitting opposite from St. Peter who expected him at the heaven's gate.

Hertzberg tried to tell the monk that he had little in common with Peter, but Thomas immediately asked again if he was in purgatory, or worse, hell. He had not recovered from the shocking change in his surroundings, and he burst out periodically in crying fits, white foam forming in the corners of his mouth.

"We can't tax him too much," Karen said after Thomas of Hemmenrode had slumped down in exhaustion. "His pulse is climbing steadily," she remarked, turning her attention to one of the surveillance screens in the control room. "We should tranquilize him before he has a heart attack. Otherwise we run the danger of a psychotic episode when he finds out more about the circumstances that brought him here. Besides, I don't think it's good for him to find out too much about the twenty-first century before he returns home."

"What, you think he'll invent the bicycle?" Hertzberg burst out laughing.

"No," Karen Baxter retorted with a solemn expression. "I'm afraid the poor man will face difficulties when he shares his experiences from the future with his medieval peers."

"Give the monk something so that he sleeps through this catastrophe," Tom said to Karen. "In the meantime, Paul and I will find a way to send him back where he came from."

CHAPTER 38

St. Martin's Day

Saturday, November 11, 1307
Chinon, France

When Gero and his companions reached the city of Chinon on the morning of November 11, 1307, they had already completed a strenuous, fourteen-day journey through the cities of Troyes, Orleans, and Tours. As Anselm remarked, they could have covered the 60 medieval miles, or 400 modern miles, with a car and modern roads in a day.

Anselm grew increasingly fascinated by the Templars' relatively sophisticated transport system, and, more and more, he began to question if anyone from the twenty-first century could imagine how well organized the so-called dark Middle Ages were. At regular intervals, they passed exchange stables, which gave the numerous messengers an opportunity to exchange horses and letters. More than a few of the couriers traveling were wearing the blue and yellow tabard of the French King. There were also countless guesthouses where one could spend the night or purchase cake, meat pies, and soup, more delicious by far than the wares offered by contemporary street food vendors.

Fortunately for the travelers, they didn't have to fear hunger or thirst as Gero's father had given them enough silver to last their entire journey. They had even been able to afford exchanging their exhausted draft horses several times for new, well-rested ones, and paying the bribes to pass through toll and way stations without difficulty.

Even before the tall fortress walls of Chinon appeared on the horizon, Gero led the troupe away from the cobbled main street of Tours and down a bumpy path to the banks of the river Vienne.

A smile flitted across Gero's lips when he saw the slow, meandering stream gleaming in the golden morning sun. The knowledge that they had safely arrived at their destination filled him with relief, despite the dangers to come. His eyes fixed on his goal, he steered the wagon down towards a small building attached like a swallow's nest to the base of the fortress. As he had done throughout the rest of the journey, Gero made a detour

485

around the local Templar commandery that stood near the St. Mexme Abbey outside the city walls of Chinon.

It was St. Martin's Day, the day when St. Martin of Tours was celebrated in France, and also the day when taxes and duties were counted.

The wagon lurched to a sudden stop as Gero navigated into the inevitable traffic jam in front of the imposing city gates. Anyone who wanted to enter the fortified part of Chinon had to undergo an extensive security check here. In a small station with a wooden roof, uniformed men collected money and recorded the names of visitors to the fortified city on ell-long scrolls of parchment.

"Where are you going?" the guard asked impatiently as Gero stepped forward to register the wagon and its passengers.

"To the castle," he answered in a monotone.

"How many are you?" asked the man.

"Seven."

The guard scribbled something on the coarse parchment. "Names?"

In a patient voice, Gero gave him the names of all the travelers.

"Documents?"

Under the guard's watchful eyes, Gero sorted through a heap of parchments and papers, like a child holding too many playing cards in their tiny hand. But with some finesse, Gero managed to fan out the documents in his hand without dropping a single one. Among the documents were a few expired passes from cities they had passed through, which they used as proof of their integrity.

"Weapons?" The guard looked cuttingly at Gero when he didn't answer right away.

"We are jongleurs," Gero explained with an expression of innocence. "We need swords and daggers for our performances. In any case, the blades are too blunt to be used in battle," he lied.

The guard wrote something down and glanced at the colorful vehicle one last time. "You may pass," he said, waving them through.

They entered the city alongside farmers and merchants. The procession of humans, horses, oxen, and wagons meandered through the narrow lanes.

Hannah crouched by the window inside the wagon, studying her surroundings intently. She held her breath for a moment as a herd of bleating goats squeezed through the narrow space between the wagons and the walls of the houses lining the lane. Now and then, she saw flashes of brilliant blue sky between the gaps in the gables, and, if she stuck her head out a little further, she could even see the castle of Chinon above the houses: whitewashed towers and roofs of smooth, black slate gleaming in the morning sun.

Gero brought the wagon to a halt in front of a narrow, multistoried, timber-framed building. An ornate wooden sign with the inscription *Ad Stellam* – To The Star – hung above its front doors.

Johan rode up to the front of the wagon. "What are you doing?" he said, eyeing Gero, who had stood up and was looking around the establishment.

"I will inquire if we can spend the night. I want Hannah, Anselm, and Matthäus to wait for us here, at least until we have an idea of how dangerous our plans are."

"What's going on?" asked Anselm, riding forward to join them.

"Our commander has decided," Johan answered, "that we should seek accommodation for the night here, and that you, your sister, and the boy should wait for us here until it becomes clear how we can best execute our plans."

Anselm shook his head in disbelief. Seeing Gero heading to the back of the wagon to open the door, he abruptly turned his horse around in the narrow street.

"What is this shit?" he gasped, staring at Gero angrily. "'Our commander has decided'? Just yesterday, the plan was to head to the castle together."

Gero stopped and turned to face him. "It'd be best if you did what I tell you," he threatened.

"And what if I refuse? I want to go to the castle with you. Did you really think I'd miss out on that?"

"Do you know what a command is?" Struan cut in.

"I thought we all had the same rights," Anselm retorted gruffly.

"If you want to win a battle, there can only be one leader, or you've been badly counseled," Struan explained in a firm voice.

Gero ignored Anselm's stormy expression and turned to open the wagon door, but just then, the door burst open, and Freya nearly crashed into him on the wooden steps.

"Is there trouble among you boys?" she asked loudly.

"Tell Hannah to pack some of her things," Gero answered grumpily. "I want her to stay here in the guesthouse with Anselm and Matthäus until we return."

Freya folded her arms firmly across her chest. "Are you mad?" she retorted feistily. "Am I supposed to deal with the soldiers at the castle alone? I can't do this without Hannah. Even though she doesn't speak French, she is beautiful. She won't just draw the guards' attention, but the officers', too. We'll need her help if we want to lure one in and weasel out information about the dungeons."

Gero sighed. "Very well," he grumbled, "but watch out for her. But the boy must stay here with Anselm."

Madame Fouchet, the innkeeper of *Ad Stellam*, looked exactly as Hannah had imagined the typical madam of a brothel to be, advanced in age, buxom, with purple-red cheeks, and a heavy layer of make-up. Madame Fouchet wore a surcoat with deep slits in the sleeves. Despite the cold weather, she wasn't wearing undergarments, granting her guests an unobstructed view of her wrinkled breasts. The white wimple that covered her thinning hair could not offset her otherwise questionable appearance.

"This is a pleasure house," Johan muttered quietly to Gero. "Do you really intend for us to spend our night's rest here? Not to mention the fact that we'll be leaving the boy behind in this den of sin?"

"Anselm will look out for him when we're at the castle," Gero answered simply.

"Ah, you want to go to the castle," crowed Madame Fouchet, who had caught the end of Gero's words.

Gero whipped the hood off his head and executed such a gallant bow that Struan found it hard to suppress a grin.

"Madame ..." Gero paused, "could you provide us with one or two simple rooms for a night's rest? We would be of no inconvenience to you."

"Of course," the old woman grunted, planting her hands on her ample hips. "I've no customers at the moment, anyway." Quickly she eyed the members of the strange troupe. When she saw Struan, she licked her lips lustfully, and a suggestive grin spread across her aged face when her eyes landed on Hannah and Freya.

"The soldiers will certainly be glad of some variety," she explained. "They haven't been able to leave for weeks. There are always either new captives marching in or important visits being announced. If this lunacy continues, all my business will be gone."

488

"What lunacy?" Gero asked in a deliberately innocent voice.

"Why, the Templars' arrest of course!" the old woman cried in amazement. "Don't tell me you haven't heard about it? Philipp of France has ordered all Templars to be arrested. Rumor has it that some of them are sitting behind bars up in the castle." Madame Fouchet winked at Gero knowingly. "The Templars are said to be sodomites," she whispered conspiratorially, and then burst into a sudden bout of laughter. "As if I didn't know any better! But I can't imagine that that would be the only reason to arrest them," she continued in a more hushed tone. "Apparently, they're harboring a secret. Idol worship, I hear. And our King is hell-bent on discovering the truth." Madame Fouchet flattened her garishly painted lips into a thin, blood-red line. "Don't tell anyone that you heard this from me," she hissed. "But one of my girls told me a few things after she was with one of the nobles. You wouldn't believe what secrets men spill in their ecstasy. They even pride themselves on the fact that they torture their prisoners for all they're worth. Those deviant dogs! Up there in the castle, they make life hell for respectable men, and down here with me, they yearn for the whip."

Having promised not to leave the guesthouse, a still resentful Anselm escorted Matthäus into one of the small, narrow rooms in *Ad Stellam*. Taking care of the boy was not his only task. Gero had also handed him the Head of Wisdom, with the instruction that if anything befell the rest of the group, he should immediately return to Breydenburg Castle with the boy and entrust themselves to Gero's father until there was news.

Gero and his companions made their way up to the castle with the wagon and horses. When they arrived at the top of the mountain, Freya sprang down nimbly from the colorful wagon. In her billowing, turquoise surcoat that sinfully displayed her breasts, she strode, light on her feet, to the soldiers who were guarding the main gates of the castle. Her long, red hair swung in tandem with her steps, and the bells sewn onto the hem of her skirt complemented her seductive appearance with a soft jingle.

The young soldier was initially so confused by the appearance of this sinfully beautiful creature that he didn't know where to look. Freya gave a peal of laughter, which only bewitched him even further, and after they had exchanged a few words, he let the peculiar looking troupe pass through the gates, completely forgetting to search the men for weapons.

In the inner courtyard of the royal castle, one of the places Philipp IV of France only stayed when he traveled south, they were greeted by loud shouts from a few bored-looking children.

Gero and his comrades were all too familiar with this less gloomy part of the fortress. They had rested here several times when they escorted the Pope on his way to Poitiers. Unlike the picturesque buildings and towers at the front of the compound, the western wing had massive cellar vaults and heavily fortified keeps. This was where the dungeon was housed. One had to cross a drawbridge over a deep, man-made trench to reach the western wing from the residential castle.

"You've come!" rejoiced the stocky steward, striding towards them with a jovial smile. His expression became brazen when he spied Hannah and Freya. "We have fifty men stationed here to guard the dungeon, and today, St. Martin's Day, is the perfect time to celebrate a little."

Hannah hadn't understood anything the middle-aged man said. Instead, she examined his exceptionally elegant outfit. He was wearing a dark green surcoat of fine velvet, embellished at the hems with gold lace. On nearly every finger was a large, flashy ring.

"What will you take as payment?" the steward asked Gero, whom he assumed to be the troupe's leader.

"A writ of escort with the royal seal would aid in our further travels," Gero replied. "After this we go to Poitiers, where we are to delight the court of the Pope."

The steward shook his head in surprise. "It's yours," he said without enthusiasm. "You really don't want any money?"

"Perhaps a little silver, too," Gero added to hide the fact that the writ of escort meant more to him than any treasure in this castle.

"What about room and board?"

"Don't trouble yourself," Gero said softly. "We're only here for one night and have already found a place to stay. Apart from that, a modest evening meal and a little hay for the horses should be enough."

"Excellent," replied the steward with a smile that revealed a few missing teeth. "If your performances don't disappoint, and your girls don't make a fuss, you'll even receive a bonus."

Gero clenched his fists in annoyance. Lord in heaven, why does every fool on earth think that a woman from a minstrel troupe is fair game? *he thought.*

Smiling, Freya stepped up to distract the steward from Gero's displeasure. "Rest assured, my lord. We will not disappoint you." Turning to look at Hannah, she asked, "Right?"

Freya had taken Hannah by the hand and smiled at her encouragingly. Hannah smiled back in confusion, while Gero could only suppress his disgust with effort.

"Very well," the steward declared, "you will perform just before sunset."

Dusk had already begun to fall. In the castle's great hall, a loud band of men had gathered in their various uniforms. The best seats, directly in front of the musicians and next to the few women, had been reserved for the soldiers in the black tabards and brown leather vests. At the back of the room, the royal guards in their blue and yellow tabards pushed and shoved to find their seats.

Gero's heart beat wildly as he plucked his lute to strike up the first song with Johan, who was alternately beating the drums and playing the hurdy-gurdy. Struan, who lacked any sort of musical talent, had been tasked with watching over the horses and wagon out in the sprawling courtyard.

Freya had appeared on a small, improvised stage in a gleaming green surcoat after the melody began. She was swaying with the rhythmic music like a belly dancer. She had slit her dress up to her hips and Johan looked down at the ground in agony when he noticed the men's lustful gazes fixed on the swell of her breasts and her firm thighs, which were exposed with every provocative gyration.

Unlike Freya, Hannah was determined to keep a low profile. She was glad that she had chosen an ocher-colored dress that didn't grant the men any lewd glimpses of her body. She wished that she could hide her face from the gawking audience with a veil, but Freya had only given her a net embroidered with pearls to tame her chestnut curls and frame her captivating beauty.

On the steward's orders, Hannah went around the hall and offered the guests, already drunk, candied fruit on a pewter plate, stoically enduring the soldiers' attempts to grab her bottom or touch her breasts. Occasionally, someone hissed a comment at her, and Hannah was only too glad that she couldn't understand anything.

The evening seemed to fly past, and even the gentle ballads that Gero played from time to time to calm the audience were met with rousing cheers.

In honor of St. Martin, and to raise the men's spirits even further, the castle steward had had dozens of geese slaughtered, which had been sizzling on huge spits since that afternoon. Between performances, servants distributed bread and meat to the boisterous crowd.

While Gero and Johan were encouraged to play more pieces for a dance, one of the soldiers dressed in brown and black approached Freya, who was still out of breath from her last performance, to offer her a cup of wine. *He is a good-looking guy,* Hannah thought, *perhaps in his midtwenties,* although it was difficult for her to guess the ages of people from this era.

"Madame," he said, flashing Freya a charming smile. Freya smiled back brightly, looking slightly relieved that her supposed victim was at least pleasant-looking. The young man bowed down to her, pushed her red hair aside, and whispered something in her ear.

Hannah's gaze fell on the soldier's curly, chin-length hair, and she was suddenly reminded of Tom. She constantly wondered what had happened to him and Paul, and whether the two of them were trying to bring her and Anselm back to future.

Smiling, Freya said something and pointed to Hannah, at which the soldier looked over and seemed to notice her for the first time. He grinned broadly and put two fingers between his lips. A loud, piercing whistle rang out over the music, and a few of the men nearby turned to where the noise had come from. The soldier signaled something over the throng of uniformed men, and then a tall blonde man broke away from the crowd.

Freya talked with both men for a minute, and they appeared to come to an agreement about something. Then she steered the two expectant-looking soldiers towards Hannah and introduced them.

"This is Pierre and Michel," she said casually. "Michel is from Lorraine," she continued, nodding at the blonde man, who was staring at Hannah from a pair of close-set blue eyes. "He speaks German. The two of them are captains of the Gens du Roi," she added solemnly, as if to emphasize the men's importance.

A little later, Hannah found herself at the exit with a second cup of wine in her hand. Michel wouldn't stop talking to her. He had been constantly edging closer to her, and couldn't keep his hands to himself. Without answering him, she searched around for Gero, but he was too far away and too busy with his performance to notice her pleading looks.

In confusion, Hannah saw Freya let Pierre cover her neck in kisses as they stood half-hidden in a corner of the room. Laughing, she eased herself away from her admirer and whispered something to him.

"We've decided to take a walk," Freya declared chirpily, pulling her companion over to Hannah. As Pierre conversed with Michel, Freya took the opportunity to explain her plans to Hannah.

"Don't worry," she whispered to her. "I've gotten what I wanted. He's showing me the dungeon."

"Don't leave me alone here," Hannah pleaded uneasily.

"Don't worry," Freya murmured. "I have to do this, or I don't know how else we'll find out where the Templars have been locked up. Nothing will happen to you if you stay here with Michel and keep him company. It won't occur to him to follow us."

Hannah tried to say something, but suddenly the blonde man from Lorraine was standing next to her announcing with a crooked smile that he wanted to accompany his comrade and Freya on their stroll, and that he would not do so without Hannah's presence.

It was clear that Freya wasn't thrilled by this suggestion, but she didn't have a reason to object, and, in any case, Pierre seemed just as enthused by this idea as his colleague.

The blonde soldier offered Hannah his arm, and reluctantly she allowed him to escort her outside into the damp, chilly night. Freya and Pierre walked ahead of them. The soldier had laid his arm around the Beguine's shoulder and played incessantly with her curly red hair.

"Where are we going?" Hannah asked the man from Lorraine after finally summoning her courage to speak to him in Middle High German.

"You have a strange dialect," he commented with a smirk. "Pierre suggested that we show you charming ladies some once-proud men."

Her steps echoed on the smooth cobblestones. Hannah felt her heart racing, and, in her anxiety, she struggled to breathe. Michel, who was barely taller than she was, gave her a puzzled look.

"Are we going too quickly for you?" he asked.

Hannah shook her head.

"We're nearly there," he remarked as he headed towards a rectangular arcade lit by numerous torches.

Now and then, a snappy greeting sounded from the defensive wall, but neither Pierre nor Michel acknowledged them. Although Hannah had put on her warm cloak, she felt an eerie coldness as she approached one of the archways that marked the gated entrance to the dungeon.

"Seigneurs!" the young guard cried in salute when he realized with a jolt that the two high-ranked officers had nearly discovered him napping.

"Open the gate, you moron," Pierre bellowed in a manner that ill-befitted his harmless appearance. Hannah shuddered.

Pierre took two torches from the wall and handed Michel the second before they headed toward a heavy, iron-plated oak door that opened as if pushed by an invisible hand.

After they passed a second nervous guard, they reached a long, torch-lit passageway that led to a gloomy cellar.

"Scared?" Michel asked mockingly when he saw Hannah hesitating to take the first step down the steep spiral staircase. It was not fear, however, but an almost unbearable nausea that was tormenting her. The place stank of shit and urine, but far worse was the sharp scent of blood and sweat that lingered in the air.

After a few more steps, her escort suddenly froze and turned around to face her with a broad grin. Almost playfully, he grabbed her hand and pulled her towards him. "If you're afraid, you can hold on tight," he whispered, planting a quick kiss on her lips. She drew back in horror. It was not just his brazen behavior that alarmed her, but also the fact that the idiot had nearly singed her hair with his torch.

"What is it?" Michel demanded when she pulled her hand away and put a clear distance between them. "Don't you like me?"

Her heart hammered madly. They were all alone; Freya and Pierre had long disappeared into one of the many passageways that intersected at the foot of the stairs.

"Of course I do," Hannah answered, racking her brain for an answer. "But surely there are better places for a romantic adventure than this stinking cellar?"

"That's true," he replied with a grin. "But I've always wondered what it would be like to do it in a dark dungeon with a creature as ravishing as you – in front of all those languished men."

For a moment, Michel seemed to revel in her disgust, but then he broke out in raucous laughter.

"Have no fear, my love," he said. He leaned in, pulled her close, and tried to kiss her again. "You smell good," he leered as he urged her forward.

The man from Lorraine raised his torch in defense as another figure suddenly appeared around the corner and bowed to him obsequiously. The man was short, somewhat misshapen, and cursed with an unfortunate pockmarked face. A large bundle of keys jangled on his leather belt, which was fastened far too tightly around his bloated belly. His once-white shirt was stained with blood and congealed grime.

"Take us to the Templars!" Michel commanded the warden sharply. "I would like to show the lady how the Gens du Roi deals with its opponents."

Echoing from somewhere, she could hear steps, and, in the distance, Hannah thought she recognized Freya. It wasn't the stench but naked fear that hit her in the gut as she reached a row of barred cells. Here and there soft snores, and, from time to time, a ghastly moan could be heard cutting through the silence.

Michel stepped up to the bars of one of the cells. The light from his torch fell on the confused face of a young bearded man who was staring apathetically into nothingness.

"Ever seen a sodomite?" Michel asked her with a provocative laugh. "Take a good look at him! This is what a Templar looks like when he can no longer carry his banner with pride."

Shocked, Hannah looked down at the prisoner. His dark, damp hair was stuck to his forehead with sweat and dirt. Quietly moaning, he tried to sit up, holding his left arm while doing so. His expression was contorted in pain. It looked as if his arm was broken or dislocated. His body was emaciated, and his bare feet were covered in blue smudges and brand marks.

Hannah clung to the rusty bars of the cell. She longed to tell the tortured Templar that there might be a way to escape this horror. But she dared not say anything in front of Michel, she couldn't risk letting anything show on her face.

"Well, my boy," Michel called gleefully, "Philipp of France has worked your ass over real nicely there. You couldn't have done it any better yourselves."

"I want to leave," Hannah whispered, fighting with her tears.

"Don't tell me you're feeling sorry for this piece of scum?"

"No," she said, turning away. "I'm just feeling sick. I'm not used to this stench."

Dazedly, she staggered up the stone spiral staircase to the exit. Like a drowning person, she gasped for air when she finally made it outside.

"Come here, my pretty," hissed Michel, who had tailed her. He seized her arm and pulled her to him. "Let me comfort you."

As if she were a doll, Hannah let him grab her waist and kiss her.

"The show isn't over yet," he whispered, licking her ear with his hot tongue. "Now comes the enjoyable part."

"Please," she gasped in agony as she struggled to escape his grip. With a grin, he finally released her.

Their steps echoed dully into the night as he pulled her across the courtyard. Hannah thought of crying for help, but who would hear her?

Michel opened a wide wooden door to the horse stables and shoved Hannah into the aisle that divided the two rows of stalls. Swiftly, he lit another torch and placed it in one of the holders on the walls. All at once, his hands were everywhere on her body, and Hannah gulped for air as he seized her roughly and pushed her into an empty stall filled with straw. Gasping, she landed on the floor.

He crashed down on her like a hurricane, and, although Hannah had vowed to keep calm, she unexpectedly defended herself fiercely. As he ripped at her clothes, she pummeled him with punches, but her efforts merely seemed to egg Michel on even more. Mercilessly, he thrust his knee between her bare thighs and Hannah felt his hard penis threatening to enter her. Her strength began to ebb.

Suddenly, her tormenter froze as if he had turned to stone.

Carefully, she opened her eyes and found herself staring into a pair of flickering eyes that were as dark as coal. Struan was standing over her. He had clawed his hand into Michel's blonde hair and pulled his head back while holding a large dagger to his throat. A thin stream of blood ran down the soldier's neck.

Struan hissed something at Michel in French. At that, the soldier clumsily scrambled to his feet, shaking with fear. The knife still at his throat, he pulled up his pants. He had barely refastened his cords when Struan kicked him hard between the ribs and told him to get lost.

Hannah slowly stood up and nervously fixed her clothes and hair.

"You were lucky, you little whore," Michel whispered to her in German before he left. "I'm not so foolish as to challenge your protector, but you can tell him to beware if he meets me with my troops."

Only when Michel had finally disappeared did Hannah dare breathe normally again. She turned to the Scotsman in gratitude. His hand was trembling slightly as he returned the dagger to its sheath. The next moment, he drew himself to his full height and gave her a strange smile. He took a step towards her and placed his large, warm hand on her shoulder.

"Is it good?" he asked her in broken German.

"Yes. Thank you." She didn't need to say any more.

Then she fell into his arms and broke down sobbing. As she let her tears fall freely, he held her awkwardly against his broad chest, murmuring something in a language Hannah couldn't identify. Silently, he escorted her out of the stable and into the night.

Back at the banquet hall, the soldiers' rowdy voices were still at full volume and a few drunkards were staggering about in front of the entrance. Struan guided Hannah past them, holding her protectively as if they were lovers out on an evening stroll. When they arrived at their wagon, the Scotsman stopped and took out a blanket, which he wrapped around Hannah's shoulders to keep her warm. He also brought a skin of wine, offering her a sip before taking a mighty gulp himself.

Gradually, Hannah's thoughts cleared, and she began to worry about Freya. What if her new friend had met the same fate?

The music stopped playing, and a little later, Gero and Johan appeared at the exit. When Gero saw how unusually closely Struan and Hannah were standing, he ran to them as if the devil was after him.

"In God's name," he croaked, "what happened?"

Hannah began to cry inconsolably. Gero handed Struan his torch and gathered his lover into a protective embrace.

"One of Nogaret's men tried to harm her," Struan explained quietly. "But stay calm, I showed up in time."

"Did you kill him?" Johan asked shocked.

"No," Struan replied darkly, taking another gulp from the skin. "How stupid do you think I am? I just taught him a lesson."

"Where's Freya?" Johan looked at Hannah with wide, fearful eyes.

"I don't know," she replied in a hoarse voice. "She went off with a soldier from the Gens du Roi."

Before Johan could say anything, they heard footsteps.

It was Freya, appearing like an apparition. She was alone. Her hair was a little unkempt, but otherwise, she looked unharmed. Without a word of

497

explanation, she grabbed the wine skin from Struan's hands, surprising him, and took a large gulp. But instead of drinking the fine red wine, she gargled and spat the liquid out in disgust.

"What did that man do to you?" Johan yelled furiously. "Tell me!"

"I don't have to tell you everything I do," Freya retorted calmly. "After all, we agreed that we had a common goal and now we have come a whole lot closer to it."

"So you …" Johan's' voice trailed off for a second, and his eyes widened with horror. "You pleasured him with your mouth! That bastard!" he swore, without waiting for an answer from Freya. "I'll kill him if I ever catch him!"

"Johan," Freya tried to reassure him as she stroked his cheek tenderly.

"Let me go!" he spat, and pushed her hand aside.

"Johan!" The Beguine's voice took on a pleading tone. "Don't make things harder than they already are."

Freya stepped close to him, but he drew back as if she had the plague, refusing to look her in the face.

"Damn it," she swore softly. "It meant nothing, nothing at all."

Johan shook his head silently before retreating into the pitch-black night.

"He'll calm down soon enough," said Gero. "What did you find out?" he asked Freya.

"Your commander is wasting away in a solitary cell," she replied. "Two more of your Brothers from Bar-sur-Aube are in the cells directly next to him."

"Their names," Gero gasped. "Do you have their names?"

"No, but I know how to find them. Luckily for you, I've been able to find my way around the most convoluted passageways and alleys since I was a child."

"Good," Gero said. "You can tell me the rest in the inn."

"We have to find Johan," Hannah said to Gero after he had harnessed the horses. Somewhere, a tower clock rang midnight.

"I'll look for him," he said, and promptly disappeared into the darkness.

Hannah climbed into the wagon and sat down next to Freya, who sat with bowed head, playing nervously with her rosary.

"Damn it!" The Beguine sighed the rather unladylike expletive.

"I'm sure he'll calm down soon," Hannah said, trying to look confident.

Freya shook her red mane and sighed. "Will he ever talk to me again? You know, I used to work in a whorehouse."

Hannah tried not to let it show how strange this information seemed to her, but Freya noticed her amazement and misunderstood her. "Before I joined the Beguines," she added in explanation.

"Have you told Johan that?" Hannah asked.

"He comes from a devout family," Freya said. "Besides, he is a Templar with high moral standards. This can't go well in the long run."

"What nonsense!" Hannah exclaimed. "Look, I really like him, but his moral standards can't be that high, or he wouldn't have started anything with you. He's scared for you, and maybe a little jealous too."

"When you put it like that, perhaps I understand," Freya answered smiling. "Thank you," she said, standing up and climbing nimbly out of the wagon.

When Gero peered around the door a little later, holding up an oil lamp, Hannah jumped back in fear, her nerves still frayed. Faster than she had expected, he climbed into the wagon and took her into his arms.

"Don't do anything like that again," he said in a choked voice, kissing her so passionately that she had to gasp for air when he let her go. "If anything happened to you, I don't know what I would do," he continued quietly. "It's bad enough that I must bear the responsibility for my Brothers' suffering. If it pleases the Lord Almighty, I will pay for it with my life, but yours would be far too high a price."

Hannah felt her belly clench and her mouth go dry. Silently, she watched him leave her and set the wagon in motion. Gero had made arrangements with the castle steward to meet in the steward's chambers in the castle the next day to collect the evening's wages, giving him another chance to inspect the castle by daylight.

When they returned, things in *Ad Stellam* were becoming livelier. After the minstrels' performance, a few blueskirts were using their first day off in weeks to amuse themselves in the city's notorious establishment. Cautiously, Gero and his companions approached the inn.

"Oh, God," Hannah whispered in horror after she stepped out of the wagon with Freya and walked to the front entrance of the guesthouse. In the flickering light of torches, she spotted her tormentor inside the inn, flirting with a blonde girl.

Freya recognized the danger immediately, and pulled Hannah to the rear of the house. "We forgot something," she called to Gero, who had left Struan to tend to the horses and was now hurrying forward to look for Anselm and Matthäus. "We'll be right with you."

"What do we do now?" Hannah asked in a shaky voice. "What if the soldiers recognize us?"

"Be quiet," Freya hissed. "Houses like these always have a back door. We'll sneak past him. Let's not imagine what would happen if our Templars encountered that wretch."

The Beguine grasped Hannah's hand and pulled her to the back entrance. Carefully, she opened the door. In the narrow hallway, a large, shaggy wolfhound stalked towards them, growling. Hannah's heart raced. Although she wasn't normally frightened of dogs, this was a particularly fearsome specimen.

Freya stretched out her hand and spoke to the dog so soothingly that it stopped growling, and even let her scratch its head.

Setting one foot silently in front of the other, Freya and Hannah were slipping past the kitchen when suddenly the door to the taproom was yanked open. A tall, dark-haired man stumbled drunkenly towards them. Immediately, Freya recognized Pierre, her admirer from the castle. Hastily, she pushed Hannah into an alcove, but she herself could not manage to hide.

As the drunken man saw her flame-colored hair, he drew himself up. "Darling," he slurred merrily, "I knew you belonged to Madame Fouchet's stable." As he tried to reach for her, he tripped.

In two steps, Freya had slipped up the stairs. "Sorry," she teased, leaning over the railing lasciviously, "I already have a customer."

"Tell the old girl that she doesn't have a better flute player than you," he called. "Next time, I want you for an entire night. If not, your madam will be sorry."

His eyes flickered, and Hannah barely dared breathe in her hiding place. But then he left, presumably to head across the courtyard to the latrines.

"Good God," Hannah groaned softly and hurried to Freya in relief. "That was close."

"Let's get out of here," Freya whispered, taking her by the hand, and together they ran up the narrow, creaking steps.

MYSTERY OF THE TEMPLARS

Their room was on the second floor, right next to Anselm and Matthäus'. They had decided to share a room with Johan and Gero while Struan stayed behind to keep watch over the wagon. In the dim, flickering oil lamp, Freya smiled and looked at Hannah.

"It's about time we finally lay in the arms of the men we love."

CHAPTER 39

Retreat into the Swamp

Sunday, November 12, 1307

Hannah awoke to find the first rays of sunlight shining through a gap in the window shutter. She ran her hand over the straw mattress where she had been curled up against Gero. The spot where his warm body had been was now empty, and Hannah recalled that he had gotten up before daybreak to take over the rest of the night's watch from Struan.

Her eyes fell on Freya and Johan who were sharing another straw mattress on the floor. In his sleep, the redheaded Templar held his lover in a tight embrace with his cheek resting on the crown of her head.

The sight of Johan's scarred face sent a pang through Hannah's heart. Despite his disfigured features, the contented expression he wore made him a handsome man.

Hannah slipped to the window with bare feet. She opened the wooden shutter as quietly as possible, and stuck her head outside. Down in the courtyard, the bustle had already begun. Hannah breathed in the fresh air and watched Gero feed and water the horses.

Just last evening, Gero had assembled the band of travelers for a short meeting before they had gone to bed. Freya had managed to find out that Henri d'Our was a special prisoner whom his captors were anxious to keep alive, despite all the torture that he was no doubt being subject to. Every three days, a medicus was called in from the city to examine the commander and two other prisoners from Bar-sur-Aube. Additionally, every Monday, a Benedictine monk arrived from the nearby Fontevrault Abbey to read the Holy Scriptures aloud to the unfortunate men and hear their confessions.

Freya also reported that the mortal remains of the prisoners who had died under torture or from exhaustion were discarded in a pit behind the northern castle wall and burnt once a week with the rest of the trash.

With this information, Gero quickly devised a plan that, despite sounding extremely dangerous, was nonetheless met with general approval.

Without much fuss, Gero paid Madame Fouchet the fee they had agreed upon, then climbed up on the bench seat and steered the wagon away from the questionable establishment without once looking back.

Johan had ridden to the castle beforehand to collect the promised writ of escort. A little later, he returned with the parchment bearing King Philipp's seal. The document was not only necessary to enter and leave the city, but also guaranteed their safe return to the German lands.

Shortly before they reached the city gates, Gero stopped the horses and helped Freya off the wagon. The two of them headed down a dark alley, where, according to Madame Fouchet, an old widow sold rare medicinal herbs for some extra income. Even though Hannah and Anselm would have loved to explore the medieval apothecary, both and the rest of the group stayed behind to avoid drawing any more attention to themselves.

Madame Dubart, the herbologist, lived in a cellar. Her hair hidden under a tight wimple, the haggard woman was sweeping the narrow stairs of her dwelling and eyed Gero and Freya suspiciously as they approached her, hand in hand.

"Madame Dubart?" Gero called.

"I am not a backstreet abortionist, I'll tell you that right now," the old woman grunted.

Gero ignored her unfriendly remark and, with a charming smile, introduced himself and his redheaded companion. "We need your help as a healer," he explained.

Without looking up once, the old woman shook the dust from her gray-brown surcoat and grabbed her broom like a lance. Finally, with an authoritative gesture, she indicated that her customers should follow her down the stairs.

The cellar smelled of sage, lavender, and lemon balm. Under the low ceiling arches, Madame Dubart had hung numerous bundles of different herbs to dry. The plain walls were lined with wooden shelves, crammed with glazed pots and jars. Their Latin inscriptions announced their occasionally unappetizing contents: dried boar penises, frog bladders, fly shells, and spider legs stood next to numerous Oriental plants.

"So, what do you want?" demanded the old woman, sourly planting herself behind a wide oak counter.

"Opium powder, thorn apple, mulberries, hemlock, and mandrake." Gero pondered for a moment before looking at Freya for help.

"Along with deadly nightshade, henbane, and ivy," she added with a smile.

"Why do you want these things?" The old woman rubbed her sharp nose mistrustfully. "Are you trying to destroy an entire army?"

"We are minstrels and barber surgeons," Gero lied. "We want to concoct a drink that gets rid of pain and all sorts of illnesses, and sell it to our audience."

"If you want to make theriac," Madame Dubart lectured, "you won't need half of these things."

"We have a new, more potent recipe," Gero answered, drumming his fingers impatiently on the smooth polished wood. "My father brought it back from the Outremer, from the Mohammedans," he added when the woman continued to eye him doubtfully.

Only after he pulled out a silver Livres Tournois coin did the old woman set one stoneware jug after another on the counter. After she had assembled all the ingredients in a row, she stooped over with a groan and retrieved a silver tray from under the table, along with two small spoons, two silver spatulas, and an ounce scale.

"So," she said glancing at Gero and Freya. "How much do you want?"

When Gero and Freya returned to their waiting companions, Gero was holding a small leather sack and a chest with ten clay vials. They left the city, crossing the Vienne over the very same stone bridges that the English King, Henry Plantagenet II, had built over a hundred years earlier to drain parts of the nearby swamp. They headed further southeast along plowed up wheat-fields and grazed pastures.

Gero decided to seek shelter nearby in the densely forested swampland until their plan had been carried out. The sun made the numerous puddles glisten. Gnats danced about in the air, and, once in a while, a gurgle could be heard.

Sure that no soldier would stray into the swamp, Gero let his eyes sweep across the birch trees and weeping willows , then he ordered his comrades to set up camp for the night, hoping that they would remain undisturbed.

As darkness fell, a small fire was lit on a clearing, and the three knights celebrated their own holy mass under the open sky for the first time. Anselm, who had barely been able to suppress his fascination during their numerous visits to church along their journey to France, watched in awe as the three Templars lit several torches and planted them an equal

distance apart in the soft ground. After that, they rammed one of their swords into an overturned tree trunk as a sort of makeshift cross and finally took their positions in front of it.

With folded hands, they broke into a Gregorian chant that moved the rest of the group to reverent silence. Once more, Anselm became aware that Gero, Johan, and Struan weren't just fearsome warriors, but deeply devout men, whose belief in God played a fundamental role in each of their lives. In his deep, solemn voice, Gero prayed in Latin for the Almighty's blessings upon their plans. Anselm slowly began to realize that this mission could not be completed without some sort of divine intervention.

CHAPTER 40

Fontevrault

Monday, November 13, 1307

Throughout the brutally cold night, Anselm and the three knights kept watch in turns. The next morning, Gero gave his companions the day's orders, tasking Anselm with watching over the women and instructing Matthäus to look after the wagon and animals for as long as Gero and his comrades were gone.

After a simple breakfast of hard cheese, dried rye bread, and Chinon wine warmed in a kettle, Gero and his Brothers started their hunt for the monk who was scheduled to take the confessions from the Templars imprisoned in the fortress of Chinon.

The three men got ready in silence. Johan handed swords to Gero and Struan. Without a word, they each put their chain mail on over their doublets, helping each other to secure their armor.

Pensively, Anselm's gaze followed the three men as they crept silently and slightly stooped into the thick morning mist with their swords clamped under their arms.

"If the monk wants to have breakfast at the castle, he needs to hurry up," grumbled Struan, who, like his two companions, was lying on his belly in a shallow trench between gorse and blackberry bushes.

"If he doesn't show up soon, my dick will freeze off," Johan moaned.

"Stop whining," Struan grunted. "It would be worse if Philipp's soldiers discovered us. I heard the inquisitors roast your balls to make you talk."

"Quiet," Gero snapped, as Johan was about to reply.

Their eyes glued to a fork in the road, the men could already make out someone approaching in the distance. The narrow road was reinforced in some spots with wooden planks and stones so that summer travelers didn't sink into the bog. They heard the soft footsteps of the approaching traveler, who was whistling to himself like a frightened knave sent to fetch wine from a dark cellar.

"Get ready," Gero hissed. "Where's the sack?"

Johan handed Gero a burlap sack that was finely woven and so large that a person could easily fit into it. Gero had bought five sacks at the local undertaker.

Out of the corner of his eye, Johan saw Struan straighten his upper body and pull a heavy oak cudgel from his belt. "Wouldn't it be better if I did it?" he asked the scotsman with a frown. "If *you* strike, he probably won't survive."

"Don't worry," Struan murmured with a weak grin. "I'll treat him as kindly as our rabbits back home."

"We shouldn't have a problem," Gero whispered as he pushed himself through the bushes, ready to pounce. "Although he's tall, he's pretty scrawny."

"Is he alone?" Johan asked since Gero's broad shoulders were blocking his view.

"Yes, apart from his donkey," Gero answered with an amused smile.

Johan snorted. "If a donkey thwarts our plans, maybe we should start thinking about finding a new calling."

Brother Julian had already walked for four and a half hours, and the donkey he was leading was not about to endure a rider on its back in addition to the sacks filled with cabbage heads it was already carrying.

And so, the young monk was far too exhausted to notice anyone lying in wait for him. A mighty blow on the back of his head rendered him unconscious immediately. His four-legged companion, however, would not surrender so easily. It balked, trying to break away, and when Gero tugged on its halter, the Templar suddenly felt the donkey's teeth.

"Damned beast," he swore.

The next moment, the donkey kicked, nearly injuring Struan, but the Scotsman jumped aside before seizing the donkey's sensitive ears and twisting them backwards. Immediately, the animal froze and stared at him with wide eyes.

"My friend," Struan snarled. "If you don't behave, I'll personally make sure that we turn you into sausage. Have I ever mentioned how much I love donkey sausage?"

A smile flitted across Gero's face as he placed the reins around the animal's mouth, tightening them with a powerful jerk so that it could neither bite nor cry.

With their combined strength, they heaved the unconscious monk on top of the sacks of cabbage and, with a few knots, tied him tightly to the saddle. A gentle poke with the sword in the donkey's sensitive flanks made it finally relinquish its last traces of obstinacy. The animal, now noticeably more co-operative, plodded along behind the men.

When they arrived back at the campsite, Gero searched through the saddlebags for documents or other clues that would provide information about the monk's job at the castle. While it would have been easier to just ask the man, he was still unconscious, and they decided it was perhaps better that way. They tied a long strip of black, woolen fabric over his eyes, so that when they released him later, he could not reveal who had kidnapped him.

Apart from a crust of brown bread and a piece of hard cheese, the only thing Gero found in the monk's bag was a worn-out Bible. Placing the holy book aside, Gero slipped into the dark, felted wool habit that Johan and Struan had taken from the man.

"Maybe we should have given the robe to a washerwoman first," Gero joked pulling the tight habit over his broad chest.

"The stench that awaits you in the dungeon is far worse," Freya remarked.

Casually, she handed Gero a small pouch to wear on a cord around his neck. Although the pouch looked harmless, it contained five vials filled with Madame Dubart's herbs, dissolved in wine. No one could predict the exact effect the herbs would have, but Freya estimated that the contents of one vial could knock a two hundred pound man unconscious for hours. A few drops too many, however, would spell certain death.

Three vials were destined for the imprisoned Templars, whom Gero hoped to find alive in the dungeon. The fourth vial had been prepared for the medicus who regularly visited the castle, and if everything went according to plan, it would play a decisive role in rescuing the Brothers.

The fifth was an extra, in case one of the vials broke. Gero gave the rest of the vials to Johan. One of them would quiet the monk as soon as he awoke.

With a serious expression, Gero looked at Freya. "Have I ever told you how grateful I am for all you've done for us?"

"You don't have to thank me," she replied, lowering her eyes for a moment. "Preparing medicine was one of my duties as a Beguine."

When Freya looked up again, Gero was captivated by her olive green eyes.

"Besides, I was not alone at the castle," she said, motioning to the wagon with her head, where Hannah was observing them patiently. "Your friend there was just as brave."

"I know," he said and turned his gaze to Hannah. Her pretty face was tinged with a fear that affected Gero more than his own nerves did.

He tied the robe's cords around his waist and slipped into the monk's worn sandals, which, thankfully, were large enough for him. Finally he pulled the dark-brown cowl over his head and drew the hood so low over his face that he could hardly see anything.

"If you don't lift your head too much," Johan remarked helpfully, "no one will recognize you."

"If I'm not back by evening, you'll know someone recognized me," Gero replied pushing the hood away from his face.

To look like an authentic monk, he should have had his hair cut into a tonsure as well, but there was no time for that. For a moment, he gazed into Hannah's eyes. He longed to gather her into his arms, but he thought it a bad omen to part from his lover with a kiss. He would return to her, and then he could kiss her until the end of days – or at least until the day that she finally returned to her world.

Struan hastily made the sign of the cross. "May the Almighty protect you," he said quietly, hugging Gero one last time.

"Come along, comrade," Gero said to the donkey, who was calmly chewing on a turnip that Johan had bribed it with earlier. The reins tightly wound around his right hand, he pulled the animal behind him with some effort.

"Your Bible!" Freya called when he had almost left the campsite behind him. She ran after him and handed him the old book bound in pig leather.

To his relief, Gero saw that a different guard was standing at the fortress' main entrance, allowing him to enter the city without hassle. Still, he couldn't afford to take any chances. He murmured from under his hood to the guards who let him into the inner courtyard only a soft greeting of "Praised be Jesus Christ."

Although determined, Gero could not stop his knees from shaking as he walked towards the arcade in the middle of the main courtyard, which was flanked by a tall, square tower and a right-angled annex.

With the hood pulled as low as possible over his face, Gero's field of vision was heavily obscured as he crossed the cobbled courtyard. Shortly before he had reached the first arch, a boy stepped up to him to take the donkey's reins from his hand. Alarmed, Gero whipped around.

"Where is Brother Julian?" the boy asked as he looked up, scrutinizing Gero.

"He is sick," Gero replied quickly, not looking the boy in the eye.

The boy nodded. "My name is Claude," he introduced himself in a friendly voice. With a nod, he gestured to the burlap sack with the cabbage heads. "I'm here to collect the vegetables for the kitchen."

Thank Mother Mary, Gero thought, that he'd resisted the temptation to leave the sacks of cabbages behind in the forest. Before tying the donkey to a pole, he helped the boy unload them.

"I have to go to the prisoners," he murmured, taking the Bible out of the saddlebag and holding it up like a passport.

"They're already waiting for you down in the dungeon," Claude informed him. "You're late." The boy's gaze wandered to the sundial that stood in the middle of the courtyard on a small stone pedestal, but the sky was too cloudy to read the time of day.

As Gero had expected, the entrance to the dungeon was heavily guarded.

"Did you bring your report?" The young guard's expression was as cold as his green eyes. His uniform revealed that he was a member of the Gens du Roi.

Gero pulled his shoulders forward to make himself look smaller, and shook his head cluelessly, his face still covered by his hood. "Brother Julian didn't tell me of such a thing," he said defiantly.

Only then did the guard realize that the man before him was not the usual monk. "Is he sick?" he asked.

Gero nodded, hoping he hadn't given the guard any reason to doubt him.

"Tell him I need the records of the prisoners' confessions by Thursday. He was supposed to bring the report today. He can count himself lucky that Guillaume Imbert was delayed in Paris, and is only expected to return on Friday, or things wouldn't be looking good for your Brother." The soldier's face twisted into an expression of derision. "Twenty strokes of the stick await him if he doesn't obey orders. Even his abbot wouldn't be able to help him then."

Interesting, Gero thought. So Guillaume Imbert was on his way here, and they had till Friday to organize the escape. *Damn bastards*, he thought.

The king and his followers would stop at absolutely nothing to learn their secrets. But if Gero was right, it was unlikely that a Templar would make his confession to a monk from a different Order.

As Gero opened the heavy doors to the dungeon, they parted with a loud creak. The nauseating stench of blood, urine, and vomit suddenly made him gag. Freya had not exaggerated at all, and, in retrospect, Gero felt even more respect for her for daring to venture down here.

Hung on the narrow walls, torches lit his way down into the realm of despair. The cold, damp air that wormed its way through his clothes with every step made him shiver. He broke out into a cold sweat, as if the hand of death had touched his breast.

When he arrived below, he was greeted by a dungeon guard whose ill-favored appearance perfectly suited his surroundings. Noticing that Gero was not the monk he had expected, the man offered to show him the way into the jail.

From Freya's instructions, Gero knew roughly the direction of his Brothers' cells but, strictly speaking, everything here looked the same. In any case, he knew he wouldn't be left alone here. Following the dungeon guard hobbling ahead, Gero had to duck to avoid hitting his head on the damp ceiling.

He was clenching the Bible so tightly in his hand that his fingers became numb. Eventually they reached the first cell. When the guard inserted the key into one of the locks and advised him to bend down on entering the cell, naked fear momentarily gripped Gero. What if the guard had seen through his ruse and was going to lock him in as well?

"Should I leave the door open?" the man asked, as if he had guessed Gero's thoughts. "Your Brother didn't like being locked in with the prisoners. But don't worry," he continued, "the prisoners are chained, and can't harm anyone – the Inquisitor's men have seen to that."

The guard handed him a torch, and only then did Gero see a person cowering in the furthest corner of the cell.

"If you could give me a moment alone with the man," he said, quietly but firmly. "I hardly think the prisoner is ready yet to give his confession."

The guard sniggered. "He won't give it to you even if I go away," he croaked in amusement. "These Templars are cut from a special cloth. They only trust their own people, no matter how badly things are going for them. That's why Imbert won't have any success with them. And they certainly won't tell him what he wants to hear. For that, we have to turn to other methods."

"What do you mean?" Gero looked up in alarm.

"The men here will bear anything. Their belief strengthens them in miraculous ways. But when they are made to witness someone they love being tortured – a brother, sister, mother, or father, the situation is different."

"The King won't dare to do that," Gero let slip.

"Ha!" snorted the dungeon guard. "What, holy man, you don't think people like you are capable of such things?" It was probably more of an assessment than a question. "But what am I saying … " The man shook his head and finally turned away to leave Gero to his task.

Gero crouched down to enter the open cell.

"Get away!" the prisoner hissed at Gero, who crawled over to the man.

As soon as the man had opened his mouth to speak, Gero's doubt disappeared. It was Arnaud de Mirepaux. Although he seemed to have kept his sharp tongue, the Brother was in a pitiful state. He didn't seem to recognize Gero.

"Brother Arnaud?" Gero whispered cautiously, slipping closer to him on his knees. "It's me – Gero. Don't you recognize me?"

Despite the dim light, he could see Arnaud raising his head in disbelief, his sallow face and dark eyes etched with confusion. Cautiously, Gero stretched out his hand and touched his comrade's shoulder. He fought against the desire to embrace his Brother, his tears rendering him momentarily speechless.

"Lord Almighty," Arnaud murmured, unable to comprehend what was happening. "You can take away all my strength, but please don't take my mind," he whispered, his lips quivering so badly that the hairs in his beard shook.

"It's really me, Arnaud," Gero insisted in a choked voice, raising his torch so that his Brother could see him better.

"By God's will," Arnaud gasped in disbelief. "It really *is* you! What in the world are you doing here?" Still doubtful, he glanced at the dark-brown robe that Gero was wearing.

Gero quickly gave him a short explanation, though Arnaud didn't seem to understand everything he was saying. Nevertheless, Gero pressed a vial into his hand. "Have no fear, Brother," he whispered conspiratorially. "Drink the whole bottle tomorrow after breakfast, and then just wait."

"Breakfast?" Arnaud whispered and grinned fatalistically. "I haven't eaten anything that deserves that name in weeks. No, Gero, I have no fear." He raised his head and looked around. "Things can't possibly get any worse than wallowing here in my own shit. Even death would be salvation."

"Don't talk like that, Brother," Gero chided gently. "Where is our commander hidden?" His fear that Henri d'Our would no longer be alive made his voice quiver.

"He is two cells away," Arnaud whispered. "After they almost tortured Francesco to death about two weeks ago, they put the rest of us together in the same row. Still, we are forbidden from talking to one another."

"Francesco?" Gero was nearly at a loss for words.

"Don't worry," Arnaud reassured him. "He's alive. They let him go, and let him take his mother and sister with him to Navarra. But don't ask me why. The old man must have agreed to some sort of ultimatum that will run out one of these days. So, you've not come a day too early."

"Who else is here?"

"Besides d'Our, just Stephano de Sapin. He's next to d'Our at the end of the hallway. They've moved all the others to Troyes. And in case you don't know yet, they've carried off our Grand Master to Corbeil. Two weeks ago, he apparently confessed to the Order's guilt. They'd forced him to witness two Brothers from Payens being skinned alive. He was left with no choice."

Gero swallowed, speechless with horror, not just because the circumstances were so horrific, but also because everything corresponded with what he had read in Hannah's books.

Abruptly, Arnaud paused and massaged his left arm while wincing in pain. "They put me on the rack," he explained, wheezing. "They stretched my body to get me to confess the Order's secrets."

"You have me to thank for that," Gero muttered guiltily.

"What nonsense are you speaking, Brother," Arnaud said softly. "How could you know what happened?"

Gero spared both himself and Arnaud an answer.

"What are you planning?" Arnaud asked. "Are more of our Brothers outside?"

"Just Struan and Johan," Gero whispered. "But have faith," he reassured him, seeing his look of doubt. "With God's help, we will free you from this hellhole."

Arnaud raised his arm weakly.

"As discussed," Gero said simply as he crept out of the cell on his knees and shut the door behind him.

Hastily he pulled the hood over his head and straightened himself with effort. He let the guard lead him to Stephano de Sapin, to whom he handed the second vial.

Finally, Gero arrived at his commander's cell. Unlike Arnaud and Stephano, Henri d'Our had not retreated into the back of his cell, but instead had positioned himself near the bars.

"I've brought you a new confessor," the dungeon guard said in a mocking voice. "Brother …" The man paused as he realized that he didn't know the name of the substitute Brother from Fontevrault.

"Gerard," Gero declared, pronouncing the "G" like a "J".

D'Our looked up at him from below. As if struck by lightning, the commander from Bar-sur-Aube stared into the sky blue eyes of his trusted Brother. He had to summon all his martial discipline to hide his astonishment.

He nodded contemptuously. "Fine with me," he murmured. "If he's less obnoxious than his predecessor, he can stay. But I want you to make yourself scarce," d'Our said to the dungeon guard. "Or did you think I'd make my confession while you're standing nearby?"

"I'm the last person who wants to stand in the way of your confession," the guard croaked. "See it as an act of divine providence that God is offering you a replacement for Brother Julian. This might be the last chance you get to cleanse your soul before Imbert sends you to hell."

Then he turned and left.

"What in the devil's name are you doing here?" d'Our whispered in a commanding tone once they were alone.

Gero was taken aback by the tone of his question. He hadn't counted on d'Our being overjoyed to see him here, but his commander could still have shown a bit more enthusiasm.

"Does the word 'CAPUT' mean anything to you?" Gero asked instead of answering d'Our's question.

"Shh …" d'Our hissed, placing a finger on his split lips. "Have you gone mad? If you had followed my commands, the Brother from the High

514

Council would have been able to turn back the wheels of fate, and we wouldn't be sitting in this cellar!"

"It is not my fault that things turned out differently from what you intended." Gero felt his anger rise. "Your intermediary is dead. No ..." he corrected himself, deciding to tell the truth. "Before I could even carry out your mission, I was transported seven hundred years into the future, and could only look for the Brother upon my return. But what he planned on doing was even more unbelievable than what I experienced in the future."

D'Our stared at him incredulously. "You were there? In the future?" he stammered.

"Yes, November 2004 – to cut a long story short," Gero confirmed, and said no more. It would have taken too much time to explain everything.

"Will they help us?" Hope glimmered in his commander's eyes.

"Help us?" Gero shook his head. "With what?"

"You really have no idea of the significance of your mission," d'Our sighed. "For a hundred and fifty years, we've been waiting for someone from the future to contact us again so we can change history and prevent the downfall of the Order."

"Nothing was changed," Gero said, showing no emotion. He seriously wondered what his commander was getting at. "In the year of our Lord 2004, the Order is gone. To be precise, it was dissolved in the year 1312, when Pope Clement V issued the Bull *vox in excelso.*"

"2004?" D'Our slumped down as the hope in his eyes was extinguished like a candle in the wind. "And the boy?" he pressed on. "Did you at least manage to get the boy to safety?"

"He's waiting outside the city gates on the other bank of the Vienne."

"By God's will, Brother Gerard, have you lost your mind? How could you have let this happen?"

"That's a damn long story," Gero retorted harshly. For the first time in his life, he didn't care about showing his commander deference. He took a deep breath before he found the courage to continue without raising his voice. "With all due respect, sire, if you had used your wisdom to warn us in time, we would've been spared much suffering and bloodshed, and perhaps we could have even saved our men and the Order from a fate of death and destruction."

D'Our gave a deep sigh. "As easy as it might seem, it is not." Guiltily, he glanced up at Gero. "So what do you have planned, and why have you returned?"

In a few quick words, Gero explained what had happened and that he now had a new problem on his hands in the form of two time travelers.

"They're stranded here," Gero said, trying to explain Anselm and Hannah's situation. "I don't know how or if they can return home with the help of the Head."

"Don't tell me you've brought the Head here, too?" D'Our looked at him as if he had just announced the Apocalypse.

"What else could I have done?" Gero argued. "Brother Ronan accidentally killed himself, while he was fighting against me and apart from you, I don't know anyone else who knows anything about this thing."

"This knowledge has already become my downfall," d'Our moaned. "How do you think I managed to save Francesco? I've sold my soul. Imbert gave me an ultimatum. If I don't tell him what the Head can do by Friday, he will torture the rest of them to death in front of my eyes."

"King Philipp?" Gero exclaimed. "Why does he know about it?"

D'Our snorted in derision. "He doesn't know. He has a hunch," the former commander of Bar-sur-Aube continued, "I can't bear to think of what would happen if the Grand Inquisitor got his hands on Matthäus …"

Shuddering, Gero drew out a vial from his robe. "It seems as if you now have to fall back on the plan of a subordinate," he remarked. "Do what I've told you to, and we can at least save a few lives."

Gero imagined that Jesus had probably not felt any less miserable on the evening before his crucifixion. The potent mixture that he had given his comrades would make them appear dead after they had drunk it. Freya, or so Gero hoped, was experienced enough to concoct the right strength of dose for the effect to last at least twenty-four hours without harming the person who drank it.

Now, Gero would have to give the medicus the same mixture, and Anselm, who was the only one who had not yet been seen at the castle, would certify the deaths of the prisoners in his place. After that, Gero hoped that the corpses would be thrown into the waste pit, where they could easily rescue them. He didn't want to think about what would happen if they were discovered, or if his comrades didn't regain consciousness at the right time. A person could stay unconscious for at most three days before dying of thirst.

Suddenly, the dungeon master appeared next to Gero, just mere seconds after he had left d'Our's cell, and escorted him to the exit.

"Did they talk?" The Gens du Roi soldier who had let him into the jail grabbed Gero's sleeve as he tried to leave without a word of farewell.

"They barely said anything," Gero answered, hoping that the man would let him go without further questions.

The guard looked at him through narrowed eyes. "You were down there far longer than your Brother," the guard said sharply. "They must have said something."

"Yes, certainly," Gero replied cautiously. "But nothing worthwhile."

"I decide what's important or not, not you," the soldier announced, blocking Gero's path as he tried to leave.

"They confessed …" Gero stopped, lowering his head as if embarrassment was the reason why he had fallen silent.

"What did they confess?" his opponent urged.

"That they constantly think of naked women who spread their thighs lustfully and long to be taken by them."

The young guard looked at him with rapt attention. "And? Do they fantasize about doing it with each other, too?"

"No," Gero answered darkly.

Suddenly, the soldier yanked his hood from his head. "Your voice sounds familiar."

Gero felt his heart pounding wildly as he resisted the temptation to avoid the man's piercing stare.

"I've seen you somewhere."

"This is my first time at the castle," Gero answered. "I just joined the Benedictines a few days ago. I haven't even had the time to have my tonsure cut." As if to prove it, he lowered his head, and as he looked up, he took the chance to pull the hood over his head again.

"Very well. You may leave," the guard finally said, and snapped his fingers.

Gero bowed courteously. His heart still pounding, he strode out into the courtyard to fetch the donkey.

Upon his return to the swamp Gero felt embarrassed to be greeted with his companions' heartfelt embraces and he struggled to avoid bursting into tears as he reported the fate of their imprisoned Brothers.

In the meantime, the Benedictine had regained consciousness. Despite his strong protest, Johan had given him the mixture in the vial. Then he had covered him in warm blankets and placed him in a small tent not far from the wagon.

Gero stowed the monk's habit behind the tent. With a ladle, he scooped cold water from a bucket and poured it over his head to scrub away the stench of the dungeon with a piece of soap. He was still completely naked when Hannah appeared behind the wagon to bring him two linen towels.

"Thank you," he said taking the towels.

She bent down to gingerly lift up the monk's robe and folded it neatly. As she straightened herself and turned around to face him, he was standing in front of her, one of the linen towels casually slung across his hips. Tenderly, he took her in his arms and kissed her.

She let the habit fall, and blissfully pressed her body against his, her hands wandering over his muscular back that was still damp and cool.

His mouth glided up her neck. Through the thin fabric of her chemise, he grasped her breasts and his breath quickened as his gaze fell on the closed wagon.

"Come with me," he said.

As Gero shut the wagon door behind him, Hannah sensed that he wanted more than to just make love to her. Readily, she threw her arms around his neck and stumbled backwards onto a heap of clothes that cushioned her fall like a makeshift bed.

Gero went to his knees slowly. As Hannah looked up at him, lying between woolen blankets and surcoats, he pulled the linen towel off his hips and approached her with unbridled desire. He ran his cool fingers up her legs and tenderly stroked her bare upper thighs that peeped out from underneath her hem. Hannah spread her thighs eagerly and trembled under his caresses.

"I've wanted to do this for two long weeks," he whispered hoarsely. "And now I know that I shouldn't waste another moment."

With a soft gasp, he pushed into her as her sensitive bud began to blossom under his skilled fingers.

"I love you," he stammered breathlessly as she pulled him down to be even closer to him.

She could feel his heartbeat as her breasts brushed against his upper body and his mouth found her lips. Then he straightened himself up a

518

little and smiled dreamily as he continued moving slowly and deeply inside her.

"No one can take away our love," he said softly, "no matter what happens."

Shortly before sundown, Freya and Hannah prepared dinner, cooking honey-drenched apple pancakes in a flat cast-iron pan over the campfire.

The sweet scent drew the men to the fire, and together they feasted on a mountain of the delicious pancakes. They passed around several goatskins of fresh red wine that Gero had bought on his way out of the city, and, despite the bleak circumstances, they hadn't felt this relaxed in a long time.

"So," Gero began. He had sat down with his companions on a fallen tree stump. "The medicus lives not far from the Church of St. Maurice. Madame Fouchet explained that he usually stays there when he isn't on call at the castle. That, too, usually happens at previously arranged times. In the evenings, though, he is always at home, and most days he uses his free time to get drunk in the brothel, and …" He paused and coughed slightly as he turned around to glance at the women. "You know what I mean," he said with a slight grin. "He is unmarried, and an old handmaid usually does the cooking for him. She leaves the house shortly after the Vesper prayers and comes back the next morning, so we have some time to convince him to write us a letter announcing his indisposition. By early morning, he will be in dreamland, after we've given him our mixture. All clear up to this point?"

Struan nodded, picking an apple seed out of his teeth with the tip of his dagger.

Anselm shivered though the air wasn't too cold. Johan, on the other hand, simply chewed casually on his last pancake.

"And now to you, brother," Gero said looking at Anselm. "The course of history depends on your talents."

Anselm nodded silently. "I've been thinking about how to do this the entire morning," he said, his voice trembling with excitement. "I'll wait in the medicus' house until they send someone from the castle to call for me. But what if the old maid comes in the morning and finds me in the house? She doesn't know me at all."

"I've already considered that," Gero answered calmly. "Madame Fouchet has a messenger boy, Frydel, to whom I gave a few juggling balls yesterday before we left. He'll deliver messages for a bit of coin. I'll commission him to go to the woman's house before she arrives and tell her that our dear old medicus doesn't want to see her that day because he's drunk. If we furnish this message with a good enough tip, we will have both Frydel and the maid dancing to our tune."

"Very good," Anselm said, sounding a little more reassured. "As soon as I've seen the so-called corpses, I will declare that their deaths have been caused by an unknown pestilence which looks as if it is advancing from the Orient, and advise that they immediately place the corpses in the sun."

"Exactly," Gero said, glancing at the rest of the group before his gaze returned to Anselm. "I hope you don't lack any skills of persuasion. And if someone asks you how you know our medicus, just tell him that you come from the German lands and studied with him in Tours for a while. You're staying with him on a visit, and he requested that you represent him."

Anselm looked at Gero in astonishment. "I didn't know there was a university in Tours."

"Gatien, the Bishop of the city of Caesarodunum, as Tours was earlier known, founded the medical faculty hundreds of years ago," Gero answered casually.

Anselm was momentarily speechless. How often on this fateful journey would he have to correct his image of the supposedly backward Middle Ages?

"Wonderful," Gero continued. "If all goes according to plan, I will buy a wagon from the local cartwright and move the unconscious medicus out of the city with Struan. We cannot afford to leave him behind unattended. He could wake up and betray us. After that, we'll wait by the city walls at the western gate until it becomes dark enough to retrieve our Brothers."

Gero turned to Anselm again. "Before that I'll come back to the portal of St. Maurice to fetch you so we can leave the city together,' he reassured Anselm.

Johan looked doubtful. He held a wine skin in his hands. Before he handed it to Struan, he took another mighty gulp and wiped his scarred lips with his arm. Then he shook his head. "Everything sounds so perfect," he said thoughtfully. "What if something goes wrong?"

"Then that's God's will," Gero said simply.

CHAPTER 41

Experimental Games

Sunday, November 28, 2004

"Dr. Stevendahl, you will succeed," Professor Hertzberg declared joyously as he stormed into the office of the new project leader the next morning. In his right hand, Hertzberg was waving a stack of papers.

"What will I succeed in?" Tom asked cluelessly.

"You'll find a way to send the monk from Hemmenrode back. Here!" the professor gasped, and threw the papers on Tom's writing desk.

Quickly the professor told Tom that, according to his research, Thomas of Hemmenrode was the monk whom Cäsarius of Heisterbach had immortalized in his miraculous fable.

"When corroborated with the Templar's claims," Hertzberg exclaimed, "everything makes sense."

A little later, Paul and Tom retreated into a secret laboratory to investigate the inner workings of the server. Professor Hertzberg, who had recently discovered a new interest in technology, watched them curiously as they worked.

All the individual components were bound together not with screws but with sophisticated plug connections instead. The energy cell, a fusion reactor hardly any larger than a cell-phone battery, ran on a small volume of distilled water.

"The energy converter is tiny," Paul exclaimed in amazement as he examined the shimmering, blue-green point in the middle of the fuel cell. The container for the water reservoir was as large as a pack of cigarettes. "Do you reckon this thing could run on saliva in emergencies, too?"

"I doubt it," Tom muttered. "Saliva has DNA in it, and would probably disrupt the programming process. The device seems to carry out a personal encoding, like fingerprint verification, when it's powered up. It might even calibrate first to check if it's possible to transfer the scanned organism into the chosen time plane."

Professor Hertzberg cleared his throat. "Have either of you ever heard of the Atik Yomin?"

The two scientists shook their heads regretfully.

"It is an artifact described in the Jewish Kabbalah," Hertzberg explained. "Presumably, this device could distil water from desert air. Descriptions of it go back to the time of the Old Testament." He glanced at Tom furtively. "What if the original owner of this device could travel to much earlier time periods?"

Tom looked up and nodded. "Since we found out that Professor Hagen got the clues he used to construct our facility from eight hundred year-old documents, I don't think there are any real limits to this whole affair."

"If we know exactly how to use it," Paul suggested, "we could have control over a far broader spectrum of things than just time travel. For instance, we could make anything we wanted materialize. And who is to say we can only transfer people with it? It could also serve as a sort of freight transporter. If tests permit, we could transfer provisions, water, and, not least, valuables from one point to another. With this thing, anything is possible."

"As long as we don't know how the various components interact, we still have to be very careful," Tom cautioned, pushing Paul's hand aside to touch the small reactor. "So much energy is contained in this small space that you could destroy the entire world in one breath."

Hertzberg gave him a piercing stare. "You think this thing could be used as a weapon?"

"Certainly," Tom declared. "Whoever owns such a machine rules the world."

"Maybe the mechanism doesn't need as much energy as we think," Paul muttered, carefully inspecting the interior of the server again. "If so, the risk would be correspondingly minimized."

"What are you getting at?" Tom asked impatiently.

"What if we're talking about a far more advanced mechanism, still similar to ours, but the main difference being that the necessary amount of energy is significantly reduced, so you don't need to energize an entire football field to arrive at the desired time, but a single molecule?"

Tom stared at his colleague through narrowed eyes, and then, all of a sudden, his face lit up. "Why didn't I think of that?" he groaned.

Paul grinned triumphantly. "Beats me."

"To put it simply," Tom continued, "that means that our descendants have managed to run this thing by simply putting their foot in the door to gain access to a neighboring time-plane. Influencing single strings is all that's needed to produce the desired controlled chain reaction. Because of quantum coherence, the strategically connected energy structures remain intact and, can be detached from the rest of the net without being harmed …"

" … and with that, the clipping of the transferred materials stays restricted to a specifically defined time-plane," Paul continued, his eyes gleaming, "as if you're opening a door with a key, and hidden behind it is an entire realm of possibilities."

"No more transferred clearings with trees cut in half …" Tom declared triumphantly.

" … instead, exactly calculated units with strings that oscillate in synchronized time," Paul completed his sentence.

Hertzberg was not able to follow the young scientists' explanations, but his enthusiasm was undiminished. "And when will you be able to send our monk back?"

"We'll have to try to as soon as possible," Tom answered, "and hope that Paul is right."

The next day, the unconscious monk's stretcher was transported into a specially equipped laboratory by a robot that was normally deployed for clearing mines.

The walls and doors of the room were both sound-proof and radiation-proof in order to prevent the timeserver from registering any DNA other than the subject's and disturbing the transmission process – or unexpectedly transporting someone into the Middle Ages.

Tom felt a little strange as he clumsily sang the Gregorian chant that would unlock the server. He had practiced with an MP3 player for hours in order to hit the notes needed to activate the system. The microphone was connected wirelessly to a computer that sent the tones into a loudspeaker specially constructed for this experiment.

As if by magic, the familiar holographic profile of an Asian woman appeared on the device's mirror-like surface. As before, a few introductory words were said, which, despite the special safety glass panels and soundproof walls, everyone present could hear in their minds. Then, uncertainly, Tom announced the intended destination and time without having to utter a single word. A little later, a blue-green holographic grid appeared, into which the robot guided the unconscious monk's hand.

The countdown that commenced set the spectators into tremendous suspense, but a garish flash of light ultimately prevented them from witnessing the man's disappearance. The only thing that they could be sure of was that he was no longer in the laboratory. Even the footage from the security cameras couldn't shed any light on whether the man actually arrived at the correct destination.

CHAPTER 42

The Medicus

Tuesday, November 14, 1307
Chinon, France

Shortly before dawn, Struan saddled the horses. Anselm, who had been observing the Scotsman for a while, turned his gaze away and began to put on the long black robe that, by sheer luck, they had found among their minstrels' clothing. The somber robe formed a medicus' typical uniform, as blood and pus could not be seen on it. Over the robe, Anselm put on his trusty long leather coat that kept him warm in the cold weather.

With a silent clap on the shoulder, Gero said goodbye to Johan. The Flemish knight was staying behind to look after the women and the boy, as well as keep an eye on the kidnapped monk whose absence would be noticed at the Fontrevrault Abbey by the next evening at the latest.

Gero didn't want to worry her any further, so he refrained from waking Hannah to say goodbye. Johan looked at Gero in concern. "If things don't run as smoothly as we hope, we will have a high price to pay," he said.

"You don't say," Gero replied gruffly.

Anselm, who had heard Johan's remark, was struck all at once by the weight of his responsibility. Persecution, torture, and the deaths of all those present would be the likely consequences if he made even one small mistake.

To avoid drawing attention to themselves, Gero, Struan, and Anselm waited patiently by the Vienne's embankment until the city gate was opened at the first cock's crow and the bells began chiming for the morning prayers. Then, the King's seal once again let them enter the city without any trouble.

The medicus lived in a narrow corner house next to the inner fortress wall and across from Saint Maurice, the only church in the enclosed part of the city. It was a gloomy part of town, for hardly any light fell into the alley, and it reeked of damp walls and brackish water. A few rats scurried across the narrow cobblestones before disappearing into a drain that led into the Viennne.

With a cautious glance around, Gero made sure there was no one to thwart their plans. Some distance away, they tied the horses to an iron ring embedded in the church's unplastered limestone, hoping that any passersby would assume that the animals' owners were in church for the early mass.

With his back pressed flat against the house's wall, Struan peered into a small window, but there was nothing to be seen. The medicus was either still sleeping or not at home, which might be problematic for them. The door to the house was unlocked. In a city like Chinon, having something stolen was a rare occurrence.

So that it wouldn't creak, Struan opened the door only as far as was necessary for him to enter. Nimbly, he slipped through the narrow opening and gestured for Anselm and Gero to follow him.

Together, they crept through the dank air of the ground floor of the house before climbing up a flight of cherry wood stairs that creaked softly despite their best efforts. A loud snore could be heard from behind an open door, revealing that the master of the house was still lying in bed.

A small, open window in the stairwell let a little sunlight in through its shutters, allowing Anselm to catch a glimpse of Struan's expression of grim concentration. Along with Gero, the Scotsman snuck onto the small stair landing that led to three different rooms. Gero turned his head to Anselm and gestured for him to stay behind. Silently, as if on command, the two Templars stormed into the room of the clueless physician. The medicus was so shocked that he did nothing. A moment later, with his eyes covered, mouth gagged, and hands bound behind his back, the gaunt man was led by Struan into the small hallway.

Anselm's heart hammered in his chest. He stared at the scrawny figure who was standing on the stair landing, shivering. With his black, shoulder-length hair, and naked save for his braies, he looked like Jesus on the cross.

"Forward," Struan growled, giving the captive a light shove.

With Struan behind him, the medicus stumbled his way down the stairs.

"If you play along, no harm will come to you," Gero assured him.

"But if you don't," Struan hissed, "Jesus will celebrate his next birthday without you."

The medicus gave a muffled grunt that could be interpreted as agreement. Unimpressed, the Scotsman maneuvered the physician into the sitting room, where he forced him to sit in a chair in front of a large oak table.

"I'm taking off the gag now," Struan announced threateningly. "If you dare scream, I'll cut your throat."

The medicus nodded hastily, which the Templar acknowledged with a satisfied smile. After Struan had taken the gag out of his mouth, the captive told the men where parchment, goose-quill, and ink were to be found.

In order to make space on the table, Struan shoved aside a plate of leftovers and an empty, brown stoneware cup, shooing away a few fat flies that had been feasting on the remnants of some cheese.

Struan took an apple from a fruit basket in the middle of the table, and bit into it heartily. The medicus slumped down in fear. Threatening torture if he dared to look up, Gero began to take off his blindfold. Then he ordered the medicus to dip the quill into the silver inkpot and dictated word for word what he was to write.

"I, Medicus Etienne de Azlay, declare that my good friend, Medicus Anselmo de Trevere, shall be my representative, as I myself am ill and cannot fulfill my duties for the period of my illness. Written and signed on the day of St. Lawrence in the year of our Lord 1307. Signature."

Mistrustfully, Gero watched the medicus scrawl his name. Out of a stack of papers, Gero took a single page and studied it closely.

"Should you try to use anything other than your usual signature," he said, holding out the document to the medicus, "I will check it against this document, and cut off a fingertip for every failed attempt you make."

The medicus nodded and completed his signature without looking up.

As Gero was about to replace the blindfold on the frightened man, his gaze fell on a worn, leather bag in the corner of the room. "What is that?" he asked harshly, pointing at the bag.

"I … I can explain it to you," the man stammered, his gaze fixed firmly on the tabletop. "But cover my eyes first. I don't want to look at you. I know that you'll kill me if I do."

In a trembling voice, his eyes now covered again, he explained the assorted medical utensils in the bag to Gero and his companions. Anselm was amazed. The various lancets, delicate forceps, scissors, and a sharp, handy silver axe all looked rather advanced to him.

In a small, linen sack, they found sewing supplies: catgut and fine silver needles of various sizes in a red, felt booklet. There were also rolls of white linen, sheep's wool compresses filled with a mixture of dried liverwort and alum powder, as well as a plain wooden case containing small, different-colored, wax-sealed stoneware vials.

"Do I have to know what this is used for?" Anselm asked innocently, holding up a vial.

"No," Gero decided. "If we start to distribute medicine, it won't end well."

"I don't know what your plans are, sir," the medicus whispered hoarsely, "but if you're trying to enter the castle in my place, you should know that the steward is waiting for a medicine that I must take to him as soon as possible. It's a mixture of pulverized boar penis, hop blossoms, fly shells, and the dried slime of a brown toad."

Anselm's face twisted in disgust.

"Taken with stallion piss during a full moon, it increases your potency," the medicus croaked. "It works wonderfully if you want to deflower a virgin. Equipped with this, you can easily take seven women at the same time. But it also helps against hair loss. If he asks you about it, it's in the small green bottle."

"Fascinating," said Struan, who was still looming over the medicus. "But we're far more interested in what you did with the Templars."

"I only examined them," the pale man answered in a whimper. "Nothing else. They enjoy the best of health …" He paused abruptly as it became clear to him how much of a lie this statement was. "Well," he added lamely, "they're still alive at least."

Gero nodded to Struan, who opened one of the vials they had brought with them and gave it to him. Unsympathetically, Gero set the brew to the medicus' lips.

"Drink!" he ordered the man, whose limbs were shaking with fear.

Gasping, the medicus turned his head to the side and pressed his lips together.

"Drink it now!" Struan snarled, and seized the physician's bony shoulder so tightly that he yelped in pain.

"You're going to kill me," the medicus moaned in despair, trying to open his lips only as wide as he needed to speak.

"If we wanted to kill you, our blades would have done so long ago," Gero explained serenely. Then he added sharply, "Now do what I've told you to do!"

Slowly, the man opened his mouth just wide enough for Gero to pour the liquid down his throat.

Anselm watched the man's Adam's apple bob up and down. A choked cough followed, and tears trickled down from his blindfold. A few sharp breaths later, he slumped over in his chair. Struan grabbed him and laid him down almost gently on the wooden planks.

"Now it's your turn," Gero said, and turned to Anselm with a frighteningly neutral expression. Anselm was shaking with nervous excitement, and suddenly felt an urgent need to pee.

After Gero had left the house to attend to the old maid and the wagon, Anselm and Struan waited for a messenger from the castle to appear and request the medicus' service.

Anselm was shivering, but whether it was from the cold or fear, he could not say. Struan seemed to notice his unease, and he stood up to light a fire. Sympathy wasn't his true motivation, however, but the realization that every house usually kept a fire burning in the early morning hours, and that the neighbors might wonder why there was no chimney smoke on this particular day. After lighting the fire, the Scotsman kneeled down next to the unconscious man and placed his ear on the man's chest while grabbing his wrist.

"I can barely hear his heartbeat," the Templar muttered in concern. "We should carry him back to bed."

Anselm nodded uncertainly. He wondered how they would transport the medicus up the narrow steps, but then Struan simply grabbed the man like the carcass of an animal and heaved him onto his left shoulder. Without Anselm's help, he climbed up the creaking steps as the medicus' arms bobbed up and down on his broad back like the limbs of a marionette.

Anselm was considering whether to follow Struan, but before he could decide, someone pounded on the door, and a second later a boy of about fourteen stood in the room, staring at him in surprise.

"Where is the medicus?" gasped the unexpected visitor breathlessly.

With a swift glance, Anselm inspected the boy's poor clothing. Apparently, he was neither a page nor a squire .

"The medicus is sick," he announced calmly. "You will have to make do with me."

The boy didn't seem to hear him, and wrinkled his forehead. "I've come by order of the castle steward. It is absolutely urgent. Where is the medicus? Is he in bed?" Without waiting for Anselm's answer, he stormed up the stairs.

For a moment, Anselm was too surprised to follow the boy. Then he heard a choked cry that he couldn't make sense of immediately. Had the boy discovered the medicus, or had Struan immobilized him?

Anselm took a deep breath and hurried up to the second floor. Struan was nowhere to be found.

"I did say that he was sick," Anselm remarked, stepping behind the boy who was staring in astonishment at the medicus laying motionless in the bed.

"He doesn't look sick at all," the boy replied, staring at the man's waxen face. "He looks dead!"

"He isn't dead, he's just lost consciousness," Anselm explained.

"And who, in the name of all things holy, are you?" The messenger boy glared at him in outrage.

"I am his friend," Anselm answered, trying to sound convincing. "I'm representing him as a medicus until he is … until he is well again."

"You're a medicus? Then let's go!" the boy yelled, sounding a little relieved. "It's not me you'll have to convince, but the steward."

Before he followed the boy down into the sitting room, Anselm glanced stealthily around again, but Struan had disappeared like a ghost slipping through a crack in the wall.

When they arrived on the ground floor, Anselm picked up the medical bag in his shaking hands and went outside with the boy. Just before they left the house, Anselm noticed the certificate that the medicus had written for him. Instead of rolling up the parchment, as was the usual practice, he folded it hastily and stuck it in a side pocket of his black woolen surcoat.

While they had been inside, the morning sun had reached the narrow alleys by the city walls, but the air was still bitterly cold. The boy ran down through the city, and Anselm followed him on foot, leading his horse by the reins. But after a short while, the gap between him and the boy was already so huge that he decided to mount the horse and follow the messenger on horseback.

As they approached the castle, he steadily grew more uneasy. He was a man from the twenty-first century. It was insane to pretend to be a medicus from the Middle Ages. And in the event of him actually succeeding, what if someone found out that his letter of recommendation was falsified? Despite all his knowledge, he knew nothing about the actual customs of this era and the responsibilities of a medicus. If he was honest, despite his fascination with the Middle Ages, he had always regarded medieval people as sword-swinging barbarians. Now he was increasingly discovering that he had completely underestimated them.

The view of the castle confirmed his suspicions. Like all the castles that he had seen till now, this one too appeared elegant and well maintained. The paths were neatly cobbled, the towers symmetrically arranged, and everything was bright and cleanly plastered.

The boy was waiting for him at the path leading to what would later be called the clock tower. But right now, everything looked different from what Anselm had experienced of the city in his own time. The tower was not oval, but round, and there was no clock on it. Later on, Joan of Arc would call this place her home, recognize the Dauphin of France, and spend a few happy years at the fortress among her followers. But as of now, she hadn't even been born, and Jacques de Molay had never been imprisoned here, although he would spend a few years here if Gero and his Brothers didn't succeed in changing the course of history.

The morning sun blazed against the bright walls, and Anselm felt momentarily dizzy, his fear growing by the second.

To his relief, the messenger made sure that they went past the guards without having to identify themselves or be searched.

"Finally! There you are!" called a loud male voice when they passed through the gate.

A pot-bellied man in a black and brown uniform appeared and pulled on the bridle of Anselm's gelding. The animal began to prance uneasily, and Anselm cautiously decided to dismount.

"Who are you?" the man gasped in surprise.

Anselm felt his lips go numb. Instead of answering, he retrieved the parchment from his pocket.

Suspiciously, the man inspected the letter. Fortunately, he could read, and asked no further questions.

"If you would follow me, please," he said, now sounding much friendlier.

Gero had tried to prepare Anselm for the dungeon, but to avoid scaring him ahead of time, he had probably been too merciful, and had left out a few gruesome details. As he followed the man through the narrow, grotto-like passageways, Anselm felt as if he was walking through the innards of a great, stinking whale. The dripping ceilings and walls were lit only occasionally by weak, flickering torches.

A sudden brightness blinded Anselm, and a moment later he found himself in a tall, arched hall lit by several fire baskets. Vaguely, he smelled fresh blood, and when he turned around, he found himself gazing upon a man's back that had been completely ravaged by wounds. Anselm realized that the man hanging on the plank like a gutted rabbit must have endured excruciating torture. A soft moan confirmed that the injured man was still alive.

Filled with horror, Anselm watched blood running from countless wounds on the man's muscular backside. How could anyone endure something like this?

Suddenly, a hand seized his arm, yanking him out of his startled state.

"Before you make sure he doesn't die, you first have to examine the figures up there," the uniformed man whispered to him.

Knees trembling, Anselm stepped up to three men who were lying lifelessly on the ground.

"Are they dead?" he heard himself say, and his voice seemed to him as if it came from far away.

His counterpart wrinkled his forehead in confusion. "I think *I* should be asking *you* that question, not the other way around."

Anselm bent down to the first man, whose face was hidden in the shadows. His distinctive white hair and the description that Gero had given him on the way here told him that this must be Henri d'Our. With his thumbs, Anselm pulled up the man's eyelid and inspected his gray iris. The pin-sized pupil didn't show the slightest sign of movement.

"He's dead," he said with conviction, almost convincing himself that it was the truth.

"Shit," the uniformed man swore. "And the others, too?"

Anselm stood up slowly and inspected the two other men. "I think so," he replied carefully.

"What does that mean, you think?" The man in the uniform edged closer to him. "Do you know or don't you?"

"They are dead," Anselm said, as calmly as he possibly could.

The man sighed, not from sympathy, but because of the substantial difficulties he now foresaw for himself. "Can you at least tell me what they died from?"

"A pestilence is the cause of their deaths," Anselm answered.

The man thrust his beefy head toward Anselm. "A pestilence?" he gasped uncomprehendingly.

Anselm felt himself grow hot. Lord, was there already pestilences in this time? Yes, leprosy and plague were well known, and had afflicted entire populations. "A pestilence that can infect anyone who comes into contact with the disease," Anselm explained with a conviction that amazed even himself. "It is dangerous and can spread like a fire in a dry bush."

"Then we should burn the dead immediately," the uniformed man decided, much to Anselm's horror. Feverishly, he searched for an answer.

"If you burn them immediately, the disease will spread with the smoke and could wipe out the entire area," he lied. "You should first lay the dead out in the sunlight. The sun will kill the disease, and then we'll have nothing more to fear."

"Where did you get this knowledge from?" the uniformed man asked him gruffly. "Are you a sorcerer?"

"No … by God's will," Anselm stuttered. All at once, he realized what dangerous territory he was treading on. "This corresponds with the latest research of the medical faculty at the University of Tours."

The soldier nodded, although Anselm's explanation still didn't seem to fully convince him. A second soldier came along. Thin and pale, with a blonde, short haircut, at first glance he didn't seem to be of any importance. Nonetheless, the uniformed man stood to attention when the new arrival turned to face him.

"Sir Guy," the soldier saluted, lowering his head respectfully and quickly stepping aside to grant his commander an unencumbered view of the dead prisoners.

Casually, Sir Guy inspected the corpses on the floor then looked sharply at Anselm.

"And with whom do I have the pleasure of speaking?" he asked in a superior voice.

"My name is Anselm de …"

"Your name doesn't matter. Tell me what your business is here." Sir Guy's watery blue eyes looked as if they could bore through Anselm.

"He is the representative of the local medicus, Sir Guy," the uniformed man said, coming to his rescue. "I'm afraid he has unfortunate news for us." With a nod, the dungeon guard gestured at the supposedly dead Templar knights. "The Templars of Bar-sur-Aube have all died of a pestilence. We have to burn them as soon as possible."

Sir Guy's expression darkened immediately. "Before Guillaume Imbert gives his orders," he snarled, "no one will be burned. Put them in the ice-cellar!"

"But Sire, the disease could infect us as well!" the uniformed man declared bravely.

"Silence!" Sir Guy roared. "Obey my orders, or I'll put you in chains, too!"

In confusion, Anselm watched how much interest the dead Templars aroused in this high-ranking official. The man walked past the row of men, but his eyes showed neither recognition nor sympathy, burning instead with hatred and loathing.

"We don't need you anymore, medicus," Sir Guy declared. A sarcastic smile spread across his face. "Unless you can bring them back to life?" He raised a mocking eyebrow.

Anselm took a step back in shock. "N … no," he stuttered hastily, and looked down at the floor. "Do you honestly think that I'd put myself above the Almighty?"

Sir Guy spat in front of him. "You have a damn loose tongue, medicus. How are you so bold as to ask me such a question?" His eyes blazed in fury.

"I …" Anselm was at a loss for words. "My lord," he tried again, bowing slightly, "I meant no offence …"

"Ah – you meant no offence," Sir Guy sneered. "Get down on your knees and kiss my boots. I want to hear you beg for forgiveness." His voice had grown louder, and two nearby guards looked up with unashamed curiosity.

Damn it, what am I doing? Anselm thought in despair.

"On your knees! "Sir Guy bellowed.

Anselm crumpled as if he had been shot, as one of the nearby soldiers kicked him in the back of his knees. *Holy Mary, Mother of God*, he began to pray silently. The next moment, he felt an iron-shod shoe on the nape of his neck, pushing his head further down to the floor so that his nose nearly touched Sir Guy's boots, which stank of feces and urine.

"I don't hear anything!" Sir Guy snarled.

Anselm couldn't make a sound, as he knew he would throw up if he took a single breath.

Suddenly, hurried footsteps echoed through the room, and someone called loudly, "Sire!"

The boot withdrew itself, and Anselm finally straightened up, gasping for breath.

"Sire," the same voice rang out again. "Your Excellency's messenger has just arrived to give you a secret message from Paris immediately!"

Sir Guy looked at Anselm darkly before squaring his shoulders and hurrying away with the guard who had called him.

Anselm struggled to suppress the urge to throw up.

"You're damn lucky," one of the dungeon guards whispered to him. "That was Sir Guy de Gislingham. He is our Grand Inquisitor's new assistant."

His entire body shaking, Anselm fought to stand up. There was no time to lose. He had to inform Gero immediately that his Brothers were not going to be taken to the trash dump, but into a kind of cold store.

After Anselm had returned to the Church of Saint Maurice, he tied the reins of his gelding to one of the iron rings and looked around. It was midday, and the sun was high in the sky. Most of the city's residents had withdrawn into their houses, and only a few beggars were loitering around the church entrance.

Suddenly he heard a soft whistle.

Gero had found shelter in the shadows near a side entrance. Anselm hurried to him and made his report breathlessly.

"Guy de Gislingham." Gero whispered the name like a grim prophecy. His eyes narrowed, and his already stern features became even stonier.

"Do you know him?" Anselm asked.

Gero smiled wryly. "He was our Brother in Bar-surAube," he said coldly. "Struan and I helped him escape back when we were attacked in our commandery by the kings' soldiers a month ago. We should have left him behind. He is the King's spy – a traitor. I once had the chance to cut the head off this snake, but I didn't because I thought it would be a terrible sin to take a Brother's life. But it was a far greater sin not to do so." Gero's voice was bitter. "Follow me!" he said, and pulled his hood lower over his face.

Making an effort not to draw any attention, they hurried to the medicus' house across the street. After they had slipped up the stairs to the second floor, Anselm was startled by a soft creak at the door. Immediately, Gero drew his hunting knife, and Anselm's heart began to pound. Suddenly, a shadow flitted across the hallway. It was Struan, who had wormed his way into a narrow wall cabinet so that he could see who had entered the house of the still unconscious medicus. The Scotsman's expression darkened further when he learned what had happened in the dungeon.

"Gislingham, that bastard," he muttered, looking scornfully at Gero. "I should have killed him back in the valley when he challenged me to a duel. It was wrong of you to spare him."

Gero let out a deep sigh, thoughtfully observing the unconscious man on the bed. "We already have enough souls on our consciences. Let's just count ourselves lucky that we didn't run into that English traitor when we performed at the castle. In any case, we have to finish what we've begun. Instead of the trash heap, our sleeping Brothers now lie in the ice cellar. To retrieve them, we need a map that shows us the passageways and catacombs under the castle." While Struan and Anselm were still looking at him cluelessly, Gero continued with a hopeful smile, "and I already have an idea of who can help us."

Frydel, Madame Fouchet's messenger boy, was not just trustworthy, but also incredibly resourceful. As Gero had expected, the small French boy knew immediately how he could get Gero what he needed.

"You are no minstrels," the boy whispered as he handed Gero a tattered parchment in a deserted alley. "Am I right?"

Gero suppressed a smile. "What am I paying you?" he asked instead of answering the boy's question.

"Two silver Livres Tournois," Frydel said hastily, and Gero could see that he was not satisfied with his response.

"That's rather pricey, don't you think?" Gero grumbled, searching for the right coins in his money pouch.

"Let's just say that it wasn't easy," the boy replied. "I *borrowed* the maps from the city treasurer, and I had to buy off his servant for that. Everything has its price, except death," Frydel declared lightly.

"That's where you're wrong," Gero replied, his features suddenly darkening. "Death costs life. But maybe *your* life isn't worth anything to you."

Frydel looked taken aback. "You know what you're talking about, sir, I can tell."

Gero pressed the coins into the boy's hand, and then placed a third one there. "So that you may *not* know what you are talking about," he said, looking the boy sternly in the eye.

"I'll be as silent as a corpse," Frydel replied chirpily, raising his hand as if he were swearing an oath. "It is a great honor to serve a Brother of the Temple."

Gero looked at the boy in surprise. "Mother Mary be with you," he said with a serious expression. "She will be able to judge the worth of what you've done far better than I." He held out his right hand to Frydel.

His chest swelling with pride, the boy shook Gero's hand with the crossed handshake, revealing that he was already familiar with the obligatory greeting ritual between the knights of the Temple.

The purchase of the hay cart they needed was a far easier affair than that of the maps. The price that Gero offered the bewildered cartwright was far too seductive, and the man immediately agreed to it. After Gero had hitched his brown horse to the wagon, he stocked up on water barrels and feedbags, along with a few sheaves of hay and straw. Meanwhile, Anselm was given the task of keeping watch for soldiers of the Gens du Roi.

As darkness fell, Gero led his horse, attached to the hay wagon, to the front of the medicus' house. With Struan's help, he carried the unconscious physician out of his house and, after hiding him between the water drums and sheaves of hay, covered him with a horse blanket. No matter what happened, they had to prevent the medicus from regaining consciousness before they had finished their mission.

Frydel's map showed that there was a secret entrance directly behind an abandoned ruin just below the castle walls. According to the map, the passageway hidden behind it led straight to the so called ice cellar. As inconspicuously as possible, they placed the cart with the medicus in it near the entrance and carried him into an abandoned goat stable. Behind bushes and a pile of garbage that they moved out of the way, they found a weather-beaten stairway that had obviously not been used in years. Struan struggled to light a candle with a fire striker and a little straw, but with two pulls, Anselm turned on the small LED lamp he had taken with him from the future and handed it to Gero so that he could inspect the map better. While Gero smiled thankfully, the Scottish Templar regarded the man from the future with a look mingled with suspicion and curiosity.

"Don't worry," Gero said, seeing his Scottish friend's unusually timid expression. "This isn't sorcery, it's a torch from the future. Roger Bacon was right. They are rather more advanced than we are in these things."

"Shortly before daybreak tomorrow we will sneak into the underground passageway," Gero decided, unrolling the parchment against the flat wall. "When we have found our Brothers, we'll carry them outside one by one and lay them on the cart with the medicus. Then we'll have nothing left to do but to wait until the city gates are opened."

Anselm nodded, and Struan growled something that no one could understand.

A guard patrolled the city until the bells chimed for midnight. They could hear his call and see his lantern from afar, but before he reached the alley in which they were hidden, he turned around. The deserted area was obviously too eerie for him.

After Gero had looked around once more, he signaled to Struan. With all his might, Struan set himself against the brittle iron door and yanked it off its hinges. They were met with an endless path of darkness, from which no sound could be heard. Gero lifted the door from where Struan had let it fall and set it back against the doorway. Now it was time to wait.

Around four in the morning, when they thought they could be sure that everyone was sleeping, Gero and Struan prepared to infiltrate the cold store.

"Here," Anselm said, handing Gero the lamp.

"Thank you," Gero answered.

He knew how to turn on the magical light even if he had not entirely overcome his discomfort with it. With a pat on the shoulder, he left Anselm behind and gave Struan the signal to set off.

The first three hundred feet led through a musty smelling passageway. Their steps echoed off the roughly hewn walls, and, with the gleaming lamp, they startled countless insects that skittered away into the cracks in the wall.

Suddenly they heard voices some distance away.

"Watch out," Struan whispered to Gero. "Sixty feet more." With his acute hearing, he was able to judge roughly how far away a noise was.

According to the map, they were directly under Fort de Coudray, where groceries were stored during the summer and, well into spring, snow was kept ready in order to satisfy the King's extravagant culinary desires.

Three soldiers of the Gens du Roi were passing the time playing dice games and holding card readings while guarding three corpses. Judging by their slurred speech, they had been comforting themselves with copious amounts of red wine. It would keep them in good spirits until they were released from duty the next morning.

Struan's eyes flickered in the darkness. Slowly the Scotsman raised his left thumb and executed a swift movement underneath his throat. They had not explicitly discussed it, but it was clear that they would have to kill the soldiers if they couldn't incapacitate them in less permanent ways.

Struan and Gero pulled the felt hoods normally worn under their pot helms over their faces. Only their eyes could be seen.

At a sign from Gero, Struan sprang out of an alcove and seized the first soldier by his head of curly hair. Mercilessly, he slammed the man's forehead against the hard oak table and the soldier lost consciousness immediately.

Unnoticed, Gero stepped behind the two other soldiers, and, even before they could shake themselves out of their stunned state, he seized both of them and smashed their heads against each other. Moaning quietly, the men sank to the floor.

From up the stairs, a tired voice floated down, as if someone had just been woken from a deep slumber.

"What's all that noise you're making, Hugo? Everything all right down there?"

Quickly Gero muffled his voice with his arm and yelled, "The card table toppled over."

"Did Jorge have a bad hand again?" the voice shouted impatiently. "You fools need to stop fighting all the time!" Then Gero and Struan could hear shuffling steps trudging away.

Struan returned his sword to its sheath. He rummaged in his leather belt-pouch and pulled out a fire striker, flint, and tinder to re-ignite the two torches that had gone out during the short scuffle.

In the meantime, Gero began to gag and bind the three unconscious soldiers. When he was finished, he searched around for the entrance to the cold store. He spotted it behind a mighty oak door. Luckily, it opened silently and with astonishing ease. Inside the room it was pitch black and frigid.

Struan stepped behind him and held a torch over Gero's shoulder and the three presumably dead Templars. The soldiers hadn't made the effort to remove their rags or even cover them in linen cloths, but, to his great relief, they had freed their limbs from their iron chains.

Silently, the Scotsman handed Gero the torch and bent over Henri d'Our to inspect him. His skin was cold and his limbs were stiff, but Struan's sensitive fingertips felt the slight pulsing of his heart at a specific spot behind his ear. After examining his two other comrades, he stood up with a smile.

"They're still alive," he said to Gero, who fought back a few tears of joy.

Hastily they laid the three unconscious soldiers in place of the Templars and began to carry off the Brothers.

First, Struan heaved his commander onto his shoulder. The Scotsman's own fate hinged upon his survival, as only Henri d'Our could honorably discharge him from the Order so that he could take Amelie as his lawful wife.

Without a second glance, the Scotsman trudged down the passageway to get outside as quickly as possible.

"Wait a minute," Gero whispered after he had lifted Arnaud de Mirepaux onto his shoulder with a soft groan. Although the sinewy, dark-haired Southern Frenchman was emaciated, he was still a heavy burden because of his height. Gero felt around for Anselm's light that he had hooked on his belt earlier. With the push of a button, he lit the passageway as bright as day.

"Go!" he whispered to Struan.

Anselm shivered with cold and excitement and only when he recognized the long shadow cast by the Scottish Templar at the entrance to the cold store did he begin to relax slightly. Gero followed closely behind his comrade, groaning. Both men were carrying what looked, at first glance, like game on their shoulders. Anselm ran up to them to help but Gero shook his head and held out the lamp to him instead. To avoid attracting any unnecessary attention, Anselm dimmed the light.

After Gero and Struan had laid the two unconscious brothers on the hay wagon, the Scotsman suggested that they give the unconscious guards the tincture from the remaining vial so they wouldn't wake up too quickly. Regardless, the King's men had to remain undiscovered for two more hours, until the city gates were opened at the cock's crow and they could take their rescued Brothers back to their campsite. Gero and Struan hurried back into the cold store to fetch Stephano de Sapin, the last of the three Templars. After what seemed like half an eternity to Anselm, they finally returned.

Quietly, Gero disguised the entrance to the cellar with the garbage that they had previously moved aside. Meanwhile, Struan hid the three motionless men in the cart, beside the unconscious medicus, spreading sacks and feed over them.

"So, we've done it," Anselm declared with relief as they set off on horseback with the cart. Now they just had to pass the city guards to cross the bridge into the swamps. "I thought it would be harder than this."

"You best be quiet," Struan whispered harshly. "Celebrating something that hasn't yet been seen to its end brings bad luck."

A moment later, two soldiers stepped in front of the already open gates and crossed their lances in the first light of day.

Gero stopped the wagon as Anselm and Struan reined in their steeds.

"You there!" called an authoritative, young voice. "Come here! I need to see your papers. Do you have any goods to declare?"

Gero tried to hurry, but the young solider stepped up to the wagon so quickly that he didn't manage to produce the royal writ of escort from the saddlebag in time.

The young soldier had already climbed up and was about to pull the blankets and feed aside to inspect what else was in the wagon, when Struan rode up, grabbed him around his waist and plucked him unceremoniously from the wagon. Unlike the Scotsman, the uniformed man had a slim, lightweight build, but he fought back valiantly.

"What are you doing?" he bellowed, struggling so wildly that he lost one of his boots, revealing a blue, felt sock that was full of holes.

"Let him go!" The elder guard's commanding voice made Struan release his victim and he crumpled to the ground.

The man's arrogant gaze was directed at Gero. But to Anselm's astonishment, Gero remained completely calm, and simply held out the King's writ of escort to the stout soldier.

"I hope you have a good reason for your rude behavior," hissed the soldier taking the paper and scanning through it quickly.

Gero hoped that the fellow could read and didn't have to search for a scribe to finally let them pass. The young soldier rearranged his doublet and bent down to look for his lost boot, which he pulled on with a livid expression. He positioned himself next to his older comrade who had just then recognized the seal of the King. Although the younger man began to protest, he waved to Gero to inform him that the entire group could pass.

"They stand under the protection of the Crown of France," declared the elder man to his younger comrade. "If you want to be an officer one day, Luc, you won't lay hands on anyone who has our King's writ of escort."

CHAPTER 43

D'Our

Wednesday, November 15, 1307

With her skirt hitched up, Hannah ran the last fifty yards to the wagon, and flung her arms around Gero's neck with such force that he nearly lost his balance, when she hugged him. Tired but happy, he returned her radiant smile and kissed her tenderly.

"Lord Almighty," Johan rejoiced when he realized that the entire group had returned to the swamp unharmed.

Anselm, on the other hand, was wearing a far less joyous expression. He looked confused and completely exhausted.

Struan raised his hand in greeting before swinging himself off his black stallion.

Matthäus, who had been grooming the rest of the horses, threw the cleaning supplies aside and hurried to Gero who embraced him tightly as the boy nuzzled himself against him. As usual, he asked no questions, though he realized that his uncle's welfare was at stake.

Suddenly Gero's expression darkened, and he pushed the boy aside.

"What happened?" he asked softly as Johan stepped up to him with his head bowed.

"The monk is dead," Johan's voice sounded emotionless, but Hannah knew that the news was affecting the Flemish Templar more than he was prepared to admit.

Gero handed the reins to Matthäus as Johan led him to a pile of branches that were stacked on the corpse to protect it from crows.

"I wanted to wait until you came back before burying him," Johan continued, bending down and brushing aside branches to reveal the body wrapped in a sack and two blankets. "Freya wanted to give him an antidote to drink," he explained, "but he flailed about wildly, and when I tried to calm him down, his eyes suddenly went wide and he stared at me like someone who had lost his mind. Then he stopped moving. It was frightening." Johan shrugged his shoulders apologetically as he registered Gero's dark look. "Freya thinks that his body might not have been able to tolerate the mixture. There was nothing we could do …" He hesitated. "He deserves to be buried on sacred ground, don't you think?"

Gero nodded thoughtfully, and then looked around. "But there's no sacred ground to speak of anywhere nearby." He looked at Johan for an answer.

"We can only hope," Johan added glancing at the cart, "that the others don't meet the same fate."

"By God's will," Gero groaned, hurrying past Hannah toward the hay wagon, "we were able to retrieve all of them. I don't even want to consider that we've saved them from the clutches of the Inquisition only to deliver them to the Lord. We need to check them now, hurry."

A little later, the unconscious Templars were lying next to the fire on blankets and sheepskins. Gero left the medicus on the wagon. They would tend to him later.

Along with Struan, who was able to sense their pulse with his fingertips, Freya examined the three Brothers again, and came to the conclusion that they were still alive. Then again, the Benedictine had only died after he had regained consciousness.

Freya heated water in a cast-iron kettle and motioned for Anselm and Hannah to help her. Carefully, they removed the tattered rags from the Templars whose emaciated bodies were covered with the marks of torture. Cautiously, Freya began to wash the first Templar. While Johan went over to help her, Hannah and Gero followed her instructions and washed the other men while Anselm prepared clean towels and clothing for them.

Hannah recognized that the dark-haired man she was tending to was the same young man with the injured arm she had seen down in the dungeons with Michel. She cleaned his face gently with a warm, damp, linen rag. Even unconscious, his features were etched with pain. His beard was teeming with lice, making Hannah recoil for a moment.

Freya, who had noticed her horror, simply smiled. "We should shave them before they regain consciousness and wash their hair with warm lye."

She beckoned to Johan, who was cleaning Stefano de Sapin's wounds.

Cautiously, he ran his fingertips through the French knight's blonde beard before nodding at Freya. "Stefano would definitely want to be shaved. He is the vainest man I have ever met."

Struan provided them with an endless supply of water and firewood and, on Freya's instructions, Hannah prepared suds from marigold soap in a wooden bucket.

A soft moan made Johan, who was crouching on his knees in front of his tortured Brother, jump up in fright. Glancing up at Gero, who was taking care of Henri d'Our, he made certain that he wasn't the only one who had heard the moan.

Freya appeared almost immediately with a sponge that stank of ammonium and, without hesitation, she pressed it under Stefano's nose.

The Templar began to cough weakly, his upper body suddenly beginning to shake, and he opened his blue-gray eyes. He blinked in disbelief when he saw Freya's red mane hanging over him, and moaned even more loudly. A moment later, he recognized Johan who was bent over him in concern.

Tears welled up in Stefano's eyes, and he sobbed into Johan's chest like a lost child who had been reunited with his mother. After he had calmed down a little, Freya held a cup to his lips, a bitter herbal drink that she had prepared to counteract the headaches and nausea that she suspected would follow the strong brew that had been used to knock him unconscious. Amidst constant coughing fits, Stefano drank it tentatively.

Hannah and Freya watched the moving sight of Johan helping his weakened Brother to sit up, tenderly speaking to him in Old French.

Gradually, the two other Templars came round as well. Henri d'Our took the longest to wake, his age and weakened state taking their toll.

Even the medicus awoke before the commander. With the doctor still blindfolded, Struan administered the medicine Freya had prepared. Afterwards, the Scotsman tied him tightly to the wagon where, after warning him to remain silent, he left him for the time being.

That evening, d'Our and the two other Brothers sat around the fire, washed, shaved, and dressed in clean clothing, warming themselves with large cups of chamomile tea. Freya had prepared a porridge of oatmeal, honey, and apples for the starving Templars. Along with Hannah, she helped the men to eat.

Fascinated, Arnaud de Mirepaux gazed at Hannah gratefully as she raised a spoonful of the porridge to his bloodied lips. "You're an angel aren't you?" he whispered with a smile.

Hannah, who hadn't understood him, simply nodded and returned his smile.

"I knew it," he said and grinned in satisfaction, though his dislocated arm and his other wounds were still causing him dreadful pain.

"I'm afraid you still have to wait for heaven," Gero said, suddenly stepping up to them. "To be safe, we first have to escape the clutches of the French devil."

"I would love to know how we even fell into his clutches." Arnaud raised his head and glanced over at d'Our, who was sitting at the fire with his nephew.

The commander's subordinates surrounded him in a semicircle. No one dared to speak to him, but they were all wondering the same thing. What did he know that he couldn't tell them, even now?

Gero stared at his commander intently. The more he knew about the Head of Wisdom and the High Council, the greater his anger became. Why hadn't the ordinary Brothers of the Order been warned of Philipp IV's intentions in time? After the conversation with his father, it had become clear to Gero that the Order had been in possession of the Head for over a hundred and fifty years, and if his father was right, the High Council had known of a prophecy about the Order's future since that time. Why hadn't they taken everything with them and fled to Portugal, setting up a new headquarter under the King there, instead of putting all their hope in Paris where things had grown steadily more dangerous for the Order? Or why hadn't they just stayed in Cyprus and, over time, secured enough land and power? Fifteen thousand well-equipped men should have been enough to send any enemy fleeing. But scattered to the four winds, they were easy prey.

Gero had too many questions, and he had waited too long for answers. He squared his shoulders and marched resolutely over to his commander. Next to the fire he stopped and looked down at Henri d'Our, who was chewing on his bread.

"*Beau Sire*," Gero said in a cutting tone that he would never have used under normal circumstances.

Anselm, who was close by, bringing new wood for the fire, paused and watched Gero with just as much fascination as the rest of his Brothers.

D'Our raised his head slowly. "Brother Gerard," he said in a shaky voice. "What is your demand?"

"Sire," Gero began again, "I think it is time you shared your knowledge with us. Every one of us has been affected by it, and we have all sworn an oath of silence. As such, I see no reason to keep us in the dark any longer about our Order's fate."

D'Our nodded slowly, but then his gaze fell on Anselm and the women.

"You can trust them," Gero said. "My friend from Trier and his brave companion come from a distant land we thought we could never reach." He nodded at Freya, who was still kneeling on the ground and tending to Stefano. "And without the young lady, Freya of Bogenhausen, who belongs to a Beguine convent that helped us escape, we would never have been able to save you."

The evening had almost turned to night, and the flickering campfire cast surreal, shifting shadows on d'Our's face.

"Very well," the commander began with a sigh, laboriously sitting up straight and making sure that he didn't move his hand with the broken fingers too much. With a quick glance, he ensured that no one was approaching the small campsite. "Bring me the Head of Wisdom," he said quietly.

Besides Gero, no one understood his command. Even Struan and Johan, who knew about the existence of the strange machine, had no idea what it could do.

Everyone's eyes followed Gero as he disappeared into the minstrels' wagon and reappeared a little later with a small gray box.

He set a red silk pillow on the floor, and placed the Head upon it like a crown. Their astonishment grew when d'Our began singing a familiar Gregorian chant.

The lid of the small box sprang up, and suddenly a shimmering, blue-green light appeared. Freya cried out in horror, and the usually unfazed Templars gasped as well.

"Nothing will happen to you," Gero reassured them hastily.

He was slightly annoyed that d'Our had not explained what the Head could do in order to prepare the others for what they would now experience. Even Anselm and Hannah looked fearful as they stared at the box and the light, spellbound. Matthäus had jumped up, choosing to seek safety with Hannah instead of Gero or his uncle.

When the small female head appeared, everyone held their breath.

Only Arnaud de Mirepaux hissed in fury, "What is this? Are we really fraternizing with sorcerers now? I always thought that was foolishness. But now I see that Philipp of France was right – we've been invoking slit-eyed demons with idol worship!"

"Arnaud, shut your mouth!" Gero yelled with a sideways glance at Henri d'Our.

He had no idea what his commander had in mind, but hoped that he didn't plan on making Hannah and Anselm vanish in front of their eyes.

As if in a trance, d'Our stared at the pulsating female head, whose chin-length black hair blew in an imaginary wind.

Instinctively, everyone shut their eyes and absorbed in their minds what was happening. In a language that everyone understood, a pleasant female voice guided them through a sprawling green valley and over deep blue rivers, until even the last of them was ready for what would follow.

In what seemed like a vision, they learned that two female scientists from the year 2151 would travel back into the past, one hundred and fifty years ago, with the intention of delivering a secret message to the Order of the Temple in 1118. They intended to carry out a specific change in the course of history, which would have far-reaching effects on the history of humanity. The Order of the Temple had been selected for this goal because precise calculations indicated that the Order's preservation and expansion beyond the year 1307 would change the face of the world in a peaceful way. Early on, the Order's leadership had already been following the balancing principle of tolerance among different faiths, and, for a while, they managed to bring these ideals into harmony with the Catholic Church. But then the dark era of the Inquisition began, and it became impossible to publicly declare tolerance of members of different faiths without putting one's own existence at risk. Had the Order not been annihilated, and had it even been able to expand its influence, there would have been neither the Holocaust nor the two World Wars, neither capitalism nor communism, no atomic threat, and no other reasons for armed conflict. The three major monotheistic religions, Islam, Christianity, and Judaism, and the religious representatives of the peoples of the East would have built an alliance under the diplomatic influence of the Order, where they not only tolerated one another, but would have even begun a peaceful co-existence. It would have been a world of trade and development, under the eyes and guardianship of open-minded, devout men and women, for the welfare of all humanity.

The impetus for this unbelievable mission was not a future generations' romantic visions of an extinct knights' order, but simply a survival strategy. The world was balancing on the edge of a knife in the year 2151. Brutal battles over the allocation of natural resources, religious wars, environmental degradation, and violent natural disasters that shook all of humanity, were tearing apart countries and sending the world into chaos. China and India, as ambitious upcoming world powers, had pumped the very last oil reserves out of the earth, and with the same insatiable policy of growth and expansion as their predecessors, had driven most of humanity back to mere subsistence. With political upheaval everywhere and an uncontrolled global population boom, all kinds of decisions were ultimately left to greedy business magnates, who bled the planet dry and reduced the human population to robotic, laboring slaves. Controlled by computer systems that were able to decrypt even the thoughts of an individual person, people were hardly in the position to protect themselves from manipulation and total surveillance. The people had long been made into marionettes who served the whims of a global market-oriented system with its control center located in the land of the rising sun.

God had long ago deserted the world. A small group of anarchistic young warriors who become scientists, however, had managed to gain access to what was once top-secret research by the American military in the depths of the now impoverished American continent. By deploying a re-engineered timeserver, they believed they had found the key to solving the global crisis. With technology based on long-lost knowledge, they embarked on a journey back into the past, with the intention of setting in motion a ripple in the time-space continuum. According to complicated calculations, their own survival in this new, alternative world was guaranteed, although if their mission were successful, they would be the only ones to remember what had been, or what might have been.

The plan ended in catastrophe, however. Instead of landing in the year 1118, they became stranded in Jerusalem in 1148. While stuck in the middle of the desert, they became embroiled in a conflict between Templars and Saracens, and, thanks to the fact that they spoke Old French, the greatly weakened Templar army took them in, saving them from dying of thirst. When they arrived in Jerusalem, they realized that their contact with their base in 2151 had been cut off. Every attempt they made at re-establishing contact was unsuccessful. In the hopes that their mission to change the world could be accomplished even without guidance from home, they struck up a friendship with the Grand Master of the Templars in Jerusalem. Undaunted and eager to learn, the wise man had absorbed whatever information they could provide him with, and for weeks, he and his most trusted men sat together in secret meetings and deliberated about what would need to be done. In the end, rationality won out: the Templars realized that the world as they knew it tolerated only a low level of progress. The Temple leaders knew that they had to use their newly acquired knowledge cautiously to avoid being denounced as heretics.

But then, a far more unbelievable secret was gradually revealed: there had already been an encounter of the Templars with travelers from a far distant future. Nonetheless, there were barely any records of this encounter, and no one could tell what purpose this mission had served.

Meanwhile, the stranded scientists' desire to return to their world became almost manic amidst the deprivation and increasingly frequent attacks from Fatimid troops on the fortress in Jerusalem. The desperate young women decided to write messages to leave behind as burial objects in the mass graves of the Brothers of the Order who had died in combat. Their hope was that when the graves were being excavated hundreds of years later, someone who was capable of building a device that could sent them back into the future would discover these messages. Hannah and Anselm were the only people who could appreciate how close they had actually come to this goal.

Just as abruptly as it had begun, the vision ended. Even sharp-tongued Arnaud de Mirepaux was at a loss for words. His mouth hung open, and he sat frozen, staring at his commander as if he were the devil himself.

Henri d'Our cleared his throat before he began to speak again. "One day, the women disappeared without a word of farewell. They left the Head of Wisdom behind, with instructions on how to use it, and with a Gregorian hymn as the password. From then on, the Order had access to detailed information about future events, as well as a diverse array of inventions and sophisticated trade systems. Moreover, if there were ever an emergency, we could go back into the past with the Head's help. But there was no coming back after that. Next to the Head, the Templars of Jerusalem found a note promising that they would do everything they could to prevent the annihilation of the Order at the designated point in time."

To everyone's surprise, Struan was the first to speak.

"Why?" His hoarse voice was quiet but unwavering, as his eyes met those of his exhausted commander. "You knew that someone wanted to destroy us. And it wasn't just two days ago, but more than a hundred years in the past. Yet ..." Struan swallowed hard as his voice faltered. "Yet you didn't think it was important to warn us in time … You let all of us run into a trap like frightened rabbits, and then let us all be skinned alive." He grimaced in contempt and despair.

"Brother Struan," d'Our began in a guilty voice. He looked around at his audience to make sure he had all their attention. "It wasn't, and still isn't, as simple as you might think. We didn't know whether history had taken another course. Initially, we hoped that the former owners of the Head would keep their promise, when they reassured us they would do everything they could to change the course of history to help us, even after their hasty departure in 1153. But then, when the catastrophe began to run its course, the High Council had to conceive of a new plan in case the prophecy of the Order's destruction was true. It was impossible to inform all our Brothers about this beforehand. Guy de Gislingham is a good reason why. Our Order has been infiltrated by spies. There are few men we can trust. Do you have any idea what would happen if the Head of Wisdom fell into our enemies' hands?"

The commander turned to Gero for sympathy, who gave him a barely perceptible nod.

"This miraculous object gives its controller the ability to overcome time and space. Just imagine if someone like Philipp IV learned of it," d'Our continued in a low voice. "For this reason, the Head was long ago relocated to a secret chamber in the Cistercian abbey of Heisterbach, on the other side of the Rhine, far away from the influence of the French kings. And although we were tempted, we only humbly noted some of the futuristic technologies that the Head offered us and used them to help neither the Order nor humanity in general. The time was not yet ripe for many of the things that were so miraculously revealed to us. We would have been burned as heretics if we had told anyone about our knowledge. Nonetheless, inventions like improved magnetic compasses, unbelievably precise cartographical data, instructions for fighting deadly diseases, and the introduction of a sensible numeric system were too seductive for us to ignore. We had to expend tremendous effort in finding explanations for all these inventions. And we had to demand strict silence from anyone in the Order who came to learn of our secret knowledge."

For a moment, the group sank into contemplative silence.

"And?" Arnaud asked. "Does this machine also know if Jesus actually died on the cross, if he was buried in the ground, or if he really ascended to heaven? Is he even God, or merely mortal like the rest of us?"

The commander felt the group's eyes fixed on him. He tried to smile, but could only muster a tired grimace. "We are all godly creations. The world … the Almighty … and everything that lives in it is comprised of pure energy. Each one of us is part of this godly light, and even when he dies, he remains a part of it. Our Lord Jesus is no exceptions there, and this machine can't change anything about that. On the contrary, it gives further evidence for this truth. Just think of the Gospels of John and his followers, which, beyond giving us a vision of the future, confirm that there is a world behind this world – even if we can't perceive it."

Gero spoke up. "Is it possible to send our friends here back into the future?" he asked in Middle High German, nodding at Anselm and Hannah, though he hated thinking about Hannah returning to her world.

D'Our answered in Middle High German as well. "We will probably have to take them in, Brother Gerard, possibly to the end of our days, as no one can travel into the future with the Head."

Unlike Anselm, Hannah exhaled in relief, and gave Gero a stealthy smile that he returned with mixed feelings.

"If you want to travel into the future," d'Our continued, "you need someone to retrieve you from there, and even then, only if the Head allows it. However, it is possible to travel from here into the past, but only to times you aren't already existing in, for it's impossible to exist in the same time twice. The Head performs a check before every journey to determine whether you are suitable for it or not. In any case, it should not be treated as a toy. We must recognize that it is a dangerous creation that can summon Judgment Day if it falls into the wrong hands."

"Was that what you wanted?" Gero asked, switching to French so that his comrades would understand him.

"To summon Judgment Day?" D'Our looked at him as if he had lost his mind.

"No," Gero said, shaking his head. "Did you intend to kill Philipp IV and his parents in order to protect the Order from its downfall and to protect the Head from him, too?"

"It was a desperate plan," d'Our admitted hesitantly, "but it was not the right thing to do. And perhaps God the Almighty used you to prevent it from happening."

"Does that mean that you're going to stop interfering with time, and let things run their course?"

"Yes, in principle," d'Our answered softly. "Still, that doesn't mean that the Order's fate has been sealed. With our knowledge about the future, we may still be able to save whatever there is left to save. If we set off tomorrow morning and battle our way through the German lands, perhaps we can still change things as far as the Almighty will allow. And I hope, in the name of the Holy Virgin, for the support of everyone here, including our two Sisters." His eyes wandered to the women, and a small smile played on his lips.

No one dared to contradict him. It could take weeks, perhaps even an entire lifetime, for them to truly understand the truths they had just learned. Silent nods went round.

"So be it," sighed the commander, and then, softly and reverently, he began the vesper prayer.

CHAPTER 44

The Traitor

Thursday, November 16, 1307

The next morning, Hannah prepared, at Johan's request, a warm drink of red wine, egg yolk, honey, and spices for the Brothers they had rescued from Chinon.

"I can ride," Stefano de Sapin declared bravely, after Gero had asked his Brethren who wanted to ride a horse for the rest of the journey, and who would prefer to ride on the wagon.

Stefan was a tall, sinewy man, and even the Grand Inquisitor of France hadn't been able to take his particular combination of stubbornness and courage from him. Still a little wobbly on his feet, he stood up.

"I'll ride too," announced Arnaud de Mirepaux. Despite the pain that still plagued him, he squared his angular shoulders.

Henri d'Our, however, said nothing. His fingers were broken, and the tight bandage to ease the swelling made it impossible for him to hold onto a horse's reins. He wasn't sure if he would ever be able to fight with a sword again.

Gero loosened the floorboards in the wagon and distributed the swords and shields they had hidden there. Arnaud hefted a gleaming sword in his hand. Gero brought out three crossbows and three new, English longbows. As the men discussed the fearsome weapons, Freya managed to pull Johan aside for a few minutes.

Arnaud, who had relieved himself close by, clicked his tongue as Johan marched past him to give Freya a warm cloak. "Can I get such a pretty maiden when we're safe, too?"

"You're an idiot," Johan snorted with a sheepish grin.

"What will you do if the old man notices your dalliance?"

"I think," Johan replied, "that our commander has more important things on his mind right now, and besides, I heard that he once contradicted Brother Augustinus, when he claimed that women represent a fundamental evil," Johan smiled. "Apparently he said, 'If women are fundamentally evil, Brother Augustinus, how do you explain why the Holy Virgin, a woman, stands at the top of our Order?'"

"And what did Augustinus say?"

"Nothing. He was speechless."

While the Brothers of Bar-sur-Aube prepared for their journey, chaos reigned at the castle of Chinon.

"Guillaume Imbert will skin you all alive!" Guy de Gislingham was livid. He strode past the lifeless bodies of the three guards who had been pulled from the cold store. "Not only did the three dead Templars disappear," he growled, "it looks as if this strange pestilence has taken these three men as well."

The officers of the Gens du Roi, who had been in charge of the dead soldiers, looked ashamed.

"Do you think the Templars have risen from the dead?" a pot-bellied dungeon guard suggested with a shudder.

"Risen from the dead?" Gislingham cried. In three steps, he stormed up to the man. "You should be hanged for your stupidity! Take another look at our guards. Someone hit them on the head before they died. Templars were at work here!" He turned around to address the twenty guards of the Gens du Roi, as well as thirty French royal soldiers.

"No one else," he continued scornfully, "possesses the audacity to steal three corpses from one of the most secure dungeons in France under the eyes of nearly fifty soldiers."

None of the men dared to utter another word.

Gislingham glanced around. "The only question is how they got inside, and how they knew where their Brethren were located." His hawk-like gaze landed on a tall, dark-haired soldier. "Pierre de Vichy, do you have any idea how someone might have gained access to one of the most important prisoners from the Order?"

Pierre snapped to attention, his discomfort steadily growing. After all, it had been he and Michel who had shown the two women the dungeons.

Michel, who was standing next to him, seemed to be plagued by similar thoughts. Uneasily, he shifted his weight from one foot to the other.

Gislingham hadn't missed his unease. "Soldier," he hissed at Michel darkly. "What is making you so nervous that you're fidgeting like a three year old?"

"I might know who was behind the attack," he answered hoarsely.

"Well?" Gislingham's eyes blazed. "Why have you only brought this up now?"

"It just occurred to me," Michel said weakly. "There were minstrels …"

Pierre felt his gut twist. Surely Michel wouldn't be so stupid as to tell him about the women?

"One of them seemed odd to me," Michel continued in a hoarse voice. "I bumped into him on my rounds in the stables, where he had no business being. He spoke a strange language."

"What did he look like?" The question came so hard and fast that Michel winced.

"He was tall, with black hair and broad shoulders."

"Who else was with him?"

Unnoticed, Pierre de Vichy shut his eyes. His heart was beating so mightily that he feared it would rattle his chain mail. *Good God*, he prayed, *please don't let Michel mention the women.*

"There was a redheaded fellow," Michel began tentatively, "who was performing with another man up in the hall. He had a badly scarred face."

Gislingham looked stunned. "And the other?" His voice was almost a whisper. "Can you remember the color of his eyes?"

Michel found the question odd, and he honestly couldn't remember the man's eyes. His goal that evening had been to celebrate his first free weekend in forever, and to get incredibly drunk. He had only been paying attention to the women, not some minstrel.

Pierre, however, was the one to speak. "They were blue," he said without the slightest hesitation in his voice. "As blue as a cloudless summer sky."

"Shut the city gates," Gislingham commanded. "Now! Until we have found the perpetrators, no one leaves, and no one comes in. Understood?" He turned to the other men. "And you," he snarled in fury, looking up at the tower of dogs, "release the beasts from their chains and gather together every man in the castle. We will comb all paths that lead out of the city, in every direction. They can't have gone far!"

Struan had already left the campsite before daybreak to take the medicus, blindfolded and tied onto the donkey's back, towards Fontevrault. Outside the swamps the donkey would be able to find its way home.

On the way back the morning air was so foggy that Struan could hardly see his hand in front of him, but his sensitive ears heard the riders and their howling dogs long before they came near him.

He spurred his black horse on. After a while, however, the riders had gained on him, closing the distance to only six hundred feet. A moment later, a crossbow bolt hissed forward and pierced his horse's jaw from the side.

With a cry of pain, the animal reared up on its hind legs and dashed off. Struan let himself slip halfway out of his saddle, pressing himself flat against the horse's belly for cover. Feverishly, he wondered which path he should take. After he had left the medicus near the road to Fontevrault, he had intended to take a path straight through the woods to Parilly, where he had parted from Gero and the others. Should he now distract his pursuers from his companions, or should he try to lure them down a false trail? In any case, his horse would not endure this torture much longer. The arrow had buried itself deep into the animal's head.

The panicking horse barely reacted to a squeeze on its flanks. In its fear, it galloped even deeper into the forest where the ground grew increasingly muddy. Suddenly, the horse staggered.

"Come on, boy," Struan pleaded. "Don't die on me! Not now!" He glanced backwards. The tree boughs were obscured by fog, and every noise sounded muffled. Nonetheless, the tracks in the soft forest floor were a clear invitation to his pursuers. The horse swayed, whipping its head to and fro, trying to rid itself of the arrow.

Behind a stone outcrop, Struan stopped. "Quiet, my boy," he whispered, cautiously patting the animal's nostrils. The wooden shaft protruded from its blood-soaked, black coat. Because the iron snaffle lay behind the arrow, he couldn't free the horse from its bridle. If he didn't manage to pull out the bolt, the poor horse would die before his eyes.

Struan opened his belt pouch and pulled out the last sealed vial of Freya's mixture, hoping it would act like a painkiller. Hastily, he opened the seal and held the animal's head in place with his arm before drizzling the liquid from the small bottle into the horse's mouth.

He waited for a moment. Finally, he sat down on a stone, and with one arm, encircled the horse's head so tightly that, despite its strength, it couldn't escape. With his free hand, he yanked the bolt, pulling out the bloody tip. The horse reared up and let out a heart-wrenching cry. Where the arrow had been was a gaping hole, as large as a coin.

Struan quickly took off his brown, hooded scarf. With the help of the bridle, he pressed the fabric to the bleeding wound but instead of calming down, the animal began to snort nervously. All at once, its legs quivered and buckled, and its heavy body slumped to the ground. With rapid, shallow breaths, the animal lay there, unable to move. It seemed the painkilling potion was too much for even a horse.

Struan unharnessed the weakened animal and loosened its saddle belt. With a sigh, he removed his sword and shield from the horse.

"I'm sorry, my friend," he murmured, "I can't do anything more for you."

He pricked up his ears for movements in the forest then stepped out from behind the outcrop to make the rest of his journey back by foot.

"Weapons down, you Scottish bastard," yelled someone through the thick fog.

Struan was more baffled than afraid when he found himself gazing into the triumphant face of Guy de Gislingham. Behind the Englishman stood at least ten French soldiers, five of whom held their crossbows aimed at the Templar.

Before the group started down the road to Saint Jacques, Gero had asked his commander what they should do with the dead monk. To deny him a burial on sacred ground seemed like a mortal sin.

"God is everywhere," d'Our reassured him. "We can't drag him through half of France just to find a suitable cemetery."

At the commander's word, Gero and Johan hastily dug a grave with the shovel that Gero had hidden in the wagon with the weapons. Covered in a sack, the corpse was carried to the grave and lowered into it as the Templars completed their ritual with soft chants and prayers. Shortly after the improvised ceremony, d'Our gave the command to set off.

They stopped for the first time in a dense oak forest near Parilly where they were to wait for Struan. The hours passed, the morning mist slowly cleared, but the Scotsman never arrived.

"I'll go find him," Johan suggested, bowing slightly in front of d'Our and looking up into his commander's face for his permission. D'Our nodded weakly, leaning on the minstrels' wagon. Only his stern expression revealed that he had once been the imposing commander of a large Templar settlement.

Hannah used the brief pause to take a short walk and relieve herself. Gero, who was busy hanging the feedbags around the horses' necks,

558

smiled at her as she disappeared behind a thick hazelnut bush. On her way back, she walked past Arnaud de Mirepaux who was leaning against a sturdy oak tree amusing himself with a game of boules. He had set an acorn some distance away as the goal, and was trying to hit it with another acorn. With a friendly wave, he called Hannah over. There was nothing they could say to each other as he spoke only Old French. Still, she pulled her cloak tighter around her shoulders and sat down beside him. With his dark locks, black stubble, and impish, dimpled grin, he looked like a typical Frenchman. He tried his best to communicate with her using his hands and feet and occasionally let out such an infectious laugh that she had to join in.

"Do you have any idea what that trickster is saying to you?" Gero asked, appearing at Hannah's side unnoticed.

She shook her head. "But he is very entertaining in his own way," she answered as Arnaud grinned at her from the side.

"Yes," Gero smirked, "that he is …" He called out a few words in Old French, and Arnaud, whose expression had darkened at Gero's words, once again broke out in hearty laughter. Stefano, who was nearby, looked up as well, and his face brightened. Somehow, the Templars rescued from Chinon seemed to have found their way back to life, perhaps grasping how much luck they had had.

Suddenly, Johan came galloping back on his horse. "They've discovered us!" he yelled as he sprang off his horse. "They killed Struan!"

"What are you saying?" Gero hurried up to him and gripped him tightly by the shoulders.

Johan couldn't control himself any longer. Tears rolled down his face; again and again he shook his head in disbelief. "The soldiers of Chinon are marching. I saw them on the road here. A second group is on their way back to the city. I saw Struan hanging lifelessly on the back of one of their horses. He was covered in blood, and neither his hands nor feet were tied. That can only mean that he's dead!"

"Impossible!" Arnaud shouted. "The Scotsman would never let himself be caught, and besides, how would they even know that he's a Templar?"

"Guy de Gislingham is at the castle," Johan retorted. "Have you already forgotten? If he sees Struan, dead or alive, he will know that it was us who freed you!"

"We have to take the women and the boy to safety," Gero said quickly, looking around until he found Anselm. "I want you to take the women and Matthäus down into the village with two horses. From there, ride eastwards to Sazilly. You have to cross the Vienne so the dogs don't sniff you out."

D'Our stepped up and raised his hand authoritatively. "They must take the Head with them," he said to Gero looking him sternly in the eyes, "and try to find their way into the German lands through Tours and Troyes. Then they'll give it to your father so that he can hide it. It is our only chance to protect it from Philipp's grasp."

"Maybe you could follow us," Anselm suggested. "I don't know if I can travel alone with two women and a child through half of Europe in the year 1307."

D'Our's gray, wolf-like eyes were fixed on him. "Listen, my foreign friend," he said quietly. "Our prospects of escape are close to zero. They will kill us as soon as they catch us."

He had spoken French so as not to distress Hannah, who was standing next to Anselm.

"Go to Breydenburg Castle," Gero added in Middle High German. "My father will take care of all of you." He gripped Hannah's hand and smiled weakly. "You have to go far away before the King's troops pick up your scent," he said quietly to her.

Freya began to cry and Hannah laid a comforting arm around her shoulders. "What does this all mean?" she asked, fixing Gero with a look of alarm.

"It means that you will live," Gero replied in a subdued voice, "but only if we part now."

Hannah loosened herself from Freya and stared at him in disbelief. "No," she gasped. "You can't possibly leave us alone. We don't know our way around here at all. Do you really think there is any point in me continuing to live in this chaos if you're not by my side?"

He stepped up to her, placed his arm around her waist and pulled her towards him. "There is a reason," he said softly, and looked at Matthäus, who was standing by the wagon, rigid with fear. "Trust me, and stay with the boy. We will join you as soon as we can." Without caring that his commander was watching, he kissed her. "I love you, no matter what happens. Never forget that!"

Numbly, Hannah stood unmoving as Gero belted on his sword. Anselm put on his chain mail uncertainly. A few steps away from him, Johan and Freya bade each other farewell. The redheaded woman looked heartbroken. Out of the corner of her eye, Hannah could see that Johan was obviously fighting the same battle as Gero. One last time, he held Freya tenderly in his arms and stroked her red hair before he kissed her.

As a sobbing Freya mounted the horse behind her, Hannah felt her sorrow deepen. She turned to look at Matthäus, who was trying his best to bid Gero goodbye like a steely soldier, when the Templar unexpectedly gathered him into his arms and hugged him tightly. With bated breath, Hannah watched Gero lift the boy onto the horse behind Anselm. As tears ran down the boy's face, Gero slapped the horse on the flanks. Somewhere in the mist, they could hear a pack of dogs howling and barking. They needed to leave immediately.

Still too startled to react, Hannah registered that her mare had broken into a slow trot. Glancing back, she saw that the men were all armed, even the Brothers who had been tortured in Chinon. Arnaud smiled wistfully at her. She lowered her head, then looked back one last time. Gero was standing there motionless, his face stony, not once taking his gaze off her.

Anselm drove his gelding along a dirt road. Hannah felt delirious, perceiving everything as if through a fog – this must be what a slow descent into madness felt like.

About a quarter of a mile later, they reached a village populated by small timber-framed houses with thatched roofs. The muddy streets were empty. A few chickens were running about, and a lone dog barked at the unexpected strangers.

Although there was no one to be seen, Anselm decided to ride around the village instead of through it. He didn't want to take the chance of anyone remembering them and giving the soldiers any clues of their whereabouts. As they passed a pond, they startled a young pair of lovers who weren't a day older than fifteen, and who had made themselves comfortable behind an abandoned duck house. Half naked, they fled behind a nearby bush.

Hannah's horse shied, but she quickly managed to calm it down again. When she turned around to make sure that Freya was all right, however, she realized that she was no longer behind her in the saddle.

"Anselm, wait!" she called in alarm, jerking her horse around.

She found Freya cowering in the damp grass not far away.

"Are you hurt?" Hannah asked as she dismounted.

The young woman shook her head in despair. "I'm not going with you."

Anselm had gotten off his horse and handed Matthäus the reins. He kneeled down in front of Freya in the grass and grasped her hands. "You can't desert us. We don't know our way and might not be able to make it without you."

"I'm sorry," Freya whispered staring blankly ahead. "I'm not going without Johan, even if I have to wait here till Judgment Day."

"That might take a while," Anselm remarked drily. "Believe me, nothing much happens in the next seven hundred years."

"Anselm!" Hannah shook her head as she bent down to stroke Freya's shoulders.

The Beguine looked at her with sad eyes. "I've already lost too much to bear losing someone I love again. If he dies, I'll have no one left in this world." Tears ran down her pale cheeks.

"Oh, Freya," Hannah tried again. "What are you saying? Gero promised that we would meet them as soon as we could."

Freya looked at her sympathetically. "He did say that," she replied softly. "But his commander said something else."

Hannah looked at Anselm in confusion. "What does she mean?"

Anselm cleared his throat sheepishly.

"What?" Hannah demanded.

"She's right," Anselm admitted. "According to d'Our, they won't have much chance of following us."

Hannah felt as if she had been hit on the head with a wooden plank. She stood up, took a deep breath, and looked at Freya and Anselm. "I don't think we should abandon Gero and his Brothers to their fate. I want to know what's happening back there. We're going back."

Anselm raised his eyebrows in disbelief. "Are you crazy?"

"Feel free to get lost if you wish," she spat angrily. "I'm going back with Freya to see if we can help." She eyed Anselm's chain mail in contempt. "Strutting around as a re-enactor with a medieval sword and acting like King Arthur doesn't mean a damn thing in this world. If you were a real knight, you wouldn't just run away."

Anselm's face grew red in fury. "You have no idea what you're talking about!" he bellowed.

"I'm talking about friendship, honor, and a clear conscience," Hannah retorted. "Things you don't seem to understand at all." Determinedly, she pulled Freya to her feet. The woman had watched the heated exchange in modern German in amazement. Then Hanna's gaze fell on Matthäus, who was looking no less confused.

"Come along, Mattes," she called, and was about to help the boy onto her horse as well. "We won't leave you behind!"

"Damn it," Anselm snorted, stamping his feet. "You have no sense of responsibility."

"Oh, but *you* do? What will we do if we can never return to our time? Do you think your tiny shreds of theoretical knowledge will help us to survive in this world? Forget it! Without Gero, we are completely stranded."

Despite her angry words, in her heart, Hannah knew that she wasn't just mad at Anselm, but Gero as well. He should have told her the truth.

Anselm turned his horse around, swearing softly, and swung himself onto the saddle in front of the boy.

"Where are you going?" he called after them as Hannah trotted out onto an open field. "If we're heading back, we should at least be a little stealthy, and not just serve ourselves to the soldiers on a silver platter."

"Please, my lord." With an exaggerated bow, she gave Anselm and his horse the right of way. "Ride on, and we will follow you."

A little later, Hannah found herself again in a small birch grove where they had a clear view of the road to Parilly.

"Dismount," Anselm commanded gruffly, "or they'll see us."

Matthäus tied the horses to a tree, and together they scurried up the slope. The fog had almost completely cleared, but the sky was covered with clouds. Behind a plateau overgrown with bushes, they heard the howling of dogs. Not far from there, they saw the corpses of a few soldiers. The five knights had entrenched themselves behind the fallen men.

"Yes!" Anselm hissed, balling his hand into a triumphant fist.

"What happened?" Hannah asked, looking up nervously.

"Do you see the trees over there in the mist?" Crawling on his belly, Anselm moved a little closer to her and bent aside a few branches that were blocking Hannah's view. "Gero and his men are over there. Obviously, the soldiers hadn't considered that the Templars would be armed with crossbows and longbows. The idiots simply charged ahead. Serves them right."

"Did we win?" Matthäus looked up hopefully.

"I've no idea," Anselm replied, "but it looks like the score's now one-nil to the Templars from Bar-sur-Aube."

"Holy Mother of God, praise be unto Mary, full of grace ..." Freya began to pray. She knelt down in the thicket and gripped her green malachite rosary.

Hannah took a deep breath. "And what should we do now?"

"Keep still," Anselm said quietly. "Maybe Gero really will keep his promise and try to meet us."

For a moment, all was quiet. Then, all of a sudden, a branch snapped loudly behind them.

Anselm sprang to his feet so quickly that he amazed even himself. With a singing sound, he drew his weapon as Hannah screamed in fear. About sixty feet away, two soldiers had shot out of the ground like poisonous mushrooms. Their swords whooshed through the air as they swung them skillfully.

"*Bonjour, mon ami,*" one of them sneered.

He stormed up to Anselm with a flood of Old French, each word dripping with hatred and bloodlust. Sparks sprayed as steel hit steel. With remarkable agility, Anselm parried his opponent's blows as if he were wielding a whip. Roland of Briey had taught him that elegance had no part in a serious fight. Survival was the only prize.

Anselm ducked, stood up, and let his sword crash down on the man's shield. The soldier stumbled and nearly lost his balance. His companion, however, charged and forced Anselm to defend himself.

Filled with new life, Freya sprang up and grabbed a nearby branch on the ground. Fearlessly, she ran to the fighters in her long hooded cloak.

Before Hannah could call out a warning, the Beguine was a few feet away from the men. At an opportune moment, she lunged, and, with a loud crack, hit the shorter of the two soldiers on the back of the head. He fell to his knees groaning. The other man jumped back momentarily.

Anselm gritted his teeth as he lunged to deal his final blow to the man kneeling in front of him. The blade pierced the soldier's chain mail and sliced through his throat like butter. Blood sprayed, and the man's neck snapped to the side like a flower stem that had been broken in half. Then he collapsed.

Anselm staggered. A sudden burst of adrenaline prevented him from losing control. As he whipped around to face his second opponent, he saw that the soldier had seized Hannah from behind and was pressing the blade of a dagger to her throat.

"Throw the weapon down!" the soldier yelled. "Or the woman dies."

564

CHAPTER 45
Jacques de Molay

Thursday, December 2, 2004
Chinon, France

It was still early morning when the motorcade of five black Mercedes vans with tinted windows and a large medical RV passed the border from Luxembourg to France on the highway towards Thionville. Paul Colbach sat beside Tom Stevendahl and Professor Hertzberg in the back seat of one of the vans, absently inspecting Jack Tanner's face in the rearview mirror.

With his dark sunglasses and cropped hair, the NSA agent driving the van looked exactly like what Paul had always imagined a secret agent would look like. The second agent, Mike Tapleton, had made himself comfortable in the front seat and was leafing through a sports magazine with a bored look on his face. His Beretta 92 FS Brigadier poked out from under his loose bomber jacket.

While Tom indulged himself with a nap, Professor Hertzberg watched over a plain metal suitcase. Humanity's greatest secret was hidden inside.

Paul still couldn't believe that the American government had actually authorized the use of the timeserver to transfer Jacques de Molay, the last Grand Master of the Templars, out of the guarded dungeon in the castle of Chinon in 1308 into the year 2004. They had been dealing with an endless stream of Pentagon specialists ever since he and Tom had worked out how to program the timeserver, thereby allowing them to target a world seven hundred years ago with pinpoint accuracy.

Though it wasn't clear that this undertaking would succeed, it was a good chance for Tom to discover Hannah's location. Hertzberg had put forth the idea that the last Grand Master of the Templars could help them unlock the timeserver's complex secrets, especially after Hagen's Lebanese friend hadn't proven very useful. Hertzberg went as far as to theorize that Molay might be able to connect the timeserver to an even more distant past, directly to the Ark of the Covenant, the greatest relic in the Old Testament.

The advantage of first searching for Jacques de Molay lay in the fact that they could narrow his whereabouts to an exact day and place using information from historical documents. Because the device was oriented to the earth's magnetic field and only worked within a radius of 100 feet, it was essential to determine a specific deployment site and time.

As they drove past, Paul glanced at Cattenom. The four cooling towers of the nuclear plant belched white steam into the sky like a cloud factory. Paul wondered how things had looked here in the fourteenth century, and what it must feel like to be suddenly transported into a different time.

It was dark by the time they reached Chinon. After parking the NSA vehicles on a forest path outside the city, armed agents prepared for the mission with military precision. General Lafour had insisted on personally commanding twenty of his best men. A line of communication with the American military headquarters in Paris had been established so that in an emergency, the agents could quickly summon additional helicopters and Special Forces. But first, the mission had to be carried out as silently and inconspicuously as possible. No one, apart from the personnel involved, could ever find out what would happen here.

At 1700 hours CET, visiting hours at the castle ended. When darkness descended, they would enter the Fort de Coudray through an abandoned wine cellar. The cliff was made of porous limestone, and had been deemed unstable ground. With little effort, NSA specialists had obtained maps of the compound's network of passages. Up until this point, everything had been planned down to the last detail, but the next task remained firmly in the realm of speculation.

Tom's entire body was shivering with excitement as he put on his black overalls at around 2300 hours. Just before they infiltrated the cellar they would have to put on black masks and armored vests like the NSA agents. When Tom climbed into the van, he felt as if he was about to rob a bank. Although he had suppressed his doubts about their mission so far, his discomfort became greater, when they arrived at the foot of the castle hill. Like silent assassins, the NSA agents opened a locked door in seconds and with an unmistakable gesture ordered him to follow them into the darkness. Tom's pulse quickened. Past piles of garbage and old storage racks, they made their way through long passages draped with spider webs. Finally, the ten agents, their commander, and the three scientists reached a gate locked with a rusty iron chain, which the agents cut through effortlessly with a thermal lance.

The steps they ascended were so narrow that only one person at a time could climb them. Tom ducked his head, all the while wondering how people in the past could have survived in such a frightful environment.

After they had climbed the first two flights of stairs, another iron gate, which looked newer than the first, blocked their way again. This, too, posed no obstacle to the NSA and Agent Tanner shoved the rusty bars aside. After two further staircases, they stood in the "Donjon du Coudray" – the prison tower where the last Grand Master of the Templars had spent his last days seven hundred years ago.

With his LED flashligfht dimmed, Mike Tapleton inspected the round stone chamber. His gaze fell on the famous stone engravings above the entrance, which were protected under a shield of Plexiglas.

"The infamous graffiti of Chinon," explained Professor Hertzberg excitedly. "Apparently they were made by the Templars during their imprisonment here."

"General Lafour, we need space to carry out the experiment," Tom said, turning to the mission's commander. "Could you and your men retreat into the stairwell until we are sure that our transfer has been successful?"

The bullish general looked disgruntled in his too-tight overalls. "And what about your safety? That's why we're here, after all. Or do you think we're just locksmiths?"

Tom sighed. "I assume that you care about your men's safety as much as we do, General. For this reason, I think it's better that you step back for a moment, at least until we can be sure that we have our target. Or do you want to risk falling within the detection radius and being transferred into the year 1308?"

"And what about yourself?" Lafour challenged Tom. "What if you suddenly disappear or transfer something dangerous?"

"In the first case, that'll be just my luck, and in the second case, I can still cry for help. From what I've seen, your men are some of the fastest around."

The General sighed. "Tanner, Tapleton, stay here. Everyone else, retreat until I tell you otherwise."

Whispering, the rest of the men left the room and returned to the so called ice-cellar underneath.

In what resembled a holy ritual, Tom set down the metal suitcase in the middle of the room, carefully removed the timeserver, and placed it on top of the closed suitcase. Now he just had to hit the right notes.

CHAPTER 46

Vendetta

Thursday, November 16, 1307

On the way down to the road, Anselm desperately pondered how he could free himself and attack the soldiers. Even if he managed to slip off his ropes, he had no weapon. If he failed, however, they would all face a fate even worse than their current misery.

The soldier on the horse in front of him led them down into the woods, tied on a rope. Anselm inspected his bound hands as he kicked up the rust-colored leaves on the forest floor with his boots. Matthäus had been tied up like a package and left lying in front of the saddle, while the soldier on his horse held a dagger threateningly against the boy's throat.

"*Compagnons!*" he bellowed across the open farmland after they had left the village behind them. "*Compagnons!*" he screamed again, when no answer came.

Then they heard a distant cry. A little later, they were surrounded by five other men in black and brown uniforms.

Hannah, already feeling weak from fear and pain, felt her heart stop when, among the newcomers, she spotted the dark hair and elegant features of Pierre, whom she had previously avoided at Madame Fouchet's.

"Well, well, well," the handsome soldier smirked as he ran his hand through Freya's flaming red mane. With a look of smug glee that transfigured his handsome features into something far uglier, he seized her by the hair, ignoring her cries of pain.

"My little flute player – who would have thought!" he gloated.

Hannah looked around in despair, but no help was in sight. About 50 yards away, she saw the corpses of the blue-and-yellow uniformed soldiers and at least ten wolfhounds strewn across the grass. Arrows were lodged in their bodies.

From afar, another troop approached and Anselm gathered from scraps of conversation that they were scouts of the Gens du Roi.

"What happened here, then?" the leader snarled.

Anselm shuddered. It was Guy de Gislingham. Anselm had recognized him right away, and now he feared that the man with the blue-gray eyes would notice him, too.

Unlike their first encounter, the Englishman looked utterly satisfied. Glancing at the captives, his gaze fell on Matthäus who lay bound and gagged on the ground.

"I knew it!" he gasped, spitting contemptuously at the boy.

Suddenly he seemed to discover something. "I can't believe it," he exclaimed. "This is our new medicus!"

Quicker than Anselm could anticipate, Gislingham lashed his riding crop at his face.

Anselm felt no pain, only a hot, burning sting and warm blood running down his neck. Hannah gasped in horror.

"Where are the others?" Guy de Gislingham yelled.

Pierre stepped forward dutifully and saluted him. "They've entrenched themselves over there in the grove of trees, sire."

"Send a negotiator," Guy ordered coldly. "Tell them that if they don't give themselves up, we'll throw the boy into the tower of the dogs, where the beasts will take revenge for their dead compatriots."

With a slight twitch in the corners of his mouth, he turned to Hannah and Freya.

"And tell them that their whores will burn alive, but only after my soldiers have had their fun with them."

Hannah hadn't understood a word, but Freya's miserable, pale face made her pulse quicken with dread. Anselm felt the sudden urge to give up and let things run their course. Bathed in sweat, he saw a rider with a white flag set off at a speedy gallop, and return barely five minutes later.

"Sire. They demand free release for the women, the child, and the man. In exchange, they'll turn themselves in. If you agree to this arrangement, they will come back with me one by one."

Gislingham nodded. "Tell them I want to see Gerard de Breydenbach first."

The soldier nodded and turned his horse round.

"Wait!" Guy de Gislingham called and the soldier looked around in surprise.

"If you want to see the next day, make sure that they are unarmed when you bring them to us."

"They won't let the women go, Brother Gerard," said d'Our softly. "I see no sense in surrendering ourselves, at least not when Guy de Gislingham is involved, let alone Guillaume Imbert. Tell the negotiator that I'll be the only one to turn myself in, but only if they release the boy first."

"Then you and the women will die," Gero answered calmly. With a blank expression, he stared in the direction of the messenger, where he was waiting for their answer at a respectful distance.

"What about the Head?" Johan van Elk could not stand the thought that his commander would so readily accept their companions' deaths. There had to be something that would bring him to his senses. Perhaps the strange device would be important enough to him to make him accept Gislingham's offer.

Gero looked up, and for a few short moments he could see the despair in d'Our's eyes before the commander again put on the steely expression of an experienced soldier.

"Johan is right," Gero said. "Gislingham will not be satisfied with you," he confirmed. "He wants me. If he sets the others free for that, we might have saved the Head. I will send the messenger back with our offer."

For a while, silence reigned as the men looked at their commander, who was still their leader, to whom they had sworn unconditional obedience.

"So be it," d'Our said halfheartedly.

The Templars let out sighs of relief, knowing that only God could help them survive their grizzly fate now. Nonetheless, to sacrifice innocent lives for their own safety would have been a shameful act, antithetical to the rules of the Order. Even during the storming of the Templars' Fortress of Acre, the knights had chosen to die in battle rather than leave innocent women and children to the Mamluks' caprice.

Hannah was on the verge of breaking down when Gero came galloping over, escorted by the messenger and without any of his weapons. They had tied his hands together, so he could only hold the reins loosely between his fingers as he squeezed his horse's flanks, signaling to the animal to stop.

When Pierre presented the Templar knight to the Englishman, Anselm watched in horror as Guy de Gislingham's face twisted into a devilish grin. Anselm didn't know why Gero had turned himself in, and, encircled by crossbows, it was impossible for him to make eye contact with the Templar.

The thickening fog and the cawing of isolated ravens only added to the ominous atmosphere, and Anselm fervently wished for the roar of an airplane overhead, or the rumbling engine of a tractor, or even the life-saving ring of a cell phone.

A soldier forced Gero to kneel before Gislingham. Despite this gesture of subservience, Gero squared his shoulders and looked the Englishman firmly in the eye.

"Let the women, boy, and man go free!" Without a flicker of hesitation, Gero made his demands. "What you want, Gisli, is between us. The others haven't the slightest thing to do with it."

Gislingham looked unamused. Like a snake eyeing its prey before devouring it, he slowly circled around his former Brother.

"*Sir Guy*," he said cuttingly. "For a traitor like you, it's always Sir Guy!"

"I wonder who the traitor is here," Gero declared coolly. "I saved your life when you were cowering behind the walls of the commandery in your pissed braies. Don't forget that."

"I'm sorry to disappoint you, Brother Gero, but I was never one of you. From the start, my task was to uncover the Order's dark deeds as an undercover spy of the King."

Gero cleared his throat loudly and spat on Gislingham's boots. Without thinking, the Englishman brutally struck him in the face. Gero's cheek split open as the plated chain mail glove collided with his flesh, and blood ran down his chin to his broad neck.

With a mocking expression, Gislingham began again. "I will let the women and boy go only when all your comrades and your senile commander are ready to give themselves up."

Without waiting for Gero's answer, he turned around and beckoned for his men to bring Anselm forward. "This fellow here," Gislingham said sharply, "will share your fate. He killed one of my best men. There is no reason to spare him the gallows."

For a moment, Gero shut his eyes.

"It was self-defense!" Anselm bellowed, beside himself with outrage.

"Teach him a lesson!" Gislingham commanded one of the soldiers.

The soldier seized Anselm and threw him to the ground, where two soldiers held him down while two others kicked and beat him. His choked gasps were punctuated by cries from the women.

"So, what will it be?" Guy de Gislingham turned to Gero again.

Gero quickly decided that there was little chance of saving Anselm. The saddlebags on his horse, however, were untouched.

To avoid provoking the Englishman any further, Gero decided to address him with cautious respect. "If you swear to me, Sire, by all things holy, to let the women and the boy leave freely with their horses, we will turn ourselves in."

"I swear," Gislingham answered with an ugly grin.

Gero knew that there was no circumstance that would justify having even the smallest amount of trust in his former Brother. But what other choice did he have? With relief, he watched Gislingham order the boy's shackles be taken off before sending him towards the grove on Anselm's horse.

Soon after, d'Our appeared, escorted by the messenger. This procedure was repeated twice with Freya and Hannah in exchange for Stefano and Arnaud. Finally, Johan came.

Gero and his comrades couldn't see what happened to the women and boy after their release. Along with Anselm, the Templars were taken to the castle, where they were thrown into the dungeon of Fort du Coudrey.

Numb and battered, Anselm let a blacksmith secure his wrists and ankles with iron bands, pull a chain through each of the eyelets, and smith the smoldering ends to another ring embedded in the wall with a hammer and a chisel. In their chains, the prisoners couldn't move more than two feet away from the cold walls, which also meant that they would have to relieve themselves nearby. Speechlessly, Anselm turned to face the walls, where the famous Templar graffiti was still missing.

It was already dark when the dungeon's plated door opened with a god-awful squeak. Gero groaned in horror as two fleshy hands pushed Hannah, Freya, and Matthäus into the bleak dungeon. The only consolation was that they hadn't chained the women and child. With a choked cry, Freya stumbled toward Johan, who had been awoken from his short, merciful sleep by the commotion.

But before they could express their outrage over Guy de Gislingham's dishonorable behavior, they were unexpectedly confronted with yet another misfortune. The door opened once again and three mighty soldiers dragged in a man, blood-soaked and half naked. Like the carcass of a dead animal, they tossed his limp body onto the stone floor. The door banged shut again and was locked from outside. It took a moment for the prisoners to recognize Struan.

"Lord Almighty! That devil!" Gero let out a muffled cry, pulling against his chains in vain.

Hannah and Freya hurried to the Scotsman. Carefully, they turned him on to his stomach. His shoulder had been pierced by a crossbow bolt, and then they had totured him brutally – whipped, broken on the wheel, and burned with smoldering iron. A weaker man would have long been dead. Freya stroked the Scotsman's blood smeared hair and felt for a pulse on his neck.

"He's alive," she said, looking hopefully at Johan, who was looking on in blank horror.

"Lord Jesus Christ, why did this have to happen?" Gero hung his head in despair.

"It's not your fault, Brother Gerard," d'Our said softly. "It is God's will. Never forget that. You are just an instrument of the Almighty."

Tears of despair welled up in Geros eyes. Hannah longed to comfort him, but she needed to help Freya tend to his injured Brother instead.

"Help me," she said to Matthäus.

Without a second thought, Hannah took off her underskirt and ripped it in two. She folded one half and placed it under Struan's head. Then she ripped the other half into several long strips, and tasked Matthäus with binding the still bleeding wounds on the man's limbs.

"What will this accomplish?" Arnaud snorted. "It's better that he dies now than tomorrow morning, when Guillaume Imbert begins his dreadful game."

The other men stayed silent.

Struan's face was bleeding, too, but his back was what most unnerved Freya. Blue-black marks stretched over his buttocks and hips, down to his muscular thighs.

"We have to keep him warm," she decided, "or he won't wake up again." With Matthäus' help, she seized Struan under his arms while Hannah lifted his legs. Together, they pulled him towards to Johan, until the injured man was lying next to his Brother. With Johan's silent consent, Freya curled up next to the Scotsman and draped her woolen cloak over all three of them.

Hannah stood up and took Matthäus by the hand. Without a word, she motioned for him to huddle between herself and Gero, so that they could all share a little warmth under her cloak.

"I'm so sorry," Gero stammered, unable to look her in the eye. His lips quivered, and she saw that he was struggling to hold back his tears in front of the boy.

"It is my fault," she whispered, and touched the wound on his face. "We were already on the road, halfway to the river. It was I who wanted to return. I couldn't just run away, knowing that I might never see you again."

Gero's chains rattled slightly as he raised his right hand and tenderly stroked Hannah's cheek.

"Let's not speak of blame, my love," he replied gently. "Our commander is right. The Almighty is the only one who guides our fate, and perhaps one day we'll know why he tested us so."

He lowered his eyes and looked between them at the frightened boy in silence. Again, his eyes filled with tears. Hannah took his arm and squeezed it tightly. She herself didn't know where her strength was coming from; maybe it came from the simple fact that she had no idea of what exactly awaited them.

Two or three hours must have gone by when a barely audible moan broke the tense silence. Struan stirred, and blinked up at Freya. She had dozed off a little, but now she was wide awake.

"Struan? Can you speak?" Johan, too, had awoken and was worriedly inspecting his wounded friend.

"Amelie," Struan whispered in a hoarse voice. "Amelie, is it you?"

Freya exchanged a shocked glance with Johan. Struan's face twisted in pain, he raised his left hand and felt for her. His fingers touched her long hair and despite his obvious agony, he smiled weakly.

"I can't move my legs. Do you know what happened to me?"

"Everything will be fine," Freya replied in a trembling voice. Tenderly, she stroked his blood-crusted black hair, unable to tell Struan that she was not who he thought she was. "You will be well again," she stammered. "Believe me."

"I love you," Struan whispered as he clenched his eyes shut. "I didn't want to abandon you and the child. I swear to you. Can you forgive me?"

"He … he's lost his mind," Johan stammered, but Freya was ready to play her role to the end. She bent down to Struan and kissed his bloody lips. "I am with you, my love," she whispered in his ear, laying her face on his damp cheek. "And I will love you until the end of time. Do you hear me?"

The corners of Struan's mouth twitched into a slight smile. "You are a stubborn woman, and a smart one, too," he said weakly. "My love, I …"

Then he sank back into unconsciousness.

With a loud creak, the door flew open and Guy de Gislingham was standing in the middle of the room like an angry ghoul, accompanied by several heavily armed torchbearers. A gust of icy November air blew into the already chilly dungeon.

Four of the guards were carrying two fire baskets, which illuminated the dark, bare cell, and thankfully gave off a little warmth. The Englishman snapped his fingers and two more soldiers carried in a flat, wooden case on a pedestal, covered with an ornate, green, brocade cloth.

As the door shut again, Gislingham stepped forward, whipped off the precious cloth and opened the wooden case. With a lingering look at his audience that reminded Hannah of a stage magician's performance, he took out a flat object, shut the case, and placed the object on top. It was the Head of Wisdom.

Hannah held her breath and even the usually stoic Henri d'Our couldn't hide his horror.

"I'm listening," Gislingham said smugly, closing his eyes expectantly.

But no one said anything. With a threatening flicker in his eyes, he nodded in Matthäus' direction, and his men quickly grabbed the boy, kicking and screaming, from Gero's side. Hannah wanted to run to Matthäus, but Gero held her back with an iron grip.

"You bastards, let the boy go immediately!" he hissed. "Gislingham, if reveling in our misfortune isn't enough for you, then take me. You can draw and quarter me, but in God's name, leave the child alone!"

"There's no need for such great sacrifice," Guy de Gislingham replied with a smile. "You just have to tell me what this strange object is."

Hannah didn't dare believe her eyes when Gero, as well as the rest of his Brothers, turned to look at Henri d'Our, asking their commander for permission to speak. But as if he had become mute, d'Our said nothing.

"That is a time machine, you asshole!" Hannah suddenly screamed in High German. "But it's certainly too advanced for a pea-brained idiot from the Middle Ages!"

Instinctively, Gero clamped a hand over her mouth, encircling her waist with his other arm before she could spring up in a fit of frenzy to attack Gislingham. Guy de Gislingham hadn't understood what she was saying, but his interest was aroused nonetheless.

"You," he addressed her in Old French. "Come here!"

"No," Gero gasped, holding onto Hannah in desperation as Gislingham's guards came to pull her away from him.

"She is not in her right mind," he called with a pleading look. "You have to consider that when she speaks."

Gislingham halted his soldiers and they let Hannah go. Gero quickly pulled her back onto his lap.

"Very well, Breydenbach," the Englishman relented with an ill-humored gesture. "Then tell me exactly what this strange object is, unless you want me to throw your squire to the dogs and let your whore see my men's cocks for herself."

Gero ran his tongue across his split lips. "Very well," he said finally, clutching Hannah's cloak. "She was speaking the truth. It is a magical artifact that allows you to conquer time."

"Brother Gerard!" D'Our hissed, "think about what you're saying."

"Don't worry, Sire," Gero assured him quietly in German, narrowing his eyes. "Believe me, I know exactly what I'm doing."

Resolutely he fixed his gaze on the harmless looking Head of Wisdom.

"Step aside," he commanded Gislingham, and, as the Englishman looked at him angrily, he added reassuringly, "It can be dangerous, and you might be shocked when it opens."

"Enough of your womanly drivel, Breydenbach. Show me!" Gislingham retorted.

Slowly but surely, Gero raised his voice and sang, with more fervor than he had ever sung in his life: "*Laudabo Deum meum in vita mea …*"

As the Head's cover sprang up, Gislingham and his guards recoiled in shock. Their eyes widened in fear as an ethereal woman's head materialized to give her silent instructions.

Gero's plan was to escape from Gislingham and his men by having the machine catapult Gero and his companions into another time. Even if they could only travel into the past, that was still better than being trapped in this dungeon, where they could only wait for certain, miserable death. When the greenish vapor appeared, Gislingham looked at him for an answer.

"Now, just place your hand inside," Gero said.

"That might suit you well," Gislingham retorted, looking uncertain and frightened, but not wanting his men to see his hesitation. "Put your own hand in!" he ordered Gero.

Now Gero had his traitorous comrade exactly where he wanted him.

"Give the boy the box," he said calmly. "Let him bring it to me."

Upon a nod from Gislingham, Matthäus obediently brought over the timeserver. "Come here, Mattes," Gero said, giving his squire an encouraging wink. "Place your hand inside and show the Sire that you're not afraid."

By now, Hannah and Anselm had realized what Gero was doing. The voice could be heard in all their heads, announcing that the server would begin calibrating the newly-entered data. Only Gislingham and his men had no idea what was going on.

"Go on, Mattes, let all our Brothers and Sisters place their hands in it. We'll show the noble lord that nothing bad will happen."

With calm composure, the boy began to present the green hand that had materialized from the vapor to each of the prisoners, so that they could place their own hand in it. With a smile, Hannah encouraged Freya, who was looking terrified, to follow Gero's instructions. Johan sensed that Gero was confident about what he was doing. If his plan worked, they could find a way out of this hellhole. With shaking hands, he lifted Struan's wrist and placed his blood-smeared fingers in the vapor.

Seconds too late, Gislingham realized that something was afoot.

"Come here!" he ordered Matthäus, after the boy's uncle, the last to do so, had placed his fingers in the green vapor. "You," he said to one of his soldiers, "do the same!"

After the man reluctantly obeyed his superior's command, Gislingham let the other guard follow suit. So that he wouldn't appear cowardly, he, too, finally placed his hand in the swirling, green fog. With a nod, he ordered Matthäus to set the object back in its original place.

"What now?" he asked, giving Henri d'Our a superior look.

But before the commander could say anything, something unexpected happened.

CHAPTER 47

Mission Impossible

Tuesday, December 2, 2004

Sucking in a deep breath, Tom turned to his colleagues. "Are you ready?" he asked.

Paul nodded reverently, and even Jack Tanner and Mike Tapleton held their hands folded in front of them as if they were witnessing a sacred ritual. In a solemn voice, Tom began to sing the password.

But suddenly, the server reacted in a manner that they had never before witnessed. Instead of the familiar woman's head, a pulsating holographic diagram materialized, oscillating wildly like the graph of an electrocardiogram.

"Incoming data calibrated," said the voice. "Target acquisition running. Calibration of DNA structures to follow in ten seconds."

"Paul! What's happening?" Tom gaped at his colleague.

"How should I know?" Paul cried. "We've never seen this happen before! Maybe it's getting a signal from somewhere?"

"We should stop the experiment!"

"We can't," Paul answered. "The only thing you can do is destroy the server, but then you'll lose any chance of getting Hannah back."

Tom stared at the rising greenish vapor, unable to decide what to do. Jack and Mike had drawn their weapons instinctively, and were aiming them uncertainly at the precious artifact, which was now shrouded in the strange blue-green light.

Before Tom could do anything, a mild shock-wave rippled through the room and the light expanded like a massive bubble, threatening to burst at any second. A sudden flash of light followed, and all at once, the room went dark.

Seconds later, an LED light flickered on. Voices were heard shouting, and Tom saw that the box had toppled over. General Lafour and his men stormed into the room. There were screams, moans, and then the voice of a woman. Lost in the chaos, Tom flattened himself against the wall and paused. It was Hannah's voice, he was absolutely sure of it. Opening his

579

eyes wide in shock, he suddenly saw the Templar rushing towards another man in medieval clothing and wrestling him to the ground.

Breathlessly, Tom watched as another stranger raised his sword and charged at the Templar's squire. There was no mistaking his intention. Impulsively, Tom ran forward, but before he could reach the boy's attacker, an emaciated man threw himself between the boy and his furious opponent. Helplessly, Tom saw the sword pierce the man in the middle of his chest.

All at once, the Templar jumped between them. Someone fired a taser but missed the man by a hair's breadth. Instead, it hit Mike Tapleton, who fell to the floor with a grunt. More NSA forces rushed into the small cell. Meanwhile, the Templar and the stranger had disappeared.

Suddenly Jack saw the glint of a sword blade in front of him, and, in his confusion, fired involuntarily. He gaped in disbelief as his opponent fell to the floor.

Somewhere in the chaos, Paul had been knocked to the ground. Crouched over the Luxembourgian was a wild, sinister figure in chain mail, brandishing a dagger. But before he could drive the dagger into Paul's chest, he was seized by the head and thrown aside. Breathlessly, Tom watched Paul's scarred savior mercilessly snap his victim's neck. For a moment he feared that they had landed in the Middle Ages.

"Tom!" cried a voice as if out of a fog. "Tom!"

Tom whirled around and found himself looking straight at Anselm Stein. At first, he thought he must have been hallucinating, but then the medieval expert embraced him.

"I don't understand, Tom," he cried, gasping. "Heaven has sent you!"

But they were still far from heaven.

"Seize them!" General Lafour thundered at his men.

The next moment, a bright light filled the room and the room fell strangely silent. Only a light moan could be heard. In the sobering light, they assessed the situation.

There were two dead men in medieval uniforms, and two NSA agents who had been cut. The elderly man who had stepped between Matthäus and his attacker lay motionless in a pool of blood. A redheaded woman was cowering against the wall in fear, holding the boy protectively in her arms. She did not dare to look up. Nearby, the man with the scarred face was tending to a half-naked, blood-soaked man, lying on the floor. Two more young men in gaudy clothing stared in disbelief at the NSA agents.

"Tom!" Hannah sprang to her feet and came running to him. Unexpectedly, she flung her arms around his neck. "Where are we?" Gratefully, he basked in the warmth of her embrace.

"At the Castle of Chinon in December 2004," he answered breathlessly.

"How did you find us?" she gasped in excitement, looking him in the eye as tears of relief ran down her cheeks. "Are we safe?"

Tom glanced towards the exit, to gauge the situation. The Plexiglas and the graffiti it protected were still there. Lafours' men had taken over control.

"Yes," he said weakly. "We are safe."

"Paramedics!" someone boomed.

Hannah whipped around. One of the marines, who had regained his composure after a brief moment of shock, was surveying the room with seasoned expertise.

Matthäus loosened himself from the redhead's embrace and hurried over to crouch by his uncle's side. Henri d'Our was dead, lying on his back with his eyes wide open.

He saved my life," stammered the boy as one of the NSA agents gently lowered the dead man's eyelids.

Hannah held on tightly to Matthäus' shoulders to comfort him.

"He threw himself in front of me," the boy whispered, "as Gislingham tried to kill me."

"Gislingham?" Hannah looked around in confusion.

Neither Gislingham nor Gero could be seen. She felt herself grow cold.

"Gero!" she screamed, her eyes darting about in panic. "Where is the server?" she demanded. "Gero was here just a minute ago!"

"Hannah," Tom said, "that can't be true." He nodded at the plain metal suitcase that Paul was holding. "We have the server."

"No," she protested. "We brought it here from Heisterbach, and now it's gone."

"Maybe it disintegrated," Tom guessed. "According to everything we know, it's not possible for the same contiguous patterns to appear in the same time plane twice." Laying an arm around her, he tried to calm Hannah down, but she pushed him away.

"And what happened to Gero?" Hannah was in tears. "You have to get him back immediately! They will kill him if you don't!"

"I don't know how to do that," Tom said with sincere regret in his voice. "I didn't transport you here. It happened all by itself. If Gero was with you, he must have been transferred as well. It worked for the others, after all. Maybe his DNA prevented his return." He didn't mention that, for a few seconds, he thought he had seen the Templar in a skirmish with another man.

As if someone had given her a death sentence, Hannah turned to her medieval friends. Johan scrambled to his feet, and, after inspecting his surroundings suspiciously, he gathered her into his arms.

Professor Hertzberg emerged from his hiding spot, and he began to attend to the other newcomers. Unselfconsciously, he spoke to them in their own language. Swiftly, General Lafour announced that he would treat the men and women with civility and respect, as they posed no threat, and instructed his agents not to handcuff them.

Paul looked on in stunned silence. After all the excitement, he was filled with a sudden urge to relieve himself. Without warning, he pressed the metal suitcase into Tom's hands. "Sorry, I'll be right back," he said apologetically and left.

He didn't want to go down into the dungeon where Lafour's men were preparing to leave. He noticed that there was another stairwell. Who would know if he relieved himself in a corner of one of the desolate rooms upstairs?

As he arrived upstairs, however, a soft moan made him freeze. Paul shone the flashlight he had borrowed from an NSA agent into the room. He nearly fell over when the light suddenly hit the watery blue eyes of a dead man. Behind the corpse, something was moving, and Paul let out a choked cry when he recognized who it was.

"Gero!" he exclaimed. "Good God, where did you come from?"

"I could ask you the same question, Paul," replied the crusader, uttering his name for the first time. "Have you seen Hannah? Is she with you?" He clutched the left side of his body with a moan.

"Hannah is down below with the others. You're back in the year 2004, but don't ask me how that happened. She'll be overjoyed to see you. She thinks you were left behind in the past." Only then did Paul notice the wound on his face and the blood seeping through the gaps in the Templars' fingers. "Jesus, what happened to you?"

"Nothing important," Gero reassured him, breathing heavily. "I had to settle an old score. To be honest, I thought it was going to be easier."

"Stay here," Paul instructed him. "I'll get help."

After carrying out the injured on foldable stretchers and packing the dead men into black plastic bodybags, the NSA agents left the tower swiftly and silently with their new wards.

Gero needed to be treated by the medical staff on site until he could be transferred to an American hospital. Hannah never left his side. Thrilled as she was about Gero's survival, her greatest worry was Struan, who, even with modern medical treatment, was still closer to death than life.

On a high plateau behind Chinon, two American MEDIVAC helicopters landed in the middle of the night on a plowed field to transport the injured Templars to an American military hospital in Germany.

As the huge, metallic birds descended, eyes gleaming in the darkness, the time travelers nearly passed out from terror. Despite his fear, Johan marveled at the large red cross on the bird's dark body.

Anselm looked at Johan and smiled as the gust created by the helicopters' rotors whipped his hair about his face. "That symbol is just as trustworthy today as it was seven hundred years ago," he called to the knight, stretching out his hand in invitation.

Johan looked at the red cross again and drew a deep breath. Along with Freya, who was clinging to him like a frightened child, he took his first step into a new, unknown world.

CHAPTER 48

Fin Amor II

Friday, December 24, 2004
U.S Military Hospital, Germany

"The only person who can help him recover is Amelie," Hannah said in concern as they left Struan's hospital room.

It had been three weeks since they had transferred him to Spangdahlem, but his condition remained critical.

"Who is Amelie?" Tom looked at his ex-fiancée quizzically.

"She was – no," she quickly corrected herself, "she is his lover. She's pregnant, and he's been blaming himself for leaving her behind in that condition."

"Couldn't we bring her here as well?" Gero asked bluntly.

He looked at Tom with an expression that was simultaneously pleading yet doubtful. He knew that while Tom had mastery over the time machine, how the machine was deployed was by no means his decision to make alone.

"I can try," Tom answered, "if the Americans play along."

"Thank you," Hannah said, giving his hand a light squeeze.

Despite his earlier clashes with Gero, Tom had finally accepted that he had lost Hannah's love to the crusader. After all, the man had risked his life for her.

After a week of intense consultations with the Pentagon, Tom received the approval to carry out yet another experiment. Hannah was convinced of the necessity of this mission, but when the time came for Gero, Tom, and a team of NSA agents to set off for Breydenburg Castle, she was still overcome with nerves.

The plan was to send Gero to his parents' castle in the year 1307 to find Amelie, whereupon he would take her to a previously arranged spot to be transferred back into the year 2004.

They had chosen the third day in December 1307 for their mission, as Dr. Karen Baxter had decided that seven months was the optimum time in Amelie's pregnancy to minimize the risk of a premature miscarriage during the journey through time.

Gero felt momentarily disoriented after the armored car dropped him off in a forest clearing in the middle of the night. But then he lifted his bright flashlight and saw the steep cliff where the castle of his ancestors had stood long ago. He felt a sudden pang of sadness for his lost home, nearly as strong as the first time he had stood before the ruined walls.

"It must have been here," he said hoarsely, showing Tom the spot where he thought the entrance to the castle had been.

"Countdown commencing," said the silent voice, and in the secluded darkness, a blue-green light flickered on.

Tom and the NSA team had hidden behind a few rocks, far enough away from the server's search radius to remain undetected. They watched in awe as Gero suddenly vanished into the light.

When Gero turned on his LED flashlight, he saw to his relief that he was standing in Breydenburg Castle's main tower.

Silently, he slipped past the costly carpets and up a narrow spiral staircase to the rooms upstairs. Everyone in the castle was asleep, for not a sound could be heard and no one was roaming the halls, aside from a white cat that sprang towards him, arching its back and hissing fearfully as Gero shone the bright, unfamiliar light in its gleaming eyes.

As he reached the chamber he thought was Amelie's, he began to pray that he would find her there. She had spent a few happy days in this room with Struan before he was torn away from her by their cruel fate.

Cautiously, he turned off his flashlight so that he wouldn't scare her unnecessarily and opened the door. The room was dark and cold. Even without light, he sensed that no one was inside. He turned away, disappointed. But as he turned around, he felt the tip of a dagger in his back.

"Keep calm, friend," a man whispered to him in a rough voice. "One move and you're dead." The man behind him raised his torch. "Turn around," he ordered harshly.

The knife still against his ribs, Gero did as he was told. "Roland?"

"Lord Almighty!" Roland of Briey nearly dropped his torch.

Dressed in a white nightgown and nightcap, he looked like a portly ghost haunting the halls.

"Gero!" He stepped back as if light had blinded him. He looked as if he were staring at the devil himself. "Don't tell me you're an apparition!"

"No," Gero reassured him. "I am of flesh and blood. But please don't ask me how I've come here. I'm looking for Amelie. Is she with you?"

"Yes, but ..." the steward stuttered, "she's not doing well. She lost the child. What happened to Struan? Is he here, too?"

Ignoring Roland's question, Gero exclaimed in horror, "She lost the child? Is she dead?"

"No! In God's name, she's alive, but worrying about Struan has nearly driven her crazy, especially as the days passed and no word arrived of your survival. It has been pure hell here for the last few weeks," Roland explained. "Ever since the Trier chapter chose Baldwin of Luxembourg as the new Archbishop, his messengers have been streaming in and out of here non-stop. They threatened your father that they will take away his fiefdom if they find out that he's hiding you or one of your comrades. You can't stay here. They're searching for you and Struan, too – more intensely than ever before."

"Take me to Amelie. Please."

Roland was much too taken aback to question Gero's request.

Before they arrived at the young woman's chamber, another figure appeared in the hallway. It was Richard of Breydenbach. At first he looked no less astonished than Roland, but then he ran to his lost son and hugged him fiercely.

"Gero! Oh, thank the Lord my prayers were heard." His voice sounded raw. "Where are your Brothers?" Richard inquired as he loosened himself from the embrace. He looked at his youngest son with eyes full of hope and anxiety.

"In a distant place, where neither the Pope nor the King of France can reach us," Gero answered ambiguous, because Roland didn't know anything about the timetravel. "I have to go back there. But first, I would like to take Amelie with me. Struan is badly injured, and he won't make it without her."

While Roland looked on in confusion, Gero's father nodded knowingly.

"Good," he said, sounding almost relieved. "Just a few days ago, we received a copy of the Bull *Pastoralis praeeminetiae*. Now Pope Clement wants to pursue the Templars even beyond France. Are you safe there? Are they treating you fairly?"

"Yes, Father. Don't worry about me. This is about you and our family. If you, mother, and Eberhard …" Gero swallowed. "If you want to follow me, just tell me. I think it would be possible."

"And am I to abandon everything here, boy? I am responsible for more than two hundred souls."

"And what if Baldwin really takes away the fiefdom? There is a prophecy …"

"I don't want to hear any prophecies," Richard cut in sharply. "I only believe in what the Almighty promises us. Now, go and get the girl. I don't want your mother to wake up and worry. I'll give her a kiss from you and tell her that you're doing well." Gero could see that his father was struggling to maintain his composure.

Hesitantly, Gero opened the door to the woman's chamber. For a moment, he stood by her bed, looking at her pale face before he stroked her cheek to wake her up.

"Gero …" she stirred, rubbing her eyes as if chasing away a dream and squinted into the light. All of a sudden, she let out a shrill scream. "Struan!"

Gero quickly gathered Amelie into his arms.

When she saw that the Scotsman wasn't with him, she began to cry inconsolably. "He's dead! Am I right? Tell me the truth!"

Gero stoked her hair. "Struan is alive," he said reassuringly, "but he needs you to survive."

"Where is he?" Her eyes shone as she looked up at him.

"Come with me," he whispered. "He's waiting for you." Escorted by his father and Roland of Briey, he carried the young woman down into the knights' hall.

Richard of Breydenbach held his steward back as he was about to follow Gero and Amelie into the castle's main hall.

"Stay back," the castle lord said darkly. "They are going on a special journey and no one must try to follow them."

As the blue-green light flared, Roland shielded his eyes with his hands. After that, there was only silence.

"Gero?" His voice echoed through the empty hall.

With a sigh of relief, Hannah ran to Gero. The retrieval team had returned to base early that morning.

"We did it!" Gero cried in joy. He was still wearing his medieval clothing. "They gave Amelie a sleeping pill. I was the first to tell Struan.

He'll be able to see her today," Gero said as Hannah flung her arms around his neck breathlessly.

"I can't tell you how happy I am for him," Hannah exclaimed, laying her head blissfully on Gero's shoulder.

Gero paused for a moment and his expression darkened. "She lost the child. While we were in France, she had a miscarriage."

"Does Struan know? How did he take the news?" Hannah looked up at Gero in concern.

"He was stunned at first, but then he said a prayer of thanks that at least his beloved was alive, and that we were all safe. I don't think anything could shock him anymore."

That afternoon, the Templars gathered in their wounded brother's room, along with Hannah, Freya, Matthäus, and Professor Hertzberg, who had organized the visit. Ever since their arrival, he had devoted himself to looking after his medieval pupils, as he had nicknamed them. Johan, Arnaud, and Stefano let out a sigh of relief when the small, white-haired man, who been firing the oddest questions at them, finally gave them a well-earned break.

Struan still couldn't stand up, but after a successful operation, he could already move his feet and toes. The physician had arranged for a second bed to be set up next to Struan's bed, where Amelie now lay, covered in blankets and sedated so that she could recover before being confronted with her new, confusing reality. The Scotsman stretched out his hand and played with her hair. Her eyes were shut, and a distant smile graced her pretty mouth as if she had felt Struan's touch.

"*Fin amor*," Struan whispered, and smiled knowingly at his Brothers.

Gero put one arm protectively around Hannah and his other arm around Matthäus.

"*Fin amor*? What does that mean?" Hannah looked up at him curiously.

"True, eternal love," Gero answered softly and kissed her, "the only thing that really matters, no matter what time we find ourselves in."

EPILOGUE

Feast of the Conversion of Paul the Apostle

"Jesus said, 'it is to those who are worthy of my mysteries that I tell my mysteries.'"

The Gospel of Thomas, Verse 62

Tuesday, January 25, 2005
Bar-sur-Aube, France

Snowflakes floated down slowly like fat feathers over the graveyard of Bar-sur-Aube. Today was January 25, the day of Saul's conversion to the Apostle Paul. Only those gathered in the quiet cemetery knew whether they themselves had experienced a conversion of any sort.

His fingers red from the cold, the priest leafed through his worn-out Bible and began to recite one of the Gospels of Thomas: "The Kingdom of God is inside and all about you, not only in mansions of wood and stone. When I am gone, split a piece of wood and I am there, lift a stone and you will find me.

"And so we leave our brother Henri d'Our in the hands of our Almighty God, who reveals Himself not only in the light of eternal life, but also in the words and deeds of our fellow men, and in the wonders of nature, ubiquitous yet mysterious."

Once again, Tom questioned whether the future had already been written in stone. Since he had begun experimenting with space and time, everything above and below had merged into a horizontal line, where all calculations indicated that neither forward nor backward existed.

Just that morning, General Lafour had informed him of the American president's latest plans. Having learnt of the world's dystopian future, the leader of the United States had decided that immediate action had to be taken. Even if far more research on the timeserver and its impacts needed to be done first, the American government had decided to put together a team that would set off from the Temple Mount in present-day Jerusalem and journey into the year 1153. The mission's objective was to rescue the original owners of the quantum server, so that the United States could benefit from their knowledge.

Lost in thought, Tom glanced over at the five crusaders, who, with folded hands, were standing silently before their commander's open grave. In their black suits and trench coats, they looked no different from the NSA agents in their midst.

Tom's mind was racing with a million questions. Would the Templars answer the call of science in exchange for the chance to save their Order? Or was there an unknown force that prevented anything from being changed? Did God have a hand in this game? And if so, would He be open to negotiation?

Professor Hertzberg listened with rapt attention as the five deep voices suddenly rang out in Gregorian chants, extolling God's greatness and benevolence so beautifully that even the priest held his breath.

Who would have thought that the mysterious Head of the Knights Templar held such a secret? Did Philipp IV really have any idea what he was after when he destroyed the Order seven hundred years ago? Was there anyone else who knew the truth? Or was the man who now lay peacefully in the cold earth of Champagne really the last link to the High Council?

Perhaps it was something divine, waiting only for the last puzzle piece to fall into place before it revealed itself. But what if the only thing revealed was cold technology, destroying everything divine?

Gero's gaze swept across the bare hills of Bar-sur-Aube's winter landscape. Henri d'Our would have wanted to be laid to rest here, in the place where he had fulfilled his destiny, even if the cemetery of the former Templar commandery was now gone.

Despite his worries for the fate of his family and the Order, Gero felt a deep sense of peace. He had doubted God, yet he was certain that, unaffected by the actions of mortals, everything between heaven and earth followed His unfathomable plan. And, in whatever way, this God had always heard his prayers.

He gripped Hannah's hand and stared at her lovingly, then shifted his gaze to Matthäus, who was standing devoutly next to her. A woman who loved him. Children. A home of his own – if he were honest with himself, he'd never wanted anything more.

The End

Afterword and Acknowledgments

Save for a few historical figures, all characters and events in this novel are fictitious. Any resemblance to real persons living or deceased and/or their conduct is entirely coincidental. Places and institutions in France, Israel, Germany, Scotland, and the United States have been altered by the author in the spirit of artistic license.

When I began writing the first drafts of The Mystery of the Templars in the Fall of 2003, my intention was to paint a historical picture of the Knights Templar that would do them justice, fantastical elements aside. I had little idea how much work would be needed, and what followed was a research marathon through countless non-fiction books, doctoral theses, websites about the Order, and several research trips around Germany, as well as to Israel, France, and Scotland.

As I was writing this novel, I was repeatedly confronted by strange coincidences, which suggested to me that elements of my story might be more than just fantasy, that, as a writer, I had mysteriously tapped into some sort of channeling process. For example, the large-scale power outage in the novel really did occur in real life. Same place and time – but, just as inexplicably, it happened after I had already incorporated the event into my story. And – three years later, I got an email with an official note, which remains a mystery to me. To this day, no one can explain it. On other occasions, I thought I had invented a historical event or name, only to find both recorded in an ancient research volume, which was unknown to me at the time of writing. How fascinating!

What is no coincidence, however, are all the dear people who have helped me make this project a reality. First and foremost, I would like to thank my Scottish friends, George and Mairi St Clair, who were a wonderful source of support with their constant encouragement to "just do it!" and Mairi with proofreading the drafts. I would especially like to thank Yan An Tan in Singapore for undertaking this labor-intensive translation – amazing! Furthermore I would like to extend my heartfelt gratitude to Dr. Eva von Contzen, professor of English literature at the University of Freiburg, who helped make the novel all the more authentic by translating the Middle High German dialogue into Middle English (no knight making a sudden appearance in the future would speak the Lingua Franca).

Also I would like to thank the Heisterbach Abbey Foundation (www.abtei-heisterbach.de), which was kind enough to provide me with a map of the former Cistercian Abbey Heisterbach's compound and underground sewage system for my research.

A sincere "Thank You" to all those whom I cannot personally thank, but who have helped me craft a story as realistic as possible by giving me all sorts of information, including the exact position of the moon on a Friday the 13th in 1307.

A big hug to my family for their most precious support. I love you.

Last, but not least, I want to thank YOU.

Thank you for your interest - I hope you enjoyed the story about the Templars of Bar-sur-Aube. If you did, please support me by leaving a review on Amazon.

Love,

Index of Characters

** actual historical figure
* fictional figures

Knights of the Templar commandery Bar-sur-Aube, France (in 1307):

Gero of Breydenbach* – Commander Lieutenant of Templar commandery, originally from Trier, German Lands
Johan van Elk* – Knight Templar from Flanders
Guy de Gislingham* – Knight Templar from Suffolk, England
Struan MacDhoughaill nan t-Eilan Ileach* – Knight Templar from Scotland
Arnaud de Mirepaux* – Knight Templar from Languedoc, France
Henri d'Our* – Commander of the Templar commandery,   originally from Lorraine, France
Francesco de Salazar* – Knight Templar from Barcelona, Catalonia
Stephano de Sapin* – Knight Templar from Reims, France

Enemies and adversaries of the Knights Templar (in 1307):

Guillaume Imbert** – Grand Inquisitor, Bishop of Paris, personal confessor of Philipp IV, and unholy ally of Guillaume de Nogaret
Guillaume de Nogaret** – Keeper of the Seals and head of the Royal Secret Police (Gens du Roi) in Paris, France
King Philipp IV of France** – Destroyed the Order of the Templars in 1307

Friends and Relatives of the Knights Templar

Freya of Bogenhausen* – Member of a Beguine convent in 1307

Amelie Bratac* – Daughter of vineyard owner Alphonse Bratac* in Champagne, 1307

Jutta of Breydenbach* – Mother of Gero of Breydenbach

Richard of Breydenbach* – Father of Gero of Breydenbach

Eberhard of Breydenbach* – Older Brother of Gero of Breydenbach

Matthäus of Bruch alias Mattes* – Young squire of Gero of Breydenbach

Wilhelm of Eltz* – Godfather of Gero of Breydenbach

Hannah Schreyber* – Bookseller, historian, hides Gero of Breydenbach and his squire in her house in 2004

Anselm Stein* (Anselmo de Caillou) – Historian and confidant of the secret Project C.A.P.U.T in 2004

Members of the American secret project C.A.P.U.T in 2004

Dr. Karen Baxter* – American molecular biologist, partner of Paul Colbach

Paul Colbach* – Computer scientist from Luxembourg, partner of Dr. Baxter

Professor Dietmar Hagen* – German Professor of quantum physics, director of the project in Germany

Professor Moshe Hertzberg* – Internationally renowned historian

General Alexander Lafour* – Head of the National Security Agency (NSA) in Germany

Dr. James Piglet* – Professor Hagen's aide, responsible for managing the research assistants' schedules

Major Dan Simmons* – Official representative of the U.S. Department of Defense

Dr. Tom Stevendahl* – Danish quantum physicist, former fiancée of Hannah Schreyber

Agent Jack Tanner* – Operations Manager of the NSA in Germany

Agent Mike Tapleton* – NSA agent, co-worker of Jack Tanner

Glossary

Chapter – Weekly meeting of the Knights Templar

Chlamys – White cloak of the Templars with red croix pattée made from worsted wool.

Commandery – Administrative seat of the local division of the Knights Templar

Cotte – Medieval type of clothing (coat, tunic) worn by both men and women

Croix pattée – Cross of the Knights Templar

Crusade – War of the Christian states of the occident against Muslim states in the Middle East in the late 11th Century and early 14th Century.

Dormitory – Sleeping chambers of the Knights Templar

Fief – An estate of land, especially one held on condition of feudal service. In a feudal system, a peasant or worker known as a vassal received a piece of land in return for serving a lord or king, especially during times of war.

Medieval mile – Approx. 7.5 miles (12 km),one hour by horse

Miswak – Arabic teeth cleaning twig

Order of the Knights Templar – One of the three large chivalric orders in medieval times. Also known as the Poor Fellow- Soldiers of Christ and of the Temple of Solomon

Refectory – Meeting and dining room of the Knights Templar

Serf – An agricultural laborer bound by the feudal system, tied to working on his lord's estate

Squire – Young man training to become a knight, servant of a knight

Surkot – Medieval long tunic, worn by both men and women

A Chat with Martina André

While visiting her son in Scotland, author Martina André talked to »be« (publisher of the digital version) about the inspiration behind her sweeping historical saga, Mystery of the Templars. Available now for the first time in English, the novel has sold hundreds of thousands of copies in Germany and has garnered rave reviews for its attention to detail. André's tale pulls from local folklore and a fascination with the fantastic.

1. Where did you get the idea to write about the Templars?

As a child, I lived close to the Cistercian Abbey Heisterbach by the Rhine river, in which a legend about a time-travelling monk has been told for almost a thousand years. As the Cistercian order had a close connection to the Knights Templar, who were allegedly in possession of a mysterious talking head with supernatural powers, making a connection to „Mystery of the Templars" was easy. Apart from that, the time travel novels by Diana Gabaldon inspired me to portray the story as realistic and historically accurate as possible.

2. If the book were made into a movie, which actors would you like to portray Gero and Hanna?

Chris Hemsworth and Emma Stone.

3. Who is your favorite character in the book?

Gero of Breydenbach, very closely followed by Struan MacDhughaill nan t-Eilan Ileach

4. Which scene was the hardest to write?

The scene in which Gero is tasked by his Templar commander to save the order. I rewrote it so many times to make it sound as realistic as possible. The rape scene in the river valley of Anglus was also difficult, because it strongly affected me emotionally.

5. What is the strangest message that you've ever received by someone who had read your book?

There were two readers who seriously wanted to show me their invention of a working zero-point-energy generator based on cold fusion, with which they could create a quantum field that makes time travel possible (as in my story).

6. If you were not an author, what would you be doing for a living?

I still dream of opening a bed & breakfast hotel with café in Scotland, serving my very own homemade cake.

598

7. What are you currently working on/writing about?

I am currently working on a sequel to the Templar series and a mystery novel about Romans and Germanic tribes. In addition, I started writing a science fiction love story a few months ago, which also still has to be completed.

Martina André can be reached via her website
www.martinaandre.com

Made in the USA
Coppell, TX
28 May 2020